THE CROW: A MURDER OF CROWS

THE CROW: A Murder of Crows

QUOTH THE CROW
by David Bischoff

THE LAZARUS HEART
by Poppy Z. Brite

CLASH BY NIGHT
by Chet Williamson

Inspired by the series created by James O'Barr

SFBC
FANTASY

Printing History: HarperPrism trade paperback January 1998

Printing History: HarperPrism trade paperback April 1998

Printing History: HarperPrism trade paperback July 1998

First SFBC Fantasy Printing: August 1998

Published by arrangement with:
HarperCollins*Publishers*
10 East 53rd Street
New York, NY 10022

Visit our website at *http://www.sfbc.com*
Visit HarperPrism's website at *http://www.harperprism.com*

ISBN # 1-56865-830-3

PRINTED IN THE UNITED STATES OF AMERICA

Contents

Quoth the Crow

by
David Bischoff

To Dean Koontz
Past, present, and future master

A flap of the wing to:
Jimmy Vines, Martha Bayless, Robin Shurtz,
John Douglas, and Jeff Conner

Prologue

I was sick—sick unto death with that long agony; and when they at length unbound me, and I was permitted to sit, I felt that my senses were leaving me. The sentence—the dread sentence of death—was the last of distinct accentuation which reached my ears . . .

. . . The thought came gently and stealthily, and it seemed long before it attained full appreciation; but just as my spirit came at length properly to feel and entertain it, the figures of the judges vanished, as if magically, from before me; the tall candles sank into nothingness; their flames went out utterly; the blackness of darkness supervened; all sensations appeared swallowed up in a mad rushing descent as of the soul into Hades. Then silence, and stillness, and night were the universe.

—Edgar A. Poe, *The Pit and the Pendulum*

The house screamed.

It was one of those bloodcurdling cinematic screams, the kind horror movie scream queens were famous for. It seemed to rattle the windows of the little rowhouse building, shake the walls. The bass aspect throbbed the foundation, the high ululation reaching up to the flat roof, shaking the gravel and tarpaper.

It sounded, Count Mishka thought, rather like Jamie Lee Curtis.

In fact, it was Jamie Lee Curtis, doubled and manipulated like a Tarzan yell. A digital stitching of classic distress from both *Terror Train* and *Prom Night.*

The youth, all dressed in black (black shirt, black boots, black jeans, black T-shirt, black earring, black nose-ring, black eye liner, black razor-cut, black scarf, black jacket—all not merely black but stylishly *Gothic* black with bits of shine and gloss on hems and edges, a little touch of glitter around Alfred E. Neuman/Prince Charles ears) giggled.

He pushed his new door alarm again.

Another female scream, this time a little bit shorter and cut off quick, as though some killer had just slashed off her head.

Brinke Stevens and Linnea Quigley? Yes, surely. Nice and sexy, even in terror. Especially in terror.

Yum.

Dusk, bleak and autumnal, settled over the snug Baltimore neighborhood. A dog barked in an alley. A woman in a hooded coat bent toward a destination. The smell of fresh tarmac hovered from a construction site a few doors down.

A gull, a little off base from its harbor environs, swooped over the line of tiny Fells Point rowhouses.

Carrying his loot under his left arm, Count Mishka, known to his parents and the government as Richard Mark Henneman, slotted the key to his house with his right hand.

The keys jingled as the door opened. The last of the prerecorded door alarm screams the Count had engineered wafted away in the shadows like dark smoke.

A cold chill seemed to blow through the house.

Richard shivered, with something more than the cold.

What the hell? he thought. *Is this house haunted?*

Cool, he thought.

The gang would approve.

For a year now Richard Henneman had allied himself with a self-described "elite" group of local Goths—that post-punk, funereally festooned subculture whose fierce rejection of mainstream commercialism was often obscured by equally rigid, narcissistic obsessions, scorched-earth cliquishness, and an unhealthy addiction to black nail polish. The Gothiques, however, had of late, become a much more closely bound unit. A unit bound not just in blood . . . but in money. Lots now. A great deal more in the future. Yes, the Gothiques were quickly becoming Goth, Inc.

And all because of a teensy little *murder.*

How delicious!

The Count's hallway was splattered with blood.

Movie poster gore.

Bloody fanged Draculas from Bela to Gary menaced. Luckless women with deep cleavage held up their arms, screaming. Alongside these posters were framed collages Richard had made of pictures Xeroxed from his favorite fan-boy genre mags, *Fangoria, Shivers, Midnight*

Marquee, European Trash Cinema, and their lesser-known brethren. Exotic movie makeup and mayhem. Decapitated heads. Eviscerated bodies. Slobbering monsters trailing guts, rarely their own.

Art, pure and simple.

Frozen moments of pure pop cinema at its zenith.

Chuckling to himself, the Count turned on the living-room light, kicked the door closed behind him, and headed straight for his holy of holies, his entertainment center. He bowed slightly to the fat Buddha above the television set. "Much incense to be burned tonight, oh Enlightened One!"

He dumped his treasures on the couch, dug out the new Iggy Pop CD; well, not so new really, as it was the *Raw Power* remixes, a twenty-year after-the-fact revision of the classic album that had been "ruined" (according to hardcore fans) by David Bowie's attempt at making it sound commercial, back when Mr. Pop was still called Iggy Stooge. The Count put the disc in the CD player and hit random play (the most important development in modern conveniences since the remote control). Immediately, Iggy and the Stooges started blaring proto-punk through his new Bose satellite speaker system.

"Rock my world, Iggy!" said the Count. He pogoed through the narrow dining room, through the narrow kitchen, where he opened the Sears Hotpoint refrigerator, pulled out a fat can of Fosters, and ripped off the poptop, letting the foam spurt up, Aussie-style. Back in the old days, he had to drink National Boh. Now the Count drank *good* stuff. "Go, Iggster, go!" He laughed, letting beer run down his mouth and shirt.

The Stooges electronically obeyed.

The bass throbbed and screeching guitars rang. The drums ripped and hammered. "I am the world's forgotten boy!" Iggy shrieked.

Iggy rocked the walls, postered with Goth rock, darkwave icons. The Sisters of Mercy, The Cure, The Mission, The Damned, and Bauhaus; newer acts like Switchblade Symphony, Laibach, Chem Lab, Attrition, Lycia, Dorian Gray, Die Laughing, London After Midnight; and even molding oldies like David Bowie (hey, Trent digs him), Kiss, and Alice Cooper (Marilyn Manson should be paying them royalties for stealing their acts) to show the catholicity of his taste.

Iggy rocked the bookcase, holding film and TV books and a few horror novels. Iggy rocked the racks bulging with plastic-covered comics. Iggy rocked the CD racks and the record stacks. Iggy rocked the multimedia racks stocked with hundreds of videos near the thirty-one-inch Sony TV and various video players, dripping with yet more videos, laserdiscs, and DVDs.

Iggy rocked *all.*

The Count's collection of pop culture and effluvia flowed out from the living room, filling the dining room. Rolling up the staircase were more piles of videos and CDs, on up to the top rooms of the house, which were also filled with bookcases, comics, posters, action figures, Japanese robots, and other arcana.

Many of these things had been stolen.

Richard was an excellent shoplifter. He'd found, as a prepubescent youth, that his hunger for comics and such far exceeded his allowance. Deft of finger, fleet of foot, and big of coat, he found his forté was in theft. What he didn't want to keep, he sold or traded, thus starting up a most wonderful collection. At the age of fourteen, he'd broken into a comic shop at night, cut off the lock on the collector's case and stolen a treasure trove of old Marvel and DC comics, even some EC titles from the fifties. By the time he was eighteen, he had so many comics and books, tapes, CDs, and records that he operated a store out of his college campus apartment, making a major killing on Image Comics (love those variant covers!) during the market's speculator boom.

Alas, he'd been thrown out of college as a sophomore for numerous offenses. Unchastened, his larcenous activities continued, refining his skills while building his stock and trading capacities—but his constant hunger for more and more loot kept his vision low, a victim of his own compulsive appetites.

Then he'd met the Gothiques, or rather, Le Salon des Gothiques, the funky basement hangout presided over by one Baxter Brittle.

His talents were quickly discerned by salon director Brittle, a boozehound artist and erstwhile editor of Tome Press, blessed with a recent inheritance (namely the Cork'd Sailor bar, home of said basement), whose own collections were often augmented by the Count's activities. Previously just a spotty nerd with a light touch, Richard Henneman's social activities increased. He achieved the identity of "Count Mishka." He even got semi-regular helmet polishing from a few of the Goth chicks attracted by Brittle's garish personality (and free booze).

However, it had only been in the last year, with his induction into the inner circle of Baxter Brittle's trust, that his monetary situation truly improved. He bought a small townhouse in Fells Point and moved the contents of his apartment and storage spaces here. True, soon he was going to have to rent another storage locker, but such was the volume of the flow of materials through his possession (some, like tonight's stuff, actually *bought*) that he was able to keep selling things and making a profit in addition to the moneys achieved from his work at Tome Press.

Iggy rocked the book vault.

The elaborate cabinet, a genuine antique of solid oak, had been a gift from Tome Press. ("For extraordinary services rendered," said Brittle.) All the locks had been refitted with modern hardware, and the interior made air-tight and moisture free, perfect for housing rare books, just like the special cases used by William Blessing for his famous Poe collection.

Iggy Pop railed on about penetration and shake appeal while the Count laughed. Shaking his head to himself, he chuckled as he inserted the magnetic key into the antique facing of the lock. He opened the cabinet and looked at his most prized of treasures. His "double-bag" items.

Behold! he thought. First editions. *Signed* first editions, a collector's best investment, guaranteed to appreciate in value. From Stephen King to Anne Rice to Clive Barker to Dean Koontz to Ramsey Campbell to Robert Bloch to Shirley Jackson to Richard Matheson, they were all here. And a nice tight copy—or better yet, an unread, signature-only copy—had more built-in security value than any 401k plan or IRA account. There was a first edition of Bram Stoker's *Dracula,* signed. Ambrose Bierce. Some nice Lovecraft. Dozens of wonderful collectable valuables, ah, yes.

Glorious stuff indeed.

However, the totally primo material he had only just recently obtained . . . The most valuable, the oldest . . . the most magical . . .

And for free!

There they were: a solid set of first editions by Edgar Allan Poe. These from an era when first printings ran in the mere hundreds, and often were just privately issued. Fruit of that terrible night of four months ago that had turned, somehow, into such a bonanza.

Even now, as he did every night, his fingers drifted over the leather spines of the old, custom-made clam-shell slipcases (valuable relics themselves) that held the fragile volumes from the corrupting influences of light and air and unnecessary handling. He felt a palpable thrill, an exquisite energy humming within these repositories of magic.

Ah, yes, who could have predicted that through a death and a burglary, such luck would fall upon his collector's head!

Tome Press was doing very well indeed, expanding by leaps and bounds. Richard Mark Henneman, being one of the Inner Circle, was now Vice President in Charge of Special Projects. Which meant, in addition to his usual cool duties of overseeing a small press turning into a large press, looking into other avenues of expansion. Being a music maven and motion picture nut, it was natural that the Count's interests should be stirred by the desire to "produce." And to judge by the idiots already doing so, how hard could it be? concluded the Count. Just today he had spoken with some film students about Tome Press making its first horror movie. And he was sure he could get one of those one-man studio "bands" like Trust Obey to do the music, then make a soundtrack deal with Projekt, Tess, or Cleopatra. The possibilities were endless.

Man, what a blast!

Touching the volumes of Poe was like getting jolts of power.

Raw power! Hey!

Goth, Inc. was headed for the stars!

"And we're along for the ride, huh, Iggy?" the Count said, closing the cabinet.

Iggy bellowed and groaned and retched in reply.

"Give me danger, little stranger," they sang together.

He took another chug of Fosters, then wiggled into the living room. He took a carefree backward half-gainer (after placing his hefty beer can on the coffee table, already groaning with Cool Stuff) onto the couch.

He grabbed one of his controls.

Aim. Press of button. Off with Iggy's head!

He hit another button and *Interview with the Vampire* zapped onto the thirty-one-inch TV screen. The Count mimed along with Brad Pitt's dialogue, then took another swig of Australian brew.

Yes, after a long day in the salt mines, it was time for a little lie-down. Then, up in time to hit Fletcher's, where Death On Two Legs, a new band he was interested in, was playing. He'd check out the babes, do a little Ex . . . have a good time shmoozing . . .

And then, maybe find a willing female (his personal goal: an honest-to-God honey from the Goth Babe of the Week website) and come back to the bachelor pad to watch trailers for sixties horror films and partake in some hot sex.

Man, talk about a perfect prospective evening!

Even as the ominous music swelled from the vampire video, the Count found exhaustion closing in on him, cushioned by the beer. Sleep was cool, but all in all, he'd rather do it during the day. Night, he'd always felt, was full of so many other possibilities.

As he slept, he dreamed he was flying on the back of a giant black bird. The creature dived and spun above foggy lands of mysterious castles, streaked with rainbows. Lightning and heavy metal music thundered in dark caverns.

Far out, he thought. *Amazing.*

Dreams were good. Even bad ones.

Maybe especially bad ones.

"After all," he mumbled hazily, rising up from his nap, "I wouldn't be in business without them."

Vaguely he reached out for his can of Fosters to jump start his neurons. His hand clenched on emptiness where the can had been.

"What the—" he said, blearily rising up.

"Looking for this?" said a voice.

A dark form stepped forward and pressed the can into his hand.

"I went and got you a fresh one, Count. Warm beer doesn't really make it when you're just waking up from a nap."

Someone else is in the house . . .

Who?

The Count looked up from his place on the couch.

A figure seemed to swim in front of him.

The light from the dining room made a nimbus around his body, but around his head there seemed a halo of pure darkness.

Somewhere (from the second floor?) came the sounds of wings, flapping.

Click.

Gears warmed from their freeze.

"Hey, man. I haven't got much worth stealing. A little money in my pocket—my TV set and—"

He turned and gestured toward the towering entertainment center.

Where there had been a brand-new Sony XBR thirty-one incher, there was now only an empty space.

"Whoa! You already *got* it."

He started to get up.

The figure leaned over.

Stuck a Heckler and Koch HK-4 in his nose.

The Count flung himself back on the couch.

He recognized the gun.

It was his.

"Oh, shit. Looks like you've got the run of the place. Guess you're going to take what you like, huh?"

"I know exactly what I want, Mr. Henneman. That is your name, isn't it, Count? Richard Mark Henneman."

The man's voice was harsh and scratchy, and somehow off . . . like a special-effects voice, pitch-shifted, controlled anger through clenched teeth.

"Yes. Yes, that's me." The bore of the gun was cold and heavy as it pushed into his nose. And it hurt like hell.

"Look, sorry to be in your way. Just take the stuff, okay? I don't care. Just don't shoot me."

"No?"

"No! That . . . would be really stupid!"

"Would it?"

"Look, are you trying to screw with my head or something? I told you to take what you like. I'll even show you, okay? Just get the gun out of my nose!"

The gun pulled back.

The figure stepped away.

It appeared to be a dark man dressed in a dark coat, but as he moved back, some of the darkness about the face seemed to fade away. It was an older man, with taut and aged skin. Dark glasses. Was he being burglarized by some retiree?

Cool!

"Look, Grandpa. I promise I'll cooperate. You can even have the gun. That cost me a pretty penny, I'll tell you . . ."

And I wish I kept it on me at all times . . . Your head would be all over the living room . . .

He couldn't really shoot, but the thought was delightful and helped keep down the fear. Mick Prince had helped him buy the gun, and was going to show him how to use it. Mick was showing the Count lots of neat new things.

The Count wished that Mick were here now.

He'd know what to do.

"You have no idea who I am!" the man yelled. "No idea!"

Without warning, the man flung his gun arm across the table, sweeping it free of the books and tapes and videos and the drug paraphernalia box.

Stuff went flying across the room.

Two glasses crashed against the opposite wall.

This sucker was *strong* for an old duffer!

The Count cringed backward. He started pushing at the couch with his feet to push himself off and to somewhere safe.

With surprising quickness, the Dark Man reached out and took a fistful of his shirt with the gun-free hand. He then hauled the Count over to the coffee table and slammed him down on top of it.

The Count was so dazed by this that he barely noticed the Dark Man's next motions. He tried to get up, but soon realized he'd been restrained. There were several belts tying him down. He could only move his head, his hands, and his feet—and those not terribly far.

"Shit! How can I show you the stuff!" he complained, not liking this turn of events, cold reality beginning to penetrate.

"I know exactly what I want and where it is," said the Dark Man. "Now, though, I need a few things I can only get from your brain."

"Huh? Information? What? Jeez . . ."

Everything seemed dark and fuzzy about the stranger. Around the room, the ceremonial candles had been lit, though above, on the ceiling, darkness held sway. The Count sensed a form, a presence up there, somehow hulking huge and ominous.

For a moment the Dark Man remained silent, perhaps to allow more time for the fuse of dread to ignite in his captive's heart.

Then he knelt down by his side.

"I have powers now . . . strange powers . . . I perceive things as I had not before . . . in life," he said, in a solemn whisper. "In life, Mr. Henneman. I perceive, Mr. Henneman . . . Count Mishka . . . that beyond the sins and minor atrocities you've already stitched into the cosmos, there are greater evils which are your destiny. Imagine, Count . . . Imagine, say, if Joseph Goebbels of the Third Reich had been earlier recognized as the villain he would become. Oh, the better world it would have been had he been excised from existence. Snip snip, go the scissors of fate, always, Count. But too often, too late for the world. I am seriously considering helping those scissors along tonight." The Dark Man pulled out a large pair of pruning shears, their newly honed blades bright in the flickering candlelight.

"Jesus! What are you going to do with *those*?" the Count gasped. "Look, I told you—"

"You have no idea who I am, do you?" said the Dark Man. "Let me inform you." He started to come closer. "I am Doctor Phibes, Mr. Henneman. I am the vilified Shakespearean actor of Vincent Price's *Theatre of Blood.* I am Peter Cushing in *Tales from the Crypt.* I am Claude Rains in *Phantom of the Opera.* I could go on, Count. Am I speaking your variety of cinematic dialect now?"

"What are . . . I don't . . . You're making no sense!" squeaked the Count.

Snip, snip went the shears.

The Dark Man knelt beside him, removing his dark glasses. Candlelight reflected on gray, scaly skin. The Count got a faint scent of ripe roadkill. He looked into the eyes, and saw something he remembered. Something just a few months back.

Then he recognized the eyes.

He opened his mouth to speak, or at the very least to scream, but nothing came out.

Oh God, oh God, oh God . . .

"I see the spark of recognition in your eyes, Richard," said the Dark

Man. He slowly put his glasses back on and then stood. "It does my soul good. I think, perhaps some good can come out of my death. And that is why I'm here. Not just vengeance, you see. Not just redemption. But for the good for future generations!"

Still paralyzed with horror and disbelief, the Count watched as the Dark Man withdrew something from his pocket. It was the remote control device for his television . . . What was he doing with—?

Click, click.

The hulking form that the Count had sensed before, up in the darkness near the ceiling, suddenly lit up.

It was his massive Sony XBR, somehow suspended by its cable and electrical wires from the lighting fixture in the ceiling. In gorgeous Technicolor, Peter Cushing's Van Helsing was holding a stake, his hair flopping about wildly, as he battled Christopher Lee's Dracula.

The huge TV set dangled six feet above Richard Henneman's head.

The Dark Man began to intone.

"'I now observed—with what horror it is needless to say—that its nether extremity was formed of a crescent of glittering steel, about a foot in length from horn to horn; the horns upward, and the under edge evidently as keen as that of a razor. Like a razor also, it seemed massive and heavy, tapering from the edge into a solid and broad structure above. It was appended to a weighty rod of brass, and the whole *hissed* as it swung through the air.'

"Quiz time, Mr. Henneman. What is the source of that quote?"

"I . . . don't . . . know . . ." the Count managed to squeeze out.

"Perhaps I should approach the subject through the media that you are familiar with."

Suddenly on the screen flashed scenes from a movie that the Count had seen. Vincent Price in a cowl. Stone steps, a dungeon . . . A bosomy woman . . .

Then, the guy from *Millennium* (cool show!) in a cowl too. A dungeon. A bosomy woman, naked . . .

"Pit . . ." he said. *"Pit and the Pendulum."*

"That's right, Count," said the Dark Man. He reached up with the shears and pushed hard on the TV set. It started swinging back and forth, back and forth.

Strobing light.

"There was Roger Corman's classic interpretation . . . and the more recent Stuart Gordon version," said the Dark Man. "And I don't need to tell you about Dario Argento's graphic quotation of the tale some years back."

Back and forth.

Back and forth.

Strobing light across the dry and dwindling skin of the Dark Man, flashing on his glasses.

"What is this?" cried the Count. "Baxter! Is this some trick? Baxter? Is this your sick and twisted sense of humor?"

Back and forth went the television, spurred on by the shears of the Dark Man.

Back and forth.

Strobing light.

Scenes from movies sprayed from its gigantic cathode ray, garish scenes from *Night of the Living Dead,* old Universal horror movies, fifties monster movies, eighties slasher movies, Stephen King movies, Clive Barker movies, forgotten movies he'd bought from Sinister Cinema and Video Search of Miami, read about in *Video Watchdog* . . .

Back and forth, they went.

Strobing light.

"Oh, what a rainbow of delight, Count! Pain and blood and horror in ninety-minute packages! Such decadent fun, don't you think? But not as much fun as joining in on my melodramatic death scene. Not as much fun as jumping on the bandwagon of my estate, barreling toward commercial hell."

"Stop it!" cried the Count. "Just cut it out!"

"Maybe. Maybe I'll let you go, if you tell me where your other royal friends are. The . . . uhm . . . Marquis I believe his name is, hmm?"

"He'll be at the Cross Club," said the Count. "Yeah. He usually hangs out there, this time of week."

"Thank you."

However, the Dark Man who claimed to be William Blessing, risen from the grave, did not release the Count from his bonds.

"Hmm. I see you also collect those paragons of culture . . . comic books." The Dark Man limped over to a bookcase and grabbed a handful.

Back and forth . . .

Swish . . . swish . . .

. . . went the Sony over his head.

"Oh, and what do I see? *The Sandman* by Neil Gaiman." He limped back and tossed the pile onto the Count's chest. "These issues feature that cute little bit of jail-bait, Death. I'll make a deal with you, Count. You explain to me what these comic books are supposed to *mean* exactly, and I'll let you go!"

"What?"

"To me it's obvious, but then I'm a professor of English. Perhaps if I got it straight from a dedicated fan I could learn some nuance I might have missed, hmm?"

The Count looked aghast. How could he answer a pop quiz with Death when there was a 100-pound television swinging above him like a wrecking ball?

"Sandman's, uhmm . . . like, this prince of dreams . . . and he . . . uh . . . goes back and forth in cool mythologies . . . and . . . like . . . uhm . . . is . . . uhm . . . cool and . . . uhm, profound . . . and uhm . . ."

"No. I didn't think you could tell me," said the Dark Man, with a slight trace of sadness. "What's the purpose of collecting something if you can't be bothered to understand it? Is it cool because others like it, or because *you* do? You see my point, no? Well, you will soon enough."

Then the Dark Man reached up and cut the power cord and cables with the heavy shears. *Snip.*

The Sony XBR thirty-one-inch stereo television came down from its pendulous trajectory with unnatural speed, as if hurled from a great height.

The Dark Man watched.

He felt no joy, no satisfaction.

But neither did he feel sorrow.

The TV's edge smashed into the bound man's face like an anvil on an apple, crushing first it (a splash of blood and brains all about), and then the end of the coffee table. With a crack and splintering and the sound of a splatting melon, the television set pushed the table down, hurling the rest of the body up, whipping it, cracking it.

Glass shattered and flew, some into the Dark Man's legs.

Though it cut his flesh, he barely registered the pain.

Electric sparks shot out from the set, and for a moment from the cut wires. Smoke wreathed the wreckage and gore.

Then with a sputtering, the electrical charge faded.

The feet of the Count spasmed, then went still.

The Dark Man stood silently for a moment.

From a pocket inside his coat, he pulled a single black feather.

The feather of a crow.

He tucked it into one of the Count's hands.

"Fly into the dark now, my foe," said the Dark Man. "Fly to where neither you nor I know."

Then he turned and departed for his next assignation . . .

. . . remembering.

* * *

. . . the first bullet stabs into his chest. Its impact is astonishing, tearing forcefully through skin, ribs, right lung, veins, arteries, then exploding out of his shirt and cashmere sweater. It feels as though a grinning demon has stabbed a red-hot poker through him, searing and scalding . . .

The demon, though, wears the contorted mask of a wild-eyed lunatic, a huge gun held out before him.

The Dark Man walked the streets of night, the streets of Baltimore, for his next rendezvous. These men had killed him, destroyed all that he'd held dear. Now it was their turn to die.

The Dark Man walked the streets of Fells Point.

. . . remembering . . .

. . . Amy! Oh, my dear God! Amy! Don't hurt Amy!

. . . burglars! Madmen! Killers!

Help! Oh, dear Jesus! Help!

All through searing manic pain as he flies against the bookshelf. Precious ancient volumes are knocked from the shelf. The smell of vellum and old paper, the odor of wax mixed with fresh blood.

The image of his assailant burns into his mind, every ragged stretch of facial sinew, every pore and bend of nose. The hard, thin lips. The thick, curling eyebrows. The granite eyes. The greasy black hair, tied behind into a ponytail with a ring of bone . . .

And, peripherally, the image of the other attacker, holding his wife. A muscular ape of a man with a buzz cut, thick brow ridge, no chin, an oozing look of lust in his piggish eyes.

He scrabbles against the shelves of his library, against the slime of himself, trying to push himself back, thinking "Save Amy, save the collection . . ."

Then the gunman sneers . . .

. . . and he knows in his soul it cannot be.

The Dark Man walked through the streets of Baltimore, his home.

Baltimore, Maryland.

He had been born here in the city, and he seemed to grow up with a sense of its history and promise. Now, he could smell the waters of the Inner Harbor to the south. Baltimore, on the Patapsco River two thirds of the way up the Chesapeake Bay. Largest city in Maryland and one of the largest natural harbors of the world. A city of American growth, American architecture, American heritage. Now, as he walked, he could almost taste, amongst the stink and the humidity, steamed blue crabs in the air, cold cheap lager, rich bay spice.

Baltimore.

A good place to die.

But no place to rest . . .

Yet.

The Dark Man walked through the dark folds of Little Italy . . .

. . . remembering . . .

The weapon explodes a second time and to his pain-heightened senses it seems to squeeze out its bullet in slow-motion amidst the halo of fire. He can feel his denial, feel himself crying "No" again, feel himself reach for some kind of inner power to push back the metal charging for him.

When it connects, the force of it smacks him back against the base of the shelving where he'd been pushed by the first. It rips and gouges and tears through his already bloody shirt into his abdomen, a buzz saw of power ripping flesh and life with abandon and spitting out raw hunks of him onto the floor. He can feel it drilling through him, cutting through his solar plexus and his internal organs with mad indifference, chewing up what is left of his life and spitting it out.

His assailant is saying something but he cannot hear it. He realizes that his assailant has been saying things all along, accusing things, but he cannot register them . . . cannot retain them.

His only thoughts are of Amy, his wife, his beloved . . .

And how powerless he feels, how consumed with pain.

Blood blood blood . . .

He falls to the floor, blood overwhelming him, blood covering his awareness.

The deep black blood of unconsciousness amidst a final thought: Amy.

The Dark Man walked the downtown streets of Baltimore.

Past the new clean walls of Harborplace, past the Aquarium and past the bright hotels, past the moon glowing in the windows of the office buildings.

But he is not dead.

. . . not yet.

He clambers from the darkness, back to save Amy, to save his collection, to save . . . save . . .

He opens his eyes and groans . . .

And he looks into the eyes of the greatest horror of all . . .

The Dark Man walked toward the Cross Club.

He heard the beat of wings and he looked up and saw a dark form, flapping through the city canyons, above the cars and late-night activity. He followed.

And as he followed the crow, the Dark Man remembered his dream.

His dream of Edgar Allan Poe.

1

I pray to God that she may lie
Forever with unopened eye . . .
Far in the forest, dim and old,
For her may some tall vault unfold
Some tomb, which oft hath flung its black
And vampyre-winged panels back,
Fluttring triumphant o'er the palls,
Of her old family funerals.

—"Irene"
Edgar A. Poe, *To the Humane Heart*

December 8, 1811

There was some kind of bird in the winter forest.

"William," Edgar had said. "William! A bird!"

A big *bird.*

A black *bird.*

Black as the dark cellar beneath the theater where he and William would hide and play while mother rehearsed. Black as the night when all the candles were out in their boarding house and clouds moved across the stars and the moon like giant wings. Black as the suit the somber Doctor had worn when he'd come to visit Mama yesterday.

"Where?" His brother William stood up from where he'd been sitting on the porch.

"There! In the tree . . ."

But where Edgar pointed now there were only branches. Skeletal branches, clacking memories of trees once filled with green and fruit and life, now barren with December's cold.

"I don't see any bird, Edgar," said William, who'd proceeded to continue playing soldiers, not including Edgar in his game.

Now Edgar stood by a window. In the room was a nurse with one-year-old Rosalie. Standing by a bed were a number of family friends, theater people mostly. William now clung expressionless to a woman who had stayed with Mama all night.

Edgar sat by the window, fidgeting and staring out at the trees. That big bird fascinated him. With its vibrant "Caw! Caw!" and its knowing eye, its sharp beak and its powerful claws, it seemed so strange and yet so forthright. Like a mystery that answered a puzzle. He tried to keep looking for the bird because what the grownups in the room were saying troubled him, even though he didn't understand much of it, and not just because it came in strained whispers.

"She can't last much longer."

"What will become of the poor children?"

"I can't help them! I've enough of my own!"

"They'll have to be separated. Such a shame. And they seem to love each other so much!"

"The poor woman. Such talent! Such a sweet singing voice. She shall sing for Jesus himself, I think."

"She is going to a better place."

Mama, going someplace? Edgar had thought. But how could that be? She was in her nightclothes, tucked very nicely in bed. No, the adults must be very wrong, for even though he was only three years old, he well knew that if you were going someplace you got dressed up . . . and at the very least you got out of bed. But Mama had been in bed for days and days . . .

True, it wasn't like Mama at all. Mama was mostly always out of bed. Mama was an actress. A famous actress, William had declared. "She has trod the boards from Richmond to Boston!" his five-year-old brother had declared once, striking a melodramatic pose. "Sirrah, she has won even the cold hearts in New York City and Philadelphia with her dulcet tones. She is simply the best actress and singer ever."

Edgar certainly knew his mother was the most beautiful creature in the world. But his mama was the one who would hold him and put on his coat and tie his shoes and tell him it would be all right when he fell down and scraped his knee. The woman who painted her face and put on frilly outfits and danced and sang in Time Tells a Tale *or cried and swooned in the melodrama* Tekeli, *or, the* Siege of Montgatz *almost seemed someone different—and yet very wonderful nonetheless.*

A flash of wing . . .

A blur of black . . .

There . . . just on the horizon of this dismal Sunday morning. Was that the strange bird?

"I wonder if her husband knows she is ill."

"That scalawag. David Poe! No one has heard from him. Left the family last year, the drunkard."

"A terrible father."

Edgar barely remembered his father. Somewhere deep inside him were memories. Somewhere deep were feelings. However, at this moment, the possibility of a glimpse of that dark avian emissary seemed the most vital matter, not the hushed chatterings of these people hovering around Mama's bed.

Where was it?

"Edgar? Edgar, come here dear. Your dear mama wishes to speak to all her children." Edgar recognized the voice. It belonged to Fanny Allan, who had taken much interest in his family. He liked Fanny, very much. She was a sweet lady. Her husband, John, however—he was stern and disapproving and frightening. Edgar wasn't sure he liked John Allan.

"I'm trying to find the bird!" Edgar said. "I know it's out there!"

"The bird can wait, sweet child," Fanny insisted. "Your mama needs to speak to you immediately."

Edgar sighed. He got down off the chair near the windowsill and he walked toward the bed. William was already there, looking sad and confused and holding Mama's hand. Another woman held Rosalie, Edgar's infant sister, who stared at her mama with big, dark eyes and uttered no sound at all.

Edgar walked to the side of the bed and leaned against it.

"Edgar?" said a soft, wispy voice. "Edgar, is that you?"

"Yes, Mama."

He didn't like the way she sounded. Mama's voice was very feminine, but it was also a very strong soprano. This voice was but a ghost of mama's, and it rasped from her mouth as though pulled through pain.

Groaning, William Blessing woke up.

He was sweating and gasping. His sheets were wet with sweat.

"Oh dear," said the sleepy voice of his wife, Amy, turning over and placing a comforting hand on his shoulder. "That awful Poe dream again?"

"Yes," said William Blessing. "The dream. The dream about the crow . . ."

"Maybe," she said softly. "Maybe you should write a nice romance novel next."

2

Gaily bedight,
A gallant knight,
In sunshine and in shadow,
Had journeyed long,
Singing a song,
In search of Eldorado.

—Edgar A. Poe, "Eldorado"

Mick Prince kicked open the door.

Fumes from booze and dope poured out into the hallway, followed by the smell of rancid food and vomit. Drawn tattered window shades leaked morning across listless bodies still drugged by night. They sprawled across the filthy living-room rug and torn-up couch, half-comatose even with the sound of doom ringing all around them.

The big man in the long coat grabbed the nearest homeboy by the ear, yanked him up, and stuck the barrel of his semiautomatic into his mouth.

"Grimsley," Mick Prince snarled. "Where?"

Drool had been leaking down the homeboy's lips. Now his eyes bugged and he started to convulse and choke. The man in the long dark coat pulled the gun out of his mouth to let him speak.

"Dunno," said the homeboy, rank with sweat and urine.

Mick jammed the barrel down again, breaking off a tooth.

"Know."

Tears and blood flowed. "Toilet, man." Muffled. "Think I saw him headed for the john!"

Mick heard the click of a weapon. He didn't wait to check the direction. He let his reflexes bounce his gun up, pull the trigger, and spray.

The first rounds caught a long-haired white boy sleeping on the couch, who jerked awake just in time to die, two short bursts taking out fist-sized divots in his chest, kicking up skin and blood. Mick yanked the bullets up higher, catching the cowboy who'd drawn the gun. Two of the rounds went wild, smashing a pink plastic bong and an ohaus triple-beam scale on the table into pieces. The next bullet smashed into the black man's skull, drilling a neat hole and slamming out brains and red. The gun hand slew off, hammering a couple of bullets into the wall. Plaster spilled.

The three other drug-heads woke up amid rotting pizza boxes, coke pipes, discarded needles, and a fine mist of blood and bones that gentled down through the cordite-laden air. One of them wore a holster top with the butt of a gun. The others seemed unarmed.

Not that it mattered.

The man in the long dark coat redirected his weapon.

Mick Prince remembered once he'd read when the forces of the Roman Catholic Church, in the late Middle Ages, had attacked the city holding the apostate Cathars. The Pope had been asked if any mercy should be shown for any of the gnostic sect, in deference to any holiness. "Kill them all," the man of the Lord had said. "God will know his own."

That Pope was not merely a wise man, Mick Prince thought. *He was one practical pontiff.*

With practiced ease, the man casually emptied the rest of his clip into the three remaining lives. The dying men jerked and spasmed, splattering blood as if invisible hooks reached down from above and played them for spastic marionettes. When the clip was empty and the gun searing hot, a trace of smoke hung above the stilled bodies like a benediction and the drab walls, ceiling, and floor had been repainted a moist, shocking crimson.

Without pausing, the man of death reached into the deep pocket of his coat, pulled out another clip and rammed it home. He'd been hired to kill the Man in this group, and though his employers would no doubt be pleased by the carnage here and the resultant terror it would cause amongst gang leaders and drug lords, his mission was not yet completed.

Mick Prince strode toward the next room, straight and purposeful, looking for the bathroom.

Mick had spent much of his life in institutions of various sorts. All these institutions had libraries. He had read the contents of those libraries. Mostly paperbacks. If he had been much of a filmgoer, perhaps he would have thought of himself as a mercenary Clint Eastwood, grim and expressionless, performing his duty in this Wild West world. However, he far preferred to think of himself as a contemporary Parker, from the crime novels Donald E. Westlake wrote under the name Richard Stark. Parker, that cool and conscienceless pro, sleek and fast and deadly.

Here is Parker now, Mick Prince thought, *moving through bare-bones prose. Modern and hip, in a pre–Quentin Tarantino noir escapade, raising himself some money so that he can take some months off to pursue a postmodern dream. Here is Parker-plus. Hitman, professional criminal—*

Writer!

Earning enough money to hole up with his notebook computer and write hard-boiled stories of naked screaming horror.

Parker, though he killed people, was not a professional assassin. Mick Prince was. He worked mostly in the drug trade, since he found there was plenty of money to be had there. When he was a rich and famous writer, perhaps he would still do the occasional hit just to keep in practice. However, he intended to get away from it professionally as soon as possible.

Mick Prince found himself wondering how his Writer's Digest School instructor was doing with his latest piece. It had structural problems, he felt, and probably could benefit from a trimming. That it was horror wouldn't help it in the current marketplace—that's what the writer guy in Pittsburgh would probably say—but that was all Mick wanted to write lately.

He moved past a dilapidated kitchen that smelled of refrigerator rot. The stench turned toilety down the hall. He was getting close.

There was a puddle of water running into the hall from a closed door. All the adjacent rooms seemed empty, windows shut.

This had to be where Grimsley was making his stand.

,Neo-Parker—relentless, machinelike—strides through the halls, the new post-Nietzche man. The best-read man in his prison, he is able to cite chapter and verse of philosophers, poets, and pulp writers. However, now, in this Zen moment, all has been jettisoned. He is now one with the metaphorical blade-gun, one with his mission. Neo-Parker, samurai-sophisticate.

Street warrior.

His honed mind tastes of the Now and prepares for the future.

The fierce Enemy awaits.

Holding his gun up and ready, Mick Prince drew in a mantralike series of silent breaths.

Then, like a martial artist in front of an audience, he lifted his metal-soled boot and rammed it at the exact proper juncture of door knob and jamb.

The rickety wooden door splintered open.

Another kick drove it back, slamming it against the side of the wall.

Mick Prince swung his gun down immediately, about to squeeze off a short burst of bullets.

Something stopped him.

The bathroom was floored in old-fashioned black-and-white tile, half torn up. Graffiti was scrawled on the walls, the medicine cabinet mirror long since shattered, and the plumbing pipes lay exposed. A narrow window, naked of curtains, cracked, lay half open.

On a dilapidated commode sat a man in a torn T-shirt. Boxer shorts hung down around his ankles. He lay back, eyes barely open.

A rubber tourniquet was wrapped around his arm. A hypodermic needle was stuck at the juncture of his elbow. His arm was blue.

Drool dribbled from the man's lips. His breathing was shallow. He was alive. He had no firearms.

Mick Prince recognized him from the picture he'd been given.

Grimsley.

The place smelled foul.

A sudden unforeseen foreboding swarmed through the man in the long coat. There was the essential touch of *something* here. Something that reached out of cell-block nightmares.

The Other.

He'd been here.

The man on the commode lifted his head. His eyelids were so wide open they seemed to have disappeared, and the skin of the man's face had contracted so much that Mick Prince felt as though he were staring at a living skull with protruding eyeballs.

"Mick," said the Other, "the Enemy is . . . *here!* I am the Enemy!"

"No," said the man in the long dark coat.

Panic gripped. He lifted his gun and flexed his finger. The nozzle spat fire. Bullets pummeled into the man sitting on the toilet. They pushed him up like an unseen force, up and up and up, ripping him into shreds of flesh and T-shirt, shards of bone and pirouettes of blood. Still Mick Prince kept his finger tight, pumping the rounds into the body, lifting him up. A protruding eye blew out, the nose cracked inward. A few more bullets and the head exploded like a firecracker up a frog's ass. He kept firing until the clip was spent.

What was left of the drug lord's body hung for a moment as though the flesh and blood were making one more attempt to reform. Then the body slid off and thumped on the floor, splashing into the pool of blood and urine.

The man in the long coat stood in the quiet for a moment, feeling his heart thump, listening to the ratcheting of his breathing.

The Enemy.

The fucking Other!

Here in Baltimore!

He had to find him . . . Track him down . . . Destroy *him . . .*

A dark form, like a pile of soot collecting into animated smudge, alighted upon the sill of the window. A beak poked through. Wings spread, balancing. Talons gripped. The head cocked and a single eye stared at Mick Prince, assaying him with dark intelligence.

The man in the long coat gawked.

A crow!

What was a goddamned *crow* doing here?

As a boy, he'd spent time on a farm. He knew that crows were scavengers, clever carrion cowards.

The crow stared at him with one eye for a moment, looking at him as though it could see through his skin and straight into his soul. For a moment their eyes locked.

It was as though the crow was saying, *I know you!*

Mick Prince felt frozen in place. He'd read his share of books, all kinds of books. A crow was never a good omen.

"Shit!"

Just because he read things didn't mean he *believed* them.

He dropped the empty machine gun and reached into his belt for his Beretta .32 Cougar semi-automatic pistol fitted with a custom-made noise-suppresser. But even as he touched the gun-butt, the bird spread its wings and leaped.

A coil of oil black and fiery eyes, it flew right for Mick Prince's face, its talons extended.

If not for his excellent reflexes, the man in the long coat would have lost an eye. As it was a claw ripped across the top of his forehead, and tore out a clump of his long hair from its moorings in his scalp.

He pulled the gun out, flipped off the safety and fired. The silenced, hollow-point rounds made a forceful *thwip thwip* sound. Plaster fell from the ceiling, raining upon him. But the black wings flapped away, unharmed.

"Damn!"

Mick Prince chased the bird, his boots hammering in the hallway. It flew quickly through the door. Mick Prince squeezed off another round, then followed it into the living room.

The drug den was a mass of sprawled dead bodies and a floor soaked in blood. At first the man in the long coat thought that the crow had gone. But then, as though to say, "Here I am!" it jumped up on the couch and stared at him again, lifting its wings as though faintly ruffled but generally going about business as usual.

"Caw!" it said, and looked at Mick Prince with defiance.

His common sense told the man in the long dark coat that he should just walk away now. His reaction before had been automatic and understandable. He'd been a killing machine and the crow hopped in front of his wheels.

Now, though . . .

Now he had completed his mission and he should just leave the place. The longer he stayed, even in this bombed-out part of town, the more likely he would be caught. What he should do was just walk out the goddamn door and bang it closed and let the crow have a feast . . . Let it have its way.

Something, though . . . Something *bothered* him deeply about that creature. It was the biggest crow that Mick Prince had ever seen, and it had a strange *presence*, a creepy *otherworldliness* to it.

Worse, it had the taint of the *Other.*

The Enemy.

For as long back as Mick Prince could remember, he had been aware of the Enemy. He had felt him prowling in his dreams, in the shadows of the day, and in the twisted motives of those who had tortured him, those who had made his life so difficult. He felt as though his soul was older than his years, had tracked across the wastelands of time on some desperate pursuit, dogged by a dark and mysterious creature he had come to know as the Enemy.

An Enemy that wished to *destroy* him.

An Enemy that wished to *consume* him.

For years he had scurried away in fear. Now, though, he had a different tack. Now he was determined to search out his foe, confront him . . .

Kill him.

"Who are you?" he said.

The crow fluttered its feathers. It hopped down to the arm of the couch and pecked its beak into the air, as though attempting some arcane semaphore.

"Why aren't you a fucking *raven*?" shouted the man in the long coat. "Quoth the Raven . . . Nevermore, Lenore! Not some goddamned stinking *crow*!"

The crow waggled its tail, as though in a kind of shrug.

"You think I haven't read my Poe?" said Mick Prince. "That overrated hack! What a joke! Some Frenchies got a hold of him . . . and whacko! The Jerry Lewis of literature! Well let me tell you . . . I'm of the old school. I say that Rufus Griswold was right. Edgar Allan Poe was a worthless drunken bastard." Mick Prince tapped his chest with the end of his gun. "And when I write, I certainly don't kneel at his altar!"

"Caw!" said the crow.

It stared directly at Mick Prince, unblinking.

"Fuck you!" said Mick softly. He lifted up his gun, trained its sights carefully upon the bird. In his mind's eye he could visualize the bullet blasting into its chest, shattering the entirety of the delicate bone structure into a black and crimson Fourth of July firework. Oh, the feathers would fly, the beak would soar!

He was just putting pressure on the trigger when the man walked into the room. He was wearing baggy pants, a ripped sweatshirt, and a Baltimore Orioles cap slung on backward. In his right hand was a Walther PPK.

"Mutha fu—"

Without a thought, Mick Prince shot him twice. Flowers of blood bloomed from the T-shirt. The man hobbled back two steps, then stumbled over a body, his arms spinning as if to lift him away from his impending death. Mick Prince shot him again and the man's head was nearly torn in half. Brains and blood made a rough new wallpaper.

Wings spread and flapped.

The man in the long coat whipped his attention back.

The crow flew toward the hallway.

Mick Prince fired at it, but the bullet went wide, smashing into a window.

The bird wheeled around, swinging back, keeping a jagged flight path. It dove down toward Mick Prince, then at the last moment swung away.

The crow lighted on the windowsill. It swung around and looked directly at the man in the long coat.

Something in the crow's gaze stopped Mick Prince from firing. There was something so *intense*, so *riveting* about that gaze—

He wasn't sure if it was the wind or if the plumbing was responsible. Certainly it was not the bird, because crows could not speak . . .

However, in truth, the thing's dark, sharp beak moved.

Not now, said the wind or the plumbing. *Not yet. Soon!*

And then the bird turned and spread its wings.

"No!" cried Mick Prince.

He lifted the gun and fired.

But the crow was gone.

Mick Prince ran to the window, shrieking.

"No, damn you! Come back!"

But when he stuck his head out, the crow was just a speck on the horizon above the spectral, twisted city, beneath a sky the color of a fresh bruise.

3

Once upon a midnight dreary, while I pondered,
weak and weary,
Over many a quaint and curious volume of forgotten
lore—
While I nodded, nearly napping, suddenly there
came a tapping,
As of some one gently rapping, rapping at my
chamber door.
" 'Tis some visiter," I muttered, "tapping at my
chamber door—
Only this and nothing more."

—Edgar A. Poe, *The Raven*

There was something on the roof.

Something big and noisy, and very, very annoying.

William Blessing's writing study was on the fourth floor of his large downtown Baltimore townhouse. Late at night, when he was at work on his new novel, *Objects Dark and All Aglow,* for Knopf Publishers, he'd been hearing something strange on the small roof.

. . . *clacking* . . .

. . . *scraping* . . .

. . . *beating* . . .

A bird? he had wondered, looking up from his computer keyboard. Had some bird made its nest up there? It was indeed springtime, and very much spawning time for the little creatures. Blessing wished them no ill. In fact, he liked the idea of birds in the city. Robins, cardinals, jays, sparrows—all were important to nature amongst the urban landscape.

Even pigeons and gulls, for goodness sake! If there was, in fact, one thing that was sincerely wrong with his beloved Baltimore in his estimation, it was the lack of trees. Often as not, when the ugly, tiny townhouses were built cheek-to-jowl in grimmer eras of the Charm City's history, trees had simply been razed, giving many neighborhoods a bleak, cheap look. Fortunately, programs had been implemented to return trees to these blighted areas and it wasn't as though Baltimore didn't have trees. Its huge parks were lush with oak and pine and cypress, the wealth of green that was Maryland's treasure that had been so terribly ransacked by industry over its history. Blessing felt fortunate indeed, not merely for the huge 1890s townhouse he owned, or for the fact that it was next to a brilliant city park, but that the entire neighborhood was filled with great, oak trees, friendly old sentinels against urban blight, a stand of nature as his front yard.

A bird then, but by its sounds an awfully *big* bird.

Now, Blessing put his galleys down and looked up on the roof.

Skitter.

Flutter.

Crackle.

Damn! How annoying. He had hoped to have a pleasant morning, and the weather had cooperated grandly, giving him one of those gorgeous spring days with low humidity, a gentle breeze, low pollen, and warm sun, gently touched with stately piles of cumulus, serene in cerulean sky.

Amy was off to Saturday classes and that new graduate student wasn't due until later this afternoon. Stephen King had messengered down his new book, hoping not just for a good review from a fellow writer but perhaps, "a caustic blurb to release some of the burden of selling too many copies from my tired back." Well, that wasn't going to be possible, because the book, a real departure for King, was truly and strikingly fine, and deserved a rave review, which Blessing hoped to wrangle space for in the *New York Times Book Review.* Worst of all, it was an accursed page-turner, and although Blessing certainly had plenty of other things to do, nothing seemed so urgent now as to get to the final page of the galleys.

Atop the highest part of the townhouse, as part of the refurbishing that Blessing himself had done on the house after the success of his third dark fantasy novel *Black Soul Descending,* had been built a balcony of sorts, which connected to a small cupola, done in grand nineteenth-century Gothic style. Together with the gables the old house already sported, this created a wonderful little retreat to take tea or beer with his friends and colleagues and view the rooftops of Old Baltimore. In fact, you could see the delightful Victorian buildings comprising the better part of Johns Hopkins University, where Blessing was a full professor in the English department. Here on this balcony, on this splendid day, he had taken his Kenyan coffee, white with fresh milk, his toast and marmalade, and had intended to have a relaxing and entrancing total immersion into Stephen King land.

Scrabble.

Scutter.

Scrape.

On principle, Blessing approved of birds.

But on the other hand, a bird making all this dreadful noise when he was trying to write or read . . .

Well, that was another matter.

He sighed, got out of his chair, and went up to the space where seasoned, carpentered wood became shingles, and the roof angled up to the several chimney pots and enclosures that lined the top of the roof. Leaning on a post, he craned his head to catch a glimpse of whatever was up there. *Must be on the other side,* he thought. He couldn't even see a hint of twigs or brambles or whatever birds used to build their nests with these days. It was tempting to just give up his place on the rooftop, go down to his library, put on some Bach or Chopin and, enclosed in a chamber of music, read. However, he intended to have a party here next week and this area was a beloved place for friends to cluster. Having a bird on the roof might or might not be a bad thing, but certainly if there *was* a bird, he'd want to be able to lecture folk about it. Besides having a fine intellect and wide knowledge on a large variety of subjects, William Blessing prided himself on his *curiosity.* He enjoyed talking at length on the wonderful oddities, academic and otherwise, that curiosity uncovered. No doubt Lincoln Holmes would be at the party and, should this bird make noise, he'd ask what sort of creature would have the effrontery to nest atop the great William Blessing's house. Blessing, without a detailed answer, simply wouldn't be Blessing, and not only would his friends be worried, but his more dangerous and jealous colleagues would whisper behind his back. "Oh, dear. Poor Bill is losing his edge!"

Blessing knew birds. He would only need a glimpse of this one to tell what kind it was. Also, if it were merely *starting* a nest, it could be chased away. Blessing surely didn't wish to chase it from eggs or babies if that was the case; but the sooner he knew what was up, the better.

Although he was forty-seven years old, he kept in relatively good shape and was able to easily clamber over the fence and then up the crease in the roof centered by an aluminum gutter. The shingles were fairly new and gritty, and the grade, though steep, was not prohibitive to climbing. He was careful though, and occasionally leaned over to steady himself on the rough shingles.

At the top of the roof, he hoisted a leg over to the other side of the arch and straddled the central point, lifting himself up to a stand. From here he could see all the way down to Camden Yards where the Baltimore Orioles played, to the large office buildings and hotels of downtown, clustered around the central point of Baltimore's renaissance in the seventies and eighties: the Inner Harbor. Mayor Schaefer had dredged the thing, then hired an architect to give it just the right look—and then proceeded to create a huge tourist attraction and centerpiece for a run-down and exhausted city. Blessing could see the restaurants of Little Italy off to the east, the Aquarium and, on the other side of the water, the Science Museum. It being Saturday, dozens of paddle boats were inching around in the blue-gray, below the masts of the old colonial warship, the U.S.S. *Constellation,* restored and polished and ready for Kodak flashes and the scampering of children's tennis shoes.

There was a puff of breeze, the smell of cherry blossoms and honeysuckle and tar. Blessing looked down to the street. The house was seventy-one feet tall, six stories including attic and roof; and while this did not sound that high, when actually staring down from the top onto the hard concrete of the sidewalk, it seemed a great height indeed.

Blessing suddenly experienced a wave of vertigo. He felt dizzy and had to crouch down to steady himself. He took a deep breath. *Maybe this wasn't such a good idea after all,* he thought. Why had he even bothered? That's what money was for: to let other people risk their necks. Get a handyman to come on up here and take a look. Experienced roof people with a decent sense of balance.

However, the dizziness passed.

Well, he told himself. *As long as I'm up here . . .*

Just ahead reared the chimney, a brave, old, brick thing with the faded original ceramic, red chimney pots, proudly tilted against the elements. And on the other side, a rustle, a clatter, a scraping.

Blessing inched forward. If he could get a little bit closer, he could peer around the chimney and get a look. At that point he would know whether or not there was a nest. If there wasn't and it was just a bird perched there for a bit, or even in the beginnings of a nest, he could scare it off immediately and be done with all this. He wouldn't even have to call the handyman and he could proudly tell Amy of his valiant exploits.

He reached the chimney. It smelled of soot and ash. Blessing still couldn't see a thing around the side of the chimney base. It was as though the damned bird had intentionally occluded itself from view.

If he could just poke his nose around the chimney, there was no way the bird would be able to hide itself. At the very least he'd be able to see the twigs and whatnot of a bird's nest and that would be all he needed to make a judgment. He could creep back down and finish the Stephen King book knowing exactly what was going on.

Suddenly, in his mind, a picture flashed: Stephen himself through a fish-eye lens, peering into his life, black horn-rimmed glasses huge.

Don't go in the cellar, Bill!

"I'm on the roof, dammit." Blessing laughed through gritted teeth. "And life is not a horror movie!"

Using the crevices in the masonry of the chimney, he pulled himself slowly up toward another stand.

Peripherally, he noticed someone walking up the sidewalk. There was a chuff, chuff, chuff of feet mounting steps.

And then an angry clang, clang, clang of the doorbell.

Blast it! thought Blessing. *Who could that be?*

Distracted, he reached to the top of the chimney for the topmost brick, not noticing that years of rain, wind, snow, and sleet had eroded it.

Blessing gripped it, pulled on it to regain his balance.

Ke-rack.

With a sickening crumble, the brick gave way.

Blessing found himself hanging in the air, wildly windmilling. He let go of the half brick and it tumbled down the side of the roof, clanking off the gutter and bashing into the top of the gas barbecue before falling off the edge into the backyard garden.

William Blessing fell the other way.

He made a desperate reach for the tin top of the roof with his right hand. Missed. His body pounded hard onto the shingles, and bounced. And he began to slide. The angle was even steeper than the side he had scaled and he well knew that there was precious little hope that the flimsy aluminum gutter that ridged the edge would hold his weight, even if he could grab it.

With all his strength, he kicked upward with his legs. His Rockports caught the rough shingles at a sufficient angle to cause friction and a temporary stop to his nasty plummet.

His left hand flung out and snagged the edge of the top aluminum strip. His left Rockport skittered off the shingle, and the fall yanked at his left arm hard, but he managed to stop his fall at the last moment.

Blessing gripped with all his might, realizing that the fall had pounded much of his breath out of him. He managed to take in a ragged gasp even as he swung up with his right hand to grab hold of the edge. His first effort failed—but the second hooked onto the aluminum firmly.

Blessing hung on, not moving for a few moments, trying to regain his breath and his strength. Once that was accomplished, he knew he could use his feet *(Thank God for Rockports—good ridged walking shoes. Yes!)* and his jeans to edge on up. Then he could wrap his arms over the edge and get a decent hold onto the roof. Then he could start edging his way back down to the balcony—not exactly a study in gymnastic competence, but at least assured of a platform of wood to prevent him from falling seventy feet.

However, just as Blessing was beginning to get his wind back and start thinking about making the effort, there was a flutter and flap.

And a "caw."

Startled, he looked toward the chimney.

From behind it emerged the largest bird that William Blessing had ever seen in the wild.

His first impression was simply of black, as though some piece had been cut out of the darkness of last night, and been hidden behind the chimney until now. Its wingspan must have been at least a yard or more as it flapped toward him. It settled on the top of the roof, just inches from his fingers, and it cocked its head at him, as though to inspect him at close quarters.

A crow.

Blessing could see that it was a crow, of the sort he would normally see winging over Maryland horse farms or perched on telephone wires in the country, scanning the fields for prey—but not in the center of town.

This close, Blessing could see that it was not all black. Its feet were gray, its talons were white, and its eyes were crimson.

"Shoo!" said Blessing. "Come on! Shoo!"

Instead of winging away however, it sidled closer, its sharp talons scratching along aluminum.

It opened its sharp beak and stared down at Blessing as it stepped toward his hands.

4

But see, amid the mimic rout,
A crawling shape intrude!
A blood-red thing that writhes from out
The scenic solitude!
It writhes!—it writhes!—with mortal pangs
The mimes become its food,
And the seraphs sob at vermin fangs
In human gore imbued.

—Edgar A. Poe, "The Conqueror Worm"

When Baxter Brittle awoke at seven minutes after noon, he found himself half-covered in blood that was not his own.

The blood was sticky and sweet smelling. It clung to his long hair like a gypsy curse. The pain of his hangover doubled as he sat looking at his hands, dazed, wondering what the hell had happened. It couldn't be real blood, he knew. Had they been spraying around some sort of homemade Halloween dye in imitation of an Insane Clown Posse concert?

Droning in the background of the "Dungeon," the salon in Le Salon des Gothiques, were the ominous sounds of Lustmord. *Fuck me,* thought Baxter. *I gotta stop putting those damned CDs on repeat.* The unnerving vibrations echoed throughout the dim recesses of the basement. Although he'd made every effort to clean the place up and decorate it after inheriting the building from his parents *(I told them they needed new tires),* and despite the gang burning incense and censer pots like crazy, the place still smelled of fungus and damp and Baltimore. Feathers and posters and chains and swords and daggers and swaths of white muslin hung everywhere, and huge candles (the next best thing to torches!)

burned in sconces, giving the area great atmosphere and depth. Hallways led to a mysterious, unfinished subbasement, an abandoned relic from the last days of Prohibition. But the ceiling was too damned low, and the altar was something out of a shot-on-video horror movie. *Garish and wretched, really, all of it,* Baxter thought. If he could ever scrape together a decent amount of cash, he'd either do this den up right—or just move away and ditch the whole Goth business. Just retire to the south of France, drink red wine, eat snails and truffles, and listen to Chopin.

He groaned and got to his knees. He was wearing his long coat, silken black on the outside, silken red on the inside. Part of his pain wasn't the throbbing hangover but from the inside of his mouth. He pulled out faux fangs and placed them on a nearby antique mahjong table he'd bought at Goodwill. *Damn!* He didn't remember putting in his Drac chops last night.

On the other hand, he didn't remember a whole lot of anything. Barney and Wilhemina had taken over the bar about nine. He'd hung around with some of the early arrivals of the gang at one of the back tables. It had been "old school" Goth night, with lots of Bauhaus, The Cure, Sisters of Mercy, and The Mission making up the spin list. He was competing with Orpheus and Hepburns, two club bars uncomfortably close by, for the city's meager Goth crowd, which included everyone from curious students and RenFest Celtic fans to confused metal-heads and old punkers. His two main DJs also worked local music shops, Modern Music and Soundgarden, and were beginning to build a following, though it was the weekend New Wave and Disco nights that did the most business.

He recalled vaguely drinking something green with streaks of blue—some sort of melon shooter, doubtless. Oh, right—there was this newbie there—a cute teenager with so much mascara and eye shadow she looked like some Gothic raccoon. Blond dye job with straggly spiked hair, torn Siouxsie and the Banshees T-shirt held together with safety pins. Obviously under eighteen, but she was so damned cute, he didn't have her carded and booted. In fact, when the gang adjourned downstairs for a meeting of the Salon, he'd instructed Baron DeBaskerville to make sure she came along. However, this was the point where memory began to shred into smoke, mirrors, throbbing electric guitars, and sonorous chants.

The rest . . .

The rest was darkness.

Baxter Brittle hoisted himself up. Damn! He had to open the bar. Hung over or not, he pulled the Saturday afternoon shift, and if he didn't let the daytime regulars in, they might switch to one of the other myriad bars near the Little Italy area of Baltimore. This was not a good cash flow time for that to happen. No, not at all.

Baxter's actual living quarters were above the bar. (The gang called the Dungeon the "Dying Quarters.") Baxter would have to take his shower there. But there was a laundry sink off in the corner, so he went over and splashed himself with some cold, brackish water. His head was pounding. His eyes were bleary. He went back to the mahjong table, and stared down hopefully. Yeah! Sure enough, there was a little vial. Just enough for a snort.

The single skinny line through a plastic straw cleared his head a little. He just wanted to get out of this hole for right now, deal with the spilled "blood" or whatever it was later. But there was a bottle of good French Napoleon brandy that should be in the Cabinet of Dr. Caligari by the Chamber of Naked Horrors altar and a swig would surely ease some of the claws digging into his neocortex. He struggled over to it, stopping a moment to put a sock in Mr. Lustmord's cavernous rumblings (oh, sweet, sweet silence) and opened the fake-walnut cabinet door. Sure enough, there was the bottle. Close to empty, but he didn't need a lot. He grabbed the bottle by the neck, pulled out the stopper, and tilted it back.

Fire and condensed wine.

The liquid burned down his throat, exploding into gentler warmth in his stomach. He could feel the raw alcohol spread its feathery fingers of comfort through his torso and up to his head, easing the throbbing pain somewhat. The comfort was so great, that he swallowed another gulp. Less impact, but still . . .

He put the bottle back, weaved around, a little unsteadily, and started back across the rug in front of the cheesy grade Z movie altar and . . .

. . . almost tripped over the body there.

It was a naked woman.

He hadn't seen her before, because she was half under the table holding sacramental dishes, goblets, and all that black magic gobbledegook. She was stretched out, spikey-haired head poking out like a bit of fading flesh amidst ceremonies of the grave.

"Oh, come *on,*" said Baxter Brittle. "Hey! You're not supposed to be here . . ." God, he could get in a lot of trouble for this! "Look, wake up!"

He reached down haltingly and pulled her over toward him.

She flopped back.

The mascara and makeup looked as though it had melted down her cheeks and temples, and her red lips looked like a pile of mashed cherries.

She no longer looked like a sexy punk-tart.

She looked like a dead little girl.

From between her small, banal breasts jutted a silver-handled blade. Even through his stunned horror, Baxter recognized it as one of the gang's ceremonial knives.

It too had come from the grade Z movie, but its origins had apparently been, like many of that movie's props, through some of the less reputable downtown Baltimore pawnshops. Before, it was one of the few items down here that Baxter had taken genuine pride in. Some of the Gothiques and he would play for hours at speculating on the true origins of some of their ghoulish, macabre collection. The pearl-and-gold-handled knife had been one of their favorites. It was from the torture chambers of Torquemada's Spanish Inquisition, surely! No—it had once belonged to one of the soldiers of Vlad the Impaler of Transylvania, fighting off the barbarian hordes! No—it was stolen from an old Buddhist Monastery of Mysteries in Nepal!

Now, though, it was just a piece of sharp metal stuck into a naked girl.

There was blood everywhere.

This, Baxter Brittle realized, was where the stuff on him had come from.

Beyond here, in fact, was a large pool, already congealing.

Hoping against hope, woozily, Baxter felt for a pulse in the neck.

Nothing but cold, dead flesh.

He drew his fingers away as though he had touched something hot. His head buzzed and for a moment, he felt faint. He staggered a bit and had to fall against the table. A goblet fell over, and thick, cold blood oozed out onto a pentacle emblem on the cloth there.

He swung around to the cabinet, grabbed the bottle of Napoleon brandy, and swallowed the last few ounces of the stuff. He let it drop from his fingers, and then he staggered away from the scene of blood, death, and more blood.

There had to be better ways of waking up.

5

And the silken, sad, uncertain rustling of each purple curtain
Thrilled me—filled me with fantastic terrors never felt before;
So that now, to still the beating of my heart, I stood repeating,
" 'Tis some visiter entreating entrance at my chamber door—
Some late visiter entreating entrance at my chamber door;—
This it is and nothing more."

—Edgar A. Poe, *The Raven*

Donald Marquette leaned against the doorbell for the third time.

He could hear the buzzing sound going through the house again. Loud enough, he thought, to wake the dead. So where was Professor William Blessing, anyway? He said he'd be available at noon and here it was . . .

Donald checked his watch.

Twelve oh seven!

Marquette felt nervous. He'd made sure he'd gotten there on time. Although he'd corresponded with Blessing and spoken to him on the phone, he'd never actually *met* him in person and he wanted to make a *good* first impression and lead this literary and educational journey off on the right foot with William Blessing, famous writer; William Blessing, brilliant scholar; William Blessing, Edgar Allan Poe expert; William Blessing, "the only truly fine writer and academic entering the fields of popular fiction" according to no less an authority than *The New Yorker* and . . . and . . .

"You're no good!" he seemed to hear his father say. "Worthless! All you do is stay in the stinking cellar and read. God! I don't think you're my son at all! You're just . . . just a mistake!"

And when his father said that, he'd wanted to kill him.

When bad things happened in horror stories, often Donald would imagine them happening to his father.

Marquette took a moment to steady himself on the railing. He realized his pulse was rising and that his blood pressure was probably going nuts. This was the moment he'd been anticipating for months and months, and he really was letting things get out of hand, really. *Steady, guy. Twenty-eight years old is too young an age to blow out a heart valve. So you're excited . . . Blessing gets his pants on one leg at a time, and probably forgets to put the toilet seat down like all men. So he's brilliant! So he could be the ticket to literary fame, fortune, and academic majesty for a humble corn-fed boy from Dubuque, Iowa! So you worship his novels, his short stories, his criticism, and his great "History of the Gothic Tradition from* Castle of Otranto *to Stephen King and Beyond"! He said he was really looking forward to working with you, and meeting you and that he'd take you for a drink (a drink!) this afternoon to Fells Point, where Edgar A. Poe himself had fallen flat on his frothing face and died.*

Donald Marquette was a tall, gangly young man who looked as though he might be more at home taking the road from Iowa to Congress with Jimmy Stewart's Mr. Smith. He had long, dark hair that he tied in the back with a bit of rawhide strap and deeply earnest eyes above a sensitive nose and thin Midwestern lips. His ears were a little too large for his head, and his hairstyle emphasized this, making them appear to stick out rather like Howdy Doody's. Marquette was grateful when his youthful freckles had passed on a couple of years ago. He wore a mustache and dark, wire-rimmed eyeglasses to counteract his distinctly innocent look and cultivate a more serious literary air. Neither a pipe nor cigarettes had appealed to him much; however, he'd long since abandoned his teenage habit of chewing bubble gum (and started watching his weight) from his first fantasy convention onward.

Now he stood on this lovely Baltimore avenue, lined with freshly bloomed tulips, bushes, and other aromatic vegetation—a block of buildings steeped in the colors of history that his hometown so sorely lacked. A breeze played with his hair and butterflies fluttered in his stomach and bees buzzed amongst dandelions in the rich green grass that bordered the old, red brick.

A twig suddenly dropped onto the steps beside where he stood.

Then, a piece of shingle fluttered down, just missing his head by a breath.

He looked up, shielding his eyes from the sun.

Nothing more descended.

His eyes lighted on his Timex, which now declared, digitally, twelve oh nine and . . .

Oh, jeez.

Noon had been the original time. Blessing had suggested that he make it at one instead.

And he'd totally blanked out on that.

Man, what a gaffe!

He was about to turn and skedaddle, get the hell out of there before Blessing (probably wearing a towel and dripping) scowled out of a window, yelling down, "Marquette, you're too damned early. Go back to the sticks, you stupid hick."

However, before he could even get one step down and away from the landing, the door opened.

"Yes?"

Donald turned around.

He recognized the man standing at the door immediately from the book-jacket photos. However, William Blessing looked a good deal more professional and focused in those pictures. Now, his hair was ruffled, his flannel shirt was untucked, and he looked . . . well, *askew* both mentally and physically. There was a bit of dead leaf on his shoulder. He was about five foot ten and, though not overweight, he clearly didn't exercise much more than his walking to school, which he was so proud of. He had light-colored eyes and a bland, even face—but even now, in his disarray, Donald could see he was a mild, friendly sort. Not angry at all. This put him at ease a bit. Marquette swung around and offered his hand.

"I just realized . . . I'm early! I'm Donald Marquette and I'll come back later in the afternoon and I'm really, really sorry to disturb you and—"

"Oh, Donald!" said Blessing. The puzzled frown became a light smile. He pushed the door open and reached out an open hand. "You are a bit early, but that's all right. Actually I'm glad of company. I'm not much good for anything else."

Donald happily grabbed the hand and pumped it. The handshake was firm and heartening, and suddenly Donald felt as though a burden had lifted from his heart.

"Are you all right, Mr. Blessing?"

"Donald . . . please . . . I told you. Call me 'Bill.' I know I'm going to be your graduate advisor . . . but we're also fellow authors, eh? Colleagues." Blessing pronounced "author" with satiric self-importance. "And we're going drinking this afternoon. God knows I could do with a beer pretty damned soon. Come in, come in, though. Would you like some coffee? Tea? I've got a pot of Kenya mix on and I'm going to pour myself a bracing cup of hot joe. Oh . . . I'll be all right. Just a bit shaken up. Come on up to the kitchen, Donald. Come right this way."

Donald found himself being led into the foyer. He'd been impressed by the house from the outside, with its newly painted front door and beautiful flower boxes and its red Victorian brick. Inside, though, it was something out of *House Beautiful.* The townhouse immediately gave the impression not so much of wealth, but *taste.* It was decorated with immaculate antiques. Fine art hung on the walls, and beautiful Oriental rugs covered gorgeously refurbished wood floors. Silver fixtures and mirrors sparkled, and, past the front parlor, in a large dining room was a chandelier that glittered above a large, highly polished waxed table. Everything smelled of Endust and carpet cleaner and furniture polish—all in all, a far cry from the drab and funky houses that Donald had lived in back in Dubuque.

"Really . . . nice place!" he found himself saying.

"Thanks. Wife keeps it shipshape . . . And I must say, before my ten-year overnight success, I really couldn't afford the army of housekeepers we put to work. Too much for me to take care of, I'll tell you. So, would you like some coffee as well?"

"Sure. Thanks."

Blessing led him back to the large modern kitchen. He pulled open a cabinet and got out a couple of fresh mugs, then poured coffee from a Braun coffeemaker sitting on the tiled sideboard.

"Milk? Sugar?"

"Just milk."

"Yep. That's the way I take it. Great minds think alike. I'll tell you, though, Donald. Before the wife moved in, didn't have all these modern appliances. I had the house and lots of the antiques but I never bothered to put them all together into a semblance of order. Amy's first project was to do the full Martha Stewart, get it all fixed up into the way you see it. Impresses other women, I suppose, and it's damned nice and convenient. But I kind of miss the scattered way it used to be. Had a kind of . . . individualistic flavor before, you know what I mean?"

"Well, being not exactly wealthy, I've lived in my share of individualistic dwellings."

"Ha! Well said, well said! But Donald, don't ever tell that to Amy. She despairs of my office, which is a disaster . . . But it's my territory and I won't let her in. Am I bad for that?"

"I think the psychological term is 'boundaries,' . . . uhm . . . Bill."

"Oh. Psychobabble terms! Love them! I've got a psychobabble talk show hostess in my new book." Blessing grinned. "Gets hung by a phone cord and electrocuted. And who says my popular fiction doesn't have literary value!"

Donald found himself laughing. He felt much more at ease. Plus, the coffee was absolutely delicious. Generally, he was an instant-coffee drinker who only took the stuff to jolt him awake in the morning, or as a stimulant while he was writing, a time when he often let his cup go cold and nasty. This coffee, though, was rich and smooth with a complex and excellent taste.

"Do all bestselling writers brew super coffee?" he asked.

"No, that's not a qualification, but thanks anyway. I like it. And God, I need it now—and maybe with something more in it. Would you come round this way?"

Blessing jerked his head and then proceeded to go through the kitchen toward the dining room. At the far end of this very large room replete with antique walnut sideboard, an amazing French-style table capable of seating twelve, was a full wet bar, obviously designed to fit exactly into the formal qualities of the room. Blessing clunked his cup of coffee onto the tabletop and opened a cabinet. The array of bottles inside could have stocked a decent-sized cocktail establishment. Blessing plucked one of them out and swung round toward his coffee, displaying it for his guest. "Just a little Irish whiskey, Donald. Bushmills. Care for a squeak of blarney?"

"Uhm . . . no . . . I'll have some beers with you, but I don't drink the hard stuff."

"Good for you." Blessing unscrewed the top and poured himself a healthy dollop, filling his large mug to the brim. "I generally don't drink this early, but I have to tell you, Donald, my nerves need to be numbed down a bit."

Blessing took a sip, smacked his lips, shivered. He looked, thought Donald, like someone who . . . well, someone who'd just had some kind of spectral visitation.

"Are you all right?" That would explain his slightly disheveled appearance.

"I will be in about one more gulp," said Blessing. He lifted the cup again, drank, put it down. "There. You know, you'd think an expert on Poe would stay away from whiskey." The man looked a bit haunted and distracted. But then he focused up again and looked at Donald Marquette. "There was this crow up on the roof."

"A crow? Not a raven?" said Donald.

"No. A genuine farmyard denizen . . . The sort scarecrows are for, only lots bigger. Well, I was up on the balcony, taking in a little of this spring sun and reading the galleys of the new Stephen King book, when I hear something up near the chimney. So me, being a total dope . . . Well, I climbed up to have a look. I slipped, and had to grab onto the top or I would have come tumbling down . . . maybe on you!" He chuckled, took another sip of his Irish coffee.

The bit of shingle, thought Donald.

"So while I'm hanging there, this crow hops out and he looks at me. Big red eyes, too. Damned scary thing! He hops over to my hands and for a minute I think, Jesus! He's going to peck my fingers with that sharp beak of his."

"Yikes!"

"Well, I think stronger words were going through my head at the time! But that crow . . . he looked me over. He *examined* me. It was like he was making sure that I was somebody. He looked . . . intelligent. He just stared at me for a few moments . . . and those moments seemed like an eternity. Then he gave a caw, spread his wings, and just flapped off. I still don't know if there's a nest or anything up there. I guess I'll get someone to go up there and check.

"But not me," concluded Blessing. "I'll tell you. Not me!"

After another drink of coffee there was a moment of silence while Blessing examined him.

The professor suddenly smiled. "Oh no, Donald. No roof climbing for you. That's not a part of the deal here." He put a fatherly hand on his shoulder and patted. "You're here as my graduate student assistant. And sub-anthologist!"

Blessing's forefinger smote the air with mock-authority.

"You're not here to chase avians marauding from my gables."

"I guess that's a relief. But if that's part of what it takes to work with a man like you . . ." said Donald. "I'd do it!"

"No, no, you just read and write and research. A little grim clerical work is about all that's going to get your hands dirty. By the way, I take it you're all settled into your new digs?"

"Yes sir. The boardinghouse you got for me is just fine!"

"I thought you'd like it. Graduate students should have someone to cook and clean for them. The ones I've had who have to do daily nuisance chores too much . . . Well, they just don't get the time they need. And with you writing your novel . . . And maybe teaching an undergraduate class! No, no, Mrs. MacDonalds's is the place. And within walking distance of the university—and here as well!"

"I really appreciate you finding it for me."

"Good, good. Now then. I'm going to pour myself a little more downer and splash on a little more upper . . . and then we'll go up and I'll give you the cook's tour."

"You'll show me where I'll be working?"

"Your place at the oars of this fine galleon, cutting its way across the choppy seas of literature? Why, yes. All my slaves have their own little cubicles in the computer division!"

Blessing immediately laughed at Donald's expression. "Just joking of course. I've got a few students I hire part-time to do files, secretarial work, and such. Amy does quite a bit as well. As they say, the writing business can certainly generate a great deal of paperwork."

"Why, yes sir!" said Donald. "You must employ a full-time helper for your fan mail alone!"

Blessing chuckled good-naturedly. "Ah, yes. The man knows his way around good, old-fashioned flattery. Always a rather exceptional quality. Come, come, lad!" Blessing cocked an eyebrow. "Enter through the gates of Edgar Allan Poe and William Blessing. Abandon all hope, ye who enter here!"

Eagerly, Donald followed, feeling very much a most fortunate fellow indeed.

Who would have known that those short stories he'd written in that creative writing class in college would have brought him *here*! He'd always loved literature, whether from the racks of used bookstores or the stacks in libraries. Being a voracious reader and enthusiast for the thrills and purposes of fiction, it was natural that he'd try to do something with it in his life. This led him toward a degree in English at Iowa University, with a side degree in education so he'd be able to teach. After college he'd gotten a job with the Dubuque school system, teaching high school English. Nights he worked on a masters degree in American literature. However, he also worked on a hobby that had started to pay: writing short stories. He'd written some mystery and science fiction, but he found his natural bent toward the horror genre. Most of his stories had appeared in smaller journals such as *Cemetery Dance, Bones of the Children, Frights* and other semi-professional magazines (several, like *Inquities* and *Midnight Graphitti,* now out of business). However, a few of his stories had made it into the *Magazine of Fantasy and Science Fiction* and other higher-paying markets (including a short-short in *Rage*, his first men's magazine sale). He'd even written one of the books in the perennial horror line based on the popular Gothic TV series, *Dark Sunset.* Unfortunately, it had been severely rewritten by the in-house editor of the series, while his own serious novel had fallen victim to the industry-wide retrenchment in mid-list category fiction. Translation: it had never sold because it wasn't "high-concept" enough and he wasn't a name-brand writer. *At least not yet,* he'd tell himself.

His masters thesis had been called "William Blessing and American

Gothic." He'd been thrilled when Blessing had actually answered the questions he'd sent in a letter. When Blessing had received the final thesis, he'd been so pleased with the results that he'd helped get it published as a monograph by a small university press. They'd stayed in contact through e-mail, and when Donald had started wondering whether he should get a doctorate, Blessing had been more than supportive. Having read and admired not just Donald Marquette's critical efforts but his short stories as well, Blessing suggested that he come to Johns Hopkins to get his doctorate and had arranged for financial help, including a scholarship. Blessing was also assembling a huge collection of Gothic fiction in three volumes: one from North American writers, one from British writers, and one from writers from the rest of the world. In addition to other editing work, Blessing thought that Donald might be interested in helping to assemble these volumes with him.

Naturally, Donald had jumped at the chance.

Teaching on a high school level was getting to be a drag. Getting a Ph.D. from a prestigious school like Johns Hopkins would make it possible to get a position as an assistant professor at a university somewhere. Also, being associated with a person on the level of Blessing, both academically and in terms of popular fiction, could do nothing but good things for his writing career.

With Blessing's help, he was accepted at the Baltimore university. He'd arrived before the beginning of the next school year in order to get settled and start working seriously with Blessing on the ambitious multivolume series.

Now, the notion of seeing Blessing's famous library with its amazing collection of the memorabilia, not merely of Edgar Allan Poe but of many other writers in the Gothic tradition, gave Donald a thrilling buzz.

Except for this strange business with that bird, it looked as though it was going to be a banner day, he thought. Blessing, though obviously troubled by the crow incident (and, naturally, by his brush with death) was a genuinely fine fellow and, although Donald was still a little nervous, Blessing's politeness and enthusiastic reception made him feel very good indeed.

What treats awaited him upstairs!

Blessing made a quick detour back to his bar.

"Come, come, then," said Blessing, pouring another drop of whiskey into his cup, this time without diluting it with first-rate coffee. He smoothed back his hair and pointed upward. There was a manic gleam in his eye. Clearly he relished showing off his home and his treasures—particularly to someone like Donald Marquette, who would appreciate them. "Let's go up to the lab and see what's on the slab."

"Lots of books, I'd imagine," said Donald.

As they passed into the hallway, approaching the staircase, the door opened.

"Ah! It's the wife!" said Blessing. He quickly downed the whiskey and wiped his mouth on his sleeve. He handed the mug over to Donald. "Do me a favor and hide the evidence, eh?" He pulled out a cough drop from his pocket, unwrapped the paper, and popped it in his mouth.

"Okay," said Donald. He thought for a moment and then walked back to the kitchen. He went to the sink and ran the hot water, washing out the dregs of the whiskey.

When he turned the water off, he heard voices from the other room: A man's. A woman's.

"I'm just glad you're all right!"

"I'll tell you one thing. No one's getting me up on that roof again! But come on up, dear. Donald Marquette's here!"

"Terrific! I've been looking forward to meeting him!"

The woman's voice was rich, sweet, mellifluous.

Marquette stepped out of the kitchen, quickly drying his hands on his shirt, anticipating an encounter with a strong, friendly woman. Probably with a touch of gray but strongly built with a gentle, mature smile and the kind of steadiness that gave a great writer and scholar like Blessing foundation and anchor in this rough world.

"Donald! I've heard so much about you," said the woman as she saw him.

Donald Marquette blinked and stopped in his tracks.

Amy Blessing was one of the most beautiful, striking women he'd ever encountered in his life.

And she was no more than twenty-five years old.

6

Out—out are the lights—out all!
And over each quivering form,
The curtain, a funeral pall,
Comes down with the rush of a storm,
And the angels, all pallid and wan,
Uprising, unveiling, affirm
That the play is the tragedy, "Man,"
And its hero the Conqueror Worm.

—Edgar A. Poe, "Ligeia"

There was a girl with a knife in her chest in the basement.

Somehow, Baxter Brittle managed to keep his hands from shaking too much as he poured himself several ounces of good French cognac into a glass of Coke.

A very, very dead girl.

Brittle drank gratefully, allowing the carbonated varroom of alcohol to separate him just a little bit more from the problem.

The familiar environs of his bar helped him as well, the touch of the field of bottles, the smell of last night's beer and cigarette smoke in the air. Fortunately, Ed the janitor had come in early as he was paid to do and swabbed the place down after last night's bacchanalia. He and the other bartenders could pretty much take care of it through the week, but on Saturday and Sunday mornings, they needed a professional.

Now the beer cans were in a black sack along the side of the road outside, with the rest of the Friday flotsam and jetsam. *Too bad the garbage collectors don't take dead bodies,* thought Baxter.

Outside it was a beautiful spring day, unfortunately. The nice thing about his bar was that it was equipped with shutters as well as windows, so he could pretty much control the lighting. Most of the time, he kept them tightly shut. Baxter took pride in the fact that, in his bar, he could create perpetual night. Right now, in fact, those shutters were closed. The only light in the room was provided by the dim overheads, a few lights in the bar, and an EXIT light to the rear of the place. However, even *this* was too bright for Baxter Brittle's delicate condition, so he was very happy that from time to time he wore shades, inside and outside, and no one would wonder why he was wearing them now. (Not just to keep out the light, but to hide his puffy, bloodshot eyes, as well.)

He tilted back the rest of the Coke and allowed the cognac entrance into his system. Then he poured himself a little more, neat, and put it upon the bar. And surveyed his domain.

Thank God no one is here, he thought.

He knew that customers would be straggling in eventually, but every moment of peace he got he needed to get his brain back in gear.

After his intimate acquaintance with blood and death, he'd managed to hobble to his upstairs apartment. The shower had been hot and welcome, going a long way toward getting him back on the road to something at least approaching sanity. A scrubbing, some shampoo, and lots of steam had led him to a conclusion.

Whatever had happened last night, there was time to deal with it.

Enough time had passed to allow certain key memories into his brain pan, the most significant of which was the fact that the girl was from somewhere far, far away; was, in fact, a runaway, if memory served, who'd just arrived in the area and knew practically no one. The others of the Gothiques, Baxter felt, were probably having a similar morning as he had. Even if any of them remembered what had happened last night, he was pretty certain that no one would go to the police. No, he had enough on them, enough power, that they'd just come in here, check things out, talk it over. That this had not happened yet did not surprise him. Many of the gang didn't even rise before the sun set. Baltimore vampires! Just as well.

After his shower, he'd put on some fresh clothes, padlocked the cellar doors, and then opened the front door. He'd pretty much figured that if he kept the bar closed today, that would be a pretty damned suspicious thing. No, better to get through today, another Saturday-as-usual, and then deal with the horror below late tonight or tomorrow. To that end, he'd padlocked the door to the cellar. Cops could hack their way through, sure, but he'd deal with that if it happened. Right now the main thing was to put on a good face, get enough drugs and alcohol into the system to appear normal, and just get on with slinging the good old booze.

He'd just about started thinking normally, without the spike of terror and anxiety rammed up his butt, when the door opened and the man all in black walked in.

He was a tall man with a muscular build, tightly wound around a large frame. He had a V-like torso and wore tight blue jeans. An expensive coat hung down from immense shoulders all the way to the heels of his black leather boots. Long hair in loose ringlets highlighted a face that could have been something chiseled out of stone. His eyes were deep-set and looked at Baxter with an amazing intensity.

"Hey, Brittle," said the man, showing strong white, wolflike teeth in a predator's smile. "How about a nice vodka martini. Shaken, not stirred. Just like you."

The smile turned into a grin.

Baxter stared at the man.

He knew this guy.

Yeah, he *knew* this guy . . . and things started falling into place.

Last night.

This man was at the bar last night!

But had he been below?

Baxter Brittle's mind churned hard, but that was all that he could come up with. It was enough, though. There was something about this man that was important. *Vital.*

Exactly what was hard to say, but making the guy his martini would buy him some time.

Baxter grinned. "Hey, man. First customer. You get a big one, small price."

"You always pay more than money for martinis," said the man. He had a resonant precise voice, rich in irony.

Baxter forced himself to chuckle. "You bet. But oh, they can go down so smooth."

He pulled out the stainless-steel mixer, dug up some shaved ice. Mucho vodka, a whisper of vermouth. Affix top. Shake, shake, shake. Quickly, before too much ice melted, he set up one of his classic martini glasses on a napkin in front of his customer. A strainer affixed to the top of the tumbler kept the ice back as he poured the clear mixture into the glass. It was a focused ceremony, and the traditional moves gave him an odd kind of familiar comfort.

"Olive or twist?"

"Didn't Charles Dickens write that book?"

"What? Oh, yes. Right." He winked at the man, cocked a finger at the man. "Good one. I'm a bit slow this time of day."

"I would think so . . . after what happened last night." The man leaned forward on the bar, his teeth going into a Jack Nicholson sort of grin. "I'll take both the lemon twist and the olive. Please."

Baxter pulled open the condiment tray, selected a nice fat Spanish olive, and squeezed a toothpick through it and the pimento inside. Then he pared a bit of lemon zest and gingerly placed it in the drink. Cautiously, he said, "I'm not sure I know what you mean."

He studied the man's face, tried to get some memory back, but there was nothing there but a vague certainty that, in fact, the man had somehow been involved with last night.

The man picked up the toothpick, waggled it for a moment in the drink, then sucked off the olive. He chewed this methodically for a moment, then drank off a half inch of the martini, still staring at Baxter with those penetrating eyes.

"I hope you won't think of me as anything but an ally, Baxter. In fact, I want to make sure you know that I absolutely harmonize with everything in your life. Only I believe I can take you in the directions you desire."

"I'm sorry. You lost me." Baxter was frightened, but he was also annoyed. "Look, I admit I drank too much last night. I don't remember a damned thing that happened after about ten."

"But you recognize me."

"Vaguely."

"Good. That's all that's necessary. Oh—and help yourself to some of the mix if you like. On me."

"Don't mind if I do."

Baxter grabbed some normal crystal, poured himself the drink, and took a swallow. The chill bite gave him a bit of relief. "What's this about—blackmail?" He sighed. "If you're after money, I'm afraid you've got the wrong guy."

The man sipped at his martini, still intently staring at Baxter. He looked like some gigantic snake, its prey in the corner, sizing it up, getting ready for a strike.

"Oh, I think we're both after money, but that might come down the line, if we can get in synch." The man leaned back, looking relaxed. "If you woke up as I imagined you did, it was to a bit of shock, Baxter Brittle. I'd like to help you with the situation that you're in."

Baxter knocked back the rest of the drink. "I'm tired of beating around the bush. What are you proposing?"

"Ever see that movie *Pulp Fiction*?"

"Sure."

"John Travolta and Samuel L. Jackson accidentally blow a guy's brains out in the backseat. The result: one messy backseat. They take the car to Quentin Tarantino's garage. The mob boss calls in Harvey Keitel, who figures out what to do before Tarantino's wife gets back. He's called 'The Cleaner.' "

"What are you saying?"

"Just call me *Harvey.*" The man smiled. "You've got yourself a situation. I can take care of it for you. It's that simple."

Baxter shook his head. "If you know I've got a situation, maybe you can tell me what happened!"

"Maybe it's just as well you don't know, Baxter. Maybe you'd sleep a lot better in the future if we just get this little matter behind you. And I'll take care of the . . . uhm . . . dead weight in your life. No one else knows, Baxter. No one really cares about the victim. I have the talent and the power to erase just about everything that might lead anyone looking for her here."

Baxter was just damned grateful there was no one else in the bar. His entire being had shut down from the moment he'd seen that knife stuck in that girl. Now something very much like hope glimmered at the back of his mind. He knew very well that this man could be some strange kind of informant. Maybe an investigator into cult activity, looking into the warped world of the Goths, and coming away with a lot more than he'd bargained for—trying to nail the heinous slaughter of a poor innocent.

No. As Baxter studied the craggy face of this man, he saw nothing but a different kind of ambition. An ambition that had already etched itself into his own heart.

Baxter pulled out a pack of French cigarettes. He took one and stuck it in his mouth. He felt a little more powerful just completing this ritual.

"Tell me your name. I need to know your name first," he said, offering the stranger a cigarette.

The man took the Gauloise and fitted it into his mouth. He pulled out a cigarette lighter from a voluminous pocket. He lit his cigarette. As he held the flame out to light Baxter Brittle's tobacco tube, Baxter could see that the lighter was made of wood and metal, carved to resemble one of the famous gargoyles of Notre Dame.

"Prince. The name is Mick Prince."

Mick Prince. Yes, he had heard that name before. Last night . . . Yes, definitely last night . . . but also elsewhere.

"You're a subscriber! A subscriber to *The Tome.* And—"

And you've sent in stories and poetry . . . The sickest, nastiest prose and verse I've ever seen in my life . . .

And I've rejected every single one.

He caught himself.

". . . and you've submitted material, I believe."

The man glowed with a kind of infernal pleasure. "That's right. Nothing that fit your purposes, I think. But that's one of the things we can talk about. You see, there's a whole new dimension awaiting you and Tome Press." A cloud of smoke billowed up past his face, obscuring it. "And I would like to show you the way."

Immediately, Baxter saw it. He bought himself some time by sucking in some thick aromatic smoke and blowing it out slowly, very slowly, through his nostrils, examining the burning end of this Gallic cancer stick.

This guy was some sicko. One of the unfortunate side effects of the various fringe groups that read the magazine he published and edited, that bought the various books Tome Press released. These were the sort of sad unfortunates Baxter had known were out there, but had always endeavored to avoid. Now though, apparently, one had managed to insinuate himself into the scene.

What had happened last night?

If only he could remember! Then he'd be able to judge better how far he could trust this dark creature.

Brittle tried to reconstruct the scene in his mind. He could imagine the Salon's sybaritic revelers, stoned and drunk both, dancing with Mr. D . . . The ceremonial knife, a lethal plaything, somehow burying itself in one of the participants, and that little slip, whether intentioned or not, could very likely spell the end not only of Le Salon des Gothiques, but to the freedom and joi de vivre of Baxter Brittle.

Had his hand been on that knife?

Had he cried out in joy to penetrate that girl so?

No. There was far too much at risk. If nothing more, the stranger knew that there was a dead body in the basement and not only didn't seem to be inclined to run for the authorities, but in fact wanted to *help*. Wanted to take away the little problem, dispose of it under the fresh pourings of some expressway on-ramp or deep in the Chesapeake Bay, weighted down by anchors, food for the crabs.

So why not? Why not let him?

A deal with the Devil?

No. Of course not. There was no devil, just as there was no God.

As Brother Crowley, dear old Aleister, said: *Do what thou wilt shall be the whole of the law.*

Well, this thou here wilt that his butt not be parked in some state institution or prison, prime young meat for predatory fudge-packers!

"You'd do this? Why?" he asked.

"I want to move to Baltimore. I want to be part of the Gothiques salon."

"Why? Anyone with any ambition gets the hell out of Baltimore. If I didn't own this bar I'd be long gone."

The agate eyes in the man glittered and twisted. "Because I think you have . . . potential. And I believe with all my soul that I can be the heart of that potential."

Again, the lips parted and he showed that strong, hard grin.

Baxter Brittle shivered at this. The darkness in the man was astounding. He tried to slip back in his memory and recall the poetry and stories the man had sent to *The Tome.* Vague recollections of twisted viscera, decayed corpses dripping, flayed children, imploring chants to forgotten gods . . . the usual litany of adolescent death-worship. But this guy's material had been different; there was a freakish intensity, an unfettered ferocity that had been, well, startling. Frightening. And if a hint, a breath of literary value had invested the work, Brittle most certainly would have published it. However, it was fairly puerile, showing no real sense of structure or rhythm or character or just about *anything* that distinguished it . . . except of course for that brutally assaultive, weirdly confessional *intensity.*

Yes indeed, this ferocious man gave Baxter Brittle the creeps.

But he also intrigued him.

And if he wanted to pull Baxter Brittle's posterior out of the crack into which it had lodged . . .

So be it.

He had no illusions. It was pretty clear what this was going to cost him. The man wrote like a fiend and valued his writings; he wanted to get published. Pure and simple. Ah, yes, literary ambition! What a charming state! Yes, yes, Mister . . . Why these poems in fact are quite fine. And the stories . . . well, I suppose they could do with some editorial polish, minor revisions for tone and consistency. However, that can be arranged. Why yes! And while I don't think we'll be able to squeeze *too* many into *The Tome* . . . let us see, there must be other possibilities. Of course! A collectors edition, signed and numbered! With illustrations by . . . who? Why, yes, Alan Clark or Harry O. Morris would be superb for the dustjacket, with one of those hot young horror artists from Chaos! Comics or Verotik for the interiors. I believe, sirrah, that we can do business . . . Oh, and again, thanks so much for hauling that spitted naked girl out of my closet. No more liquor-fed home-surgery sessions for me . . . uh-*uh*!

"Hmm. Yes . . . well, the gang is always looking for new blood!"

The man extended his hand. He wore leather gloves with the fingers cut off. Small chains twinkled.

Baxter shook the gloved hand. "Welcome to the club."

"No parties tonight, Baxter," said the man. "Stay as sober as you can. You're a lucky bastard. No one else remembers what happened last night either."

"How do you know that?" said Baxter. That was only a slight concern, as the gang had blood oaths and even if several had been present at the unfortunate, inadvertent "sacrifice," they'd pretty much all be in Baxter's state of murky amnesia. Certainly none of them would be so foolish as to go to the authorities.

"Just take my word for it, brother." He looked around. "You get any customers this time of day?"

"Yes. They just haven't straggled in yet."

"That's what I thought. Just keep the basement shut tight. I'll deal with it tonight, after you close." The man's long coat shifted and swung like curtains hiding mystery. "I'll come into the bar at midnight. Be here." He strode to the door. There he swung about and again showed that manic grin to Baxter Brittle. "It's nice to be a part of the Gothic tradition, isn't it, Baxter?"

Then he was gone, a blur of black against the Saturday morning glare.

7

True!—nervous—very, very dreadfully nervous I had been and am; but why will you say that I am mad?

—Edgar A. Poe, *The Tell-Tale Heart*

She took her hand in his gently and gave him the sweetest handshake he'd ever received in his life. That hand was soft with long, elegant fingers and a touch that he'd wanted on his body all of his life.

"Uhm . . . Oh. Yes. It's really nice to meet you too, Mrs. . . ." Oh, gakk! No. Donald Marquette's flustered mind flailed about for the right term. "Amy. Yes, Amy."

"I was about to take Donald on the nickel tour," said Professor Blessing.

Amy Blessing's eyes twinkled and her smile lilted mischievously. "Oh, I think you should charge him at least ten dollars, Donald. All that old wretched stuff is pretty hard to take."

Donald laughed and reluctantly let go of her hand. "Oh, you don't realize how much I've been looking forward to seeing that old wretched stuff." How he'd gotten back hold of his speaking facilities, he wasn't sure. Inside he still felt like an awkward teenager, tongue-tied and stunned. "And to being here, to meeting you both . . . to being in Baltimore at the university. It's all like a dream."

She giggled with almost childlike joy. "Oh, good. How nice to be in someone's wonderful dream."

Donald Marquette had never met a woman quite like Amy Blessing before. His first sight of her was like a physical blow—a blow wrapped in velvet, reaching every part of him. She was not a tall woman, perhaps five-five, but somehow her vitality seemed to make her physical presence overwhelming. She had long blonde hair, perfectly cut and resting just-so atop a simple black blouse grazing breasts sweetly poised between big and small. She wore blue Guess jeans that wrapped around a narrow waist but gave a pearish posterior room to express itself. She made her simple black Reebok shoes seem utterly feminine. A minimum of makeup managed to accentuate her pert nose, her chin was just short of sharp, and she had high cheekbones. Perhaps her most amazing feature, though, was her eyes. She had large hazel eyes filled with spark and crackle, innocence hot for experience. Every jot and lilt of the woman bespoke a bright, *alive* personality. She was simply so pretty it was almost painful to look at her.

And her eyes looked at him with frank interest, saying, Who are you? I'm very interested. I really want to know. I *care*.

Care.

Something Donald Marquette had not known much of in his life.

"Hmm. Well, no dreams are allowed here," Professor Blessing said gruffly. "Only nightmares. That's the way to riches, fame, and wealth!" He laughed with obvious irony.

"Did you find your boardinghouse all right?" asked Amy. "All settled in and everything? We've got guest rooms if there's a problem."

"Oh, no. I got here yesterday and it's been very easy. The landlady is already spoiling me," said Donald. "I guess I'm just not used to people making breakfast for me."

"Oh, such a hardship," said Amy. "Well, you'll have to get used to having meals over here, because you certainly will be invited. This project that you're working on with the Good Doctor here is just *so* exciting." Her eyes shone with delight. "I'm going to help as well, you know. I mean, as much as I can fit in . . . I'm pretty busy."

"Amy's doing some writing of her own these days, when she's not working on a masters in music. I guess you'd be out of a job if she didn't have a life," said Blessing.

"I'm afraid you'll have to put up with my practice while you work," said Amy, playfully. "I do try to keep my instrument in tune, though. As for the playing itself . . . and the compositions . . . Well, I make no promises."

Donald lunged at the opening. "Oh! What instrument do you play?"

"Piano," she said.

"Concert piano," explained Blessing. "And sometimes I think she married me just for my Steinway." He put his arms around her. She eased into his embrace with a kittenish languor, looking up at him with love, admiration, and something else even more intimate.

"Actually, darling, I prefer your organ."

Suddenly, she blushed and put her hand over his mouth, giggling as she looked at Donald.

"Oh, dear. He does actually have a very nice organ, you know, a pipe organ, like in church . . ."

Blessing blushed a little bit. "All you have to do now, darling, is to describe proportions and my male ego will be properly confirmed for our guest." He smiled ruefully.

Donald blinked with mock-bafflement. "I'm sorry. All this banter is flying right over my head!"

Both Blessings laughed. Not only did all embarrassment disappear, but some other slight rind of ice, of formality, disappeared as well.

William Blessing reached over and draped an avuncular hand over Donald's shoulder. Donald did not notice his closeness as much as the impact of the subtle flowermusk scent of Amy's hair. "Don't worry, lad. Just stick with me. You'll be able to banter with the best of us. Now what about that tour?"

"Which is my cue to go and make lunch," Amy said. "You will stay for lunch, won't you, Donald?"

Professor Blessing blanched comically and placed the back of his hand up against his forehead in melodramatic malaise. "Sigh! My secret is out. My politically correct status is kaput! I force my wife to make lunches."

She cocked an eyebrow and placed her hands on her hips. "Just as long as you don't keep me barefoot and pregnant, I guess that one will pass. So do say you'll stay, Donald. The Professor can be so very dull at lunch."

"Sure. Thanks," said Donald.

"Brilliant!" Amy tossed them both a toodle-loo wave and then strode off to be about her business. Donald had to force himself to turn away from the sight of her. He had to work hard to focus back again on what Blessing was saying as the professor led him up the old-fashioned banistered stairs. The scent of her, the feel of her in the air seemed to linger like a pleasant haunting.

"You two really are too kind. If I report this to the world at large, everyone will want to get a Ph.D. at the Johns Hopkins graduate school."

"I do believe our previous interactions have something to do with our ease with you, Donald," said Blessing convivially. "You're an intelligent, talented, hardworking young man with great promise in the field. I pride myself on being able to discern that. What's more, you have something that's perhaps just as important as all those other qualities. You have drive."

Donald found himself nodding. "I would characterize it as *relentless ambition.*"

Blessing stopped at the top of the steps and turned around, obviously struck by the intensity and sincerity and conviction with which his new associate had said that.

"Well, then! Far be it from me to do anything but facilitate the rise of our new literary star!"

Donald smiled with the fanciful irony. But a little smolder of anger touched him.

Just you wait, you smug bastard.

I'll show you.

I'll show everyone.

"I believe," Donald said mildly, "that even when he was a teenager, Edgar Allan Poe thought he would become a great poet. And I think I remember a few words in your early work, talking about your mission in life. That's why I'm here, Professor Blessing. Bill. To be in such good, aspiring company."

"Again, flattery is always welcome when honesty is involved." He pursed his lips with mock chagrin. "Hmm. I believe you're referring to that essay I wrote in graduate school, 'On the Wings of Poe.' "

"That's right."

"I was quite young and foolish then. As certain of my opinions as only the young can be. Now, I'm just foolish."

"I understand, but where you invoked Poe as your muse, saying that sometimes you felt as though you were his reincarnation. And if not—then you invoked his spirit. You almost invited possession. It was a bravura performance. A really amazing piece. Power and passion—yet in artful control. God, it made the hairs on the back of my head stand up." Donald shook his head in frank and total admiration. "Literature can just be so powerful."

"Yes. You're right about that last part. Beyond spirit. Beyond art. Beyond space and time and the petty things that weigh us down," said Blessing.

There was a moment of shared seriousness.

Donald Marquette found his new mentor looking at him in a strange and serious way. Assessing, judging, joining . . . And a shiver of dark brightness brushed across his heart. He felt a *connection.* And yet also, a *danger.* And the combination was as thrilling as the thought of Amy Blessing's lips gently touching his earlobe.

Blessing grinned again, and broke the spell. "Ah, yes, Poe! Poe! Let us now more than invoke his spirit. Let us invoke his glorious spoor!" Eagerly, he gestured his guest to follow. He took out a set of keys. Upon the next, large-framed door was an alarm box. Blessing punched in a number in the sequence of keys. The light atop the box switched from red to green, and something clicked.

Blessing inserted one of the keys from the twisted, jingling set. As he opened the door, Donald felt a soft rush of cool air.

"Uhm . . . Are you sure this isn't the H. P. Lovecraft room?" asked Donald.

"Oh, my. The witticisms keep on coming. No, no. It's just best to keep the room at a lower temperature—to preserve the collection, you understand." Blessing gestured and affected a Vincent Price imitation. "Won't you come in, honored guest. Please excuse my lack of a candelabra, but it's being cleaned."

Blessing reached in, clicked on a switch. Soft light flowed. He beckoned with a manic gleam to his eye, and thus ushered his guest in.

Incredible, thought Donald as he entered the room.

What struck him first was not so much the content of the room as its orderliness. The room itself was large, with Victorian filigree but modern tables, bookcases, and glass showcases, all immaculately lit with track lighting or underlighting to throw things into something a little more profound than three dimensions. There was clothing, spectacles, pens, combs, glasses, bottles, shoes, furniture, sketches, paintings, photographs, and daguerreotypes, all immaculately presented and labeled.

Mostly, though, there were books.

Books, magazines, manuscripts. Letters, chapbooks, writing pads.

The room was simply filled to bursting, its principal subject matter centrally indicated by a bust of Pallas, crowned by a stuffed raven; and above this, a large and beautifully framed portrait with the familiar domed forehead, the thin lips, the mustache, the dandy's clothes, and the night eyes staring out, barely surviving their own darkness.

EDGAR A. POE, was lettered in the plaque below the remarkable portrait.

"You'll have plenty of time to inspect everything closely, at your leisure," said Blessing. "Various items of clothing and artifacts of the man and his time—" He walked along, letting a finger gently stroke along glass tops. "Letters. Signatures. What have you. All the evidence of a great man's time on Earth. And also, of course, all the editions extant of all his publications, including all foreign editions of note, pirate editions, and bootleg translations. *Tamerlane. Al Aaraaf. Tales of the Grotesque and Arabesque. Collected Tales. Eureka.* First editions all."

He spoke with a dramatic enunciation, but Donald was barely listening. He went up to the glass-enclosed cabinet Blessing was indicating and simply stared. The books here were modest-looking enough, and certainly old. However, they seemed to glow with some inner light to the writer and student.

The first editions of Edgar Allan Poe.

Had he held these in his own shaky hands?

Had he signed them for admirers? Had he spilled wine on them accidentally? These were the children he'd been able to actually witness in their infancy. Even in his wildest cups, had the man ever realized how great they would become, how much they would be esteemed?

"Of course the rarest copies are protected in custom slipcases, most from Baltimore's great private libraries of the time. Specialty binding was quite the thing back then. It was common for publishers to make available uncut sheets for wealthy book lovers to take to their favorite bookbinders. Quite the status symbol back then. Exquisite craftsmanship.

"Also, I managed to track down every known appearance by Poe in all the magazines of his day. Not only in *The Southern Literary Messenger, Burton's, The Mirror, The Broadway Journal,* but all the other magazines he appeared in or edited. I generally even have representative runs of other magazines where he may well have contributed under pseudonyms, something we know he did often. I think I may have even found a few tales and poems previously not attributed to Poe." Blessing's eyes simply glowed with enthusiasm. "I'm preparing an article on that very subject now in advance of a small book. Imagine! New stories and poems by Edgar Allan Poe."

Donald Marquette was stunned. This, of course, was unheard of. Enough scholars had pored over Poe's life and times and magazines to have found such if they existed long since, surely! Half of him still disbelieved. However, the Poe enthusiast was ecstatic at the very possibility.

"What you see here, Donald," said Blessing, "is the largest private collection of its kind. It is the reason I don't have a summer home in the Hamptons!" He smiled. "I have spent far too much time and money on all this, but then, such are the fruits of being a scion of old-school money. And I mean that literally. My family has found a home in academia since before the Civil War. Many elements of my collection, and of course this house itself, come from the farsightedness of my scholarly forebears. Even with all the funds now available to me, I don't believe it would be possible to build such a collection."

His eyes grew distant, unfocused, as if gazing on some private vision. After a brief moment, Blessing turned back to Donald, smiling. "I find it . . . inspiring . . . to have so much of Poe here. I find it equally invigorating to know that I need but drive a short way to be in the presence of his gravestone, his earthly remains. It's as though all of these are parts of some arcane microphone, through which his spirit speaks to me, becomes me, serves me, as I serve the voice that found its throat in his grim and sorrowful delivery."

Blessing grinned wryly.

"Of course, it's also damned good equity."

"No. I understand," said Donald in a soft, encouraging voice. "That's not why you collected it. You collected it because it was in your blood."

"And because I could. The Blessing blessing, you might say. I've got other manuscripts and books throughout the house. And heaven knows, stored elsewhere, safely, or else even this large house would burst its seams." He walked up to the bust, and touched the excellent example of taxidermy that graced the top of it. "The collection is a hobby of mine. I used to be much worse about it—until I met Amy."

"Worse? Seems like it's a worthwhile thing to do . . ." said Donald. "I mean, you said yourself you've got the money and the time—"

"The money, anyway. No, Amy appreciates my collection. She's just put a great deal of sanity back in my life." Blessing shook his head and smiled. "Not that I was insane before. Perhaps just a little monomaniacal at times." He lifted his hands up to the image of Poe. "Oh, God, I am *so happy*! *So very happy.* I cannot imagine what I did to deserve to be *so content.* No. Content is not the right word. *Happy, Donald!* The word is *happy.* Thank the heavens Zeus and company aren't knocking around Olympus. They'd be jealous!" He caught Donald's eye, swung around, and pointed a finger at him. "Oh. Of course. I can see what you're thinking. How exactly *did* a crazed bachelor professor and scholar meet a delightful creature like Amy?" His eyes brightened. "A delightful, *young* creature. She's twenty-five years old, you know. Twenty-five!"

Dead on, thought Donald to himself.

"I met her when she was twenty-two, at a World Fantasy Convention in Providence, Rhode Island. She was in town, visiting relatives and she heard I'd be signing. She wasn't particularly a fantasy fan, and at that time I was better known as a critic and short-story writer. *Black Soul Descending* had just come out, with very little fanfare I might add, so at my publisher's behest I was there to help it along—even though the convention is limited to only 750 attendees. But somehow she'd been exposed to my work and was intrigued enough to come see what I was like." He smiled wistfully. "I instantly adored her, of course. Who knew she'd adore me, too?"

There was a bit of dead air between them as Blessing lapsed back into pleasant memories, his eyes unfocused. Donald found himself flailing about for something neutral to say. Even now, the impression of Amy

Blessing hung about him, gently yet insistently. "She was a pianist then too?" He finally ventured.

"Hmm? Oh, yes. Yes. A very good one, but what impressed me most was that she was also composing. Creativity! God, that is the greatest gift we humans have. That, and the ability to love."

"And collect!" said Donald.

"Oh, yes. Well, Amy was pretty fascinated with all this, I can tell you. But it was she who suggested that maybe I should spend more time on the creative part of my career. Try to make a serious go of it." He grinned. "In fact, after next year—in which I hope to get you all settled and at least one of our anthologies completed—I have a sabbatical. Perhaps a permanent one. We're going to rent an Italian villa on the Mediterranean where Amy will devote herself to composing—and I to writing *two*—" Blessing flung up two fingers, "—count them *two* novels. I have a new three-book deal, you see, and I'm almost finished with the first. Should have it done this summer. Then three seasons of intense academia . . . Then bliss."

"This is a year where fortune is smiling on us all," said Donald. "I can't say I've ever been more thrilled with where my life is headed."

"Then we're a fine pair, Donald. A fine pair." He looked around happily at his treasures, then rubbed his hands together. "But let's show you where we'll be working together before we go down for lunch, eh?"

"That sounds great."

Across the hallway was a sitting room. Donald glimpsed the interior as he went past. Chiffon curtains, pleasant wallpaper, antique chairs, and a couch. To one side stood a Steinway grand piano—black, shiny, elegant. The room smelled of fresh cut flowers.

"The music room, I take it?" said Donald.

"Oh, yes. I was going to leave it to Amy to show you that one. Tinkle some keys for you. You'll hear her many times, I'm sure. But come on. I've had our secretary make this space up for you especially, and I'm very eager for you to see it."

Donald followed him up another set of stairs. "How many floors does this place have?"

"Five, not counting the basement. Our rec area and bedrooms are on the fourth level. My study is on the fifth. Going up and down contributes to my exercise. That, and walking to campus."

They reached the landing of the fourth floor. "Here we have our business office and two guest rooms. This is where you can crash on heavy work nights if you like." He pointed to one of the rooms. "Or simply if we carouse too much and you can't wobble back to your boardinghouse."

Donald smiled congenially. "That's always good to know."

Blessing led him into a large room filled with desks, cabinets, bookcases, filing cabinets, and computers. Again, the smell of cut flowers (lilies?), this time mixed with the smell of laser printer toner and fresh paper. Donald could almost taste work—and accomplishment—with the aftertouch of stamp glue, in the air.

A waggle of a finger and Blessing was leading him toward a corner of the room. Donald couldn't help noticing a pile of paperback copies of *Black Waiting Room,* Blessing's second Gothic novel, sitting by a desk.

After years of toiling in the anonymous world of "serious" fiction, producing well-crafted, intellectually challenging but emotionally dry works that consistently sold in hardcover in the mid-teens, Blessing had begun to write short stories that interpreted Poe's core creative principles. Initially a self-made challenge to see if it was possible (those who can not do, teach), he gained enough confidence to try for the big leagues. *Black Soul Descending* would encompass everything he believed about the Gothic tradition. It would be his breakout book, his *Rosemary's Baby,* his *Exorcist,* his *Shining,* his *Ghost Story.*

And so it had come to pass, much to his amazement, and often time consternation, due to the demands of "the business."

Something about William Blessing's work had kicked off new mainstream interest in the Gothic tradition of suspense and horror. Not since Stephen King had the marketplace been so excited about a new writer. And, unlike King, the critics worldwide had fallen over themselves to praise Blessing's novels and short-story collections.

When asked what he owed his books' success to, Blessing had simply answered, "Accessible literary values."

Man, thought Donald Marquette. *Seven million copies in the U.S. alone! That's worth ten years any day.*

"Here you go," said Blessing, breaking the spell. "What do you think?"

The question immediately knocked Donald out of his reverie. He turned and looked at what Blessing indicated.

In a corner of the room was a brand-new desk, featuring a sparkling new Compaq computer, filing cabinet, bookcase, printer, plus an office chair obviously ergonomically designed for comfort.

On the wall was a tastefully framed picture of Edgar A. Poe. Beside it was a Picasso poster. On the desk was a bouquet of flowers, beribboned, with a card set beside it, reading: "Welcome Donald, to the hall of high literary endeavors . . . and any silly computer game you wish to play. William and Amy Blessing."

"I'm speechless," said Donald, moving forward. "Computer games. Wow!"

"Indeed. We've got you all set up. If I recall you characterized yourself as a disorganized soul. Even before Amy, I knew that a properly organized office was absolutely paramount in importance to freeing the creative soul. So we took the liberty of providing you with what you need. You may even, if you like, use this office to do your own writing. Naturally, we don't want that to interfere with your work for us, but if you're inspired . . ." Blessing shook his head, as though seized by some intense muse. "Creativity. Inspiration. We worship them here, Donald. They are our guidance, and we revere them. Do you understand? *Revere* them. So many people think that writers merely sit down and string together words and *poof!* a piece of writing. Not so!"

"Whew!" said Donald. "I can't agree with you more. And furthermore—" he said, wishing to continue the thought, but then suddenly halted in his tracks with what he saw. Set neatly between leonine bookholders was a familiar stack of magazines, and a single paperback novel. He recognized them only after a moment of shock, but then was so touched that he didn't know what to say.

"Writing is very hard," said Blessing. "You have to keep on looking at the evidence that you can do it. Hmm?"

"My published stories!" Donald laughed. "My stupid *Dark Sunset* novel. You got them all!"

"I told you I was a collector. I have my sources. You must realize, they are for viewing only. They still belong to me." Blessing smiled warmly. "And I hope, during your tenure here, that you might find time to autograph them for Amy and myself. All except that one piece in *Rage.* I'm afraid my wife might get the wrong idea." He laughed.

"You're so kind. Thank you! Of course," said Donald.

Blessing reached over and thumbed through the collection of publications. He pulled out a neatly printed magazine, with clay-coat paper, looking rather like a cross between a literary magazine and a quality trade paperback.

"The Tome," he murmured. "You've got a few stories and a couple of poems with those people," he said softly.

"Yes. And there's some interest in a collection of my work, too, I think," said Donald.

"And they're right here in Baltimore," said Blessing.

"Yes. I thought it wouldn't hurt to go down sometime and say hello. You know, fraternizing with the editors and all that."

Blessing looked down at the magazine.

On the cover was a beautifully rendered medieval-style print of Satan as a goat, squatting in a pentacle decorated with Barbie and Ken dolls in various angles and combinations of copulation. The Satan goat wore vampire fangs, shades, and a velvet Dracula cape. In one hand was an electric guitar. The other held a huge cigar-sized *ganja* spliff, the mother of all reefers.

Donald felt vaguely uncomfortable, sensing disapproval from Blessing.

"These are the folk I see all dressed up as vampires and such at some fantasy conventions," he stated blandly.

"Well, sort of," said Donald. "I'm not sure these guys really go to conventions at all. But I suppose you can call them a Goth offshoot."

"Goths. I'd always thought them rather harmless. Rather a fascinating subculture as a matter of fact." Blessing started paging through the magazine. "Spooky British rock 'n' roll. European affectations. Layers of makeup. Attitude. Leather. Oh, no, let's not forget leather. And . . . uhm . . . decadence. That's the word I was looking for. Byronic decadence."

"It's all just role-playing."

"Oh, of course. Problem with American subculture I suppose is that it doesn't provide enough variety. So young people invent their own as they define their individualism through group rituals and behavior," concluded Blessing quickly, realizing too late he had strayed into his didactic lecture-mode. "Hope they pay; the magazine, that is."

"A few cents a word."

"Hmm. Better than most of the literary magazines." Blessing looked bemused. "Interesting. Might give me an idea for an article and—" He was looking at the masthead. " 'Editor and Publisher, Baxter Brittle.' " Some new realization seemed to flit over Blessing's face. He frowned. "I recognize this name . . . Oh, yes. I got some calls and letters from this fellow. Wanted me to talk about Edgar Poe's influence on Aleister Crowley and modern-day Paganism. Well, of course, that was absurd! I told him that politely. He sent a nasty reply back, and I haven't heard from him since, thank God." Blessing shuddered. "Something about these particular Goth fans."

"What do you mean?"

"They strike me as rather creepy. Unduly so, by my lights. Maybe you should be careful if you go to meet them. Nothing wrong with literary markets, but you've got to be careful. There are some strange people out there. My secretary fortunately handles the letters from the crazies that are attracted to me, so my paranoia factor is still very low. All the same—I'd give this Baxter Brittle wide berth if I were you, Donald."

Donald shrugged. "I guess that's not the reason I came to Baltimore."

"No," said Blessing. "No, of course not. But come on up and I'll show you my *sanctum santorum.* We've just time before lunch."

"Your office!"

"Yes! I do believe that you mentioned in a letter once that you'd like to see it sometime."

"Right. I guess . . . Well, I guess I've got this feeling I'd feel inspired."

"Well, thank you . . . Sometimes I wish it inspired *me.*"

Blessing laughed and started walking away enveloped in musing haze. He'd left the copy of *The Tome* on the desk. Donald picked it up, feeling grateful to this generous and vastly talented man . . . and yet, at the same time, oddly angry.

Patronizing bastard! a voice seemed to say deep within. *I'll do exactly what I want to do, meet who I want to meet here!*

He slotted the magazine carefully back into its place and followed his mentor.

8

The old man's hour had come! With a loud yell, I threw open the lantern and leaped into the room. He shrieked once—once only.

—Edgar A. Poe, *The Tell-Tale Heart*

Above the dreaming buildings, the crow circled.

Clouds were boiling over the half moon while darkness slipped through the streets and alleys of the Baltimore neighborhood, flowing like liquid fingers, touching and erasing all.

The crow blinked its piercing brown-black red-flecked eyes.

It wheeled and fluttered, like a piece of the sky cut out from between the constellations, a section of destiny scissored from reality's fabric, lost and looking for a perch.

Down below its heady spin: movement.

The wind whirled past its ears as it flapped down. Atop an old church, half in ruin, it settled. The place stank of pigeon droppings, but the crow paid no heed.

It cocked its head, its senses ethereally alert.

There.

Figures.

They moved amongst the shadows, half shadowstuff themselves.

The crow leaned down, like a gargoyle, watching as the figures weaved and spun through an alley. A trash-can lid clattered off. Drunken laughter echoed against broken windows.

A current of cloud moved and the moon peered down again, silken light washing over the crow.

It cawed with alarm.

"Hey!" cried a voice. "What the hell is *that*?"

"Bad luck."

A whistling.

An empty can clanked against the rusted gutter by the crow's perch. Alarmed, ancient instinct overriding indistinct mission, the crow leaped back into the air, its large wings grabbing hold of the air and pushing up, pushing up, flapping back into the sky, and back between the stars . . .

. . . for now.

"Fucking sky vermin!" said Mick Prince, clapping his gloved hands free of any muck they might have collected.

With a half-aware chuckle, Baxter Brittle watched as the big bird exploded into flight. A feather floated down, backlit by the moon. The empty can clattered onto the cobblestones of the alley, rolling over toward Count Mishka's foot.

"Kick the can!" said the figure in dark leather, eyes black with makeup and long hair flowing in tangles about his narrow face. He booted the can toward the Marquis de la Cinque, who caught it on one of his black jacketed arms.

"Hey! Have a care!"

Count Mishka lifted his pale face toward the moon and laughed wildly. Wracked by this amusement, he wobbled, finally having to fall against the alley wall for support.

That bastard is somehow more fucked up than I am, thought Baxter Brittle.

"A crow!" he repeated, looking back up. The bird had been swallowed up by the darkness. "What's the problem with a crow?"

Mick was standing stiff, like some romantic statue. His hands were clasped together into fists, held up against his chest as though preparing for the first part of some arcane martial arts move.

His huge coat billowed up in a breeze, filling up like the sails of some phantom ship.

"I despise crows," he whispered through clenched teeth.

The man's intensity was a gas! Baxter could feel the drugs dialing in harder, and his brain seemed to be swelling up like some hot-air balloon billowing, gently flowing upward toward the skies to look down upon this grand jest called Earth.

Cool it, man, he told himself. *Don't puncture yourself on the stars!*

"I wish," said Mick, "I had my gun. Would have blasted it right off that fucking spire." He spat the words like pieces of ripped flesh. His stillness was rapture. His presence was catharsis. Baxter Brittle suddenly felt surging drugs kick *through* . . .

Something.

The detritus of the destruction drifted up high, higher, highest, spinning his brain up into a vortex of consciousness. He felt as though he was rising up and up on the wings of the crow, up past the planets, past the constellations, into the arcs of Olympus and Valhalla, up through the dizzying verandas of the Cosmic . . .

All to the delicious smell of rotting orange rinds, the scent of whiskey in the litter, pounding and thrashing to a Nine Inch Nails soundtrack.

He could taste the blood of delirious pleasure/pain in his mouth and it was, oh, so grand.

Like the crow he soared, to the industrial pulsebeat, to the Ecstasy-meth-morphine-cognac cocktail in his brain, to the rhythms of his heart, this ratcheting soundtrack. He gazed at the gang, the roving Avengers des Gothique at three-thirty A.M., a touch of fall chill in the air, Baltimoring.

Guided by Mick, the Arch Deacon himself, the Cleric of Chic.

Hovering so, in Mick's rock 'n' roll presence and yet somehow apart, Baxter felt he could look back at the past months with absolute clarity and see the crystalline *rightness* injected into the veins of night.

What a spirit!

What a dark and powerful spirit was Prince Mick, oh Royal Fellow!

Good to his word—that unfortunate girl's body had been thoroughly "cleaned," never to be heard of again. Baxter knew. He'd scoured the papers for weeks afterward. Nothing. Zilch. Brittle was a stone-free man, and the truth was, he hadn't had even the *foggiest* notion of how to deal with that *knife,* much less the body that held it to its bosom.

However, more than a deliverance, Mick the Man had been a godsend. Exactly which dark god, Baxter hardly knew or cared; he didn't have to. All he knew was that suddenly the salon was stocked with the best drugs, and business in the bar was up so much he'd hired new people, including a manager. Now he could devote his full time and attention to writing, editing, and publishing. *The Tome* and Tome Press were prospering like never before. The first new book had been Mick's *Hatescrews in Your Corneas, Baby,* a collection of the prose and poetry he'd so stupidly rejected before (its print bill subsidized by Mick himself). The deluxe limited edition (illustrated by T. M. Caldwell) had sold out and the trade edition was moving along quite well. True, no mass market publishers seemed particularly inclined to take it on, but then Baxter didn't really expect them to, didn't really *need* them to.

Next step would be a trade paperback anyway, and he'd already contracted with Publishers Group East to handle that for him. Mick was finishing his first novel, *Decapitation Nation,* and with the new funds from the expanded publishing efforts, Baxter would be able to produce even more fine works.

Now that Tome had a real publishing program up and running he'd found the independent specialty bookstores more responsive, stocking his backlist and some even paying on time! He'd made sure to get on-line listings with Amazon.com and the web-stores from the major chains, and now his press was getting reviews and notices in the college papers and alternative journals.

Also, he was able to do his first favorite thing.

Party down, Beelzebub!

Oh, the glorious times they'd had in the cellar. No more dead naked runaways, uh-uh. But lots of other kinky stuff, real Anton Levey action. Mick had introduced strange (and messy) new rituals based on the *Golden Dawn* material. It had been a bit hard to accept it initially. Oh, yeah. First some chickens, then rabbits, a pig here and there, then up to goats and sheep. There had been some accidents along the way, but hey—whatever words Mick was intoning when he did the slicing and dicing (oh! bright!), they were for sure working some kind of major juju on the fortunes of *The Tome,* the Cork'd Sailor, and life in general.

Dark angels!

Finding that young stiff in the middle of his hangover had been the low point of his life. (And what a waste of perfectly good pussy, he'd later concluded.)

Now he was arcing up toward the high point.

And, ah! What a ride!

"Baxter!" snarled Mick.

Baxter Brittle, wobbly-hobbly and adrift in his trance, managed to tug his consciousness back in, plant his billowing gray matter back into his brain pan.

"Yo!"

Baxter turned toward the Prince and blinked. The man's thick, strong face was startling in its present visage. The eyes bugged. Veins in both temples bulged. The teeth ground audibly. The neck cords bulged. Without warning the dude's right hand shot out and gripped Baxter's shirtfront, pulling him into the stink of garlic and French cigarettes.

"I can feel him. I can feel him near, Baxter." Even in the dim light of the moon and the halogen bulbs, Baxter could see how bloodshot Mick's eyes were.

"The Enemy, Mick," cried Count Mishka.

"I sense him. He would devour my soul—I must tear out his heart first and split its sinews. I must snap it up in my mouth and gnash the ventricles and spit them into the dust. I must be sure that his spirit is shredded and sinks into the netherparts of creation."

Baxter suddenly remembered.

Oh, yeah. That was why they'd gone out on the town in the middle of the night. Lying about in the cellar, blasted on drugs and drink, speakers thumping with Usherhouse and Sleep Chamber, Mick up and hollered: "He's *out* there!"

He, of course, being the Enemy. The Anti-Mick. Whether Mick's obsession was delusion or not, there was in fact some other *something* out there freaking him bad. Following him. Making him swear he'd get it before it got him. Now, paranoia was fine, of course. Baxter Brittle had always thought, even in his idealistic days before the Bad Thing with his parents (he'd *told* them to get new tires, he was almost sure he had), that just because you weren't paranoid didn't mean people weren't out to get you. But Mick . . . Jeez, Mick would go just bugfuck crazy sometimes, feeling that presence . . .

"That's why I came here, man," he'd admitted once, wild-eyed. "I felt Him all my life. All my life I've been running. I don't know who or what he is. I'm tired of running. I'm making my stand. I'm here and I'm going to get the bastard! I'm facing up to him. That's my wall I have to get through. Get through to get to my destiny. Do you understand, Baxter? And you're going to *help* me. You *do* understand, right?"

Sure Baxter understood. He understood that when Mick was happy, things went well. When Mick wasn't happy, things got real ugly. So when Mick decided it was time for a little jaunt, a hunting in the supernal night, zapping along on dope-fueled dreams, Baxter Brittle figured it was best to go along with him.

"There!" gasped Mick, angling a finger across the street. "Over there, beside those castle ruins. I *feel* him. Dark knights under my liege. *Avaunt!*"

With a billowing of that great coat of his he leaped out and across the street.

Baxter motioned the attendant members of the gang forward after their Prince, hoping that not much would happen. He could feel himself starting to spiral down, a headache taking deep root, and he hadn't brought the proper medications for a soft landing. *Well, get this over with,* he thought. *And then back to the opium pipe . . .*

With uncommon speed, Mick had dashed across the street and was now stealthily slinking along a brick wall, a shadow fading into darkness.

Huffing and puffing, Baxter and the others found themselves at the edge of the alley.

They peered into the murk. Baxter found apprehension beginning to crawl up his spine on fat spider legs. Something was wrong here. Something was *real* wrong.

"Here!" cried Mick's distinctive gravelly voice. "Come here!"

There was a rustling, a clanking of boxes.

"You!" The voice was harsher now, edged with broken glass. "I found you!"

An electric light beam flicked on. The strong spike of light stabbed across the alley, bounced, steadied. There was a grunt, a clatter of cans and bottles.

A groggy voice growled from a pile of refuse. "Hey man! I'm just tryin' to get some goddamned sleep. Leave me the hell alone!"

"Sleep?" cried Mick. "MacDuff hath murdered sleep!"

"Wha—"

"You have persecuted me long enough, you foul cur! Get ye back to the Hades where you belong."

Baxter and company were now close enough to see what was going on. Mick was holding a flashlight on the intersection of ground and adjacent wall, a bunch of cardboard boxes. Huddled there amongst rags and newspapers was a bum in an overcoat and beard that reminded Baxter of every other homeless schitzo he'd ever seen passed out on the streets. Christ, why couldn't they ship them all off to D.C. where they belonged?

"What the shit you talkin'—" the rheumy, smelly man was saying. He got up to his feet, an empty bottle of Thunderbird rolling away from under his legs.

"Mick!" said Baxter. "This is just some derelict!"

Too late.

Mick stepped forward, and kicked.

The toes of Mick's black thigh-high boots were silver with reinforced metal that flashed in the bouncing electric torchlight. A sickening thunk and an *"Oof!"*

The tramp gagged, gasped—then blew chunks all over the diseased alleyway.

Wine and bile and rotting Wonder bread . . .

. . . and blood.

Something in Baxter clicked. He stepped forward and put a restraining hand on Mick.

"Hey man! Chill!"

Mick pushed him back, pointing down at the retching man. "You see. He attempts to spit poison at me! Do not underestimate the wiles of the Enemy. Now you must help me. You must help me *remove* my Enemy! Now. Hold this!"

He handed Baxter the flashlight.

Then, from the folds of his coat, he drew something out. Something that gleamed harder and sharper in the shaking light.

A black, eight-inch tensile butterfly knife.

"Begone, filth!" said Mick.

Before Baxter could say or do a thing, the knife blurred in Mick's hand, the blade diving in, doing its wet, messy work. The bum managed to get off one gurgly scream before red gushes burst from his neck and torso.

Mick stepped back, his blade and hands dripping with blood.

The bum twitched and splurged and shuddered.

"Now," said Mick, turning toward the gang, "prove your loyalty to me. Send him off! Stomp him, trample him, kick him so hard he'll go soaring off through the other side of the afterlife, never to return."

"Mick . . . Mick . . ." said Baxter. Head spinning, reality chipping. "I can't . . ."

"Sure, Mick," said Count Mishka.

"Cool, man," said the Marquis.

They stepped forward and started playing soccer with the bum's bloody head.

Baxter couldn't move. He just stood there, frozen.

"What's wrong?" said Mick. "What the fuck is wrong with you!" The butterfly's blade waved about wildly, splattering blood onto Baxter. "Do it. *Do* it!"

Fear wrapped its prickly thorns about Baxter's viscera. He wanted to run, get away from this far-past-madness.

He dare not, he knew. For Mick Prince would just as soon bury that knife in *his* spine. Baxter could almost feel the blood-hot shaft touching his nerve stem now . . .

Clearing the way for him, leering in the light, the Count and the Marquis stepped aside.

Separating his sanity from the rest of him, Baxter allowed his body to step forward and kick the prostrate body.

It squelched and oozed. Dead meat.

Baxter stepped back. "To the butt of the netherworld, Mick. And shat into oblivion," he made himself say.

Mick grunted. "Bastard!" he cried. Hawked up phlegm. Spat on the just-dead meat. Then he stood back, taking in great, victorious gulps of air. "Yes! Yes! Freedom. Freedom at last!"

Silence.

Ponderous silence, broken only for a moment by what seemed to be a flap of wings.

"Give me the light!" said Mick.

Baxter gave it to him. Mick took it and flashed it onto the gory mass on the alley floor.

Mick sighed with disgust.

"Tricked!" he said. "Tricked."

"What?"

Mick shrugged. "Not him. Not the Enemy." He plunged a fist into the air. "I'll get you yet, you bastard!" He turned. "Come on. I need a drink."

He swung away and stalked off.

Giggling, the Count and the Marquis followed.

Reeling, Baxter Brittle could do nothing but follow.

Wings seemed to beat softly in the air above him but he dared not look up into the night sky, blackening again.

9

I dwelt alone
In a world of moan.

—Edgar A. Poe, "Eulalie—A Song"

. . . *wings beating softly in the night sky* . . .

Away from the alleyway, the crow flaps.

It flies toward the harbor, where boat lights glitter. Fog is rolling in, thick, creeping on catarrh feet, smelling of the sea, smelling of dead fish.

. . . *wings beating softly in the day sky* . . .

The crow wheels and caws, flying into another date, dipping down through sunlight. It perches atop a chimney pot, above the smell of tar.

It watches as the man named Marquette enters the bar known as the Cork'd Sailor. It blinks and stands a lonely vigil. The sun sets, the stars wink on. Traffic snarls and jerks in the streets and laughter and music wax and wane.

After the full moon is set, at the bottom of night, the writer known as Marquette leaves the Sailor, books in hand . . .

. . . weaving ever so slightly.

The crow caws and leaps toward the stuff between the stars.

. . . *wings beating softly in the summer sky* . . .

The crow dips and swoops.

The black bird flies past the Washington Monument, past Johns Hopkins University and the smell of hot dog and pretzel vendors and the rustle of oak leaves.

It flaps down and lands upon the roof of a townhouse. It peers down upon a balcony and a table. The young writer named Marquette and Amy Blessing sit across from each other at a table, eating salads and drinking wine. They talk intently for a bit. Then the young woman laughs and puts her hand across the table and touches the young writer's hand. He clasps her hand, smiles and lets go.

With a caw, the bird leaps up for the stuff between the clouds, moving forward, forward . . .

. . . *wings beating softly in the autumn sky* . . .

The buildings of Johns Hopkins poke up, venerable and sturdy, from the coloring leaves. A cool current carries the crow as it sails down toward the sidewalk.

There, holding a large briefcase, warmly wrapped in a cardigan sweater, puffing on a pipe, strides the man known as Professor Blessing.

The crow flaps down and sits on a park bench—staring intently through one side of its face, brown eye on the professor.

The professor stops, looking intently at the crow.

"You!" says the professor, stopping.

The crow says nothing.

"You're the one that's been hanging around my house, aren't you? Ever since spring."

The crow says nothing.

"Well, all I can say is that I'm just grateful you aren't a raven!" He laughs and shakes his head. From his case, he pulls out a half-eaten bag of Chee-tos. The crow cocks its head, almost inquiringly.

"Okay, okay. So I've got some bad habits. Look, let's make a deal. You take the rest, you don't tell my wife, okay?"

He dumps the Chee-tos onto the pavement.

The crow regards them for a moment.

Then it hops down from its perch and begins eating the Chee-tos.

"You know, if I was more of a believer in such things, I'd say you were trying to tell me something, Crow. You are a mythological symbol, did you know that?" He folds his arms. "Well, you don't seem to want to kill me. If you wanted to do that you could have just pecked my hands when I was hanging so stupidly on my own roof, hmm? Got something to say, Crow?"

The crow does not say anything. It merely eats another Chee-to and peers up intently.

It is not time.

"Well. Have a nice day, chum. Hope you have as good a life as I do."

Laughing, the professor turns and, whistling, proceeds on his walk back to his hearth and his home.

The crow eats more Chee-tos until the man disappears around the corner.

Then he flaps up again into the stuff between the Victorian spires of Johns Hopkins.

. . . *wings beating softly on the winter air* . . .

Dusk has come to a snowy January. Ice crystals twinkle below streetlamps. The smell of roasting chestnuts rises up from street vendors.

The crow flies to a townhouse. Lights glimmer warmly from a window. The black bird settles down upon a window box.

Inside, in a large office are three people: Professor Blessing. Donald Marquette. Amy Blessing.

They are talking.

The crow watches intently.

. . . *wings beating softly on the air of otherwhere* . . .

Soon.

Soon.

10

And travellers, now, within that valley,
Through the red-litten windows see
Vast forms that move fantastically
To a discordant melody,
While, like a ghastly rapid river,
Through the pale door
A hideous throng rush out forever
And laugh—but smile no more.

—Edgar A. Poe, "The Haunted Palace"

The fist pounded into the man's face.

Mick Prince could hear teeth break. A spout of spit and blood gushed. The man's head snapped back and the wooden chair in which he was tied creaked as it tilted, then thumped back onto the floor. The bound man whimpered and moaned. Mick could smell his sweat, could sense the pain and fear. His nostrils widened, taking in the sensations.

However, this was merely peripheral to the main subject of his attention. The man with the knuckle dusters. The torturer. Something about him . . .

A black man in an Italian suit held up his hand. Brass-knuckle guy took a step away as the Suit leaned in toward the prisoner, careful not to get his nice clothes soiled with blood.

"So, homeboy. Hear you been messin' on other turf."

They were in an abandoned warehouse. Night hung outside, like protective padding. A boom box spat up Mack 10's latest west-coast gangsta rap, alongside the five other gang guys who served as audience. Mick had wondered why he'd been brought here. Now he knew why.

Homeboy's eyes bugged, livid with pain. His face had already begun to swell. "Shit. That's a lie, Cobra!"

"Oh?" The sleek, short-haired man in the Italian suit stepped back to where a table had been set up. He pulled a forty-ounce bottle of Cobra malt liquor from the ice and poured the amber stuff into two long-stemmed wineglasses. He handed one to Mick. Mick hated the stuff, but he took the glass from the Suit. You want to do business with the Man, you drink what he drinks. "Oh, yeah, sucka! You know, that could just be real true. But you know, that don't mean, though, it couldn't be true. Money, man . . . Money has a way of fuckin' up a man's mind. Makes him forget his bloods, huh?"

"I don't forget you, bro!" said the man tied to the chair. "Man, we go back a long ways."

"Yeah. A long ways. So I won't be killing you."

The man whimpered a bit, as though with relief.

"Just gonna fuck you up a bit, see." He looked over at the big white man. "Theodore. Give the man a little more metal, please."

Then he nonchalantly lifted the glass to his lips and sipped.

Theodore stepped up.

Mick figured him to be late twenties, early thirties, but with a face that had a lot of life's hard road ground into it. A face that looked forty. The man had an ex-Marine vibe to him, a blond jar-head feel. He was wearing black chinos cinched tight over a narrow waist and a knit shirt that showed off rock-hard abs, a large body builder's chest, and thick ropey triceps and biceps. *Must've kept up his exercise routines from prison,* thought Mick.

The man appeared Nordic. Maybe, when he was younger, he looked like the sort whose pictures Hitler yanked off to. Now, though, he seemed wizened and grizzled. An experienced pro. His eyes were not dull, though. They glistened with intelligence. They did not seem to be taking any particular pleasure in this task.

Theodore pulled the steel-clad fist up and slammed it into the sitting man's abdomen. The man jerked over. He coughed up blood and gasped and wheezed. Theodore lifted his fist again, clearly targeting the face. This time the other side.

"No!" screamed the man. "No more. Okay, okay, I sold a couple bricks on the side. Shit! But it was DelRoy . . . DelRoy, he told me how to do it. DelRoy's on the take from the D.C. Crips!"

"Shee-it!" One of the young men in oversized pants, oversized sweatshirts, and floppy-tongued tennis shoes stepped back and pulled a gun. "I ain't gettin' my fuckin' face smashed. None of you assholes move an asshole hair, I'll make holes in you, I swear. Big muthafuckin' holes!"

"DelRoy, man. I was wonderin' about you," said the Suit. "Shit, man. Why?" The Suit seemed calm, as though this happened all the time.

Mick's adrenaline was spiking though. Hell, he just wanted to make a deal for the Tome boys with the homeboys, not get his shit blown up in a family gang fight.

"You gettin' weird, man! You gettin' big-time shit. You bringin' in white trash. You bringin' in Mob shit. Man, I'm thinkin' about gettin' my black ass outta Baltimore. Maybe down to Miami. I ain't done nothin' to hurt you, man. So leave me the fuck alone and let me—"

The sound of the gun echoed through the warehouse.

A fat hole appeared in the black rebel's forehead. Brains and bones and blood sprayed out the other side, leaving a fine red mist to settle onto the floor's sawdust. The man's semi-automatic tumbled from his fingers, clunking onto the floor. The black dude buckled, folded. Went down. A basketball shoe spasmed off a foot.

Mick swung around.

Theodore stood, holding a smoking Coonan .357 Magnum in his left hand.

"Ambidextrous," he said.

"God *damn*!" The Suit smiled, then let out a good-natured laugh. "Man. You expensive, but you *worth* it."

He went over, pulled a bottle of malt liquor from the ice. "Shit with this." He tossed his glass away and it smashed into a distant wall. He upended the bottle and glugged down a few swallows. When he was finished, he offered it to Mick.

"No, thanks. Still working on this," said Mick, holding up his half-full wineglass.

Cobra shrugged, pulled out a fresh bottle. "I figure you ain't here to have a gun waved at you. Maybe a little nervous, eh?"

"I don't get nervous."

"You a stone man, huh? You Clint Eastwood."

"The Man with No Name."

"Yeah, that's why I don't put names on my bullets. Shit, yeah. You white boys, always gotta show what a big pair you got. What do our Latin brothers call them? *Cojones? Huevos?*" He took another sip of the malt liquor, then nodded at the others. They hurried over and dug out the remaining bottles for themselves, looking decidedly uneasy, despite their street faces. "So Mr. Eastwood, what you want from the Cobra?"

"Peace, brother—just like that old song says. You see, I'm contemplating a career enhancement, having just recently relocated to your fine city. The group I'm working with is expanding, part of which includes some light dope trafficking. I heard you were the Man in Baltimore so I came to pay the Man his proper respect."

"You got that right, and I likes how you say it. You honest, but what's this group you're talking about?"

"A start-up entertainment company. Small press publisher. Magazines. Books. Get into music and movies down the road."

"Say *what*?" The boss man shook his head, as though to realign his hearing. "What kind of magazine? What *kind* of books? None of that kiddie stuff, right?"

It took all of Mick's self-control not to laugh. "No," he said patiently. "Dark fantasy."

"What?"

"You know, horror books, like Stephen King. Vampire stuff. Noir."

"Far out!" said Theodore, though not part of the conversation.

Mick turned.

The big man was smiling. The smile looked strange on that big face.

"You're kidding me, right?" said Cobra. "Really running a front for porno and blow. I got no problem with that, we can deal."

Mick tried it once more. "Sure, there's some dope on the side, but just club stuff, party favors. Basically this is a legit operation, with great opportunities for moving cash around, clean it up, hide it from the Feds. Then we'll move on to the top dollar side of the street: music, movies—show business."

"A Death Row Records thing I can understand. But books, man," said Cobra, shaking his head. "Where's the money in that? Unless they hollow, got something else in 'em."

"I take your point, but as the good reverend doctor said, I have a dream. I see a real growth potential here, which no one has had the vision to exploit yet." He smiled. "And best of all, we're not going to be in the street, carrying guns and shooting people." He gave a quirk of a grin. "What we've got is a real peaceful operation. All legal—" He tapped his chest. "Except my part. Which is why I'm here—"

Cobra shrugged. "Hmmm. The money cleaning sounds interesting." He gestured at the fallen hoodlum. "You gotta know though—I don't take no shit."

"Wouldn't have it any other way," said Mick, grinning.

"Okay Clint, my man. We'll be talking. Come on up to my crib. Tomorrow. And like the Thelonious Monk song says: 'Round Midnight.' "

"Cobra!" said the man tied in the chair. "Hey man. I'm cool now, right?"

Cobra held up a finger toward Theodore.

Theodore took off the brass knuckles.

Then tossed his gun to his right hand, aimed, and fired.

The bullet *thunked* straight through the bound man's heart, crashing out the back of the chair, splattering the floor with torn fleshy debris.

"Yeah," said Cobra. "You cool like that, bitch." He turned to the others, who stared, trying not to be affected by the sudden carnage. "Looks like we got ourselves the human wreckage of a turf war, people." He snapped his fingers. "Get these traitors out to the right place and maybe they'll lead the six o'clock news tomorrow night, make their mamas proud."

Mick watched all this without flinching or reacting. It was rather interesting, observing without participating. Mick always enjoyed it.

Cobra patted him on the back. "Later, Clint." He waved toward the hired gun, Theodore, who holstered his weapon and followed his employer.

However, the big man stopped by Mick.

"Horror, huh?"

"That's right."

"I like horror books. Horror movies. Crime fiction and all. This kind of job . . ." He shrugged. "Relaxes me."

"I know."

"Maybe we can have a drink or somethin'. After Thelonious Monk time, ya know?"

"Trade some used paperbacks?"

"Yeah. Sure."

Mick shrugged. "Nothing better to kill time in prison."

"Nothing I found."

Mick nodded. "Okay."

The muscular man nodded and gave a strange smile.

Then he trooped off after Cobra.

Mick checked his pants and shoes, making sure no blood had splashed on them.

Then he walked casually toward the other exit of the abandoned warehouse. *Books,* he thought. *They sure can bring people together.*

11

I presume every body has heard of me. My name is the Signora Psyche Zenobia. This I know to be a fact. No body but my enemies ever calls me Suky Snobbs.

—Edgar A. Poe, *How to Write a Blackwood Article*

"This is the most ludicrous idea I've ever heard!"

Professor William Blessing stared down at the letter and slapped it, as though to knock some sense into the thing.

"I don't know, dear," said Amy, smiling brightly. "Donald's talked to me about it and I . . . well I think it's rather an *interesting* idea." She laughed with a naughty gaiety. "Of course, I guess, I'm prejudiced—being bought off and everything."

Blessing glanced up at Marquette. His assistant and protégé was smiling too, but uneasily. "Exactly what have you got to do with this, Donald? I know you're associated with these people. Obviously they know you're associated with me . . . but I'm still confused."

"Uhm . . . Bill . . . Perhaps you haven't read it properly," suggested Donald. "I've only looked at Amy's copy, and briefly. So perhaps if you read it again . . ."

"Okay," said Blessing. He was feeling very odd about Donald and this letter just added to the load. However, as Amy had often told him, he had a tendency to fly off the handle.

One breath.

Two breaths (deep).

"Very well," he said, utilizing his full professorial plumage to prevent any sign of weakness or fluster. "I'll just read it out loud, then, shall I?"

"I think that's an excellent idea, Bill," said Amy. She bounced over and put an arm around him. "And just remember, you always promised to help make me famous."

"Famous!" He had a strong urge to say "Balderdash," but bit his tongue. Too much nineteenth-century reading was infecting his vocabulary. Instead of commenting further, he reached over to his office desk, grabbed a set of the numerous reading glasses he kept around the house, fitted them on, rattled the letter, and began reading:

Dear Dr. Blessing,

I'm sure you've heard of me—or at least the line of books I edit. My name is Roscoe Mithers.

Yes! That Roscoe Mithers, the editor of the *Dark Sunset* series of books for Paperback Gems. Ah, yes! Based of course on the television series and movies (which you doubtless watch, since I can see much influence in your own very excellent writings, although I honestly think you should watch the vampires closer on *Dark Sunset* for better lessons on that particular creature of the night!) and regularly ranked on the Walden and B. Dalton bestseller lists right along with your worthy efforts.

One of our authors, Donald Marquette (*Flowers of Torture,* number twenty-two in the *Dark Sunset Extreme* line) has informed me that not only is he under your tutelage in matters of the Gothic and supernatural, but he is assisting you in editing a new series of anthologies of horror greats.

As you no doubt are aware, the *Dark Sunset* TV series, its spinoffs *Dark Dawn, Dark Day Dawning,* and *Ricardo the Vampire Lover*—along with the top-grossing movies—over the past ten years have kept the horror field alive in the world's mind. How else would your well-deserved popularity have found its right audience?

Naturally, you were one of the first people I thought of when we were able to convince the Dark Powers That Be (heh heh) of the potential efficacy of this project:

The Dark Sunset Anthology.

This would be a thick trade paperback volume (which will doubtlessly be immediately snapped up by book clubs and thus see hardcover release) containing original stories based on the most popular characters of the series: Rupert the Zombie, Hilda the Sorceress, and of course, Ricardo the Vampire.

We'd love to see a story from you. In fact, I have even

made the arrangement with the Dark Powers That Be that if you were willing to write a story for us, you could place it in the universe of one of your novels. (Rather like King having Ricardo visit Castle Rock, true?)

Naturally, we're looking forward to Donald's story as well. However, he tells me that you have a charming wife who dabbles in fiction. We would most certainly welcome something from her. Or, since we understand that you're a busy man, perhaps a collaboration!

We who work with *Dark Sunset* have always been amazed at the power it has for millions of readers and viewers. Just the other week I was at a *Dark Sunset* convention and once more, I was astonished at how this phenomenon so well-embodies the fruition of the Gothic and horror tradition in modern culture!

We hope you'll join our growing throng!

Fangs!

Roscoe Mithers

P.S. For your reference (and collection) I am enclosing under separate cover the latest batch of our *Dark Sunset* books, including the exciting launchbook of a new Young Readers series, Backbone Shivers, *A Monster's in My Lunchbox*.

When he finished reading the letter, there was silence for a moment.

Finally, William Blessing chuckled half-heartedly. "Okay. I understand now. This is a joke! A kind of preemptory April Fools' Day guffaw."

He couldn't help noticing the hurt look on Donald's face. "No, Bill. It's not a joke. That's the editor who bought my *Dark Sunset* book. And he's talking about me doing more, at twice the money as before."

"To say nothing of a story as well," said Blessing, unable to keep a barb out of his voice. "Hmm. All right, I was just hoping it was a joke. That's all."

Amy had started to frown. "Bill, really. That was a very important step for Donald, that book. And it's not like he's been able to sell the other novel he's written. It's given him the confidence to forge ahead. You don't have to be so negative!"

Blessing checked himself.

Invective had been on his tongue. He held himself in, leashing the words "puerile," "asinine," and "joker." However, he had to make one small comment.

"It would seem that this . . . Roscoe Mithers . . . is . . . uhm . . . very involved in his occupation."

"Oh. Right. Sorry about that!" said Donald. "Roscoe's been a fan of the show since day one. This is like a dream come true for him, editing these books. He really sinks his heart and soul into the job!"

"To say nothing of his fangs." Blessing shook his head sorrowfully, reigning back his anger totally. He just felt vaguely depressed now. "I apologize. Of course you can write a story for the collection, Amy. You're getting very good. And naturally, Donald, you're going to. You are already becoming a very fine writer. This whole experience has clearly just propelled your abilities even further than I expected. I guess I had hoped that you'd have set your sights a little higher than *Dark Sunset* material."

"Aren't you being just a little bit pompous and elitist, Bill?" objected Amy, hands on hips, not at all pretty in her miff, but rather beautiful instead. "I mean, come down from your ivory tower! This is a fun series, fun books. Bill, I watch the show and we've seen the latest movie together!"

"Purely because you dragged me to it!" said Blessing. He could feel his ire rising again. He couldn't believe that his own wife was challenging him on this matter, right in front of Marquette. "Look, I teach popular literature! I know all about popular literature. Do you know how many novels and stories were published in the nineteenth century that are forgotten now? And better fiction than anything in the *Dark Sunset* series. In my opinion, this rush of commercial books, cashing in on dubious trends by publishers, and now the corporate puppeteers of modern publishing, is helping along the gradual desiccation of Western culture. Decline and fall, people. And you want to join in the madness? Well, that's jolly good for you, but the very notion of someone having the nerve to ask me to write something of . . . of . . . this . . . this . . . *drivel* . . ."

"Uhm . . . maybe I'd better not bring up that other thing, Amy," said Donald, looking sheepish.

"No," said Amy. "You have every right. And you promised you would."

"But—"

"Very well. I will."

"What *are* you talking about?" demanded Blessing.

"Mr. Mithers suggested that if you weren't interested in writing a story for the anthology, that maybe you'd do a blurb for it, Bill."

"What?"

"You know, Bill. A little something nice about the book . . . or even the series. You do it for your other friends. Dean and Peter and Stephen and Clive all get blurbs from you. What about one for Donald and your wife. Hmm?"

Blessing saw red.

He turned around and walked to a bookshelf. He leaned against it, breathing slowly and deeply, trying to get his composure back.

Finally, he turned.

"You know, one of the things I've always commented on concerning the life of Edgar Poe was that although he wrote a great deal in his life, he was only able to do a comparatively little amount that he really cared about: his poetry and his tales, *Eureka* . . . maybe some of his criticism . . . The rest of his time was spent doing magazine hackwork. Oh, the torture the man must have felt in that alone, along with the other miserable parts of his life. Can you imagine what he might have accomplished if his horrible foster father John Allan had believed in him? If he'd gotten a really fine education, if he'd found a nice teaching position like Longfellow? Or even if some moneybags had seen his value and simply become a patron? No, he had to work in a pathetic and squalid industry full of sentimental bullshit fiction and formulaic emotion and style.

"Well, Poe had to do that. And what little he was able to write in his short life *triumphed.*

"But now the hackwork, the silly sensationalistic nonsense of popular taste, of puny capitalist minds has perverted the goals of the tradition that he so well modernized. And what do we have? *Buffy the Vampire Slayer? Xena?* And God help us, *Dark Sunset.*"

He sighed.

"And you think I would affix my name to the kind of stuff which I abhor!"

Blessing could feel his blood-pressure rising. *It was like a sacrilege! A defiance of everything he stood for!* However, there seemed nothing that he could do to stop himself. He had to vent. *This point was central to his existence. Didn't they know that?*

Amy rolled her eyes. "Oh, for heaven's sake, Bill! No one's trying to compromise your integrity when you can do it so much better yourself. So just forget it, okay? Forget it."

She looked at him, and the anger flashing in her brilliant hazel eyes startled him.

"Sorry, Bill," said Donald. He looked stiff and pained, obviously feeling awkward and upset to be in the middle of this kind of conflict.

Anger control, man. Count to ten.

He did so, quickly, moving his shoulders within his cashmere sweater, loosening his tie, letting the blood flow a little better. "I guess you struck a sore point."

"I'm really sorry. I didn't think you'd like the idea much," said Donald. "But I guess, well . . . we figured it was worth a try."

The look on his face said, *We sure didn't realize you'd blow a gasket.*

"I suppose I do have strong feelings on the subject," Blessing said. "But I'm afraid that I have to stick to my principles." He cleared his throat, hazarded a look at his wife. "Look, dear. I'm sorry. You can do what you like. You have the right. I just don't want to be roped into something like this. I have far better things to do with my time, and I have better uses for my good name and what I have achieved in academia and literature. Mainstream success doesn't mean a person had to stoop to the lowest common denominator to get it."

"But it usually does, that's for sure." Amy fumed. "God, Bill. You can be such . . . such an *asshole* sometimes!" Amy threw up her hands. She turned around and stalked from the room, clomping down the hallway and then the steps.

Looking startled, Donald seemed about to follow.

"No, no," said Blessing. "She'll be all right. She's probably just gone to take a walk or call one of her girlfriends and talk for a couple hours. I'll make it up to her."

Marquette seemed uncertain.

"Look, I'm sorry to be such a jerk, eh? Stick around. There's something I need to talk to you about anyway." Blessing could still feel the adrenaline coursing his veins like razor blades. He stepped over to his desk, pulled open a drawer, and yanked out a half-full bottle of Johnnie Walker Red and two glasses. "Join me for a drink?"

Marquette, for once, did not seem hesitant about hard liquor at all. "Sure."

"There's the lad." Blessing poured unhealthy amounts of Scotch into both glasses, slopped one over to Marquette.

"To Poe!" he said, repeating the toast he and Marquette would use when they went out drinking beer.

"To Poe," said Marquette, without quite the gusto.

Then Blessing tilted a good two ounces down his throat. The liquid dragged raw, tasty fire with it and splashed into the sour cauldron of his stomach. Immediately, he could feel the warmth spread out on little feelers of calm and hinted oblivion.

Oblivion? Was that what Edgar Poe had sought? A surcease from the overwhelming agony?

If he truly was the reincarnation of Poe, then he would know that, wouldn't he?

He looked over to his assistant and protégé. Donald was handling that liquor as well as he. It was already half gone.

A little shiver of dread touched him.

A little too close to what I want to talk to him about . . .

These nine months with Donald Marquette had been good ones. The man learned incredibly quickly. He absorbed like a sponge, and worked hard. The first volume of the anthology was almost put to bed, Marquette's doctoral work was going well, the articles he was writing on the "Manifestations of the Gothic Tradition in Modern Prose" were not only well-researched, but contained keen insights. Plus, he was churning out fiction as well, as though inspired by listening to Blessing's rambling seminars and actually watching him write and then revise. When he lectured, Marquette was always close and focused and extremely attentive.

He reminds me of a younger me, thought Blessing. *Only slightly off, a bit askew . . .*

And then, there was that latest story.

Not only was it very good indeed but its style and comprehension of tropes and allusion played against its taut and powerful plot, and was very much like something that William Blessing might write.

This was a little startling, but rather gratifying in most ways. No, what was disturbing was another matter entirely.

Blessing took another sip of his drink, then put it down. Marquette clutched his, however, as though anticipating something unpleasant approaching. It still had a jigger or so of Scotch left, but Donald eyed the bottle, as though he was thinking about asking for more. Blessing could already see the alcohol in his eyes.

"Donald. Tell me again about that ambition of yours!" said Blessing, affably.

Donald's eyes burned. "What? You mean literary immortality?"

"Yes. That's not such a bad goal, is it? It was Poe's, you know. Even when he was far younger than you, he thought he was great. Of course, *Tamerlane* is hardly the greatest of poems, but it showed huge ambition, no?" Blessing regarded his drink. Set the glass down and sighed. "You're good," he said, getting up and walking over to his thick, leather bag. "A damned good writer. And getting better. Much too good to waste your time on juvenile stuff like *Dark Sunset.* I mean, if you need money . . . Well, I'd increase your wages . . . Hell, I'd pay for your room and board and computer supplies, if that's what you need. But *Dark Sunset* . . ."

"I guess it gives me confidence," Marquette said tersely. "It stretches me, exercises me, and to see my name on the bestseller lists . . . That's part of the dream."

"Hmm. Well, we can talk about that later, I suppose." Blessing unlatched the bag, pulled out a hardcover book. "Oh, by the way, congratulations." He put the book down. *Dreaming Demons,* proclaimed the title. *Stories Dangling on the Edge,* by Donald Marquette.

"The Tome Press, I see," said Blessing.

"Oh. Yes. You got one. It's just come out. I was going to give you and Amy a signed copy," said Donald, still looking a little apprehensive.

"You've been down there. Haven't you? You've hung out with them."

Marquette shrugged. "Sure. I went down for a few business meetings."

Blessing shook his head. "Okay. I just wonder why you didn't think about some other press."

"Well, frankly, no regular publisher is taking horror short story collections."

"Why not another, more reputable small press? Why *this* press?"

"They wanted to publish me." Marquette finished his Scotch. "Simple as that, Bill. Plus they're local. I can be more involved. And they're no less reputable than Necro, Subterranean, or Terminal Fright. The small press scene for horror is not like it was in the eighties, when Scream/Press, Underwood/Miller, Dark Harvest, and a dozen others were fighting the good fight. There's just not a lot of options now."

"Well, I hope it doesn't hurt your reputation." Blessing took a deep, pained breath. "And I hope that it doesn't hurt mine since we're associated together."

"I don't understand. Tome is doing extremely well lately. They've already shipped half their first printing, and a trade paperback is in the works. What's wrong with that?"

"The same thing happened to the horror field last time," responded Blessing. "Some warped writers thought they could use it to hype their own private psychopathology. And some editors thought that what people liked about Gothic literature—which is the term, as you know, that I far, far prefer—was the pure nastiness of it. These disturbed, misguided people simply wanted to screw with readers' brains, foist off their private hells of pornographic violence as some kind of statement. That's my take on the Tome people. And I might add that I've been hearing disturbing things about them from other sources. Whispers of Satanic blood rituals. Evil stuff, Donald. We, as serious writers, have a great deal of license but we need to carefully watch our lives—for many, many reasons."

"Hmm," said Donald. "They seem all right to me. A little way out, perhaps. Extreme Goth, they call it, but they do care about literary quality. They're really quite serious."

"I don't doubt it. But seriousness of purpose alone does not ensure

12

One night as I sat, half stupified, in a den of more than infamy, my attention was suddenly drawn to some black object, reposing upon the head of one of the immense hogsheads of Gin, or of Rum, which constituted the chief furniture of the apartment. I had been looking steadily at the top of this hogshead for some minutes, and what now caused me surprise was the fact that I had not sooner perceived the object thereupon. I approached it, and touched it with my hand. It was a black cat—a very large one—

—Edgar A. Poe, *The Black Cat*

"Pray for me," said Donald Marquette. "For I am a soul damned as no soul has been damned before."

The group exploded with laughter.

Donald grinned, took another drink of his beer, and shrugged. "That's the message the good professor believes he found buried in the works of Edgar Poe."

"Kinda like a Captain Planet secret decoder ring, huh?" said Count Mishka. The Count wiggled his fingers, displaying the numerous baubles he wore himself, more colors amongst his long, lavender, sparkle-encrusted fingernails.

"Or Batman!" said the Marquis. The Marquis was in a retro New Romantic phase, aping the looks of Gary Oldman's Dracula and Alan Jorgensen of Ministry. Tonight he wore a purple velvet coat, flowery dress shirt (only a few wine stains so far), and the requisite black crushed-felt top hat, wire-rim glasses with purple lenses, and shiny black nail polish. He was seriously considering going for hair extensions next week. The look seemed to be working for him.

The group around the table snickered at these remarks.

"Pretty damned loony, if you ask me," said Baxter Brittle, at the head of the table in an elaborate Victorian high-backed chair. He lay stretched out along the arms, legs a-dangle on one side, snuggled up to a goblet on the other. Baxter had effected an Oscar Wilde persona lately—lids drooping, dark hair winged over his forehead, baggy Edwardian top-coat and black pants above spats. "Love old Oscar's fashions all right, it's that cock-sucking business I don't go for," he would say routinely, lest anyone get the wrong impression about his bedroom orientation.

The murky odor of wormwood drifted up from a jewel-spangled goblet. Baxter had been drinking absinthe lately, having found great success in concocting a homebrew version of it for the bar. Thanks in part to Trent's *The Perfect Drug* video, the exotic liqueur, with twice the potency of vodka, a mild hallucinogenic property, and a coolness factor hyped by association with such artist types as Hemingway and Rimbaud, was making quite a comeback with the young Goths.

Donald Marquette scowled into his British-style imperial pint of Old Peculier beer, another new addition to the Sailor's distilled fares. He was getting very fond of the high-alcohol brew with the strange, rich taste.

Damn the bastard, he thought. *I'll show him! I'll show the arrogant asshole!*

"Yes, it's going to be the subject of a new article," he said, after another dark, yeasty quaff. "And the funny thing is that he's so high up in the academic and literary and *popular* pecking order, that people are going to take him *seriously.*"

"Here's a chap," said Baxter, sloshing his absinthe lightly, then pinging the side with a fingernail so that it rang like a little bell, "who should be taken down a peg or three!"

"You might say he puts the *Poe* in *poseur,*" quipped the Marquis, going for a droll George Sanders tone (having given up on doing Peter O'Toole or James Mason with any credibility).

Donald smiled, then sighed.

Yeah. Exactly. The Poe in poseur.

He could feel the beer murmuring around in his veins, and the dope they'd done before down in the basement turning his brain into an Escher study. It felt good. Damned good. *Down a peg. You bet! Arrogant jerk!*

"There's more," he said.

It was a Wednesday night at the Cork'd Sailor, "lounge" night, and not terribly successful with the irony-deficient crowd Baxter was forced to cater to. *(Cocktail Nation, my ass!)* But still the air was bluish-gray with smoke. It smelled of cigars and the cordite of matches, and of bar rags. Donald liked it, though. It was dark and comforting, with all manner of Victoriana and pictures cluttering the walls. The rows of spouted liquor bottles against the bar mirror looked like a lovely glass garden, glittering in the muted lighting. Though closer to Little Italy, the place tasted of the exotic funk of Fells Point, and Donald Marquette had fallen in love with it, almost as much as he had fallen in love with Amy Blessing.

"More?" drawled Baxter, blearily looking up at his author.

"Yes. He hit the roof when he saw my collection from you. He's pretty much figured I've been down here, hanging out. He wants me to cut off all relations with you guys. No more stories in *The Tome,* no more books from the press . . . And I suspect that if he finds out I even drink at your bar anymore, he'll boot me."

Even as he said the words, Donald steamed.

Like he had any other *outlet!*

With his workload, he had to be able to blow things off with friends once in a while! Professor Adolf Hitler Blessing was acting like Donald was a teen, and Blessing his dad!

In fact, Donald only came down here, generally, on weekends. It had all started innocently enough, with a few business meetings. But when the contract for the story collection had been signed, Baxter had started inviting him down to the bar on weekends and giving him free drinks. Donald had gotten to know his clique, who had all read his stories and *adored* them. He seemed to be somewhat of a celebrity amongst them. They hung on his words, especially when it came to literature. Initially, Baxter had wanted him to be an associate editor, "To get some kind of class into this rag, dear boy!", but Donald had demurred. No, far too much *else* to do. However, he *had* been honestly flattered, and the respect they gave him had made him feel not only good about himself, but more at ease with all the . . . er . . . *flamboyant* aspects of Le Salon des Gothiques.

In fact, he'd rather developed a taste for their liquor. And even a few of their drugs. He kept that intake down. Just for special occasions, actually. Party time and all that. However, with his heavy workload, he sometimes found himself taking a tab or two of the more stimulating items they provided him with. And damn, if it didn't rev him up, allowing him to work a great deal and sleep little. In his opinion, it also actually *improved* his writing. It cut something open inside him, allowing his raw creativity, yes, his *genius,* to flow out.

Cruising with the Goths.

It was great, great fun. True, that Mick bothered him sometimes—

something in his eyes, and manner and dress. *And the man's stories.* Donald had to admit that Blessing hit the nail dead center on that one. Both Mick and his prose were hard, driven, strange, and resonant with menace. Yes, Mick had even inspired a couple of his better recent stories. He was just kind of grateful now, in what would probably be the last visit here for a while, that Mick wasn't around.

"Oh, goodness," said Baxter. *"How very annoying."*

Yes. Annoying enough, Donald noted, for the bar owner and publisher/editor to actually rouse himself for his torpor of world-weary dissipation.

Something, in fact, was sparking in his eyes, like the end of a broken power line.

"No," Baxter said. "I don't think I care for *this* bit of news one bit."

Donald found himself not merely flattered, but moved at Baxter's response. He often thought that the Goths merely patronized him, because he amused and diverted them. If he had to go, he'd pictured them saying, *Well, au revoir, baby.*

Now though, a little *frisson* of connection touched him.

They actually valued *him.*

Actually liked *him.*

Donald Marquette had always been a bookish sort, never very successful with girls or other people. He even still felt stiff with the very friendly, but pompous and somehow too formal William Blessing. His bonhomie with the scholar and author he often had to fake. Basically, the main reason he was there was to advance his knowledge, training, and above all, his career.

Certainly, he'd never been associated with people who had been anywhere near as self-possessed, self-assured, and hip.

These Gothiques, though. They were . . . well, *cool.* And he liked the fact that they thought *he* was cool, too.

That was, as they might say, a major *buzz*!

Baxter Brittle stroked his chin. Then he got up, stuffing his flask of absinthe in one of his oversized pockets. "Come, Inner Core. This is a serious matter indeed. We must descend to the *sanctum stinktorum* and cogitate."

With a casual air of consummate presence and mastery, he rose. The Count and the Marquis followed. Presuming that he also included, Donald got up and followed.

However, halfway to the door they were stopped by the arrival of a young man and woman, attired in elegant Gothic vampire attire—save for the fangs.

"Baxter Brittle," said the young woman, holding up a hand gloved in black silk.

"That is, indeed me," Brittle said, giving a polite half-bow. "How may I be of service, Lady Jessica and Prince Knowlton?"

The young woman, a spunky, almost punky sort with multicolored hair, stepped forward in front of Baxter. "Something weird is going on with your people, Baxter."

"Pardon me?"

"Look, I like the Goth scene as much as anyone. Maybe more," said the slender girl. "But there's stuff going on here that we're not very happy with."

"Oh? How so?"

"Some perfectly straight people I know have turned into drugheads in the past six months," said Lady Jessica earnestly. "I'm not some naïve, 'Just Say No' hypocrite either, but this is getting too serious. It's not fun anymore. And the Prince came home last night with blood on his cape!"

"Mercy!" said Baxter Brittle. "A vampire with a little blood on him. Dearie me." Brittle wobbled a little, obviously the worse for his absinthe habit.

"I don't remember a thing about the whole night!" said Prince Knowlton. "Man, that scares the *shit* out of me!"

"This salon thing used to be cool decadent fun, not just degenerate drinking and drugging," stated Lady Jessica, accusingly. "Most of us get up on Monday morning and go to work or school or whatever and deal with the normal world. I'm sorry about your parents and all, but we don't have inheritances to live off of. That's fine, but you guys are digging down too deep in the darkness." She shook her head. "Too deep."

"Please," said Baxter. "Brevity is the soul of wit. I'm afraid you're not being very witty."

"We're leaving the Gothiques," said Lady Jessica. "We're starting up our own group. Me and Knowlton and a few others. We're getting *out* of this scene and away from *you*."

Baxter held a spread hand to his chest. "Gasp! You've cut me to the quick!" he said, sarcastically. "Am I really so bad, mad, and dangerous to know?"

"Come on, Prince," said Lady Jessica, taking him by the arm and leading him away. "Let's get out of here."

"Ooooooh!" called Baxter after them. "Going to have a vampire tea party, are we? Make sure to hold your pinkies out!"

Donald found himself laughing along with the others.

"Couldn't stand the heat, then," said Baxter, gaily. Suddenly, however, a hard cast came to his face. He looked at his core group, at the

Marquis, at the Count, and at Donald Marquette, and he said, "You guys can, can't you?"

They all nodded. Yes, they could stand the heat.

Yes, thought Donald. *I can stand it. These are my friends. These are the kind of people I've been looking for. And if they play with darkness . . . well, so do I.*

So, really, do we all, in our heart of hearts.

That was a line from one of his stories, and he knew deep down it was true.

The group jangled through the bead curtain at the back of the bar, through the kitchen, as Baxter drew out his keys from his pockets—then down into the Dungeon.

Even though Donald had found the cellar "salon" ornate, clever, and well, rather kinkily mystical the first time he'd been down some months before, now . . .

Well, now, with the financial state of Tome Press improving by leaps and bounds, so was the opulence of this den of dissipations. Baxter Brittle had purchased a number of spectacular Oriental rugs which now draped over the floors, adding richness and luxury. Elaborate antiques had been added to the mix, and beautifully framed artwork. Necklaces and crosses and symbols from the darker side of the esoteric and the occult dangled hither and thither, sparkling and shiny in the glow of flame from thick aromatic candles. The dense, rich smell of incense, along with the ruminations of Baxter's French cigarettes, lingered. Tallow and tobacco and frankincense—and the aftersmell of exotica and alcohol.

Baxter led them round a large and gorgeous old teak table with elaborately curved chairs. He fluttered his hands. "Sit! Sit!" He pulled his bottle and goblet out and placed them at the head of the table before him. "Libations, my brethren?"

They all chose beer. Baxter blithely pointed to the icebox. "You may retrieve your own."

Donald pulled out another bottle of Old Peculier.

They settled back.

"Cosmic think tank, gentle people!" said Baxter. "We have a dilemma. On the one hand it is very good indeed that some of our members are leaving. However, we must watch carefully to be sure they keep their mouths shut." His eyebrows waggled a bit at that one. "However, we have a friend here who does not wish to disassociate yet finds he is professionally being forced to by his mentor."

"William Blessing!" said the Count.

"A powerful figure to cross!" noted the Marquis.

"Perhaps we should invite Blessing to join!" suggested the Count.

"I have long since made overtures," said Baxter. "The good professor lives in an ivory tower, it would seem. He scoffs at us. He despises us. So easy to do when you have barrels of money, cauldrons of success. And yet, brethren, do we not drink from the same well? The literature and the philosophies and the emotions that travel through our gray matter, through our very veins—it travels through William Blessing's. Our friend Donald Marquette acknowledges it. We acknowledge it. Others acknowledge it. And yet, clearly Blessing is a necromancer who denies his spells stink of sulfur. He believes himself impervious, powerful, and aloof from the delightful vapors of night that cloak us."

Baxter was silent.

The candle flames beside the table flickered as though a phantom wind whispered through the room.

"Perhaps," said the Count, "someone should wake Blessing up."

"Yes," said the Marquis. "He should wake up and smell the tea!"

Donald was about to correct the elaborately attired and coifed fellow, but one look at his three-quarters dazed expression changed his mind. "That's all very well to say," he said. "But at the moment, all the people I'm meeting, all the publishing ins I'm getting . . . I mean, New York publishing, that is."

"Nothing to sneeze at, chum," said Baxter. "But there's the *Dark Sunset* stuff! Remember."

"I'm afraid he wasn't thrilled with that, either."

"Hey!" said the Marquis. "That's my favorite!"

"I admit to being partial to it myself," said Baxter. "But let's face it—they could get *Star Trek* writers to hack out that stuff and it would still sell to the *untermensch.*"

"Hey," said the Count. "I *like Star Trek* books!"

"Well," said Baxter. "We can't all have good literary taste." He leaned over, stroking the bridge of his nose as though coaxing out inspiration.

Donald sipped at his beer. It seemed very bleak to him. He'd have to just throw himself harder into his work. It was damned tough being around the household, suffering Blessing's eccentricities. God, the man liked to talk, and all the talk was generally pompous and self-absorbed. Smile and scrape, Marquette. Kiss his hairy ass! Lo! The Great Authority pronounces and exposits. Pay heed to another tedious rumination!

Worse, though, was being around Amy.

He'd fallen hard for her the moment he'd seen her, and it just got harder as time went on. Man, it was *so* difficult to get near her, and not put his arms around her and kiss her forever. She was such a *tactile* person. She loved to touch him. Lately, she'd hug him from time to time. The touch of her breasts against his chest or arm was electric. The warm scent of her perfume was ecstatic. At Christmas, she'd actually kissed him under the mistletoe. On the cheek, true, but still . . .

She's so hot for me, he thought, gurgling down more amber liquid. *Maybe she doesn't realize it yet, but she most certainly is!*

If only he had more *power* in the situation.

If only . . .

Suddenly, footsteps began to trudge slowly down the steps.

Baxter Brittle looked up from his mire of thoughts. "Now whoever could that be?"

The swirl of a long coat.

The pound of leather boots.

The coat lengthened into the long and black frame of Mick. He carried a bottle of Courvoisier in one hand. The other one gripped a fancy riding crop. He slapped the banister with it as he descended.

The candle flames guttered. It somehow seemed colder—with the touch of the bay fog and the stink of rats and seagulls arriving with this man.

Behind him came another set of boots, this time not touched by the edge of a coat. The scuffed black of the boots rose up into a fluid transition to black leather pants. As these legs descended farther, Donald could see that the pants were ridged with silvery studs. Up and up they went to powerful buttocks, tight across a codpiece crotch. Up further to a tight belly, open past the navel to show ridged abdominals. A leather shirt, up yet farther to huge pectorals and heavy shoulders and a football player's face, heavy and dull. Hooded in more black leather, more studs.

"Come, Theodore," said Mick. "Don't dawdle. I can't guarantee this crowd won't bite—" He smiled grimly. "—but I'm sure you'll like it if they do."

Mick turned to the others. "Gang. This is a new recruit. This is cousin Theodore. He wants very much to become a Literary Light. Hmm, Theodore?"

The heavily muscled man grunted.

"A brew, Theodore?" said Mick.

"Becks."

"Why surely—go and help yourself. The refrigerator over there is very well stocked."

The big man lumbered over to the icebox, while Mick sauntered over to the table. He slapped his riding crop down gently onto the tabletop and then sat down in a chair.

"Council meeting without me?" he asked, slowly and suspiciously. "Something the matter?"

Baxter fell back and laughed with a maniacal edge. "Not any more."

Mick's brow knitted. "What the fuck is that supposed to mean?"

"Your arrival is a solution," said Baxter. "I believe I have an idea. Indeed, a *wonderful* solution!" His face, previously dark and unfocused, now simply beamed as he turned his gaze to Donald. "And not only will it further you in the estimation of our dearly beloved Dr. Blessing, and allow you to continue your frolic with us—but it shall further our cause—immensely!"

At this point, Donald was willing to listen to anything.

He took another drink, folded his hands together, then leaned over to listen.

13

Open here I flung the shutter, when, with many a flirt
and flutter,
In there stepped a stately Raven of the saintly days of yore;
Not the least obeisance made he; not a minute stopped or
stayed he;
But, with mien of lord or lady, perched above my
chamber door—
Perched upon a bust of Pallas just above my chamber door—
Perched, and sat, and nothing more.

—Edgar A. Poe, *The Raven*

William Blessing had always heard about these kinds of evenings. However, in his bachelor life, he simply had scoffed at them. Foolish sentimental prattle, he'd thought. Nonsense and humbug and general propaganda conjured up by society to strike down independence, stick the bit in the male mouth and keep it hauling those genes across the dismal fields of time, toward certain, total winter.

Now, though, sitting here, Blessing realized that not only was this business rather pleasant, not only did he feel content in a way he'd never felt before.

But he felt happiness.

Pure unalloyed happiness!

The glow of the crackling fire in the hearth cast a wavering warmth of peace over him. The rich smell of the burning cedar blended perfectly with the pots of potpourri that Amy had gently simmering under candles. The taste of cocoa in his mouth had just the right edge with that touch of whiskey he'd put in the mix. In his hands was a very well preserved nineteenth-century beautifully illustrated and designed copy of Charles Dickens's *Nicholas Nickleby,* the book he was savoring at calm moments these days, away from the literary rapids and in a timeless backwater of magical words and eternal characters. It was a comfortable Saturday night in February, and he and his beloved were tucked away in their safe and snug house, away from the snow and the wind that puffed and howled beyond the window.

The fire popped.

He looked up at the flames, feeling a moment of alarm, then, seeing that all was well, and that only a small spark had jumped out from the fire and was now fading on the tile, looked around.

The truth was, of course, that all this contentment—no—*happiness*—was because of the person who sat across from him in the other armchair, her knitting put aside and now deeply immersed in Jane Austen's *Mansfield Park.*

Amy.

His very own Amy.

He couldn't help, now, but just sit and gaze at her. She was so very beautiful, and her beauty touched off something deep in him, something resonant and pure and . . . well, yes . . . holy. For although there was youth in that beauty, even when there was not, maturity would take its place and perhaps create even more beauty than now.

They used to joke that his Poe obsession had gone too far. That, like Edgar, who'd married his thirteen-year-old cousin, William Blessing had taken a child bride. Of course, even when they had begun corresponding and speaking on the telephone after that first weekend together at that fantasy convention (chaste! a first in such an experience for bachelor Blessing), it had become obvious that in certain emotional ways, it was Amy who was the more mature. Then, a few months after the excitement of marriage and honeymoon, constant togetherness, flowers, billets-doux, and all the other heartbeats of joy, the jokes stopped. For very quickly and comfortably they settled into a tight domestic unit of passion, love, and understanding. There was this amazing *connection* between them that transcended age or flesh that was merely celebrated by sex. To Blessing, Amy embodied all the best of poetry itself, from her beauty, to her taste, to her musical gifts—to her sweet and gentle soul. In fact, this had been something at the back of his mind since he'd first seen her shy smile, and every once in a while he would write verses about her with an old-fashioned quill pen, its feather shivering as he scratched. When the book was full, he was going to wrap it in a red ribbon and lay it upon her pillow before some journey.

God, how he loved her!

He peered up again from his book to admire her fine features, as he often did these peaceful reading evenings, and he found her looking at him oddly.

"Amy, is everything okay?" he asked.

"Yes. I think so. I think so, Bill."

"You look . . . troubled."

"Hmm. I guess I've been having difficulty reading. I'm a little worried."

"About what?"

"I don't know. Just this . . . this feeling."

He got up and put his book down. He went over and knelt by her chair, put his arm around her. She smelled of jasmine tonight and Earl Grey tea. Her hair was lustrous in the flickering flames of the fire. "Are you still upset at me about that little spat last week?"

"What? The *Dark Sunset* thing?" She laughed softly. "Why? I won. I'm going to have a story there, despite your snooty upper-class priggishness." She wiggled his nose gently. "And I have to confess, I'm not at all upset that you suggested that Donald not associate with those Goof people."

"Goth, dear. Goth."

"I know." Her eyes twinkled. "I know."

"It's not that I disapprove per se of groups getting dressed up and acting strangely, although I don't think I ever did that when I was younger."

"No, you were too busy writing footnotes."

He smiled, acknowledging the joke. "It's just that I've read these people's publications and they rather bother me. I guess I've unfortunately managed to get myself a good reputation—though how on earth I don't know—and I have to be very, very careful. Do you understand?"

"Certainly. Donald doesn't seem to mind very much. Although I do wish he'd find himself a girlfriend or something. That's what he needs. Maybe we just keep him too busy. I've been trying to introduce him to one of my friends from the Peabody, but he doesn't seem interested."

"Is that what you're thinking about now, Amy? Donald?"

"Well, no . . . lots of things I suppose." She bit her lip, looked at him sadly, and placed a hand to his cheek. "Bill. Sometimes I think we're both . . . both just too busy. I wonder if our lives aren't just eating us up."

"You think we need a vacation?"

She laughed. "Oh, you know me. I *always* need a vacation. No." She bit her lip. "I've been thinking. The years are passing. I know I'm young . . . but you—"

"I'm aging rapidly?"

"No, no. I guess I'd better just spit it out. I know we've talked before about . . . about having a family . . . and put it off. But now I think if we wait too long . . . Well, you'll not really appreciate children. And who knows?" She smiled bleakly at him, tears glistening in her eyes. "Who knows what the future holds? I'd like to, maybe, enjoy . . . grandchildren with you . . . and all that other stupid and sentimental nonsense." She sniffed and turned away. "This is just too much. One year I'm reading Herman Hesse and listening to Kurt Cobain. The next, I want to start knitting booties for grandchildren and planning retirement cruises!"

He laughed, deep feeling moving within him.

So many of his emotions had been buried or stunted before he'd met Amy. Now there seemed a rich harvest of them—he felt as though he owned a Matisse's garden of wonder and life, the bountiful spectrum of love in all its colorings and art.

"Oh, dear. Age creeps into the mix, finally."

"I'm sorry," she said. "You know that I don't feel comfortable not expressing my feelings."

"No. That's perfectly fine," he said. "You're not just talking about your feelings. This is logical fact that you're facing. And we've got to face it together."

"I was worried you'd be mad."

"What? That I'd be so vain as to not acknowledge that I'm getting to be an old geezer!"

"You're not old. That's not the issue."

He chuckled. "No, of course not. I know." She had turned away. He reached over and pulled her head around. He kissed her gently on one cheek. "Darling, you're perfectly right. There's absolutely no reason we shouldn't have children. Immediately. I guess I've just been so very selfish. I've wanted to have you all to myself as long as I could."

Her eyes were filled with wonder and delight. "Bill! You're serious!"

"Well there is the little matter of where we'll find the money . . . But you know what they say. When it comes to kids, you always scrape together just enough."

She spoke in a baby voice. "I can write a *Dark Sunset* novel, Daddy!"

Then she hugged him.

She held him so hard, it felt as though she were trying to melt into him.

And if that were at all possible, the way William Blessing felt now, it would have been perfectly all right with him.

He held her close, and the firm softness of her, the heady fragrance and warm essence surrounded him in a nimbus of erotic sensation. They kissed, and somehow it was the sweetest, tenderest kiss he'd ever experienced.

The next thing he knew they were entangled passionately on the floor, fire hot beside them. He could feel his love for her burning hot as the coals in that hearth. And far longer lasting.

"Well, darling," said Blessing. "Even Charles Dickens pales in interest compared to you." He pointed upstairs. "And you know what? Despite what you say, I think I'm a bit too old to be rolling around on the floor. I think I'd far prefer to work toward pregnancy in our nice warm and very expensive bed."

"Spoilsport," she said, laughing.

Athletically, Amy Blessing hopped to her feet and helped Blessing get up. He mimed creaky rheumatism and then wobbled and hobbled as Amy led him, chuckling and amorous-eyed, toward the steps that led up to the bedroom.

Halfway up, the doorbell rang.

"Who could that be?" said Amy, looking vexed.

"Couldn't be Donald," said Blessing. "He's got a key and can let himself in. Besides, he never bothers us on a Saturday night."

"I think you should just ignore it, Bill. Come on." She tugged on his arm. "Let's just not be at home."

"No. It's obvious that we're home. It could be something important." He gently disengaged himself and gave her a reassuring smile. "Look, go on up. I'll deal with whatever it is and I'll be up immediately."

"No. I'll wait for you here." She crossed her arms, looking vaguely vexed at his insubordination.

"It's a snowy night. Maybe someone had an accident or got stuck outside and needs to use a phone," he said. "One has certain neighborhood responsibilities."

"In the middle of a city? I'm not so sure," she said.

Amy was a suburban girl, and she tended to be a bit nervous about living in an urban environment. This was a fairly safe neighborhood, though, and Blessing couldn't imagine street criminals out and about in the snow. Icy sidewalks and roads made for a slippery getaway!

Besides, he didn't even have to open the door to see who was out there.

At the front door, he clicked the security monitor on.

"Hello," he said through the intercom system. The TV monitor fuzzed into life, lived a moment as a flipping horizontal colored band, and then became a blur. Snow must be covering the lens outside.

"I'm so sorry to bother you, but there's been an accident out here. I need to call a tow truck and perhaps the police."

It was a woman's voice, teeth a-chatter slightly with the cold. Blessing could hear the whir of the wind and the clattering slap of hard snowflakes. He could almost feel the bite of that chill in her tone.

But no image.

Damned snow. He usually didn't mind snow, but at times like this he wished he lived in a milder climate. The east coast could be pretty damned vicious. Why this woman had chosen his door to knock upon, he didn't know. But he felt obliged to perform his humanitarian duty and help her out.

Quickly, he tapped out the off-alarm code, then twisted the door lock, unlatched the latch, and pulled the heavy oak door open.

Immediately, the cold air blasted in, hard and nasty, carrying with it a flurry of flakes.

"Exactly what hap—" he began.

Immediately, he saw that it was no woman who stood out there, but a large man in a long coat, a monolithic black form against the less-black swath of outside snow.

Before he could even think about trying to slam the door closed, the man stepped in and drove a fist into his solar plexus with the precision and speed of a veteran boxer.

Stars mixed with the snow. He gasped out a choked cry and dimness clouded his vision. He doubled over with the blow, fell into the big form. The big man walked him back into the foyer.

Blessing felt he had been split in half.

"That's right, Professor Blessing," said a voice from behind the man who'd attacked him. "Give us a little room, so we can get out of the cold."

The pain was beginning to creep from his abdomen up to his chest. He seemed to flicker in and out of consciousness as the other man stepped in from the scatter of snowflakes and slowly eased the door closed behind him.

Long, long coat.

Naked fingers sticking from black gloves.

Hard chin.

Smirk.

"There we go. That's better," he said in a biting whisper. "Now then, Professor. There's no reason for anyone here to get hurt further, although we certainly have the instruments available to sufficiently accomplish that task."

"Yeah. Like fuckin' knives and guns," snarled the man in black.

"Oh, and a few other choice items, I suppose," whispered the man in the long coat. "We're professionals, you see, and we enjoy our work. Now, we understand that you have a most remarkable collection, containing quite a few items of value. Is that true, Professor?"

The breath wheezed from Blessing's lungs, carrying no words.

"I said—" The man pulled his hair back and glared face-to-face at him. Blessing smelled alcohol, garlic, and something nastier on the man's breath. "I said, Professor, is that true?"

Blessing managed a harsh "Yes."

Enough adrenaline had charged into him now that he was focusing. The thought that occurred to him was not fear for his collection of Poe—but rather for his wife.

Amy.

They mustn't hurt Amy!

"Yes. Please. Force isn't necessary," he managed. "You may have whatever you like."

"Why, there's a smart man," said Long Coat. "All the same . . ." He nodded.

The dense, tall thug with a face like a battered Marvel comic character grabbed Blessing from the rear, yanked his arms back, and easily held his wrists together.

A jab of pain shot up to Blessing's shoulders. It felt as though they were trying to pull his arms out of their sockets. Unconsciousness beckoned, but as if he anticipated this, the big man eased the pressure.

"Excellent. Now. We can make this very quick and, if not painless, then at least not as agonizing as it might be," said Long Coat. "Please, Professor. Show us to your collection. We presume it's somewhere upstairs, true?"

"Yes," Blessing said.

"Good. Slowly and easily . . . up we go. But not too slow. We get very impatient."

Neither man wore a mask, and as his senses sharpened back up, Blessing took in every detail, every scar, every bend of nose and hair follicle he could, imprinting it on his memory.

You are making a mistake, he thought. *You will be caught. You will not be able to get away with this.*

This was the thought that kept him going, that kept his mind from snapping and rebelling. Kept it away from *This can't be happening,* firmly on *There will be justice!* and *I must protect Amy.*

They hustled him up the stairs.

"Now, show us which door and then let us in," demanded Long Coat.

Blessing thought about offering them money or whatever valuables he had if they would only leave, but he knew that would accomplish nothing. Clearly, they knew what he had, and were intent on their goal.

He'd always known that so many valuables were vulnerable. But he'd only thought that incidental burglars might fall upon them. He'd never imagined that someone might want all those first editions and other collectibles badly enough to make it a special job. How could they hope to resell, to make any money off of that kind of heist?

Yet clearly, this was the purpose of the duo. That they, in the end, would not be able to get away with this seemed obvious. Blessing was concerned about the preservation of the items he had paid so much for and so revered; however, his life and Amy's life were far more important. He'd do whatever they asked.

They reached the second floor when Amy came out of the bathroom. "Bill. Is everything—?"

As soon as she took in the sight of the men with Blessing, alarm registered on her face. She turned and started to hurry away.

"Amy. No!" Blessing cried after her.

Long Coat sprinted after her. There was no contest. He caught up with her on the first stair step, flung an arm around her waist, and yanked her back.

She yelped.

"Shut up, bitch!" he said. He shook her like a dog shakes a rabbit.

"Don't hurt her!" cried Blessing.

Amy stopped struggling. Long Coat dragged her back to the door.

"No one's going to get hurt if you do what we say. Understand?" He gave Amy another shake. Eyes wide and terrified, she nodded. She looked over to Blessing and showed relief that he didn't seem hurt.

"They just want the valuables in the Poe room," said Blessing. "I'm going to let them have them."

"A good liberal policy, Professor," said Long Coat. "Now please . . ." He pointed at the alarm. "Would you do the honors?"

"I would if I had a free hand."

"Of course. Just remember, we're more than capable of hurting Mrs. Blessing here. Try something and that's exactly what will happen."

The big bruiser was still hovering over Blessing as he rubbed some circulation back into his hands, then applied himself to the alarm box. A few finger-punches later, and the red light winked off.

He put his hand in the right pocket of his pants.

"Careful, Professor," said Long Coat.

"I'm just getting my keys."

"Fine."

Blessing drew the keys up. Jingling. He showed them to Long Coat, then selected the correct one.

Inserted it.

Twisted it.

Pushed the door open.

A cool draft pushed out of the room as the door opened, with it the smell of old leather and paper. He reached in and turned on the overhead light.

The group walked in.

As soon as Long Coat stepped into the room and looked around something changed.

Previously, he'd been wearing a self-satisfied smirk. Now, though, he looked vaguely confused. Disoriented. Troubled. Perhaps even frightened.

"Oh, man," he whispered.

"What gives?" said the other man.

"Hold the woman," said Long Coat.

The bruiser immediately obeyed, stepping over and grabbing Amy. "Hey, she's a babe. Smells damn good, too."

Absently, Long Coat reached into the pocket of his coat. His hand came out, holding a gun.

"Son of a bitch!" he said.

He started quivering. He turned around and looked at Blessing, his eyes had turned red and bloodshot.

Up came the gun. The bore was the blackest, coldest thing that Blessing had ever experienced.

"You!" said Long Coat.

"What?"

"No!" cried Amy.

Instinctively, despite the fear that ran through him, Blessing turned to his wife.

The big man had been distracted from the proceedings. His proximity to comely female flesh had apparently triggered more immediate desires than the need to rob. His bullish nostrils were wide, and he had his mouth buried into Amy's neck, a thick hand over her right breast, kneading it roughly.

"Get away from her!" Blessing cried. With no regard for his own safety, he stepped over and swung his fist into the big man's face. The blow hurt Blessing more than it hurt the man, though he did attract the fellow's attention. He looked up and glared defiantly, raw lust in his eyes.

Despite the pain in his fist, Blessing was about to punch again, when a hard blow smacked him on the back of the neck. Reality jumped and jarred. Blessing popped in and out of consciousness as he stumbled over to the other side of the room then bumped into a set of books.

He crumpled to the ground, trying to cling to awareness.

Stay awake! Stay alive!

For Amy's sake!

The next thing he knew, Long Coat was standing over him, straddling him, gun out and brandished.

"You!" he snarled through clenched teeth. "You are my Persecutor!"

"What?" said Blessing.

The cords on the man's neck stood out, and veins bulged on a sweating forehead.

"Finally, I confront you!" said Long Coat. His eyes wobbled wildly. "You shall trouble me no further—"

"Get that beast off my wife!"

Blessing started to get up.

Two bullets put him back down.

The pain was sharp and blunt and radical.

Darkness came swiftly.

And it was no friend.

14

Then this ebony bird beguiling my sad fancy into smiling,
By the grave and stern decorum of the countenance it wore,
"Though thy crest be shorn and shaven, thou," I said, "art sure no craven,
Ghastly grim and ancient Raven wandering from the Nightly shore—
Tell me what thy lordly name is on the Night's Plutonian shore!"
Quoth the Raven, "Nevermore."

—Edgar A. Poe, *The Raven*

It was a brilliant plan!

Absolutely *brilliant!* thought Donald Marquette as Baxter Brittle's Volvo chugged through the frosty streets. The snow was coming down so hard now it blurred the streetlamps. Marquette wore no gloves and so he kept his hands warm at the car's hot-air vent as he sat in the front seat.

The Marquis had been ordered not to drink that night, so he negotiated the street, with the help of the car's heavy-duty snow tires. Baxter Brittle and the Count were in back. The whole interior of the car smelled of the sickly sweet scent of the absinthe that Baxter had insisted on drinking, despite Marquette's request that he remain sober. He wore a Victorian-style fur coat, and seemed fascinated just watching the dance and swirl of the snow as it rushed down out of the sky.

"Nice night for peace and joy, eh?" Baxter slurred. He started crooning, "I'm dreaming of a white post-Christmas!" in an off-key warble.

"This is the place," said Donald. He pointed. "And that's the house."

"Park! Park!" said Baxter. "This is going to be a lark!"

"Sure," said the Marquis, peering around through the nearly opaque air. "All I have to do is to find an empty spot, okay?"

Donald shot his cuff and examined his watch. "Well, don't be too fancy about your parallel parking. We're just about at the meeting time."

He himself, though not drunk, was not entirely sober either. Although he'd suggested that sobriety was best in this particular situation, he found his excitement and nerves had been a bit much to take, while waiting back at the Sailor. No one seemed to mind that he'd had a few beers, or that he'd slipped a bottle of vodka in his pocket. Just in case, he'd told himself. He could always chuck it.

A fabulous plan!

Even as the Marquis fought with the wheel to back the Volvo into a space, snowflakes battering the windshield only to be swept off by the swishing wipers, Donald Marquette could hear Baxter Brittle's voice drawl, back in the basement below his bar:

"A simple plan, indeed!" he said, waving his cup of drink about happily in one hand and pointing toward Mick and Theodore. "We have before us the solution. Here: two rather large, rather frightening men. Aforesaid men bust into the Blessing establishment with a maximum of menace but a minimum of actual violence. I trust that you two are up to this so far," he'd said, eyeing the guys in black.

"Sounds like fun," Mick said, mildly.

"Yeah. Cool," said Theodore.

"Excellent. So far, so good," Baxter Brittle had continued. "Now then. Along comes our hero, young Donald Marquette. Why has he arrived on the doorstep of the Blessing residence on the fateful Saturday evening? Why, to mend a rift. To prevail upon the Blessings to directly deal with the subject of controversy! The illustriously bad influences themselves! The Gothiques! To that end, representative members—to wit, myself, the Marquis, and the Count—have accompanied him, carrying with us offerings of peace and perhaps books to be signed."

His finger smote the air melodramatically.

"But wait! Wait. There seems to be trouble! Yes, the Blessing homestead, with its wonderful collection of Poe artifacts, is in trouble! And, being brave and valiant citizens, and very, very *good* Goths, we come to the rescue.

"Bam! Pow! Whack! Out you baddies! Take this, take that!" Baxter Brittle had become so enamored of his scenario, that he arose and started whacking the air with fisticuffs.

He huffed and puffed as he shadow-boxed. Then he gave one climactic whack, whirled around, and spread his arms in glorious celebration.

"Behold, the villains are vanquished. Off they go, escaping into the night. But the Poe collection and the brilliant Professor and his Missus are safe and sound, thanks to our valor. Our heroes, they shall say." He picked up his absinthe. "Thank you, Donald! Thank you, Gothiques. Clearly, we should reconsider our stand concerning you. Let's reconvene at a peaceful time, have a few drinks, and be pals!"

Baxter had turned to Donald.

"And you, Mr. Marquette . . . why, we value you so much now, that we have no problem at all associating with such fine people!"

He'd grinned.

"So you see! Very simple but very effective. And who knows what value Tome Press might receive? An exclusive edition of an obscure William Blessing work? Why yes! What a good idea, Baxter Brittle. You are a genius." He bowed. "Thank you! Thank you all so very much!"

They'd all had a few more drinks to toast the proposition.

To Donald, it was perfect.

Not only could he consolidate his position with the Blessings, he could also still hang with his friends—perhaps even gain status with the gang. Perhaps his own line of books! Anything was possible! The only limit in this kind of situation was imagination, and his imagination was . . . well, literary and therefore limitless.

The banging of the wheels against the curb, the squeak and squeal of rubber against ice. They were parked. He pushed his way out, into the blast of raw cold. He pulled out his bottle. Nothing like vodka to warm the soul. He took a bracing swallow, another, and then placed the bottle back into his pocket.

"This way."

He led them up to the front stairs of the townhouse.

The street was a winter wonderland. Icicles hung from the branches of trees in a bizarre imitation of fangs. Snow was piled high on cars. The large range of townhomes squatted under the burden of ice and snow, like frozen giants.

From somewhere above in the darkness from which the snow materialized, a sound emerged.

A caw!

Donald looked up. A piece of night seemed to flap away up there. Then the smashing of snow on his face made him look back down.

Baxter Brittle had a bit of difficulty navigating the snow, but with the help of the Count and the Marquis he managed not to slip and slide. A sorry bunch of saviors. Fortunately, the villains were in on the game and would fall and flail and then fly away. A minimum amount of force would bring a maximum amount of effect.

Donald led them up the icy steps. He had to grab the railing to keep himself upright. The door was closed and locked, of course, and presumably the alarm system was off. He didn't bother to knock. He could claim that he'd tried to knock and, upon getting no response and being concerned, had simply brought out the keys the Blessings had given him and used them. "Thank goodness you did that" they'd say, and that would be that.

The lock clicked.

The door squeaked open.

Donald walked in and was surprised at what awaited him.

Silence.

He held up his hand to the others. "I don't hear anything."

"Look, this is a pretty solid house," said Baxter. "If they're ransacking the Poe room by now, we wouldn't hear it. Let us in! I'm dying of cold."

Donald walked in farther and the others followed. He walked toward the steps that led to the second floor.

Thumps.

A muffled cry.

More thumps.

"Okay. We'd better go up," he said.

He swallowed and found himself nervous and frightened, even though there should be nothing to be frightened of.

"Look," said Brittle. "We hear bad noises. We grab weapons. Boys! There's a kitchen. See what you can do." The Count and the Marquis scurried off into the kitchen, while Baxter Brittle looked around the room. He pointed toward the fireplace. "Yes. We hear noises. We grab fireplace utensils as weapons. Perfect!"

Baxter got the shovel, and Donald the poker.

The Count and the Marquis emerged from the kitchen with a cleaver and a chopping knife. Fortunately, they were in normal clothing tonight, looking like nervous young men dealing with burglars extemporaneously, and that was exactly the impression that was needed.

They made their way upstairs.

The door to the Poe room was open.

The thumping had stopped though.

"You first," Baxter whispered. "You're the hero."

Donald nodded. He raised the poker and proceeded into the room.

In the middle of the room, sat Mick, coat and legs flailed. He was staring at a gun he held in his hand. Upon sensing an approach, he looked up. Glazed eyes focused. He smiled at Donald like one possessed.

"Mine Enemy is Dead!" he whispered harshly. "Finally! Dead! I can rest at night! No longer pursued!"

Alarm filled Donald. He stood transfixed, staring at Mick, not knowing what to do.

Then Theodore arose from behind a table. His face was flushed, and his eyes looked sleepy and slaked. His pants were halfway down his powerful thighs. "Man," he said. "What a gas!"

Donald stepped over to him. Behind the table lay Amy Blessing, clothes half torn off, bloody and unconscious. Donald didn't have to ask what Theodore had been doing to her.

"Oh, my God!" he said.

He lost control of his grip on the poker and it dropped from his hand, thunking onto the rug.

Baxter Brittle staggered in, looked at Mick. "Dear me," he said. "Mick! Mick!" He made a naughty-naughty gesture with his fingers. "This was not in the plans, Mick!"

"He's dead! The Enemy is dead!" repeated Mick.

"What?" asked the Count, breathlessly. "He *killed* Blessing!"

Killed Blessing?

The words reverberated in Donald's mind. Part of him simply walled up, denied it. Another part drove him to action.

"What are you talking about, Mick?" he demanded, almost on the point of hysteria. The horror of Amy's naked bloody body was bad enough. But Blessing—murdered? "Where is he?"

"Hell! I have boosted his soul straight to Hell—away from me. An infinity, an eternity—away!" Mick leaned his head back and laughed.

Dire realization flowed through Donald like a raging fever. He instantly understood that all the uneasy feelings and dark suspicions he'd ever had about Mick were just mild doubts compared to the reality standing before him. The man wasn't a writer with a few odd personality quirks, but a true-to-life sociopath, a for real deranged killer who just happened to dabble in fiction when not out skull-fucking his latest victim.

Donald looked up and around.

Legs.

He saw a pair of legs, beyond a high-backed Victorian chair. Donald hurried over. The legs were indeed attached to Professor Blessing. His body lay half-propped by a dump of fallen books, beneath the raven atop its bust of Pallas. Two bloody holes were in his chest, and he was still and stiff and apparently quite, quite . . .

Dead.

Dead!

Donald Marquette could feel his whole world fissuring and crumbling as he neared the fallen author, looking down at the blood that dribbled down his chest, staining the floor, rendering it sodden with dark red.

He spun around.

"You *idiot*!" he screamed at Mick. And turned to Theodore, stabbing a finger. "Why did you *do* this? This was not . . . *not* in the plan."

Baxter Brittle shook his head forlornly. "Oh, dear! Oh, dear me!"

"Hey!" said the Count. "Cool stuff here, though!"

"Yes!" said the Marquis. "We may as well take it now, huh?"

"You were supposed to just scare them!" screeched Donald. His voice lowered plaintively. "And then we were going to come . . . to . . . the . . . rescue."

"Enemy . . . gone . . ." said Mick, wearing a silly grin and laughing. "Enemy . . . kaput! Enemy—*banished*!"

Donald was about to run forward and kick that damned gun out of Mick's hand. Then he had to check on Amy. Yes, if Amy was all right, just unconscious, this whole nightmare could possibly be survived. Could possibly—

Something grabbed his pants leg.

His heart jumped up his throat.

He wheeled around.

William Blessing's eyes were open. He leaned forward and was grabbing hold of Donald Marquette's pants leg so hard his nails dug into his leg beneath.

"You!" Blessing croaked. "You did this . . . Donald. *Why?*"

As he stared down in shock and horror, something went cold deep inside Donald Marquette. Glacier cold, ancient cold. The whole scene seemed to slow, to freeze, like the re-run of a winning touchdown. The frigid Donald Marquette observed, analyzed, made the logical and totally inevitable decision.

"You . . . will . . . *pay,*" gasped Blessing, inching forward, hand reaching out as though for Donald's throat. *"Pay!"*

Donald grabbed the bust of Pallas, the stuffed raven tumbling off as he raised it high above his head. His mind screamed *No Dad,* you'll *pay!* as he drove the bust down with all his might upon the head of Professor William Blessing.

The head made a sickening cracking sound.

Blessing issued no other sound. His hand lost its grip on the pants leg and his body splayed back onto the floor, adding a larger splash of blood to the carpet. The bust of Pallas rolled off and lay facedown upon the floor.

Stunned at what he'd done, but nonetheless still coldly convinced that he'd had no alternative, a different, deader Donald Marquette turned and looked back.

"I had no choice," he said in a monotone.

"The Enemy . . . wasn't dead," said Mick. He turned his head toward Donald, new respect and gratitude in his eyes. "You . . . killed the Enemy."

"Oh, dear," said Baxter Brittle. He took out his flask and polished off a swallow. "Oh, dear me!"

Donald walked around the table to Amy Blessing. He knelt down and felt for her pulse.

Yes. It was there. She was still alive. Mercifully unconscious, but still alive.

"Listen to me now," said Donald, suddenly feeling totally sober and in command. "Take as much of this stuff as you can carry. There's no one outside. No observers, but still we must be careful. We will all go . . . and then I will come back and discover this scene. Understood?"

The others nodded.

"Quickly now!" said Donald. "And I'll show you what's worth the most."

Mick's gun had a silencer. There was no sign of alarm from the adjacent houses. Good. They just might get away with this.

They had to.

It was Donald Marquette's only hope.

But if they did *get away with it . . . if it was believed that the Blessings had been the victims of random drug-crazed burglars . . .*

Donald looked down at Amy Blessing, sprawled and bloody but somehow still beautiful.

Amy's mine!

So, he thought, taking out a rag to start cleaning off fingerprints, was a great deal more.

Outside, Donald thought he heard the flap of wings.

He ignored it.

15

Mimes, in the form of God on high,
Mutter and mumble low,
And hither and thither fly—
Mere puppets they, who come and go
At bidding of vast formless things
That shift the scenery to and fro,
Flapping from out their Condor wings
Invisible Woe!

—Edgar A. Poe, "The Conqueror Worm"

The rest was *not* silence.

Professor William Blessing woke up.

The first thing he was aware of was muted light, coming through tinted windows. He looked up and realized that he was in a huge room below a rotunda. In the top of the rotunda, some kind of white bird was fluttering, trapped. As he focused, he could see it was a dove. A dove flying from perch to perch, looking for a way to escape.

He looked down.

He sat upon an old wooden chair. Underneath was a beautiful tile floor. Around him were lines of desks. Reading desks, with no occupants. Upon the circling shelves were books and magazines and newspapers.

A library, then.

He was in a beautiful old library.

It smelled of that delicious combination of worn leather and paper, of silence and concentration. Dust motes danced in a shaft of light, like unbound atoms intellectual, dancing in the halls of knowledge.

He was wearing a dark suit of Victorian cut. It was silken and comfortable. As he turned around, he saw, beside a large circulation desk, still untenanted, a drinking fountain. His mouth was dry, so he got up and got a drink. The water was cold and refreshing, but brackish.

When he arose from his drink, he turned and saw that there was a man behind the highly polished wood desk. He too wore a Victorian coat along with odd spectacles, mutton-chop sideburns, and a black bow about the neck, tied with a Byronic flair. He was an elderly man, but there was something familiar about the shape of the head, the stare of the eye.

"May I help you?" the librarian asked.

"I . . . I don't know why I'm here," said Blessing.

"Surely you are here to use the library, sir," said the man. "May I see your library card?"

"Of course." Blessing checked his pockets, but found nothing in them. "I don't seem to have one," he said.

"Well, then!" said the man, still dark and ruminative. "Obviously you are here to obtain one. Allow me to help you. Step up to the desk, if you will."

Blessing obeyed, still feeling confused and disoriented. The man in the dark suit and tie and domed forehead reached underneath the counter and pulled out a piece of paper.

"Your name, sir?" asked the librarian.

"William Clark Blessing."

"Date of birth?"

"Uhm . . . December fifteenth, nineteen-fifty."

"Date of death?"

Blessing blinked at the old librarian. "Excuse me . . ."

"I need the date you died, sir. If you're going to check in or check out of the library, or even use it, I'll have to have all the proper information." The man looked faintly impatient and piqued. But there was something else in his eye: a kind of fury. A challenge.

"But I'm not dead! I don't know what you're talking about."

"No memory of death. Hmm. Not uncommon," said the librarian. "Well, I suppose there might be something in the records that could help. I have your name. Let me see what I can do." He sighed, then gestured about. "Here are the current periodicals. You're not allowed into the stacks or the other reading rooms or the crypts without a library card. However, please feel free to peruse our journals while you wait. I'm sure we can get all this sorted out, please be patient with us."

Blessing was not so much patient as bewildered. The whole experience had the skewed reality of a dream, but all the sensations and validity of reality. "Thank you," was all he could say.

"If you'll excuse me."

The clicks from the librarian's heels echoed up into the rotunda. Blessing looked up. That dove was still flapping up there. Looking for an escape. But the windows all seemed closed.

Blessing walked over to a stack of newspapers and magazines neatly displayed upon the table.

His eye was immediately caught by a headline.

HORROR WRITER SLAIN—MYSTERIOUS SERIAL KILLINGS CONTINUE.

He read the article. Dean Koontz had been killed, despite extraordinary security measures he'd taken following the deaths of Stephen King, Peter Straub, Clive Barker, and the first, William Blessing.

The paper was *The Washington Post.*

The irony! Dean always claimed *not* to be a horror writer.

Blessing felt oddly aloof.

Detached.

He felt as though his emotions were someplace distant, his brain itself not quite fitted properly into his skull but floating up above him like a helium balloon, oddly fitted with new sensory apparatus he had no idea how to engage.

Next to the *Washington Post* was a copy of the *New York Times.*

Idly, he flipped back to the bestseller lists.

There was a book at number one on the hardcover list by himself that he had never written. Number five was a novel by William Blessing and Donald Marquette. Number twelve was a novel by Donald Marquette.

Blessing turned to the paperback bestseller lists.

Number one was *William Blessing Presents Classic Dark Sunset.*

Number three was *William Blessing's Spook Nook: Goblins Ate My Shorts!*

Number five was *Soul Bite: William Blessing's Short Stories, Volume Two,* edited by Donald Marquette.

Number ten was another novel that he'd never written.

Randomly, he paged through the magazine. He noted an advertisement for *William Blessing's Magazine of the Outre* and upcoming novels by himself and in collaboration with Donald Marquette.

Slowly, very slowly, he could feel something like emotions. They trickled in from the floor, like flames slowly warming first the bottoms of his shoes and then, upward, toward his abdomen.

Next was a copy of *People.*

He paged through this. Toward the front, he recognized two people in a picture . . .

The title of the article was "The Blessing Heritage."

The caption of the photo read, "Newlyweds Donald Marquette and Amy Blessing, widow of William Blessing, relax in their Maryland estate."

There was another picture on the next page of Amy Blessing in a riding outfit upon a thoroughbred. The next page had a photo of Donald Marquette sitting near a stack of hardbacks, paperbacks, movie posters, and videos.

Blessing read the article carefully.

In it, he learned that somehow additional novels he had written had been "found" after his death. Some were stand-alones, but others had to be finished. Also there were notes for many, many series, a few screenplays, and enough jottings concerning high concepts and plots to keep several writers busy for many years. Many of his books had sold to the movies, and he was now considered to be the most popular horror writer of all time, surpassing even Stephen King, who, alas, had left no unpublished works after his untimely death and who had specifically requested that his name not be merchandised.

In the works, according to Marquette, after the launch of the Blessing magazine, were a line of William Blessing Halloween masks and William Blessing *Spook Nook* action figures.

Marquette also promised a television series, a comic book line, and the possibility of a Blessing theme park. Right now, he was working on special logos and emblems, based on ancient symbols, for a series of William Blessing designer plates and Franklin Mint mugs to be sold only on QVC.

The article said, " 'I even had a paper company call me. They wanted to get merchandising permission to use Blessing logos on toilet paper.' Marquette, brushing back his long locks from his healthy tanned face, leans back and laughs. 'But I had a few fundamental problems with that!'

"Nonetheless, upon contacting Esquire Paper, *People* learned that Marquette, President of Blessing Enterprises, apparently has approved William Blessing Presents Edgar Allan Poe toilet paper, featuring illustrations and text and poetry from that famous American author, as part of their Bathroom Reading line."

The article also noted the booming success of Tome Press, associated with Blessing Enterprises, and the wild parties and antics of its Baltimore members at a popular series of conventions and concerts promoted by that organization. A new record label, Tome Records, was in development, as well as a movie and television production company.

"When asked if he thought that William Blessing, a noted scholar and academic whose bestselling dabblings in fiction were intended merely to be a side-career, would approve of the use of his name in such intense merchandising, Marquette replied: 'I don't even consider that an issue. The work of deceased great men belongs to history. As an academic myself, I see my role as making sure that William Blessing's name is firmly chiseled into the stones of literary immortality.'

"And, along with the immense wealth and fame that his present work brings him, would Marquette like to be a literary immortal?

" 'Hey. Why lie? I'm just a humble scribe . . . But every man jack of us would like literary immortality. But I tell you, that's not what matters to me the most, and if it happens it's because of what Blessing bequeathed to me. What makes me happiest is my beautiful, dear wife Amy, who William Blessing left behind.'

"And if there was one thing he could say to William Blessing now, what would it be?

" 'That I'm keeping Amy happy.' "

When he finished the article, William Blessing closed the magazine. The room seemed to have changed colors. He looked up and saw that clouds had passed over the rotunda, jabbed with lightning. Thunder rumbled, and spatters of rain could be heard against the glass.

William Blessing went back to the circulation desk, where the old man waited for him, holding a small laminated card. There seemed a nimbus of gloom around his head, along with a grin that seemed more rictus than amusement.

"I remember now," said William Blessing.

Above the sound of rain now was the flapping of wings. Not just the dove's, it would seem. A darker pair.

"Ah, yes. I found the records. Most unfortunate circumstances. I've already inked something in on the certificate. If you'll just sign in, you can make this wonderful, quiet establishment your home and roam the halls of books or rest in peace, as you may desire."

"There is unfinished business," said William Blessing. He could feel emotions rising up to his head, out to his hands.

And the emotion was rage, strong and pure.

"Well now, I suppose we all leave behind unfinished business, Mr. Blessing."

Blessing raised his hands and his head to the lightning and thunder. He saw the dark form, chasing the dove.

"It is me," he said. "I am the crow."

Above there was a furious screeching and scrabbling. Pain and anguish shrieked and echoed through the rotunda. Lightning flashed, showing coal black ripping cotton white.

A small body fell, flopping and spasming upon the desk, splattering blood.

With one final jerk, the dove died.

Flapping down came the bird of black, the killer.

It stood beside its victim, eyeing the librarian and Blessing, challenging. Dark crimson matted its beak and breast.

"Quoth the Crow," said William Blessing.

Intuitively, Blessing reached out his right arm to serve as the creature's perch.

16

Regarding, then, Beauty as my province, my next question referred to the tone of its highest manifestation—and all experience has shown that this tone is one of sadness. *Beauty of whatever kind, in its supreme development, invariably excites the sensitive soul to tears. Melancholy is thus the most legitimate of all the poetical tones.*

—Edgar A. Poe, *The Philosophy of Composition*

The melancholy strains of a Beethoven piano sonata drifted down from the top of the large townhouse.

"Delightful," intoned Baxter Brittle, beaming up toward the roof and chandelier. "She plays so very well!"

"At this point," said Donald Marquette with a bite to his tone, "I think I'd rather hear *Roll Over Beethoven.* That's all she does. Play mournful classics. When I work here, I have to put on headphones."

"Healing takes time," said the Marquis, inspecting the place settings, glasses, silverware, and silver serving dishes one last time. "There. I believe that all is in readiness."

"Wait!" said the Count. "We forgot to uncork the wine. This is very fine wine. It needs to breathe—"

Baxter Brittle picked up the large bottle that they'd been working on, eyeing its diminishing contents analytically. "Well, tell it to take deep breaths, because we'll be drinking it very, very soon, I think."

Brittle was not wearing his Oscar Wilde outfit.

In fact, he was dressed conservatively, in a nice coat and tie and loafers. Only his long hair attested to his usual look, as was the case with the Count and the Marquis. No trappings of decadence, those sartorial affectations were tonight in abeyance. Now they were just neat twentysomethings attentively making sure that all the dinner preparations were made. The rich smells of exquisite Italian food, heavy on oregano, basil, tomato sauce, virgin olive oil, and the crisp texture of fresh-baked bread floated above all like a promise.

The wine was all red.

Donald himself wore new casual clothes: nice slacks, a faint blue shirt, a tweed jacket from Saks Fifth Avenue. They felt good, and the recent influx of money he'd bought them with felt good, too. The expensive Calvin Klein cologne he wore now gave him just a jot more welcome self-confidence, aided by the two glasses of wine he'd already consumed.

He was limiting his alcohol intake, though.

Tonight was *the* night, and while he wanted his nerves to be slightly coated, he wanted to be very far from blotto. He'd ordered the Count and the Marquis to restrict their intake as well. With Baxter though, it didn't really matter, since his tolerance was quite high and wine was like water to him, compared to his beloved absinthe. The evening would end long before Baxter Brittle's intoxication would cease being pleasant and charming.

"One question, my boy," said Baxter, looking blearily up over his vintage burgundy. "Why Italian?"

"This is Amy's favorite," said Donald. "And Blessing loathed all forms of Southern Italian food. Allergic to the spices, I think. They never had it."

"Good thinking!" said the Count. "I got it from the best place in Little Italy."

"My mouth is watering, man!" said the Marquis. "I love Neapolitan food. I've already sampled the cheese—and it is to die for!"

"Unfortunate words," said Baxter Brittle. "Cannoli for dessert, I hope."

"Oh, yes. Absolute tops!" assured the Count.

"Mmm. Lovely and decadent," said Baxter. "Well, all seems to be in place. Perhaps you should go up and fetch our hostess."

Donald nodded.

Yes. Yes, it was time.

He straightened his jacket in the living-room mirror, then ran a comb through his hair. He took a deep breath, then went up the stairs.

The Poe room was double locked and boarded up. It hadn't been entered since he'd had the inventory done, to determine what had been stolen. Since her return from the hospital, Amy had not been able to even look at the place, much less go in it. It was she who had more or less walled it up. This was unfortunate, since Donald could have used what was left in the room—quite a bit, actually—to good purpose.

But, he thought as he slowly and methodically took the stairs step by step, *assuming tonight works out, there's plenty of time for that.*

A Chopin etude commenced, lovely, but slower than it should have been. Not surprising, really. Everything about Amy was slower than it should be these days. He was just glad, though, that she was reasonably functional and not in some mental institution.

Surprisingly, despite all the death and blood and rape, things had worked out far better than Baxter Brittle's original plan.

They'd hustled boxfuls of books and letters and Poe collection items out to the waiting cars. The others had sped away to store it and lie low. Then Donald had returned to "discover" the horrible scene. He'd called 911. The cops had arrived. They bought his story, and if any evidence pointed toward him, Amy Blessing's tale upon awakening two days later immediately refuted it. A manhunt began for the burglar/ killer and the burglar/rapist, but they could not be found. Tome Press had provided sufficient funds to send them off for an extended "vacation."

It was only during the aftermath, however, that Donald Marquette learned about his true talents. With the police detectives he had been perfect, the grieving student, the horrified protégé—but that had only been practice for the outstanding performance he gave for the media.

Suddenly, with the spotlight upon him, Marquette became Fred Astaire, dancing away gracefully and capturing the hearts and minds of readers everywhere. Blessing's latest books, already selling well, shot to the tops of the bestseller lists. Movie proposals turned into production deals. Rights were sold to countries that had not yet bought them. And Donald Marquette, his name now inseparable from the famous slain horror writer (and scholar!), had easily sold that languishing novel and contracted for another as part of a two book deal at a very respectable sum, a healthy portion of which he had pledged as a reward for information leading to the arrest and conviction of Blessing's killer, and the recovery of his ravaged Poe library.

Of course, considering who the killer truly was, he knew he'd never have to pay out.

Minor chords from the piano waxed and waned as he entered the room. He'd put a vase of cut flowers on the Steinway today, and they smelled fresh and nice. However, this close to the scene of death, the place still held the faint odor of old blood. Not entirely a bad smell . . . mixed with the scent of Amy's shampoo. She didn't wear perfume anymore, and had taken to dark, drab clothing, but to him it made her look more beautiful.

Now, as she sat on the bench, softly playing the keys and working the pedals, she seemed very pale and precious, a breath of weary life in a frozen picture.

He leaned on the piano, just within range of her peripheral vision, adopting an attitude of intense listening. When she finished the Chopin piece, he clapped softly. "Very nice."

She smiled wanly. "Thanks, Donald."

"Hi."

She nodded and then shuffled through the leaves of music on the holder.

"Has any chance any fragrance drifted up from the kitchen in the past hour or so?"

She blinked. "Oh, dear! Are you making dinner? I forgot!"

"Yes. Would you believe, rigatoni bolognese with some nice Italian sausage thrown in for balance? Antipasto for starters and a fresh spinach salad to get some green in. And for dessert: cannoli." He comically acted out a role of a waiter ticking off the specials. "Oh. And a fine vino rojo."

She brightened a bit at all this. Just a shade, but it did seem to light the room just a notch. Never much of a drinker before, she'd taken to consuming more red wine. In part, this was one of the reasons for the Italian meal. Red sauce needed some red wine. It would encourage her to drink.

"Sounds good." She stared off, looking remote and slightly troubled. "Wasn't there something else?"

"You've forgotten the extra treat. I've invited the Tome folks."

"Oh, yes. Your funny friends." She smiled a bit.

"It will certainly take the onus of conversation off of us. Baxter was just at a British convention, and I do believe he's chockfull of gossip."

She nodded, but just sat, looking spacey and disoriented.

She'd been like this, to one degree or another, ever since she'd woken up. It was as though the pain of her husband's death and the trauma of rape had, if not turned her socially autistic, then at least turned her partially oblique to the rest of existence. The doctors claimed she was perfectly fine physically, but would probably take a long time to heal emotionally. Donald had sworn to help make sure this psychological event occurred rapidly but naturally. All the doctors involved, all her friends and family, knowing how close Donald had become to the Blessings, seemed confident that if anyone could break through the shell that Amy Blessing had erected about herself, it would be Donald Marquette. In the meantime, though, Amy was quite capable of ordinary day-to-day business decisions involved with running the Blessing estate, insurance, et al. She just performed them perfunctorily, with no spirit or joy involved. Four months after William Blessing's murder, things were a bit in stasis concerning his books. There was a new one due for publication next month, but the one he'd been working on was only half finished. And his stories and articles and notes—no one knew much about them. Amy kept them locked away, even from Donald, who was still hard at work on the anthologies under Blessing's name.

That was part of what tonight's dinner was about.

"Yes. The gang is quite hungry. They've been swilling wine and munching chips and enjoying your piano for the past half hour. They'd like to know if you'd play for them later . . . but right now, I suppose, we should eat before the pasta gets cold."

"Of course." She pulled the top of the piano closed. "I don't want to keep people waiting."

As she got up, he offered her his arm.

She took it and sighed. "How symbolic, Donald. You know I depend on you for your support. I don't know how I would have gotten along without it."

"I feel honored to do whatever I can," he said. "You are a very important part of my life. In fact, my work now . . . and you." He paused, as though choking slightly with emotion. "Central. Absolutely . . . central."

She reached over to touch him. "Yes," she said in a small voice. "It's been so hard. So very hard."

He feigned a difficult recovery. "Hard. Yes."

He patted her hand.

This was the trick of course . . .

To show her grief and emotion, to draw *her* out. Thus, a bond was achieved. Thus they harmonized. And, gradually, he could take that composition into musical lands of his choosing.

This was a part of the strength he'd discovered in himself—the ability to withdraw into a cold, judgmental, and analytic shell deep within himself and play his emotions like a puppet master. Yes, in truth, he still had deep feelings for this woman. But now that the goal seemed more obtainable, he recognized the lustful aspect, the possession aspect.

He had goals now. Love and desire were all just a part of the mix.

Goals.

Yes.

He heard a distant snigger inside himself.

Donald Marquette once thought that if he hurt anyone, he'd never be able to live with himself. He wasn't particularly religious; he just always thought he had a sense that morally, he would be paralyzed. Now, though, that he'd actually *killed* someone . . . Well, to tell the truth, it wasn't that bad. There were occasional pangs of guilt, but they were growing less and less. And as the actual *rewards* of Blessing's passing began to kick in, Marquette became more and more grateful to Mick and especially to stony old Pallas, who had crushed Blessing's skull. A talented, learned man, certainly . . . but as he reviewed Blessing's personality more and more, Marquette realized well and truly that his original idol worship had blinded him to the man's outrageous faults.

He really had been a total *bastard.*

"I guess this conversation isn't very good for the appetite," he said. "Maybe we should just try and enjoy the evening."

He took her down to the Gothiques and all that red wine below.

The dinner was a great success.

The food was delicious, the wine was sturdy and on the right side of ten-percent alcohol.

The Count and the Marquis were loquacious and in fine fettle, prattling on about this and that in their cultural world. Baxter Brittle was charming and witty, making sure to make Amy feel a part of everything, even though she actually contributed very little in the way of words.

Marquette was very attentive, too, without being obtrusive about it. He smiled at her often and made sure that her wineglass was always full. By the time the cannoli (absolutely delicious!) were finished, Baxter had even been able to tweak a smile or two out of her.

At the behest of all she agreed to play the piano for them, after coffee.

During coffee (with cognac for Baxter, and yes, a wee drop for himself and a slightly greater tipple in Amy's cup) Donald Marquette began to bring up the subject which was truly the reason for the whole occasion.

He began casually, and had made sure that he'd dropped references to William Blessing from time to time the entire evening.

"You know, I think that we should just be grateful," he said, lifting his hands expansively. "Grateful to our departed friend for this house, for what he has left behind. None of us know how long we have upon this Earth. To be able to leave something behind, something of worth. Now that is truly something to be thankful for."

"Here, here," said Baxter, raising a glass as though in toast. "I for one shall cherish my special editions of William Blessing's work."

"Me too!" said the Count.

"And I!" chimed in the Marquis.

Amy shook her head, clearly withdrawing. "I don't know if I can ever read anything he wrote again. There was so much pain and anguish in his work, so many dark things in a man who was such a good man, a man—I thought—of light."

"Hmm. Well, you are the literary executor, my dear," said Baxter Brittle. "You inherited yourself quite a task, along with all the financial boons of an ongoing literary enterprise."

"Well, I for one have sworn to myself," said Marquette, nobly, "to dedicate a part of my life to preserving the legacy that he left. I'm even thinking of a biography." That was one of the cues for the prepared speeches.

Silence ensued.

He turned, annoyed, to Baxter Brittle, who was in the middle of pouring the dregs from a wine bottle.

"Baxter," he said, a slight wake-up edge to his voice. "What do you think? A William Blessing biography!"

As he was sitting across from him, he managed to give the foppish fellow a swift jab to the shin.

Baxter started. He barely managed to keep from spilling his wine.

Amy, still detached, didn't seem to notice any change.

"Biography? Oh, yes! Biography! What a splendid idea!" He took a few sips, letting a moment pass. He furrowed his brow thoughtfully. "But you know, it's not as though William Blessing's legacy has to be wrapped up with a biography . . . It occurs to me that his influence upon literature, upon history in fact . . . well, has a good deal more . . . potential!"

Right on cue, the Marquis asked, "What do you mean by that, Baxter?"

"Why, simply that there are short stories to be collected . . . letters to be published. Heavens, there might even be a couple of early novels hiding somewhere that Blessing never published. Plus outlines and notes . . . the unfinished novel . . . heaven knows what else." He turned a sympathetic smile toward Amy. "I can understand why all association makes you so sad . . . but . . . No. Never mind. I shouldn't even bring it up."

Brilliant! thought Donald. *Nicely played.*

Amy's interest, though still clouded with melancholy, had clearly been pricked.

She leaned toward Baxter. "No. Go ahead, Baxter. Please. You're full of clever ideas."

"Well . . . it just occurs to me that Donald here . . . Donald Marquette knows more than just about anyone else about your husband's work. Who better to lay the responsibility of co-literary executor . . . or perhaps, if you want to simply get out from under the responsibility, the *total* literary executor."

Amy blinked.

Donald watched her closely. She wasn't saying no, but she wasn't saying yes, either. Her expressions were quite difficult to read these days.

He decided to try Baxter's tactic.

"I don't know . . ." he said, hesitantly. "That would be so much . . . responsibility."

"Of course it's up to Amy," said Baxter. "But it seems to me you're already doing a great deal of work with what Blessing left behind."

Amy nodded. "That's true." She looked over at Donald. Reached over and touched him with a hand. "Would you do it, Donald? I realize that you have your own things to write . . . but it seems to be a wonderful idea to me. It would take the responsibility from my shoulders, and help to continue William's place in literature." She squeezed his arm. "I know you can do it. What's more, I trust you."

"You know, I'd like to . . ." said Donald. "But how can I? I mean, Bill's will and all . . ."

"Oh, I know some law," said Baxter. "Amy would just have to sign a few papers."

Amy nodded. "I'd be happy to. And I know that, considering these circumstances, William would want this as well."

"I think it's a great idea!" said the Count.

"Yes," continued the Marquis. "And you're a good writer! Maybe you can even finish that novel . . ."

Donald shrugged eloquently. "I'm overwhelmed." He turned and looked soulfully into Amy's dark, mourning eyes. "But of course, I'll do the very best I can."

"Good," said Baxter, rubbing his hands. "Well, that's settled then. Now, Amy, you promised a few pieces on the piano. I've been looking forward to that the whole dinner."

Amy nodded and slowly arose from her seat.

As he ascended the stairs behind her, watching her cute butt wiggle upward, Donald Marquette knew exactly what song he'd request to celebrate, if he could.

We're in the Money!

17

The boundaries which divide Life from Death, are at best shadowy and vague. Who shall say where the one ends, and where the other begins?

—Edgar A. Poe, *The Premature Burial*

When he awoke and made to rise, William Blessing hit his head on the lid of the coffin.

The coffin was lined with cushioned velvet, so he didn't hurt himself. In fact, what he felt didn't seem to quite correlate with what he remembered of pain. Nonetheless, it was disturbing and disorienting.

The closed coffin was dark beyond dark, and while it was roomy for a coffin, a few movements of his hands and feet determined that it was, in fact, a coffin. It smelled of damp earth and mildew and rot.

Naturally, his immediate conclusion was that he'd been buried alive. This did not bring up reflections or meditations upon Edgar A. Poe's *Premature Burial.*

It brought out extreme claustrophobia, total consuming terror.

The scream built up from instinct and came out loud and overwhelming.

However, the force of it startled him enough that his reason was engaged, and he paused.

The gun, the shots . . .

Donald Marquette with the bust of Pallas, bringing it down upon him, hard . . .

His reason said, a still, small voice in the darkness, *You're dead.*

Then he remembered the library. Then he remembered the librarian, the bloody dove and—

"Are you going to snooze down there all night?" asked a distinct voice. It did not seem to be coming through his ear, but directly to his mind. Nonetheless, it seemed to have timbre and tone—and a vaguely Brooklyn accent.

He remembered the crow.

"What . . . What is this place?" he asked.

"A fine and private place, Doctor," said the voice. "But none, I think, do here embrace."

"I've gone mad," he said.

"Oh, you're mad, all right. That's why you're here."

"Where?"

The voice sounded exasperated. "Six feet under! The narrow house! A sepulcher, a tope, a stupa. A cist, a tomb. Doctor, you're in a coffin in your grave! Some fun, huh?"

Oddly, although he was aware of panic deep inside of him, there was something that prevented it from taking control. His powerful cognitive abilities, yes—but also another emotion.

Anger.

Hot anger, cold anger, all the varieties of anger there were. The anger stretched from his mind and stitched together the sinews and bones and flesh of this resurrected body. It lit the fires of his being and it pumped the stuff of revenge through his veins that once held blood.

He knew now that he had been resurrected. The truth came with a surety that was as overwhelming as it was calming.

"I have returned from the dead," he said, matter-of-factly.

"Dead on, fellow! Welcome back!"

However, he was still in a coffin, below the earth a good distance. And it seemed like a very bad place to start. He did not seem to be suffocating, and he did not seem particularly hungry—but this was no place to remain for any length of time.

"Who are you?" he asked.

"Come on, don't ask stupid questions. Get your butt outta there. You've got work to do," said the voice.

"How?"

"Come on! You're the horror writer. How do revived corpses climb out of graves? Hmm? Transporter beams? No, let's try another one. How about *digging*? Duh!"

"I'm back from the dead through some supernatural agency," he said.

"Well, it sure ain't the employment agency."

"Can't I get out of here through some supernatural manner?" Blessing objected.

"Look, man. You're supernatural already, okay? You think a normal human being could dig his way out of a coffin? Just take my word and give it a try."

Even as he contemplated the voice's words, he could feel he was different. He felt as on the verge of alien senses, occult powers. The fibers and molecules that constituted his corporeal form now seemed charged with some offbeat energy.

Blessing pulled his hands up. He wiggled his fingers in the darkness before him, imagined them—

Saw them.

Even though it was pitch-dark, he saw his fingers. They seemed to glow with some supernal light. He was intensely aware of every wrinkle in the knuckles, every hair follicle, every fingernail. He noticed that they had grown very long; now they almost looked like talons rather than nails.

He lifted them up to the cool of the cushioned silk that lined the coffin.

Pushed.

The lid seemed to give way a bit. Dirt spattered through the opening casket. He could feel the pressure of the ground above, but somehow it did not seem oppressive. It felt . . . altered.

"There you go!" said the voice. "You've got the idea. Keep on! Keep on!"

Straining only slightly, he pushed the casket lid up farther and yet farther. The dirt began to tumble in upon his face and body. It tasted of humus and rocks and worms. It smelled of memories, despair, and regret.

The dirt fell upon William Blessing, but it was no dirt he'd ever experienced before. Rather than dense, it seemed merely opalescent, fluid, like some dark water. He pushed up and it gave way slowly, as though recognizing his mastery of the tomb, his triumph over the graveyard. He began to push himself up and through it, slowly but steadily pushing up and up on a gravelly stairway toward the surface.

"There you go!" cackled the voice. "You've got the knack. Comes naturally, doesn't it?"

He dug upward, upward, and then, reaching up again, he could feel his hand push up through the sod, whip past wet grass into the cold night air. The effect charged him with raw power, and the rest of his ascent was speedy. He emerged into the invigorating midnight air, breathed in the dank mist, and hauled himself from the hole where those he loved had imprisoned him.

Dirt spraying from his hair and face, he flopped onto the ground, gasping and heaving, the night swelling about him like a symphony of silence.

"I said you could do it!" piped the voice. This time not in his head, but in the near darkness. "Bravo."

He spat out dirt and coughed. "Just like an E.C. horror comic," he said bitterly, feeling bile not just in his mouth but throughout his being. He twisted his head toward the voice. "Does that make you the Cryptkeeper?"

"No, no. No such obvious antecedents for me. In fact, perhaps if I weren't very much real, I might make my home in some graphic novel. French, preferably. *Oui! Bon soir, monsieur.* Welcome back to this delightful planet. Are we ready to rumble?"

Blessing pushed himself up, unsteadily got to his feet. Around him he could see tombstones rising up, white beneath a smear of moon in a cloud-flecked night. His joints creaked like chains around an agonized soul. The place stank of history and moiled with ennui.

"Where are you?"

"Try your headstone, sirrah!"

He willed his eyes to focus, and the supernal light clicked on again, as though he were wearing infrared goggles. Although the graveyard it revealed was like no other cemetery he'd ever imagined, let alone seen.

Still, he *recognized* it.

Stunned, he stumbled and fell onto the gloaming loam, knocking his head against a rock. He looked up. There, chiseled upon marble were dates . . . and his name.

"Most Beloved . . . Rest Well, Much Loved . . . Never, Never Forgotten."

His fingernails scrabbled up and clicked along the words.

"Amy," he whispered. "Amy."

"You'd think she'd have thrown in some Latin, huh?" said the voice. "Or Greek. One of the classic languages. Classy stuff. You know both, don't you?"

"Yes," said Blessing, distractedly.

"*Kyrie Eleison,* pal. And on the fourth month, he arose from the grave and yea, he did kick some ass!"

Blessing, irked, looked up.

The gravestone was in the form of a large Celtic cross. This must have been Amy's idea, as he never cared much for crosses of any kind. He'd always joked that all he'd wanted in his crypt was a notebook computer and a modem line.

At the top of the cross, peering down with intense dark eyes, was a large crow, radiant with blackness.

"A crow," he said, thoughtfully. "A crow . . . One of the most ancient of mankind's symbols."

"So I know what you're thinking. Heckle or Jekyll?" The crow cocked its head. "Neither. This is no cartoon, Blessing. This is Reality Noir. You're here for a reason. I'm here to help you. Period."

Blessing turned around and looked at his environs. He recognized the cemetery. It was the celebrated graveyard where none other than Edgar Allan Poe was buried! Of course! Since he'd bought himself a plot here (as a part of his Poe collection, more than with the actual intention to inhabit it) of course he'd be buried here.

"Help me," he said, slowly. "Help me."

"Yes. Help you set things . . . right," said the crow, suddenly stark and serious. "There is only chaos in the universe. But chaos randomly also creates order. And order can be retrieved from entropy, that road back to chaos . . . by that ultimate creation of order . . . Will. Consciousness. Self-awareness." The crow's voice cracked into a harsh, defiant whisper. "And though, in the end, chaos shall swallow all . . . will can control what it swallows. For will, when it is truly strong, can stand apart from chaos . . . from death and nothingness . . ." The beak snapped. "For a time. For a short time only."

Time.

A short time.

Blessing looked out upon the place of his interment.

It looked like the portrait of a graveyard that Vincent van Gogh might paint, in monochrome with breaths of azure and surreal spirit wafting. Phantom land, allusions upon illusions. Three dimensional slipping into the fourth . . . rotting and desiccating and losing its bony grip upon life, symbolism, and architecture.

Rust to dust.

Sashes to ashes.

Man lives but a short time . . .

. . . nasty, brutish, and short . . .

. . . rounded not even by a dream.

"If I cannot have the dream," said Blessing, "I shall have the nightmare."

He began to walk slowly through the groundfog, the quickened corpse upon a mission . . .

And soon he heard the wings of his avian familiar flapping behind him.

18

. . . the unseen figure, which still grasped me by the wrist, had caused to be thrown open the graves of all mankind; and from each issued the faint phosphoric radiance of decay; so that I could see into the innermost recesses, and there view the shrouded bodies in their sad and solemn slumbers with the worm. But, alas! the real sleepers were fewer, by many millions, than those who slumbered not at all; and there was a feeble struggling; and there was a general sad unrest; and from out the depths of the countless pits there came a melancholy rustling from the garments of the buried.

—Edgar A. Poe, *The Premature Burial*

The city was alive.

For the first time, Blessing saw Baltimore as a living, breathing beast. Sweating mist now, breathing from its sewers, snoring through its telephone wires.

Smelling of smokestacks.

Tasting of destiny.

As he hobbled away from the dreamscape cemetery, the skewed streets seemed to warp and twist away from van Gogh into Picasso. Pieces and bits separated, tenuously reconnecting, like a multicolored lava lamp of triangles and squares and rectangles as well as of blobs and spheres.

"I don't know," he gasped. "I don't know where—"

Behind him, wings on air.

"Focus, Blessing. Remember. Imagine."

He stopped and leaned against a brick wall. He closed his eyes.

Baltimore.

My city.

When he opened his eyes again, he saw streets and buildings and neon lights again. Streetlamps burned halogen. Stoplights clicked.

But nothing seemed quite straight. All was slightly off, surrounded with varicolored nimbuses. There was a music in the air that had no sound, a vibration that was silent. He could sense these things, see these things with senses he'd never experienced before.

At an open avenue, he halted and looked down a hill. Spread out before him lay a view of lower downtown Baltimore. The harbor sparkled and glimmered, the buildings stood in exaggerated relief against one another. The sky seemed a vast cauldron of galaxies chased by violent shocks of clouds. Streaming above the hyper-real asphalt and concrete, the transdimensional brick, were grotesque shreds of faces, mangled remains of bodies with eyes in buttocks or mouths in chests, swimming in the air aimlessly. Occasionally a large mass of jumbled claws and fangs would, like some shark pouncing unsuspected upon a school of fish, fall upon a mass of ectoplasm and gobble it up, then sail on malevolently, searching, cruising, continuing the food chain in this fractured spirit world.

"There you go. You're starting to get it," said the crow.

Blessing shivered.

He looked away, staggering into an alley.

The crow lighted beside him, looked up. "Hey. Come on. There's work to be done."

"I . . . I just have to compose myself."

"Of course. You're decomposing!"

"God! God!" he said, looking at his hands in the light, half expecting shreds of rotten flesh hanging on skeletal phalanxes. His hand seemed perfectly formed, though. Again, he saw every detail of the hand down to the whorls of his fingerprints. He lifted the palm to his nose. He could smell no corruption.

He looked down at the crow.

"Look, don't ask me! Your will just reassembled your self. But believe me—you can't keep it together forever," said the black thing, scuttling along the ground, flicking its tail about and lifting its wings a bit, as though reshuffling its feathers.

"How long do I have?" Blessing asked.

"A few days. Longer? Who knows?" said the crow. "But you must keep your resolve. Lose your passion, lose your anger and resolve, and you shall become what you were."

"Heavens! I need a drink!"

"A little preservative never hurt!" said the crow. "I believe if you turn the corner just up there, you could well find what you're looking for."

Blessing pushed himself off the brick wall and tilted himself in the direction the crow indicated.

The crow lighted upon his shoulder. "Hope you don't mind if I take a little ride from time to time."

"No."

"Better ask any questions you might have now. I don't think they let crows into bars. Just Old Crows."

"What?"

"Whiskey."

Blessing did not respond. Maybe he'd left his sense of humor back in the grave. Or it had been segregated into the part of him that was now the crow.

As he rounded the corner, he saw the bar that the crow had promised. It was a neighborhood bar with no name displayed; just a huge neon sign showing a martini glass.

"I don't know . . . I don't know if I can do . . ." he said, stopping, ". . . what I must."

"What? Take a drink? I believe you've done that once or twice before," said the crow.

"You . . . know . . . what . . . I . . . mean."

"Hey. They've got an off license here. Grab yourself a bottle or two. Buddy, whatever it takes. Right?" Blessing reached the entrance to the bar. "I get off here. See ya!"

The crow leaped off his shoulder, and flew away into the night.

William Blessing opened the door and went into the bar.

It was one of those seedy downtown bars kept alive by regulars during the week and hard weekend drinkers; the sort of bar that would have had free lunch jars in the thirties and forties. A couple of men below a cloud of cigarette smoke were talking intensely in one of the booths. Two solitary drinkers sat far apart from each other on the long, cracked, wood bar. The bartender sat on a stool by the cash register, smoking a cigarette and reading the *Sun*. No one registered his arrival as he walked through the door.

Blessing felt apprehensive.

This was the sort of bar he had generally avoided. The cheap booze and depressing atmosphere reminded him too much of the specter of alcoholism that hovered over drinkers. As a student of Edgar A. Poe, he well knew the long-term hazards of drink. *The curse of the writing class,* as he used to joke to his students.

Also, Blessing felt self-conscious. He was dead, after all. How would the living deal with him?

However, his appetite for strong drink had been resurrected along with the rest of him. He *needed* that drink, and here he was.

He sat down at the bar. The bartender winged the paper closed and came over to him, eyeing him oddly.

"Hey bud! Just come from a fancy ball or something?"

He looked down at himself. Of course! He was still wearing his graveclothes—his best tuxedo. It was his wish that he be buried in it. "Makes me look so good!" he'd put in his will and testament.

"Uhm. Yes, as a matter of fact. A dry dinner party. I desperately need something stronger than iced tea."

"You came to the right place. What'll you have?"

"Double Old Crow," he said. "Water on the side."

"Sure."

As the bartender went to grab one of the spouted bottles perched in front of the bar-shelf mirror, Blessing reached down for his wallet.

His hand found only empty pockets.

Of course! No one was buried with money, at least not any more. He had nothing to pay for his drink with.

The bartender returned with the double shot glass and the water.

"That'll be three-fifty," he said.

"I seem to have left my wallet . . . uhm . . . in my car. Do you mind if I go and—"

"Sure. I'll guard your drink."

Embarrassed and frustrated, Blessing nodded and walked out of the bar, wondering what he could do to get money. He'd just have to give this whole drink business up.

Perched on a parking meter outside was the crow. In his beak was a hundred-dollar bill.

Blessing, surprised but gratified, reached over and took it. "Thanks."

"Thought you might be needing a little shambling-around money. You wouldn't want to *leave tomb* without it," said the crow. "Never showed you that on *Creature Feature,* did they? Resurrection can be such a bitch!"

"Maybe I will get that bottle," said Blessing.

He walked back in and handed the bartender the hundred-dollar bill.

"Jeez," said the bartender. He was a pudgy, fiftyish man with a little squib of a mustache and a receding hairline. "You ain't got anything smaller?"

"Look. I'll buy a whole bottle, okay?" said Blessing.

He noticed that the two men looked up from their beers at this interchange. They both looked deader than he was.

The bartender shrugged. "We're talkin' an extra . . . ah . . . twenty bucks."

"That'll be fine."

"Seems like I oughta be able to make some change now," said the bartender, smiling a bit with the added business. He walked over to the cash register as Blessing settled behind his drink. He took the drink half down in one swallow.

Waited.

For a moment, he simply couldn't taste it. But then, as though just waking up, his taste buds came up to speed. His throat stung, and the familiar warmth spread through him. Only oddly tinged with other things he could not place . . .

Nonetheless, there was still that hint of oblivion and relaxation, and he welcomed it. He took in some water, which was cold and much needed as well. By the time the bartender returned with his change and the wrapped bottle, he'd finished the rest of his drink.

"Another please," said Blessing. "And more water as well."

"Must have been a hard night," said the bartender.

"You don't know."

The bartender poured another double Old Crow, and then placed a fresh glass of water beside it.

Blessing sipped at both, taking his time, reflecting on what the crow had said.

Mission.

He had a mission, and he well knew what it was. He had only a short time in which to accomplish that mission. The fires of the drink mixed with the fires inside him, the relentless drive that must have driven him up out of the grave.

Justice!

Revenge!

However, even as the fires raged, the tranquilizing effect of the alcohol eased the broken glass-on-nerves that seemed to line his spirit.

He closed his eyes.

Ah, to rest!

To let go!

To have that peace of mind where there is no mind.

He could feel the very stuff of the bar throbbing in sympathy. As he breathed in the last of the whiskey, the stale fumes around him joined into the chorus.

Relax, they seemed to say. *All will be nothingness soon anyway. All comes to dust and oblivion, eventually. Join the lucky already there.*

Peace, Blessing. Comfort and joy and the sweet, sweet darkness. Light is the lie. Darkness is the truth.

He sighed and put down the whiskey glass. Oh, to taste fully of that sweet drink again.

The River Lethe and its calm currents of . . .

He opened his eyes.

There was something in the whiskey glass.

It was a nose.

Automatically, he reached up to his face.

Where his own nose had been once, was a hole.

He looked at his hands. The nails were cracked, the skin slowly drying and graying even as he watched.

No!

No, this was too soon!

He poured his nose into his left hand, then smashed it back onto the hole where it had been, holding it there. Then, with his other hand, he grabbed the change and his brown-bagged whiskey and hurried out from the bar into the night.

The slap of the cold air, the panic, and the fear seemed to arrest whatever was happening to him. However, he could still feel the skin of his face begin to draw back from his teeth and eyes.

"No!" he gasped. "No."

He halted in an alley. He put the bottle of whiskey down and felt up to his cheek. Skin was beginning to split. The hand came away green and slimy, slick with pus and . . .

What?

Embalming fluid?

Even as he stared at the mess in his hand, noxious in the distant amber glow of the streetlamp, he felt something hard and insistent poke into his back.

"Okay, asshole. Hand over your cash and you'll make it to morning."

The voice was brisk and demanding.

There was no question about what was in its owner's hand.

Again he saw the gun in the hand of Long Coat.

Saw it fire.

Felt *it fire, two bullets slamming into him.*

"No," he said.

He turned around.

He recognized the man as one of the drinkers at the bar. Must have figured nice dress, big cash—easy pickings. Then followed him out, hoping to catch him in some ill-lighted place.

"Jesus!" cried the man.

He fired the gun.

Blessing felt it merely as a small smack into his abdomen. There was no pain as such. Just a light tap, exploding the rage deep down inside of him.

"Scum!" he cried.

Blessing knocked aside the gun, then pulled the whiskey bottle up and slammed it against the man's head. The bottle broke and splattered the man with whiskey, blinding him. He tried to bring the gun back, to fire again.

Blessing found himself with amazing speed, power, and dexterity, driving the broken neck of the bottle into the torso of the mugger . . .

. . . straight through to the other side, all the way up to his forearm.

Blood gurgled from the man's mouth. He spasmed, head back, light in his eyes dimming—all, to Blessing's perception, a kind of slow-motion freeze.

Blood pumped onto his arm.

Blessing, in a trance, let the mugger hang limp for several long moments (the weight did not seem great) . . . and then simply lowered his arm. With a squelching sound, the man slipped off, flopping onto the ground in a messy heap.

The smell of blood and whiskey was intense. Blessing lifted the red-streaked bottle and sniffed. He felt invigorated. The night seemed to explode with a resonant electrical charge, humming, harmonizing with his anger, his indignity and sorrow . . .

His rage.

He looked down upon the dead man and felt himself Justice personified. This vile hunk of detritus would no longer trouble the living. As he stared at the cooling carcass, he saw the cankered soul leak out, tiny and shriveled, to join the spirit-fog of the night.

He had performed a service. This validation imbued Blessing with renewed purpose. He could feel power coursing back into him . . .

Resolve.

A dark-winged form hopped onto the body. It dug its beak into the steaming entrails, pulled out a tangly bit and swallowed it.

"Mmm. Guts flavored with whiskey. What a treat," said the crow.

"I must . . . be about my work," said Blessing.

"My, my," said the crow, peering up at Blessing's ruined face. "Lost a bit of inner fire, did we? Looks like *you're* off the sauce for the duration. That is, if you want to put things right. That is, if you think that, all in all, you'd rather not see your killers enjoy a prosperous old age molesting kiddies on the rides at Blessingland!"

Somehow, the rage got stronger.

"That is, if you don't want your betrayer doing the double-backed Big Nasty with your wife thousands of times . . ."

Blessing moaned and howled.

He threw the bottleneck against the wall. It shattered into minute pieces.

"There you go. That's the spirit," said the crow. "I'm here to help, William. Only to help."

"My face," said Blessing. "My nose—"

"Yes, yes. A little reconstructive surgery is in order. I do hope you saved your fallen proboscis."

Blessing looked down. Yes, it was still in his left hand.

"Good. So then, looks like your face is getting a little—shriveled, too. Well! Good thing we happen to have some nice fresh protoplasm here to aid in your reconstitution."

"How . . . ? I don't—"

"Leave that to me. We've got to fix you up for tomorrow morning, don't we? You don't want to have Amy see you without your nose."

"Amy? What?" Blessing said. He could feel his being wrench at the very thought. "Why?"

"You must find the name and address of at least one of your assailants, true? Also, I believe both you and the librarian would appreciate the Poe collection being restored to its proper room. A little bird has told me that our dear friend Donald Marquette has introduced several members of his new club—members involved with your death—to Amy." The bird paused, cocked its head thoughtfully. "Besides," it said in cold tones. "You need to remember what you've lost, Blessing. Or more will fall apart in this mission than your nose."

"Yes," said Blessing, no longer allowing reflection or hesitation into his mind. "Yes."

William Blessing knelt down by the steaming body of the man he had just killed and, with his long sharp nails, did as the crow instructed.

19

On this night, *Mrs. Poe,* lingering on the bed of disease and surrounded by her children, *asks your assistance; and asks it perhaps for the last time.*

—*Richmond Enquirer,* November 29, 1811

"Good. You are all here, then," said Eliza Poe. "All my children. All my loved ones. I need to speak to you now." The death-pale woman's voice was low and very sad.

It took little Edgar Poe's mind off that big black crow somewhere outside.

Edgar was confused, but he kept quiet and listened. He always listened when Mama spoke. She always had good things to say.

The room seemed somehow darker, even though there were lanterns and candles about. Colder, even though there was a well-stoked fire in the hearth. It smelled of camphor and tallow and the black tea with cream that the grownups were incessantly drinking. There was a stack of small cakes and jam near the teapot, but Edgar didn't really want any, even though blackberry jam was his very favorite and he hadn't had much for breakfast. Somehow, he just wasn't that hungry.

Above the sea of wool-patch quilt, Eliza Poe's head seemed sunk deep in the white linen of the feather pillow. Her dark hair had been combed out so it formed a kind of unearthly black halo about her head. All of her was pale, a deep white shade of pale, the pale of worms that Edgar had found under rocks—except her cheeks and her lips, which were colored a cherry red. She had dark black eyebrows and the biggest eyes that Edgar had ever seen—big, dark eyes that had always seemed so full of life and curiosity . . . but now, they held nothing but sadness.

Still, when they turned to Edgar, a little spark kindled in them. Edgar felt momentarily happy, for he saw the caring and attachment his Mama felt for him. There were times when he sensed that the world was a cold, nasty place, filled with cold, nasty people and not a great deal of fun or joy. However, he always felt, even in these bleak moments, that he was a fortunate soul, for in this world there was always, for him, the deep warmth and caring that Mama held for him.

"Oh, Edgar," she said in her little voice. "Your Sunday tie is crooked."

"Yes, Mama," he said, and attempted to straighten the thing. He made a botch of it, and one of the old ladies had to help him.

"There. That's better," said Eliza Poe. "Come closer, Edgar."

Edgar stepped beside William, who quietly relinquished both his place and his mother's hand. Eliza Poe stroked her son's dark hair, and then let her fingers drift fondly down his face, touching his high cheekbones, his sensitive lips and noble nose, his strong chin.

Her hand was cold and clammy and Edgar felt a shiver run through him. He felt alarmed and felt a need to cry, but he knew he had to be brave for his Mama and he clamped back the tears.

"Dear Edgar, there can be no one who doubts that you are my child," said Eliza. "For you have my eyes."

"Yes, Mama."

"Have you been good for our dear friends?"

"Yes, Mama."

"No, he hasn't," said William, suddenly. "He keeps looking for a crow. All he can talk about is crow . . . crow . . . crow."

His mother turned her eyes back to him. "Edgar, you must not dwell on dark things. Do you love Jesus, Edgar?"

"Yes, Mama."

"Jesus is the Son of Light, and there is no Darkness in him. Look to Jesus, Edgar. And always pray to God."

"Yes, Mama."

Eliza Poe took several long, difficult breaths, and closed her eyes, as though fortifying herself. Then she opened her eyes and began to speak:

"Children. I'm afraid there will be difficult times ahead for you," she said in a weak voice.

It was not the best of times.

It was not the worst of times.

It was the end of 1811.

Soon England would make another final and weak attempt to regain her lost colonies, but already America had identity and power. Its cities were growing, its sense of itself as a nation was getting stronger. Having only just formed its more perfect union, the States were having difficulty thinking of themselves as a country, but the idea was sinking in and most tradesmen were prospering. With its fine ports, the Atlantic seaboard was beginning to grow in wealth, and people flocked for work to the brave, new, and beautiful cities. Needing entertainment, this new society looked to theater and music, and one of its most popular young actresses was Eliza Arnold, who had been born into an acting family and took to the waters like a swan. She had married young to another actor named David Poe. Unfortunately, though filled with plenty of bravado and ambition, Poe was not a very good actor. His reviews were generally dismal, and he took to drinking. Alcohol at the turn of the nineteenth century was a generally acceptable libation—so much so that office workers often had snorts of whiskey at eleven A.M. breaks called "elevenses." However, drinking before breakfast was not thought to be a good idea, and David Poe did not seem to be able to control his bouts with the bottle. When failure as an actor loomed, he simply packed up and left the family.

Eliza had soldiered on.

Now, though, at the age of twenty-four, Eliza Poe was on her deathbed.

She'd been ill for months. Some said she'd never been quite the same since the birth of little Rosalie, that the fever that had taken her might have let go had she not been weakened. Without the income from her career these past months, the family had become destitute. Only the kindness, hospitality, and sheer Christian goodwill from friends such as Fanny and John Allan had kept them from starving.

However, young Edgar really understood little of this. He felt sad that Mama did not feel well and seldom rose from bed; but she never stopped touching him and holding him and professing her love for him, and this in a way was an improvement on the times when her life was a bustle from stage to stage, from social affair to rehearsals, when he seldom saw her. And it had done him good to see the sheer pleasure that his presence gave her; it made the solemn little boy's feeling of self-worth bloom.

"Difficult?" asked William, "That is the word Papa used. Things are always difficult in the 'noble profession' of acting."

"We cannot count on your papa for even proclamations anymore," said Eliza Poe. "We must all fall upon the kindness of others . . . And I must fall upon the mercy of God."

She blinked and seemed to faint a moment, but then rallied, whispering to herself. "No, Eliza, no. You must speak to the children. Speak to the children."

One of the women gave her some nasty-smelling medicine from a big silver spoon, then tilted some hot, milky tea down her throat. Her awareness flickered back on, and once more she was able to address her children.

"I am going away," she said. "Jesus is calling me."

Edgar said, "We will come, too!"

"No, child. Only I can go."

Edgar was suddenly very upset with Jesus. Jesus, who had before been such a friendly and sweet fellow . . . Not letting him stay with Mama. It seemed very wrong . . . Very wrong indeed, and Edgar intended to let Jesus know this in no uncertain terms when he said his prayers tonight.

"You and William and Rosalie must grow up and do good works and become fine people. You must love God and love Jesus and love your fellow man."

As Eliza spoke, Edgar felt suddenly cold and alone. This was not the Mama he knew who would comfort him; she was becoming like the lecturing ministers at churches they had attended, cold and distant and aloof, filled with words and precious little kindness or comfort.

Eliza spoke to them for a while, reciting Bible verses and instructing them on matters of morality and goodness. Edgar could not help noticing that the others in the room, the grownups in their stiff, starched outfits and their high collars, all smelling of rough soap and self-righteousness, would nod occasionally and add stern but approving amens to Eliza's instructions to her children.

Eliza then kissed Rosalie and whispered in the nurse's ear. She then beckoned William to come closer and kiss her cheek. William did so. She whispered something into his ear and he nodded. William's face had gone white and confused tears brimmed on his eyelids. Edgar wondered if he had caught Mama's fever; he surely hoped not.

"Edgar. Please. Come here."

Edgar neared and looked into his mother's eyes.

. . . black feathers . . .

. . . flapping . . .

. . . flapping . . .

. . . like wings of some dark angel.

Edgar backed away. His heart hammered in his chest. He felt he must get outside. There was no air here . . . Nothing to breathe but black feathers and . . .

The little boy took a step and rammed directly into the leg of a man. He felt thick, hard hands descend upon him. He looked up and found himself staring into the granite face of John Allan. "Boy!" said Allan, in the same masterly way that he spoke to his slaves. "Do your duty. Go to your mother!"

Terror added heartbeats to his confusion, but the words turned him back, and he found himself close to his mother again.

"Edgar," said Eliza. "I want you to remember me."

. . . remember . . .

. . . remember . . .

The word echoed in his mind.

"You are so young . . . I fear you will forget the mother who loves you so very much. To help you remember your mama, Edgar, I am giving you a miniature portrait of myself . . ."

. . . remember . . .

"Some letters I wrote which I feel hold some of my soul and perhaps even some literary quality, for you love reading and poetry and stories so . . ."

. . . remember. . .

"Lastly, Edgar, I am giving you a watercolor sketch of the Boston harbor. Do you remember Boston, Edgar? It's where you were born . . ."

. . . remember . . .

"It is where your mother found her best and most sympathetic friends, several of whom are here today."

Eliza's hands were cold to Edgar's touch. She smelled odd as well, and Edgar had to fight for the composure that he sensed his mama needed from him.

Mama said more things, but they made a great deal less sense. There was a great deal about Jesus and God and charity and strength and love and honor, but there were also words that made no sense together, spoken in a feverish whisper.

Finally, Eliza Poe was quiet.

A woman felt her wrist and then put a mirror to her face and nose.

"God bless her and God be thanked," she said in a stolid tone. "Her passing was peaceful."

There was some quiet weeping from Fanny Allan, but John Allan's face was like a statue. "I suppose we shall be stuck with the middle brat, then," he muttered.

Edgar couldn't understand what the fuss was about.

Passing? What did that mean? Mama hadn't gone anywhere! She hadn't gone to heaven to see Jesus. There she was . . . Looking as beautiful as ever. Sleeping . . . Couldn't they see? She was just sleeping!

"Edgar, William," said Fanny Allan. "Your mother has passed on. Kiss her now to speed her with your love."

Obediently, William went to the bed, leaned over, and kissed his mother's lips. He seemed to be in some sort of trance.

Then it was Edgar's turn. He had to be lifted onto the bed. He looked down upon his mother's pale face and he said, "Mama. Wake up."

"Blast you, child," barked John Allan. "She's dead. Can't you see? Now kiss her and let's be done with this. I've a business meeting to go to."

Edgar cringed at John Allan's voice. He touched his mother's face.

Somehow, she seemed warmer than before. He kissed her lips and they too were warm. "Very well, Mama," he whispered, "I will not give away your trick."

Then he heard a sudden rapping.

He turned around and looked toward the window. There on the sill, on the other side of the windowpane, stood the crow. Its wings were spread, and the dark span cut off what little sunlight bled through the overcast sky. The feathers flapped against the glaze—a skittering of claws and peck of beak and then the creature flapped away, disappearing once more into the cloudy, barren unknown.

"Look, Mama!" said Edgar Poe. "I told them! I told them . . . A great black bird!"

But his mother said nothing.

Nor did she speak again or hold him or kiss him or smile and laugh and sing her lovely songs.

Never.

Never.

Nevermore.

"Nevermore," moaned Donald Marquette.

He woke up breathing hard. He felt disoriented.

The dream.

He'd had that damned dream again.

"Poe," he said, reaching for the glass of water by his bedside. "I'm sick of Poe."

A guilty conscience?

Maybe. He rejected the thought. There were things to be done, hard things to accomplish if he meant to achieve his goals. Guilt was something he simply could not afford.

The cup was cold. He sipped at the chill liquid . . .

. . . and spat it out.

Damn!

It tasted like blood.

20

Take this kiss upon the brow!
And, in parting from you now,
Thus much let me avow—
You are not wrong, who deem
That my days have been a dream;
Yet if hope has flown away
In a night, or in a day,
In a vision, or in none,
Is it therefore the less gone?
All that we see or seem
Is but a dream within a dream.

—Edgar A. Poe, "A Dream Within a Dream"

Amy Blessing was drooping over a fresh mug of coffee in her kitchen, when the doorbell rang.

Amy had never liked coffee terribly much, before William was killed. She'd far preferred tea. When she and Bill had gone for their trip to England last year, they had returned with mountains of different teas she'd bought at Fortnum and Mason's in London. Darjeeling, Earl Grey, Lapsang Suchong, English Breakfast, Irish Breakfast, oh, and so many more, kept fresh in splendid tins. She also had tea from various provinces of India and China, splendid, first-rate, very expensive tea.

Now, though, she mostly drank coffee.

When she drank fresh-ground coffee, now, she felt warm and invigorated . . . and close to Bill. She could sip on the aromatic stuff sweetened with milk and just a breath of sugar, close her eyes, and she'd be with him again. The memory of his musky aftershave seemed closer, the touch of his voice, the taste of his skin in rumpled bedclothes, his protective *presence.*

She knew that she'd withdrawn, but she knew no other way of dealing with her loss. At the end of a brilliant, fun career in college, she'd thought she had her whole life mapped out. Professor William Blessing had been a stunning surprise. The college girl would have been horrified at the notion of marrying a man over twenty years older. Perhaps the writer part would have been romantic to that person, but the academic part? Oh, no! Stuffy, theoretical, painfully dull—this was not what she'd envisioned for herself. No, a life vaulting across oceans and continents, passionately pounding concert pianos, chased by exciting foreign men with burning eyes and a terrible need to bury their sensuous lips in her long, flowing hair. Yes, that was what she'd seen. Then, settling down, a life-mate, family; a musician, yes. Someone to duet with constantly.

William Blessing, of course, had been a bit of a veering off course, but every bit of it had seemed *right,* indeed almost *fateful.*

Fate, though, it would seem, had deadlier things in store.

If only Bill hadn't had to keep his Poe collection in his home and make it common knowledge. If only he hadn't insisted on keeping his professorship and living downtown, exposed. With his money, they could have had a nice big house in a guarded community, away from the threats that plagued people who did not distance themselves from the human viruses that plague society . . .

If only . . .

The bell rang again.

She went to the control wall.

After that horrible night, when he couldn't convince her to move out of the house, Donald had insisted that the security of the townhome be beefed up. This was costly, but his argument was that there was plenty of money still in the bank, and only so much life remaining in the house.

Part of the new security system (along with barred windows and an impenetrable first floor and basement) was a video system that monitored all of the house's entrances and windows and much of its interior. In a kitchen nook was one of the control areas. Amy went to this, carrying her cup of coffee with her like a talisman.

She switched on the monitor.

The screen showed a man in a hat, dark glasses, and a long coat, his collar pulled up around his neck and up past his chin. Spring in Baltimore had been breezy and a little chilly, but not *that* cold.

Still, it was morning, and the clothes and hat looked top quality and the man hardly looked threatening. No reason to call the police.

She turned on the audio. "Yes," she said, voice monotone. She could still play music, but she could not get up enough energy to make her voice musical again.

"Mrs. Amy Blessing?" said the voice. It seemed harsh and muffled, but somehow strangely familiar.

"Yes."

"I wonder if I might . . . might speak to you?"

"Go ahead."

"In person."

A shiver of dread went through her.

That night, when Bill answered the door . . .

It was ten forty-five in the morning. Donald had come into the office bright and early, but then had gotten a phone call and had to go out for some sort of business meeting.

She was alone now, and had no intention of going to the door and talking to anyone in person. She wanted the safety of two thick doors and many locks between herself and the world.

"I'm afraid that—"

"I understand your position," said the man. "With your recent . . . tragedy, you are very cautious. However, I can assure you, I mean no harm. And I must speak to you. I have come . . . from a very long distance . . . to speak to you."

The man's voice, previously staccato, suddenly seemed filled with emotion.

"Who are you?"

"I am . . . I am Delmore Blessing."

"You're related to Bill? I've never heard of any Delmore . . . He never mentioned . . ."

"I am . . . a distant older cousin . . . Our contact was . . . rather infrequent, I fear. However, when we did correspond we shared ourselves and our secrets. There was much trust between your husband and me." He paused. "I have to speak to you of . . . of things."

She was flustered. She hesitated. "How do I know you're really my husband's cousin? How do I know anything of the sort? I've never seen a letter of yours or answered a phone call."

"You may ask me what you will about William Blessing and I can do my best to answer. But please let me say that my time is very short. May I start out by telling you . . . that your husband . . . He loved you very much. He wrote to me that on your recent wedding anniversary he gave you a poem he had written for you, and that at the end of every month he would give you a clue to the puzzle the poem presented. For the poem would lead you to a secret place and there would be a prize of prizes there. A heart of hearts."

She could feel her heart beat harder.

The memory of that poem opened something inside of her.

She welled up, full of pain.

Full of endless joy . . .

She found that there were tears in her eyes.

She had not cried since the day of William Blessing's funeral. And though the tears burned her cheeks, she welcomed them. For at least it meant that she could feel again.

"You . . . You know about that poem? No one could have known. How could—"

"I taught him to write poetry, you see," said the man who called himself Delmore Blessing. "And I gave him some early lessons in prose as well. I . . . I gave him his first book of the stories and poems of Edgar A. Poe. So you see . . . we were very . . . very close . . . a long time ago."

No one else could have known about that poem.

Her next question should have been, she supposed, why this mysterious relative of William's had not called first. She'd never even heard of him, now he suddenly appears!

However, he looked so uncomfortable out there. And he had been close to William. He *must* have been.

And wouldn't that make her closer to her dead husband . . . just being near this man?

"All right," she said. "I believe you. I'll be right there."

She turned off the monitor and went down to the front door to allow the strange but marvelous man to enter.

21

A dark unfathom'd tide
Of interminable pride—
A mystery, and a dream,
Should my early life seem;

—Edgar A. Poe, "Imitation"

"This is most disturbing," said Donald Marquette.

"I gotta say, Mister," said the cop. "Never seen anything or heard of anything quite like it. But then, this is a damned crazy world. You never fuckin' know nothin'. Truth is stranger than fiction. That's what I say."

"Who else knows about this?" asked Marquette, an odd and eerie sensation of dragging chains across his backbone.

"Just the caretakers."

"And where were they?"

The policeman's name was Daniels. He had a donutlike rind of fat around his belt and sweat stains on his blue shirt. There was a bit of snot hanging out of his nose. *Baltimore's Finest,* thought Marquette. "That's the strange thing, Mr. Marquette. This graveyard's got security up the yin yang. I mean, it being the resting place of Edgar Allan Poe and all. But the security—the patrol boys I talked to from last night—they didn't see nuttin'."

Marquette looked down at the ground.

It looked as though a hole had been dug in the grave and then filled back in, badly. There were clumps of dirt in the grass, leading away toward the cemetery's gate. The bright, new, expensive Celtic cross at the head of the grave was untouched, unharmed. Funny. In a case of vandalism, you'd think that would be the first to go.

"Have you examined the coffin?"

"No. Got to dig it up. That's why we called you. We wanted to know if you knew anyone who'd want to dig Mister Blessing up. Him bein' a horror writer and all . . . Gotta have a lot of strange fans. I heard tell of one time, that Stephen King guy was signin' autographs. Guy comes up, slashes his own hand and asks King to sign his book—in blood."

"That was Clive Barker," said Marquette.

"No shit! I knew he was a fan, but man . . ."

"No, no. It was Clive Barker's autograph session."

They'd called this morning to tell him about Blessing's grave being desecrated. He was just damned happy they hadn't gotten ahold of Amy, the lumbering jackasses. He'd gone down straightaway to investigate, telling Amy he had a business meeting.

Grisly business.

"Oh, yeah. Shit, I don't read that kinda stuff anyway. Me, I stick to straight mysteries. I like reality. Know what I mean?"

"Well, I suppose we're going to have to exhume the coffin to make sure that nothing's been down to it or Doctor Blessing's remains," said Marquette.

"Well, that ain't in the area of police duty, Mister."

"I'll check with the cemetery officials to make arrangements. Should there be charges, the Blessing Trust will handle them. I just want to thank you, officer, for letting us know so soon about this nasty business."

"Yeah. Sure. Just doing my job."

"And doing it very well indeed."

The policeman wobbled back to his squad car and headed off, doubtless to the nearest donut shop for lunch.

Donald Marquette went and dealt with the cemetery officials. Since there was no outward evidence of anything missing, there would indeed be a fee for exhumation. Marquette did not argue. The soonest this could happen was tomorrow morning. Not to Marquette's liking, but then he didn't particularly care to grab a spade and start digging himself.

When he had finished these dealings, he found a telephone booth and called Baxter Brittle.

Baxter was not in the Tome Publishing office, which was not surprising.

Marquette tried his personal number, and got a messaging service. Again not surprising. This was very early for Baxter.

However, there was another way, short of actually going over and rousting him out of bed. After that terrible, ultimately wonderful night that everything had changed, Marquette had made Baxter see that communications had to be immediate between them, should anything arise.

They had special phone lines installed, and had bought cellular phones. As Baxter hated his, he'd asked that Marquette avail himself of all other means of communication before going for the cellular. In turn, Brittle had promised to keep the channel open. At all times. No flicking the switch to off. No submerging the device beneath his pillows. No simply ignoring it (something that would be very hard indeed, as Marquette had made sure he bought him the model with the most annoying ringer).

Marquette reached into the pocket of his jacket and pulled out his phone. Clicked it open. Stabbed the pound key, which was programmed to immediately dial Baxter's number.

It rang for a long time, but finally Baxter's voice, heavily distorted, came over the line.

"Yes, dear boy."

"Baxter," said Marquette. "Are you straight?"

"I am immensely hungover. In a moment, with a sip and a pill, I shall be straight enough."

"No. Don't. Wait. Talk to me first."

"Very well. Something important, I presume."

"If it wasn't, I wouldn't be bothering you. I keep my promises, Baxter."

"Glad to hear that. Sorry to hear of problems. What seems to be the matter?"

"Mick and Theodore. They're back in town, right?"

"I did mention that last week. Indeed they are. Fit and tanned from their Caribbean adventure."

"I still wish they hadn't chosen to come back to Baltimore."

Whenever they spoke via the phone lines, they were careful not to be too explicit, keeping to generalities as much as possible. Paranoia seemed a useful state when dealing with such delicate matters as covering up murder and robbery.

"Be that as it may, they have their uses." Baxter Brittle's voice was full of pain and emerging annoyance. "Please do get on with your subject matter, dear boy."

"A certain grave has been desecrated. I just wanted to make sure that certain friends didn't have certain odd vices."

There was a silence.

Then a short bark of a laugh.

"Maybe the occupant arose on the third day and ascended into heaven. I always thought he had a bit of a Christ complex."

Marquette's voice was harsh. "This is no time for smart remarks of extremely poor taste, Baxter. Check up on this. Now. Do you understand?"

"Certainly, dear boy. However, I don't think we exactly have to panic about this."

"There's no panic involved. Just precaution."

"Fine. Fine. Now can I go and partake of my eye-opener?"

"Just get back to me, and sooner rather than later."

"Must I use this hateful device?"

"No. I'll be back at the office."

"Best news I've heard all day, dear boy. *Ciao!*"

Marquette clicked off.

He found himself drifting back to the graveyard, and the disturbed grave. He stood by the cross thoughtfully, staring down at the troubled dirt and grass.

Marquette shook his head and laughed.

All this was giving him a *great* idea for a short story.

Feeling much better, he walked jauntily back to his car, hands stuck in the comfortable silk-lined pockets of his sporty Italian jacket.

22

It was many and many a year ago,
In a kingdom by the sea,
That a maiden there lived whom you may know
By the name of ANNABEL LEE;—
And this maiden she lived with no other thought
Than to love and be loved by me.

—Edgar A. Poe, "Annabel Lee"

Dr. William Blessing, risen from the grave, stood at the door of the house where he had once lived and waited for the living to answer.

The crow was gone, nowhere to be seen. Just as well. After a miserable night on a park bench, it had come to him holding several more hundred-dollar bills in its beak. He'd shuffled into a downtown department store, bought new clothes and some makeup.

Staring into the men's room mirror, looking at his flaky, cracked, dead-man's facial skin, he'd splashed on pancake foundation and then, on some strange whim, color-penciled in clownlike smile lines, clown sparkles about his eyes.

On reflection, he decided that perhaps this was not the proper disguise.

He simply used the pancake to cover some of the more egregious of facial scars and fissures. The work with the fresh flesh of last night had filled in the cracks off his reattached nose. Still, even with the pancake, he looked older than when he had died.

Thus, from the foundation of dead William Blessing, grew the (supposedly) living Delmore Blessing, distant (but letter-close) cousin.

Standing outside now, in these clothes, waiting for the door to open, whatever served him for a heart now seemed to pump harder in him, his excitement at seeing Amy again was so great.

The sound of her voice over the speaker had nearly paralyzed him. He was grateful he'd been able to speak and tell his story, let alone do it with sincerity. Fortunately, his appearance and voice had altered sufficiently to mask his essential identity.

Steady, fellow, he told himself.

This reunion is purely for informational purposes.

But, oh!

Her voice had sounded so sweet and sad. He'd had a mad urge to just let out the truth.

Amy! I'm back! Risen from the dead to set things straight!

However, he knew he could never tell her who he really was. He had left her once . . . but he had not intended to. How could he tell her who he was when he very well knew he'd have to leave her again . . .

Soon.

So very soon.

The door opened.

He could see her cautiously peering out, a chain still latched between the door and the frame.

Oh, she was so beautiful. He thought his heart would break, so immense was the feeling that swept through him.

He stood back as far as he could, his hands, empty, at his sides. He tilted his head.

"Hello, there."

"Hello," she said tentatively.

"I thank you so much for trusting me," he said. "Again I am so sorry I didn't tell you I was going to come to Baltimore. In fact, I did not know myself until yesterday. I thought that it would be an opportune time to present myself to you, explain who I am and also tell you how you might help me . . . And how I might help you."

"I just wish that William . . . Bill . . . had told me that he had a cousin . . . who he corresponded with . . . and told such personal secrets."

"I am very embarrassed. But you see, it is necessary to tell you these things . . . in order to see that I mean you no harm." He smiled and he could feel his makeup and his dry, tense skin crack with the facial movement.

"Harm? No, of course not. It's just that—"

"Oh, yes, I understand perfectly."

"Please come in."

"Thank you."

She unlatched the door and stood back.

As he entered, it took every fiber of his being not to embrace her. Not to hold her close, to have her life in his arms again. To have again, so close, what he had lost.

He walked in and stood in the foyer. Almost automatically he had wanted to go up to the bar to make coffee, but he stopped himself, waiting obediently for instructions.

"Would you like some tea or coffee?" asked Amy.

"Yes, thank you."

"This way."

As he adjusted to being in the presence of his beloved again, Blessing had a realization.

She wasn't the same.

There was some spark missing in her. She seemed to shine less brightly now. That biblical bushel was hiding her candle.

And no wonder.

He could feel the rage build inside him. There would be no danger of parts falling off him here. In her presence, and with his anger aflame, his will would be strong.

Amy led him to the dining room table.

"I have a pot of coffee on. A Kenyan blend I like. Would you care for some of that?"

"Coffee? Not tea?" he asked.

She looked at him oddly. "Yes."

"Oh, I'm sorry. William mentioned your passion for exotic teas. It's strange to find you drinking his preference."

"I feel . . . closer to him with coffee," she said. "Besides, it helps keep me awake. I've been sleeping so much lately."

"Sleeping, I understand, is good for healing," he said. "But coffee would be fine, thank you."

She left. As he waited for her return, sitting in his own dining room, he found tears coming into his eyes. He had never really liked this dining room. He'd always felt it was too . . . too . . . American looking. He far preferred European-style dining rooms. Now, though, there was no place else he'd rather be.

Blessing choked back his tears.

When she returned with a tray, she set it down and turned to him.

"Why don't you take off your glasses?"

"Oh . . . ah . . . these," he said, touching his dark tinted glasses. "My eyes are . . . ah . . . very sensitive to light."

"Oh. Like Vincent Price in *Tomb of Ligeia,*" said Amy matter-of-factly.

"Oh. Uhm . . . Yes. One of Roger Corman's classic Poe movies," said Blessing.

Amy began to pour the coffee. "Bill thought it one of the better ones."

"Yes. Scripted by Robert Towne, not Richard Matheson, the writer most closely associated with Corman's Poe cycle. I must confess that Charles Beaumont's version of *The Haunted Palace* has always been a favorite of mine." Blessing found himself chuckling. "Of course, that was really from an H. P. Lovecraft story, which could be why."

"You are a Poe fan, aren't you?" said Amy.

"As I said, I introduced William—"

"I think the one we enjoyed the most together was Corman's version of *The Raven* . . . though of course it didn't have much to do with Poe, either," said Amy. "I just loved Peter Lorre as the Raven."

"Yes, of course. Though I must admit that talking birds are getting old with me lately," said Blessing.

He added milk to his china cup of coffee.

"You take it with milk. Just like Bill."

"It seems to run in the family."

"Well, I can see the family resemblance."

"Yes. That was remarked upon the few times we actually were together."

Blessing took a self-conscious sip. He could feel the warmth, but distinguished no flavor. His rage grew.

"You said you needed to speak to me."

"Yes. I live in Vancouver, British Columbia. When word reached me of William's death, he had already been interred . . . I am so sorry I was not at his funeral."

"I'm not sure I was all there, either," she said.

"Perhaps I might have comforted you. William's violent and sudden end left much unsaid. I do not know what was happening between you at the time . . . only know that whenever he wrote me in the last few years, William could not stop talking of you . . . and his feeling for you. He loved you very, very much."

"You don't need to remind me of that. I know that," she said. "I never, ever doubted that . . ." She sighed. "I loved him. I still do."

"Love lasts beyond the grave."

"Yes," she said. "I know that now."

There was a moment of silence.

"William always hoped to share everything with you," said Blessing finally. "But he said there was much of his life that he had not told you about. Nothing terribly exciting . . . Just minutiae, you understand. I'm here, I suppose, to help fill that gap. I'm here to let you know things, small things perhaps, but relevant things, I think, about your departed husband." He sighed. "Of course, if this is too painful to you . . ."

He looked up, despite his misgivings.

Amy Blessing was staring at him.

There was a light in her eye. A light that had not been there before.

"Yes. Yes . . . I *would* like that," she said. "Please go on . . ."

Blessing took a sip of his coffee. He told his wife things about himself that he had not told her before, that he had been too busy to tell her. Somehow, their life together had been left incomplete in ways that were not necessary. Even though he'd been very much in love with her, he was not a practiced hand at intimacy, and now, he wanted to leave her with more of him.

He told of some of his failures, how his first stories had never found publishers. How he'd had a bad year in college, before he really was thoroughly sure of his literary mission in life. He told her of bad relationships, of silly, stupid things he'd done. He'd told her all the wonderful things during their too-short marriage. While he was alive he hadn't brought out all the warts; he felt, now, that this was unfair to her. Amy should remember him the way he truly had been.

Finally, an hour later, realizing that he had more to say but feeling a great weariness of the soul, he could not muster any more out.

"I'm sorry. That is all I can manage to remember now," he said. "I'm sure that William told me more . . . but perhaps I can tell you at a later time."

He looked at her again, expecting her to look disappointed. Disappointed at the woefully flawed man she'd married. Maybe, perhaps, a little relieved that she'd been saved from a lifetime with him.

Instead, she seemed happy, even through a slight sheen of tears.

"Thank you. This really . . . really means so much to me," she said. "Somehow I feel I know Bill . . . better now."

He nodded. "That is good."

"But you must stay! You can rest if you like . . . There are plenty of guest rooms."

"No. I have a room in a hotel here in Baltimore."

"Please! Check out and stay here with me!"

"I'm afraid that would be impossible. Please . . . don't ask me why."

"Very well. As you wish."

"I must go now. I will . . . call you. And tell you when I can return."

"I shall look forward to that."

"There is one more matter," he said. "I wish, during my stay here, to contact certain people. Personal business, you understand. Literary business. These are members of a group involved with an effort called, I believe, Tome Press?"

"Oh, yes! Tome Press. Of course. My associate Donald Marquette works closely with them. He can help you there, I'm sure."

"Actually, I cannot tell you why just now. You must trust me. I must be very secretive, which is why I am so happy we could speak like this, Amy. Please humor me. I would far prefer to get this information from you, and leave anyone else out of the matter."

She looked slightly baffled, but nodded. "All right. I suppose if that's the price I have to pay to get more of these lovely facts about William out of you, then so be it."

"You have information on how I can get in touch with these people?"

"Yes. I have a few cards they left me. As a matter of fact, I obtained them just recently, at a dinner party."

"I'm sure, if you could just let me borrow them . . ."

"Certainly. I've no real use for them. Do you need them now?"

"Yes. I fear I must be going."

"Very well."

She went into her office and returned with several cards, all of them fancily embroidered and embossed with occult symbols.

He took them and got up to leave. It was a wrenching business, but he could feel himself cracking inside. He needed to leave before the fissures were too deep.

"I thank you so much . . ."

"It's I who wants to thank you," she said, and before he could do or say anything, he found that she was hugging him. Her warm and giving flesh against his felt like electric bliss. The smell of her—baby powder and woman-scent—jolted him like nothing spiritual or physical he had ever felt before. She was soft and tender, the curl of her hair brushing against his cheek, the *life* in her a febrile dynamo of possibility and wonder and boundless illumination in a dark and nihilistic universe.

For a moment he thought he would literally melt into a pool of tears. He managed to hold himself together.

"I'm so glad you came," she said. "Please promise me you'll come back."

"I promise," he said.

Gently he removed himself and left, Amy's farewell lingering in his mind like the grace notes of a great symphony.

He found himself walking aimlessly down the road, the cards she had given him gripped in his hand. He felt dazed. Was it the sunlight? He didn't know. He felt as though he were a denizen of the night, unearthed into the day—and yet, the sunlight did not burn or corrode him, as it did Christopher Lee in Hammer's classic Dracula films. He felt somehow just the opposite: as though the sunlight imbued him with greater power and understanding. True, he was a creature of the night now. But that did not mean he hated the day.

Eventually, he found himself on the campus of Johns Hopkins University.

He sat down on a bench under the shade of a tree.

Absently, he watched as students passed by. He caught sight of a few young men and women he recognized. People he taught. God, but they were young and fresh and vigorous. He regretted now how harsh he'd been with some, how little he tried to know them. Perhaps, if he had tried to understand them, they would have better understood him. He could have buried himself in the life of the university, that sacred trust. Written under a pseudonym. Avoided this nonsense of death and resurrection.

Had a normal family.

A young man, carrying a Dean Koontz paperback and a 16-ounce bottle of soda, settled down against a tree. He eagerly started paging through the book, finding his place, intently becoming absorbed.

Slowly, as Blessing watched this young man, something dawned on him: He looked like Amy a bit, with his curly hair, the dark eyebrows, the chin.

He looked a bit like William Blessing.

This student could have been their son.

Gripping the business cards in his hand, Blessing had to leave the bench, to stalk through nastier, grimmer areas of town, remembering the last intentions that he and Amy had, before the atrocities had been visited upon them.

They shall pay! he thought.

Through vengeance shall all be redeemed.

23

I could no longer doubt the doom prepared for me by monkish ingenuity in torture. My cognizance of the pit had become known to the inquisitorial agents—the pit whose horrors had *been destined for so bold a recusant as myself—*the pit, *typical of hell, and regarded by rumor as the Ultima Thule of all their punishments.*

—Edgar A. Poe, *The Pit and the Pendulum*

The Cross was a new club.

It was one of those clubs born from somewhere else, settled in for a time to the throbs of dance music, glitter, poppers, fumed on alcohol and the endless night hours, and probably destined to either move on to some other address—or simply die a spastic, unnatural death.

It was down an alley in the heart of downtown Baltimore, amongst office buildings, stores, and restaurants long since shut up for the evening. No neighborhood here! Tucked away in a canyon of concrete, terrible and raucous noise could be made way into the wee hours. With no peace to be disturbed, there could be no misdemeanors committed.

Of that sort, at any rate.

On the other side of the entrance was a fire exit. Supposedly only emergency was cause for it to open, but tonight, as on many other nights when the club became too hot or the groaning bathrooms were too full with carnal activity, one of the nightclubbers stepped into the dimly lit area formed by stone steps and brick basement access door.

This was Evelyn Nichol, Marquis de la Cinque to his brethren.

Lordy, lordy, he thought as he put his sweaty face into the cooler air. *Hot in there for a work night!*

Ev pulled a pack of Virginia Slims from the sleek black purse at the side of his red plastic jacket and lit it with a Zippo marked with a death's head. He added some pollution to the Baltimore air of the alley, already foggy and surreal at the edges.

His head was swimming! Man, much too much swirl of lights. Too much jackhammer music, aggressive and mean, NIN, Prodigy, Ministry, et al, a pummeling megamix of anger and despair. Too many drugs, too many drinks, too much dancing.

Now he relaxed, rocking on his stiletto heels, letting cool air rise up his mini-skirt to lower the temperature of his tight, tight panties. He smoothed out his nylons carefully, admiring again his perfectly formed calves, his excellently turned ankles.

The funny thing was, although he preferred guys personally, the Marquis looked much better when he was in drag. Especially when he applied makeup. He had the precise *something* that put the *trans* in transvestite.

Yes, he'd admit merrily, *Rocky Horror made a* big *impression on me!*

Used to be, back before the Gothiques, Evelyn Nichol made most of his money as a prostitute. Getting guys off was pretty easy, and it was always fun pretending you were a woman. Unfortunately, it was all ultimately pretty gross and rancid and yucky, with all that disease threat, so when he started making decent dress money with Tome Press and company, the tricks were the first to go. He liked the hip-shaking part and the wig-shaking and the flirty part, but all that groping and grunting with deep voices, all that savage love business, just went the way of all flesh.

All right! he thought, thrusting his hands up toward the sky as though to tap some kind of power latent therein. *A whole new world awaits me! Too long has my nose been on the ground! Now my eyes are on the stars!*

The Marquis was finding a different kind of power. He was discovering that he had abilities in administration. Imagine! At Tome Press, with its burgeoning businesses and way-relaxed office codes, he could be a top manager, helping guide the company through the exciting prospects that its association with the Blessing estate would bring. What a rush it had been that fateful night when a rich man went to death, and the Gothiques shot to greatness! And he could *still* go out and party any damned way he pleased.

No.

Correction.

Partying was *mandatory!*

Partying was part and parcel of the whole Tome Press philosophy. Already, part of the drug business that Mick Prince was bringing in meant going out to parties with select business associates. It was all this wonderful, Byzantine stuff and it was exciting, powerful, and, best of all, lucrative.

God, he was not only getting the best drugs now . . .

He was getting the best dresses!

What a fucking wonderful fantasy life, thought the Marquis, letting the rich and stimulating tobacco smoke fill his lungs, then gush through his nostrils. And all it cost was a squashed big-egoed head.

Yes, and the darker stuff. That was choice. He had no doubt that the dark stuff was part of the reason for the increased revenue, increased success. *But you know what?* he thought to himself.

The dark stuff was a gas, just by itself.

The Marquis grinned to himself and flicked the cigarette away.

Time to head back for a little boogying. Then, see if I can pick up a pretty little something to take home for later . . .

"Mr. DeMille," he whispered, patting his wig. "I'm ready for my close-up!"

He reached for the door to push back through into the noisy, delightful din, but then was stopped.

A hand reached down from above, hooked into the back of his dress, the back of his bra, and pulled.

The Marquis felt as though some crane hook had gotten hold of him. There was hardly time to even gasp as he was hoisted up onto the street level and then heaved over the side of metal rungs.

"Hey. What—"

Another hand grabbed him.

An arm readjusted around his neck and somehow managed to tie some kind of gag around his mouth. He was then dragged, kicking and groaning, down the alley and across a deserted street.

The Marquis lost both heels in the process.

Adrenaline pumped through him. Was this some kind of drug thing? *Oh no,* he thought, *were all the accounts caught up? What the hell was going on?* He knew that Mick Prince was back in town. Was this some kind of *joke*?

Something smelled bad. It smelled of blood, bad meat, something gone off—

The next thing he knew, he was being carried past a construction post marked DANGER. He saw a Caterpillar roadgrader, hulking like a giant insect in the night. The smell of asphalt and dirt and sewer pipes drifted in the air.

Suddenly, the Marquis found himself staring down into a dark hole. Below, deep, deep down, he saw vague forms of spikes poking up from the bottom of building foundations. His abductor pushed him out—

"No!" he cried, voice muffled.

And then he dangled, feet kicking, above the chasm.

"Yes, I'm afraid so, Ev. Pardon me—Marquis."

Fear filling up his head, the dank air from below sailing up his dress, the Marquis managed to get a grip on himself. He tried to speak but could get nothing decipherable past the gag.

What he was trying to say was that he had money in his purse. His attacker didn't seem to care much about that one way or the other.

" 'In the confusion,' " said the Dark Man, " 'attending my fall, I did not immediately apprehend a somewhat startling circumstance, which yet, in a few seconds afterward, and while I still lay prostrate, arrested my attention. It was this—my chin rested up on the floor of the prison, but my lips and the upper portion of my head, although seemingly at less elevation than the chin, touched nothing. At the same time my forehead seemed bathed in a clammy vapor, and the peculiar smell of decayed fungus arose to my nostrils. I put forward my arm and shuddered to find that I had fallen at the very brink of a circular pit, whose extent, of course, I had no means of ascertaining at the moment. Groping about the masonry just below the margin, I succeeded in dislodging a small fragment and let it fall into the abyss. For many seconds I hearkened to its reverberations as it dashed against the sides of the chasm in its descent; at length there was a sullen plunge into water, succeeded by loud echoes.' "

"Mmmph!" said the Marquis.

"Do you know why this is happening, Marquis?" asked the Dark Man.

"No," said the Marquis, muffled.

"Do you know who I am?"

"No," said the Marquis, again muffled.

"Well, perhaps I won't tell you. What difference does it make whether you know or not? You are but a bit of dimness, I think, in the greater darkness."

The Dark Man was quiet for a moment, as though considering.

The Marquis felt a wash of vertigo, despite the fact that he wasn't looking down.

He could *sense* the fall below him.

Finally, the Dark Man spoke.

"That quote. Do you know where that's from, Marquis? Tell you what. Answer me correctly and perhaps you won't go tumbling tonight, hmmmm?"

The Marquis nodded violently.

The Dark Man parked his feet against the edge.

Man, this was one powerful dude to be capable of this, the Marquis thought.

"Scream and down you go instantly," said the Dark Man, who immediately lifted the gag.

"First, tell me . . . Marquis. Where is your good companion Baxter Brittle this fair evening?"

"At home. At his bar."

"Yes. That is what I thought. Just ascertaining. Now then. Your answer. Where is the quote I gave you from?"

The Marquis shuddered.

A bit of asphalt broke off and clattered down the artificial cliff.

"Clue. Gimmee . . . clue."

"You are a demanding fellow. Shall we say . . . from a famous horror story?"

The Marquis blinked.

He'd never read all that many horror stories, a fact he'd always been afraid the rest of the Gothiques would discover. It looked like that worry would soon be over.

"Uhm . . . *The Shining*?"

"Wrong," said the Dark Man.

He slipped the gag back on.

And pushed the leaning man over the chasm.

The Marquis, falling, screamed.

It felt as though he fell forever. Abruptly, though, he impacted and it felt as though a fist from below had punched up from the darkness, directly into his gut.

The darkness filled with red, and the dressing-room curtain slammed shut.

When he awoke, the Marquis felt a vague but overwhelming pain, but mostly a feeling of nothingness below the level of his chest.

He felt a liquid lapping at his face. He smelled clay and brackish, dead water. He tasted blood in his mouth.

He tried to move, but could not. It was as though a giant high heel were stepping down on him from above, pinning him onto the ground.

Suddenly, just a few feet from his face, a match lit.

The Dark Man stood there, his face in half-shadow, regarding the fallen Marquis.

He intoned: " 'While I gazed, this fissure rapidly widened—there came a fierce breath of the whirlwind—the entire orb of the satellite burst at once upon my sight—my brain reeled as I saw the mighty walls rushing asunder—there was a long tumultuous shouting sound like the voice of a thousand waters—and the deep and dank tarn at my feet closed sullenly and silently over the fragments of the House of Usher.'"

The Marquis opened his mouth. He felt blood leaking out. "Who . . . are—"

"You don't get it yet? Those books you stole . . . Part of the loot . . . ?" said the Dark Man.

"The Poe books," the Marquis gasped.

"Don't worry. I got them back today. I have . . . ways."

The match went out.

Amidst the faint buzzing in his ears, the Marquis heard a squeaking sound. A slithering sound.

Another match was lit. This time, it was much closer. "You don't recognize me yet? But of course not, how could you. You've probably never met a man who's come back from death for vengeance, have you?"

There was some kind of squeaking nearby, at the edge of the fitful light thrown by the match. The stunned pain in the Marquis's head gave way to realization. He rejected the thought as soon as it came up, but the name escaped his mouth all the same.

"Blessing?"

"That's right, Marquis. That's right. It would seem there are, in fact, forces of justice in this universe . . . If you want them enough."

The Marquis twisted his head away and tried to move again. He looked around and saw the reason for his immobility.

He had been impaled on a thick concrete reinforcement wire at the bottom of the construction site into which he'd been pushed.

"Help . . . me. Call . . . 9 . . . 1 . . . 1 . . ." he gasped. "Help!"

"You know, Marquis. The end of *Pit and the Pendulum.* Do you remember what happens there?"

The Marquis groaned.

"Of course you don't. You don't know anything about Poe. You don't care about Poe. Those first editions meant nothing to you except money. Well, the character in the story, Marquis, is a prisoner of the Spanish Inquisition. Torquemada and all that. In his dungeon, he's tortured with the pendulum . . . a sharp thing that goes back and forth, back and forth, as it descends. But there's also the pit. He almost falls into the pit, you see. However, he does not . . . But I've always wondered what would have happened if he had. Would he have been swept away by an underground river? Or would he have simply lain there, dying, gnawed upon by big fat rats with razor teeth?"

The match went out.

Louder, he could hear the squeakings, the slithers. The scratch of little feet.

"Hungry rats," said the Dark Man. "Good night, Marquis. Sweet dreams."

Something nipped at the Marquis's ear.

The muffled screams were like music. Darker than darkwave, harder than hardcore.

In the alleyway, Blessing leaned against brick and listened, composing himself, regaining energy. Two down: the Count and the Marquis. Four to go.

A black form flapped down from the sky, settled down on his shoulder.

"Crow . . ." he said. "Crow . . . I can . . . do things . . . There are . . . forces about . . . I reach out . . . and control . . ."

One more final phlegmy screech, and then the pit was quiet, a bit of mist seeping out, like escaping spirits.

"Sure. Like I say . . . Will. That's what's keeping you together," said the crow. "Pure willpower. Your love survives. And your rage—" The crow tilted his beak, regarding the edge of the pit. "Hmm. Wonder if any pickings are left. I could use a small nibble—"

"Do I have enough . . . will . . . for one more . . . tonight?" said Blessing.

"What? I certainly hope so . . . Your nerve is up. I'd say go for it."

"I don't know . . . I don't . . ." Blessing looked at his hands. "I'm a murderer now."

"More like a special messenger doing the job of the Universe, that's all," said the crow. "Just doing your job, one most people never get a chance at. So don't get all self-doubting, guy, or that nose is going to come off again. And maybe those ears. You want to see Amy again, don't you?"

Blessing said nothing for long moments.

"There are things I can do . . ." he said, finally. "No human should have the power to do. Am I damning myself by my own anger?"

"Think of what they took from you—more than Amy, more than your life—your full and rightful place in history. And they would ruin it with garbage," said the crow. "You have much to settle, yes, William Blessing. But you are also a servant to the furies who, without you, might find justice in methods less satisfactory to you."

"I . . . I . . ." said Blessing.

"Kill the bastards," said the crow. "And leave their souls to the mercy of the darkness they serve." The crow flapped away into the night.

William Blessing nodded and walked into the harbor fog again, looking for a bar.

24

The thousand injuries of Fortunato I had borne as I best could, but when he ventured upon insult I vowed revenge. You, who so well know the nature of my soul, will not suppose, however, that I gave utterance to a threat. At length I would be avenged; this was a point definitively settled—but the very definitiveness with which it was resolved precluded the idea of risk. I must not only punish but punish with impunity. A wrong is unredressed when retribution overtakes its redresser. It is equally unredressed when the avenger fails to make himself felt as such to him who has done the wrong.

—Edgar A. Poe, *The Cask of Amontillado*

"Either this wallpaper goes, or I do!" said Baxter Brittle, looking up from his booth at the back of his bar.

The remains of bad carryout Chinese food—kung-pao shrimp, moo goo gai pan, and greasy egg rolls—lay on the table before him. He lifted a bottle of Newcastle Brown Ale and dripped the last few drops of the frothing stuff into an old-fashioned dimple mug. Everything smelled of sesame oil and he was burping up hops and malt and in general felt a little on the wrong side of queasy. Before him was a fabulous horror novel from a brilliant young writer who wanted him to issue a special edition several months before his regular publisher put out the trade version. Baxter fully intended to soon be big enough to publish original novels by known writers, not just short story collections and limited editions—crumbs from the tables of New York mainstream houses. *Shit,* Baxter thought, *all it takes is money, and that commodity was becoming much more common around the Tome offices.*

Ah, yes, life was good.

But he still didn't like the wallpaper much back there. Kind of yellowing *fleur de lis.* He made a mental note to have it taken down, maybe leave the natural wood (properly treated, of course) to accentuate the array of knickknacks and paraphernalia and framed pictures.

Business was slow at the bar. The bartender of the night, cleaning some glasses, laughed. "Do you know all the Oscar Wilde quips, Mr. Brittle?"

"Yes, and I have a few of my own. But only half-wits rely solely on fully original material. We full-wits know enough to plagiarize as much as possible."

"That is," said the mustached young man, "the sincerest form of flattery."

"I believe even the esteemed Edgar Allan Poe did a bit of that even while he pointed his finger at others," said Brittle, thoughtfully. He looked down at the mess before him. He suddenly realized that he needed something stronger than British ale, and he needed to drink it somewhere other than here. "Say Joe, dear fellow," he said, getting up. "Would you be so kind as to clean the rest of this up for me? There's a good deal left you might wish to save for your lunch tomorrow. Don't say the owner of the Cork'd Sailor bar is not a generous man."

The bartender bowed deeply with an ironic flourishing bow. "Oh, thank you for the scraps, oh, master."

Baxter Brittle arose, straightened his long coat, and collected the soy-sauce stained manuscript before him.

"Oh, and Joe. I may be expecting late company. There might be a man in a dark coat arriving. His name is Mick. Please allow him entrance to the cellar. I may be distracted by this stunning bit of fiction . . . and *other* things, and not have the wherewithal to let him in."

"You bet, Mr. Brittle." Joe went over to the far end of the bar, where a group of students seemed interested in ordering another round of beers.

Baxter Brittle headed for the door to his private lair. *Ah, the comforts of one's little piece of exotica,* he thought as he smelled the familiar scents of sandalwood and hash oil, candles and rosewater, as he descended. The place was getting to look more and more like a Maxfield Parrish painting, noted Baxter as he turned on the lights. All Roman columns and satin curtains and filigrees, a-splash with bright Oriental rugs and Grecian urns filled with peacock feathers. Where there had once been merely ugly plush orange and brown thrift-store sofas there were now divine divans and fine fainting couches and silken pillows by the score.

Alas, where this very special basement had once been party central for a more sociable Gothiques and associates, now, with business purring along so well, the very reason for all this added finery was causing it to be used less. Baxter Brittle was simply too busy dealing with his growing Tome Press empire. Often as not he wasn't at the bar, but rather down the street in the new offices Tome had rented to accommodate the new personnel. More and more, now, Baxter simply used this delightful place as a retreat, a place to relax and submerge himself in his peculiar dalliances.

He put the latest Planet Dog dub collection on the new surround sound system. Pulsing heartbeat rhythms took over the room.

Baxter's head bobbed to the bass line. "And now for a cocktail!"

He licked his lips and went to the altar.

The altar had prospered and multiplied also with the fortunes of Tome. No longer did it sport merely a few cheap Magickal symbols, a pentacle here, a Goat's head there. Now it was a veritable pantheon of gods and saints and demons, from Hitler and Shiva to Lucifer and Jeffrey Dahmer. Large votive candles flickered. The sweet-and-sour smell of communion wine lingered about fallen goblets. Baxter lit a few more candles, then put a couple of joss sticks in a fat Buddha's lap and lit those as well.

"These ought to burn your balls, brother," he told the somber Buddha.

He selected his own favorite sort of incense—a lovely Cuban cigar, an El Presedente no less—from a humidor. He lit it from one of the scented candles.

Then he pulled open the cabinet below the altar.

Lined up neatly were hand-marked bottles of absinthe.

He selected one, then went to the sink of the new built-in kitchen/bar. He poured the stuff into a goblet, sniffed it . . . ah! . . . and saluted the gleaming altar, and in fact the entirety of his domain.

"I fear that I have only one way of dealing with temptation," he announced. "Yielding to it!"

The digital drumming from the sound system gave an approving flourish. The high-test alcohol didn't take long to hit his system, giving him that amazing, illegal glow, both sedative and psychedelic, that was the delightful province of absinthe. Oh, he'd have to give it up eventually, tone down to wine and beer. Absinthe not only made the heart grow fonder, but it could kill you over protracted use. The burden of success would no doubt save him, Baxter thought. Who had the time to get stoned all day when there was so much profitable work to be done? However, not right now, not quite now. Now he would enjoy the richness the liquor gave the colors in his life, the deadness it gave whatever conscience he had left in his psyche.

He took the manuscript and goblet and plopped down in a favorite comfy chair in front of his private little hearth, the delightful candlelit altar. He was feeling much better now, evened out. He looked at the candlewicks doing their eternal dance and felt the hypnotic comfort of the smells and the wormwood and the calm of knowing that rewards of work and ambition were being showered upon him.

Ah, yes, money was nice but it was the things—the comforts and the futures you could buy with money—that were the best.

There were some things, though, that money simply couldn't buy, that Baxter Brittle had now.

Next to him was another recent addition: a sturdy, custom-made bookcase, polished oak, leaded glass enclosed. He gazed inside, saw his Gurdjieff books, first editions all. His Aleister Crowley books, his ancient volumes of forgotten lore. But central, yes, most important of all, were the books and magazines and documents that occupied the upper shelf, all to themselves.

Having some knowledge of the field, he'd been very quick about making sure he got the very best of the spoils of that fateful evening at the Blessing household. Not even dear Donald Marquette did as well as he, even though doubtless Donald appropriated a larger number of volumes. Even in his cups, as he most certainly had been that evening, Baxter had been able to pick and choose most artfully.

Now, he gazed upon his prizes.

It had been in his own self-interest to help Mick and Theodore and even the Marquis sell their portions of the spoils. He'd only taken a small fee for facilitating the deals with a handful of west coast underground dealers, book fair pirates (invariably fat and malodorous) who paid cash and never asked questions. He himself could have made a pretty penny on what he'd taken, but like rare artwork, Blessing's rarest treasures were well-known in the scholarly and collecting circles, and very heavily insured, no doubt. In that respect, the books might as well be radioactive, far too dangerous to be moved, but housed in his special bookcase, they provided Baxter with a constant source of . . . well, he wasn't sure just what exactly, for once words failed him, but he knew he definitely liked it.

He loved to admire his plunder by candlelight. Muse upon the meaning, meditate upon Poe. Bask in the heat of history and genius.

He took another long sip of his absinthe and considered, with mirth, the irony of it all.

Poe! Oh, how poor and destitute the man had been. And yet he'd *invented* forms of literature that had made *fortunes* for those who simply followed the formulas he'd created, the way he'd used words.

What was it that he'd read once about Poe's principal contribution to literature? Oh, yes—and it wasn't something Baxter had actually considered, yet it was most certainly, upon reflection, quite true.

The critic had pointed out that Edgar Poe was the first writer of fiction who had introduced the use of the full gamut of the devices of poetry into prose. Rhythm, meter, sibilance, assonance, tropes—you name it—Poe had dumped the whole bag of tricks into his stories. This was why, even when you read the tales today, there was a certain modernity of style, despite the nineteenth-century trappings. This, after all, was because Poe created a style that continued on to this day.

Vaguely, as he stared at the volumes before him, Baxter Brittle wondered if he should re-read Poe.

Maybe, once he was able to parcel out more responsibilities of the Press and its growing concerns . . . Maybe, he'd start writing again. Yes, business had consumed him so much . . . There was a whole industry being created here, under the brilliance of dear Donald Marquette's editorial guidance, and Mick Prince's unique ideas on marketing.

Why not claim a piece of the literary pie himself?

Lesser writers than he were certainly scattered on the bestseller lists, idolized by readers around the world . . .

Idolized . . .

Baxter Brittle wondered what that kind of fame would be like. Delicious, certainly. Quite, quite delicious . . .

Suddenly, a breeze shuffled along the tops of the candles, snuffing them out.

The room was suddenly full of wispy shadows.

Baxter looked around.

He felt a draught. A chill.

A presence.

"Who's there—?"

He tried to rise to his feet, but he'd gulped more absinthe than he'd intended and found himself too drunk to leave his chair, at least not without extra concentration.

He fell back, blearily peering into the darkness that had swept the rest of the room.

A figure stepped from the shadows.

"Hello, Baxter. Enjoying your new acquisitions, are you?"

Baxter squinted. "Mick? Mick, is that you?"

He'd called the fellow earlier to arrange for a meeting. Yes, surely this must be Mick, playing some sort of ghoulish prank.

Naughty fellow.

"Come over and have a drink, Mick," said Baxter. "I know you don't particularly enjoy absinthe, but I'm sure I can find something more to your taste."

The figure stepped forward. It was wearing a dark coat, but nothing as showy or attention-demanding as Mick Prince's. Ahead of the figure wafted an odd smell. Once, on one of their drunken larks, the gang had visited an abattoir on a field trip. Tanned hides, rotting carcasses, bones, and animal glue. A camera had caught some of the more interesting images available of after-death, bizarre juxtapositions of light, dark, and the inclinations of death. But the starkest memory that Baxter still retained was the smell, a strange otherworldly yet very immediate valentine from the dead to the living. A thing of instinct and promise, as though this odor were intoning: "We are the flesh beyond flesh now. The reverberations of blood. The resonance of what was. Take your time or not. You will join us soon."

Somehow, above the smell of the incense, and the taste of the absinthe, Baxter detected a breath of that now.

"No, Baxter. Not Mick. And nothing to drink, thank you."

The figure stopped. Folded its arms together. "Someone you requested to meet once. Perhaps I should have been more attentive at the time and responded. Perhaps things would have been different then. Then again . . . perhaps not."

The blur in Baxter's mind prevented thought from moving very quickly. "How did you get down here?" he said, realizing that the visitor was a stranger.

"There are ways I have now . . . abilities . . . things I can do now . . . *Now.* Such a qualitative sort of word, don't you think? My now, is not very long. In fact, in a very real sense, my now is a projection of the past, a lingering shadow."

Baxter was confused, but the whiff of decay he'd caught triggered alarm, an automatic fear. The fear cleared his head enough to allow him to rise to his feet, still gripping his absinthe.

"Who are you?"

Even as he spoke, he put his goblet down and stepped back a bit.

"Someone I don't think you ever expected to see again, Baxter Brittle. I am here for two reasons."

Baxter inched back toward a chest. He pulled one of the drawers open, slowly and unobtrusively put a hand back into it. He'd always been paranoid about intruders into his sanctum sanctorum, and he had taken precautions. Now, it would seem, those precautions had been wise. He sensed immediate danger, strong danger. However, fortunately, he was still too drunk to panic.

Just get hold of it, he thought, bleariness lifting only slightly. *Grab it, and things will be fine. Just grab it and everything will be absolutely fabulous.*

The guy was talking. Talk took time, which was good in this situation. Baxter knew that even if he had to report this particular adventure, a corpse would not be a particular problem. After all, this would be a situation of *self-defense,* right?

"I don't know what you're talking about. Then again, I don't know who you are, do I?" asked Baxter.

The figure stepped forward.

Its face was lit by a convergence of candlelight and halogen.

Pale and ashen was that face. Slightly cracked and shriveled, but still handsome. There were dark glasses around the eyes, but the man took them off.

The eyes were dark but familiar.

The realization of the intruder's identity stunned Baxter so deeply that for a moment his hand paused in its search. His mind rebelled against accepting the image being relayed to it.

"Blessing?" he said.

"That's right, Baxter."

Baxter Brittle found himself giggling. "But this only happens in particularly odious and banal stories!" he said. "I simply won't accept it."

"I had the same thought, myself, Baxter. But then, perhaps, we are both simply odious and banal characters, hmm? Trapped in some shlocky, tossed-off pennydreadful, acting in a dreary tale by a writer more desperate even than we are!"

Baxter couldn't help himself from chuckling. "No, I'm just hallucinating." He shook his head.

"A bit of undigested gruel? No, I'm no Jacob Marley, Baxter Brittle, come to summon ghostly redemption. And I know Ebenezer Scrooge. And you, sir, are no Ebenezer Scrooge." The Dark Man shook his head sadly. "No redemption involved here, Baxter. Merely . . . retribution!"

Donald Marquette's call.

. . . *the grave* . . .

. . . *disturbed* . . .

And now, here was a man dressed in dark clothes who looked very much like William Blessing.

Baxter Brittle had always been an atheist. His dabblings in dark things were always, he thought, an exercise in psychological self-manipulation. An amusement, a method of hypnotic control over self and others. The powers were all, he'd felt, on the inside, and through ceremony and ritual could be unlocked. All the peripheral stuff was whimsical rococo window dressing. Interior decoration.

If nothing else, then the black arts had always been a good excuse to drink and use drugs.

Now, though, here was evidence that he'd been wrong.

His mind bent.

But it did not break.

"Oh, dear me," he said. "Come back from the dead for revenge. But why on me, dear boy?"

His hand rummaged farther back in the dresser drawer.

"You helped steal my wife from me, my wife . . . my entire life," stated the man, baldly. "You seek to steal my good name. And you also have something that belongs to me—that I'd like back."

"And what, Mr. Corpse, would that be, pray tell?"

"What you stole from my library."

"What? You're going to take it back to the grave with you?" Baxter chuckled. "Not much light to read by, dear boy."

"You may do me a favor, Baxter."

"A favor? Why, of course."

"Tell me where I can find the man named Mick Prince."

"Certainly." Baxter gave him the address where Mick was staying. "You'll find Theodore Melvins there as well. They're the ones you're after, Blessing. Not me. Mick shot you. Theodore raped your wife. Me . . . I just wanted to be your friend! It was all a ruse. I just wanted to know you!"

"But it was *your* plan."

"My plan. Alas, gone wrong. But I assure you, my intentions were good. Oh, yes, my intentions were very good indeed."

The dark man named Blessing stood still.

Baxter's fingers touched his gun. His hand closed around it, finger finding the trigger.

But he paused, waiting to see what this . . . this . . . *whatever* was going to do.

"Intentions are pavement, Baxter Brittle," said William Blessing. "You're already on the road. It is my duty to give you a small push."

Damn, thought Baxter Brittle.

He pulled out the gun and fired.

There were scant feet between the two of them. Aiming was not difficult. A quick succession of three shots pounded into the Dark Man. Baxter saw bits of flesh and clothing rip out of the man. However, William Blessing did not fall.

Rather, he simply stepped forward, grabbed the gun, and twisted it from his attacker's hands.

"Sorry, Baxter. You've just made things more difficult for yourself."

Baxter gasped and turned away.

The Dark Man's free hand swung, casting Baxter Brittle into darkness.

He awoke in gloom.

There was a faint pain in his head, but mostly he felt the continued effects of the absinthe. He was still drunk.

For a moment, Baxter Brittle was fogged and perplexed.

Where was he? His back was against some kind of rough wall, and he was sitting. There was a slight glow coming from the darkness above. There was a scraping and clacking, muted, beyond the darkness before him.

Then, it all came back to him.

The Poe books. The gun . . .

William Blessing, risen from the grave, standing before him.

"No," he said.

As he made to get up, there was a clanking and clinking. His hands and feet were restrained. God, what were these?

"Chains?" he gasped, with disbelief. "Where am I?"

He heard scraping. A slap of something wet.

The glow of candlelight in a crevice of the darkness above him.

" 'At the most remote end of the crypt,' " intoned the voice, " 'there appeared another less spacious. Its walls had been lined with human remains, piled to the vault overhead, in the fashion of the great catacombs of Paris. Three sides of this interior crypt were still ornamented in this manner. From the fourth, the bones had been thrown down, and lay promiscuously upon the earth, forming at one point a mound of some size. Within the wall thus exposed by the displacing of the bones, we perceived a still interior recess, in depth about four feet, in width three, in height six or seven. It seemed to have been constructed for no especial use within itself, but formed merely the interval between two of the colossal supports of the roof of the catacombs, and was backed by one of their circumscribing walls of solid granite.' "

"Stop it!" cried Baxter. He found himself laughing maniacally despite himself. "Where . . . where is this place . . . ?"

There was a scraping, as of a trowel working with cement.

"Very, very handy, this," said Blessing. "You're in your unfinished subbasement—"

"Subbasement?" Baxter blinked in the gloom. Yes, he could smell the damp and the fungus and the cool cellar smells—and something more . . .

Old rot. Dead flesh. Ancient corpses of rats, perhaps?

"Yes. The work was pretty much done for me. I just availed myself of it."

Scrape, scrape.

Clink, clink.

"Did you recognize the source of my recitation, Brittle?"

Baxter laughed drunkenly. *"Cask of Amontillado."*

"A perfectly constructed story, don't you think? I could not help but seize the opportunity presented here to act it out."

Brittle kept panic at bay, giggling.

He was still alive, and if alive, there was certainly hope.

Moreover, there was something that Blessing—or whoever this madman was—could not have known!

Carefully, so as not to jingle his chains too much and let his captor know what he was about, Baxter Brittle crept his hand into the inner jacket of his coat pocket.

Yes.

There it was.

Snug and safe in there was a hard bit of electronics. Baxter Brittle chuckled to himself. Oh, Donald, my boy! Marquette, my lad, he thought. Thank you!

His cellular phone.

He could call for help on his cellular phone.

He laughed. "Walled up alive!" said Brittle. "How original." He let his hands fall back. "My question is now, Blessing . . . or whoever you are . . . where's the Amontillado, then?"

A flicker of light. Baxter could see that there was just enough room to slip one more brick in the wall.

Eyes, lit by candlelight, stared through, directly at the captive.

"No Amontillado, I'm afraid, Brittle. No, something much more to your liking. I took the liberty of installing several bottles of what appears to be your favorite drink."

Baxter laughed. "Absinthe! You left me absinthe . . . Oh, the quality of mercy!" He looked around. "Unfortunately, I can't see a thing!"

"By your side, there is a candle with some matches."

"You are most kind."

" ' "For the love of God, Montressor!" ' " quoted Blessing.

" ' "Yes," I said. "For the love of God!"

" 'But to these words I hearkened in vain for a reply. I grew impatient. I called aloud.

" ' "Fortunato!"

" 'No answer. I called again—

" ' "Fortunato!"

" 'No answer still. I thrust a torch through the remaining aperture and let it fall within. There came forth in return only jingling of the bells. My heart grew sick; on account of the dampness of the catacombs. I hastened to make an end of my labor. I forced the last stone into its position; I plastered it up. Against the new masonry I re-erected the old rampart of bones. For the half of a century no mortal has disturbed them. *In pace requiescat!*' "

"Bravo!" said Baxter Brittle. "Excellent. Far hammier than Vincent Price's reading. A true accomplishment."

His chains jingled as he clapped.

"Farewell, Brittle," said Blessing.

The last brick began to slip into place. Then, abruptly, it stopped. Was pulled back out. The eyes peered in again. "Oh, one more thing. You might have some company."

"*Ciao!*" said Baxter.

The brick was pushed into place, cutting out what little light there was in this dank tomb.

Baxter fumbled about immediately for those matches and the candle. Reaching out, he found the candle. He gripped it. He could feel the wick. His hand patted out, looking for the promised matches. At first he felt nothing, but then, as his hand moved outward in a wider arc, his fingers touched a box that clattered when he touched it.

He grabbed and pulled it against him, doing as best he could, considering the iron bracelets he wore.

With the darkness descending, for the first time, he felt as though the alcohol was wearing off. He could feel stark, glaring fear threatening at the base of his spine.

Baxter really, really needed a drink.

Especially knowing that drink was absinthe.

Yes, he would light the candle. He would find the promised bottles of his brand of Amontillado. And, then, unlike poor Fortunato, he would be able to get out of this prison. All he had to do, after all, was pull out the cellular phone and call Marquette. Should Marquette not be available . . . hmmm. What? Members of the gang? Yes, perhaps, but if worse came to worst, surely he could just call 911.

Hello. This is Baxter Brittle. Help. I've been walled up alive!

Carefully, Baxter pulled out a match. He held the matchhead against the side of the box, struck it on the flint. The flare was magnificent, a beacon of hope, and the smell of sulfur was delicious. Carefully, eagerly, he guided the flame over to the top of the candle. Touched down.

The wick came to life almost immediately. It cast a bold bright light across the expanse of the compartment.

Baxter held the candle up for better illumination, and he immediately saw the bottles that had been promised.

They were held between the arms of a corpse, obviously long dead. The flesh was decayed, and bones showed through, but there were enough features left, primarily the hair, to make it familiar to Baxter.

That, and the ceremonial knife still stuck in the chest.

The punk girl! Oh, jeez, when Mick had said he would take care of the body, he thought he'd meant drag it out and dump it in the bay or something—not entomb it beneath his own bar!

The eyes were rotted out, leaving dark obscene orbs staring out above a twist of cartilage that had been a nose. Those orbs stared forward, directly at Baxter, as though saying, "Here you are, Baxter. Come and get your drink."

A paroxysm of panic hit Baxter. He lost hold of the candle.

It fell to the ground and the light flashed out, filling the tomb again with darkness.

Silence shrouded him then, except for the sound of his beating heart. Like Poe's *Tell-Tale Heart:*

. . . a low, dull, quick sound—such a sound as a watch makes when enveloped in cotton.

It grew louder—louder—louder!

And the harsh sound of his own terrified breathing.

"Hey, Party Guy," he thought he heard a voice from the very throat of night. "Let's get Gothic!"

Then he heard the sound of a bottle breaking against the wall, the slither of a knife sliding from between ribs . . .

I left you some company, Blessing had said.

And the stirring of old bones and dry flesh, rasping toward him, were like the flapping of the wings of some bird of prey.

25

And then came, as if to my final and irrevocable overthrow, the spirit of Perverseness. *Of this spirit philosophy takes no account. Yet I am not more sure that my soul lives, than I am that perverseness is one of the primitive impulses of the human heart—one of the indivisible primary faculties, or sentiments, which give direction to the character of Man. Who has not, a hundred times, found himself committing a vile or a silly action, for no other reason than because he knows he should not?*

—Edgar A. Poe, *The Black Cat*

Donald Marquette's cellular phone rang.

Marquette was standing at the window, staring down at the street pensively, sipping strong coffee and milk, feeling as odd as he'd ever felt in his life, when the insistent annoying beep, beep, beep whined from the technological wonder in his pocket like the motor of an artificial heart.

It was morning at the Blessing house. Outside, it was a moody day, warm and muggy, with dark rain clouds threatening. The air smelled like storm.

Donald had arrived early to start work. He hadn't been able to sleep well last night. What drowsing he'd experienced had been charged by nightmares he could not exactly remember. So he'd come in early and started business up. He didn't think he'd be able to write any fiction today, something he did at home. No, there were practical matters to be taken care of today, especially since he was now in control of the Blessing literary estate, the Blessing name . . . everything. Amy fortunately no longer came into the office. It held disturbing memories for her. There was a secretary, but she was out today.

Donald Marquette flipped open the cellular phone.

"Hello?"

On the other end, silence.

Some kind of grating, an echo . . .

"Hello!" he said again, exasperated. His nerves were such that he wanted to just cut off all communications.

That, of course, in the present situation, would be extremely unwise.

"Oh. Sorry! Donald! It's Roscoe! Roscoe Mithers!"

Donald's heart skipped a beat. "Oh, yes. Mr. Mithers. Good morning."

"Just call me Roscoe, Donald. I hope you don't mind that I called on this number. I got voice messaging on the other services and you did say this was your private line . . . I thought that would be appropriate."

"Yes, yes. That's fine. Glad to hear from you so soon."

"I got your proposal, of course. And I've got some ideas myself. But I want to tell you from the very outset . . . I'm very, very interested. Like Ricardo the Vampire says, it's something I can sink my teeth into! Now, I'm having a meeting this afternoon with higher people. I'm going to present these ideas, and a few of my own. I think that there's a very good chance we're going to be able to start up a very lucrative program here, and with our corporate tentacles in every media, every merchandising area, every licensing possibility—I think we can come up with an excellent arrangement. Of course, we'd have to work out the details with your agent, but I think we'll be able to handle that."

Of course he could have taken the Blessing properties elsewhere. There were also contracts to be fulfilled. The anthologies, the novels . . . but there were other possibilities, and in Roscoe Mithers, Donald Marquette saw other opportunities.

"Have you had a chance to look at the other material, Roscoe?"

"Yes, I have, Donald. What can I say? It's excellent. You know, I can't pretend this isn't giving me a real opportunity for my own career. Naturally, I'd very much like to publish your solo efforts as well as the proposed collaborations with the Blessing material—"

Yes!

"—and since it will be under my auspices, I'll put just as much elbow grease and promotion into those solo efforts."

Yes! Yes!

"But I can't do anything until I get the okay from above, as well as input from sales and marketing."

"I understand, Roscoe. When will I hear from you?"

"Either late this afternoon or tomorrow morning. In any event, on the other side of the meeting."

"Thank you, Roscoe. I'll look forward to your call."

"Right. Thanks, Donald. Go with the Golem!"

The connection ended.

Marquette was always fairly irked by the way that Mithers always related everything to the *Dark Sunset* universe. Personally, the only reason he dealt with that putrid material was for the money and the career advancement. But Roscoe Mithers was exactly the sort of guy who could do for Marquette what he wished done: wed his name inseparably with that of William Blessing.

From this launching pad (also highly lucrative!) could his own work take off into the stratosphere.

Donald Marquette.

A good name to see regularly on bestseller lists!

The call lifted his spirits. He sat down in the leather chair, feeling a rush. He swallowed the rest of his coffee, letting the caffeine push him into a kind of elevated trance.

All kinds of possibilities, he thought.

The future was boundless.

The cellular phone rang again.

He picked it out of his pocket faster this time, wondering if it was the New York editor again.

It wasn't.

"Marquette?" said a terse, gruff voice.

"Yes?"

"Trouble."

"Mick?"

"Yeah. Man, somethin' goin' on. The Count and the Marquis, man. Fuckin' wasted. And I can't find Baxter. He's just . . . gone. No sign of him, and he didn't pack or take his passport."

Marquette gawked at the receiver. "Wasted? I don't understand."

"Dead. Big-time dead. Like . . . like in one of my stories."

He'd never heard Mick Prince sound like this before.

Unnerved.

Scared.

"Something's going on, man. I can feel the vibes," Mick stated. "Theodore wants to leave town again, and I'm thinking that's a damned good idea."

"Dead?" said Marquette. "How—"

Mick told him.

"Police won't come to you," he said upon finishing. "I heard about it because they tried to find Baxter and we were at the Tome office. Got out damned fast, and we gotta keep goin' before they think to pin these fuckin' bodies on us. Hey man, Baxter ever tell you about . . . about any enemies that Theodore and I never knew about? Some other Goth crew or something?"

What about your *enemies?* thought Marquette. *You're the over-the-edge mad-dog psycho who pushed us into this.*

"No. But then, you were involved before I was."

"Shit, man. Don't lay this on me."

"Look. This shouldn't be dealt with through the phone lines."

"Shit. Jeez. You're right." Marquette could hear the paranoia in his voice. "You want to come here?"

"Yes. But I've got to deal with some things first. Can you guys stay put for a while?"

"Yeah. Sure. But don't be too long."

"Look, Mick. All I can say is, hang tough. There's too much at stake."

"Yeah. Like a fuckin' *witch,* burnin'."

The connection was severed.

What had he meant by that?

Marquette felt dizzy. He leaned against a desk. Distantly, he heard the doorbell buzz. He sat down. Someone else could take care of that. Someone else . . . He had to assimilate all this . . .

He'd thought that the violence would end after that dreadful night. He could live with the excellent consequences, yes, but he was not by nature someone who preferred violence or enjoyed it. He'd always felt that violence was the instinctual response of the uncreative mind and had vowed to leave that part of things, if any, up to Baxter and his cronies. That night . . . he really hadn't been himself.

Baxter, missing.

The Count and the Marquis . . . dead?

And the disturbed grave . . . That must have been a clue. There was someone stalking them. Someone perhaps who knew that Blessing's death was more complex than surface presentations. Someone from left field. Someone out of the blue.

He could call the police, he supposed. But there was too much he'd have to tell them. Too much that implicated him in the burglary, the rape, the death . . .

No. He'd have to deal with all this himself.

On the verge . . . On the verge of the ambitions of any writer. Success, wealth . . . fame!

Maybe even literary immortality.

When he was in high school, the yearbook staff had asked him about his goals in life. The answer that appeared below the smiling youth in the Dubuque High yearbook was: "I want to be a world-famous writer!"

Donald Marquette slapped the desk.

"No," he spat.

It was so close he could taste it.

Nothing would stop him.

Nothing!

Suddenly, the intercom buzzed. "Donald?" came Amy's voice. "Donald, are you up there? There's been the strangest delivery."

"I'm sorry, Amy," he said into the speaker. "I can't look at it now. I have to go out for a while."

26

Then, methought, the air grew denser, perfumed from an unseen censer
Swung by Seraphim whose foot-falls tinkled on the tufted floor.
"Wretch," I cried, "thy God hath lent thee—by these angels he hath sent thee
Respite—respite and nepenthe from thy memories of Lenore;
Quaff, oh quaff this kind nepenthe and forget this lost Lenore!"
Quoth the Raven, "Nevermore."

—Edgar A. Poe, *The Raven*

He checked his nose, his ears, his appendages.

All seemed firmly in place.

The wealth of blood and flesh last night had been a boon. The morning had dawned on a healthier than ever undead man. He fancied that now, sitting here in the park within sight of his townhome, he could smell the spring flowers that grew in rows here, feel the warm pressure of the sun against his cracked, gray skin.

As though I were really alive, thought William Blessing. *As though I were truly human, and not this vengeful husk of faux-life, shaking a bloody fist at eternal night.*

There came a flapping.

The crow settled on the bench beside him.

"What a champ!" said the crow. "You've got him rattled all right. Murderer Marquette is heading toward the graveyard. Maybe with a stop at the hardware store for a spade, first, eh? Plenty of time to go and talk to Amy."

"Talk to her one last time," whispered Blessing. He bowed his head into his hands. "Suddenly I'm so tired of this. The pain never ends, and this won't stop it."

"Whoa there, chum," said the crow. "Do I hear the sound of your nose falling off into the drink? You've gone too far to turn back now! You have to pick up the backbeat, amigo! You haven't even settled with your murderers yet, to say nothing of the brute who raped your wife . . ." The crow's voice filled with venom. ". . . or the assassin who wants to do the same to your art!"

"Marquette," said Blessing. Cold, raw fury filled him again.

"You didn't notice him pawing her as much as he could? The laughter between the two . . . The chemistry he tried to evoke? On some level, Master Blessing, you must have smelled the rank lust oozing from the monster when he was around your wife. Hmm? Just one more reason to heave old Pallas, eh? The student deposing the teacher."

Blessing nodded. "Yes."

"So go and do what you must. Why?" said the crow. Its eyes flashed and its beak snapped. "*Because you* must!"

William Blessing rose from the park bench and headed for the townhouse.

The crow flapped off in the opposite direction, to follow the progress of their enemies.

The boxes were scattered about the living room, all open now.

Amy Blessing held the carving knife over them.

She stared down, still stunned at what they held.

The books . . .

The magazines . . .

The letters and the artifacts . . .

The Poe collection . . .

It wasn't all here. Something instinctual told her that. But the bulk of it was, the corner-stone items.

They'd been placed in boxes, taped, and then put through a local messenger service.

When she called Donald down, she'd thought he'd be as astonished and happy as she was. Instead, she thought he was going to fall over with shock. He'd turned the whitest shade of pale she'd ever seen on a face. He'd helped her with another package then disappeared into the dining room. She thought she'd heard the clinking of glasses. Drinking so early in the morning? No, surely not. That wasn't like Donald at all. Although, in truth, he had been drinking more lately. Well, then again, so had they all—she included. All that wine!

Then Donald had said he was going down to the messenger service to see who sent the books. Then, perhaps, to the police. That had sounded quite reasonable to Amy.

She leaned over a box. The comforting fragrance of ancient vellum and old print touched her, made her feel astonished and filled with awe.

The buzzer sounded again. She was happy to hear the voice of William's cousin come over the speaker system. She let him in immediately.

"The most astonishing thing has happened!" she told him. "Look."

The man looked much the same. For some reason, though, he seemed stronger now, missing that hint of frailness.

He knelt down by the books. Touched them.

"Yes," he said. "Good. Very good. They are home now."

Amy had the oddest feeling. "You don't seem surprised to see them."

He stood, holding a copy of *Tales of the Grotesque and Arabesque,* smoothing his hand over it in a cherishing fashion. "I told you there were things I had to do in Baltimore, Amy."

"You . . . *You* sent these books?"

"I recovered them. Yes, Amy. I trust you will take care of them now. Place them back in the collection where they belong."

"Of . . . of course . . . But how . . . ?"

"I cannot tell you that. Just be assured, I am working to preserve that which your husband strove so hard for. And I have more yet to do—"

"Well, I must say that I'm happy to see these books back. William loved them so . . . and I have feelings for them myself. But more than that, William had hoped to save them for posterity. For a foundation . . ."

"That is what you must remember, Amy. Yes, he spoke of that to me, when he wrote."

"Look. Let me make you some coffee or something . . . You must stay . . . You must tell me about this. And you must talk to Donald. He needs to meet you."

"No coffee. I must go," said the man. "However, Amy, there is one more thing I must tell you. Something that your husband meant for you to know . . . Something that he meant for you to have."

The man in the dark coat quietly told her.

27

"Keeping now steadily in mind the points to which I have drawn your attention—that peculiar voice, that unusual agility, and that startling absence of motive in a murder so singularly atrocious as this—let us glance at the butchery itself . . . "

—Edgar A. Poe, *The Murders in the Rue Morgue*

Mick Prince swung a lamp into a mirror. The glass smashed, sending down dozens of shards to rain down onto the opulent antiques of the subterranean lair. The strong scent of ropy incense in the air. A flash of candle, a stir of tassels.

Mick Prince's chest heaved. "Damn him, the fuckin' bastard. He'd better have my money here someplace."

Theodore Melvins tossed back a swallow of wine from a bottle he'd found in a corner. "Maybe he just took off with all the money."

"I'll find him," said Mick.

"Maybe . . . . maybe he's dead like those other geeks."

"I'll find him," roared Mick Prince. "And then I'll fuckin' kill him again."

It has to be here! thought Mick Prince, ripping off upholstery from a couch. He pulled out the knife from his boot and started attacking pillows. Stuffing flew, but nothing more was revealed.

Once, when drunk (a common enough condition for Brittle), Baxter had mentioned that he kept "reserves" for emergencies, scattered hither and thither. Especially now since his financial condition had improved, those reserves should have swelled. The previous day when they had talked, and it had been suggested that maybe Mick Prince and Theodore Melvins might best leave town again, Baxter had promised Mick money that he'd owed him. Mick was supposed to drop by the previous night to discuss strategy and pick up that money. It had also been his full intention at that point to reveal his major plan to Baxter, and thereby obtain *more* funds to begin executing that plan. Mick was particularly annoyed to find Baxter gone, possibly having absconded with the seed money for a huge fortune, when he, Mick, was just on the cusp of a brilliant endeavor. The little crimes and drug money that he'd brought into the business had been good for him and certainly for Tome Press. Now, though, with stone deadly muscle like Theodore, Mick Prince realized that he had to think *macro.*

"You see, B.B.," he was going to say, familiar hand draped over his comrade's shoulder, the mug of ale in his fist strengthening the bond. "It's very simple. Now that Tome, in conjunction of course with our good friend Donald Marquette and the estate of William Blessing, is starting to produce products and our fortunes are particularly tied to these books' placements on the bestseller lists, I figure, what's the best way to make sure we get a healthy market share. Hmmm?"

And Baxter would have shaken his head woozily, breathed some absinthe into Mick's face and said, "I don't know, Mick."

"Why, eliminate the competition, of course! Clear the way for our success. It's quite simple, really. With my talents for burglary, and Theodore's mercenary soldier talents, and our conjoined talent for murder . . . why, all we have to do is to pay . . . uhm . . . visits to other writers of horror literature whose books perform as well or better, and then remove them from the planet! Of course, we'll make sure to get signed first editions before we kill them and I'm sure pillaging their homes will be extremely remunerative. But the main thrust of our mission would be to follow the traditional American capitalist dictate: Bury the competition!"

And Baxter Brittle would have said, "Oh, excellent idea, dear chum. Please, *please* obtain souvenirs for me. Just don't have anything *personally* inscribed!"

Mick Prince had come up with the idea while he and Theodore had been in Antigua, laying low and living high. It seemed the perfect area for improvement of the literary business. Mick wondered why organized crime hadn't thought of it first. In fact, when it worked, maybe this would be the beginning of a new force in media. Yeah. Drugs, racketeering, prostitution, gambling, and bestsellers! Sheesh, it was *brilliant!*

And then he'd be able to sell his own novels to big publishers. Yeah, that was what Donald Marquette had promised. He could be a part of that new line that was being proposed: *William Blessing Presents: Sliced Eyeballs* by Mick Prince.

Oh, man, what a *rush* that would be!

"Find anything?" he called across the room.

"Shit, no," said Theodore. "Just a bunch of bottles and old crappy videos!"

"Keep on looking. There's gotta be somethin' down here!"

Mick went over to the altar. Crazy Baxt venerated this place. Maybe he felt that a plastic Satan was going to protect his stash!

"Sorry, bro," said Mick Prince to the picture of the pentagrammed goat hanging on a curtain. "Need some dough."

He cast his arm out across the altar. Idols and icons crashed to the floor. He pulled off the red altar cloth. Below this was a cabinet. Mick began to rifle the drawers.

Yes, yes. Now that the Enemy was gone, the world was his oyster, Mick thought.

Ever since that night at the Blessing house, when he discovered the true reason he was in Baltimore, he felt like a free man. Mick Prince had always been aware of some Other—some terrible enemy—ever since his days in reform school. He'd never known his parents—probably just some whore and her john had always been his theory. But still, he hadn't ever done well at the orphanages, and foster parents just weren't his bag. It was only when he got busted for dealing at the age of fourteen and got stuck in a reformatory in the San Francisco Bay area that he realized that he loved to read. And what he loved to read were wild and creepy and crazy stories, nonfiction and fiction. Man, he was just as happy with the Marquis de Sade as Clive Barker, with books about the Holocaust or the Khmer Rouge as Stephen King, and he devoured them all.

It was a good hobby, yeah.

Most outlaws (and that was what Mick Prince considered himself—an outlaw) just diddled their time away, gambling and womanizing or whatever. What a waste. Man, reading was the thing. You could do it outside the pen, or inside the pen, it didn't make any difference. Books were books and you could read 'em fuckin' anywhere.

Mick pulled a drawer so hard, it pulled all the way out and off its track, spilling candles all over the floor. Mick picked one up, lit it, and pushed the flame back into the shadowy recesses to check if there was anything hidden back there.

Nothing.

Shit!

A black rage flung itself over him. He started kicking and smashing away at the altar, splintering the balsa and plywood. Abruptly, the spell was over as soon as it had begun. Now that the Enemy was dead, Mick had better things to do than scrounge around for spare change.

He had goals!

He had *dreams!*

The Enemy had seemed to haunt his dreams as long as he could remember. A dim form, hidden in the shadows, that always made things go wrong in Mick's life.

Of all the horror stories and tales of mystery Mick had read, the ones he'd had the most trouble with were those of Edgar A. Poe. Once he'd read a biography of Poe. Man, what a bastard the guy had been! No wonder he'd had so many enemies. The figure that Mick had identified with the most was the literary executor, Rufus Griswold. Good ol' Rufus had told the truth about Edgar, all right. The A. in the middle wasn't really for "Allan." It was for *asshole.*

Too bad he'd already sold his share of the Poe collection, though. He sure could use the funds right now!

"Hey, Mick!" said Theodore from across the room. "We got company!"

"Baxter?"

Mick's shout was half-anger, half-relief.

Man, if that was Baxter Brittle, that would solve a shitload of problems. They could get the money they needed and *vamoose,* amigo! Adios Baltimoron *muchachos!*

"No, pard. Ain't Brittle."

Mick spun around. His long coat twirled and his brow furrowed deeply.

A man stood in the shadows beside the entrance to the subterranean lair. He was dressed in black and his face was in darkness.

Something else moved farther back in the dimness.

"Who are you?" Mick demanded, sauntering forward a step, chest stuck out, using his deepest and most intimidating tone. "How the *fuck* did you get down here?"

"I walked down the steps," said the figure. "As to the first question—Mick . . . That is your name, yes? Mick Prince?"

"Yeah," said Mick, trying to figure out what the hell to do in this situation.

A forefinger pointed toward his big, gruff, scar-faced partner. Theodore had gotten more tattoos and piercings on their recent "vacation." Earrings dangled from him now like baubles on some muscle-slab Christmas tree.

"And you . . . you're Theodore."

"What of it?" said Theodore.

"Yes. I recognize you both. I'd hate to be dealing with the wrong people. That just wouldn't do. No, not at all."

"Look buddy, you want to tell us what this is about?" demanded Mick. "We got work to do!"

"Looks as though you're doing some of my work for me," said the man.

He stepped forward.

The man was in dark glasses, despite the low light. His hands were beneath a dark coat.

"I'm the dead man whose wife you raped, Theodore," he said. "Let me apologize in advance for the lack of imagination here."

An arm lifted from the coat, holding a Heckler and Koch. The scabby finger tightened on the trigger, banging a slug straight into Theodore's crotch.

Theodore screamed.

He doubled over and fell to the floor, writhing.

"Shit!" said Mick.

He pulled his knife up.

The gun swung over to cover him.

"I wouldn't do that, Mick. I'd just stay where you are for now and let me deal with Mr. Theodore here. I can't quite decide if I should let him go on with his life without male apparatus . . . or send him to Hell without male apparatus. Any thoughts, Mr. Rapist?"

All that came from Theodore were agonized moans.

"As you wish, sir."

The gun swung again.

This time the bullet tore apart the man's head. Blood and gray matter splattered across the floor like a wash of particularly vile vomit.

"Now that's my kind of body piercing, Theodore," said the Dark Man.

Theodore's body shuddered, spasmed, kicked—then was still.

Mick Prince flinched. He stepped a pace back, trying to figure out what to do.

Dead man? The guy had said he was the dead man?

What the fuck was he talking about? Mick Prince didn't know yet, but that the dude had killed Theodore was pretty clear, he could see that, no problem. His experiences with street and prison violence, as well as other delightful modes of self-expression, put him in good stead. Wasn't there some quote about keeping your head when others were losing theirs?

So Mick just raised his hands up to show he held no weapon. He knew he needed to buy time. Then he might be able to do something appropriate. With time, he might be able to wax Mr. Mysterioso here.

"Shit, man! I ain't got a beef with you, whoever you are!"

"You don't? Then why did you shoot me?"

Then Mick Prince got it.

Didn't make a lick of sense, but he got it.

This son-of-a-bitch *thought* he was William Blessing!

That must be the case. Because no fuckin' way could this motherfucker actually *be* Blessing! He himself shot Blessing—and then watched as Marquette, bless 'im, bashed his skull in with that bust!

"Buddy, when I shoot people . . . they're dead. Real dead."

"No argument there, Mick . . . I'm dead, all right. Real dead."

"You? You're William Blessing?"

"Correct. Who else would know his murderers in an unsolved case—except for the murdered man himself."

"Oh, man." Mick's mind kind of *twisted* at the very notion—but he kept his calm, his cool, and his belief that deep down, there had to be some kind of explanation here. In the meantime, the number-one priority was to keep on breathing. "So . . . you just . . . pushed up out of the grave, got yourself a gun, and went after the people who you thought had killed—"

Then he got the buzz.

It was in the air . . .

The electric charge he got late at night, when his extra senses caught wind of that scent . . .

That *smell* of the Other. . .

The Enemy . . .

Mick froze, unable to move, even though he wanted to. Here he was, staring at a guy who'd just shot his buddy—who claimed he was a corpse come back to life.

And suddenly, every bit of him told him that this was the *thing* that he'd been dreading all his life, the force that haunted his dreams, his anathema, his nemesis.

Still, he hung tough.

He'd been tough all his life, and he intended to stay tough.

"So then," he managed to growl. "Back from the dead, you say. Well, that gun's alive enough for me."

"It works. That's the important factor."

Something clicked in Mick's head.

"Shit. You're the guy that killed the Count . . . And the Marquis, too . . ."

"I have a mission, yes."

"And Baxter . . . What about him?"

"I'm afraid that Baxter went the way of all flesh as well."

"Okay, damn you. I been expecting this all my life. I could feel you creepin' around my brain since I was a kid, gunnin' for me. Why—I don't know. Maybe you made me what I am. I just got one question for you."

The Dark Man didn't respond.

"Just tell me, shadow man, who was my real mother? Why did she give me away? I figure you must know." Mick's eyes betrayed his own surprise at saying these unbidden words.

"That's two questions. And I'm afraid you're mistaking me for a therapist. I'm your undertaker."

"Then what are you waiting for? Do it and quit wasting my time."

"You're pretty tough, aren't you, Mick?"

"Yes," said Mick. "Tough as you want."

"You scared now?"

"Shit, no!" Mick spat the words.

"I like your bravery, Mick," commented the Dark Man. "I like your attitude. So, tell you what. I'm going to give you a chance. You look like a street-fighting man."

Mick felt a glow of pride despite himself. "Damned straight."

"You beat my boy here, I'll let you out of here alive!"

"Your boy?"

" 'As the sailor looked in,' " the Dark Man quoted, " 'the gigantic animal had seized Madame L'Espanaye by the hair, (which was loose, as she had been combing it,) and was flourishing the razor about her face, in imitation of the motions of a barber. The daughter lay prostrate and motionless; she had swooned. The screams and struggles of the old lady (during which the hair was torn from her head) had the effect of changing the pacific purposes of the orangutan into those of wrath. With one determined sweep of its muscular arm, it nearly severed her head from her body.'

"So," said the Dark Man, "First test, then. What's that quote from?"

"Sure. I read that. *Murders in the Rue Morgue.*"

"Excellent. You'll be familiar with my boy, then."

The Dark Man stepped aside.

Shuffling up from the gloom came the movement that Mick had noticed before. A hulking presence, a congruence of form and darkness . . .

And masses of hair.

It was an ape. A primate . . . an orangutan.

Bulgy and ugly and awkward but unusually big and powerful looking.

"What do you say, Mick? Beat my boy here, you get to go."

"Then bring him on, I got better places to be," said Mick.

The Dark Man stepped aside.

Gangly and menacing, the orangutan moved forward, long arms outstretched, smelling of offal and wildness. Mick was glad of the lump he felt in his boot—his butterfly knife—a street-fighting tool if there ever was one.

The orangutan grimaced and peeled its lips back, turning to the Dark Man as if to receive instructions.

Mick quickly retrieved his knife, bringing the blade out in one fluid motion.

But with a lightning-fast swipe of its massive arm, the giant ape knocked the blade from Mick's hand, breaking his wrist in the process.

Grabbing his wrist, Mick bit back a howl of pain.

The ape took a slow step forward. Showing its sharp yellow teeth as it brought up a massive hand. In it was a jagged straight razor.

Then, in his mind, Mick heard the ape speak. A strangled low rumble, the inchoate voice of the Other, splintering his last coherent thoughts.

Mick, old friend, the ape said, *I'm going to fuck you up.*

When it was finished, the orangutan stepped back from what had once been a man, tossed its sharp instrument aside, and stepped back into the shadows again.

The shadows shifted.

The figure that re-emerged was no longer a primate, but a raptor. A crow.

"Plenty of material over there to work with, if you need a little cosmetic surgery," piped the creature.

"I'll consider it," said William Blessing.

"I'd take it if I were you. You're looking a little rough."

"That's the way I'm feeling."

"There's one more for us to deal with, and then we're through and you can rest."

Blessing nodded.

Yes. Rest. He had only one more bit of justice to mete out. He'd told Amy what he had to tell her.

From time to time during their living relationship, he'd written poems for her. Some he'd given to her. Others, though, he'd kept back and collected into a volume, because they seemed to be of a thematic piece. She'd never even known about that volume, let alone read any of the poems, before he'd been killed.

He had them hidden behind the *Complete Works of William Shakespeare* and volumes by Keats and Shelley.

This was the information that he'd given to Amy, in his role as his own mysterious cousin.

"Ah, c'mon," said the crow. It fluttered down to the mass of corpse, sipped a little blood, pecked a little flesh. "No telling if you're going to see Amy again. Want to look your best. Dip in! It will put some color in your cheeks!"

The crow returned to its sacramental repast.

Just on the edge of the pool of blood, William Blessing knelt.

His kneeling, though, had nothing to do with prayer.

28

"Prophet!" said I, "thing of evil!—prophet still, if bird or devil!—
Whether Tempter sent, or whether tempest tossed thee
here ashore,
Desolate yet all undaunted, on this desert land enchanted—
On this home by Horror haunted—tell me truly, I implore—
Is there—is there balm in Gilead?—tell me—tell me, I implore!"
Quoth the Raven, "Nevermore."

—Edgar A. Poe, *The Raven*

The grave was empty.

Donald Marquette stared down at the casket that the workers had pulled up out of the ground. What he saw appalled him.

The coffin had filled with dirt, which of course had been dumped out. Its lid had been busted through, splintered in half, torn apart.

"Damnedest thing I ever did see," said one of the diggers, scratching his head. "Looks as though the corpse bashed itself through from the inside!"

The sun had just set, and a breeze fluttered leaves of a nearby tree. The place smelled strongly of overturned earth and diesel fumes from the coughing truck on a nearby road.

"Impossible, of course," continued the worker, a coarse-looking man who smelled of beer-laced sweat and cigarettes.

"I should hope so!" said another of the men, stepping back.

"Impossible. Obviously," said Donald Marquette. "What is important is that the grave has been defiled and the body *stolen.*" He turned to the night-shift cemetery keeper, a grizzled old coot munching on a bacon, lettuce, and tomato sandwich. "How do I report this to the proper authorities? Not that idiot beat cop I dealt with yesterday."

The old guy wiped off some mayonnaise from a bushy mustache. "Don't know. This ain't ever happened before, as far as I know." He took off his cloth cap and scratched a tuft of hair on a generally balding dome. Dandruff and dead skin flaked down. "My guess is, the night police have their hands full with live people. You're going to have to file a report tomorrow, I suppose." He shrugged. "And talk to the day people as well."

It had taken Marquette all day to get this project started. Only because of his persistence, and his willingness to pay extra money, had the grave been dug up this quickly. And despite his anger at the policeman last night, now he wasn't so sure that having a bunch of cops nosing around was really such a good thing. It would surely mean more questions about the events surrounding Blessing's death.

As the cool of the evening seemed to caress his bones like slimy tentacles, it was everything he could do to hold himself together. And a new thought began drumming at the back of his head like a scrap of music repeating itself incessantly:

What if Blessing had *pushed through the lid of that coffin?*

What if he was back, returned from the grave, to avenge his wife, to restore his scattered Poe collection, to drag those who killed him back with him?

Absolute nonsense, of course.

Utter foolishness.

Something was going on, yes. With the Count and the Marquis dead, Baxter missing, and now *this* staring at him, the pattern could not be denied.

But surely this was the work of some living group, perhaps some rival group of death-obsessed Goths, or just Baxter himself, or any one of a hundred possibilities. When you ran with a morbid bunch like the Gothiques, was it any wonder that a body would get dug up now and then? Big joke! Ha ha! Sheesh, maybe it was even the nut-case *Dark Sunset* editor, or even Blessing's publisher. He could see the headlines now:

HORROR AUTHOR'S DECOMPOSING BODY DISCOVERED IN *NEW YORK TIMES BOOK REVIEW* OFFICE.

Great publicity!

Yes. What was that philosophical and scientific principle?

Right. Occam's Razor.

The simplest solution to a puzzle was usually the *correct* solution!

And surely a body with two bullets in its vital organs and a smashed-open head, declared way dead and filled with embalming fluid, was not a likely candidate to liberate itself from a strong oak box six feet under heavy rock and dirt!

"I can't deal with it tonight?" he asked the groundskeeper.

" 'Fraid not," said the man. He spat out a wad of chewing tobacco on the ground. "Funny business. Horror writer, wasn't he?"

"That's right," said Marquette.

The limbs of the trees were knocking together now. The breeze had stepped up to just-approaching-wind status. Dark clouds were rolling across the stars and the moon, more storm weather. Nothing unusual in a place where the weather is moody and fitful; but all the same, not a comfortable experience in a graveyard.

"Mister Poe been here a century and a half. He never tried to get out of his grave," said the cemetery man.

"As far as you know," quipped one of the diggers.

"Usually, people come out of graves cos they're pissed off," said another of the men, resting on his spade, smiling with the joke. "Wonder what Mister Poe would want to come out of his grave for?"

"Royalties, most like!" sniffed the keeper. "Poor fellow died a pauper. Not like Mister Blessing here. No sirree, Bob. I seen the funeral party, I seen the casket. Mister Blessing was a rich man. He didn't need no royalties to take with him into the afterlife."

A flash of anger fell upon Marquette.

"All right. That's enough of that!" he said. "This is a crime scene. Blessing's grave has been despoiled, violated, and the body taken. It's a sick desecration, and I'm going to find out who's responsible." His voice was snappish and deep. Marquette had discovered he'd gained in authority and stature these past months. Killing someone had certainly matured him. "It looks like rain. I want you to put plastic and a tarp here. There might be evidence for the police."

"Right," said the keeper, understanding and agreeing. "I'll keep an eye out for wandering corpses, too!"

"Just direct him back here where he belongs!" replied the joker.

Marquette swirled around and stalked off.

Whatever was going on, he didn't like it. He'd already told Mick and Theodore to clear out. There was danger afoot, he could feel it in the air.

A shudder ripped through him as he headed back for his car.

A fat raindrop splatted onto his head.

No, it was time to get to safer territory. Time for that vacation he'd been promising himself. He could deal with business through phone and fax from some other location just as well as from here. At least until all this blew over.

Problem was, he also had to convince Amy to leave. What was a danger to him could well be a danger to her. And there were many, many reasons he wanted to keep Amy Blessing alive and healthy.

Because he *loved* her?

Was that what it was? he thought as he hurried through the gates of the cemetery and ran for his car. Cold rain slashed from the sky.

As he opened the door of his new BMW, and slipped into the fresh new-car smell, Donald Marquette smiled grimly to himself.

Yeah.

Love was always *such a useful word.*

A loud clap of thunder rumbled outside.

Amy Blessing awoke.

She was sitting at the table of the Poe collection room, the book mashed against her chest. She felt the salty wet of tears on her cheeks. The laser-printed pieces of paper, which William had bound carefully into the book himself, were still slick. Her hair was loose and tangled. She smelled of herself, mixed with the scent of the candles she had lit around her on the reading table, by a copy of the Sunday *New York Times* which she'd been looking at here last week, to be close to William and that which he held dear, despite the troubling memories the room held.

She'd fallen asleep.

She'd brought the book she'd found, the book of poems that William had meant to give her, down here to read in this special place, the place that William had filled with the poetry of the author who had meant so much to him.

The candles she'd lit, smelling of lavender, were nearly to their end. She'd only been asleep for a short while. Why?

And then she remembered.

She looked down at the page the book was open to. The poem there, a short one, spoke of the time they had spent in a rustic cabin by a beautiful lake. She had cut his hair one morning after a delicious breakfast of blueberry muffins. The cabin still smelled of the fresh-baked stuff, and she felt alert and awake and aware with the taste of the bracing Earl Grey tea she sipped. Looking out at the blue of the lake, the green of the evergreens, and the bright red of berries on a bush by the veranda, he had told her that he had just experienced the true meaning of eternity. Eternity, he said, wasn't measured from birth to death, wasn't linear at all. You had eternal life, if your life was full of life's true deepness. Each moment of Now was an eternity. But the key, he said, was truly being in love, and regarding the beloved in the beauty of that moment.

Forever.

Forever was lateral, for those in love.

And William said then that he was truly and eternally in love with her. Forever and ever. Then and now.

That sentiment had been gorgeously reflected in this poem, and she'd been overwhelmed with emotion. She cried and cried, leaning into the singular book as though to be nearer to it. Cried into her folded arms.

And there, she'd fallen asleep.

She closed the book and rubbed her eyes. She felt odd.

"No more of these tonight," she whispered to herself. She would take it with her and place it on the spare pillow on the king-sized bed upstairs.

William's pillow.

There, she could read another poem tomorrow, if she felt up to it.

The night seemed very thick outside and bleary. Then she realized that it was raining, and it was the thunder that had awoken her.

A haze of lightning brightened the window. Flickered. Faded away.

A moment.

Thunder again.

She had a pot of tea and a teacup before her. Gone cold, of course. She picked up the cup.

She still felt odd. Very odd, indeed. Something seemed very off. She'd been dreaming the strangest dreams, none of which she could remember. They seemed cut off by some gauzy, opaque curtain. Half-recalled forms seemed to move beyond that veil, none tangible . . .

She still felt very *close* to William. It was as though his death were the dream, and she was just waking up.

The pain of the rape, the trauma of that evening—whole chunks of it she simply couldn't remember. Like some alcoholic blackout.

Repression, the psychiatrist who'd treated her had said. Perfectly normal and healthy. The way the mind deals with things too horrible to accept. She'd never heard the shots that had killed William, or seen which of those dreadful men picked up that bust of Pallas and brought it down on her husband's head.

She'd woken up in a hospital, already tapped into drugs. She still took anti-depressants. All her friends and family had been so kind, but still, with all their support, she seemed to move in a kind of half-lit, shadow-floor of an alien ocean, from the time she had learned that William was dead. She sometimes wished she hadn't decided to stay in the townhouse, but then she couldn't imagine leaving it either.

Another burst of lightning, this time brighter. It threw a wash of light over the end of the room. A part that had once been in darkness.

Something was wrong there.

Something was *very* wrong with that end of the room!

The melancholy and sadness, the *lost* feeling was swept away in a spurt of adrenaline. Amy arose, went to the side of the room, and turned on the overhead electric light. They were track lights, positioned to subtly illuminate key elements of the collection. The farthest away had been angled to throw a spot directly upon the bust of Pallas with the stuffed raven perched upon its head. The bust, though, had been taken away by the police to fingerprint and use as evidence. The raven had been taken away as well, to where Amy wasn't sure and hadn't cared to ask.

Now, though, there they were.

The white marble head statue of Pallas Athena, the Greek goddess of wisdom.

The black bird.

Undamaged. Defiant.

As she stood gawking at this (had Donald put them back there? If so, *why*?) Amy heard the door bang loudly on the first floor.

She heard the pounding of feet, coming up the stairs.

"Amy! Amy, are you here?"

It was Donald's voice, loud.

Quickly she went to the door of the collection room, and opened it.

"Donald!" she called. "I'm in here."

The whole house was lit up. He'd turned on all the lights. He hurried up the stairs now, his eyes wide, looking definitely disheveled.

"Amy? Are you all right?" he asked.

"Well yes, I guess so . . . I'm very upset, though."

He grabbed her by the shoulders and breathlessly asked, "What's happened?" He looked past her, into the library. "What are you doing in *here,* Amy?"

"The bust of Pallas. The raven . . . Did you put them back here?"

"What?"

Donald swept past her into the room, eyes targeting the back area. Amy watched as Donald, shocked, noticed the re-erected statuary. Then he noticed the boxes that she had returned to the room. The boxes of books that she had opened and carried up here and not unpacked.

He drifted over to these, bent down, let his hand touch the spines of a few books.

When he turned back to look at her, his eyes were full of surprise, even shock.

"These books . . . These are . . ." Donald shook his head as though to realign jarred portions of his brain. "I mean, these were part of the stolen collection . . ."

"Yes. Yes, isn't it amazing? They came after you left this morning!"

she said. "They've been returned to where they're supposed to be. But I have absolutely no idea where the bust and the raven came from. You didn't—"

He shook his head, still trying to put something together. "No. No, Amy." He stepped over to her, touched her arm. "But those books delivered here this morning. Do you have any idea who—"

Donald noticed the handmade book of poems on the table by the candles. He stepped over and turned the book over.

"A book of poems by William Blessing. I wasn't aware of these!"

"No. William had intended to give them to me . . . His cousin told me about them."

"Cousin?" said Donald. "I didn't know about any cousin who was in contact with you."

"Yes. His name is Delmore Blessing. They hadn't had much contact lately. He knew a great deal about Bill that I didn't know," said Amy. "Delmore's the man who retrieved these books."

"Retrieved . . ." said Donald. "But . . . how?"

"I don't know."

"How do you know . . . this man?"

"He came by . . . yesterday. He introduced himself to me. We talked. I wanted to tell you about him, but he said not to. Not right away, anyway. He said that you two would meet in due time."

Donald gripped Amy by both of her forearms. He looked deeply into her eyes with an intensity she'd never seen before.

"Amy," he said. "Listen to me carefully. You're in great danger. I may be in danger as well, by association."

"Danger. But why? How?"

"Some madman—perhaps this man who has visited you, I don't know for certain—is committing atrocities here in Baltimore. Atrocities associated with William Blessing."

"Atrocities? What do you mean?"

"There have been . . . murders! And Bill's body." He looked away, biting his lip, looking vastly indecisive. "It's—"

"My husband's *body*? What about my husband's body? Tell me!" she said, almost on the verge of hysteria. "Tell me what's happened to my husband's body!"

"It's been stolen from his grave."

"What!"

"Yes. I'm notifying the proper authorities. But tonight . . . listen carefully . . . tonight we should go someplace else. Away from here. I don't feel that you are safe in this house."

She still couldn't quite comprehend what Donald had said. "Stolen

. . . stolen from his grave? But why? Who would want to *do* such a thing!"

"Amy, your husband had a very long life before he met you. There could have been secrets he kept from you. God knew what strange associations he had. Maybe he wronged someone . . . Maybe there was some sort of . . . I don't know . . . *curse.* That we can discover later. But right now, I am convinced that you must pack some things very quickly. I'll take you to a hotel, get you your own room, and I'll take one right beside you. Maybe notify the police for security. I don't know, but what I feel absolutely certain of is that *we must get out of this house*!"

"But I live here . . . And I have to guard . . ."

"I'll notify the police. We can even hire a security person or something, Amy. Everything in this house will be safe. But I feel that *we* must get *out*!"

Something deep inside of her not only rebelled against the notion of leaving the house, but made her look at Donald Marquette in a new and altered fashion.

A little voice spoke in the back of her mind:

Who's truly been keeping secrets?

"If we're worried, why can't we just call the police from here, have them check on us?"

"I'm not comfortable with that alone, Amy," he said, shaking his head insistently.

"Well then—if there are security men to be hired, Donald . . . Can't we hire them from here? Can't we just have them come over *here*?" She gestured about. "This collection, these books and memorabilia, they were so important to William. Now that they're back, I don't want to risk losing them again."

"These things are worth *nothing* compared to you. To your safety, to your *life.*" Donald looked terribly stressed, as though something that had been weighing on his mind for a time was beginning to exert the full extent of its pressure.

Amy shook her head. "Why is my life threatened? I don't understand, Donald. Before I leave my house, I have to know exactly why you think that I'm in danger!"

For a moment, Donald was at a total loss for words.

"This man—this so-called cousin of William's—it sounds strange to me. He could be the one who's the danger. He could be a *madman*!"

"If he wanted to be *dangerous* to me, Donald," said Amy defiantly, "he had his opportunity on two separate occasions! Now I demand that you tell me everything you know. Why do you think I might be in danger tonight?"

Amy was beginning to feel as though she were coming out of some kind of fog. And what she was seeing was different than she'd ever imagined it would be. Before, she didn't want to know anything but the drugged stupor of melancholy that padded herself away from existence. Now, though, she felt herself emerging from sleep to discover a very strange world indeed. "Tell me. I need to know!"

Donald opened his mouth, but nothing came out. His eyes darted about, but they seemed filled with panic and indecision, not any kind of answer.

Then a voice spoke from the doorway.

"Yes, Donald. Perhaps you should tell her."

29

"M. Valdemar, can you explain to us what are your feelings or wishes now?"

—Edgar A. Poe, *The Facts in the Case of M. Valdemar*

"Be that word our sign of parting, bird or fiend!" I shrieked, upstarting—
"Get thee back into the tempest and the Night's Plutonian shore!
Leave no black plume as a token of that lie thy soul hath spoken!
Leave my loneliness unbroken!—quit the bust above my door!
Take thy beak from out my heart, and take thy form from off my door!"
Quoth the Raven, "Nevermore."

—Edgar A. Poe, *The Raven*

His heart had been pounding, pounding, pounding in his chest, and his ears seemed to be ringing, ringing, ringing with a dizzy tintinnabulation of disjointed words, fears, and jumbled emotions.

However, when the words came from the doorway, they were like a cold hand of night slapping him across the face, and pulling Donald Marquette into an attentive focus.

He swung his head over to the door.

Standing there was a man in a dark coat. He wore a hat, pulled down over his brow. The lapels of his long coat were pulled up over the lower portion of his face. In between, dark glasses obscured most of the rest of his face.

Donald Marquette found words.

"Who are you? How did you get *in* here!"

Panic and fear seemed gone, erased in a flood of adrenaline. He seemed in control again. But he sensed nothing but threat from this figure in the doorway, and something deep, instinctual and competent, some survival instinct took over him.

Amy did not respond with the same kind of alarm.

"Delmore," she said, stepping forward. "I'm so glad you're here. You were right! I found that book of poems . . ." Amy hurried back to the desk, pulled up the book to show the stranger. "You see?"

"I'm so glad," said the Dark Man. "Did you have the opportunity to read any yet?" His voice softened discernibly.

"Yes! Oh, yes, they're *wonderful.* It's like . . . It's like they've brought William back to me. I can let him go now because I know how he truly felt. I can let him go, because I know how much he'll always be in my heart."

The Dark Man nodded. "That is how, Amy, he . . . he would . . . he would have . . . liked it . . ."

Donald Marquette heard the voice breaking . . . as though with tears . . . or something else.

"This is the mystery cousin, I take it?" Donald said, voice freighted with suspicion.

"Oh, yes. I'm sorry. Delmore, this is Donald Marquette. William's colleague. He's stayed on, to help with the estate . . . and deal with so many things."

"Yes, of course," said the man. "William wrote about him." His voice hardened. "In fact, it is Donald with whom I wish to speak. That is why I have come back tonight, Amy. I had hoped not to disturb you. Perhaps you might want to go and occupy yourself with things upstairs. Your piano? Work? It's a shame it is such a wet and dreary night outside. You might go visiting a friend. Still, I'd be willing to call you a cab."

Fierce doubt arose in Donald. "Does this concern the Blessing estate?"

"In a way, yes," said the Dark Man.

"Then why have Amy leave? She is still directly involved. I have nothing to hide from Amy in my dealings concerning the estate. She should stay if she likes."

The Dark Man shook his head. "I would prefer it if she went—"

"Amy," said Donald in a taut, hard voice. "All these things I spoke of—the reasons I wished for us to leave this house until we know we are safe—they have begun with the arrival of this man. I fear that this is the man behind it all. This is the man we should fear!"

"But . . . But *why*?" Amy turned to him, emphatic. "He's told me so much. He's somehow restored the stolen books . . ."

Donald turned to the man who called himself Delmore Blessing. "The body of William Blessing is missing from its grave. Is it *you* who took it?"

The Dark Man held out gloved hands, imploringly. "Amy. Please. You *must* go!"

Amy shook her head, her eyes becoming hard. "What? Is that true? Are you the one who took William's body? Are you the one who's been causing so much alarm from Donald? Is this true?"

"Trust me, Amy!" The man's voice was teetering toward despair. "Go! Go, I say! Now!"

"William always told me, the truth is the hardest, yet it is the best. It will always bond together the good, and destroy the evil," whispered Amy. "Are you evil, Delmore? Are you bringing evil to the memory of your cousin?"

"No, Amy! No, I swear."

The Dark Man held up his hands imploringly.

"Then what is the issue that you cannot reveal in front of me?" she demanded.

Donald heard a strength there—a strength that he had not heard in Amy Blessing's voice ever before.

"Yes," demanded Donald, already doing mental calculations on how he could get some time to himself to call the police. Dash into another room and quickly tap out 911 on the cellular in his pocket. He wished he'd called some kind of security patrol before he'd even gotten here. "What is it that you don't want to reveal to Amy about yourself?"

The Dark Man swung toward Donald Marquette. He suddenly looked like an animated statue, aloof and cold—and yet still burning with something intense.

"Very well. You leave me no choice, Amy. I wished to spare you, but I am running out of time."

Slowly, the man removed his hat.

Then he lowered his collar.

Lastly, he took off his dark glasses.

The man's features were vague, waxy, and rough. Like a modern sculptor's impressionistic version of a face rather than a face that any normal human being wore. Bits of skin were flaking off, and scablike protrusions grew on the cheeks and neck. Marquette could see that one of the ears was half gone, and the other one was bent at a strange angle.

The eyes, though slightly milky, burned with identity and personality.

A personality that Marquette recognized, and yet could not bring himself to accept.

"In the future," said William Blessing, "I want you to think of this as a dream. A dream, Amy. Do you understand? I do not want it to be included in your scheme of reality."

"I don't . . ." Her voice came out choked and aghast. "I don't understand. You look . . . You look even more like . . . your—"

"There is no cousin, Amy," said the Dark Man. "I am William Blessing. It's me, your husband. There is . . . unfinished business. I have somehow been given . . . another short chance—" He turned to Donald, and those eyes burned hard and fiery. "—to make things right again. To preserve my legacy . . . and you . . . from further atrocity."

Donald Marquette shook his head adamantly. He could feel madness nipping at his heels, but the strong thing in him, the vital thing that had taken control, that had preserved him in times of catastrophe, returned again.

"No, Amy. It's a trick. Some sort of trick. This can't be William Blessing. William Blessing is dead!" he shouted.

The Dark Man shook his head sadly. "I never claimed to be alive, Marquette."

The Dark Man took a shuffling step toward him, holding out a pointing, accusing forefinger toward him.

"I killed them all, Donald. Your cronies, the Gothiques. I destroyed them and the blight they were going to present to my house . . . and perhaps to literature. Vengeance? Perhaps. Justice? Definitely! And now it is with you I must settle."

"William . . ." said Amy, voice trembling. "Bill . . . ?"

Donald took a step back, but before he could get far, the Dark Man rushed forward.

A cold, waxy hand clamped around Donald's throat.

"No!" shrieked Amy. "No!"

The arm and hand were unbelievably strong. This close, in his grip, with the smell of the grave clinging to him, and the sense of otherwhere defiant and strong, Donald could not deny—despite the rational side of him in strong objection—that this was William Blessing.

Choking, he reached out and grabbed at the face. A chunk of skin flaked off.

Strangling, gasping, Donald grabbed at the arm that held him, trying with all his might to pull the hand away from its grip around his windpipe.

"It was this villain," said the Dark Man. "This villain, Amy, who killed me. This noxious traitor who we took into our home—who we *trusted*—who introduced the forces of chaos and corrosion into our lives!"

"Help . . . Amy!" Donald managed to squeeze out of his windpipe. "Call . . . police!"

"No!" shrieked Amy Blessing.

Donald's vision was growing red and dimmer as he struggled desperately. He caught sight of Amy's movement. Beside the doorway was an antique chair. A chair, it was claimed, in which Edgar Poe had once sat. Amy grabbed this chair and ran toward them. Her face a mask of inchoate emotion, she slammed the old wood against the back of the man who claimed to be arisen from the dead.

With a loud crack, the antique flew apart.

The death grip upon Donald's throat disengaged. He flung himself back, away from his attacker, holding onto his throat as though to yank breaths through it into his famished lungs. He staggered, falling against the table.

Gun! Why hadn't he thought to get a gun!

The Dark Man stood, not so much harmed as astonished by the attack.

"Amy!"

"People don't come back from the dead!" Amy cried. "They just *don't.*"

"But it's me . . . Amy . . . It's me . . . Bill."

Amy's words were high-pitched with stress and disbelief. "If you are indeed my husband, then my husband was not killed! I did not witness his death," she said. "But if you *are* Bill . . . then it's a Bill that has gone *insane*! Bill Blessing would never, ever hurt anyone. Ever. He was a gentle, *civilized* man. Not . . . not some *monster*!"

The Dark Man staggered a bit. He moved his arms in an ungainly, spastic, uncertain manner as he moved around toward Amy Blessing. "Amy . . . you don't . . . understand."

Donald was reminded of Boris Karloff as Frankenstein's monster, groping pitifully toward light and compassion.

A strip of skin from his face fell off onto the floor.

The strong part of Donald Marquette, the survival part that *comprehended* things, suddenly understood on a deeper level than his mind ever could. It *sensed* the being's true character, the truth of its statement, the dire danger it posed, the structure of meaning this imprinted on the dark underpinnings of the universe . . . What it meant to him . . .

And how he could intervene to save himself.

The survival part, the dark instinct pushed back the sheer horror of the moment, and dove in to the attack:

"She's right!" said Donald. "You can't be Blessing! Blessing would never, never murder wantonly. Blessing would never cause pain! His work said as much! Yes, death and destruction was in his writing—but it had the moral structure of comedy, of tragedy, of the great things in man. Not the utter banality of revenge plays, the melodrama of lesser artists!"

The Dark Man turned toward the speaker.

Donald caught the bleak glimmer of doubt in his eyes.

A larger piece of skin flaked from his temple, flopping down onto the floor. Some kind of crimson goo began to leak there on that face, as though from a pestilent sore.

Yes! thought the instinct. *That's it!*

"No!" said the Dark Man. "Punishment! There must be punishment . . . prevention!"

"You're mad! Mad, whoever you are! Prevention of *what?*!" He sidestepped a lunge of the Dark Man and stepped beside Amy, holding her around her waist in a comforting way. She grabbed him, held on to him, terrified of this dark specter before them.

"You need help!" said Amy. "Let us call help for you . . . whoever you are!"

"Punishment," growled the Dark Man, more of a bent creature now, a grim shadow of Basil Rathbone playing humpbacked Richard the Third. He scrabbled forward slowly, but his gait now seemed hamstrung. More of a hobble. "Prevention!"

"I've done nothing to harm Amy! I've done nothing but good for the memory and the estate of William Blessing. His books will continue to be popular because of my work. His name will remain on the bestseller lists, his stories and novels taught in schools. He will be remembered for posterity . . . kept alive by the values of good and virtue and love which he epitomized in his best work," said Donald Marquette. "Whatever you are, you are an instrument of insanity, a black and squalid thing, bringing destruction upon the true friends and believers in the legacy that William Blessing left!"

The Dark Man held out a hand.

"Please! Don't hurt us!" said Amy. "Whoever . . . Whatever you are . . . know that William Blessing was full of love and goodwill. Not murder and vengeance!"

Two of the lower fingers of the outstretched hand fell off, lying in pieces on the floor.

"Amy . . . No. I must . . . There are forces: Destiny. Love. Memory. Justice. Will. Forces that must hold back . . . the Evil . . . the Darkness . . . I have returned to fight the darkness. I have returned . . . *for love*! For love of you. For love of my art . . . *For what my work stands for!* Value! Virtue! Art! Beauty!" He moaned toward the ceiling. "Oh, Time. Poetry! Oh, Muses. Give me the words I need to *convince*!"

"Haven't you read the articles, monster?" said Donald Marquette, just the right amount of irony in his voice to be venomous. "Gothic writers are gentle people! They are civilized. They shape the darkness to bring forth the light. Besides, William Blessing . . . or whatever part of you *thinks* it is William Blessing, this whole business reeks—reeks of the recklessness and crassness of the exploitive literature that you so despised! Weren't you more a proponent of the subtle? Of *quiet* horror? All this . . . Blessing . . . poor fellow . . . It's straight out of a cheap horror movie!"

The Dark Man gurgled.

He shook and shuddered.

Part of his face began to cave in. The whole left side started melting off, showing dark skull beneath. Tiny white maggots began to squirm through the eyeballs.

Will! the voice of the dark instinct told Donald. *It's losing its will!*

"Amy," the thing gasped, bubbling pus through its gash of a mouth. "Am—"

The jaw fell, dripping down like an overheated candle, and splashing and clacking onto the floor.

The Dark Man's nose fell off, more corruption oozing out.

The stink of rot advanced before the thing.

Amy groaned. Her grip around Marquette loosened. She wilted away from him.

She'd fainted.

Amy collapsed in a heap onto the floor, unconscious.

"You inconsiderate bastard!" spat Marquette. "Look what you've done!"

The remaining, unruined eye swung down and stared at the woman, lying lovely on the floor. A long moan emerged from the creature, origins deeper than any mouth or throat or diaphragm.

"You know, Blessing. She never really loved you," said Donald. "She told me that . . . Yes . . . She merely had some sort of strange father fixation on you. Something psychological. You truly were deluding yourself."

The will . . . he heard the voice in his mind. *Kill the will!*

"Yes, Blessing. She told me that. And we flirted—even while you were alive. Behind your back. We flirted. And we giggled. And we kissed! Did you know that? Those, sweet, sweet lips touched mine." Marquette chuckled throatily. "And I could tell . . . Oh, I could tell . . . that she lusted for me. And that when your old, old loins couldn't squirt anymore, it would be mine that she would want . . . *Mine!*"

"No . . ."

The corpse continued its messy deterioration.

"You know, Blessing, you are some sight! Like that Wicked Witch of the West in *The Wizard of Oz!* Only I didn't use water on you . . . I used *Truth*!"

With a sigh of escaping gases, the bones of the dead man gave way, and the decomposing heap collapsed upon itself, leaving a heap of crepuscular material amidst the mass of clothing that remained upon the soiled rug.

For a moment, Donald Marquette just stared at the horrendous pile of corruption on the rug.

Gone! said his dark instinct. *Pffft!*

Then Marquette began to laugh.

The laughter started deep down inside him, as though from the dark instinct itself. It crept up from his spirit, through his soul, into the nether parts of him. Up and up and up, it moved through his body to his throat and his mouth and came out dark and maniacal.

A cosmic joke!

The famous horror writer—

—returned from the dead!

And there he was: a bucket of greasy guts spotting the Oriental rug!

"I've won!" he said. "The midwestern boy truly makes good!"

The pile of slop said nothing at all.

Giddy hilarity filled Marquette.

"And here's the biggest joke of all, Blessing! You became horror's biggest cliché! What do you think of that! A cover from a pathetic comic book! Something out of a schlocky movie!"

The pile of shattered bone and moribund gore did not reply.

His laughter was the dark instinct's relief; he felt high from it. He felt as though, finally, he had discovered himself. Felt his destiny. Alcoholics had their Higher Power; he had his Lower Power. And now it reverberated within him like a song that had just found its singer. Its power simply filled Marquette with the thrill of discovery, puissance of purpose—and a rapidly growing euphoria that was raw with passion, need, and desire. Feeling death glide by his eyes seemed to pump lust from his glands with a heady rush.

He looked away from the pile of death. (Oh, what other truths were there of life that he had denied! The vistas before him because of this were so much broader than simple creativity and wealth. What brave dimensions awaited!) Amy Blessing came into view. Her prostrate body was astonishingly carnal, her long hair flashed out with erotic abandon, her mouth half open as though sucking the member of some invisible incubus.

He reached out his hand and touched the firm yet soft roundness of her buttock, covered with dress. Then, experiencing a thrill sharper than he'd ever known before, he let his hand drift under her long, woolen skirt, past her thigh, beyond the elastic band of her panties . . . And made acquaintance with flesh as soft and sweet and electric as any he had ever known. The secret . . . the forbidden . . . the best . . .

"You see, Bill," he said. "It is whimsical fate—fate and destiny involved here. I am truly the superior writer! However, in usurping your world . . . merely obeying, I might add, the laws of nature in the process, I shall burst forth into the greatness that is due me from the springboard of your accomplishments . . . and drag your work with mine into history. I think, posterity would have just as soon forgotten you. My work, I promise, will be remembered. And I shall write it in the utmost of luxury and success."

He could feel the pulse in his temples quicken. The smell of Amy was thick in his nostrils, and he could feel need building in him, turgid and complex. Withdrawing his hand from Amy's skirt, he began to unbutton her sweater.

He laughed again.

Amy remained unconscious; he sensed that she would remain so for some time. It was impossible now to control himself, and it seemed to be the nature of his dark instinct to mock the vanquished.

So be it.

"Oh, and thank you so much for finding Amy for me as well. I don't know if years of combing through the world would have found a flower so sweet to plant in my bed!" He pulled the sweater aside, exposing a black lace bra. Not white! My, how he had tossed and turned at night, unable to sleep, imagining this moment.

A little peek! A little feel! What harm would it do? Then he would wrap her back up as nice as you please, tuck her into bed, put some wine and pills on the nightstand, and come tomorrow tell her a terrible tale about how she had overdosed and had cried out in her sleep with dreadful nightmares. Dreadful!

"My, my, Billy boy! What a lucky fellow you were. What sweet fruit to taste. What a bouncy little bundle we have here! You don't mind if I take a little preliminary sample, do you?" He giggled. "Of course not. Then I shall simply sweep you up and the nasty bits that remain of you. And the authorities will never, ever discover the mystery of what became of the stolen body of William Blessing. But they truly won't care much.

Besides, it will simply augment the legend. Yes, I shall make sure that the *National Enquirer* gets a hold of the story. HORROR WRITER'S GRAVE DEFILED! And every supermarket will start stocking your paperbacks at the checkout line!"

He pulled back the black lace.

The nipple of Amy's right breast was perfect. Absolutely perfect! Pink and saucy, bright and pert.

His fingers trembled slightly as he reached for it.

His fingertips brushed across the nipple. The feeling was electric, utterly what he had dreamed it would be. He could sense the blood rushing to his loins.

"Soon, Blessing," he said. "Soon I shall be sucking on this sweet bud. Soon—"

Something closed around his ankle.

Gripped.

Gripped very hard indeed.

"What?"

He swung his head around and down, startled.

Around the bottom of his pants leg was a hand. Half flesh and half skeleton. Yet even as he looked down upon it, aghast, he could see the sinews and the flesh reassembling, growing back into a full hand.

Beyond the hand, a half-face pulled itself back together over a leering skull. Pieces of skin wiggled like a sea anemone. Veins and arteries materialized, skin reassembled, hair appeared from a protoplasmic stew.

"No!" cried Marquette.

He raised a fist and struck at the grinning skull. The spine cracked and the head swung back, off its precarious perch. He was in the midst of lifting his left foot to push the grip of the dead thing's hand off his ankle when a sudden "Caw!" squawked from another part of the room.

He looked up.

There was the bust of Pallas, returned. However, what was on top of the bust was far more alarming. The stuffed raven had returned as well, perched above the head—now it was blurring and growing and turning blacker, blacker, even as its wings spread.

The raven became a crow.

Reddish-brown eyes ignited.

The bird launched. Flapped and flapped. Slammed into Marquette, pushing him back.

As the crow wheeled around in the room, Marquette's hand came away from his face bloody. He struggled again with the leg, finally knocking the dead man's hand off. He rolled, got on all fours and started for the door.

The crow wheeled around again.

Instead of attacking, though, it fluttered down between Marquette and the door.

You're not going anywhere, pal, the crow seemed to be saying.

Marquette paused for just a moment.

Then he plunged ahead toward the door, driven by the voice of his dark instinct which demanded immediate evacuation.

The crow stood firmly in place, glaring at him.

He made to kick it out of his way, but even before his foot began to fly, he was grabbed from the rear by an arm, ropy with exposed muscle and half knitted-together skin. The arm pulled him back, back, and he smelled the grave again, though this time it was a different smell, a different grave:

His grave.

Donald Marquette was flung against the table. Papers and books stacked there flew. He made a superhuman effort to push himself away, driven by panic and every last bit of power left to him. However, the less-than-human creature kept him pinned.

"I brought something along with me from your friend Baxter Brittle's chambers," said the reassembled corpse, grating harshly into Marquette's ear.

Marquette saw a flash of metal as the thing appeared.

He'd seen it on Baxter's absurd altar. It was an elaborately detailed and curlicued knife. A knife often used for animal sacrifice—and who knew what else.

A ceremonial knife.

"No!" cried Donald Marquette. "You can't do this . . . Can't—Please . . . *Please* . . . *!*"

"No, no, Donald," the voice said harshly. "You don't understand. You're going to get your wish! I promise. You're going to get exactly what you wanted!"

The knife arced in a silvery trail as it swung around.

It buried itself, hilt-deep, into Donald Marquette's lower abdomen.

The pain raged molten and fierce.

Donald watched with disbelief as blood spurted across the scattering of papers on the desk.

The images began to flicker, strobing before him. He looked down and saw the unhuman hand pull the knife up, watched as his viscera spilled out upon the paper. With disbelief he saw it was the *New York Times Book Review,* opened to a certain familiar page.

"There you go, Donald," the undead voice snapped in his ear. "You always wanted to be on the *Times* bestseller list, didn't you?"

And then, the dark instinct reached up to claim him, enfolding him, like deep bay fog upon a Fells Point alley.

William Blessing held the body until he felt its spirit flee. Then he let it and the knife go. Donald Marquette, quite dead, fell against the table, then, dragging the knife along with him, flopped down onto the floor.

The crow fluttered onto the table.

"The last one," said William Blessing.

"The last one," agreed the crow.

"I can . . . I can rest," said Blessing.

"Yes," said the crow. "And I can move on . . . and do what I must do."

Blessing looked at his hand. The skin was back on. It still looked a fright, but it was certainly a hand again. He reached up and felt at his face.

Yes. Reassembled, for the most part.

And yet, with his mission accomplished, he could feel his will diminishing again. He had reserves, he knew, but he did not want to leave himself as a splattered ruin within his own home.

No, he had another home now. A home in a cemetery, where he truly belonged.

"I must return to my grave," said Blessing.

"As we all must, eventually," agreed the crow. "But nothing lasts forever. You'll see."

William Blessing turned and looked down at his wife. Amy lay a-sprawl, still unconscious.

"I cannot leave her like this, with these memories."

"No," said the crow. "You have the power to make things right, Blessing."

William Blessing nodded.

He went to his wife. He bent and pulled her sweater back on, rebuttoning it. Then, carefully and reverently, he reached down and pulled her up to him.

William Blessing carried her upstairs. He laid her down in their bed. He let her head rest gently upon the pillow. Now that his rage was slaked, he only felt love. The love burned bright inside of him, holding him whole.

Amy's beautiful hair spread out upon the embroidered pillow. She took what breath the dead man had away. She looked like some fairy princess, resting, awaiting the kiss of her prince.

He rested a hand upon her brow.

"Rest, Amy. Rest for a full day. Dream. Remember me as I was. Do not recall what I had to become."

He could feel these powers move within him, gentling down upon his wife.

Emotion moiled inside William Blessing.

"I'll let you go now, Amy," he whispered. "When you awake from your sleep, the horror will be gone, and you will heal, soon. Soon. Then . . . Then . . . I leave you only my name, if you still want it . . . a blessing. A blessing for you to get on with your life, knowing the value and meaning and beauty you gave to mine."

William Blessing leaned down and, with decomposing lips, kissed the flushed cheek of the living.

As they moved past the office, heading back toward the grave and eternity, the crow took its perch upon Blessing's left shoulder. Then the phone rang.

For some reason he did not know, William Blessing stopped and listened.

"This is Blessing Enterprises!" said Donald Marquette's cheery voice from the answering machine. "We're not in right now, but please do leave a message after the beep."

Beep.

"Donald!" said a voice. "This is Roscoe Mithers! Yes, yes, I know it's late, but the meeting went late and then I had a private dinner with the publisher. This is the most exciting day of my life. They loved *all* your ideas! And I had a few of my own! The department heads were all there, and it just so happened that the top creative executive from the media division was in New York on business from the Coast. There is *vast, vast* interest in fully exploiting the William Blessing name and association. We're talking not just books, but movies, television, videos, merchandising, licensing . . . The action figure rights alone are going to be a breakthrough! The ideas for your collaborations with the Blessing name sent everyone into ecstasy. And they want me to be the editor on it all!

"Best of all, though, I have another idea that I ran past the publisher at dinner that he's approved immediately: a line of William Blessing *Dark Sunset* books, that you can create. Crossover, Donald. Synergy! Brilliant marketing, huh? The possibilities are endless. So please, please, I need to talk to you. Call me immediately anytime tomorrow at the office or even tonight, at my home. You have the number. Wake me up! No problem. Jesus, Donald! I had no idea how far this was going to go! You're a genius. I owe you! May your sunsets always be da—"

Blessing picked up the phone.

"Hello, hello?" said Mithers. "That you, Donald? I knew if I rambled enough you'd finally pick up. How much did you hear?"

"Enough," replied the dead man.

"Hey, this isn't Donald. Who is this?"

"The keeper of William Blessing's literary heritage. Donald Marquette had to resign his position."

"That was rather sudden," said Mithers, not trying to mask his doubts about the situation, if he was being hoaxed in some way.

"A matter of grave importance suddenly arose and he found himself unable to perform his duties."

"But we had a deal. It was being worked out," objected Mithers.

"He signed a contract? A letter of agreement?"

"Not exactly, but a deal's a deal."

"Yes, I suppose it is. Even a deal with a devil. Especially so."

There a long silence as Mithers tried to frame a response. He was getting a bad feeling about this. The odd voice on the telephone seemed half-caked in wet dirt. *Damn creepy,* thought the editor. He could almost imagine that a zombie, or some other dead thing from the *Dark Sunset* pantheon, was actually on the other end of the line.

"Mr. Mithers," the eerie voice continued, "any agreements you might have thought you had with the Blessing estate are revoked and rescinded. Do you understand?"

"Frankly, no, I don't. Just who are you? Where's Marquette? This doesn't make any sense."

"But it does, Mr. Mithers. Perfectly. Here, let me make it clear to you."

A shock wave of horror reached out through the phone lines, through the digital optical cable, striking Mithers in mid-breath. A barrage of death images assaulted his mind. His hand gripped the phone so tightly the plastic receiver cracked. All he could do was tremble as Death in all its forms boiled through his brain, freezing his blood. He began to whimper, spittle appearing at the corners of his mouth, as hot and cold blasts of fear shot through his soul.

You see why it's impossible to continue with your projects? the voice seemed to say from behind his left ear. *It would be very hazardous to your health. Now sleep.*

As if dropping from a gallow's pole, Mithers gasped and fell to floor, unconscious.

Back in Baltimore, the crow flapped onto the desk. "Impressive," it said to Blessing. "You're really getting the hang of this undead avenging stuff. Too bad you weren't killed by a lynch mob."

"Think he'll get the message?" asked Blessing, placing the phone back in its cradle.

"He won't know why exactly," replied the bird, "but just hearing your name will invoke a particularly personal brand of terror in Mr. Mithers. He'll be contemplating a career change in the very near future."

"Yes. A career change. I could use one as well," said Blessing.

He stopped at the Poe collection room to take sustenance from what remained in this dimension of Donald Marquette. One for the road.

Then William Blessing continued shuffling toward the night outside, toward his rendezvous with the grave.

Epilogue

And the Raven, never flitting, still is sitting, still *is sitting*
On the pallid bust of Pallas just above my chamber door;
And his eyes have all the seeming of a demon's that is dreaming,
And the lamp-light o'er him streaming throws his shadow
on the floor;
And my soul from out that shadow that lies floating on the floor
Shall be lifted—nevermore!

—Edgar A. Poe, *The Raven*

1849

He felt the bay fog, rolling in heavily upon him as he lay in the Fells Point alley.

As he woke, the tremors hit him violently. The cold, the horrific *cold*! It knifed through him mercilessly. The man shook violently as he agonizingly got to his feet and dragged himself across the cobblestones.

His teeth chattered.

The smell of sea and rot was heavy and wet upon him. He felt waves of hot and cold and violent horror toss him into paroxysms of hot and chill, hot and chill . . .

Shivering, he staggered out and saw the fog moving over old buildings and piers, the languid movement of dark water . . .

Above a horse-drawn carriage, he saw a huge, dark bird, flapping away into the mist.

Ahead of him a man in a top hat and a suit with a waistcoat walked arm in arm with a woman in a bonnet carrying a frilled umbrella. The street smelled of horses and an open-air marketplace.

As he staggered out toward them, his knees gave way. Shivering and gasping, he splashed down into a muddy rainpool.

Even shortened, his legs could not support him. He fell forward, and unconsciousness swarmed around him, like angry pieces of winged night.

My name? came a voice. *What is my name?*

And another voice answered, but he could not hear.

"Sir! Are you all right?" asked the man.

"Yes," he insisted, somehow dragging himself up. "Yes, I am merely . . . wet. Taken with cold from these accursed rains. A drink! A drink is all I need. To warm myself. Could you direct me, sir?"

"Why yes. Across the way is Gunner's Hall. Today is election day, so there will be plenty of folk polling there," said the man. "You may find drink . . . And help as well, if you need it."

"Yes," he muttered as he turned and headed blearily toward the building that the man had indicated. "Away from my enemies . . ."

As he staggered toward the hall, the Fells Point fog seemed to pour into his mind again . . .

"Mr. Poe," called a voice. "Drink this, Mr. Poe. You need to drink this water."

He came awake to the fuzzy images of a man dressed in black with large sideburn whiskers, proffering a glass of water. He was immediately filled with the ache and ravage of fever and sweating. Seeing that he was awake, the doctor pressed the glass of water against his lips, dribbling some onto his parched tongue. Much of it splashed down his mouth, landing upon his bedclothes.

Poe, he thought. *My name is not Poe!*

But if it was not Poe, he thought, shaking with the alternating chill and the stabs of pain, then what was it?

Another splash of water into his mouth, and then he was allowed to lie back upon his pillow. He smelled lye and sickness in the air: He was in some sort of primitive hospital.

As he drifted off, snatches of memory came to him . . . all bathed in spasms of pain and dismal melancholy.

Virginia, dead of tuberculosis. A long, tortuous death.

The long and dreadful battle with alcohol, that angel of easement against the torture of a life filled with penury and loss . . .

Alcohol, that devil of distress, casting him into headache and heartache, soul-searing pain and fretful depression . . .

The occasional island of liberation of verse and story, review and article in a sea of ache and trouble.

This was his pitiful life.

And it was, he realized, the life of Edgar Allan Poe.

The man shot up in the bed, gasping. "But I am not Poe!" he screamed. "What am I doing here?"

"I am Dr. John J. Moran. You are at Washington Medical College in Baltimore," said the man. "You were found in a semi-conscious state at Gunner's Hall. You're very ill. You've been babbling."

He tried to get out of bed. He was immediately surrounded by attendants. He had to get back home, back to Iowa . . . back to work.

"Back to work!" he cried out loud. "Back to work! I must succeed as a writer! That is my life's goal!"

The forms around him pushed him back, holding him down. "But you *are* a writer, sir. And a well-known poet as well. Now be calm, sir! You must be still. It is not good for your condition to thrash about so!"

The strong hands of his attendant soon gave way to straps which tied him to the bedposts and prevented all but the most useless of movement.

As dimness approached, he heard the doctor whisper, "The sad and hopeless ravages of demon drink has him in its jaws."

No! he thought. *Rabies! Poe died of rabies!*

And I am not Poe!

No, I am Donald Marquette!

But he could not speak these words. Dimness and oblivion reached out, grabbed him. All he could do was babble.

He seemed to be afloat in a sea of darkness and confusion. He was too baffled and delirious to be capable of regret or reflection or repentance for the blood and the pain he felt heavy upon him.

Only once more did he emerge from his confusion.

"Lord help my poor soul!" he gasped, his head moving back and forth.

Hearing the words come from his mouth he recognized them. Poe's last words. He opened himself and readied for the blessed relief and nothingness of death.

Death, instead, came upon black wings.

It carried him off, swirled him around like a sailor clinging to a piece of shipwreck, spinning around in a maelstrom. Down, down, into a deep, dark center . . .

And that center suddenly came alive.

Blinking, he found himself staring out of a window. Beyond the window were the empty forests and fields of a bleak, late fall. Dark clouds hung in the air. The smell of camphor and dusty gloom surrounded him. He felt a heaviness in his chest.

The black bird that had brought him here flapped up onto a porch, perched there. It stared at him with eyes of crimson and piercing brown.

"A bird!" he found himself saying. "I told you! See the black bird!"

The reflection in the windowpane was of a child.

He was staring out of the eyes of a child!

"Edgar!" said a woman's voice. "Come away from there. Come and sit by your poor, dead mama!"

"Blast," barked the stern voice of a man. "I can see this one's going to be trouble."

He turned around.

On a bed, surrounded by people dressed in the costumery of the early nineteenth century, was a dead woman.

Somehow Marquette knew it was Poe's mother.

His mother now as well . . .

He remembered his dream . . . His nightmare.

This year, then—the thought came uncontrollably—would be, what . . . 1811? 1812?

What was he doing here?

But even as the thought came, so did the overwhelming hint of an answer.

A woman came up beside him. "It's a crow, John. There's a big, black crow out there!"

"Well, chase the cursed thing away," said the nasty, grim man. "It's a bad omen!"

The soul of Donald Marquette stared out of the eyes of Edgar Poe to the creature that had carried him here.

Trapped!

He was trapped in the body of a man, doomed to agonies and melancholy and wretchedness beyond imagining!

Trapped in some sort of infernal time loop!

To live and die . . . and live again . . .

In this accursed being . . .

The final revenge . . .

For his sins . . .

He thought he heard the crow speak to him.

"You're a world-famous writer now, Donald," it said, a snap and bite to its eerie voice. *"Just as you always wished!"*

He leaned against the windowpane, icy and dark, and he managed, for a moment, to speak through this child, knowing that he would never be able to do so ever again, nor influence his environment or host.

Merely *suffer.*

"Pray for me," begged Donald Marquette of whatever fate had brought him this hell. "For I am a soul damned as no soul has been damned before.

"How long!" he asked the crow, knowing his time of full awareness was almost over. "How long, crow!"

The bird cocked its eyes and for a moment those eyes became human eyes. Eyes that had lost things beyond telling.

How long? cried Donald Marquette's screaming soul. *How long?*

And the bird opened its mouth to speak.

Quoth the crow:

"Evermore!"

The Lazarus Heart

by

Poppy Z. Brite

for Caitlín

When I have sex with someone I forget who I am. For a minute I even forget I'm human. It's the same thing when I'm behind a camera. I forget I exist.

—Robert Mapplethorpe

There is a dark side to the human soul that is filled with conflict and torment. It is a side of the human soul that few people are brave enough to explore.

—The priest who said mass
at Mapplethorpe's funeral

Acknowledgments

Thanks to John Edward Ames, Jennifer Caudle, Jeff Conner, Richard Curtis, Christopher DeBarr, O'Neil DeNoux, John Douglas, Christa Faust, Neil Gaiman, Caitlín R. Kiernan, Rich Miller, James O'Barr, Jeanne O'Brien, Edward R. Pressman, David J. Schow, John Silbersack, Jimmy Vines, and Leilah Wendell.

1

Down through that part of the evening that is neither night nor day, the big black bird comes, finally, to the old cemetery in the old city on the river. Such a long flight back from the places where the dead wait, marking time until they've forgotten what time is, until they've forgotten even themselves and nothing remains but these earthly stones and the moldering skeletons they signify, and even these will pass in time.

The crow descends through the low, thin clouds that have lingered behind an afternoon thunderstorm, fading blue sky traded for gray. A woman walking along Prytania Street hears the bird's grating cry, looks up to see a violent smudge of ebony against the summer twilight, crosses herself, and walks a little faster past the crumbling walls of Lafayette No. 1 Cemetery.

Maneuvering between magnolia branches, brushing against stiff dark leaves like dripping dragon scales, the crow follows instinct and duty. With nothing that could be called thought, but with something more than the simplest bird impressions, the crow understands the immediate and undeniable task before her. She understands the terrible things that must be done before she can return to the clarity of her carrion life.

And so the crow finds the smallish mausoleum near the center of the cemetery. The pale gray marble is fresh and polished, not yet blasted by the delta sun and angry Gulf storms, a modest jewel tucked between its ancient, weathered neighbors. Around it are monuments placed over the course of more than a hundred and fifty sweltering years, fallen crosses and angels with broken wings, inscriptions worn smooth as silk. And then this newcomer, at once tasteful and decadent: a tomb that speaks of the wealth of its dead, but speaks also of their otherness.

The crow lights upon the vaulted roof, her talons gripping the slippery bronze acroterion above the sealed door. The acroterion is cast in the reclining form of a pretty young man, hands bound above his head, ankles bound as well, and a gag tied tightly across his mouth. His head is bowed, his eyes closed in perfect supplication. The crow shifts nervously, impatiently, from one ebony claw to the other. Standing on the bronze boy's shoulder, the metal still years away from the streaking stigmata of verdigris, she caws once more: for herself, for the dim uncertainty she feels. Then she folds her wings, and the resurrection begins.

So much damage to a corpse after death, the slicing ministrations of pathologists and undertakers. Because this man died violently there was an autopsy, organs removed, divined, dumped back into their cold cradle of meat and bone. The application of glue to seal eyelids and hold fingers together, lips sewn neatly shut, caustic chemicals painted on or pumped into this body sealed beneath the crow. All these things she must undo before the soul can be returned, and the bird carries the knowledge of these tasks in her skull, knows them now as she knows the sweet, greasy smell of roadkill on summer asphalt miles away, as she knows the simple routine of her life.

A silent flash of lightning far away, toward the swamps where the storm has retreated. The crow blinks her weary eyes and pecks once at the bronze sculpture. The sound echoes softly through the necropolis around her. There's a faint scratch where her sharp beak struck the burnished metal, and she pecks at the boy's shoulder again.

It makes a sound she can feel through her feet, a sound that reverberates within the marble confines of the mausoleum, growing louder in the dark spaces along the walls, louder still inside the newest coffin on its granite pedestal, amplified instead of dulled by passage through stone and steel.

Selective, though, this magic. She has come for one man, and one man only. The man who sleeps beside him will hear nothing, his ill-used, pieced-together body remaining in stasis, indifferent to what has begun. The crow's dagger beak strikes the acroterion a third and final time, and now there is movement inside the mausoleum, inside the newest coffin.

The thread that holds the dead man's thin lips closed tugs itself free, drawn out through needlepoint incisions, and falls away. The cyanoacrylate that holds his eyelids closed, that holds his fingers together across his chest, becomes brittle and then becomes no more than dust. These things are simple though, and the crow shudders, captured now in the dark and irreversible process she has started.

The long incisions in the abdomen reject their stitches also and begin to heal, flesh knitting as if in time-lapse photography. The crow cries out again, giving up parts of herself to the accelerating restoration of the body below, life chasing death. Even the bird's mind understands the wrongness in these actions, the violation of an order more primal and sacred than all the religions of mankind, but she is helpless to withdraw. She huddles on the mausoleum roof and feels her life borrowed, the measured draining of her life for the working of these magics.

There are escape clauses built into the fabric of the universe, undeniable rules that have brought her here. The crow knows none of this, only that she should be moving, flying swiftly and high and far, far away from this soulless place where the memory of life lies pinned beneath heavy stone.

Still more stitches ravel, and the body bleeds not blood but an acrid hemorrhage of embalming fluid, milky spray from opened arteries. The heart is shocked rudely back to life, pumping alien liquid through desiccated veins, and this time the crow does not caw, she *screams* as the body beneath her expels four gallons of embalming fluid into its coffin. A pulsing stream from the carotid, from an incision in the upper arm and another in the groin, until the circulatory system is completely empty, purged, and the Lazarus heart pumps only formaldehyde-stinking air.

As the open arteries knit themselves closed again, another trick is turned and the crow trembles on her perch, sick and maybe dying; she would believe herself dying if she understood death as such. Blood from the genetic memory of pickled cells, water from wine, pours from the heart to fill the parched pathways of arteries, veins, and capillaries. The crow spreads her wings in sudden panic and pain, black feathers against the growing night, as the lips of the dead man part. Collapsed lungs heave, then expand and contract, forcing more bitter fluid out past his rouged lips, fighting to draw precious breath for the first time in five days, coughing, vomiting death. The crow folds her wings again, hurting, but this part is done, at least; this part is over.

The bird crouches on the immaculate bronze victim and listens and waits for whatever has to happen next. Far away, toward Lake Pontchartrain and restless waters the color of bad coffee, there is the gentle, threatening sound of thunder.

He has no memory of waking, only the sudden, jolting knowledge that he is awake, the impossible pain of the first breath. There's something filling his mouth, and his cold tongue struggles to push it aside, to spit out the sodden, cottony mass. His eyes are on fire, like when he was a child and caught pinkeye and his mother held a warm washcloth to his face to soften the crust that sealed his eyes shut. If she were here, she might do that for him now, might take away his confusion and pain.

But she is not here. Jared Poe, who knows little else, knows this much: that he is alone, beyond alone, somewhere more solitary than alone can ever be. Smothering in that certainty, he exhales, a jagged, rattling sound that could be final breath instead of rebirth, and he opens his eyes.

Even the diffuse light around him is blinding after so profound a night, after such complete and perfect darkness. Jared Poe shuts his eyes again, tightly, before the glare burns away his thin lids and leaves him helpless to stare into it forever.

I was dreaming, he thinks. *I dreamed I was flying.* A useless little thought mired in so much agony, the pain that soaks every inch of his body, coalescent with the stinking wetness around him. His chest heaves, a sudden, involuntary gasp, the contraction of too many unused muscles at once. His back arches as the air is forced out again. Something vile fills his throat, fluids driven from his lungs or stomach or both, now spilling out of his mouth.

I was flying above New Orleans with black wings, he thinks. The next gasp makes him bite his tongue, a little harder and he might have bitten it in half. His mouth fills with cleansing, living warmth, iron-water taste to wash away the bitter burn of chemicals. He rolls onto his side, coughing, reaching for the shreds of dream already fading, slipping from him before he can be sure they were even his. *Flying above New Orleans,* and then a clearer thought, like drawing that first breath again—*I was dead.*

Jared Poe screams inside his coffin, puts the oxygen forcing its way into his unwilling lungs to good use. He screams against the hateful flood of memory, the images that follow from what he cannot deny—*I was dead.* Flashpowder revelations as unwanted as the life flowing back into him and the death leaking out. The big Cuban motherfucker with the .35 Magnum tattooed on his right arm, the Virgin Mary on his left, and when Jared looked down, the hand shoving the sharpened spoon into his gut. Pushing it in, the metal going deeper and deeper, twisting. Another scream and the sound of steel bars sliding shut inside the carefully constructed hell of Angola. Lockdown. Jared's stiff hands clench. He pounds the padded satin walls of his new prison.

A little farther into himself and the stale library smell of the courthouse comes back, the condemning sound of the gavel and the vindicated mutter of the crowd as the verdict was read aloud, the doughy fat woman with ill-fitting dentures who read the words to the judge, all the faces he didn't know.

"That's far *enough*—" Jared Poe is making words with the screams, with his fury and the impact of his fists against the walls of the coffin. "That's fucking far enough! I don't want to see any more!"

But there is so much more to see, so many more little supernovas going off behind his eyes, and every explosion is another secret he wants to keep from himself, another piece of the almighty shitty puzzle he's trying not to solve.

The cigarette and sweat smell of the police car, the handcuffs biting into his wrists. "We ought to just drive over to Algiers," the cop in the passenger seat said. "You know that, Henry? We ought to just drive this faggot pervert son-of-a-bitch right over the river and let him suck on a gun. Blow his murdering brains out." The cop behind the wheel just laughed, is laughing still, like the frantic wings of black birds in burning cages, and Jared feels the metal of the coffin begin to buckle around him.

But not yet, for here comes the last and worst memory. He's climbing the stairs to their apartment on Ursulines, his and Benny's apartment, and he doesn't want to see but it's already out before there is any hope of denying the acid rush of images. His key wrestling with the stubborn lock, the door swinging open on so much red, red like lipstick and roses and carnations, oh, God just let it be *anything* but what he knows it is. The groceries he's carried from the French Market slipping through his arms, scattering across their foyer that smells like a slaughterhouse. The same smell as the time he did a shoot in a slaughterhouse, the red stench that had stayed in his nostrils for weeks afterward.

"I won't, I won't, I won't," he mutters, a helpless litany to gods he has never believed in. *"I will not see this again."*

The coffin bursts, shatters like something made of Elmer's glue and Popsicle sticks, and Jared is falling. A very short fall to the stone floor as hard, as cold and senseless, as the sight of Benny scattered across their bed, his hands and feet still neatly trussed, thoughtful Boy Scout knots joining wrists and ankles that are divided from everything else, from the careless litter of limbs and organs . . .

"Oh, fuck, oh, fuck me," Jared whispers through ragged sobs and oily tears that drip from his face and pool on the marble floor. "Benjamin," he sighs, and there is more pain in those three syllables than his body could ever hope to contain. The coffin shrapnel raining down around him clatters like brittle bones or jackstraws.

He isn't sure how much time has passed since he opened his eyes, since he began to breathe again. The tiny stained-glass window set high above the mausoleum door has gone from the darkest shades of green and cobalt blue to black, so he knows only that it's night now. Another night in this little city of the dead, and night in the world of living men beyond.

Jared sits with his back against the stone wall and stares at Benny's coffin. This is all he has done for all the minutes or hours he hasn't bothered to count. He hasn't been able to bring himself to touch it, the mahogany glinting faintly in the gloom, the brass and rotted spray of flowers on its lid. He doesn't need to touch it to know it's real.

There comes the faint, sharp sound of scratching overhead. Jared looks up, realizes he's been hearing the sound all along, ignoring it the way he has ignored the aching emptiness in his stomach, the dryness in his throat. The way he has ignored everything but Benny's coffin, still sitting undisturbed beside the ruin of splinters and twisted metal that was his own.

Jared closes his eyes again. There are no more tears left in him to cry, only the hurt that rolls over and through him in endless ebony waves, battering him as smooth as the stone at his back. There is only hurt and loss and the bottomless, churning anger.

As he sits listening to the restless sounds above, busy little claws like Morse code or impatiently drumming fingers, Jared begins to comprehend that it is precisely this anger he must embrace now. This anger that will get him up and moving, that might hold some purpose. There can be no response to the loss he has suffered, no sane answer but oblivion, and now that's been stolen from him too. But the rage is a thing beyond him, a thing that wants out, a hungry beast that can be fed and sated.

All these things he hears hidden in the scratching at the roof of the mausoleum. Now he remembers the dream of midnight wings, the dizzying dream of flight, and he rises on legs as stiff as scarecrow sticks. He stands in the dark and listens to his heart, to the faint rumble of traffic on damp streets, and the black bird calls to him.

If the door to the mausoleum was bolted, the crow has seen to that too, and as Jared pushes at the metal he feels the first hint of a physical strength he never knew in life. The tall door swings open as if it is made of plywood, disused hinges squealing loudly for a teeth-gritting instant. Then there is only the gentle sound of the light rain again, gathering on the roofs of the voiceless inhabitants of Lafayette Cemetery.

Jared looks back once, his eyes running over Benny's elegant coffin and the shattered mess where his own lay, before he steps out into the night. He pushes the door shut so he can't see anymore, so that nothing can get in. He lingers there a moment, his face pressed against the cold, wet metal, taking some vague comfort in the steady warmth of the raindrops. Then the bird caws, loud and harsh, and he turns around. The four steps leading up to the mausoleum are decorated with a scatter of votive candles and flowers in various stages of wilt and decay. *Someone still comes here,* he thinks. Lucrece, and maybe others—perhaps the core group of fans he retained after the incident, what the press called the "sicko contingent."

The bird lands on Jared's shoulder, damp feathers pressed against his neck as if there were some shelter there. The night stretches out before him, past the cemetery walls, stretches the way a great sable tomcat would stretch. Something out there is vaster and more confident than this fetid city and its infinite corruptions, perhaps even vaster than his loss.

Jared begins to listen to what the bird has to say.

Sometimes, like tonight, the man in the big house by the river calls himself Jordan. There is a river called Jordan in the Bible, and he likes the names of rivers. Sometimes he calls himself Joseph Lethe, for another river and what it means, and sometimes he's Stanley Hudson. But these are secret names that he never tells anyone—except those few he's chosen. Those he's sure will never be in a position to spread the word, to give away his names carelessly, like telephone numbers on filthy fag-bar rest room walls.

The newspapers do not know his names. To them he is the Bourbon Street Ripper, a flashy moniker earned for the first one the cops found, years and years ago. He is sure that name sells more papers than any of his real ones could. Lies always sell better than the truth. He always reads about what he has done in the papers, but he never saves the things he reads, the official police comments and the wild speculations of illiterate journalists. That, he thinks, would be like taking a trip to Manhattan and buying an I ♥ NY T-shirt.

Death is not cheap, despite what the world may believe or how it behaves. It is actually quite expensive; he has been able to finance his research only because his mother left him drilling rights to some land in Texas. Perverse to the end, she'd waited until after the oil bust to die, so there was not an enormous amount of money from the sale of the land. But it is enough. His needs are not great, except where his research is concerned. He will not cheapen death.

From his high window, the man who is Jordan tonight can see the river winding silent and powerful through the stormy night, a fat brown snake sliding between the levees. The most powerful thing in the world, a river like that.

He waits for another flash of lightning and closes the curtains before the thunderclap. There is unfinished work here, and he cannot remember what distracted him. Something at the window or down in the streets, but whatever it might have been, it's gone now and the one he brought home with him is waiting. He doesn't always bring Them home, only the very special ones, the ones who have gone all the way and so deserve more time, more attention. The ones that have the most to teach him about what They are, what abominations They have become.

Like *this* one: stretched out on the shiny steel operating table in the highest room of his house on the river. It watches him as he turns away from the window, watches him with wide eyes that are still very aware. He is always amazed at Their tolerance for physical and psychological pain. Another part of the mystery, another thing that excludes them from humanity and makes Them so dangerous.

But not half so dangerous as he. No, not even one quarter *that* dangerous.

This one, for example. This one with the Louisiana driver's license that claims its name is Marjory Marie West, that has an F recorded for its sex. This one that he's already started upon, but still it watches him, alert, aware, as if waiting for a chance to escape. As if there could ever be such a chance. Even though he sliced out its tongue before the Demerol wore off, cauterizing the slippery stump so it wouldn't bleed to death. Even though the tongue floats in its neat jar of formalin in plain sight. It's still hanging in there, this *thing,* and this is important.

The man runs bloody latex-gloved fingers through his oily black hair, pushes his straggly bangs from his flat blue-gray eyes. He selects a scalpel from his tray of surgical instruments. Some of the instruments he has ordered from medical supply houses or bought as sets in antique stores. Others he has made himself, the ones he couldn't buy because no one's ever needed them before.

On the table, it watches him, this sexless creature that would hide itself in the world of men and women, the black and white world of opposites and opposition. He knows it is not merely evil, knows that's the sort of shit a crazy man might think. There is no evil. Rather, it is *alien,* viral, and he must be careful in his campaign if he is to succeed. If the world is to be free of these monstrosities once and for all.

The man who is Jordan tonight checks the restraints, the strong leather straps and steel buckles. Soon he will pull back the sheet, all that hides its impossible body now that he has removed the deceiving clothes. And it watches him, and the thunder growls its useless protest from somewhere above the house beside the river.

Just because the man keeps no scrapbook doesn't mean he has no memories. A scrapbook would be tawdry, tasteless. There is nothing tasteless about the records he keeps in his head.

It's been seven years, seven long red years like a bolt of scarlet lace, since the sweltering August morning when his work first made headlines. That one had been a cross-dressing hustler known on the streets of the Quarter only as Josie, barely nineteen, though "she" could have passed for twenty-five. Most of what he left was found stuffed into three garbage cans outside a tourist bar on Bourbon Street. *Most* of what he left, because it had taken a lot of blood to cover the walls of the filthy alley next to the bar. There had been no witnesses, but plenty of talk from the two garbagemen who found the dented cans crammed full of meat, and photographs of the parts he left hanging from a fire escape like strings of Christmas popcorn.

That wasn't his first, of course. Only the first that he'd wanted Them to see.

"There comes a point," he wrote in one of his yellow legal pads, "when you must show a little of yourself to the enemy in exchange for Their fear. Fear must surely weaken Them."

So four days later he left a second body in a hotel on Rampart, a fat transvestite named Petey, plump discard floating facedown in a tub of soapy water and blood, naked except for his precious lingerie and high heels. A hotel maid found this one. When the police were finally done with her, the man had read, she moved back to Chicago. Petey's real name turned out to be Ralph Larkin, a happily married father of three who ran a hardware store in Metairie and was a long-standing member of a local chapter of the transvestite "sorority," Tri Ess.

The man can still remember how Petey begged for his life, how he swore he didn't know anything about the Invasion or the Cabal or even the Gay Mafia, but They all lie. Even the pretenders, the hetero pricks hiding hard-ons inside satin panties, the ones who only want to dress up in ladies' clothing and know they'll never be fit to cross over. Jordan suspects that they are all controlled by implants, nanites hidden in the sinus cavities or the rectums, miniscule robots that would look like BBs or bird shot, if he could ever find one. Jordan suspects that the nanites are programmed to teleport out of any body that is captured or killed . . . or perhaps they simply dissolve, leaving no trace.

It's almost midnight now, and the transsexual on the operating table has lost consciousness again. He has broken ammonia ampules beneath its nose three times already, shocking it back into the world, but this time it may be slipping away for good. He sighs, lays aside the speculum and the long probe with fishhooks soldered along its length, and looks down at his notes. A dark smear of gore mars the close-ruled yellow paper, making it hard to read what he's written; Jordan knows he'll have to copy the page over again later.

Its chest abruptly expands, sucking air, revealing the faint crescent scars beneath the breasts. The scars no one is supposed to see. But *he* sees everything. When it exhales, there's an uneven, wet sound from its chest. Its eyes flutter weakly open to gaze at him one last time. This one is very, very pretty, but he quickly and expertly pushes aside anything like sympathy. He's done enough experiments to know that the compassion and regret he sometimes feels are just chemically induced reactions, triggered by genetically engineered pheromones excreted in Their sweat and tears.

"It's not too late," he says, although that's a lie, of course. It has been too late for this one since he bought it a drink just after sundown. "It's not too late to come clean. I can be merciful."

And then it's gone and Jordan is alone in the room, and there's nothing for him to think about but the smell of its bladder emptying on the tabletop.

His memories are as clear as the words he puts on paper.

Sometimes, when the answers he seeks seem forever out of reach, the memories are his only comfort. Reassuring memories of his resolve and his boldness and the harvests of his dedication.

Hardly a week after the fat man in the tub, Joseph Lethe picked up one of the Quarter gutterpunks, a baby queen he lured into his car with a vial of crystal meth and drove all the way to Arabi before he pulled over and put a bullet in the kid's head. He never asked for a name and the boy never volunteered one. The boy was wearing tacky thrift store drag, '70s retro polyester and a black wig that fell off when Joseph pulled the body from the passenger seat. He chained the corpse to the rear bumper of his car and drove unpaved back roads through the bayou until nearly dawn, the lonely places between cypress and tall whispering grass, no one to see but the birds and alligators. He'd wrapped the raw and featureless thing in plastic and left it under an oak in Audubon Park.

After that, he decided to become Jordan again for a while, as he watched the city begin to draw the connections he'd left for it to make. As he watched the fear settle over the Quarter's gay populace like a theater curtain falling halfway through a film. He walked the streets and *smelled* the fear, like fresh pomegranates and old gardenias, as it ripened.

So there could be no mistaking his message, he did one more. A postoperative female-to-male transsexual, castrated, its surgically constructed genital abomination sewn up inside its mouth. That one had read his signs well enough, had even been interviewed by a local TV news crew investigating the Ripper slayings. That one had claimed there was someone preying on the city's transgendered community, a serial killer. Seeing that made Jordan proud: He hadn't been misunderstood by those that mattered. Never mind that the police were so fucking apathetic or incompetent they couldn't find their reflection in a mirror. The point was that *They* understood. They would spread the word that They were no longer free to infiltrate the city unopposed.

He'd meant to stop then, to slip back into his old habits. Taking the occasional strays and freaks, the ones that would never be more than missing persons, missing but not *missed.*

But the fleshy, sweet smell of Their fear was intoxicating. Now, sometimes, he thinks that might have been a trick to lure him into the open: an actual chemical They secreted to addict him. Given enough time, after all, even the cops might come around. It had been like trying to put toothpaste back into the tube when he tried to stop the public displays. Instead, he hunted farther afield and less often. And the years rolled by and he has learned. Even if Their numbers have not diminished appreciably, at least They know that *he* knows.

And he knows that They are afraid of him, because if They weren't, he would be dead by now.

Jordan finishes cleaning up the vivisection table, runs all the instruments through the autoclave and puts away the new tissue samples, some floating in jars of formalin, others stored in Tupperware containers and stashed in the antique refrigerator rumbling noisily to itself in one corner of the room. After he has wrapped the transsexual's body in blue plastic garbage bags and duct tape, he returns to his seat by the window.

The man with river names opens the curtains again and looks down at the black crook of the Mississippi, the glittering lights of the city reflected in it. Later he will carry the body out to his car, but first he will allow himself time to reflect on what he has seen tonight. And the other things on his mind, the dreams he's started having: dreams of flying high above the infected city of New Orleans. Dreams of black feathers and a familiar face he can't quite seem to place.

A barge on its way to the Gulf of Mexico flashes a slow beacon, and he watches without blinking as it passes in the rainy night.

When she has finished her small dinner, the olives and French bread and dry bit of tuna fish, Lucrece clears the table, puts her dirty dishes in the sink, and sits down again, very still in the straight-backed wooden chair, watching the clock above the stove until the sun goes down. There's been rain off and on all afternoon, and now it's on again, spitting against the roof of the apartment. The sound makes her sleepy, so she listens a little harder to the music from the stereo in the next room, Nick Cave like worn velvet wrapped around rusty gears growling "Do You Love Me?" So much sadness in that voice and those words, but so much courage too.

When the shadows have grown big enough and dark enough to fill the courtyard outside the window, Lucrece leaves the kitchen. Her bare feet are almost silent on the hardwood floors as she walks along the short hall leading to the big front room that looks out onto Ursulines. The persistent dark has found its way in here too. She takes a book of matches from the glass-block coffee table and lights a sandalwood-scented candle. The warm pool of light pushes the night back to the dusty corners of the room, and Lucrece pauses at her gaunt reflection in a mirror, the huge mirror in its ornate cherry frame, something Benny found in an antique store on Magazine Street and gave to Jared for his thirtieth birthday.

Lucrece cautiously touches her pale face, traces the hard lines of her high cheekbones, her full lips painted the same kohl black as her eyelids. She can see that the circles under her eyes have gotten a lot deeper since the last time she noticed, or maybe it's the way she's holding the candle. In this light she looks so much like him, the same pallor that Benny spent years cultivating. Lucrece wears it honestly, the dues of so many months spent away from the sun, of near-fasting. She has to close her eyes and turn away from the image in the mirror, the ghost-reflection of the woman her brother wore like a change of clothes: she cannot bear to see that reflection alive and breathing while he lies so cold and alone.

"Jesus," she whispers, standing motionless for a moment as the sickening blend of déjà vu and vertigo slowly fades. She concentrates on the sound of the rain, on the words Nick Cave is singing in the dark apartment.

Benjamin and Lucas DuBois were born in Pike County, Mississippi, in a town so small and ugly it was usually left off the maps. Identical twin boys born to a girl too young and frightened to care for them, and so when she finally ran off to Pensacola with a traveling evangelist, they went to live with their Great-aunt Isolde. She owned a rambling derelict of a mansion just off what passed for the town square, a house built twenty years before the Civil War and showing every sun-bleached decade of its age. Their mother never returned for them, though sometimes she sent postcards. These were almost always gaudy religious scenes: their favorite was a 3-D picture of the burning of Sodom and Gomorrah. Hold it one way, and you could see a pair of wicked-looking spire-topped cities crumbling beneath angry skies; turn it the other way and the Hand of God hovered over a fiery orange mushroom cloud.

When she was a girl, Aunt Isolde had gone away to college in

Starkville, and she taught the twins how to read and write before they turned four. She read aloud to them from the books that filled her house—*Treasure Island* and *Wuthering Heights,* all of Dickens, *Dracula* and *Ivanhoe* and Mark Twain. She taught them history and the lives of the saints, geography and a little French. In return, they wrote plays and acted them out for the old woman, raiding trunks for costumes, improvising their sets from the musty Victorian furniture.

One Christmas, the year they turned twelve and Aunt Isolde turned sixty-three, the twins performed two scenes from *Antony and Cleopatra.* They learned all their lines by heart and even made costumes on an old Singer sewing machine they'd found in the attic. Lucas played Cleopatra, and for the death scene they used a live rat snake they'd caught hibernating in the cellar. Aunt Isolde was delighted, shouting, "Bravo! Bravo!" until she was hoarse.

More Christmases passed, and the pretty boys grew into prettier, disturbingly perfect teenagers, their hair dark as anthracite coal and their eyes the muted green of dogwood leaves at midsummer. They hardly ever left the house and its vast, overgrown yard except to run errands for Isolde, and they knew the rumors the people in town whispered behind their backs. How unnatural it was for two boys to be raised by an old spinster lady in her creepy old house, not even attending a public school, much less church. The townspeople had never liked Isolde anyway, because she'd kept herself apart from them even as a young girl, had spent too much time with books and not enough with boys.

Sometimes, as the twins were walking quickly along the red-dust road that connected their house with the rest of town, other children would hide in the bushes and throw rocks or dried-up cow pies at them, calling them sissies and weirdos. Lucas always wanted to run, would tug at his brother's shirt sleeve and beg him not to stop, not to listen. But Benjamin did listen, and sometimes he stopped on the path and hurled the rocks back. Once he hit a boy named Jesse Aderholdt in the head and Jesse and his friend Waylon Dillard chased them all the way back to the house. When they reached the rickety old front gate, Lucas crying and screaming for help and Benjamin yelling at him to shut the hell up, Isolde was waiting with a baseball bat. Jesse and Waylon stopped in the road, stood safely out of reach shouting profanities while the old woman led the twins inside.

"You dried-up old cunt," they yelled. "You goddamned old witch! You *better* protect those little queers or we'll kill 'em." Then Waylon Dillard shouted that his daddy was in the Klan and, if he wanted, could have their house burned to the ground. Eventually they went away, skulking back toward town. But Lucas lay awake that night, thinking about fire. When he did drift off to an uneasy sleep just before dawn, he dreamed of men in white sheets on horses, and crosses burning.

The summer the twins turned sixteen, Isolde died of a heart attack in her sleep. After the funeral, which no one else attended but the priest, some women came to the house with a sheriff's deputy and said the twins couldn't stay there alone. They were still minors, and they would have to go to foster homes—maybe two different foster homes, because it would be hard to find a family who'd take two teenage boys.

"We're gonna let you boys stay here until we talk to the social worker in McComb. Give you time to get your things together and all," the deputy said. That night the boys took a few clothes and books and all the money Isolde had kept in a mason jar beneath the kitchen sink. Benjamin used kerosene from the toolshed to start the fire. They left the suicide notes Lucas had written nailed to a pecan tree.

They hid for a while in a blackberry thicket atop a hill half a mile south of town, held each other and watched the red glow of the burning house rage against the midnight sky, wiping out the stars. There were sirens, and Lucas imagined he heard men shouting. Neither of them said a word.

After a while they crawled out of the briars and walked away, through the woods to the highway. The twins hitched a ride as far south as Bogalusa, where they bought bus tickets all the way to New Orleans.

The bedroom that was her brother's, and her brother's lover's, has become Lucrece's church. After their grave, this is her holiest of shrines, and one by one she lights the dozens of candles until the room is bathed in soft golden light. Then she sits in her corner beside the canopy bed: another uncomfortable chair. She folds her arms about her chest, hugs herself tightly. She's put everything here right again, everything just exactly the way it was before the long nightmare began, the one she still hasn't woken from. The black-and-white photographs on the wall are the portraits Jared took of Benny in his latex and lace wedding gown, the corset underneath pulled so tight that Benny looks like an insect, so fragile, so easy to break.

These were the centerpieces in Jared's first big gallery show, the one that snagged him a write-up in the *Village Voice,* that caught the attention of collectors as far away as Amsterdam and Berlin: people with money to spend on art.

There were photographs of Lucrece in that show too, of her and Benny together, but she couldn't look at those anymore. Jared had posed them together, the twins as inverted mirrors, dressed in restraining costumes that recklessly, elegantly swapped their genders back and forth, that rendered them even more interchangeable than the work of their genes. By the end of the first shoot, eight hours on nothing but cigarettes and bottled water, Lucrece was nauseous, dizzy, and less certain of her tenuous identity than she'd been in years. She started crying and Benny held her until the world bled slowly into focus again.

Now she's staring at the photograph above Benny's dressing table, the steel frame shining dully in the candlelight. Benny stretched out on a rough and crumbling concrete floor, his head turned so sharply to the side his neck might be broken, a satin blindfold hiding his eyes, his blackened lips parted ever so slightly. Sometimes Lucrece wishes for the strength to tear the photographs from the walls of the room, to burn them and this whole goddamned building with her inside. Set a cleansing, erasing fire, as she and Benny had done so long ago. In the life before, two lives before, when she was still a frightened teenage boy called Lucas on the run, with the future stretching out endlessly in front of them. Now the future is a cinder-block wall that she could touch if she had the nerve, a cold dead end to the ever-narrowing avenue of her life.

But Lucrece knows she doesn't have the nerve, the strength to make that final gesture, to close the distance dividing her from her brother and put an end to the loneliness. She has the strength to bear this pain forever if necessary, and the strength to hold these memories, and she will ask nothing more of herself.

The clock on the chiffonier ticks off the last minute before midnight. Lucrece sits up straight and continues to pretend that she's only waiting for Benny to come home.

The setting sun was a hazy fireball sinking into the vast expanse of Lake Pontchartrain as the bus carrying Benjamin and Lucas crossed the causeway they thought would never end. It was like something from a fairy tale, something from one of the books gone to ash in Isolde's library, a bridge spanning the gap between their childhood and the dangerous, wonderful city that lay ahead.

At that moment Lucas leaned close to whisper into his brother's ear the only thing he'd ever kept from his twin, the one secret so heavy he'd never imagined it would ever become words and cross his lips. But he understood that there was a wild magic in this crossing, and if he didn't speak it then, it might stay locked inside him forever. And after it was out, Benjamin only smiled his easy smile and kissed his brother on the cheek.

"Did you think we didn't *know*?" he said, and Lucas was too shocked to answer, too overwhelmed by his confession and Benjamin's casual response, by the world slipping past so fast outside the window of the bus. "Well, we knew. We thought you *knew* we knew."

Lucas managed to shake his head.

"Jesus," his brother sighed, an exasperated sound, but he was still smiling. "You can be a dense little thing, can't you?"

"Then you don't hate me for it?" Something slipped across Benjamin's face so fast Lucas almost missed it, anger put back in its black box before it could do him harm. Benjamin shook his head. "We're both freaks, Lucas. We're nothing like these others . . ." he whispered, motioning at the people in the seats around them. "And that's our power."

Lucas closed his eyes. As the bus rolled off the causeway and into New Orleans Benjamin whispered an old story, one they had invented together years ago, about two identical fairy brothers, changelings left for human children and taken to be raised by a kindly old woman in a house full of riddles and dust and fat scuttling spiders.

Lucrece is almost dozing in her chair when the tapping at the window begins, the French windows behind the bed and all its black linen drapings. At first she thinks that the sound must be coming from the door in the other room, someone knocking at the door to the apartment, someone wanting in, and she whispers his name before she can stop herself.

"Benny?"

Then the sound begins again, sharp, like small stones hurled against the glass, almost hard enough to shatter it. Lucrece stands up. Her legs are weak and the small hairs on the back of her neck are prickling, a cold sweat blooming wetly beneath her dress, across her forehead and upper lip.

There comes a rumbling sound like thunder, except Lucrece knows it *isn't* thunder; it is much too contained and close for thunder. It rolls slowly across the roof, and she looks up at the ceiling as the windows are blown open by a sudden violent gust. The candle flames flicker, and the room fills with the smells of rain and hot wax and ozone.

"Benjamin?" she says, louder this time. The storm seems to draw its breath, and for a moment there is only the sound of the rain coming in the window, falling on the bed and floor, peppering her face.

And then the sound of wings, and she almost screams as the huge crow lights on the headboard and the windows slam themselves shut behind it.

"Jesus Christ," she gulps. The bird caws loudly as if in reply, puffs out its black feathers and shakes tiny beads of water all over the damp bedspread. As it cocks its head to one side, beak like an assassin's dagger, Lucrece wonders what her sorrow has conjured from this haunted city, what dark spirit might have come to wonder at her vigil.

She takes one step toward it, leaning forward. The crow blinks and caws again, spreads its ebony wings. Lucrece steps back and crouches at the edge of the bed.

"Who sent you?" she asks. "Who sent you to me?"

"Lucrece," a voice behind her says, a voice as familiar and as alien as anything she could ever imagine, a voice that carries everything it's felt and everything it's seen wedged fiercely between every word. She's too afraid to turn and see, her heart going mad inside her chest, but she knows that despite her fear she will *have* to turn around sooner or later. Like Orpheus or Lot's wife, never mind the penalty of seeing. The not-seeing is a thousand times more horrible.

"Jared," she says, whispers more quietly than a whisper.

"Is it . . . ?"

"Yes, Lucrece," he says. "Yes," and she turns to see.

Jared has been following the bird for what seems like miles, down the wet streets of leering, suspicious faces and cars that honked when he didn't get out of their way. He thinks that the bird has put something inside him, a burning thread so bright it could blind him and blot out the rest of the world, a hungry cutting thing that has dragged him through the storm to this place he never would have come on his own.

When the crow led him to the Quarter, he'd stood for a while across the street from the apartment, silently watching the bedroom window through the rain. He wondered at the dim flickering light visible through the lace curtains, at who might live there now that he was dead. Then the bird leaped into the air from its perch on the lamp post and the wire coiled inside Jared pulled taut again, and he followed the black wings.

Downstairs the security door was standing open, so that anyone might walk in off the street, any crackhead with a gun, or thief, or killer. He'd pulled it shut behind him and the iron bars clanged hard and hollow like the door to a prison cell.

And now he stands in the doorway of the bedroom where Benny died, and Lucrece is on her knees in front of him. The crow is watching him from the bed. He feels the wire in his soul slacken and he swallows, still tastes the chemicals, still tastes stale death like a hangover, an aftertaste like old vomit and alcohol and cigarettes.

"Why?" he says. The voice seems to come from somewhere nearby, but not really from his throat or his tongue. Jared can think of nothing else worth asking, nothing else that could possibly matter except that one word, "Why?" and so he says it again.

Lucrece seems incapable of answering him, stares unbelieving and speechless. She looks so much like Benny it hurts to see her there, Benny's impossible, identical female twin. Jared feels as if he's falling, holds on to the door frame for some support, but there's nothing to combat the vertigo sucking at his bare feet. The apartment, this fucking room, kept like an altar because she's too weak to let go. The bird seems to smile, and he wishes his hands were around its neck.

"*Why,* Lucrece?" he says in a mean growl that he can feel as well as hear. Jared closes his eyes, presses his forehead hard against the wall. He marvels that he feels the pressure of the hard wood against his brow. "What have you done to me?"

"Jared," she says again, repeats his name like something holy. When he opens his eyes, she's rising very slowly to her feet, moving as slowly as a dancer underwater. She extends one hand tentatively toward him and he feels his knees begin to buckle, so he grips the wall more tightly.

"You should have left me *dead,*" he moans, the rage rising from his guts like puke, rage almost smothering his words. He slams his head into the door frame and Lucrece screams.

"You should have left me dead. I *am* dead and you should have left me dead."

"Jared, I didn't *do* this," she says. He knows all her courage comes from the fear that he might hurt himself again, might damage her precious voodoo prize from the grave, so he smacks his face against the wall. Something cracks and he leaves a dark smear of blood on the white paint.

"Yes, *you did*! You and your fucking magic games, Lucrece . . . you sent that fucking bird to dig me up."

"Jesus, *no,* I swear . . ." She's coming toward him as if her fear doesn't matter, as if there's simply no alternative left for her. Jared almost feels sorry for her, almost ashamed, if there was any way for him to reach those feelings through the suffocating anger. The candlelight glints off the tears running down her cheeks, off her bright, wet eyes. Then he is falling, finally, but he falls very, very slowly. Sinking, so that by the time she crosses the room, he's huddled with his broken nose squashed against the wall, tasting his own blood.

"God, Jared." Lucrece puts her arms around him, pulls him close to her. He can smell her, tea rose and spice, her clean dress, her sweat, her fear crackling around him like an electric current. She holds him very tightly and when she speaks her voice sounds as weak as an old and dying woman's.

"I've *never* lied to you, Jared. You *know* I've never fucking lied to you . . ."

"But why, Lucrece? Jesus Christ, *why*?" Then there's a sudden, stabbing pain between his eyes, a raw and grating sound, and the flesh on Jared's face feels more than alive. It has begun to move and shift, and he thinks of maggots first, that maybe his skull's full of maggots where his brain used to be, and now they're eating their way out through his face. There's an audible *pop* as skin and bone and cartilage writhe. He sees that Lucrece has covered her mouth with one hand.

"Oh, Jared," she whispers, her voice swollen with terror and awe. He reaches up, expecting to find a thousand tiny larval bodies spilling from his nostrils, a cold gush of rancid fluid. Instead there's only his nose, his perfect, unbroken nose. Not even a drop of blood, and Jared stares at his fingertips as if they've betrayed him too, as if this is just another lie.

"What's happening?" she asks, her voice as brittle and jagged as a broken light bulb. He can only answer by pushing her away, shoving her so hard she loses her balance and sprawls over backward as he fights his way back to the solid, incontestable wall.

The crow is still watching him from the bed. Jared imagines that he can *see* its hold on him, the shining wire running from its livid breast to his heart, strung like fishing line, the hook buried so deeply inside him he can never dig it out.

"*You,* you black motherfucker!" he screams. The bird blinks at him. "*You* did this, didn't you?" Jared's hands grab frantically at empty air, grappling for a link as intangible and undeniable as memory. "Let me *go*!" he screams, struggling to his feet. "Send me back where I belong!"

The crow only caws once, an annoyed, impatient sound, and hops a few inches farther out of his reach.

"Jared, please, stop." Lucrece is reaching for his ankles, sobbing as he kicks her unwelcome hands away. "Can't you *hear* what it's telling you? For God's sake, stop and *listen* to it, Jared."

But something inside him has burst, something ripe and festering, and the dark, acidic fury is out before he knows it's found a way. It pours from him in a wild and mindless flood and he tears a picture from the wall, only dimly aware of what he's holding, and hurls it at the black bird. The frame crashes against the footboard and explodes in a shower of glass and splinters.

Now he *is* staring into Benny's eyes, at the face in the ruined black-and-white photograph staring back at him. The shot that was printed in the *Voice,* Benny with his hands bound behind his back, out of sight, and the softest hint of a snarl on his lips. The figure against a shadowy backdrop, blazing wings stretched wide behind him, stark projected wings that seem to grow from Benny's bare shoulders. Jared named the photograph

The Raven, and Benny complained how obvious that was, and that it was a very dumb joke.

"Oh." His voice is just another bit of flotsam thrown out in the scalding cascade. "Oh, fuck you."

"Please," Lucrece says, begging now. Begging him to please stop as he seizes the Tiffany torchère by the door and throws it like a spear made of bronze and stained glass, driving it through the center of the photograph. And he smiles for the crow now, a vicious razor smile so wide he thinks it might split his head in half, will surely slice open the corners of his mouth. The bird squawks and retreats to the safety of the headboard.

"You think that's funny? Huh, you think that's fucking funny?"

Then Lucrece is standing in front of him, putting herself between him and the crow, and his anger switches focus in the space between heartbeats.

"Get out of my way, bitch."

"No," she says, her voice low and firm and sounding male now, the way it sounded when Jared first met her and Benny at a gallery opening uptown. "No, I won't. Whatever's happening here is happening for a *reason,* Jared."

"No, *Lucas,*" he says, all the emphasis he can find loaded on top of that discarded name, such a simple, easy weapon lying there conveniently. Lucrece flinches but doesn't move. "It's just a fucking *joke.* Just a goddamned sick joke on all of us, by a sick-ass, twisted universe. Don't you get it, *Lucas*?"

"You know it's not," she says, glaring, and the heat gathering behind her eyes is almost a match for his anger.

"Jesus, you never did have a sense of humor." Jared turns away from her and rips another of his photographs from the wall, smashes it against the floor. The glass and steel cut his hands and they heal immediately, like flesh in a time-lapse film. He turns around again slowly, raising his palms so that she can see the gashes sealing themselves closed. So that he can see the look on her face.

"Then please, darling, by all means let me refresh your memory." Jared moves so fast he knows Lucrece doesn't see it coming, shoves her stumbling back into the bed. He drives words at her like nails, each one sharper and harder than the last, as if his voice alone could crucify.

" 'But the Raven, sitting lonely on that placid bust, spoke only . . . that *one word,* as if his soul in that one word did outpour. Nothing *farther* then he uttered; not a *feather* then he fluttered—' "

Lucrece slaps him, the sound of her palm loud against his cheek, and Jared pauses in his recitation long enough to laugh at her, long enough to savor the stinging sensation her hand has left behind.

"Leave me alone," she growls. Jared slaps her back, hits her hard and she trips over the lamp and falls onto the bed. And he remembers now how good the violence can feel, the cleaning release, and he leans low over her like a movie vampire.

" 'Till I scarcely more than *muttered:* Other friends have flown before—' "

Lucrece drives her knee into his crotch and uses her other foot to push him off of her.

"I said to *leave me alone,* you son of a bitch!"

Jared releases her, falls in a heap at the foot of the bed, crumples next to what's left of the lamp and *The Raven.* Lucrece rolls off the bed, breathless, expecting another attack and ready for it this time. But Jared doesn't move, just stares blankly at the photograph, at the torn ghost of Benny still trapped inside the remains of the frame. The crow silently watches them both from its perch on the headboard.

"I didn't kill Benny," Jared says, speaking to Lucrece or to no one at all, his anger spent for the moment. The sound of his voice makes her shiver despite the adrenaline hammering through her veins, such a flat and hollow sound, like someone speaking from the bottom of a deep, dry well.

When she answers him, she speaks as carefully, as soothingly, as she can manage.

"I know that, Jared."

"Yeah," Jared says, "I know you do." He starts pulling the photograph out of the broken frame, brushing away powdered glass from the image of his murdered lover, her murdered brother. The crow caws again, flaps its wings loudly, but Jared doesn't look. Instead he stares down at beautiful, lost Benny.

"Jared, you *can* understand what it's saying, can't you?"

His head turns very slowly toward her, as if he's reluctant to look away from the photograph for even a moment, as if he's afraid it might dissolve. His eyes are as far away and empty as the sound of his voice, and she wants to hold him again, wants release from all these months she's spent alone, no company but her own selfish, devouring sorrow. But Lucrece does not move, glances instead at the bird.

"It's brought you back," she says, "to find out who did do it, and stop them from ever doing it again."

The crow seems to regard her warily, maybe a glimmer of mistrust in its small and golden eyes, and so she says to it, "Am I wrong?"

"No, Lucrece," Jared says, answering before the bird has the chance. "You're not wrong. I can hear it too. I don't want to, but I can hear it just fine."

"I can help you," she says, still watching the crow, the mistrust mutual now. "If I can understand what it's saying, then I can help you. I know things about what happened to Benny, things they wouldn't let me say in court."

The crow flies the short distance to the foot of the bed and perches on the footboard above Jared, looks from him to Lucrece and back to him again, its eyes as sharp as its beak, somehow nervous and confident at the same time.

"I can't let you get involved in this, Lucrece," Jared says, hugging the photograph to his chest now, stroking its smooth surface as if there is something there more precious than mere paper.

"Bullshit," she answers. "I'm *already* involved."

He can't think of anything to say to that, nothing that would convince her, but he knows well enough that she can't follow where he has to go. So Jared Poe sits quietly on the floor of the room and listens to the rain falling outside on Ursulines and the less comforting rhythm of his Lazarus heart.

2

Detective Frank Gray has been watching the Weather Channel for the last half hour, too drunk to give a shit that he's seen the same local weather report three times already, too drunk to bother changing it over to something else. He takes another long swallow of Jim Beam directly from the pint bottle and returns it to the safe cradle between his legs. At least the bourbon still feels the way it should, the only thing left in his life that hasn't found some way to betray his trust. It burns reassuringly in his belly, adds its part to the mist he keeps between himself and the world.

There's a tropical storm somewhere in the Gulf, a great spinning swirl of white against blue on the satellite photographs. He's managed to understand that much. But the storm and any threat it might represent are far away from him, like everything else, like the rain drumming steadily against the window of his shitty apartment. Frank takes another drink from his bottle, sweet fire in his mouth, blazing down his throat. He closes his eyes when it reaches his stomach, and in the drunken darkness the hustler is there waiting for him.

The kid *said* he was twenty-one, and Frank knew it was a lie but didn't push the issue. He'd gone into the bar after his shift for a beer, the first drink on his way down into the long drunk of the weekend. It was a nameless place on Magazine Street, just a sign that read BAR and a neon four-leaf clover over the door, neon beer signs in the dark windows, Patsy Cline on the jukebox. Frank ordered a Bud and was sipping it at the bar when he noticed the kid watching him from a corner booth, sitting there alone, an army surplus duffel bag occupying the seat across from him. When he looked back a few minutes later the kid was still there, still watching him. There was a bottle on the table, though he didn't seem to be actually drinking from it.

And then the kid smiled at him, a practiced shy smile, and looked back down at the table, picked at the label of his beer bottle.

The pushy, nervous voice in his head said, *No, Frank. We don't shit where we eat, man,* but he'd learned a long time ago how to keep that voice in its place. It was only another minute or two before he went over to the kid's booth.

Up close the kid looked a little bit older than he had from the bar. Blond hair shaved down to his scalp, Huck Finn freckles under his eyes and across the bridge of his nose. His eyes were the vacant blue of an October sky.

"Hi," Frank said. The boy said hi back to him, looked up for just a second, a quick smile for Frank before he went back to picking the label off the half-empty bottle of PBR. Frank pointed at the duffel bag and asked, "Coming or going?"

"Coming," the kid answered. "I just got in from Memphis this afternoon. On the bus."

"Memphis, huh," Frank said, and before he could say anything else the kid whispered, "So, you want a blow job, mister? I'll blow you for twenty bucks."

Frank glanced over his shoulder, automatic caution. The place was empty except for the two of them and an old woman sipping a Bloody Mary at the far end of the bar. The bartender was on the phone and had his back to them.

"Jesus, kid, you don't waste any time, do you?"

The kid shrugged, pulled the rest of the label off the brown beer bottle. "What's the point in beating around the bush?"

"I might be a cop," Frank said.

The boy smiled, smoothed the ragged label on the tabletop. "Oh, you're not a cop. You don't even look like a cop. I've given cops head before, and you don't look like a cop to me."

"Really?" Frank sipped at his own beer, glanced over his shoulder again. The old woman was saying something he couldn't understand to the bartender, who was still on the phone and ignoring her. "Maybe you should be a little more cautious."

The boy sighed then, looked up at Frank, and all the flirt and pretense was gone from his face, a hint of annoyed impatience at the corners of his mouth.

"Look, man. I gotta take a piss. If you want a blow, I'll be waiting for you in the john, okay?"

As the boy stood up and pushed past him Frank stammered, "Yeah, uh, sure," but the kid was already halfway to the rest room door.

If asked, Frank Gray would be hard put to think of anything he had ever wanted but to be a cop. He spent his childhood on a steady diet of television police dramas, everything from syndicated episodes of *Hawaii Five-O* and *Dragnet* to *Starsky and Hutch* and *Baretta, Police Story, Mod Squad.* These were his cowboys, his heroes, his models of what was good and what was masculine.

And, if asked, he would also be hard put to remember a time when he was not attracted to men: these men in particular, with their navy blue uniforms and shining badges and forceful self-assurance. He never passed through a time of sexual confusion, the tentative courting of girls he wasn't actually attracted to, the belated discovery that men and only men were the proper object of his sexuality. Everything was clear from the beginning, and he never saw any conflict between the objects of his lust and his desire to be a cop.

But this naïveté did not even survive his academy training. He didn't need anybody to pull him aside and tell him, "Frank, faggots are not welcome on the force." He saw the hatred in his fellow cadets and recognized it for what it was, absorbed an acute awareness of the silence he would have to keep like priestly vows of celibacy if he was to have both these things, sex with other men *and* the badge, without having to endure any lessons firsthand. He saw others who were not so sharp, and that was enough for Frank.

By the time he came on the New Orleans PD as a beat cop in the Fifth Ward he understood the fine line he would have to walk, and he kept his arms out straight, placed one foot carefully in front of the other. Shortly after he entered the force two officers were busted after trading leniency for sexual favors from male hustlers in the Quarter. Before their subsequent hearings and dismissal Frank saw the *other* things that happened to them—the threats and beatings and humiliation—and he took note.

Four years later he was promoted to the rank of homicide detective, four long years he'd spent walking the walk, talking the talk, and satisfying his hungers with his hands and pornography, and even the pornography was a big risk. He knew that, and he kept his magazines in a locked strongbox in the back of a closet and never bought anything from the local newsstands or porn shops. Everything arrived at a post office box he kept in Bridge City under a false name, sexual care packages in anonymous brown paper, the magazines and videocassettes that served as surrogates for anything like actual companionship or satisfaction.

He learned the masquerade, the smoke-and-mirrors game, and

prided himself that no one suspected a thing. He dated fictitious women. Whenever the guys were going on about some woman or another, Frank was always right up front, his lines as well rehearsed as any actor's on opening night. "Oh, man, did you see the titties on that bitch?" somebody would say, and Frank would clutch at his crotch and grin on cue. He knew every queer slur and joke, excelled in the phony swish and lisp and limp-wristed pantomime. He had looked the other way on more than one occasion when he saw cops beating up on fags. The machismo was just another part of his uniform, after all, just as easy to put on and take off again as his hat and shoes, and if there were ever doubts, well, that's what confession was for.

It was all easy enough to rationalize. If they'd just show a little fucking self-restraint, if they'd act like *men,* nobody would know and this shit wouldn't happen to them.

But sometimes he would catch a glimpse of his thin face in the bathroom mirror or a store window and there would be only the mask, no vestige left of the man hiding underneath. He would have to stop then, would have to lean against a wall or sit down until the vertigo passed. There was a ballooning sense that he was somehow slipping out of himself, that the man he saw reflected had already consumed the *real* Frank Gray. And even this was something small enough to dismiss. Shit, it was a stressful fucking life and he couldn't expect *not* to feel it every now and then. He told himself it was just something else that came with the territory and if he had to have a few drinks before bed to keep the nightmares away, so be it.

The boy in the bathroom stall smelled like sweat and sunlight, and Frank tried hard to concentrate on those delicious smells instead of the sour stink of urine and deodorant cakes. He sat on the toilet seat, his hands savoring the soft bristle of the kid's scalp, holding back, wanting it to last, knowing it might be weeks before he allowed himself anything this wonderful again, weeks before he was desperate enough to risk it.

When he finally came, Frank leaned over and kissed the kid's scruffy hair, tasted salt and Vitalis. Tiny bursts of orgasm still lingered somewhere between his dick and his brain, and he didn't want to open his eyes, let in the ugly light of the rest room, the uglier reality of his situation.

"Jesus, I *knew* you were a fucking cop," the kid said, and when Frank did open his eyes the kid was holding his service revolver, had slipped it from his ankle holster and was pointing it at Frank's chest.

"So, since you went and *lied* to me, maybe I got a little bit more coming to me than just the twenty, huh?"

Frank swallowed, his mouth and throat gone suddenly dry, feeling like a goddamn fool, stupid enough to let this punk catch him off guard, his pants around his ankles and his shriveling dick dripping cum into the toilet bowl, the barrel of his own gun aimed straight at his heart.

"Just give that back to me before someone gets hurt, okay?" Like he really thought there was any chance of that happening.

The kid shook his head and smiled, used the back of his free hand to wipe his mouth, careful not to take his eyes off Frank.

"What?" Frank asked him, fear and exasperation fighting for control of his voice. "You think you're actually gonna shake down a policeman with his own fucking gun and get away with it?"

"Do all the other little piggies know you're a faggot?" the boy said. Frank punched him hard in the face, sent him crashing backward into the locked door of the stall. The revolver tumbled from his hand and clattered loudly on the filthy tiles. He grabbed the kid by the collar of his T-shirt, slammed his head hard against the door. The boy slumped into a whimpering heap. Frank moved slowly, reaching for the gun with one hand and pulling up his pants with the other. He shoved the .38 back into its holster before he stood up and kicked the kid once in the stomach, once in the face for good measure.

"You stupid little shit. If I ever see you again . . . if I ever so much as fuckin' *see* you again, motherfucker, they'll be dragging the river for the parts the alligators didn't want. Do you understand me?"

The kid coughed out a mouthful of blood and Frank Gray kicked him in the guts again.

"*Answer* me, fucker."

The boy managed a choked strangling sound and half a nod. Frank kneeled beside him and stuffed the twenty he'd earned into a back pocket.

"I'm going back out there, and I'm going to finish my beer. You're going to stay right here for a while." Without waiting for a response, he left the kid curled fetal and moaning beside the toilet.

Frank takes another drink from his bottle and watches the lazy counterclockwise spiral of the storm tracking across his television screen. The weatherman points to the tattered delta and barrier island coast of Louisiana and says something Frank can't hear because he's turned the sound down all the way. It's better to hear the rain, he thinks, better just to listen to the fucking incomprehensible rain.

He's always heard stories of hustlers robbing cops, stealing guns and badges when the cop wasn't looking, or trying to blackmail them later on. *Fuck that,* he thinks drunkenly, remembering the fear and surprise shining like a fever from the kid's eyes. *Fuck that to hell and back again.* But there's another voice in his head, the voice that tried to stop him from speaking to the boy in the first place. Sometimes the alcohol muffles it to a whisper, but now it's loud and it says, *Yeah, it's easy for you to talk that macho crap now, Frank Gray. But you were ready to shit yourself today, weren't you, buddy?*

Frank fumbles for the remote control and turns the volume back up until he can't hear anything above the meteorologist's nasal voice.

The heavy drinking began a couple of months before his promotion to detective, when Frank was still just a beat cop working the Iberville projects east of Canal Street. His partner was a young black woman named Linda Getty, a rookie he'd been working with only a few weeks when they got the call, what he would always remember as the Bad Call. It was a rainy Shrove Tuesday and for Frank that afternoon would mark the moment that his descent began, his piecemeal disintegration to this place of self-loathing and boozy rot.

"This domestic shit is the worst," Frank said. Linda nodded, flicking the butt of her cigarette out the window of the squad car as he answered dispatch.

"Yeah, we're only a couple of blocks from there now," he said into the radio handset, and turned the car around. Now, whenever he thinks back on the four or five minutes before they reached the maze of tenements bordering St. Louis No. 1 Cemetery, it always seems that there was some vague sense of foreboding, something more urgent than the usual dread of getting himself in between two people who hate each other as bad as married couples can. But that's probably bullshit and he knows it, like someone seeing St. Paul in a bowl of gumbo just before they almost choked to death on a crab shell, making something out of nothing for the sake of consolation.

"I know you must have heard this a hundred times in training," he said to Linda, talking fast like he always did when he was nervous, "but this mundane shit is a hundred times more dangerous than, say, robbery calls or drug busts. At least you go into those *expecting* someone to take a shot at you or something. Shit like this, you just never fucking know what to expect."

"I hear you," said Linda, trying to sound tough and sure of herself. The way that Frank remembers it, he wished she really did.

A small crowd had already gathered by the time they pulled up outside the graffiti-covered red brick building, people in the muddy yard and a few standing in the street looking at something on the blacktop. Distrusting, resentful faces turned toward them as they got out of the car. Frank remembers thinking that at least the rain had stopped.

"What the hell you gonna do about this?" a woman said, a short woman almost as wide as she was tall, with mint-green curlers sprouting from her hair. Frank could hear a man's voice from one of the apartments, loud and crazy.

"You folks need to go on home," he started, and then he heard Linda gasp, the sound someone makes when they've just seen something a hundred times worse than they've ever imagined anything could possibly be.

"Don't you be tellin' me to hush up and go away," the fat woman scolded, strident, angry. "I done asked you what you gonna *do* about this!" But Frank had already turned his back on her, was staring at Linda standing on the other side of the car, one hand over her mouth and her voice filtered through her fingers.

"What is it?" he asked. "What's wrong?" But she was already pointing at the thing he'd noticed in the street as they'd pulled up to the curb. *A fucking dead cat,* he thought. *Jesus, she better not be pulling this scene on me over a goddamn dead cat in the fucking road.*

Linda fumbled for her cigarettes, lit one and inhaled frantically to keep from vomiting, a trick he knew well. "Frank," she mumbled, "Oh, God. Oh, *look* at it."

He stepped around the back of the patrol car, trying to keep his eyes on the restless onlookers and the general direction he'd heard the man's voice coming from, trying to get a better look at whatever his partner saw lying in the street.

It wasn't a cat. He saw that a second later, a glimpse of the small brown body between the figures huddled around it, naked skin and sticky red smeared across the blacktop. The baby was maybe six months old, and Frank didn't have to ask to know that a car had run over its head.

Linda was leaning against the car, coughing, repeating, "Oh, God, oh, God," over and over like a prayer between puffs, like maybe there was some way to forget what she'd just seen, a trick that would allow her to *unsee* it. Someone in the crowd laughed then, a dry, hard laugh that Frank remembers as clearly as the broken body. And then the first gunshot and he could move again, the spell broken. He remembers yelling at Linda to get her shit together, pull it together right *then* or he was going to kick her fucking ass.

"I'm sorry," she whispered, wiping her mouth and reaching toward her holster. "But Jesus, Frank . . ."

"There ain't nothin' you can do for that poor child," the fat woman shouted at them from the other side of the patrol car. "You best be worryin' about the ones he *ain't* killed yet." And Linda glared at the woman, squinted through the tears leaking from the corners of her eyes, spilling down her cheeks.

"Listen to the lady," Frank said. He leaned past his partner into the car, trying to sound calm as he grabbed the radio mike. "Hey, we need some fucking backup out here!" He paused before going on, took a deep breath, and wondered if the operator could hear his heart pounding away in his chest, could smell the blood and adrenaline straight through the radio.

The man who had fired the shots was waiting for them on the second floor, had barricaded himself inside with his girlfriend and her three children. One of the kids was the dead baby in the street—the fat woman had told them that when Frank had finished radioing for backup. The guy's name was Roy and he'd been smoking crack all day. The fat woman had also told them that. They both drew their guns before starting up the iron-and-concrete stairs to the second floor, where they crouched just past the top of the stairway, Linda pressed flat against the wall, Frank a few feet closer to the door, a lot more exposed.

Almost five minutes had passed since he'd called for assistance and they still hadn't even heard so much as a siren. Frank's hands were sweating, slick around the grip of his pistol. They could clearly hear the man and woman inside, screaming at each other, and the terrified voices of the children, but there had been no further gunfire. On the way up Frank had glimpsed movement through a broken window. He'd guessed it was the same window from which the baby had been tossed.

"Shit," Linda hissed behind him. "Where the fuck *are* they, Frank? We shouldn't even be up here without backup."

"Just shut up a minute, okay?" he snarled at her, bracing himself against the iron railing, setting himself up for a clear shot if the door to the apartment opened and there was *anything* at all in that asshole's hands.

When he shouted to the people inside, he could hear the strain in his voice, the fear coiled there. It made him feel almost as sick as the sight of the dead kid had, the tire tread pattern pressed into the pulpy mess where its brain and skull had been.

"Roy? Roy, can you hear me in there? This is the police. Put down your weapon and open the door before anybody else gets hurt—"

"Hey, fuck *you,* motherfucker!" a male voice boomed from behind the door. The black paint was coming off the metal door in big, ugly flakes, and Frank could see a lighter, older shade of black revealed underneath. He remembered these details so clearly.

"I ain't doing *nothin'* for no goddamn City of New Orleans cops! You gonna get your lyin' cracker ass back into your police car and leave me the hell alone or I'll blow this bitch's brains out!" And then the woman screamed again.

"Jesus, Frank, where the hell *are* they? They shoulda fucking been here *twice* already."

He didn't have an answer for her, but he knew they were in over their heads.

"I don't know, *okay*?" he whispered, struggling to sound calm against the panic gathering in his belly, filling his insides like cold lead. "But we're going to have to back off and just wait . . ."

"Back off and wait for *what,* Frank? Nobody's coming, and he's ready to kill those people in there. There are *children* in there, for Christ's sake."

"Hey, motherfucker!" the man's voice boomed again, a ravening, mad-dog voice that Frank knew there could never be any reasoning with. No answer to that voice except force, force enough to kill before it would back down. "Are you deaf or what? I *said,* get the hell off the goddamn stairs or I'm gonna pop this bitch in the fuckin' head!"

"It doesn't matter," Frank said, speaking to Linda as loudly as he dared. "There's nothing we can do by ourselves." He called out to the man behind the door, "Okay, Roy, we're going to back off now and leave you alone just like you said. But I want you to do some—"

And then the shotgun made a sound like thunder trapped inside a metal box and wanting out, tearing its way free, and the black door was blown completely off its hinges. There was no time for them to get out of the way—Frank saw that at the same instant he saw Roy raising the Mag–10 Roadblocker for another shot. The woman was sprawled at his feet. Frank could see that she'd been caught between Roy and the door when the monster Ithaca semiautomatic had gone off, that the blast had cut her in half. Roy was covered in the woman's blood, and the air was thick with smoke and a settling crimson mist.

"Stay down!" he screamed at Linda, stealing precious seconds to aim before he fired his revolver twice, both shots catching Roy cleanly between the eyes. The huge man jerked backward and his spasming fingers squeezed the Roadblocker's trigger one last time, but the shot went wild, blowing a hole in the ceiling above his head, adding plaster dust and more smoke to the haze already billowing from the doorway of the project apartment. Roy stumbled backward, tripped over a coffee table, and fell dead to the floor.

"Mother Mary . . ." Frank whispered, but he couldn't even hear his own voice for the ringing in his head, the smothering echo of the shotgun.

"Are you okay back there? Linda, are you okay?" She didn't answer, but he was already up and moving, advancing on the doorway, the barrel of his .38 not moving from Roy's prostrate form. He'd fallen backward and both his feet were sticking up in the air, his expensive athletic shoes soaked in blood, his own blood and the woman's.

Frank stepped carefully past the buckled, broken door; the hole blown in the center was as big as his fist and he knew it was fucking amazing he wasn't a dead man. He stepped over the shredded mess slumped in the door, something that had been a human being hardly a minute before. The floor was slippery and he steadied himself by leaning against a wall. That was covered with blood as well, and his hand came away red and sticky. There was no sign of the other children. Frank guessed they were hiding somewhere in the apartment.

"Linda, I could really use your help up here," he shouted, leaning cautiously over Roy's corpse. "We gotta find these kids."

He noticed that there were two neat punctures just above the bridge of Roy's nose, a widening pool of blood and gray matter on the floor beneath his head. Both of his eyes were wide open, staring blankly up at the ceiling or God or his killer. The shotgun was still clutched in his hands.

"Linda? Did you *hear* me?"

When she finally answered him it was a weak, uncertain sound. He looked slowly over one shoulder, reluctant to turn his back on this crazy man even now, even when there was absolutely no way he would be getting up again. Frank stared out through the clearing fog of smoke and dust, the doorway of the apartment gaping like a ragged exit from some backwater recess of hell.

Linda was sitting at the top of the stairs, her back against the brick wall of the building, surrounded by a spreading puddle of her own blood.

"I think I got hit," she said, her words already mired in dulling shock. "Frank, I think the bastard shot me."

Frank almost slipped in the dead woman's intestines on the way out, barely managed to catch himself. Even from a distance he could see the blood jetting from the wound in Linda's thigh, bright red arterial gouts in time to her heartbeat, spilling her life out onto the dirty concrete. Linda was staring at the wound dumbstruck, as if it amazed her, as if it was the most incredible thing she'd ever seen but no *part* of her, nothing that could have happened *to* her.

When he reached her Frank dropped to his knees and looked at the hole, her brown skin and pink muscle chewed to hamburger. He had no idea how the blast could have missed him and caught her until he saw the jagged piece of shrapnel sticking up out of the wound, a piece of the door that must have sailed right by him.

"Listen, I've got to get you an ambulance," he said, stripping off his shirt for a pressure bandage. "And while I'm gone you're going to have to keep some weight on this." She nodded listlessly. *She's gonna fucking die right here,* Frank thought as he wrapped his shirt tightly around the hemorrhaging wound. *She's gonna bleed to death right here before I even get to the fucking car to call for help.*

"I think I'm okay," she slurred. "It doesn't hurt that bad. I think I can walk."

"Shut up, Linda," he said, tying the sleeves of the shirt, finishing the bandage. "If you don't sit still and keep pressure on this leg you're not gonna have to walk anywhere ever again. You'll have angels to carry you wherever you want to go."

She looked at him, blinked, and smiled, a stupid junkie kind of smile. Then she was pulling something off her finger, pressing it into his blood-smeared right palm.

"Please, Frank," she said, "tell Judy I'm sorry, okay? Tell her I still love her. You'll do that, right?"

He stared down at the ring, a simple white gold ring, trying to understand what she was saying to him.

"If something happens . . . if I don't make it . . . you tell Judy I said I was sorry." Linda folded his fingers closed around the wedding band.

Frank took a deep breath, knowing there was no time for his surprise or the pampering of his own fears. The bandage was already soaked through. He put both her hands on it and pressed down hard, and she almost passed out. He slapped her cheeks until she was conscious enough to keep her own hands over the shotgun wound.

"You keep your hands right there, Linda, and you're gonna be just fine. Ain't nothing gonna happen to you if you do what I say. Do you *understand* me?"

"Yeah," she said, sounding very faint and far away from him. "Yeah, I know what you mean, Frank."

"I'll be right back, I *swear.* I'm only going as far as the patrol car, okay?"

"Yeah," she said, and he left her there and descended the steps to the crowd of people still milling about in front of the building. The fat woman with the green curlers looked at him and grinned, showing a bright silver tooth right up front.

"You leave anyone alive up there, young man?" she asked him as he stepped between their bodies. He didn't reply, ignored them all. It had started to rain again while he and Linda were upstairs and he felt the drops cold against his skin, washing him clean. He gripped the ring in his hand and walked toward the car, praying to no God he believed in that he could at least reach it before he puked, praying that he could get help before she died alone up there.

As he reached the curb there was the sound of thunder off toward the river, a rumble like muffled shotgun fire, and the urgent wail of approaching sirens.

Linda Getty didn't die, but she almost lost her leg and would walk with a limp for the rest of her life. Frank visited her only once in the hospital, when he returned the white gold ring to her. Linda accepted it as if she were taking back a confession. She was in fact doing something very much like that, Frank knew. Linda resigned from the force while she was still struggling through physical therapy, and Frank moved effortlessly up to homicide.

But not before he learned that there had been at least two squad cars within minutes of their location in the Iberville projects that afternoon. Both had reported engine trouble to dispatch when the call for assistance had come in over their radios. And when Frank got back to the station that day, he found that someone had spray-painted DYKE in fat red letters across the front of Linda's locker and taped used and bloody tampons to the locker's door.

He stood looking at it for a while, his old familiar fear of discovery wrestling an outrage he'd never felt before, not in all those times when he'd gone along with the idiot queer jokes or turned the other way when someone was roughing up a fag, all those times he'd played along for fear of arousing suspicion and drawing the bullies' wrath his way.

He stared at the desecrated locker and saw Linda Getty slumped limp against that wall, her life pumping out of her, the blood staining her blue cop pants black. She hadn't even fucking cried, had calmly slipped the ring off her finger.

Tell her I still love her.

The ring was still tucked in his shirt pocket, and the sticky blood staining its smooth metal surface was so much like the crimson graffiti slur splashed across the locker door. Later Frank would know that if each man is given only one moment when redemption is somewhere within his reach, that moment in the locker room had been his, his one chance to change the course of his life. A handful of seconds when everything was suddenly made so clear, as simple as the resigned tone of Linda's voice coming through the pain and shock.

And then Donovan said something behind him, "You gotta be careful who you ride with, Frank," just like that, and the anger rising inside him was drowned in the fear, the cold, watery fear that had put out so many fires before and would smother a thousand more. Frank turned and faced Joe Donovan, a heavyset man with acne scars, and the words were on his lips, the *right* words, but when he spoke they slipped away and all that came out was, "Yeah. Yeah, I guess you can't be too careful, can you?"

"No," Joe Donovan said, "you sure as hell can't, buddy." He smiled with the reaffirmation that he was speaking to one of his own, someone who understood that sometimes sacrifices had to be made for the sake of maintaining a greater purity. "It wasn't nothing personal, Frank. You know that."

"Yeah," Frank replied, "yeah, sure."

So the next day, hung over and exhausted from long hours filled with drunken nightmares where he was forced to face down Roy the psycho crackhead again and again, Frank went to see her and return the ring. When he arrived there was another woman in the room, a skinny white girl with a jewel in her right nostril and tattoos on her arms. Linda whispered something to the girl and she left them alone, glancing suspiciously at Frank as she passed him on her way out to the hall.

Linda's eyes were as glazed with the painkillers as they had been with pain the day before, her voice flat and raw, sludgy. She blinked at him and attempted to smile. Frank fished the ring from his pocket. He'd washed the blood off it, and it shone dully in the white light of the hospital room.

"Thank you," she croaked.

Frank shrugged. "No problem. Hey, they treating you all right in here?"

"Everything a girl could ask for." She did smile then, a tired and honest smile that made him glance down at the scuffed toes of his shoes.

"Well, you let me know if you need anything. I gotta get back to the station. All the goddamn paperwork from yesterday. You know how that shit goes." She nodded, then reached out and touched his hand.

"Frank, you did know, didn't you?"

He didn't answer, looked nervously from his shoes to her to the door, just wanting to get the hell away.

"No," he said, and that part was the truth, he hadn't.

"Shit. I'm sorry. I thought everybody knew."

"You just rest and get better, okay?" he said. The girl came back then and stood in the doorway, silently announcing that his time was up.

"Thanks," Linda croaked again. "You saved my ass out there."

"Hey, just doing my job, right?"

"See you soon," she whispered as the drugs pulled her back down toward unconsciousness, releasing him, his duty done. Frank made it all the way to the elevator before he started shaking so badly that he had to sit down.

He often dreams about Roy the psycho crackhead these days. A very simple dream, a short-subject sort of dream where he's watching from somewhere outside himself but still close enough to smell the gunpowder and his own terrified sweat. The details are always so much clearer than anything was that afternoon in the projects, edited and retouched for his viewing pleasure. The loud, mechanical sound of the Roadblocker ejecting the spent shell and chambering the next, the one with his name on it. The parchment yellow nicotine stains on Roy's teeth. The blue-gray loops of the dead woman's exposed intestines.

Sometimes in the dreams it all goes down the same way it did the first time and Roy takes two in the head before he can get off another shot. But sometimes it goes other ways—Frank's revolver jams, or he's one second too slow, or his aim is just a few inches too far to the left or the right—and old Roy gets his second chance after all. The blast never hurts, or at least Frank never remembers the pain when he's finally awake and dripping cold sweat in the safety of his bed. There's only the impact, the mangling, bone-crushing force that takes his breath away, drives him backward and over the flimsy railing.

Sometimes he falls for a long, long time, like Alice dropping down the rabbit hole to Wonderland. And sometimes he only seems to fall for an instant before he jerks awake. But so far he's never hit bottom.

Frank Gray finally changes the channel on the cruddy thirteen-inch Zenith he got from St. Vincent de Paul's and finishes the bottle of bourbon to an episode of *The Untouchables* he's seen at least a dozen times before. Through the sleepy alcoholic fog cushioning his brain the scratchy black-and-white violence is comforting, the screech of tires and ricochet of machine gun bullets as reassuring as a lullaby.

He has to piss but thinks he can hold out a little longer, at least until the next commercial break, before he stumbles off to find the bathroom.

The pressure from his bladder reminds him of the kid from the bar, Huck Finn sucking dick for twenty dollars, makes him remember the surprise on the boy's face when he punched him. Like they all think it's gonna be so goddamn easy, having your cake and eating it too, taking advantage of someone and then robbing them in the bargain. He wishes he'd hauled the kid in for soliciting. Let him scream about faggot cops all he wanted, no one would have ever believed him anyway. At least it's nice to tell himself that, and when he's this drunk he can almost believe it, can almost pretend no one whispers behind his back or snickers or suspects him of being anything but one of the boys.

Frank closes his eyes as the credits roll, thinks maybe he can put off pissing long enough for a nap. Outside the rain falls from a black sky, and the sound of it follows him down to a deep and mercifully dreamless sleep.

3

An hour until midnight, and Jared and Lucrece sit together on the floor of the bedroom. Lucrece has carried away the broken pictures and poured herself a glass of scotch. The crow watches them from the bed. Sometimes it squawks loudly, as if it's preparing to announce something urgent; each time they turn and watch the bird, waiting for something more, until it's clear it has nothing else to say for now.

Occasionally Jared begins crying again, deep, racking sobs that seem as if they will tear him apart, and Lucrece holds him until they pass and he is silent.

"I don't understand what I'm supposed to do," he says. Lucrece looks at the big black bird, guarded reproach in her eyes as if maybe she thinks it hasn't done its job and she'll have to fill in the blanks it has left.

"What has the crow told you?" she asks Jared. He just stares at the bird on the bed, watching its vigilant eyes. In a little while he answers her, speaking slowly, as if he's uncertain of the words or the way they fit together.

"Because there are scales and Benny's death left them unbalanced." He stops, remembering a statue of Justice outside the courthouse where he was sentenced to die, the ageless bronze woman blindfolded and holding her sword and balanced scales. The memory of her and the sick irony there makes him laugh.

Jared sneers at the bird. "No," he says. "It's more than that. If all that was required to bring back the dead was a little injustice, the fucking graveyards would be empty."

The crow caws in response.

"It's not the injustice," he says to Lucrece, to himself and the bird. "It *can't* simply be the injustice, *can* it?"

"Then what?" Lucrece whispers, afraid Jared knows the answer, more afraid he doesn't. She knows, has heard it in the bird's grating voice; she could tell Jared but knows that he should be the one to see it for himself.

"Fuck you both," he mutters, and she holds his face gently between her hands. His skin is cold. The coldness hurts her like a bad memory, or a memory so good it hurts to recall.

"It's your pain, Jared," she tells him, not letting him look away from her eyes. "It's your pain that is creating the imbalance, your pain that has to be satisfied before order is restored."

"That's bullshit, Lucrece . . . do you even know how ridiculous you sound?"

She ignores him. "Not just the pain, though. Your love for Benny. That's part of it too. That's the part you were supposed to carry with you to the other side. It's the pain and anger that you were supposed to leave behind. There's no room for them among the dead."

Jared pushes her away then, the sneer dissolving into hateful laughter, an ugly, predatory sound that Lucrece would hardly believe is human if she weren't seeing it come from his lips.

"There's no room for *anything* among the dead, Lucrece, except the hungry worms."

She cannot look him in the eye now, cannot face the ebony glimmer there. She knows that it's part of what he has become, part of what he will have to do if he is ever to find peace, but that knowledge makes it no easier for her to face.

"You can hear the crow, Jared. You know I'm telling you the truth."

He doesn't say anything. When she raises her eyes and looks back at him Jared is watching the bird perched on the footboard of the bed. His lips are pulled so far back that his teeth look like fangs, bared for fresh meat.

"An avenging angel," he snarls. "So the gods can rest easy and still keep their hands clean. Is that what you're saying?" The bird ruffles its feathers and shifts from foot to foot.

"That's all there is to it, *isn't* it? Find the bad guys and make them pay, so my niggling soul doesn't disturb the spooks roasting down in hell."

The crow tucks its wings close to its body and huddles as if it expects Jared to strike it.

"Yeah, well, you tell me what good that does Benny, you black-hearted son of a bitch. You tell me that it's going to *fix* what some depraved motherfucker did to Benny and *maybe* then I'll want to play along with your little game."

Lucrece can feel his fury in the close atmosphere of the bedroom, more immediate than the storm outside, can feel his anger crackling through the damp air around them.

"Nothing's going to help Benny, Jared. Unless you can find peace and return to him, nothing's ever going to help Benny." The last part catches in her throat like broken glass, but she knows it must be said.

"Right now Benny is *alone,* Jared, alone in the cold and the dark, waiting for you to come back to him."

And she braces herself, ready to feel his fist or ready to put herself between him and the bird again. But Jared sits very still and stares at the crow, the muscles in his face relaxing by almost imperceptible degrees.

"Ah, *God,*" he says softly. She wants to hold him again, wishes there were words that she could say.

"But that's not all, Lucrece. If you can hear what he's saying, then you *know* that's not all."

"Yes," she says, because she can understand the bird voice, its shrill, uneasy mind, the way she understood the thoughts that Benny never spoke to her out loud, the way she knew when his dreams were troubled.

"You're supposed to know who killed him," Jared says to the crow, spitting out the words like a bad taste in his mouth. "That's the way it's supposed to work. You drag me back here and *show* me. But you *can't* show me the killer, can you? You can't show me shit!"

Lucrece risks one hand on Jared's right shoulder and he turns on her, the glare meant for the bird. She thinks maybe she can see hell locked up in those eyes, the pupils dropping straight down forever.

"I'm right, aren't I? It doesn't know, any more than the goddamn police knew."

"The crow is doing what it was made to do, Jared. Whatever else is going on here, it's just a crow and there are limits to its . . ." and she pauses, knowing how she must sound to Jared, pragmatic, irreligious Jared, that this is all just a bunch of crazy voodoo nonsense to him.

"There are limits to its powers. There's something else going on here, something that's getting in the way, that we have to figure out and get around."

Jared buries his face in his hands and she thinks that he's about to cry again. That would be better than the anger, something she understands more intimately. She's spent all her life since her brother's death in the company of sorrow. She has become sorrow's most cherished concubine.

"I don't understand any of this," Jared says.

"And you mustn't waste your time trying," Lucrece replies, hoping that there's at least a little solace in her voice now. "You can get lost if you spend too much time trying to understand how this could be. You have to simply accept that it is."

"How do you know these things, Lucrece? Can you just tell me that? Can you tell me why *you* understand what this fucking bird is saying?"

She pauses again, knowing the answer but afraid to turn it loose, faced suddenly with her own fears and self-doubts. Knowing that her response will bind her to this mystery with knots that no fingers, mortal or undead, can ever unravel.

"Yeah," she answers at last as she takes her hand from Jared's shoulder and begins unbuttoning the front of her dress. "I think that maybe I can." She pulls the dress down past her thin white shoulders, revealing the severe black silk corset underneath. Lucrece turns around so that Jared can see her bare shoulders.

"I had it done about a month after Benny's funeral," she says. "I hoped that the pain and the healing would help *me* begin to heal some . . ." Her voice trails off as she feels his eyes on her back, tracing the intricate pattern of scars there. The picture the scalpel drew into her skin, the cutting that she meant to be a raven, after Jared's photograph. But the artist only had a picture of a crow to work from and didn't confess that he'd cheated on the design until later, after the gauze and surgical tape were hiding his fresh, weeping work.

"I think that's why I can hear your crow, Jared."

"Oh, Lucrece," he says, and his fingertips graze the crisscross of puckered white tissue.

"It helped a little," she says, and pulls her dress back up, hiding the cutting. "Maybe it's going to help a lot now. Maybe it's going to let me help you."

Jared rises and stands above the crow, and the bird cranes its neck to look up into his face.

"If you brought me back here for nothing, you bastard," he says, "I swear that you'll die very, very slowly."

"I think it's time to cut the macho bullshit, Jared," Lucrece says, her fingers working the last of the dress's pearlescent buttons. "And if you care, it's a she."

Jared glares down at her, uncomprehending, and the crow caws softly.

"The *crow,*" Lucrece says. "It's a *she.*"

Jared rolls his eyes. "Pardon me," he says.

The crow tells them that there's a little time then, and so Jared rests awhile in Lucrece's arms and listens to the rain, coming down harder now, playing the roof of the building like a perfect and soothing percussive instrument. He closes his dead man's eyes and tries to pretend that these are Benny's arms around him instead of Benny's twin's. She strokes his hair with her long fingers, fingers like Benny's grown softer and more hesitant, but close enough for the game in his head.

"I want to get this awful jacket off you," she says. "And this shirt." He is still in his funeral clothes, slit up the back for the morticians' convenience. "And then I'll find something else for you to wear."

Jared Poe met Benjamin DuBois at a gallery in the Warehouse District, a ramshackle barn of corrugated steel, punky masonry, and bare concrete floors set so close to the river that the air smelled like mud and rotting fish. It was a performance thing and he'd only gone because it was a friend's boyfriend's show and he'd run dry of excuses. With very few exceptions he'd always found performance art either a horrific bore or simply horrible, a last, pretentious refuge for talentless wanna-bes desperately trying to gouge a niche for themselves. Most of the time he'd end up feeling embarrassed for the performer, embarrassed for the audience trying to understand whatever foolishness was being acted out for them, and so uncomfortable that he'd sneak out halfway through the show.

And the scene that night was no exception, certainly not the worst thing he'd ever seen, but bad enough to make him wish he'd just made up a story about car trouble or leaky plumbing and stayed home. The artist stood on a small stage in the center of the warehouse, wearing nothing but an old alligator hide and a pair of expensive-looking loafers, reading aloud from the *Wall Street Journal.* Fortunately there was a bar and Jared stayed close to it, downing shots of tequila and trying to keep a straight face. But the mask became increasingly difficult to manage as the guy in the alligator skin droned on and on and the Cuervo worked its way through Jared's bloodstream to his brain.

In an effort to distract himself he began eavesdropping on a couple standing a few feet away from him, near the edge of the crowd. Jared had noticed right away how much they resembled one another, and the woman was so tall he thought maybe she was really a drag queen. They were speaking loudly to each other, almost shouting in order to be heard over the stock quotes being read through the microphone onstage, the nasal voice booming from speakers rigged high along the rusty walls. Both were dressed in impeccably tailored leather and latex Victorian costumes, their skin as white as chalk and their hair like black satin. To Jared they looked like some fetish freak's vision of Jonathan and Mina

Harker, an unlikely juxtaposition of the prim and perverse, but they wore that vision well no matter how unlikely it might be.

"This is surely hell," the woman said. Her voice seemed to confirm Jared's suspicions about her gender.

"No, no," the boy said, leaning close to her ear and still having to shout. "This is a lot worse than *that.*"

The boy wasn't exactly Jared's type. He'd always gone for the well-muscled submissives, the hard but yielding bodies that could take whatever loving tortures he might happen to devise. He'd always found the goth end of the SM and fetish scene a little tedious, too much window dressing for his particular tastes. But *this* boy was something different, something so unexpected with his high, sharp cheekbones and hooded eyes, and Jared was taken completely off guard by the stirring in his jeans. He asked the bartender for another shot of tequila and took a cautious step closer to the pair.

"Hell has better acoustics," the boy was shouting.

"And something worth hearing," the woman shouted back.

"Not impressed, I take it," Jared said, just loud enough to be heard, and they both turned and regarded him skeptically from kohl-smeared eyes.

"Oh, don't tell me," the boy said, one index finger held up for emphasis. "He's this poor, misguided fuck's lover and we've offended his feelings."

"Or maybe he's just a critic for some rag," his companion said. Jared realized, now that they were facing him, that the pair were identical twins.

"No," Jared said, smiling, playing the good sport to their jibes. "He's just the poor schmuck who didn't have any place better to be tonight, that's all."

"Oh," the boy said. "That's better. Then we don't have to make polite over this drivel." Jared shook his head, took a sip of his tequila before responding.

"Hardly. Can either of you make heads or tails of what's going on up there?"

The boy glanced back toward the gator-clad nude and shrugged. "Well," he said after a moment, "we're of two minds on the subject. *I* think it's all an unfortunate misunderstanding. The real artist was held up in traffic or mugged or something, and *this* guy is just some unmedicated street person who conveniently wandered in. The similarity between his delusion and this crowd's expectation was so profound that no one's noticed yet. My *sister,* on the other hand, thinks it's a brilliant metaphor for the creeping gentrification of the—"

His sister interrupted him with a sock in the arm, not hard, but he made wounded sounds and rubbed at his shoulder. "Do you have a name?" she asked, holding out her gloved hand to Jared as if she expected him to bow and kiss it.

"Oh, yeah. Sorry." He shook the extended hand. Her leather glove was as supple as silk and her grip through it was firm but not mannish. "Jared. Jared Poe. I'm a photographer."

"Jared *Poe*? P-O-E Poe?" the boy said, still rubbing his shoulder and glaring sidelong at his sister. "That's a joke, right?"

"Nope," Jared replied, finishing his drink. "I'm afraid it's not. That's my real name."

The sister took a dramatic step back, spread her arms wide, and cleared her throat loudly before she began to speak, her voice broad and deeper than the unfortunate voice blaring through the speakers. She held her head high as she spoke, her eyes focused somewhere past the dust and rafters overhead, and delivered each syllable with stage-perfect diction.

" 'But the Raven, sitting lonely on that placid bust, spoke only
That one word, as if his soul in that one word he did outpour.
Nothing farther then he uttered: not a feather then he fluttered—
Till I scarcely more than muttered: "Other friends have flown before—" ' "

Then a hippie standing behind them turned and shushed her. The boy rolled his eyes and muttered, "Oh, *please,* like you might miss last week's pork futures." The hippie scowled and turned back toward the performer.

"That was actually very good," Jared said, and the boy regarded his sister with eyes that were somehow jealous and proud at the same time.

"Lucrece is such a terrible show-off," he said.

"It's better than listening to that idiot," Jared said, using his empty shot glass to point in the direction of the Wall Street gator boy.

Lucrece sighed and offered Jared half a smile. "Well, that's a pretty sorry excuse for a compliment, mister, but thanks anyway." And then the hippie hissed, *"Shhhhhhhhh,"* louder than before, and her brother stuck his tongue out in response.

"If you *people* aren't interested in the show, maybe you should go elsewhere," the hippie said.

"He has a point," Jared told the twins. "If I have to listen to any more of this crap I think I'll puke."

The hippie shook his head as he turned back toward the little stage. "I honestly pity people like you, who aren't open to new experiences."

"Oh, Jesus in a Ford pickup," Lucrece said, and she took her brother's hand and Jared's and towed them both through the haze of cigarette smoke and the whispering press of bodies toward the loading ramp that served as the gallery's only visible entrance and exit, leading them out into the night.

Outside, the sultry air felt almost cool after the crowded warehouse. They walked northwest along Market Street, away from the river and its fishy miasma. When Jared suggested that maybe this part of town wasn't the best spot for a stroll after dark, Lucrece laughed a soft, low laugh and asked him which part of New Orleans was. The brother, whose name he still had not learned, produced a small silver flask of brandy they shared as they turned off Market and wandered between other derelict buildings, crumbling red brick walls and tin roofs separated from one another by streets neglected so long they were more pothole than asphalt.

The heady combination of the booze and the company of the twins distracted and disoriented Jared. Soon he was uncertain precisely where they were. Nothing looked familiar, or rather everything looked *vaguely* familiar—some corner of the warehouse district that hadn't yet been made fit for yuppie habitation but had for the time being been left as a decaying signpost back to an era when the area had bustled with the noise and activity of forgotten industry.

"Where the hell are we going?" Jared asked finally, and he could hear the slur that had crept into his voice somewhere between the tequila and the brandy.

"What difference does it make?" the boy said, but Lucrece answered, "Our place. It isn't far now."

They came to the mouth of a narrow alley half barricaded with the husks of two burned-out cars and an abandoned refrigerator. As the twins slipped ahead of him, forsaking the weak cover of the streetlights, Jared paused, leaned against the hood of one of the old cars, and tried uselessly to clear his head. He'd never been far enough north to have walked on thin ice, but he thought it must feel something like this, uncertain steps taking him farther and farther from safe and solid ground. The boy turned and looked back at him from the shadows, the darker slice between high, dark walls. "Are you coming or not, Jared? It's not safe out here alone, you know?" He sounded impatient and amused, distantly petulant, and Jared realized that his dick was hard again. Hard for this pretty, taunting goth boy dressed up like some William Gibson version of 1890s London, and probably hard for his haughty bitch twin as well.

"Really, Jared. Benny's right. There are bad people out here." The voice came from somewhere close behind him. He spun around too fast, almost lost his balance, almost fell face first onto the broken pavement.

Lucrece was standing by the old refrigerator, although he could have sworn she'd been the one in the lead, had already disappeared down the alley in front of her brother.

"How . . . how'd you do that?"

She just smiled at him.

"Like I said before," Benny sneered from the alleyway, "she likes to show off. She read a book once, that's all."

Lucrece stepped past Jared, still smiling her secret smile, taking his hand again, and the three of them walked together into the gloom.

Jared's eyes are closed and he hasn't spoken for almost an hour. He is letting the memories settle down over him like silt on a muddy river bottom, like the rain falling out on Ursulines, falling on the roof and windows of the apartment. Lucrece has found a silver comb and is combing his long hair out across her lap.

"You have to tell me everything you know," he says at last, and the teeth of the comb hesitate, lingering in their gentle progress across his scalp.

"It's not much," she says after a moment. "I expect it's not much more than you know already, Jared."

He opens his eyes and watches Lucrece's face carefully as he speaks. "Harrod knew that I wasn't the killer, didn't he?"

She flinches when he says the DA's name, summoning the image of the gray-eyed prosecutor, John Henry Harrod, as shrewd as a butcher's cleaver or the grin of a hungry cartoon wolf.

"I honestly don't think Harrod really gave a fuck one way or the other. He needed a murderer and you were convenient. Nothing personal . . ."

"Bullshit," Jared says, closing his eyes again, knowing the acid tone of his voice hurts her and not wanting to see more pain on her face, knowing he's a coward to look away and looking away anyway. "Harrod was taking care of two birds with one stone. Get rid of the faggot artist and make all the faggot voters happy at the same time."

Lucrece begins combing his hair again, long smooth strokes as if she might still have a chance to calm him, to bring some stingy bit of comfort. Very softly she says, "The killings haven't stopped, Jared."

Now he does open his eyes again, stares speechlessly up at her, unbelieving, as she continues.

"The television and newspapers aren't making much of it. They're trying to play it all down, I think, calling it a copycat killer. No one wants to think there could have been a mistake, especially since . . ." She pauses, turns her head toward the bed and the crow still perched on the footboard.

Jared finishes for her.

"*Especially* since the man they already put in prison recently got three inches of sharpened spoon shoved in his guts and is buried in Lafayette Cemetery."

"Yeah," she whispers, and the black bird caws.

The twins lived on the entire upper floor of one of the two buildings that flanked the alley. Jared looked back the way they'd come, the dirty, dim light at the far end of the alley, while Lucrece unlocked a steel fire door with an old-fashioned brass key from her purse. Beyond that there was a staircase hardly wide enough for Jared to climb without having to turn sideways. There was another steel door at the top, this one with a small peephole and three deadbolts. Lucrece selected more keys, slid back the bolts one after another, and the door made a dry gritty sound as it swung slowly open. She felt along the wall just inside and flipped a switch, turning on a string of naked incandescent bulbs strung up high among the rafters.

"Jesus," Jared muttered as he followed Benny across the threshold. "Wow. You guys don't do things halfway, do you?"

"What would be the point in that?" Benny asked, but Jared wasn't listening to him, entirely too amazed at what they'd made of the second story of the old warehouse—the refuse of a city turned into impossible elegance, garbage molded into the most unlikely opulence. There were pieces of junked cars and unidentifiable machinery welded into tables and cabinets, semitranslucent curtains of expertly pleated plastic hung for room dividers, broken glass mortared into the walls, glittering like jewels. The only piece of furniture in the place that seemed to be serving its originally intended purpose was a huge canopy bed near the center of the loft. Everything was lacquered in shades of black and red that glimmered wetly under the lights.

"Have a seat," Benny said, pointing Jared toward an armchair near the bed. "We'll get drinks." Jared obeyed, too drunk and stunned to do much else. The chair was upholstered in a deep crimson crushed velvet and its spindly frame had been fashioned from human-looking bones held together with epoxy and metal rods.

"Are these real?" he called after the twins, who were standing on the other side of one of the polyurethane curtains, indistinct, murky figures appearing to move beneath cold and oily waters.

There was the sound of ice cubes and Lucrece called out, "Yes, of course they're *real*." Jared stared down at the chair's armrests—long bones that ended in skeletal fists, one turned upward toward the ceiling, the other grasping for the bare floorboards.

"Real bones are a lot easier to come by in this city than artificial ones," Benny added.

"You know," said Jared, talking now because his voice was better company than his imagination, "there are people who would think this was some pretty sick shit."

Benny slipped through an invisible slit in the plastic, a drink in each hand. "And what about you, Jared *Poe*? Are *you* one of those people? Do *you* think this is some *pretty sick shit*?"

Jared accepted his drink, straight whisky over ice, sipped at it tentatively. Benny sighed loudly and shook his head. "Go ahead, silly. It's not laced, and we didn't bring you here to poison you."

The amber whisky burned pleasantly going down, a brand he didn't recognize, probably something more expensive than the stuff he was used to drinking.

"It is very, very impressive," he said, taking another swallow from his glass.

"Which?" asked Lucrece, who'd come up silently behind him. "Our apartment or your drink?"

"Whichever," Jared answered.

"We made most of it ourselves," Benny said, sitting down on the corner of the big bed closest to Jared. "Oh, but not this, of course," and he patted the bed. "We found this in an antique store on Magazine Street. Saved up for months, but it's been worth it . . ." He let that last thought trail off ambiguously.

Lucrece sat down beside her brother and sipped from her own glass. Again Jared was struck by their resemblance, male and female reflections of the same exquisite face.

"So, Mr. Jared Poe, what is it you photograph?" Lucrece asked as she slipped an arm around her brother's waist.

"Well," he said, watching their every move. His erection was beginning to become uncomfortable, and he shifted in his chair of bones and velvet. "That depends on whether I'm trying to pay the bills or not. If the rent's due, it's mostly weddings and babies . . ."

Benny made a disgusted face and rolled his eyes.

"And the rest of the time?" Lucrece prompted.

"The rest of the time, well . . . I've been putting together a portfolio of nineteenth-century cemetery sculpture and architecture." Jared paused, then went on almost reluctantly, an ashamed or guilty admission: "And sometimes the people I find hanging out in cemeteries."

"Ah," Benny said, his eyes suddenly brightening, eager. "See, Lucrece? I knew he wasn't just another loser art fag."

"Yeah, well, I wouldn't be quite so sure," Jared said, frowning. "You ever noticed how *many* people there are out there taking pictures of the local bone orchards?"

"The *question,*" Lucrece said, speaking not to Jared but to her brother, "is whether or not he's any good."

"Whether or not his *heart* is in it," Benny added. He finished his drink, set the glass on the floor at his feet. The ice cubes clinked faintly against each other.

"What do you mean?" Jared asked, and Lucrece shrugged.

"Anyone can point a camera and click, Jared," she said. "Fucking Yankee tourists on the sight-seeing buses do *that* every goddamn day of the week. The question is, whether or not you genuinely *understand—*"

"—the dead," Benny said, completing her thought. "After all, it's *their* houses that you're putting down on celluloid and paper, right?"

Jared watched Benny's eyes a second before answering, feeling suddenly lost and stupid, in too deep or maybe even completely out of his element. Benny's eyes were the same guarded, brilliant green as his sister's, the green of uncut emeralds.

"Right," he said at last, only half remembering the question. "Right."

"Because it isn't enough to *appreciate* the dead," Benny said. "To simply steal their likenesses and call it art. There has to be an—"

"—understanding," Lucrece said, and Jared realized their habit of finishing each other's sentences was beginning to give him the creeps.

"Any genuine aesthetic of the dead requires, no, *demands* that the artist treat them as something more than mere objects. They must be seen and portrayed as dynamic opposites of life, not empty vessels devoid of anything but the power to make us nervous, afraid of our own mortality."

"And he calls *me* the show-off," Lucrece said, distractedly stirring the ice cubes in her drink with one finger.

Jared was busy trying to process what Benny had said through the alcohol clouding his mind. He shook his head.

"No, I mean, that's really, um, articulate . . ."

"Yeah, ain't it amazing that someone can be this pretty *and* smart too?" Lucrece purred, smiling as she touched an index finger, wet with whisky and water, to her brother's lips.

"But surely we didn't bring him all this way just to talk shop, did we?" Benny asked her, and she shook her head and kissed him lightly on the cheek.

Jared's face felt suddenly hot, flushed, and he knew that he was blushing, and that the twins could probably see that he was blushing.

"That would be terribly, *terribly* rude," Lucrece said, and Benny turned his head, kissing her full on the lips now. The bulge in Jared's jeans responded as if an invisible line had been attached to the end of his penis and someone had just tugged at it sharply.

"I don't know," Benny said, pulling away. The stark light caught in a thin string of saliva linking their lips. "Maybe he's not up to it. Maybe we're wrong and he *is* just another poseur . . ."

Jared swallowed hard, his mouth and throat suddenly very dry. He wished his glass wasn't empty but wasn't about to break this moment by asking for a refill. He squirmed nervously in his strange chair.

"Or *maybe* he's not into boys," Lucrece said, her voice full of mocking regret, and her tongue flicked across Benny's lower lip. And then Benny whispered slyly, mischievously, "Or *maybe* he's not into girls."

"Bingo," Jared said. He'd set his glass in the upturned skeleton hand and covered his lap with his hands, embarrassed at his own embarrassment.

Lucrece sat back, scooting a couple of feet away from her brother, her face an almost comic mask of exaggerated rejection and disappointment. Benny let her go, but his eyes followed her retreat longingly. "Not even girls who used to be boys?" he said.

Jared caught the slicing, flinty edge of the question before Lucrece slapped her brother. It wasn't a playful slap, and the sound of her hand against his skin was very loud in the apartment.

"Bitch," she hissed, and Jared thought there was the faintest, calculated hint of a smile at the corners of her mouth.

"Touché," Benny said.

There are strings everywhere, Jared thought, *not just on the end of my dick.* This scene was something the pair had rehearsed over and over again, he realized, perfected in privacy and practice.

"Never mind," Lucrece said, getting up off the bed. "Fortunately I like to watch. You don't mind if I *watch,* do you, Mr. Poe?"

"Then you are identical twins?" he asked, wondering if perhaps that was pushing her too far, if maybe this spot really was too sensitive for Lucrece and he was blowing his chance at Benny. But she just shrugged, tossed her hair to one side, and said, "Once upon a time."

"Sometimes," Benny said, removing his leather overcoat, "I think my sister will never forgive me for not making the transition with her. For ruining the set, as it were."

"You never had the balls," Lucrece said, and now she *was* smiling, a careful, secret smile that said there was so much here that Jared could never even hope to understand half of it. "You never had the fucking balls."

As Benny began unbuttoning his vest Jared got up from the bone chair, moving slowly, as if he was being scored on every action and reaction, and joined the male twin on the bed. Lucrece left them alone briefly to pour herself another drink, then returned with the bottle and took Jared's place in the chair.

Jared rubs at his temples, wishing it were anything as simple as pain throbbing there. He stands above the crow and the bird looks back up at him with mindful, eager eyes. Lucrece is still sitting on the bedroom floor behind them, holding the silver comb.

"Where am I supposed to start?" he asks, the question posed to the bird or Lucrece, to himself or all three.

"I'm not sure," Lucrece says. When Jared turns around, she's holding strands of his dark hair between her fingers, staring at them. *The way someone might clutch a holy relic,* he thinks, and the thought makes him feel sick to his stomach. *What am I to her? What does she think I've become?*

"I think you're supposed to find Benny's killer and stop him. I think that's what you've been brought back for."

"And Harrod and the cops and that fucking judge, what about them? Aren't they part of this as well?"

Lucrece's eyes reluctantly release their hold on the precious strands of his hair, refocus on Jared standing at the foot of the bed. The bed he shared with her twin brother. The bed Jared first saw in that warehouse apartment so long ago. Lucrece's eyes look as hard and old as New Orleans itself, as wet as the night.

"I'm not sure, Jared. Maybe. But maybe not. The *crow's* supposed to know what happens next, and for some reason it doesn't."

"They set me up," he says. The bird looks away, pecks at the dark wood of the headboard.

"I think we have to be *sure,* Jared, before you do anything that can't be undone."

"Did the fucking cops bother to be *sure* before they arrested me? Before they told the goddamn papers *I* killed Benny? How sure were *they,* Lucrece?" He hears the sour, jagged tone wrapped around his words, the anger cranking itself up a notch.

"I don't think that you can punish everyone, Jared. A lot of people did a lot of stupid things. I think that you have to concentrate on what started it all."

"But you don't know that, do you?"

She sighs, a broken sound like a death rattle.

"No, Jared. I don't know that."

Jared turns away from her, away from the useless bird, and there's his reflection watching him from the mirror above Benny's dressing table—a dead man's pallid excuse for a doppelgänger, its skin like cold ashes. But there *is* fire there as well, bright vengeful coals in those dead and living eyes.

"Please, Jared. Just give me a chance to find out what I can. There are people I know who might be able to help."

Jared steps closer to the mirror and his reflection takes a step to keep up with him. There's a white Mardi Gras mask hanging limply from one corner of the glass, dangling by its elastic strap. Jared picks it up, stares into the vicious, clownish grin molded into the creased and wrinkled leather. The mask has a smile no human face could ever manage, its thin scarlet lips curled back upon themselves, a black smear across the empty eye sockets like the face of a rabid raccoon. Jared bought the mask for Benny from a street vendor, their last Mardi Gras together, and he remembers Benny's emerald eyes glaring at him through those slits.

"Yeah," Jared tells Lucrece as he slips the jester mask over his own, crueler face. "You talk to your witchy friends and see what they say. I'm not going to hold my breath, but you go ask."

Now his eyes fill the space meant for Benny's, his own eyes like last night's fire that only needs to be stirred, that only needs a little tinder to become an inferno again. There's nothing else in his face any more alive than this mask, nothing else but his eyes worth showing, so he leaves it on.

"In the meantime, I have some questions of my own, Lucrece. And I know the people who have the answers."

4

The gutterpunks clustered around the gates of Jackson Square talk quietly among themselves, as secretive as any cabalistic order. The rain has slacked off a little, enough for them to slip out from under the eaves and doorways and huddle by the tall iron gates. They've come together in the lee of the cathedral, this evening no different than any other, waiting for the commencement of another night's petty dramas and business transactions. Some of them are homeless and some of them only pretend to be because they envy the independence and self-confidence, the freedom, of those who are.

"But, I mean, you know, you don't think he's some kind of pervert?" the tall boy in the long black dress, the boy who calls himself Michele, asks the others, glancing back over his shoulder at the man lingering outside the Presbytere.

"Jesus, will you please get some kind of fucking clue?" The girl who answered him lights a cigarette, exhales expertly through her pierced nostrils, and squints past the smoke at the man standing very still in front of the museum. "No offense, Mikey, but have you bothered to look in a mirror lately?"

"You ain't exactly David fuckin' Duke yourself," one of the boys says, and they all laugh. "You ain't, like, Jesse Helms's fuckin' dream girl yourself."

And Michele glances again over his lean shoulder at the man in the expensive raincoat. "I bet you he's got money," he says. "I bet you he's got a lot of money."

"You gonna blow him or you gonna roll him?" someone says and they all laugh.

"Beggars can't be choosers, Mikey," the girl taunts, then she goes back to reading a ratty paperback novel she's been carrying around for days. There's only one enticing word, *Silk,* printed across the cover, and the face of a white-haired girl staring out through a dream catcher.

Michele knows they're all still waiting for him to prove himself, to show that he's really one of them, not the new kid anymore. This is his first week on the streets, but already he likes it better than his old life in Shreveport. At least this way he gets paid and has some say about the men he has sex with instead of waiting terrified for his stepfather to stumble into his room every night, drunk and so loud there's no way his mother *couldn't* hear. But never a word from her, never so much as a question, her denial as thick as the Max Factor she caked on her face every morning to try to look twenty-five instead of fifty, as thick as the gray shroud of suburban despair he escaped with a stolen credit card and a bus ticket south.

"Gotta learn to take it like a man," his stepfather liked to tell him if he dared to cry. "It ain't no different than the way the world's gonna treat you. It ain't no different than the goddamn world."

"Watch and learn, Robin," he tells the girl. They all laugh again as he steps away from the crowd, feeling immediately more vulnerable, separated from the pack, on his own. The man in the raincoat notices him and smiles tentatively, drops the cigarette he's been smoking to the cobblestones and crushes it out under the heel of one of his loafers.

It can't be more than ten yards from the gates to the spot where the man is waiting for him in front of the Presbytere, a short obstacle course of tourists and street performers, but the walk feels at least three or four times that far. Michele is sweating by the time he's standing beside the man.

"You're very pretty," the man says, and Michele smiles cautiously for him. "But I'll bet you hear that a lot, don't you?"

You think I'm stupid? the bold, streetwise voice in his head asks the man, the big, brave voice he's spent the past five days cultivating. *You think I don't know you tell that shit to every boy you want to sell you a little head?* But he bats his eyes, just once, shy like the brainless girls at his old school preening for the jocks. "No. No one ever tells me that."

"Well," the man says, "it sure as shit is a cruel old world, then, ain't it?" and in that instant the man sounds so much like Michele's stepfather that he almost backs out, puts his tail between his legs and runs back to the safety of the others, still watching him from the gates.

"Yeah," he says instead. "Yeah, mister, sometimes it sure is."

Robin watches from her seat on the stone steps outside the square as the man leads Michele into the narrow alley between the Presbytere and the cathedral. Part of her feels sorry for him, the same part that feels sorry for them all. *The weak part,* she reminds herself, and so she keeps her thoughts to herself and concentrates on the rap music thump-thumping from the boom box at her feet.

When they're done the man gives Michele a twenty and grunts as he wrestles his zipper closed again. Michele wants to spit, wants to get the flat, briny taste of the man out of his mouth. *Nice girls swallow,* he thinks. He doesn't remember where he heard that but thinks maybe he saw it on a T-shirt once. He's still on his knees, and the old cobblestones of Père Antoine Alley reek of rotting garbage and magnolia leaves and the piss of all the drunken tourists who've ducked into the alley to relieve themselves. The stones hurt his knees and he gets up slowly, checking to be sure he hasn't run his hose.

"I meant what I said," the man says. "I mean about you being pretty and all. You shouldn't even be out here on the streets. You should get yourself a decent job doing drag or something, you know? These streets will mess you up, kiddo. No one stays as pretty as you if they stay out here very long."

Then Michele is alone, watching as the man walks quickly away from him toward the bright lights and noise and forgiving anonymity of Royal Street. Michele feels something cold against his face and he realizes that the rain's started again, just a light sprinkle so far, but there's thunder too and he knows it'll probably be pouring again in a few minutes. He looks down at the twenty in his hand, the crumpled wad of paper and green ink, and he thinks if he only had one of these for every time he went down on his fucking stepfather, shit, he'd have an apartment in the Pontalba.

He's heading back to the square, eager to show Robin and the others that he didn't wuss out, even more eager to be out of the stinking alley. Then the thunder rattles the sky above him again, rumbles like the growl of something vast and predatory, and Michele decides that he's at least earned a cup of coffee and ten minutes or so out of the weather. Just a short break before the next john, he tells himself. Maybe he'll buy Robin a cup too.

"Does the thunder scare you, Michele?" someone says, someone standing somewhere behind him. He spins around, stares into the shadows crowding the empty length of Père Antoine.

"No," he answers the darkness, and his voice sounds very small and vulnerable, not the big street-voice at all.

"Not even a little?" the voice asks, insistent and unconvinced. "All that power above your head, like the sound of the sky breaking. That doesn't frighten you?"

"It's only thunder," Michele says, straining to see the speaker, and then the thunder comes again: closer, more immediate, as if it's heard what he said, his casual denial of its authority, and is angry.

"Then you're a very brave little . . . girl," the voice replies, and the speaker steps out where Michele can see him. Another tall man, wearing a black windbreaker, his hair soaked, hanging across his face in stringy wet hanks. Michele cannot see the man's eyes.

"Do you *want* something, mister?" Michele asks. This time at least he almost *sounds* like he has his shit together, almost sounds the way he imagines Robin would. Never mind that this guy is starting to seriously creep him out, that the urge to just turn and run back to the safety of the gates of Jackson Square and the company of the others is so strong it's almost impossible to stand his ground.

"I want . . . ." the man begins, but his voice is lost in another clap of thunder.

"What?" Michele takes one step backward, wishing now that someone would come along, a bum or a haunted-streets tour or even a fucking cop, *anyone* to interrupt, to break the spell and get him moving.

"I want to talk to you, Michele," the man says. "There are things happening tonight that you and I must talk about."

"I don't have *time* for talk," Michele replies. "I have to make a living." When he turns around, the rain-dulled lights of the square seem so close. Just a few steps and he'll be among people again, back out in the open.

"You'll be paid," the man says behind him, "if that's what you're worried about. You'll get what you've got coming to you. For your time."

"No thanks, mister," Michele says. "I think you've got the wrong person." Now he actually is walking back toward the others, and he's amazed at how much brighter the lights are after only a single step away from the man's oily, vacant voice. He's already beginning to feel a little silly at letting himself get spooked so easily, knows how Robin would rag him if she found out. *You gotta get a thicker skin, girl,* he hears her say, *if you're gonna be turning tricks in the Quarter. There's a whole lotta weirdos out there . . .*

There is the deliberate sound of footsteps behind him then, and a sudden pricking pain at the base of his neck. *I've been stung,* he thinks, *Jesus, I've been fucking stung,* remembering once when he blundered into a nest of angry red wasps behind his grandmother's garage. And then the light is far away again, farther than he ever thought it could be. In another moment it is gone and he's alone in a cold and perfect darkness.

* * *

The man who wears the names of rivers knows that he is no longer like other men, that some part of his fearful work has changed him forever and he can never return to the simple, painless life he lived before. Sometimes the knowing of this hurts him so badly that he sits alone in a dark room for hours and cries for the loss of himself. It is a terrible thing, he knows, to have had so little say in the course of his own life, to have had so many things decided for him before he was even born. To be a soldier in an army of light and blood so secret that there can never be any acknowledgment of his achievements or failures, not even the most fleeting contact with his brothers and sisters in arms, for fear of discovery.

The invaders are everywhere, and Their agents are everywhere. A moment of weakness, one slip, could mean much, much more than the mere loss of his life. He has dreams where someone (never, never him) has been weak, one of the other nameless, faceless soldiers working secretly in the corrupting cities of the world. In the dreams They walk the streets without fear, spreading the androgyne contagion, and the sky burns with the roaring engines of Their warships.

He often wakes from these dreams screaming, curled in his sweat-soaked bed, the choking smells of diesel and burning flesh still hot in his nostrils. But he does not resist the dreams; he understands that they are an integral part of his vision, part of what keeps him strong and certain and pure. He writes down the smallest details of each dream, everything that he can recall, in special black notebooks he keeps in a windowless room in the center of his house.

For almost a week now there has been a new dream, and he knows that it means there is even less time than he'd thought. He has powerful black wings in this dream, the wings of a fierce avenging angel, and they carry him high above the blazing, dying city of New Orleans. The streets below are filled with fire and lakes of blood that burn like gasoline. The writhing bodies of the creatures in Their truest form, Their primary aspect, cling to every wall and rooftop, Their smooth and sexless bodies white as bone beneath the night sky, the wet red holes between Their legs like the beaked jaws of squid or octopi. In the dream Their voices have joined together into a single, hideous wail and Their black and swollen eyes watch jealously as he passes above Them. The end of the dream is always the same, the part where the man with river names looks over his shoulder at the shadow of the crow falling swiftly across the land.

Michele wakes up in a place that smells like disinfectant and mold and latex. He's lying on a bare metal table and there's insane light, white and blinding light that stabs at his eyes and makes his head hurt even worse. He's dizzy and sick and only wants to go back to sleep. Michele closes his eyes, shuts out the hateful light, and then the voice says, "It's time for us to talk, *Michael.*"

He's trying to think of what to say, something nasty and appropriate—something Robin would say—when he hears a brittle, snapping noise. Suddenly his sinuses are filled with the scorching reek of ammonia. He coughs and gags as the last merciful shreds of oblivion are driven from his reach and there's nothing left but the light hanging above him and the cold against his bare skin. And the voice.

"There," it says. "You can understand me now?"

Michele tries to answer but his mouth and throat are too dry, not a drop of spit, and his tongue feels two times too big to be of any use.

"Just nod if you understand what I'm saying," the voice says, so Michele nods. He has realized that his hands and feet are tied firmly to the table with wide leather straps. Then there is a glass of lukewarm water being pressed to his lips and he swallows a mouthful.

"The sedative does that sometimes. It'll pass soon and you'll be able to speak."

The glass returns and this time Michele takes a deeper drink, notices that the water tastes faintly of chlorine, like swimming pool water. But it feels like heaven going down his aching throat. As soon as the glass is removed he tries to speak, but there's only an unintelligible rasping wheeze where the words should be.

"Like I said, it'll pass," the voice of the man tells him. He can dimly make out the man's form now, glimpsed through the glare of the light and his tearing eyes.

"Where am I?" Michele croaks. The form moves back a little, out of the glare just enough that its face begins to solidify, its features begin swimming slowly into focus. A thin and haggard face, a face of a very tired young man who looks years older than his age. Michele blinks again, then sees the man's eyes, flat blue-gray eyes like a stormy January afternoon sky, eyes at once cold and filled with the threat of violence.

"I ask the questions," the man says matter-of-factly.

"Is this . . ." Michele begins, but he has to swallow, his tongue working up a few precious drops of spit to wet his throat before he can continue. "Is it a hospital?"

"No," the man says. "But I did say that *I'll* be asking the questions, didn't I? You should save your strength. You're going to need it, Michael."

"Don't . . . don't call me that." Michele closes his eyes, remembering the face from Père Antoine, the rain-bedraggled hair and the sting in his neck, fear rushing up to overwhelm the confusion. It doesn't matter where he is, he knows. He's somewhere bad, somewhere *very* bad he shouldn't be.

"It *is* your name, isn't it? It is the name your parents gave to you." Now there is a small black flashlight in the man's hands. He uses it to examine Michele's eyes, just like a doctor, but Michele knows now the man isn't a doctor.

"It's not . . . my name anymore," Michele tells him, and closes his burning eyes when the probing fingers and black flashlight are taken away. "My name's Michele."

"But that's a girl's name, and you're not a girl, are you?" the man asks.

Michele ignores the question, as he has so many times in the past. "What are you going to do to me?" he asks. The man sighs loudly, and Michele feels the sudden gust of the man's breath blow cool across his bare chest.

"I am going to ask you questions."

"Is that all you're going to do? Ask me some questions?"

The man doesn't answer this time. Michele pulls cautiously at the straps at his wrists and ankles. The hard leather cuts into his skin like the blade of a dull knife.

"There's no point in trying to get loose. I'd just tie you down again. You must know that."

Michele stops wrestling with the restraints and moves his tongue across chapped lips that taste like sweat and lipstick. He swallows again, careful to be sure he has control of his voice before he speaks.

"If you weren't afraid of me," he says, "you wouldn't have tied me up in the first place." In response the man makes a sudden, dry sound that's part cough and part angry huff, then slaps Michele hard. Michele's head snaps sideways, smacks roughly against the cold metal tabletop. His mouth fills with the taste of his own blood.

"I have to take precautions, *boy,* but don't underestimate me, and don't overestimate yourself." The man pauses and Michele can tell that he's panting now, his breath coming out fast and hard, furious staccato gasps and wheezes like a winded animal or a frustrated old woman.

"If I thought you posed *any* immediate threat to me or to anyone else I'd have killed you in that fucking filthy alley. There could have been cyanide in that needle, if that's what I'd wanted, just as easy. *Easier.*"

The man pauses, gasps and wheezes his exasperation, and because Michele doesn't know anything else to say, because he's already pretty sure there's no way he's going to walk away from this, he says, "You're crazy, aren't you?"

Growling, the man lunges into the glare of the surgical light so that its glow crowns his head like a mad saint's nimbus. He seizes Michele's face in both his huge, clammy hands, one for either side, his thumbs poised above Michele's eyes like snakes readying to strike. The man's face is only inches from Michele's now, muscles straining against the rage inside. The man's breath smells bad, like rotten vegetables and wintergreen mints.

"You're going to have to do a lot better than that," he says, and his words seem to cling wetly to Michele's cheeks in spatters of spittle. "Jesus! Do you really think I haven't *heard* that before? You think that's all it's going to take to mess with my head?"

The man's hold tightens, his hands like a vise, steel jaws winding themselves closed. Michele thinks that maybe they could crush his skull like a punky old melon if that was all the man wanted, if he wanted this to end so soon, so easily. But Michele knows that the man doesn't want it to be over yet, that what the man wants could take a long, long time and be a lot worse than dying.

"It's just that I've known crazy men before," Michele says, having to strain against the grinding force of the man's hands to move his mouth. "They sounded a lot like you."

"*July second, 1947,* motherfucker!" the man screams into Michele's face, as if that's supposed to mean something to him, supposed to explain all this away. "July second, 1947, you deviant little son of a bitch! You *tell* me what the fuck fell out of the sky that night if you want to live! If you even want the *chance* to get out of here alive!"

Michele swallows and thinks of his stepfather and his shitty little life in Shreveport, thinks of the freedom he felt stepping off the bus into New Orleans, of Robin and the others. He closes his eyes.

"They have medication for people like you," he whispers. The hand on the right side of Michele's face releases its grip and there's a brief moment's relief from the pain before the fist smashes down across the bridge of his nose and the world mercifully swirls away again.

The man stares helplessly down at the broken, bleeding thing he's made of the pretty boy's face, the blood oozing bright from the nostrils, spilling to the shiny silver tabletop to make scarlet pools on either side of his head. The unconscious face still painted like a carnival mask, mocking him with its lie of femininity. Mocking his weakness, the sad fact that he could be so easy to manipulate. Even after all his work, all his careful tests and observations, that he could be made to doubt himself so easily. He looks down at the blood smeared across the knuckles of his right hand, his fingers still clenched, his nails digging themselves into his own flesh. The red stain of the boy's tainted blood says, *You are so weak. You are so very, very weak.*

The man steps away from the examination table and almost trips over a chair. It was such a risk, taking two in one night, first the transsexual, dead now and awaiting its burial, and now this molly boy, not even a larva yet, just a fucking child whore playing dress-up. And the man knows he's not *ever* supposed to bring anything back to the house except the ones who have gone across, all the way across. He's broken one of his own most sacred rules because of the dreams and the things he saw from his window, the bird-things in the clouds above the river, above the city. Because he needed answers and he was too afraid to wait.

You get scared and you get sloppy, he thinks. *You get sloppy and then you get dead.*

"July second," he says quietly, and laughs a cold laugh at his own stupidity. His hands rub nervously back and forth across his trousers. "This one doesn't even know who I am, much less does it know July second. It doesn't know *shit*!"

He paces around the table, circling the boy like a hungry but indecisive shark, wondering how he ever thought this child could be of even the slightest use to him, knowing that it was a choice made from necessity, from blind desperation. If only he could drive the awful dream images away long enough to think more clearly or if he could figure out why it feels like something has changed tonight. Why after so many years of careful, painstaking planning and plotting the rhythm of Their movements, rhythms as predictable as tides or seasons or the phases of the moon, why suddenly *everything* seems so utterly changed. He cannot even remember precisely when he was first cognizant of this new sense of urgency, sometime after he brought the transsexual into his house, sometime after the tests and questions began.

Something from the sky, perhaps. *The thunder?* he thinks, trying to remember what he'd asked the child on the table about the thunder and if it might have been important. The man glances at the clock on the wall and realizes that fully three quarters of an hour have passed since he knocked the boy unconscious. *How? How could it have been that fucking long?* He checks his watch to be sure.

The man stops circling and stands very still. He closes his eyes, concentrating on a calm, small place he keeps hidden deep in his soul, a spot so deep They could never find it. *Something for a rainy day,* he always thinks whenever he needs to remember that part of himself, and right now the rain is drumming hard and icy against the window of the room. There's peace in that space inside him, or as close as he will ever get to peace again. If he can have only a shred of that peace, he can get this shit under control again. And control is all that matters.

The man stretches the calm into something bigger and wraps that thing about him. He stands and listens to his heart and the clock on the wall, the rain coming down outside and the wet, uneasy breathing of the boy on the table. And slowly, but as steadily as the ticking cadence of the sounds filling his ears, he begins to see the simple solution written in the incontestable language of his resolve.

The man first saw Jared Poe two weeks after he'd killed the female-to-male transsexual who'd been interviewed on television. He'd always believed in providence, or something that might as well be providence, so he understood when he saw the flier thumbtacked to a bulletin board in the French Quarter coffeehouse. He was having a cup of black and bitter African coffee at his usual spot in Kaldi's when he noticed the piece of paper, black ink photocopied onto marigold yellow paper and stuck up alongside a dozen other fliers advertising rock bands and lost cats. He pulled the piece of paper off the wall and read it while his coffee cooled enough that he could drink it. PAINED EXPRESSION was printed large across the top in a severe Gothic script. Beneath that was a photograph, poorly reproduced, of a figure on its knees, head bowed. Someone else stood above with a bullwhip. The man was unable to identify the gender of either person.

He smoothed the flier out flat on the top of his table and read it carefully, repeatedly, so he would be sure not to miss anything important. Besides the heading and the photograph, there were a couple of paragraphs clipped from a review in *The Village Voice* announcing the discovery of "the worthy successor to Robert Mapplethorpe, Jared Poe of New Orleans." The article went on to describe the photographer's work as "sublimely twisted" and "derived but certainly not derivative . . . [Poe] understands the subtleties to be mastered in the complete deconstruction of gender and gender roles." There was a Warehouse District address printed below the photograph, a gallery called PaperCut, dates and times. The man, who was still calling himself Joseph Lethe then, folded the flier neatly and slipped it into the front pocket of his shirt.

The next Saturday he took a cab to the opening of Jared Poe's exhibition. PaperCut wasn't a *real* gallery, of course, just an empty old warehouse with a little (and *only* a little) of the grime scraped away, a sign hung discreetly out front. Inside were maybe fifty or sixty people and a maze of pegboards on which Jared Poe's sepia-toned photographs were displayed, each matted on brown paper and framed in rusty steel or shiny chrome.

Joseph Lethe stuffed a five into the Lucite donation box by the door and kept to the fringe of the scattered clots of people milling through the exhibition. His heart had started beating fast when the taxi driver had turned off Felicity onto Market Street, and now he was drunk on the adrenaline and his racing pulse. Here he was, walking among Them and Their acolytes, androgynous bodies in latex and leather and fishnet stockings. Faces painted white as skulls, eyes as dark as empty sockets. Bits of metal and bone protruding from lips and eyebrows, jewelry like the debris of an industrial accident. They took no notice of him, the assassin in Their midst, just carried on with Their preening and posing. He had never felt half so powerful as he did at that moment, surrounded by the enemy and so clearly invisible to Them.

Joseph Lethe had brought one of his yellow legal pads and a mechanical pencil. He stood before each of the abominations hung from the pegboards, astounded and entranced that They would allow Themselves to be displayed so openly, Their perverse likenesses put down on paper, flaunted. He made careful notes on the photographs, recording their titles and exhibition numbers, writing concise but careful descriptions of each and every one.

When he realized that someone was watching over his shoulder he turned around fast, one hand spread protectively over his notes. The intruder was a tall creature disguised as a woman, scarecrow-thin and pale as chalk, as if every inch of exposed skin had been airbrushed the same matte white. It was wearing a ratty black T-shirt with the sleeves and collar hacked away, skintight black stretch pants that revealed no evidence of its genitalia, if indeed it had any to conceal. There was a single red dot painted between its dark, thin eyebrows, like a Hindu woman's *bindi.*

It smiled, showing perfect, even teeth, and said in a velvety voice that was neither masculine nor feminine, "Do you write for a newspaper?"

"No, no," he replied, surprised at how calm his voice was, no trace of the panic welling up inside, the fear that he had been discovered after all. "I'm just a student."

"Oh," it said apologetically, and blinked once.

Its eyes seemed wrong in no way that he could put his finger on. He looked quickly back at the photograph he'd been busy examining when the creature had interrupted him.

"He really is very good, isn't he?" the creature asked. "I mean, he's not just another bullshit wanna-be taking fetish snapshots for the lookieloo norms."

"Yes," Joseph Lethe agreed coolly, careful not to sound *too* enthusiastic. "He is good. He is, well . . ."

The creature finished for him. "Genuine," it said conclusively. "He is genuine."

Joseph Lethe stared intently at the photograph, praying the thing behind him would go away, that its curiosity was sufficiently satisfied. This print was titled *Skylla and Kharybdis.* Like most of the others he'd looked at so far, it showed two murky figures, one on either side of the picture. The figure on the left had both its long arms flung wide, its head back and its small breasts bared. The figure on the right had its back turned to the first and was curled into a hard knot of muscle and shadow. Something small and hard and indistinct hung between them, suspended on a taut piece of wire.

" 'God or man,' " the creature behind him whispered, " 'No one could look on her in joy.' "

"What?" he asked. "What did you say?" He turned to face it again, but already it was moving away from him, inserting itself seamlessly into a small cluster of bodies farther along the aisle of pegboards.

He wiped at his forehead and realized for the first time how hot it was in the warehouse, that there was no air-conditioning, only huge and ancient-looking fans rotating slowly high overhead. He was drenched in sweat. Joseph Lethe clutched his yellow legal pad and moved along to the next print.

This one was titled *The Pleasures of Teirêsias* and was the first that he'd encountered with only a single figure, or what he at first *mistook* for a single figure. He leaned close and could see that it was in fact a double exposure, with two bodies occupying the same space. He thought perhaps there was a male body superimposed over a female, but it was hard to be sure. Both forms were draped with strips of raw meat and the viscera of slaughtered animals, and the figures stood in a dark slick of blood that had run down their naked bodies and pooled about their bare feet. Only their faces were clear, unblurred by the photographer's trick, their two heads, male and female, turned in profile to the left and right, respectively.

And he realized something else then. All the photographs so far had shown the same couple, a boy and a girl whose features were so perfectly matched that they had to be brother and sister, maybe twins. He felt a small chill across the back of his neck like a sudden gust of cold air. Joseph Lethe wiped at his sweaty forehead again, wiped his hand on his pants, and wrote down the title of the photograph.

Past a final divider of pegboard, toward the back of the gallery, there was a folding table set up where wine was being served in Dixie cups along with dry-looking slices of a white cheese on wheat crackers. Joseph Lethe knew better than to eat or drink anything here, so he ignored his parched throat. But he did approach the table and the people gathered there, all talking excitedly at the same time. He hung back at the edge, waiting for a good look at the artist himself, who was seated at the table. It had taken Joseph Lethe a little over an hour to complete his catalog of every photograph on display, forty-three prints altogether, and he held his legal pad tucked safely under one arm.

Shortly after he'd realized that the same two models had posed for all the photos, he'd begun paying attention to the titles. There was clearly a pattern, and patterns were always the key to understanding, to putting a new part of the intrigue into context. Most of the titles had been taken directly from Homer, *The Iliad* and *The Odyssey,* the rest named for other random bits of Greek mythology. Only one broke the pattern, so he knew it must be the means of access to this cipher of light and shadows. The crucial photograph had been given the incongruous title *The Raven,* a reference to the poem, he assumed, and a pun as well—Jared Poe's *The Raven.* But Joseph Lethe also suspected that indicated that the poem would prove to be the Rosetta stone for the entire exhibition.

The Raven showed the male model only, his face made up like a woman's. His hands had been bound with electrical tape and insubstantial wings somehow had been made to sprout from his skinny shoulder blades. It was the only photograph in which either of the models had been permitted to look into the camera. One corner of the boy's rouged lips was turned up in a snarl or sneer, an animal expression of threat or defiance, and his eyes sparkled with a wicked, secret glee—like the eyes of the creature that had spoken to Joseph Lethe minutes ago, simply *wrong* in a way he couldn't yet explain. He'd made a note to concentrate more on Their eyes in future examinations.

A breach opened in the crowd and he could see that Jared Poe was busy talking to a plain-looking woman taking notes. He was nothing like the monster that Joseph Lethe had prepared himself for, none of the expected cross-dressing or physical modification. The photographer appeared to be in his mid-thirties, maybe a little older, dressed simply in a black T-shirt and blue jeans. The only notable thing about his face was a two- or three-day growth of beard. However, there was only a fleeting second or two for Joseph Lethe to wonder that a man who appeared so normal could be behind the profanities he'd just witnessed, a moment of surprise before he noticed the figures seated just behind and to either side of Jared Poe.

They were the strange brother and sister from the photographs. There could be no mistake about that, and he felt as if he'd seen something he wasn't supposed to, as if he should look away or hide his eyes.

He prayed that the shock of seeing the pair in the flesh had not shown on his face.

The woman was seated on the left and the boy on the right, holding the photographer's hand tightly. The models were wearing matching black dresses, simple clinging things that showed off the lines of their bodies, the scant differences of muscle and fat that distinguished one from the other. They *were* twins. He was certain of that now, and he was almost as certain that they were identical twins as well, although he knew that natural opposite-sex identical twins were a biological impossibility. Then the woman raised her head and looked straight at him and there were those eyes again. That indefinable wrongness in her outwardly friendly glance. The sudden heat he'd felt earlier in the evening returned, washing his skin in goose bumps. He flinched, barely managing not to look away. He felt as though she were peeling him with those eyes, removing the onion layers of clothing and skin and deception to see what lay underneath. Joseph Lethe felt sick and dizzy.

"You don't look so good," a voice said. He knew it was the creature that had spoken to him before, knew that there were *two* pairs of those terrible eyes on him now, probing his body and mind and soul, and that knowledge made him want to run. The sensation of those eyes made him want to take steel wool and borax to his skin to be rid of their touch.

Instead he stood very still and kept his eyes on the female model. She smiled at him, a gentle smile that he knew was meant to put him at ease, to lull him into a false and treacherous sense of security, but he knew also that she'd seen the truth. She understood precisely who and what he was, and in a moment she would stand and point, or whisper into the photographer's ear . . .

"You don't look well," the creature said more loudly, somewhere very close. "Would you like something to drink?"

"I'm *fine,*" he replied, turning away, pulling himself free of the female twin's gaze. He imagined fishhooks imbedded just below his skin yanking free as he moved away from her, tiny bits of himself clinging to rusty metal. She would reel them in, would have them as proof of his existence. As he walked quickly back through the aisles of pegboard the photographs seemed to peer out at him now like accusing gargoyles, hungry sentinels that might spring to life at any moment to tear him to ribbons.

But he made it past them, through the door and out into the warm and sticky night. Joseph Lethe kept moving until he'd put a full block's length between himself and PaperCut, the things gathered inside, and those hideous photographs. Then he stopped, breathless, leaning against a telephone pole, his sides aching and the panic beginning to fade by degrees. He looked up into the summer sky, past the halo of streetlights and into the dim splash of stars, pinpricks so far away and all that hellish nothing in between. He shuddered, remembering the twin's eyes, her expression of smug triumph. It would come back to him again and again as surely as the constellations spread out above the delta and the winding Mississippi. It would be with him forever.

He'd fucked up, had allowed curiosity to make him careless, had walked straight into a trap set for him and him alone. It was so plain now, so fucking *obvious,* an elaborate banquet of misinformation and red herrings that They'd known all along would be irresistible to him. They'd drawn Their one nemesis out into the open, and now They'd seen his face, knew the smell of his fear.

From now on his work would be different. It would no longer be the simple game of him picking Them off at his leisure. He had become, in a single reckless evening, the hunted as well as the hunter. That They had allowed him to escape was an indication of nothing more or less than Their deserved confidence that They could take him whenever They were ready.

Joseph Lethe closed his eyes and became Stanley Hudson, hoping that the switch might buy a little of the time he needed. He kept his eyes shut until his breathing and pulse had slowed almost to normal again. Then he removed the folded sheet of yellow paper from his pocket and stared down at the photocopied excerpt from the *Voice* article. It only took him a moment to find what he was looking for, the brief mention of the photographer's studio apartment on Ursulines Street.

Stanley Hudson refolded the flier and returned it to his shirt pocket. He glanced one last time in the direction of the gallery and disappeared into the night.

Stanley Hudson spent almost a whole week locked away in his tall, dark house by the river, eating nothing that he had not purchased in a can and carefully microwaved first. He spent a week studying his explicit notes on Jared Poe's photographs, a week trying to find some way to turn the tables back to his advantage, to unravel the net that had been cast so expertly over him.

Maybe, he decided, the photographs weren't entirely useless after all. The exhibition itself was an act of misdirection, of that much he was now certain, but the individual photographs might still prove useful—*if* he could read between the lines, if he could even discover which lines to read between. He suspected that the answer lay in the placement and composition of the last print he'd seen, *The Raven.* It was meant to throw him off the track, but maybe in that act of bravado They had shown something far truer of Their nature than all of his experiments could ever hope to reveal. If he only had the actual print in his possession, or even a Xerox, if only he didn't have to work from memory and his ultimately inadequate notes, he might begin to understand its significance.

When he felt that he could wait no longer, that every day he spent huddled over his notes was another nail driven into the lid of his coffin, Stanley Hudson packed the simple, deadly things he needed into an old leather satchel he'd bought years ago in a junk shop, all the sharp and shining things that would be required, all his needles and wire and surgical thread. But because this move against Them was not meant merely to demonstrate his superiority, not meant merely to eliminate the immediate threat to his life and mission, he also packed an assortment of specimen jars and preserving fluids. Because in Their desperation to entrap him, They had carelessly revealed one of Their most terrible perversions of the natural order, and his work required that he must never forget his role as a scientist as well as a soldier.

The very last thing that went into the old satchel would serve no greater purpose than to show Them that he was not the fool they'd mistaken him for, that They had given him the clue that in time would be Their downfall. He laid the two pages he'd sliced from his thick paperbound edition of *The Unabridged Edgar Allan Poe* on top of the rest. Then Stanley Hudson snapped his black bag shut.

He waited until he was sure that the photographer was gone, that he wasn't just *pretending* to have left the apartment, before he stepped out of the recessed doorway where he'd spent most of the morning and crossed Ursulines. It took him only a couple of minutes to pick the lock on the wrought-iron security door, would have taken him half that long if he hadn't had to keep checking to be sure no one watched. The tumblers clicked and rolled beneath his skillful ministrations, and he eased the door open slowly so it wouldn't clang against the wall of the small entryway before the stairwell, shut it even more carefully behind him.

The stairs were wooden, so he slipped his shoes off and climbed them in his sock-clad feet. There was only one door at the top, and he breathed a hushed sigh of relief that there was no chance he'd be breaking into the wrong apartment. He pressed his ear against the door and listened, past discordant strains of rock music playing loudly inside and the thumping of his own heart, for some sign that he'd guessed correctly, to be *sure* he hadn't gone to all this trouble for nothing. After a moment there was the unmistakable sound of footsteps, someone walking across the creaky pine floors on the other side of the door, and Stanley Hudson went to work on the deadbolt.

* * *

"I don't . . . know . . . what you're talking about," Michele slurs, his voice thick and syrupy from the numbing drugs the man has given him to keep the pain to a dull and distant roar. Michele has begun to think of the pain as The Pain, as a starving, fire-eyed thing with too many heads and too many mouths, chained to a wall, and the chain slowly coming free of the masonry. It seems now as if The Pain has been with him all his life. He knows now that there is only one way it will ever finally tear itself loose and gobble him up, like the Big Bad Wolf and he's just Little Red Riding Hood with an Adam's apple and a dick and there will never be peace anywhere again except in the acid darkness of its belly, the dissipating pit of its gut.

"I don't know . . ."

The man stops cutting then, abruptly, as if he's finally accepted that Michele is telling him the truth. The scalpel clangs loudly into the metal tray with all the other instruments and the man's red latex hands pass between Michele's eyes and the parts that have been cut loose and hang on hooks above the table where he can see them, has to see because the man took his eyelids right at the start.

"Of course you don't, child," the man says gently. Then he is filling a syringe with a clear liquid. He plunges the needle into the exposed muscles of Michele's abdomen, and The Pain lunges forward one last time. The sounds of its claws and the crumbling stone are very loud, drowning the raw world of meat and steel.

"But even unknowing pawns have their uses, Michael," says the man. Then he whispers indistinctly, something that sounds like "Forgive me," before The Pain opens its jaws wide and Michele slips easily, gratefully, down its gullet.

Stanley Hudson had thought he would find both the twins waiting in the apartment above Ursulines and was disappointed that there had been only the boy. It was the girl who had recognized him, who had violated him with her smirking, triumphant stare. But he would catch up to her later, he told himself, when he was finished with the boy named Benjamin.

He paused in the room where every surface was stained in complementary shades of red and black, paused and corrected himself. He would catch up to *it* later. Benjamin had told him everything he wanted to know, had confessed how his identical twin brother had gone to Trinidad, Colorado, six years earlier for the surgery, the final step in the conversion, surrendering its humanity for whatever dark rewards They promised Their disciples. *It is approximately 260 miles due south from*

Trinidad, Colorado, to Roswell, New Mexico, he absently reminded himself, glancing once again past the slaughter on the canopy bed to the print of Jared Poe's *The Raven.* The dead boy still stared out at Stanley Hudson from the photograph, but any menace that face might have harbored had been negated by the cleansing rites of the knife.

He leaned down, reaching into the leather satchel at his feet, and removed the pages he'd cut from *The Unabridged Edgar Allan Poe.* He silently counted the lines as he scanned the opening stanzas of the poem. When he reached the twenty-sixth line, he marked it with a yellow highlighter pen he'd found earlier in Jared Poe's office. And then he read the line aloud.

" 'Doubting, dreaming dreams no mortal ever dared to dream before . . .' "

Twenty-six times two, he thought, *is fifty-two,* and he counted down to line fifty-two and subtracted six lines, one for each year since the living twin's conversion, and read line forty-six out loud as he traced over it in neon yellow.

" 'But, with mien of lord or lady, perched above my chamber door—' "

Stanley Hudson sighed wearily and stared again at the photograph watching him from the other side of the room.

" 'With mien of *lord or lady,*' " he repeated slowly, satisfied that his message would be understood, that They would know he'd caught on, had made all the appropriate connections. He stood and walked around the end of the bed, stepping carefully over the boy's bowels and kidneys, the upper portion of his liver, and used a piece of Scotch tape (also borrowed from Jared Poe's office) to stick the highlighted pages to the blood-speckled glass protecting the photograph. Then he left the yellow pen in the mess heaped in the center of the bed, removed his surgical gloves, and went to the apartment's bathroom to wash his face.

That night when Jared Poe was arrested for the murder of his lover, Stanley Hudson had just allowed himself to become Joseph Lethe again. He watched the news reports on the old black-and-white television in his kitchen while he ate his dinner of canned beef stew, listened to the anchorman's account of the boy's grisly death and a short interview with a New Orleans homicide detective.

At first he felt jealous and angry, jealous that the credit for *his* work was going to the deviant photographer, though that was what he had intended. But then the reporter asked the detective if there was any connection between the death of Benjamin DuBois and the Bourbon Street Ripper killings, and although the detective refused to comment,

Joseph Lethe had seen the hopeful, guarded glint in the cop's eyes. As the anchor segued into a story about an alligator attack in Bayou Segnette, he chewed a mouthful of mealy beef and potatoes and reminded himself that there were more important things than his pride.

By killing the twin he had scored a double victory against Them, had taken not one acolyte but two. Because now the photographer, who had been chosen to spread Their monstrous images, to subliminally disseminate Their lies through his perverse "art," would be locked away in prison, useless. And if the police believed that Jared Poe was also responsible for the other killings, then it bought Joseph Lethe a lot more time. He washed the stew down with a sip from a can of warm Canada Dry ginger ale and allowed himself a cautious smile.

Joseph Lethe wraps the boy whore's body in garbage bags and binds them together with a whole roll of duct tape, until the mess is contained in a neat package. Because this one cannot be buried conveniently in the yard, because the yard is only for the ones that have gone completely across, he carries the body down all the flights of stairs that lead from his examination room to his garage and dumps it into the trunk of his car.

The thunder growls, reminding him of the storm and his visions. He opens the garage door and stares out into the storm-haunted darkness. There's still an hour left until dawn, plenty of time for him to finish the job. The fear and confusion, the dangerous uncertainty that plagued him earlier in the evening and threatened to erode his will, are gone now, washed away by the meticulous, familiar ritual of the boy's vivisection.

High above New Orleans a brilliant fork of lightning stabs down at the world. Joseph Lethe sees the outline of a gigantic ebony bird spreading its wings wide above the rain-lashed city. A *sign*, he thinks, and a warning too. That something is coming, something new and terrible sent to stop him. Something that he must lure into the open so that he can confront it, destroy it, as he destroyed Their plans against him a year before. He closes the trunk, checks to be sure it's locked, and gets into his car.

5

"No," Lucrece says, but Jared is already through the bedroom window, following the crow. He doesn't pause to consider the unseen force that threw the windows open as the bird fluttered cawing above the bed. And he does not pause to question gravity or the distance down to the street; he moves now on instinct alone, an instinct that either he's carried back with him from the grave or flows into him from the crow. He hears the French windows bang closed behind him, shutting out the storm again, shutting out Lucrece. There is a faint sense of vertigo, not of falling but of the risk of falling, and the commingled flapping from the long tails of the latex frock coat and the bird's broad wings.

Then there is a flat and solid rooftop beneath his feet. Jared turns, looking back toward the apartment. He can see dim, unsteady candlelight behind the curtains. He imagines movement on the other side, Lucrece coming to see if he's lying broken on the street, but the crow caws again, a harsh, demanding sound. Jared looks away, stares instead down at the bird perched on the edge of a sagging, leaf-clogged gutter.

"What now?" he asks.

The crow shakes herself, throws a crystal spray of raindrops from her feathers. She peers up at him, her eyes eager, impatient but indecisive.

"That's what I thought," Jared says, tasting the rain on his lips, the faint oily taint of petrochemicals in the drops. "You're turning out to be pretty goddamn useless, you know?" The crow blinks, squawks again, as if to say, *I already dragged your sorry dead ass all the way back from hell, didn't I?* She shakes herself a second time and looks south toward the lights of Bourbon Street.

"You can't find the guy who killed Benny, and you don't know why.

Well, while you're figuring it out, I have some other scores to settle. Any chance you can help with *that*?"

The bird looks away.

"I think you have to," Jared says. "Maybe you're not *supposed* to, but I can make you. Because you know where they are, and you know they damn well deserve it."

The crow huddles into herself and emits a small, mournful croak. He sees that she is shivering, but he is no longer capable of anything like pity, least of all for this black bird that dragged him out of oblivion.

The rain is cold, though, and he does wonder a moment that he can still feel cold. Then another wave of loss and anger washes over him, a thousand times more chilling than the storm, more bitter than the polluted rain. Hurt so big and heavy it can only cripple him or drive him on.

"Is that *all* there is to keep me moving?" he whispers, suspecting that the bird doesn't have the answer but needing to ask anyway. *The loss and the anger,* he thinks, fingering the words like bullets, and says, "I'm wasting time, aren't I?"

The crow replies by spreading her wings and hopping from the rain gutter into the air above Ursulines Street, heading away from Bourbon. Jared lingers only a moment, glances one more time toward the apartment before he follows, moving like something only a little more substantial than shadow across the roofs and the empty spaces in between.

At first Jim Unger thinks he has screamed himself awake, but Julie's still asleep beside him, so maybe the scream never made it out of the nightmare, out of his throat. He's shivering, drenched in slick, cold sweat. He fumbles in the dark for his cigarettes on the bedside table, lights a Camel, and inhales deeply, checking the LED readout on the clock radio. It says 3:37 A.M. in squarish phantom-green numbers. Unger takes another drag off his cigarette. His head is still too full of the dream, the red cascade of images and sounds, and his heart is racing as though he's just run a marathon.

In the dream he was back in the apartment on Ursulines, the one where his part in the arrest and conviction of Jared Poe began. Except *this* time he was the first one through the door, the first one to see the blood and viscera dripping down from the walls and ceiling. In the dream he was the one to find the pages taped to the photograph and he was standing there, reading them out loud, just the highlighted lines—he can't remember them now, but in the dream they were so fucking clear—and someone was snapping pictures. The flash went off like white bolts of lightning, one after another, and he asked whoever was doing it to please fucking stop so he could fucking concentrate.

And then there was the sound of something at the window and he turned to see. Behind him the idiot with the camera was still snapping away, *flash, flash, flash,* and he heard Fletcher saying, "Jesus, Jimbo, don't open it. Don't let it in here," and Vince Norris said, "Well, ain't this some pretty faggot shit we got here? Fuckin' *sick* sons of bitches, if you ask me."

"Shut up," he hissed, reaching over the bits of human body scattered across the bed, reaching for the windows to open them, to let it in so it would stop making those *sounds,* like the night coming apart at the seams, like a thousand sharp beaks or claws working at the glass.

"Jesus, Jimbo," Fletcher said. "You *wanna* let it in here with us? Is that what you want?" But his hand was already grasping the blood-smeared handle, already pulling one of the windows open wide. From the other side came an irresistible grinding force, and a sudden wet flood of entrails and feathers flowed in over the headboard of the bed. He caught a fleeting glimpse of something else out there, something vast and restless on scaly stilt legs before he woke up, the scream dying on his lips, mercifully taking any impressions of the thing outside the window away with it.

Unger gets out of bed, careful not to wake his wife, not to interrupt her dreams. He crosses the room to the coat hook on the back of the closet door, the hook where he always keeps his shoulder holster and service revolver. He takes it out and checks the chambers, all six loaded, then slips it back into its leather cradle.

Just the simple action helps a little, makes him feel more real, more grounded. He takes another drag off the Camel and looks over his shoulder, across the room toward the single window hidden behind the ugly purple drapes that Julie brought with her when she moved in. He can hear the rain pounding at the glass, enough like the sound in his dream that he makes the connection. A few seconds later there's a flash of lightning.

It's been almost a week since he got the news about Poe, how some big Cuban had cut him open and he'd died before anyone in the prison infirmary was able to stop the bleeding. *Good fucking riddance,* he said. *Saves the taxpayers the cost of juicing the pervert bastard.*

"You're a coldhearted SOB, James Unger. Anyone ever bothered to tell you that?" Pam Tierney had said that, and he looked at her and smiled, thinking, *Yeah, bitch, and everyone in this department knows you're a fucking bulldyke,* but all he said was, "Honey, I don't get paid to be a sweetheart."

"Well, you'd sure be one sad, penniless motherfucker if you did," she said.

Detective Jim Unger sits down on the floor beside the closet door to finish his cigarette, within easy reach of his gun. He counts the seconds between each flash of lightning and the thunderclaps that come after, and he keeps his eyes on the window.

He'd been on the force almost ten years, had spent the last four of those on homicide, and in that time Jim Unger had seen some pretty awful shit. Gunfights, knifings, strangulations, an ax murder, bodies hacked up and dumped into the bayous to be chewed on by gators and crawfish—he'd once seen the corpse of a woman that a perp had tried to dissolve in a bathtub full of muriatic acid. But nothing, absolutely *nothing,* had prepared him for what was waiting in the bedroom at the top of a squeaky stairwell near the corner of Ursulines and Dauphine that muggy August afternoon. And nothing ever *could* have.

Vincent Norris was still his partner then, lanky white-haired Vince who'd moved from the wastes of north Texas to New Orleans to be a cop, who talked like a bad actor in an old cowboy picture. Vince had never learned to laugh at all the sick shit they had to deal with day in and day out, had never managed to set up that necessary buffer between himself and the job.

They reached the scene way ahead of the coroner, just minutes after a hysterical old woman had flagged down a patrol car. That was almost three months before Vince had his nervous collapse, or whatever the hell the doctors finally decided to call it, and left the force.

Vince phoned him once from the hospital in the middle of the night, his voice groggy from all the tranquilizers they had him on. He spoke quietly and very slowly, hesitantly, as if he was afraid someone might overhear.

"How you doin' out there in the real world, Jimbo?" he asked.

"Doing fine, Vince," Jim replied. "Doing just fine. Are they treating you all right in there?"

There was silence from the other end of the line, so long that finally Jim said, "Hey, Vince. You still with me, pal?" And Vince came back, but now he was whispering.

"They're giving me these little *pills,*" he said, "Three times a day, Jimbo, these little red *pills,*" and he paused again. Jim could hear the muffled tattoo of footsteps in the background before Vince continued.

"They don't help," Vince said, and now Jim was straining to hear him. Vince didn't just sound like he was whispering; he sounded like he was speaking into the telephone from the bottom of a very deep well, as if someone had dangled the receiver over the side of a pit and Vince's words were crossing all that darkness.

"I can still see it, Jimbo," he said. "I can still see what was up there."

Jim swallowed, his throat gone almost too dry to speak. There were goose bumps on his arms, like an allergic reaction to what he was hearing.

"You gotta trust those doctors, Vince. They know what they're doing," he said, trying for Vince's sake to sound as though he believed what he was saying.

"It takes a little time, but you'll—"

Click. The line went dead. Unger sat there for a while, sipping Scotch whisky and staring at the silent phone.

When Jim Unger was a rookie a desk sergeant told him, "You let all this bullshit get to you and you'll be picking petunias off the wallpaper." He had taken the advice to heart. He'd spent the years letting the things he saw, the atrocities that human beings were capable of doing to each other and to themselves, numb him, build up a thick callus around his soul. And maybe that's why he would only have nightmares about what they found in Jared Poe's apartment.

There were two squad cars outside when he and Vince arrived, their lights washing the darkening street red and blue. Vince went up the stairs first. A cop named Fletcher met them at the door to the apartment.

"You guys better brace yourselves good," he said, " 'cause you ain't even gonna believe this one." Fletcher looked green, and he must have seen the unspoken skepticism in Jim's eyes, because he said, "My partner's in there puking. I *ain't* kidding you. This one is un-fucking-believable."

That was when Jim first noticed the smell, the cloying stink of blood and shit and raw flesh, the way he imagined a slaughterhouse might smell. Vince covered his mouth with one hand and mumbled, *"Je-sus."*

"I almost think someone used one of them wood chippers on the body," Fletcher said, shaking his head as he led them through the stinking apartment to the bedroom.

"Oh, goddamn," Vince Norris muttered, and he managed to get out of the doorway to the bedroom and halfway to the bathroom before he vomited, so at least he didn't contaminate the scene.

"I *said* I wasn't fucking kidding," Fletcher said defensively, and stepped aside so that Jim could get a better view.

Jim almost asked where the hell the body was, but he stopped himself as his first impression began to fade. A better question, he realized, would be where the hell the body *wasn't.* The walls, the furniture, the floor, the goddamn ceiling, *everything* was painted with a sticky, wet veneer of human gore. It was like looking into the belly of some bizarre and gargantuan creature whose insides just happened to resemble a bedroom. The only things he could recognize as actual human parts were on the big canopy bed: the victim's feet and hands, tied to the bedposts with nylon cord that might have been white once, but was now the same crimson as everything else.

He turned away, fighting his rolling stomach, determined not to be sick. "That's not even fucking possible," he said to Fletcher.

"If you'd asked me half an hour ago, I'd have agreed with you one hundred percent."

"I need a cigarette." Jim moved back toward the front door, trying to put some distance between himself and the smell. Vince was on his knees now, dry-heaving, and that sure as hell didn't help any. Jim leaned against a chair and lit one of the menthols he kept for the really bad cases, inhaled the smoke and stared at the floor and the scuffed toes of his shoes. The taste of the cigarette did little to mask the blood-and-vomit reek filling his nostrils.

"Where the hell's everyone else?" he asked Fletcher, exhaling. "There were two cruisers out there."

"They're downstairs with the old lady," the beat cop replied. "The one who found it. She lives downstairs. I think maybe she owns this place."

"She found that?" Jim asked.

"Yeah. There was blood dripping out of her fucking ceiling, if you can believe *that* shit. She came up to see what was going on, found the door unlocked. They're trying to keep her calm until an ambulance gets here."

"But she didn't see anyone else up here? Just . . . that?"

"Not that she's told us about so far."

Jim sighed, breathed out smoke that tasted like cough drops, and looked over at Vince.

"You gonna be okay over there?"

Vince wiped his mouth with the back of his hand, started to answer, nodded instead.

"I know the coroner's office is just gonna *love* the mess you've made on the floor," Jim said.

"Fuck 'em," Vince muttered. Then he was gagging again.

"Find him a wet towel or something, will you?" Jim said to Fletcher. They heard the ambulance, and Jim took another drag off his cigarette.

"You may as well take your time, boys," he said.

There was the sound of a toilet flushing from behind a closed door that Jim assumed led to the bathroom. A moment later the door creaked open and a younger officer he didn't recognize stepped out. The kid's face was the color of old feta cheese.

"Think you're gonna live through this?"

"Maybe," the kid replied, smiling weakly. "Maybe not." Vince slipped quickly past him and shut the bathroom door again.

When the paramedics started up the stairs Fletcher played interception and routed them back to the old lady's place. They gave her oxygen and a mild sedative, but nothing so strong that she wouldn't be able to talk when the time for questions came. The coroner's wagon arrived shortly after the ambulance. Jim Unger had stepped outside, hoping the night air would drive some of the fetor of the apartment from his nostrils, where it seemed to have taken root like a creeping red fungus. There'd been very few times when he'd thought of the air in the French Quarter as fresh, but this was one of them. After the abattoir upstairs, the ever-present background scents of sewage and river water, ripening garbage and mildew seemed familiar and soothing.

The coroner was a heavyset third-generation Irishwoman named Pam Tierney. Jim Unger knew she considered cops a necessary evil at best, thugs who were only there to keep her crime scene from getting trampled before the *real* detective work could be done. He'd actually seen her slap a policeman's hand for touching a coffee cup that lay near a body. "Just keep your hands in your pockets," she'd said. "I don't think that should be too hard for a bright young man like you."

She stood in front of him now, peering expectantly at the windows of the second-story apartment.

"Word on the radio is you got something special waiting for me up there."

"Oh, I think they ordered this one just for you, Tierney," he said, making no effort to hide his feelings for the woman. Jesus, half the ward knew she was a fucking dyke, that she was currently shacked up with some artist chick from New York City.

"So what are we waiting for?" she asked impatiently, and he shrugged his shoulders, flicked the butt of his third menthol into the gutter.

"Ladies first," he said, and followed her up the stairs, praying silently that this would be the day that old blood-'n'-guts Tierney finally took a ride on the porcelain bus. When they reached the door to the bedroom, Jim didn't look in again, stared back instead at Vince and Fletcher loitering about the living room. Vince still looked way too sick to care, but Fletcher rolled his eyes, shook his head.

Pam Tierney didn't say a word for a good three or four minutes, just stood very still, staring into the blood-soaked room. When she did turn back to Jim, the only sign that the sight had affected her was a loud, exasperated sigh.

"Wow," she said softly, and laughed, actually fucking *laughed,* a short, dry, unhappy sound that made Jim Unger want to hit her.

"Any particular thoughts as to the cause of death, Detective?" she said, stepping around him, heading for the kitchen.

"How about a goddamn hand grenade?" Fletcher said as she passed him and Vince and his partner. The partner was sitting on a black leather sofa, looking through a photo album.

"Yeah, Fletcher. That's a real good one. You must've been working on that one all afternoon." Then to the partner, "Hey, what the hell are you doing?"

The kid flinched and looked quickly up at her, startled, his eyes wide as those of a little boy caught with his arm up to the elbow in a jar of Oreos.

"Unless you're some sort of freak of nature and were born without fingerprints, I'd really like you to put that down and get up off the couch. Can you do that for me?"

"Better listen to her, Joey," Fletcher said. "Her bite's a lot worse than her bark."

But the young cop had already set the photo album back on the coffee table where he'd found it and stood up so fast he looked like some sort of mechanical wind-up toy.

"Thank you," Pam Tierney said, and disappeared into the kitchen.

"What's her problem?" the kid asked.

"Her girlfriend's probably on the rag this week," Fletcher said.

At that moment Tierney's two assistants reached the top of the stairs, both of them loaded down with cameras and cases of forensic equipment. They stood in the doorway, looking lost and wrinkling their noses at the smell.

"Where's the body?" one of them asked, and everyone, even Vince Norris, started giggling.

"If you girls will try not to touch anything for about five minutes," Jim said, "I'm gonna have a few words with the Dragon Lady in there."

He found Pam Tierney at the stove, emptying a package of Community Coffee into an iron skillet. The gas flame licked at the bottom of the pan and the air was already redolent with the rich, scorched smell of burning chicory and coffee grounds.

"What the hell are you *doing*?" he asked her, staring dubiously at the skillet.

"The guy who trained me up in Baton Rouge used to do this whenever we got a real stinker, especially the ones that had been underwater a while. Personally, I think it smells a whole lot worse than what's in there," and she motioned toward the front with her head. "But I can't have everyone puking all over the place while I'm trying to work." She adjusted the flame beneath the skillet and fanned the dark smoke toward the ceiling.

Jim coughed, squinted at her through the haze.

"Are you gonna try to tell me that shit in there didn't bother you?"

Pam Tierney turned to face him. He noticed that her eyes were watering, but he assumed it was from the sizzling coffee grounds.

"What do you *want* me to do, Unger? Barf all over the floor like the Three Stooges in there? Fuck yes, it *bothers* me, but I'm the one who has to go back in there and pick through whatever's left of that guy."

Jim glanced back toward the bedroom. "I think it was a woman," he said. "There's black nail polish on the fingernails and toes," but Tierney shook her head. She left the stove on and squeezed through the narrow entrance to the kitchen, edging past Jim Unger. She barked some instructions to her assistants and they began setting up, unpacking. Then she turned back to Jim, still standing in the door to the kitchen.

"Come here a second, Sherlock. I want to show you something."

Jim groaned, but he walked across the room to where she was standing at the edge of the bedroom, pointing down at something lying near her feet on the gore-smeared floor.

"You ever seen one of those on a girl?" she asked him. Jim bent closer for a better look before he realized that the sausage-sized lump of meat on the floor was a penis with a small bit of the scrotal sac still attached. The head had a large stainless steel ring through it. Jim Unger felt the hot rush of acid and half-digested lunch forcing its way back up from his stomach and dashed for the toilet.

"That's what I *thought,*" Pam Tierney called out after him, just before the smoke alarm in the kitchen went off.

As Jim Unger lights his second Camel a flash of lightning illuminates the room like noonday sun. Two seconds later the thunder catches up and the concussion rattles the windows of the house. On the bed Julie stirs. "What was that?" she asks.

"That was just thunder, honey."

"Oh," she says doubtfully, then, "Why aren't you asleep?"

"I had a bad dream." Though it is the simple truth, it sounds wrong coming out of his mouth. *You thought you heard something. That's what you meant to say, wasn't it? That's what you* wanted *to say.*

"Oh," Julie says again, sounding more convinced this time as she rolls over in bed, turning her back on him.

"Just take it easy, Mrs. Poche. We're not in a hurry here," Vince said for the fifth or sixth time. The old black woman stared out at him through the fish-eye lenses of her spectacles. Jim Unger was losing interest, was staring through Mrs. Poche's lace curtains at one of Tierney's ghouls snapping photographs of the sidewalk.

"Shouldn't I call my lawyer?" she said again. Vince shook his head.

"You're not a suspect, Mrs. Poche," Vince said.

Why not? Jim asked himself. *Why the hell not?* It would make as much sense as anything else here.

"We just want to know if you saw or heard anything unusual this afternoon."

The old lady stared at Vince as if he'd sprouted a second head from the middle of his chest, then rolled her dentures back and forth in her mouth.

"There was *blood* drippin' outta my *ceilin'*," she told him. "I thought that was pretty damn *unusual*."

"She's got you there, Vincent," said Jim, closing the curtains. The downstairs apartment smelled like dust and medicine, the miasma of age, and it was starting to depress him.

"If you'll just tell us anything else you saw, ma'am, it'd be real helpful," he said to Mrs. Poche. She looked away from Vince, locked her bewildered gaze on Jim instead.

"It was awful," she said again. "I'm just glad none of my grandbabies were here. Can you imagine if they'd had to see somethin' like that?"

"Ma'am," Jim interrupted, trying to sound polite but losing his patience, "did you see anyone come in or out of the apartment *before* you went upstairs?"

The old lady frowned and rolled her dentures.

Jim looked back up at the maroon stain on her living room ceiling. It was about as big as a large pizza, and he guessed it was situated somewhere just below the foot of Poe's bed. There was a much smaller, matching stain on the floor; sooner or later, the guy on the sidewalk would be in to photograph both.

"All I saw was Mr. Poe, and it's his apartment, so I don't see nothin' unusual about that. He comes and goes all the time."

"And what *time* did you see Mr. Poe leave?" Vince asked her, pretending to write down everything she said on the memo pad open across his knee.

"Oh, wait a minute now. If you're thinkin' Mr. Poe had anything to do with this, you're wrong, young man. Mr. Poe, well, he's a prissy boy, but he wouldn't *kill* nobody. *'Specially* not Benny. Benny was his fella, you know?"

"What time did you see Mr. Poe leave the apartment, ma'am?" Jim asked, still staring at the stain on the ceiling. The room upstairs had been unbearable, but the dark stain seemed to have the opposite effect; his eyes kept coming back to it.

"Ain't nothin' at all wrong with bein' a prissy boy," Mrs. Poche said, crossing her wrinkled hands on her lap. "That's what Oprah said."

"Yes, ma'am," Vince sighed. "She's entitled to her opinion. But didn't you *see* or *hear*—"

"What I *saw* was all that *blood* drippin' outta my *ceilin'*," she said, pronouncing each word slowly, as if she'd decided the two detectives were hard of hearing. Then her front door opened and Fletcher said, "Come on, guys. I think we got him."

The first time Jim Unger saw Jared Poe, the photographer was sitting handcuffed in the backseat of a patrol car, staring straight ahead as if his eyes were focused on something far away that no one else could see. If those eyes had been empty, blank, it might not have bothered the detective, but they weren't. They almost seemed to glimmer in the shadows, and it was difficult to look at his face for very long.

"Another car picked him up all the way over on Conti," Fletcher said, "just wandering around talking to himself. He won't talk now, but his driver's license says he's Jared A. Poe and gives this place as his home address."

The man in the back of the patrol car didn't respond to the sound of his name. The front of his white T-shirt was stiff and crusted with blood, as were his jeans. His hands and arms were the color of dried rose petals.

"He's gotta be our perp, Jim," Vince Norris said. "The old lady said the boyfriend's name was Poe."

"Has he been Mirandized?" Jim asked Fletcher, and the beat cop shrugged.

"Probably, but what's the point of asking this fag anything? He's a total veggie, Jimbo."

"He's *gotta* be the fucking guy," Vince insisted. "Just look at all that fucking blood on him. You think he got that from a nosebleed or something?"

Jim stooped down next to the open door of the patrol car, close enough to smell the drying blood that soaked Jared Poe's clothing.

"You've been placed under arrest," he said, "on suspicion of murder. Do you understand these charges, Mr. Poe?"

Jared Poe blinked then, just once, and turned his head slightly toward the three officers. "I understand," he said. His voice came out brittle, like thin glass. "I understand," he repeated. "You think I killed Benny."

"Holy fuck, Batman, the fruit can talk," Fletcher said, and laughed.

"Vince, will you please get him the fuck out of here before he blows this," Jim said, trying not to look away from Jared Poe's glimmering eyes.

"I'm right, aren't I?" the man in the back of the car asked them. "All of you think I did that to Benny."

"Listen, buddy." Jim leaned closer, trying to sound calm, trying to sound reasonable. "What do you expect us to think? We know he was your boyfriend and you got blood all over you. We got a witness that saw you leave the crime scene. I'm guessing we're gonna run some tests and we're gonna find out that blood came out of the guy upstairs. Now, if you *didn't* kill him, you better tell us where all this red stuff came from."

"I didn't kill him," Jared Poe said. He closed his eyes, turned away from the detective.

"Oh, yeah? Then I'm the goddamn Sugar Bum Fairy," Vince Norris sneered.

"Detectives," someone called, and Jim Unger looked over his shoulder. The guy who'd been taking pictures of the sidewalk earlier was standing in the door to the stairwell. "Pam says she's got something up here you guys ought to see right now. What do you want me to tell her?"

"Tell her to hold her fucking water," he shouted, and the guy disappeared back up the stairs. Jim looked at Jared Poe, who still had his eyes closed. There was blood on his face, too. Long streaks of it, like Indian war paint, and a dark smudge across his lips.

"You could make this easier on both of us," he said, but Poe didn't answer him. When Jim slammed the door of the patrol car a second later Poe didn't even flinch.

"Get him out of here," Jim said to Fletcher, and then to Vincent Norris, "Come on. Let's see what kind of nasty shit the Dragon Lady's got waiting for us this time."

"Fuckin' wacko," Vince said for the third time as Jim handed the plastic evidence bag back to Pam Tierney. Inside the bag there were two pages torn from a book, "The Raven" by Edgar Allan Poe. A couple of lines had been marked with a bright yellow highlighting pen.

" 'With mien of lord or lady . . .'?" Jim Unger read out loud. "Is this even supposed to make *sense*? Like he was leaving us a message or something?"

"Maybe," the coroner said, frowning down at the pages. "Or he was trying to tell *himself* something, or the dead guy. Shit, who knows. I'm not a psychologist."

Jim glanced at the framed photograph again. Tierney or one of her boys had removed it from the bedroom. Now it sat on the floor, leaning against the coffee table. There were crusty streaks of gore on the glass, partly obscuring the image inside, the winged androgyne snarling for the camera. They'd found the poem Scotch-taped to the front of the picture, and Jim didn't really give a shit *what* the killer was trying to communicate with the highlighted passages. There was an excellent partial thumbprint right in the middle of the sticky strip of tape.

"If the print matches, I'd say it's a pretty safe bet you got the right guy," Tierney said.

"Yeah," Jim replied. "Well, let's all just keep our fingers crossed." He glanced over his shoulder at the bedroom. Someone had turned on a floor lamp in there, and he could see the shadows of the men still working through the mess, shifting patches of darkness straining to pass for human, shadows stretched from floor to ceiling, as fluid and insubstantial as ghosts.

The next morning Jim Unger and Vince Norris questioned Jared Poe in a stuffy interrogation room that smelled like floor cleaner and stale cigarettes. What was left of the victim still awaited them in Tierney's office in the basement of the Criminal Courts Building. The autopsy was scheduled for one o'clock. With any luck they'd have a confession by then.

"Okay, Mr. Poe, let's just try to make this as painless as possible," Vince said, lighting a Pall Mall and blowing smoke at the tiled walls. "I can't say I slept real fuckin' well last night and you sure as hell don't look like you did either, so I think we'll all be better off if we skip the bullshit."

Jared squinted at the detectives. There were dark circles under his bloodshot eyes, like bruises, and the fluorescent lights in the room lent his skin a sickly greenish cast. He was unshaven and dressed in prison denim, a shirt that looked too large with a big stain on the front.

"That blood we took off your hands and clothes matched up with the victim's, Jared," Jim Unger said, placing a manila folder on the table between them. "And we have a shitload of fingerprints *and* a witness who puts you at the scene of the murder. We *know* you killed Benjamin DuBois, Jared. Are you absolutely sure you don't want a lawyer present before we—"

"I said I don't need a lawyer," Jared replied, blinking at them.

"Yeah, I know what you said. But I have to be sure—"

"I didn't kill him." Jared closed his eyes, shielded them from the light with one hand. "I don't need a lawyer."

"We've seen the scratches on your back, Mr. Poe," Vince said. "What do you think we're gonna find under Mr. DuBois's nails?"

Jared Poe answered slowly, as if he was having trouble remembering how to talk, or what words were for.

"We had sex yesterday morning, before I left," he said without opening his eyes. "I didn't kill Benny."

"Then how did you get his blood all over you, Jared?" Jim asked, pushing his chair back from the table a little, trying to see Jared's face better.

"I *found* him," Jared said, and swallowed hard, like someone who was trying not to cry, or throw up. "I found him and I was trying . . . I was . . . Jesus . . ."

"So you admit you were there?" Vince asked. He was standing closer to Jared now, leaning on the table, the cigarette's filter clenched between his teeth. Jim thought he looked like a cartoon vulture.

"I was at the CAC. The Contemporary Arts Center on Camp Street. I'm . . . I was going to have a show there. I was there all day taking measurements."

"But you just said that you and Mr. DuBois had sex that morning," Vince interrupted.

"Yes, before I left."

"But no one *saw* you there? There's no one to corroborate what you're telling us?"

Jared moved his hand so that the bright light washed freely across his face again. "No," he said after a moment. "No, I don't think so. But *why* . . . why do you think I would ever hurt Benny?"

"You tell us, Jared," Jim said, and Vince clicked his tongue loudly against the roof of his mouth.

"I don't have time for this crap, Mr. Poe," he said. "And Detective Unger here, he doesn't have time for this crap. You think a jury's gonna buy any of this? We've seen those pictures you take. That's some pretty twisted shit, Mr. Poe. It looks to me like you have a real hard-on for hurting people."

Jared Poe closed his eyes again.

"So how's it gonna look to a jury, hmmm? Normal guys who don't like to fuck other men up the ass, who don't get their jollies taking obscene pictures of boys dressed up like women? You know, I worked vice two years and I've never seen anything one *tenth* as disgusting as that stuff."

Jim Unger held up one hand to silence Vince, to signal that it was his turn now. Vince grunted and turned to stare at the one-way mirror on the other side of the room.

"You can't tell us you'd never hurt Benny, can you, Jared? Because you hurt him on a regular basis. Isn't that right? Every time you fucked him you hurt him. Benny *wanted* you to hurt him . . ."

"What's the point in my telling you anything at all, Detective?" Jared Poe asked. His weary bloodshot eyes made Jim Unger want to look away. "You've already made up your minds. The only thing you want to hear from me is a confession. All that's going to satisfy you is to hear me say that I did . . . that I did *that* to Benny."

"Seems pretty fuckin' reasonable," Vince said without turning around. "Under the circumstances."

"But it's never going to *happen,* Detective."

"Then you better have another good long think about that lawyer, Jared," Jim said, standing up, sliding his chair back under the edge of the table. "Because regardless of what you *say* or how many times you say it, you look guilty as sin to us. And I'm betting you're gonna look just as guilty to the DA's office and a jury."

Vince dropped the butt of his Pall Mall to the floor and crushed it out with the toe of one shoe. "And we ain't talking about life in prison, Mr. Poe. We're talking about death by electrocution. You do understand that?"

"Come on," Jim said, reaching for the doorknob. "Let's give him some time alone. I'm sure he's gonna figure this all out sooner or later. A man can't be up to his ears in his own shit and not smell something sooner or later."

Jim Unger finishes another cigarette and stubs it out in a ceramic ashtray the color of dead sunflowers, something Julie's niece made in school, a bright present filled with butts and tobacco ash and burned-out matches. There's another flash of lightning and he thinks about turning on the television. Maybe the weather reports would take his mind off the dream, off these things he shouldn't be remembering anyway, gnawing over like a dog with an old meatless bone. The storm is real, solid, *immediate,* the sort of threat he can at least comprehend, not like these haunted patches of memory trapped inside his head or the lie that there was something more he could have done for Vince Norris.

The news of Vince's suicide reached Jim the day after he heard Jared Poe was dead. It had been months since Vince's release from the hospital, but his mind was still broken, barely held together from day to day by pills and biweekly visits to a therapist. He was living with his mother in Slidell, and Jim had kept promising himself he'd do more than check up on him, that he'd make the drive across the lake and spend an afternoon with Vince. But he'd put it off and put it off and finally the call came from a friend in the St. Tammany Parish Sheriff's Department. By the time Jim got to Slidell they'd already taken Vince's body away. There was only the blood he'd left behind in his bedroom and his mother, sitting alone and staring vacantly out a kitchen window at a backyard gone wild with dandelions and polk salad. There were still a few cops on the scene too, and one of them, a detective named Kennedy, took Jim aside.

"There's something in there I need your opinion on," he said, pointing down a long gloomy hallway toward Vince Norris's room. Jim had already looked in the room and he didn't really relish the thought of going in there again.

"What? Look, I don't really—"

"I know he was a friend of yours," Kennedy said. "That's why I was hoping you could help make some sense of this."

"Make sense of *what*?" but the detective was already on his way back down the hall, back to the room where Vince Norris had cut his own throat with a jagged shard of broken mirror. And Jim followed, wanting to be back in his car and putting as many miles between himself and this house as he could, as fast as he could.

The detective led him through the bedroom door and Jim was trying to tell him again that he'd already been in there, had already seen everything there was to see and didn't care to see any of it again, thank you, when Kennedy pointed at the low ceiling and then crossed his arms.

"That," he said, and Jim looked up.

The grade-school crude outline of a bird, a huge bird with wide outstretched wings and a beak like a dagger, had been traced onto the ceiling directly above the bed. The blood was already dry. Jim Unger stood speechless and staring, dizzy. Suddenly the room seemed cold.

"No note or nothing. Just this," Kennedy said. "We think he did it with his fingers, before he cut his throat. All the fingertips on his right hand were scraped raw."

"Can you keep this out of the report?" Jim asked, unable to look away from the unsteady maroon smears across the white plasterboard, remembering Vince's tranquilized voice over the telephone: *I can still see it, Jimbo. I can still see what was up there.*

"If you know something about this, I'd like—"

Jim interrupted before he could finish. "I'm asking you if you can *please* keep this out of the fucking report." The hot surge of anger broke the spell. He turned away, better to see Vince's blood soaking into the shit-brown shag carpet and the bed.

"But—"

"Just say yes or no, Detective. But it doesn't mean anything, okay? Vince wasn't well. He had bad dreams."

There was a long silence between them while the other detective watched Jim, then glanced back at the grisly outline on the ceiling.

"Yeah," Kennedy finally replied. "Yeah. What the fuck. You got it." Jim said thanks, or he meant to say thanks, before he stepped back out into the hall. And there was Vince's mother, waiting for him, blocking his escape. She wore a dead woman's face, too much sorrow in her eyes for anything like life.

"You *tell* me," she said, and she sounded old, old as the festering swamps and the skies above them, old as the first mother who ever lost a son. "Vincent was so afraid and he wouldn't ever tell me or his doctors what he was scared of. But you know, don't you? I want you to *tell* me."

He could have told her, could have sat her down and told her about his own bad dreams, about the dripping red nightmare they'd walked into on Ursulines, details he suspected Vince had never shared with anyone. And it might have made a difference.

"I'm sorry, Mrs. Norris," he said instead. "I swear to God I wish I did know, but I don't. I'm very, very sorry." Then he stepped past her and didn't stop moving until he was out of the house and across the weathered concrete driveway to his car. He looked back then, just for a second, and she was watching him from between the living room drapes, her accusing face grown as old as her voice had sounded.

He doesn't turn on the television, but leaves Julie sleeping on their bed and goes downstairs to the living room. He removes his revolver from its holster and takes it with him. He doesn't like to be too far away from it anymore.

Outside the house the storm is battering the city. Jim thinks he'll just sit in the kitchen and have a beer and watch it for a while through the bay windows, hopes that the alcohol will be enough to make him sleepy again. He has a prescription bottle of Valium in the medicine cabinet, little blue bits of calm, but he doesn't like to use them, doesn't like their unreal, detached brand of comfort.

The rain is making a sound like giant fingers drumming against the roof as he pops open the can of Miller and sits down. The gun lies on the table in front of him and he stares past it into the wet, storm-lashed night. The beer feels reassuring going down and he drains half the can in one long swallow.

"You gotta get it together, Jimbo," he whispers, wiping his mouth. The night outside is lit by another brilliant flash of lightning. A split second of daylight pours over the world and he freezes, the can halfway to the tabletop, the back of his other hand still damp with beer and saliva.

What the fuck was that, before he can prevent the thought, before he can tell himself it was only a trick of the sudden light shining through the driving rain, just a mistake made by his tired eyes. The thunder rumbles overhead. Jim Unger puts the can down, picks up the .38, and steps around the table to the window.

What the fuck do you think *you saw out there?*

"Nothing," he says out loud, "absolutely nothing at all," but then the lightning comes again, crackles above the Metairie subdivision and makes a liar of him. Because what he *thought* he saw is still standing a few feet from the kitchen window, staring in at him through bottomless cat-slit eyes. Eyes punched into a grinning harlequin face, wrinkled flesh the color of something that's been in the tub too long.

"Holy *Jesus* . . ." he whispers. He brings up the gun, but the thing outside is faster, much faster. The glass shatters, explodes around him in a roar of wind and a drenching diamond spray of slicing glass and rain. Jim feels the gun slip from his grip, hears it clatter across the linoleum as he tries to protect his face from shards of flying glass. Above the noise of the storm and breaking window panes there is another sound, a frantic fluttering, the terribly familiar sound of angry, black wings. *I'm still dreaming,* he thinks as he stumbles backward into the table.

"Detective Unger," a voice says from somewhere very nearby, a voice that seems to weave its substance from the cacophony of unseen birds.

"Who the fuck *are* you?" Jim screams into the night sweeping through the broken windows. His arms and the backs of his hands are cut and bleeding, and he can taste blood in his mouth. But none of it hurts, not yet. There's no room in him for anything but the fear, a hundred times more demanding than the pain from any mere physical wound could ever be.

"I know it's been a while," the voice says. He realizes that it too is familiar. "But it hurts to think you could have forgotten me *already.*"

"You stay the fuck away from me," Jim growls, trying to sound cool, trying to sound like he's not about to shit himself. He glances at the floor for some sign of the dropped .38, but the lights above the sink have started to flicker and the floor is covered with glass and water that catch the unsteady light and wink it back at him, making it impossible to find the gun.

"You don't seem very glad to see me," the voice says, coming now from somewhere behind him. Jim turns his back on the gaping hole where the window used to be, and the thing with the smirking harlequin face is silhouetted for a moment in the flickering light before it bleeds away into the shadows.

No way, no fucking way any of this is happening, Jim tells himself. It is a hollow reassurance at best.

"I've got a gun, you weirdo son of a bitch," he says, and takes a step toward the door that leads from the kitchen into the carport. There are things out there he can defend himself with, sharp things.

"No, Detective. This time *I* have the gun." Suddenly there is cold metal pressing hard against his temple.

"Don't waste precious time asking yourself *how,*" the voice says, speaking directly into his ear now, and he knows there's no point anymore pretending that it isn't the voice of Jared Poe. No point pretending the dead man isn't standing in his kitchen with his own fucking gun pressed to his head.

" 'Cause *how* doesn't matter right now. All that matters is whether or not I think you're telling me the truth."

He's shoved into one of the chairs, one hand on his shoulder as cold as the barrel of the .38, one hand as hard and indisputable as tempered steel forcing him to sit when every muscle in his body is telling him to run.

"I think you remember how this works, so let's try to make it as painless as possible," the voice says. Then strong fingers are tangling themselves in his hair, pulling his head back so he's staring straight up into the pale grinning face. Now he can see it's just a cheap Mardi Gras mask, not a real face at all.

"You're not Poe," he says. "If you're Poe, take off the mask, you fucking coward."

"Wrong," the white face says without moving its lips, and the butt of the pistol comes down fast across the bridge of his nose, cracking bone, tearing cartilage. Warm blood spurts down his chin. Jim Unger screams as the searing pain fills his head, but a thunderclap devours the sound.

"Now, see what you made me do?" The barrel of the gun is already jammed against his temple again. Jim gasps and more blood spills out of his nostrils and into his mouth, gagging him.

"You *knew,* didn't you?" the man behind the mask asks. "You knew I wasn't the one who killed Benny."

"Bullshit," Jim Unger coughs, spitting out a mouthful of blood and snot, blowing a finer drizzle of gore from his broken nose. His eyes are watering and it's hard to see the mask, just an alabaster smear now against the flickering dark.

"Don't lie to me, you fucking pig." Now the gun is pressed against the tip of Jim's chin, pointing upward. "I have no reason in the whole fucking world not to pull this trigger and blow your brains out, so don't you fucking *lie* to me."

Jim hears the weakness in the voice then, the strain of anger. A chink that might let him past the mask, might even give him a chance if he doesn't screw it up.

"What difference does it make?" he asks. "Even if we didn't get the killer, we got another sicko off the street, right?"

"You really think this is all some sort of fucking *game,* don't you?" The hand holding the gun is trembling with rage that wants out, anger like a starving dog on a very short leash.

So much anger can make a person careless. Jim swallows, hating the bitter, salty taste of his own blood.

"Either way, I was just doing my *job,* right?" he says.

"Wrong," Jared Poe snarls back at him, a voice that could be Jared Poe's if such a thing were possible. The gun is suddenly past Jim's lips, chipping teeth as the stubby barrel is forced across his tongue. Thunder rushes from the sky to cover the deafening boom of the gunshot.

Four blocks west of Jim Unger's house Jared finally stops running, collapses into a row of oleander, and lies staring up into the rain, the belly of low, roiling clouds stained orange by the Metairie streetlights. Benny's mask is still clutched in his right hand. The rain has already washed most of the cop's blood off him, washes his own blood from the hundred scrapes and gashes left by his dive through the window.

Is there anything he could have said that would have stopped you from killing him? he thinks, but it sounds like Lucrece asking the question, Lucrece speaking from behind his eyes.

"What difference does it make?" he asks her, knowing that there won't be an answer. The crow lights on the ground beside the oleander bushes and Jared turns his head so he can see her. The water rolls off her black feathers; a single raindrop catches on the end of her beak and hangs there like a jewel until the bird shakes it off.

"And where were *you,* bitch? I thought you were supposed to be here to help me."

The bird caws and spreads her wings, blinks her golden eyes in a way that is somehow indifferent and accusatory at the same time. Not that

Jared has to rely on anything as subtle as body language. Her voice would be impossible for him not to hear, not to understand.

"Yeah? Well, fuck you too," Jared says, and rolls over again to stare into the storm.

6

After Jared and the bird have left her alone in the apartment, Lucrece sits at the window and watches the rain filling the gutters on Ursulines. She knows that she should be moving, should be asking the questions that Jared's impatience and rage have kept him from considering, not sitting on her ass while what little is left of her world careens toward fresh disaster. But she feels too stunned, entirely too overwhelmed.

There's a limit, she thinks. *Even for me, there must be a limit.*

Since Benny's death her life has become a downward spiral toward a despair so complete and crushing that it could be the lightless bottom of the ocean, that absolute pressure on every inch of her body and mind and soul. She wasn't even given a chance to grieve for the loss of her twin, her bright shadow, before she had to begin fighting to save Jared's life and was thrown into the merciless arena of lawyers and police and courtrooms. And the press too, because it was just too good a story not to smear across every paper and tabloid and television news broadcast: the transsexual sister pleading for the life of the accused homosexual murderer of her cross-dressing twin.

When the police were finally finished with Jared and Benny's apartment, she was the one who scrubbed her brother's blood from the floorboards and windows, the one who dragged the gore-crusted mattress away and painted the walls that could never be cleansed of their stains. She felt like a traitor, covering over those last lingering traces of him. She was the one who handled Benny's funeral when the coroner's office finally allowed what was left of him to be entombed in the plot Jared had bought the year before in Lafayette No. 1.

And Lucrece did almost all of it by herself, because while Jared had attracted plenty of art-crowd hangers-on and wanna-bes, the three of them had very few actual friends, people willing to stand by her through the shitstorm of publicity and pain that her life became in the days after Benny's murder. Those days that had turned to long months of the same droning, unrelenting hurt.

When the trial was over and Jared was sitting on death row at Angola, Lucrece was left to stand guard over the apartment. She gave up the old place in the Warehouse District. The only hope remaining in the world was that some overlooked bit of evidence would free her brother's lover before his execution left her finally, irrevocably, as alone as someone could become.

Against that day she had nothing but Jared's pearl-handled straight razor and the knowledge of her limits, the certainty that she would not be left lacking an out, a way to stop the pain when it was clear that there was nothing left for her to do. When there were no more stingy strands of idiot hope to dangle from, no more far-fetched fantasies of justice to keep her reeling from day to day.

Then Jared was killed in some sort of brawl, a fight with another inmate, or maybe he was simply attacked; she still isn't clear on the details. They didn't matter, anyway. All that mattered was that the end came a whole lot sooner than she expected and Lucrece was caught off guard. Jared was supposed to die after all the slow and impersonal rituals of legal execution, after the obligatory appeals and protests. Instead he bled to death in a prison exercise yard. Or so she was told. The news reached her in a midnight phone call from one of Jared's attorneys. For a long time afterward she sat staring at the telephone as if maybe it had been a mistake, maybe in a moment someone would call back and tell her no, it had been a *different* Jared Poe, sorry for the confusion. Or even a practical joke. Lawyers could be pretty sick fuckers, after all, and she'd have gladly forgiven them and laughed, she would have actually fucking *laughed* at that point.

Eventually she went to the bathroom medicine cabinet, where she kept the razor, and she sat on the toilet seat and stared at it the way she'd stared at the phone. She wasn't afraid of dying. If she ever had been, that fear had been stripped from her. Lucrece folded the blade open and it glinted dully in the dim bathroom light. She even made a couple of tentative cuts along her arms, preparing herself for the pain of the deep longitudinal slashes that would be necessary to ensure permanent oblivion.

But then someone had whispered into her ear, so close that she could feel cold breath against her cheek. A single question from a gentle voice so much like Benny's that she let the razor slip from her fingers and clatter to the tile floor.

Who's gonna bury Jared if you go?

It might have been in her head, the product of a traitorous or cowardly imagination, a hallucination manufactured in a last-ditch effort to save her own hopeless life. But she waited, very still, patiently listening for anything else the voice might have to say.

"Haven't I done all that I can do?" Lucrece whispered back to the empty apartment. "*Haven't* I?"

There wasn't an answer, although she sat there on the toilet seat for almost an hour longer, listening to the murmuring background noises of the creaky old building, the street sounds of the Quarter going on about its business around her. Without her, if need be. Eventually she picked up the razor and folded it closed, returned it to its shelf in the medicine cabinet. She was damned to a few more days of life, a little more sorrow, by the image of Jared's lonely funeral, the casket being carried into the mausoleum and no one in attendance who wasn't paid to be there.

Outside the storm howls like a hungry giant. Lucrece puts one hand out flat against the windowpane. It feels like she imagines herself, polished flat and smooth, transparent and cold as the rain beating against it from the other side.

Why did I have to keep going after *the funeral? That's a fair question, isn't it?*

But there are no more answers now than there were that night when she sat with the open razor glinting at her feet. Only the mindless storm and the indifferent night, the sound of her heart, a restless reminder of her own irrelevant mortality.

If Lucrece had been any less warped by the world and her time in it, if she had not already been forced to accept so much loss and horror, then Jared's return might have been one step over the limit of what she was capable of enduring, the part of the story where the author loses her to disbelief and she closes the book for the last time. As it is, it only feels like the next impossible episode in a story that has grown ever more ridiculous since the day she was born into a body that wasn't even suited to her most basic needs.

That's the only truth she can read from the rhythm of the rain against the window, the only divination to be gleaned from the interlacing paths of water down the glass. Just the cruel, simple fact of her continuing survival and the comfortless understanding that there is still something left for her to do before she can finally let go and follow her twin.

"Please, Jared," she says, pulling her hand back from the window, letting the curtain fall back in place to hide the storm. "Give me the time I need to figure this out. Don't make me have to be here for nothing . . ."

And the thunder makes a sound like an old man laughing.

The Eye of Horus is a couple of blocks west of the apartment, a tiny curiosity squeezed in between a gallery and an antique store specializing in art deco lamps. By the time she reaches it Lucrece is soaked despite her black raincoat and umbrella. She stands dripping beneath a candy-striped awning, peering into the shop's single dusty window. The glass is decorated with two carefully rendered Egyptian hieroglyphs, stylized hawks bracketing Gothic letters that spell out the shop's name. Lucrece used to come here often, with Benny or alone, when she was still designing clothing, used to buy what she needed in the way of feathers and bird bones from Aaron Marsh, the proprietor.

Sunrise is still a couple of hours away and the French Quarter is idling, drowsy, most of the soggy night's revelry over but the new day as yet undelivered. Lucrece raps her cold knuckles against the door again. A bell on the other side jingles faintly, but there's no sound or movement from within the darkened shop. She's starting to shiver. She stomps her feet against the sidewalk, realizes that the rainwater has gotten into her boots as well. She knocks harder, rattling the little stained-glass panes set into the door.

"Come on, Aaron," she says, "I *know* you're in there somewhere." She bangs at the door again.

This time a dim, yellowy light flickers on somewhere toward the back of the Eye of Horus and there are stumbling noises. Someone curses. A moment more and she hears the click of a deadbolt being turned before the door opens a crack, still held by a safety chain. Aaron Marsh peeps out at her cautiously, like a rat, his scraggly white beard and blue eyes bright even in the shadows.

"What the hell do you want?" he growls past the chain. "Do you have any idea what *time* it is? Go away or I'll call the police."

"I'm sorry, Aaron," Lucrece says. He recognizes her then, repeats her name a couple of times and makes a disgusted, inconvenienced snorting sort of sound.

"Lucrece," he says. "Lucrece DuBois? What do you want?"

"I need to talk to you, Aaron. About crows."

Aaron Marsh snorts again, the noise a surfacing hippopotamus makes.

"I thought you were *dead,*" he says gruffly, suspiciously, and Lucrece shakes her head.

"No," she says. "That was my brother. But that's why I'm here, because of Benny."

"But you just said that you wanted to talk about crows," he says, squinting to get a better look at Lucrece. His arched eyebrows are the same bristling snow white as his long beard.

"*Please,* Aaron. I'm freezing to death out here." She stomps her feet again, not entirely for effect.

He mumbles something to himself that Lucrece doesn't understand, but unfastens the chain and opens the door the rest of the way, stepping aside to let her pass. He's wearing a paisley housecoat and slippers, and his eyes are sleepy and alert at the same time. Lucrece steps gratefully into the musty, warm shop. Aaron shuts the door behind her, locks it again. The air smells like old feathers and dust bunnies, cedar and pipe tobacco—gentle, nostalgic odors from a time when her life made sense.

"You're dripping all over my floor," Aaron says, and of course she is, the water streaming off her raincoat and her hair onto the red and gold Turkish carpet. The dim lamplight from the back of the shop makes Aaron look only a little older than he actually is, somewhere on the brittle edge of sixty. He makes Lucrece think of a slightly deranged Walt Whitman. He takes her coat and holds it gingerly between two fingers, drapes it across a brass coat hook nailed up near the door, points to another hook from which Lucrece hangs her umbrella.

She glances about the Eye of Horus, which doesn't seem to have changed much since her last visit at least a year and a half ago. Rows of tall oak and walnut display cases and bookshelves line the walls, cases filled with painstakingly mounted skeletons of eagles and herons and a hundred different species of songbirds; taxidermied wonders, stuffed owls and ducks and a flock of extinct passenger pigeons, and his most prized possession in a case in the center of the shop, not for sale at any price but he can't resist showing it off: a stuffed dodo. There are jars filled to overflowing with peacock and pheasant and ostrich feathers, drawers occupied by every conceivable sort of egg, each carefully drained of its embryonic contents and protected in beds of cotton and excelsior.

Before he moved to New Orleans sometime in the nineteen fifties, Aaron Marsh was professor of ornithology at a small-town university somewhere in eastern Massachusetts. And then there had been a sex scandal, a flunking student who got revenge by confessing to the dean or headmaster or whomever that he was Aaron's homosexual lover, and Dr. Marsh was out on his ass. So he'd come south, to a warmer, more forgiving place less prone to witch hunts, and he'd opened the Eye of Horus.

"Well, would you like some tea?" he asks grudgingly, but most of the crankiness seems to be gone now. "A hot pot of green tea will warm you up."

"Yes," she says. "I'd like that very much, thank you." Aaron shuffles past her toward the curtain of amber beads that separates the shop from a narrow flight of stairs leading up to his apartment overhead. Lucrece follows slowly behind him, admiring Aaron's treasures even through her mental fog of cold and fear. She passes the big dodo standing its silent, perpetual guard like a character from a Lewis Carroll story. Its glass eyes seem to watch her skeptically, ready to pounce if she makes a wrong move.

When Lucrece reaches the bead curtain Aaron is already at the top of the stairs speaking softly to someone. It hadn't occurred to her that he might not be alone, and she wonders if they'll have the privacy she needs to ask her questions. The stairs creak loudly beneath her wet shoes.

"I think you'll live," Aaron mutters. "Now go back to sleep and stop being such a bitch."

By the time Lucrece mounts the last arthritic stair to the short second-floor hallway Aaron has disappeared into the kitchen at the other end of the hall. To her right the bedroom door is standing open and there's a lamp burning on a small table by a huge, sagging canopy bed. An annoyed-looking young man is sitting up, blinking at her.

"It couldn't wait until morning?" he asks.

"No," she replies. "I'm sorry, but it really couldn't."

The man makes a dismissive gesture with one hand and lies down again, covers his head with a pillow.

"I'm sorry," Lucrece says again, feeling awkward. Then Aaron is calling her from the kitchen and she can hear water running, filling a kettle. "Just ignore him," Aaron shouts, but she pulls the bedroom door closed and it creaks louder than the stairs.

The strong green tea does warm Lucrece. She sips her second cup while Aaron rambles on about the shop, holds the little china teacup in both hands and rolls it back and forth between her palms. The taste and smell of the tea is nostalgic too. She wonders if there's a thing left in the world that hasn't become tainted by her sadness.

"But you wanted to talk about crows," the old man says at last, peering at her from under his eyebrows as he blows on his own steaming cup of tea.

"Yes," she says, setting her cup on the table. "What do you know about crows and the dead, about crows and ghosts?"

Aaron frowns and tugs at his beard.

"You got me out of bed at four A.M. because you wanted to hear fairy tales?"

"It's very important," she says, stealing a glance at the grease-stained clock above the stove. It reads 4:20. She wonders how long Jared's been gone, where he might be now. *Or maybe I imagined the whole goddamned thing,* she thinks. *Maybe I'm just a crazy woman wandering around in the rain talking about birds.*

"Mythology and folklore are not my areas of expertise," Aaron replies, and slurps his tea.

"But you must have picked up a lot in your studies. You must have heard a lot of strange things."

"*Strange* things," he says, and laughs, closing his eyes a moment as if savoring the flavor of the tea or losing himself in some bit of memory. "Everyone sees and hears strange things, Lucrece. If they live a little while and keep their eyes open. Especially when one is a young boy in New England. Or an old man in New Orleans."

"Did you ever meet Jared Poe?" she asks, afraid she's losing her nerve. "Benny's lover, the photographer?"

Aaron narrows his eyes, blows on his tea again.

"You said crows."

"I know," Lucrece replies.

"I met him once," Aaron says, setting down his cup. "And I know he was killed in prison. I heard that on the radio a week or so back. The Bourbon Street Ripper killed in a prison brawl."

"Yeah." Lucrece begins to wish she'd gone to someone else. Someone more inclined to believe ghost stories than this outcast scientist, this snowy-haired man who might have invented doubt for his own particular pleasures.

"What's he got to do with crows, Lucrece?"

"Jared came back home tonight," she says, just like that, the whole thing out at once before she can change her mind. "He came back, with a crow."

Aaron Marsh doesn't say anything, just stares down at his cooling tea, the antique china cup decorated with cobalt blue sparrows painted beneath the cracked glaze.

"Why would I make something like that up, Aaron?" Lucrece whispers.

"That's not for me to say." Aaron sighs loudly and folds his hands in front of him. "In India the crow is the bird of death. Many cultures make that connection. It's natural enough, since crows are carrion-feeders. Crows are seen to feed on the dead, so we get legends and traditions of the crow as a sort of guide for souls, escorts between the land of the living and the land of the dead . . ."

"But does anyone ever mention it working the other way round?" Lucrece asks him, and he looks up at her. His eyes are almost the same shade of blue as the birds on the little teacups.

"I suspect that you have acquaintances better suited to answer a question like that," he says. "There's no shortage of occultists and spiritualists in this neighborhood."

"But I trust *you,* Aaron, because I know you won't just tell me what I want to hear, or listen to me and only hear what you want to hear. You're a scientist."

"I *was* a scientist," he corrected. "Now I'm an old homo who sells pigeon feathers and powdered chicken bones to would-be voodoo priestesses."

"And apparently spends a lot of time feeling sorry for himself," Lucrece adds, not bothering to hide her growing impatience and doubt.

"Yes, well," Aaron says.

"I'm sorry to have bothered you." She gets up to leave, not wanting to waste any more of his time or hers, but Aaron immediately motions for her to sit down again.

"I *can't* tell you a great deal," he says. "But there's a German. Weicker, I think . . ." He worries at his beard. "Hell. Hold on a minute. I'll be right back."

Lucrece sits back down as Aaron stands and leaves her alone in the kitchen. She sips her tea and listens to his footsteps moving along the hall and then down the creaky steps to his shop. The man behind the bedroom door calls out, "What the fuck does she *want,* Aaron?"

"I said to go to sleep, Nathan," Aaron Marsh calls back, his voice muffled by distance and the storm, the rain drumming endlessly on the roof, a car passing out on Dumaine Street. He sounds a lot farther away than just downstairs. In a few minutes her cup is empty, only a few black specks of ground tea leaves left in the bottom. Soon she hears him on the stairs again, and when he steps back into the kitchen he's carrying a dusty old book bound in black cloth with faded gold printing on the cover and spine.

"I was right," he says. "Weicker. *Der Seelenvogel in der alten Literatur und Kunst.*" Aaron holds the book up so she can see the title printed on the cover, even if the German doesn't make any sense to her. "He writes a good bit in here about birds as death spirits and images of death, images of the soul, psychopomps and what have you . . ." He trails off, flipping through the brittle old pages.

"And crows?" Lucrece asks.

"Almost all the Corvidae. Crows, ravens, rooks . . . many of them are often portrayed as death birds. Ah, yes, here." He begins to read aloud, tracing a line of text with one finger. " '*In habentibus symbolum facilis est transitus.*' "

"I don't speak Latin either," she says. Aaron frowns at her, a very professorial frown, as though she hasn't done her homework or has been caught passing notes. But he apologizes and then repeats the line in English.

" 'For those who have the symbol, the passage is easy.' " He pauses, then adds like a footnote, "The passage from the land of the living to the land of the dead."

"And what's the symbol?" Lucrece asks him, but he only shrugs.

"That depends. It could be many things." He goes back to the book. "Weicker records something here, a bit of a fairy tale that he thinks may originally be Hungarian or Wallachian." Aaron reads slowly now, translating for her as he goes. " 'These people once believed that when a person died, a crow carried their soul to the land of the dead. But sometimes something so bad happens that a tremendous sadness is carried with it and the soul cannot rest. Then sometimes the crow can bring that soul back to the land of the living to exact vengeance against those responsible for its disquiet.

" 'So long as the spirit pursues only those responsible, the crow protects it from all harm and it is invulnerable to harm by man or beast or any other evil spirits. But should the spirit turn aside from this narrow path, the crow may be forced to abandon it and the spirit will be left to wander the living world alone, forever, as a ghost or revenant.' "

Aaron pushes one finger at the bridge of his nose, force of habit, adjusting glasses he isn't wearing as he closes the book and lays it on the table between them.

"So," he says, "in this instance I suppose the symbol is the soul's pain and that pain's connection to the living."

"Jesus," Lucrece whispers, and stares down at Aaron Marsh's black book.

"It's only a *fairy tale,* Lucrece. These same people thought that the souls of suicides came back as vampires."

For just a second she wants to tell him more, tell him every detail of Jared's appearance in the apartment and the thoughts she read in the crow's nervous bird mind. Wants someone else, *anyone* else, to know the things she's seen and felt. The second passes. There might not be much time if she's going to help Jared.

"Thank you, Dr. Marsh," she says, sliding her chair away from the table. "It was very kind of you to try to help and I'm very sorry for waking you and Nathan . . ."

"A fairy tale, Lucrece. That's *all,*" he says. She smiles for him, though it feels like a sickly grimace.

"I should be going now," she says. For a moment he looks uncertain, as if he might be thinking of calling a doctor or the police. But she steps past him toward the hall and he follows, mumbling about the storm, what he's heard about it on the radio. Together they descend the creaky stairs and walk back past the moth-eaten dodo in its glass and maple prison. Aaron opens the door for her while she's putting on her wet coat and retrieving her umbrella.

"Be careful," he says as she steps across the threshold, into the rain blowing in under the awning.

"It's only a fairy tale," she tells him. He nods, a small, optimistic nod that says he at least wants to believe she means what she's telling him. "I'll be fine."

And then he says good-bye and the door to The Eye of Horus jingles shut again and Lucrece is alone on the wet, dawn-hungry street.

It's hardly an hour after dawn, and if Frank Gray has had worse hangovers, his head hurts too badly to let him remember them. His partner is driving. As the police cruiser turns right off Canal onto St. Charles, rain hits the windshield so hard he's amazed it doesn't crack. His head feels that brittle, as if simple drops of water could break it into a thousand pieces. His stomach rises and falls like the gusting wind.

"*Christ,* Wally," he says, his voice ringing inside his head, bouncing off the walls of his crystal skull. "See if you can *miss* one or two of those potholes, okay?"

Wallace Thibodeaux has been his partner for over a year, a burly gray-haired black man ten years his senior. And Wallace Thibodeaux hates drunkard cops almost as much as he hates dirty cops. He has told Frank so on more than one occasion.

"So what was it last night, Frank?" Wallace says, squinting to see through the rain, using one hand to wipe away some of the condensation clouding the inside of the windshield. "Gasoline and turpentine? Aqua Velva with a Drano chaser?"

Frank stares out at the white-columned houses lining the street, half obscured by the driving rain, and grunts for an answer.

"Well, sir," Wallace says, "if you got anything in you left to puke up, you better get it done before we get to the park, 'cause I got a feeling this one's gonna be bad."

"I'm fine," Frank says, and rubs at the throbbing place between his eyes.

"Yeah, you *look* fine. Fine is just exactly how you look." A streetcar rumbles past, a blur of red and green and spinning wheels, and Frank moans.

"You drive like an old woman," he says. "We're getting passed by fucking streetcars."

"I can't see shit, Frank. In case you haven't noticed, we're having a goddamn hurricane."

Frank remembers passing out in front of the television, remembers the Weather Channel and the pretty white swirl of clouds on the blue satellite photos of the Gulf of Mexico. "Oh, yeah," he groans.

Frank half dozes for a few minutes. When he comes to, they're passing Tulane, its not–quite–Ivy League facade of respectability like a shield against the corruption and slow, inevitable rot pressing in from all sides. Wallace pulls in behind a tomato-colored Honda and parks, stares across the street, past the streetcar tracks, at the entrance to Audubon Park. There are already four patrol cars parked on the river side of St. Charles, probably more inside the park. The rain dulls their strobing red and blue lights to something Frank can stand to look at.

"You sure you're gonna be okay, Frank?" Wallace asks, buttoning his raincoat. "I don't wanna have to be explaining why you're puking all over the place."

For an answer Frank opens his door and steps out into what seems at first like a solid wall of falling water, rain that would make Noah proud. He is soaked to the bone in seconds. But the cold and the wet make him feel a little more alive, and he thinks that maybe he can deal with this after all.

Wallace has an umbrella but the rain's blowing right up under it. They cross the neutral ground, splashing through the ankle-deep puddles and swollen gutters, and they stop at one of the patrol cars. The cop in the driver's seat cracks his window an inch or two.

"Did we beat the coroner?" Wallace asks the man inside the car. Frank looks up into the rain, opens his mouth, and sticks out his tongue like when he was a little boy. But the rain doesn't taste the way he remembers, tastes faintly of oil or chemicals, and he spits on the asphalt.

"Yeah, I think so," the cop tells Wallace. "But I better warn you guys, if you ain't heard already, this is a messy one. I mean a real gut-churner. I'm just glad it's fuckin' rainin' and the sun's not out, know what I mean?"

"Yeah," Wallace says. "I know what you mean." Frank spits again, but the chemical taste of the rain clings to the inside of his mouth like fried-chicken grease.

The cop rolls his window up again and Frank follows Wallace into the park, between the masonry pillars framing the park entrance. The rain begins to taper off to a simple, steady downpour.

The fountain is only thirty yards or so into the park, marble and concrete and a verdigris nude for a centerpiece, a bronze woman balanced on a bronze ball, her arms spread wide as if she has summoned this storm for her own secret purposes. There are two bronze children at the edges of the fountain, small naked boys astride turtles, one on either side of the woman. The fountain has already been cordoned off with bright yellow crime-scene tape strung along an irregular ring of wooden barricades. The tape flutters in the wind, ready to tear free at any moment and go sailing away into the voracious storm.

Frank and Wallace flash their badges. One of the beat cops nods and steps aside just as a particularly strong gust seizes Wallace's umbrella and turns it inside out.

"Fuck," he says, and Frank manages a small laugh that makes his head throb.

"You were getting wet anyway, Wally."

But Wallace just frowns humorlessly down at the ruined umbrella and tosses it to the ground, where it shudders and rolls about in the wind. The black umbrella makes Frank think of some sort of bizarre alien bat. He looks away, steps over the crime tape, and gets his first look at what's waiting for them in the fountain.

"Jesus H . . ." Wallace turns away, coughs into his hands. But Frank cannot look away. He stands staring at the pink-red water and the raw, floating things in it.

"Pretty amazing, huh?"

Frank only nods, doesn't turn to see who's spoken.

"Who got here first?" he asks, swallowing hard, struggles against the nauseous acid rising into his throat. It's only a matter of time until he loses, but at least he can say he fought the good fight, and maybe Wallace will cut him a little slack for the effort.

"Me and my partner. We didn't touch nothin'," the cop says. "Of course, with all this goddamn rain, I'm not sure that's gonna matter a whole hell of a lot."

"Who made the call?" Frank asks, biting down hard on his lower lip, a little pain against his rolling stomach.

"Right there," the cop replies, pointing beyond the fountain to an old man in an expensive-looking raincoat and green galoshes. He's sitting on a metal park bench holding a shivering Chihuahua on a leash. The dog is also wearing a raincoat, banana-yellow plastic. The pair are completely surrounded by cops with umbrellas, huddled protectively above the old man and his little dog.

"He called 911 about half an hour ago."

Frank holds up one hand to silence the officer and takes a step closer to the fountain.

"They ain't paying me enough for this bullshit," Wallace says somewhere behind him, but Frank can't look away from the water stained the color of cherry Kool-Aid. It's almost like one of those 3-D puzzles, a senseless collage of reds and blacks and whites, and if he could just look at it the right way it might resolve itself into something human, something that might have once been human. A blue-gray loop of bowel, a mat of black hair like a patch of some strange algae, teasing bits that almost make sense of the whole.

"There's some Hefty bags over there," the cop says, and nods toward the gnarled oak on the other side of the fountain. "They've still got some blood and stuff on them, so I'm thinkin' the killer must have used them to haul all this mess here and dump it in the fountain."

Someone tugs at Frank's sleeve. He jumps a little, but it's just Wallace, one hand still covering his mouth and nose, only glancing at the fountain.

"Let's step back a minute, okay, Frank? Give yourself a break. You're starting to look kinda green . . ."

He pushes Wallace's hand away. Only one more step to the edge of the fountain and he's looking directly down into the stew of rainwater and meat, bone and gristle, organs and muscle hacked apart like butcher's scraps. The wind gusts hard enough that for a second Frank thinks it will lift him like a stray newspaper and toss him high to snag in the branches of the craggy trees or carry him far above the city, far away from the atrocity spread out before him. But when the wind dies down again he's still there.

"Jesus, Frank. *Please* . . ." Wallace moans. Frank blinks, wipes the polluted rainwater from his eyes. That's when he sees the writing scrawled along the top edge of the fountain, the clumsy leaning letters in something black and greasy, something the storm can't wash away. Words a foot wide, so that he has to walk around the fountain to read it all. Wallace trails close behind him, cursing Frank and the goddamn weather and the sick son of a bitch who would chop someone up and leave them floating in a city park.

"Poe," Frank says. At last he can look away, as if he's passed some sort of test. He stares up through the swaying limbs into the storm clouds rushing overhead.

"What the fuck are you talking about?" Wallace gags on the last word and has to turn away.

" 'On the morrow *he* will leave me,' " Frank begins, repeating what he's read in the oil-black graffiti, reciting now from grade school memories. "It's from Poe. You know, 'The Raven'? By Edgar Allan Poe? 'On the morrow *he* will leave me as my Hopes have flown before.' "

"Whatever . . ." Wallace starts and stops, swallows before he can finish. "Whatever you say, Franklin." Then he steps away from the fountain, steps back across the barrier of tape, and vomits into the grass. Frank doesn't move, doesn't take his eyes off the clouds. In a moment he realizes that his head has stopped hurting.

In the kitchen of his big house by the river the man who is Jordan today finishes his breakfast of canned corned beef hash and canned creamed corn as he listens to the radio. The old portable Sony on the counter is the only radio in his house, and he's carefully wrapped all of it except the bent rabbit ears in three layers of aluminum foil, has drawn the appropriate symbols on the foil in red and black Magic Marker so he's absolutely certain there's no danger of errant signals or amplified cosmic rays or subliminal telepathic waves getting through to him from the Outside. He always keeps it tuned to WWOZ 90.7 because jazz is the only music he likes, the only music he's relatively certain is free of Their influence.

But now he's listening to the news, mostly reports on the tropical storm that's about to be upgraded to a hurricane. Hurricane Michael. He thinks how appropriate that will be, vengeful heaven sweeping across the Gulf of Mexico toward the seething Babylon of New Orleans. If he really believed in God or gods, he might think of the storm as a divine reinforcement sent to counter the black bird-thing from his dreams and visions. But he is not a religious man, so the metaphor and its abstract comfort will have to suffice.

Jordan scoops up another forkful of the sweet yellow corn and listens as the soothing male voice reports the discovery of a body in Audubon Park just after dawn. No details. No whisper of the time and skill he expended on the boy, but Jordan has come to expect that sort of carelessness. They're afraid to tell the truth, afraid to scare the masses living always between the rock of Their occupation and the hard place of his resistance.

"Sources indicate that the body was badly mutilated, but New Orleans police have declined to confirm or deny this information at the present. They have also refused to comment on whether or not there may be a connection between this crime and the Bourbon Street Ripper slayings."

That gets a cautious, guarded smile from Jordan, a self-satisfied smile that makes him feel a bit ashamed. *Someone's noticed,* he thinks. *They can try to cover it up, but someone* always *notices.*

"In possibly related news," the report says, "the body of Detective James Unger of the Sixth Ward's homicide division was found this morning in his home in Metairie, dead from a single gunshot wound to the head. Sources close to the police department report that Detective Unger may have taken his own life in the wake of his partner's suicide five days ago, though the possibility of foul play has not been ruled out. Both detectives were responsible for the arrest of Jared Poe, who was convicted of the brutal murders that became known as the Bourbon Street Ripper slayings.

"In sports today, the Saints lose their first preseason game—"

Jordan gets up and switches off the radio. He stands by the kitchen counter listening to his heart thudding in his chest, and his head feels light and heavy at the same time. What wrinkle in the game is this? Both the detectives dead, the detectives who had so expertly and unwittingly diverted any suspicion from Jordan, who fell for the clues he left behind in the Ursulines Street apartment. They were dutiful foot soldiers in his war. They got Jared Poe off the street.

They got the fucking pervert killed, Jordan thinks. *That's what they did.*

He knows he should have seen this coming. Dirty little reprisals for his recent actions, and surely something to do with the visions of the black, wicked thing above the city. The thing that is so close now he can feel it watching his every move. Payback for Jared Poe's death, Their prized evangelist lost to Them, and *someone* has to suffer.

"Fuck," Jordan whispers, his voice unsteady, and he looks down at his hands. They've gone the color of cottage cheese and developed a tremor, but he isn't sure whether he's afraid or just excited that his campaign has drawn such powerful forces out into the open. Perhaps it is even pride that They could fear him so much. That he has hurt Them so badly and They have not attempted to take Their pound of flesh from him, have struck out instead against innocent and ignorant pawns. Men unknowingly in his service, soldiers taking the heat, buying him a little more time.

In the end it will all come down to timing. He knows that. Jordan turns away from the radio and begins clearing the table.

By eleven o'clock Tropical Storm Michael has graduated to Hurricane Michael and the television and radio stations have begun talking about evacuation procedures, breaking into soap operas and talk shows to track the storm's steady westward swath across the Gulf. Satellite pictures of a great white spiral with an ocean-blue cyclops eye, a vast organism of cloud and wind and lashing rain, rushing past Mississippi toward the Louisiana delta, the swamps and the wide, dirty river, all the bayou towns with flooded streets and downed telephone lines. Even the dark ancient powers nestled between rotting cypress stumps and moldering Vieux Carré rooftops take notice of this force and steel themselves against its arrival.

7

The world's coming undone, Frank Gray thinks. The thought frightens him so badly that he tries to pretend it's just something he heard someone say once, nothing *he's* responsible for. But that's not the way it feels to him, standing beside his partner in Detective James Unger's kitchen with the storm whipping back and forth beyond the all-too-insubstantial walls of the Metairie house.

In the last twenty-four hours the world has somehow begun to unravel away around Frank like an old sweater, a few loose threads neglected too long and now the whole thing's coming apart at the fucking seams. Something that started with the kid in the bar maybe, the bathroom blow job gone crazy, the first step on a crooked trail that has somehow led him here.

"We should get going," Wallace says. Frank turns to look at him. Wallace looks sick, scared, fed up with this long day of blood and wind that's only half over. "Our asses got no business even bein' way out here."

That was true enough. But when the news about Unger came in from dispatch Frank had to see for himself, to hell with jurisdiction. He knew how important Jim Unger's testimony had been in convicting the man the NOPD sent up for the Bourbon Street killings. And now here's Unger, lying on the floor of his own kitchen with his brains splattered like tapioca all over the linoleum.

"What the hell's going on here, Wally?" Frank asks, but Wallace just sighs and stares out the shattered bay windows. The kitchen is drenched from the blowing rain.

"Jesus, Frank, it's not our case. It's not our goddamn problem what it means."

"Maybe not," Frank says.

"Ain't no fuckin' maybe about it, Frank. This is *not* our turf and Unger is *not* our case."

Frank stares back down at the body sprawled on the floor, still half seated in a chair tipped over backward so that its bare knees are aimed at the ceiling, the butt of the revolver protruding from what's left of its mouth.

"We got enough trouble of our own to worry about with that bullshit back at the fountain."

"Just think about it a second, Wally—"

But Wallace has him firmly by the arm and he's already leading Frank out of the house, past the annoyed-looking Jefferson Parish cops and the ambulance in the driveway, back to their car, parked by the curb.

"You didn't even *like* that son of a bitch, Frank," Wallace says as he opens his door. Frank's still standing in the rain, staring back at the house, trying to put the pieces together in his head. Trying to find a resolution for the basic contradictions and apparent coincidences bouncing around in his skull. Finally Wallace tells him to just get in the goddamn car, so he opens the passenger door and slides in as the Ford coughs noisily to life.

"So you gonna tell me what that was all about?" Wallace asks, pulling away from the dead man's house. The wipers come on, swiping like skeletal wings from one side of the windshield to the other, but they're practically useless in the downpour.

"I'm not sure," Frank says.

"Come on, Frank. Don't make me beg. My ass is cold and wet and I'm not in the mood for it today."

The entire world, unraveling like an old sweater, Frank thinks again. Never mind the care, the paranoid calculation, that he's put into keeping it all together for so long.

"Do you think Jared Poe was the Ripper?" he asks as Wallace stops for a red light.

"Do I . . ." Wallace begins. Then the light changes, a vivid blur of emerald green through the rain. They cross the intersection carefully, heading back toward I-10 and the city.

"Oh, I see," Wallace says, wiping condensation from the windshield with one hand. "You think Jim Unger poppin' hisself has something to do with this morning."

Frank wants a cigarette but he knows that Wallace is trying to quit and so he doesn't reach for the half-empty pack of Luckies in his shirt pocket.

"First," he says, "Poe goes to prison and the killings don't stop. I mean, yeah, okay, they stop for what? A few weeks or a month?"

"You ever heard of a copycat killer, Frank?"

"That's what I thought too. But that shit about the poetry they found with Benjamin DuBois's body, that never showed up in the press, Wally."

"You've lost me, Franklin," Wallace says as the Ford glides up the entrance ramp onto the interstate. "Man, I cannot see *shit* out here."

"There was a copy of 'The Raven' by Edgar Allan Poe found with DuBois's body. Some lines were marked . . ."

"You're sayin' that shit written on the fountain was from the same poem."

"Yeah," Frank replies. "It was."

"And you want to know how the copycat knows about the poem from the DuBois case."

Frank fishes the Luckies from his pocket and punches the car's cigarette lighter. "I'm sorry, man," he says, but Wallace shakes his head.

"It's been what, a week since Poe was killed up at Angola, right?" Frank says, taking a cigarette from the pack and putting the rest back in his pocket.

"Yeah," Wallace answers, cracking his window. The air rushing in makes a loud, unpleasant sound, and they both flinch at the icy drops of rain sucked into the car. "That's about right."

"And the next fucking day Vince Norris cuts his throat. Vince Norris was Jim Unger's partner."

"Vincent Norris was also as crazy as a loon, Frank." Wallace makes circles around one ear with an index finger.

"Then we get the body in the park this morning . . ."

"If you wanna call that a body," Wallace says, and swipes at the windshield with his hand again.

". . . along with a line from 'The Raven,' and barely an hour later we hear that Jim Unger's dead."

"So now you're thinkin' maybe it wasn't Colonel Mustard in the library with the wrench after all."

The cigarette lighter pops and Frank lights the Lucky Strike from its glowing red-orange coil.

"You're the most sarcastic fuck I've ever met, Wally," he says, trying to sound as though he isn't afraid, as though none of this shit's getting through his defenses. Frank exhales and looks out at the storm, the clouds, and the wind-tossed trees. The wind buffets the Ford and he can tell Wallace is having trouble keeping the car on the road.

"It's one of my finer qualities," Wallace says with a grin. "Keeps me from havin' to go suckin' on my own rod, like the recently deceased Detective Unger back there."

Frank takes another deep drag off his cigarette and watches the clouds, remembering what the storm looked like on the Weather Channel satellite photos.

When Jared opens his eyes the crow is still huddled on his shoulder, crouched close to his face as if maybe she can steal body heat he doesn't have to give.

"Where are we?" he asks her. The crow makes a soft bird sound deep in her throat.

It's still raining. Jared is starting to think that maybe it's been raining forever and his memories of sunlight are as unreal as his memories of life. He hasn't been asleep, but he feels as though he has dreamed. He doesn't remember leaving the row of oleander bushes in Metairie, but the street signs tell him that he's back in the French Quarter. The cobblestone street shimmers under an inch of water, a straight and narrow river fed by the sky and gutters and the crystal cascades falling from the roofs. He wants to lie down in the street, imagines the water carrying him away in small bits and pieces, taking apart his body and mind, all the pain, until there's nothing left but a greasy, iridescent stain. Before long that would be gone as well.

"Hey, mister!" someone yells. Jared sees a black face gazing out from an upstairs window. The face floats and bobs inside a rectangle of shadow framed in pink stucco, and then the man shouts at him again.

"Ain't you got the sense to come in outta the rain? Ain't you heard there's a hurricane comin'?"

I ain't even got the sense to stay dead, Jared thinks. *What do you expect from a zombie that ain't even got enough sense to stay dead?*

"And why you dressed like that? This ain't Mardi Gras, you know! Hey! Your bird's gettin' wet!"

Jared waves at the man, turns away from the window. Rain rolls off Benny's black latex frock coat and is lost in the downpour, drips from the jester mask that Jared doesn't remember putting back on. He wades to the sidewalk and stands in the minimal shelter of an awning outside a shop that sells herbs and voodoo potions. There are no lights on inside the shop. Jared stands there a moment, staring at his reflection in the shop's display window.

Deep into that darkness peering, long I stood there, wondering, fearing . . .

Jared touches the sharp chin of the leather face hiding his own. His reflection follows his example.

"You gonna get washed away, mister!" the man shouts behind him, and then laughs, a hoarse braying laugh. "Michael gonna wash you *both* all the way to the sea!"

A long black car rolls by, parting the river that flows down Toulouse Street, spraying the sidewalk and Jared as it passes. He turns, catching a brief glimpse of the driver through the Oldsmobile's window. The face is narrow, pinched, with hollow, hungry cheeks; that face tugs at his lazy memory and now Jared knows why he's come back to the French Quarter. Knows a name to put with the face: John Henry Harrod, the district attorney who personally handled his prosecution, the man who sat on the other side of the courtroom and nailed together his doom from scraps of coincidence and lies while Benny's murderer walked the streets somewhere, unpunished, exonerated by default, and free to kill again.

The Oldsmobile turns into a private driveway and Jared and the crow are alone again. For the moment, at least, the man in the window seems to have lost interest in them.

"I bet that son of a bitch isn't on the agenda either, is he?" Jared asks the crow. He already knows the answer before she replies.

"Then we'll just take another little detour while you're figuring out exactly who the hell *is,*" Jared says. The bird responds with an earsplitting *caw-caw* that makes Jared's head ache.

"Fine with me. Thanks for finding the asshole—I can take care of the rest myself." He reaches up and brushes the bird off his shoulder. She flutters under the awning for a second before flying away through the rain toward the rooftops.

"Hey, man! There go your bird!" the face in the window shouts. Jared ignores him, walks to the spot where the car turned in, a black iron gate set into a high brick wall. Jared grips the bars and presses his face to them, stares through a thick grove of windblown banana plants and rhododendrons. He can see the Olds, parked and empty now, in front of a cottage almost completely hidden by the garden. The storm makes wet flapping sounds in the big leaves of the tropical plants, sounds like the desperate flippers of deep-sea things beached and drowning in air.

Just like prison, he thinks. The thought makes him take a step back from the bars. No, sir. *Not* just like prison. Nothing is ever going to be just like prison again.

And scaling the wall is more of an idea than an effort, a problem he solves without knowing or caring precisely how. But he lands slightly off balance, slips, and realizes too late that someone has taken the precautionary measure of studding the top of the wall with jagged shards of broken glass, translucent teeth secure in cement gums, glass that slices his hands as he falls. Jared lands in one of the rhododendrons and clutches his injured hands to his chest. There's a deep gash across his right palm and a puncture straight through his left. The blood flows out as if from stigmata and is immediately thinned by the rain, diluted before it drips to the broad green leaves and the dark and muddy earth.

A ghost that bleeds, he thinks. *What fucking good is that supposed to be?* He squeezes his palms shut, squeezes hard against the pain. The big leaves overhead bestow a little shelter from the storm and Jared lies there until he finds the will to get up, the will to keep going. It helps to recall the thin face from the black Oldsmobile, the face from the courtroom, so he stares up into the angry sky and thinks about John Harrod.

Eventually, inevitably, they put Lucrece on the stand.

Early on, when his own attorneys had suggested her as a character witness, Jared had flatly refused. When they'd asked again, he had threatened to change his plea to guilty unless they shut up about her. No way he was going to put her through that. "And besides," he'd added bitterly, "she's just another freak for this fucking sideshow. What good is one freak's word in defense of another freak? We're all in this together, you know?"

So it was the prosecution who finally put Lucrece in the center ring, District Attorney John H. Harrod, who'd backed former Ku Klux Klansman David Duke in his 1991 bid for the governorship of Louisiana. Who'd more recently made political allies of Ralph Reed and his Christian Coalition and who'd gone as far as pledging to "clean up" the Quarter. Of course, he hadn't actually done much in the way of fulfilling that pledge: just a couple of porno busts staged for the media, the arrest of one shopkeeper who sold glass pipes, more hookers and hustlers spending the night in lockup. Harmless token gestures amplified by the press and nothing much more, until one of the highest-profile homicide cases in the city's murder-haunted history had fallen into his lap. A string of brutal killings apparently committed by a man one local radio pundit had already labeled "a pornographer of the sickest sort, masquerading as an *artiste.*"

The fact that all the killer's victims were drag queens, cross-dressers, or transsexuals made the matter a little delicate. After all, Harrod couldn't very well be seen as defending the sort of perverts he'd promised to rid the city of. But it had taken only a little semantic footwork to fix that. The very fact that New Orleans harbored the sort of deviant individuals who attracted sexual predators like Jared Poe was surely proof in and of itself that the city needed to be cleaned up.

And Lucrece had been only a little more grist for his political mill, one more life he could ruin in the name of wholesome family values. So he put her on the stand, the prosecution's last witness before they rested their case against Jared Poe. His lawyers objected, claiming Lucrece was irrelevant and prejudicial and still too grief-stricken by her brother's death to possibly be of any help to anyone. The judge overruled the defense's objection. Lucrece did as she was told, swore on the Bible she didn't believe in, sat up straight, and tried to make a brave face for John Harrod.

Harrod lingered over his papers a moment, pretending to ponder some detail or another, giving the jury time to get a good look at Lucrece. She'd dressed as conservatively as her wardrobe permitted: a plain black dress with a long skirt, her hair pulled back into a neat chignon. She had removed the omnipresent black from her nails and lips and wore none of her usual jewelry except a simple garnet ring that Benny had given her years ago.

It made Jared sick and furious to see her put on display like that, straining to pass as normal for a lot of norm motherfuckers who had already made up their narrow minds about her. To see her going through hell to try to save his ass when this trial was just a nicety anyway. He stood up, wrestling free of one of his lawyers.

"Please don't do this, Lucrece," he said, but the judge was already banging his gavel, calling for order. There were hands on Jared, pulling him back down into his seat.

"It doesn't matter *what* you say, Lucrece," Jared pleaded. "They'll make it mean whatever they want! Whatever they need it to mean! You can't save me!"

"Oh, Jared," she whispered, close to tears, and then the judge threatened to have Jared removed from the courtroom if he couldn't control himself. That was enough to shut him up, the thought of Lucrece being left alone with Harrod, alone with his manipulating questions and innuendo and no one there who gave a shit what he said or did to her.

Harrod glanced at Jared and smiled, and Jared bit a ragged hole in his bottom lip to keep himself from telling the DA to go fuck himself.

"So," Harrod said, straightening his tie, "*Ms.* DuBois. You're the *sister* of the deceased, correct?"

Lucrece swallowed once and said, "Yes," very quietly.

"Excuse me, Ms. DuBois, but I didn't quite hear you and I'm afraid the rest of the court may not have heard you. Could you please repeat your answer?"

"I said yes," Lucrece said, and Harrod nodded.

"Thank you, Ms. DuBois. But the truth is that you weren't always Benjamin DuBois's sister, isn't that correct? You weren't *born* his sister."

Lucrece didn't answer this time, looked nervously down at her hands and then out at the crowded courtroom.

"Ms. DuBois? Do you need me to repeat the question?"

"No," she said. "I heard you."

"But you didn't answer me, Ms. DuBois." Harrod took a step closer to the bench. "Were you *born* Benjamin DuBois's sister?"

"I guess that's a matter of opinion," Lucrece replied.

"Isn't it true that the name your mother gave you at birth, your *Christian* name, is Lucas Wesley DuBois?"

"I changed my name. Legally," Lucrece said.

"When you stopped being Benjamin DuBois's brother and decided to be his sister," Harrod said, looking toward the jurors' box as he spoke.

"Mr. Harrod, I *am* a transsexual. I underwent sex reassignment surgery years ago. Is that what Jared's on trial for? My sex change?"

There was tense laughter from the crowd and Harrod smiled again, nodded, and turned to face Lucrece.

"No, Ms. DuBois. I just wanted to be sure that these men and women understood your relationship to the deceased, that's all."

"I was always Benny's sister," she said.

Speaking straight to the jury, Harrod responded, "I guess that's a matter of opinion." He was rewarded with a second round of laughter.

"Now, Ms. DuBois, how would you characterize your relationship with the accused?"

Lucrece hesitated a moment, aware that every question was a snare, every answer a weapon to be used against Jared.

"Jared is my brother-in-law and friend," she said.

"He's your brother-in-*law*?"

"He was . . ." and Lucrece stopped, took a breath, and continued. "He *is* my brother's husband."

"But not *legally,* Ms. DuBois," Harrod said. "Because marriage between two men, two *homosexual* men, is not legal in the state of Louisiana. So Jared Poe cannot possibly be your brother-in-*law,* now can he?"

Harvey Etienne, one of Jared's two attorneys, stood up and objected. He tapped the eraser end of a pencil against the table as he spoke.

"Your Honor," he said, "this line of questioning is immaterial. Unless I'm mistaken, homosexual marriage is not on trial this afternoon."

The judge frowned gravely, peered down at Harvey Etienne through his thick bifocals.

"I see no particular harm in allowing counsel for the prosecution to pursue this line of inquiry as long as Mr. Harrod does eventually get to the point."

"As I will shortly, Your Honor," John Harrod assured the judge.

"Then proceed, Mr. Harrod," the judge said, and Harvey Etienne sat down again.

"So . . . your brother and Mr. Poe were *not* married—"

"Benny and Jared *were* married," Lucrece growled, interrupting Harrod. "I don't give a shit what the fucking state of Louisiana says, they were married."

"Ms. DuBois," the judge said, leaning his black-robed bulk toward Lucrece, "I would strongly caution you to watch your language in my courtroom."

"I'm sorry," she said, not sounding it one bit.

Harrod coughed dryly into one fist and continued.

"Then, Ms. DuBois, would you say that you respected your brother's relationship with Mr. Poe the same as you would any *legal* marriage?"

"Of course I did. I *do.*"

"Because in your opinion the homosexual union between your late brother Benjamin and Mr. Poe was as sacred as any legal, state-sanctioned marriage, am I correct?"

"Yes," Lucrece hissed. Harvey Etienne put one big restraining hand on Jared's shoulder.

"Tell me, Ms. DuBois, do you believe that adultery would be a violation of that union?"

This caught Lucrece off guard. *"What?"*

"Just answer the question, Ms. DuBois," Harrod said, standing very near her now. "Do you believe that a marriage, even an illegal homosexual marriage like your brother's, would be violated by the sin of adultery?"

"What are you trying to get me to say, Mr. Harrod?"

"All in the world I want from you, Ms. DuBois, is a straight answer to my question."

She watched him for a moment in silence. Jared could see how hard Lucrece was breathing, could see the fire sparking in her pale green eyes. Harvey tightened his grip on Jared's shoulder.

"Because if you *do* hold that union sacred, Ms. DuBois, I'd be very curious to know how you justified your own relationship with Mr. Poe."

John Harrod was resting one hand on the oaken rail of the witness stand, his eyebrows arched in expectation of her answer and a smug, victorious smirk on his lips. He bent close to Lucrece and spoke as low as he could and still be heard by the entire courtroom.

"I'm waiting, Ms. DuBois. I'm sure everyone in this room is waiting to hear your answer."

"*Objection,* Your Honor," Harvey Etienne said, standing again but still pressing down hard on Jared's shoulder. "This is immaterial and prejudicial, and the state has offered no evidence whatsoever to substantiate such a charge."

"Come on, Ms. DuBois," Harrod urged through a big Cheshire-cat grin. "Just tell the truth. That's all I'm asking you do. Just tell us the truth."

"Your Honor!" Harvey Etienne shouted, and the fat judge struck his gavel three times in quick succession. It made a sound like gunfire. He wiped one sweaty hand across his exasperated face and turned toward Harrod.

"I presume this *is* leading somewhere, Mr. Harrod," he said.

"It goes directly to motive, Your Honor." Then, looking over his shoulder at Jared and his lawyers, he added, "*And* I have witnesses. Witnesses who will attest to knowledge of a sexual relationship not only between Lucrece DuBois and Jared Poe, but between Ms. DuBois and her own brother."

"You're a sick, hateful son of a bitch," Lucrece said. Leaning slightly forward in the witness box, she spat in his face. There was a brief shocked silence in the courtroom.

"That means a lot, Ms. DuBois," Harrod said at last, taking a handkerchief from his pocket. "Coming as it does from a confirmed sodomite such as yourself."

Jared lunged across the table, dragging Harvey Etienne after him, and the court exploded in a turmoil of shouting and camera flashes.

"You leave her the fuck alone, you bastard," Jared screamed over the pandemonium. "You leave her alone *now* or I'll fucking kill you."

Then Etienne was hauling him backward across the table, scattering briefs and legal pads. An expensive briefcase clattered loudly to the marble floor and vomited more papers. There were other hands on him, pulling him back toward the chair where he was expected to sit still and listen while John Henry Harrod lied and twisted the truth to fit his needs, while he hurt Lucrece. Jared lunged again and was rewarded with the sound of his collar tearing.

But Harrod had turned his attention away from Lucrece, took one cautious step toward Jared.

"It is true, isn't it, Mr. Poe? It's true that you killed Benjamin DuBois because you'd decided that you *really* wanted his sister and neither of them could keep their hands off each other. You were *jealous,* weren't you, Mr. Poe?"

"Shut up!" Lucrece screamed from the stand. "Please make him shut up!"

Jared tore free, tumbled headfirst off the other side of the table, and was on his feet in an instant. He caught a fleeting glimpse of one of the court bailiffs, and there was a sudden crushing pain across the back of his skull. As he fell there was only the sound of Lucrece crying and, much farther away, the wood-on-wood crack of the judge's gavel.

Angola Prison lies at the end of State Highway 66 by a sharp bend in the Mississippi River, surrounded on three sides by deep and drowning waters, hemmed in on the fourth by the rugged, rattlesnake-infested Yunica Hills. Eighteen thousand acres of Louisiana wilderness set aside for the punishment and rehabilitation of evil men and crazy men and men who are simply too stupid not to get caught.

As in so much of Louisiana, so much of the South, time has *almost* stood still here. Angola is not so different than the day it opened its gates in 1868, barely three years after the Confederacy surrendered at Appomattox. A vast cotton and soybean plantation on the banks of the river, hidden away from the rest of the world by all-but-impenetrable stands of oak and slash pine, a world with its own secrets, rules, and deadly rituals.

Jared Poe arrived at Angola on a muggy October day, an afternoon still plagued by summer's heat, but the sky was a bright autumn blue. As the bus carried him through the front gates Jared craned his neck to look back the way they'd come, straining for one last pointless glimpse of lost freedom through a wake of exhaust and red clay dust.

The jury had needed only two hours to find him guilty of Benny's murder, two hours to decide how and where the rest of Jared's life would be spent. The judge had taken even less time to decide how it would end.

Death row wasn't far from the front gates, just past watchtowers four and five, four concrete walls the same sickly green as pistachio ice cream or Irish Spring soap. Jared wondered if they'd always been that color or if the merciless delta sun had faded them as it did men.

There was nothing notable about his arrival, a dull ceremony of chains and keys and paperwork that concluded with Jared being led to his cell through a gauntlet of six barred doors; above one of them someone had painted DEATH ROW in tawdry crimson, on the off chance, he supposed, that a man might think he was somewhere else. Abandon all hope, ye who enter here, and all that good shit. The air in the cell block smelled faintly of vomit, disinfectant, and tobacco smoke. Finally they locked him into the six-by-eight-foot cell that would be his last home. "Get used to it," the guard said as he slammed the door closed and electronic locks clicked solidly into place.

Jared sat in silence for the first five minutes, staring down at his prison-issue shoes, waiting for some small part of the nightmare to begin to feel real to him. When a voice whispered his name from the cell next door, he got up from his bunk and walked to the bars.

"Did someone say something to me?"

"Yeah, I said something to you, faggot," the voice replied in a heavy Hispanic accent. "You that Poe motherfucker, ain't you? You that fag sonabitch we been seein' all over television, ain't you?"

"Yeah," Jared answered. "Yeah, I guess I am."

"Yeah, well, you just listen to me, Anglo. There ain't no television celebrities in here. So you might have been some bad-ass spooky voodoo sonabitch down in New Orleans, but in here you just another piece of white meat waitin' your turn to ride Gertie. *Comprende?*"

And then someone down the row of cells was yelling, "Why don't you shut your wetback mouth, Gonzalez? I got a fuckin' migraine and all I can hear is your big fuckin' mouth jabberin' away down there."

"Hey, man! *Fuck* you!"

"No, Gonzalez, fuck *you*! Fuck you *and* your burrito-eatin' whore-bitch of a mama!"

Jared went back to his bunk and sat down, listened until Gonzalez and the other man got tired of yelling at each other, then listened to the other sounds, all the captive sounds inside the cement box. Eventually he began to make a mental list of the ways someone could kill himself in here if he *really* wanted to, if there was finally no other sane choice left. He stopped at fifteen.

The long weeks became months, days creeping by at a caterpillar's pace, but then so many of them were gone and Jared was at a loss to explain how the monotonous routine of television and pasty, tasteless meals could have devoured so much time.

He was allowed to leave his cell only for brief showers and calls from his lawyers, who made uncertain promises about his appeal. Lucrece called only once and he made her promise never to do it again. Never mind how much hope he might have gleaned from the sound of her, he would not have it.

"Christ, Jared," she'd said, "I can't just let you sit there and fucking rot."

"Neither of us has much of a choice in the matter. I love you, Lucrece, but *please* don't do it again." Then he'd hung up on her. There was no room for hope in this shithole. That's what those sloppy red letters over the door on the way in were meant to remind you, just some illiterate fuck's hateful idea of a joke, the allusion to Dante surely accidental, but Jared had learned a long time ago that intention and message do not always go hand in hand.

Jared also got three short trips a week outside the pistachio building, a handful of minutes at a time in the exercise yard so he could stare through the fence at the forested hills on the other side or the empty sky overhead before the guard herded him back inside again.

One day he'd been half asleep in his bunk, had been rereading a tattered Clive Barker paperback and dozed off, and then Gonzalez was calling him, a loud whisper through the concrete. Jared got up and found the small polished piece of metal that he could hold between the bars for a mirror so he could actually see Ruben Gonzalez while they talked.

"Hey, man. They took Hector." Jared watched the blurry reflection of his neighbor's face in the scratched and dented surface of the mirror.

"When?" Jared asked, because he was expected to ask, not because he actually gave a shit. Hector Montoni had been convicted of raping twelve children in Baton Rouge and Biloxi, of murdering the last three. He'd made videotapes of every one of the assaults.

"Jus' about fifteen minutes ago, man," Ruben said. "He's *over* there by now. He's in the death house by now." Gonzalez stepped away from the bars, out of the range of Jared's mirror. For a while he mumbled prayers in Spanish.

Jared went back to his cot and picked up the copy of *The Great and Secret Show,* read one paragraph before Ruben started calling him again. This time Jared didn't bother with the mirror. He lit a cigarette and sat down on the floor beside the bars.

"Two thousand volts," Ruben Gonzalez said. "That's a lot, huh? That's a whole lotta juice to shoot through someone, ain't it?"

"Yeah, it is," Jared said.

"They say it tears *holes* in your body, man. They say it jumps right outta your eyeballs like lightning and blows off the ends of your fingers. Jesus fuck, why don't they just fuckin' shoot us or somethin', you know? Somethin' a little more humanitarian."

"Humane," Jared corrected. "Something a little more *humane.*"

"Hey, screw *you,* you faggot sonabitch. You just sittin' over there so goddamn cool, man, like a fuckin' ice cube 'cause you got them fat-cat lawyers workin' for you, right? 'Cause you ain't used up all your appeals."

"Maybe," Jared said, and took another drag off his cigarette, blew smoke through the bars.

"*Maybe?* What kind of macho bullshit is that, man?"

"*Maybe* I just don't give a shit, that's all."

Ruben laughed a humorless laugh on the other side of the wall.

"Yeah, right. You gonna give a shit when they come to drag your murderin' faggot ass out to that van and drive you off to the death house. You ain't gonna be sayin' maybe then, asshole."

"Maybe not," Jared said, and crushed out his cigarette against the floor.

"Fuck you, man." Ruben Gonzalez fell quiet for a while then, five or ten minutes, and eventually Jared heard him praying again and went back to his book.

A few months later Jared Poe was led out to the exercise yard for the last time. It was a sweltering late-August afternoon filled with mosquitoes and the threat of rain, thunderheads piling up off toward Weyanoke and the state line farther north. He stood near the fence watching the clouds, not smoking, just breathing cleaner air into his lungs, washing a little of the prison out of him with air that smelled like pine sap and sunlight.

And then the guard disappeared, the first time that had ever happened, and Jared was left alone. For the first time since the judge had read his sentence Jared felt an icy twinge of fear in his gut, a sudden rush of goose bumps along his exposed arms. He stood with his back to the fence and watched the dark doorway leading back into death row. It yawned back at him like an open mouth, the toothless mouth of something ancient that could swallow a man whole and leave no trace but his absence.

When the Cuban stepped through that black hole Jared knew this was a setup. He didn't have a fucking clue who the big man was or what business there might possibly be between them, but he *knew* it had to be a setup.

The man stood by the doorway a moment, staring across the gravel yard toward Jared. His dark eyes were filled with something that transcended hate, something that had lain a long time in the shadow of that gaze, getting fat on bad memories.

Even before he saw the stainless-steel glint of the sharpened spoon in the man's hand, he knew the Cuban was there to kill him.

"Why?" Jared asked. The man raised his head a little, flared his nostrils wide as if he were sniffing the air to get Jared's scent, to be sure he had located a proper object for his hatred and the damage it could do.

"You're Poe. You're the queer bastard that killed all those people in New Orleans," he said.

Jared had long ago become too used to the presumption of his guilt, far too numbed to the denial of his innocence, to bother contradicting the Cuban.

"I'm Jared Poe," he said.

"You killed my brother," the man said, and took a step closer to Jared. "You killed my little brother and left him floating in the river like garbage for the fish to eat."

Jared caught a glimpse of the guard watching from just inside the doorway, a pale figure in the gloom, his eyes much too fascinated by what was about to happen to look away.

"I didn't kill your brother," Jared said, surprised at how calm he sounded, how steady his voice could be with his death standing only a few feet away. "I know you're not going to believe me, but I didn't kill anyone."

"Liar," the man said, spitting the word out like a bitter taste, and then he mumbled something else in Spanish that Jared didn't understand. He moved quickly, and even if Jared had been inclined to run, even if what he'd told Ruben Gonzalez all those months ago had been a lie, there would have been nowhere to go. So Jared took one small step backward and braced himself.

The Cuban's makeshift dagger went in just above his navel, made a little popping sound as it punched through skin and muscle to the vital organs underneath. The Cuban pulled the blade out and drove it back in a second time. Jared's knees buckled. He could feel the warm blood pumping out through his T-shirt, soaking into his jeans, spilling like piss down his leg. He saw it red and sticky on the man's hand and dripping in dark spatters to the white limestone gravel.

"I didn't," Jared whispered, sinking to the ground. "I didn't kill anyone."

"No, man," the Cuban sneered. "That ain't why they put motherfuckers in here, for doin' nothing to people."

The Cuban turned and walked away, left Jared kneeling in the dirt and blood, his life pouring out of the hole in his belly. He looked up once. The Cuban was gone and the guard was still standing in the shadows, watching, smiling. Jared fell over on his side, starting to feel the pain in his guts through the shock, and in a little while someone called for a doctor.

He supposes some people in his present situation—if in fact anyone has ever *been* in this crazy situation before—would have gone back to Angola and killed the Cuban. Jared cannot see the point. The Cuban was as much a force of nature as this storm, a happenstance that killed him before the state of Louisiana could. Mostly, though, he can't imagine killing the Cuban because he doesn't blame the guy for killing him. The Cuban had genuinely believed he was killing the man who'd tortured his brother to death. In his place, Jared would have done—*would* do—the same.

* * *

Jared stands on the roof of the little cottage behind the glass-studded wall. The roof is only slightly pitched, and there is a skylight that must have been added fairly recently. The rain falls on him, a thousand tiny hammers every second, and rushes around his feet on its way to the overflowing gutters. The lightning and thunder dance above the city, all flash and bluster.

Jared kneels beside the skylight and looks inside.

In a room painted the color of dead violets John Harrod is fucking a black girl up the ass. She grips the shimmering silk sheets in both hands and bucks in time to Harrod's thrusts. Her mouth is open, but Jared can't hear her over the storm. Harrod's lips are curled back to show his perfect white teeth, the tip of his tongue protruding between them like a bit of some invertebrate trying to escape its shell.

Jared puts one hand against the glass. *You bastard,* he thinks. *You goddamned hypocritical bastard.* There are suddenly too many things in his head at once, images of Benny and the trial, the thing that the killer left of Benny, the Cuban and Lucrece and a smiling portrait of John Henry Harrod with his wife and two children. Jared pushes slightly against the skylight. He can feel that it would break very easily.

The crow lands on the skylight and caws loudly at Jared, loud even over the roar of the storm. The wind rips at them both, threatens to pluck them from this rooftop and fling them into the taller buildings, press them flat like stray leaves or newspapers against the old brick walls.

"What the fuck do you want?" Jared sneers at her from behind the mask, a sneer to match Harrod's down below. The crow tucks her wings close to her body, huddles against the glass, making a smaller target for the wind.

"I *have* to do this," he tells her. "That motherfucker isn't going to get away with what he did."

And then he hears Lucrece, her voice as clear as if he was back in the apartment with her, as if she were standing in front of him with no wind to rip away the sound.

"This isn't going to bring Benny back to you," she says, and the big black bird cocks her head to one side.

"So now you're a fucking ventriloquist?"

The crow loses her footing and is blown a few inches across the slick glass.

"It doesn't *matter.*" Jared isn't sure whether he's speaking to the crow or Lucrece or both, and he doesn't really care. "Because of Harrod, the monster that killed Benny is still out there somewhere . . ."

"You can't do this," Lucrece says as the crow struggles to keep her grip on the skylight, her tiny claws skating on the glass. "Killing Harrod will only make a monster of you too, Jared."

He laughs at her, that she could possibly be so fucking naive after all she's seen, after her life and her brother's death. The laugh feels good, like he's coughing up something poisoned, something burning deep in his belly.

"Get a clue, babe. Haven't you looked in a mirror lately? We're *all* monsters."

"You can*not* do this, Jared," she says again.

"Watch me," he replies. With one arm he sweeps the crow aside, gives the wind a helping hand. The bird flutters away into the murky sky.

Jared smashes the skylight, one punch and it shatters just as easily as he imagined it would. The glass and the rain pour down on Harrod and his whore. Jared follows right behind.

He lands on his feet beside the bed. The woman is already screaming. There are jagged shards of glass protruding from her back and buttocks, and she's frantically scrambling away from Harrod, clawing her way toward the bed's wicker headboard. Harrod turns to face Jared, his trousers in a pile around his ankles and his wet, uncircumcised penis dangling loose inside its condom, already going limp, shriveling up like a salted slug.

"At least you wore a goddamn rubber, you filthy pig," Jared says. He's still laughing, practically giggling now; whatever's broken loose inside him is still getting out, a fury he's carried to the grave and back, and the laughter seems to make as much sense as anything else. "Wouldn't want to risk AIDS. That's a fag death."

"Who . . . who . . . who . . ." Harrod says, the word coughed out through the perfect, astonished O of his mouth.

"Wrong bird." Jared snickers and shoves Harrod, presses one hand against the man's bare chest and sends him stumbling backward to crash against a vanity. Bottles of perfume and tubes of lipstick clatter to the floor. One of the bottles breaks and the room is instantly filled with the sickly, funereal smell of flowers.

"Who . . ." Harrod says again. Now he has one arm up to protect his face.

"You're a slow learner, aren't you, Mr. Harrod?"

"Get out of here!" the girl on the bed screams. "Get out of here, motherfucker! I'm calling the fucking police!"

Jared ignores her and steps past the foot of the bed. Harrod is cowering in front of the vanity, nowhere left for him to run. His breath is labored, uneven.

"*Look* at me, John Harrod," Jared says. He is trying hard to stop laughing. He bites down on his tongue, but that's funny too. Harrod peeks up at him, terrified eyes peering past the shelter of his hairy forearms, and that's absolutely fucking hilarious.

"I know a rhyme, John Harrod. Just a little nursery rhyme my mother taught me. You're not afraid of a little nursery rhyme, are you?"

"Get out of my house!" the woman screams behind him. Harrod doesn't say a word.

" 'There were three crows sat on a tree,
They were as black as black can be.
One of them said to his mate:
What shall we do for grub to eat?' "

"I *said* to get the fuck out of my house, you fucking weirdo! *Now!*" Jared hears the box springs creak behind him. He leans over and punches Harrod, feels the bridge of the man's nose break. Blood gushes down Harrod's chin, falls in bright spatters to the polished floorboards. Harrod gasps and cups his hands together to shield his wounded face.

"Sorry. But you really weren't paying attention, were you? I don't have all day. There's a hurricane coming . . ."

"Who the hell *are* you?" Harrod whispers. He sounds as afraid as Jared has ever heard anyone sound, a complicated, suffocating sort of fear that Jared is gratified to hear.

"Well, that's the question, now isn't it? But where was I?" Jared scratches his head like the Tin Man in *The Wizard of Oz.*

"What do you want?" Harrod begs. "Just please tell me what the fuck you *want!*"

Jared finishes the rhyme:

" 'There's an old dead horse in yonder lane,
Whose body has been lately slain.
We'll fly upon his old breastbone,
And pluck his eyes out, *one by one.*' "

Harrod begins to cry. Jared kneels next to him in mock concern. "Jesus, that's an awful thing to teach a little kid, don't you think?"

Harrod makes a choking noise and looks at the blood in his hands.

"Now maybe if she'd read to me from the Bible like your mother must've done for you, maybe then I'd have turned out to be a *good* man just like you, Mr. Harrod."

"All right, you asshole, I've had *enough* of this shit!" Jared turns toward the naked woman on the bed just as she pumps the huge shotgun in her hands. There are shells scattered like candy across the rumpled sheets.

Jared drops to the floor and rolls away from the bed, away from Harrod. The boom of the gun is deafening in the small bedroom, thunder trapped and wanting out. Jared knows he's been hit before he even stops moving. He staggers to his feet as she's reloading, ejecting the spent shells and slipping two new ones into the chamber. There's a hole in his side as big as an orange and he gets a whiff of his own ruptured bowels.

"Jesus Christ, Harrod. Where'd you *find* this bitch?" Jared dives for the bed. The woman raises the shotgun, takes aim down the long double barrel, but a fraction of a second later he's wrestling the gun from her hands. She screams again and slides to the floor.

"This hasn't got anything to do with you, lady, so stay the fuck out of it and you're not going to get hurt."

Seeing his chance, Harrod kicks the tangle of his pants away and makes a dash for the door. He is gone before Jared can do anything but curse his pale, skinny, fleeing ass.

John Harrod slams the door behind him as he exits the cottage, the pièd-a-terre where he's installed a succession of women for three years now, mostly blacks and Latinas. The storm seizes him immediately, broadsides him. He slips down the front steps and lands in a muddy heap between the Oldsmobile and the house. His ears are ringing from the shotgun blast and his mouth is full of blood from his broken nose.

He almost panics when he reaches for the keys and his fucking pants aren't even there, but then he remembers the extra set tucked above the sun visor. He slides in behind the wheel and pulls the door shut, locking out the storm and the crazy son of a bitch in the white Mardi Gras mask.

John Harrod folds down the visor and the keys tumble out into his naked lap, cold metal against his bare thigh. He tries to start the car with the trunk key on his first attempt and it takes him a moment to find the right one. His heart is ticking off the seconds like a countdown. Then there's a sharp scratching sound and he squints through the rain beating down on the windshield. There is a big black bird standing on the hood of the car, staring in at him.

There were three crows sat on a tree,
They were as black as black can be . . .

"Oh, God," he mutters. He turns the key in the ignition and stomps the gas pedal. The car roars to life momentarily; then the motor coughs, sputters, and dies. The crow spreads its wings and caws loudly, hops toward him, and pecks at the windshield.

Harrod turns the key again, mashes the accelerator to the floor. This time the engine only chugs weakly a couple of times before it's quiet again. The Oldsmobile begins to fill with the smell of gasoline and he knows that he's flooded the engine. When he glances out the windshield the bird is gone. Harrod breathes a nervous sigh of relief and tells himself to calm down. *No way that fucker could have gotten the gun away from Tonya without getting his face blown off,* he thinks. *All you gotta do now, buddy, is calm the fuck down.*

And then something dark drops out of the sky and crashes down onto the hood of the Olds. The car rocks violently from the impact. Where the bird was seconds before, the man in the grinning white mask stands now, pointing the Remington shotgun straight at Harrod's head.

And pluck his eyes out, one by one.

Harrod screams, opens his mouth wide and screams like a woman, as the man turns the gun around and slams the butt against the windshield. It cracks, spiderwebs, and on the second blow caves in, spraying Harrod with diamond bits of safety glass. The rain and wind spill through the hole. Harrod reaches for the .38 he keeps hidden beneath the seat.

"Benjamin DuBois!" the man howls above the wind. He's stooping now, peering in at Harrod through the hole he's made in the windshield. "What does that name *mean* to you, you fucking coward?"

"It means you're a dead son of a bitch," Harrod says. He shoves the revolver through the hole and pulls the trigger and the gun goes off in the man's face.

"Fuck," Harrod grunts, wiping blood from his eyes, blinking through a blurry, red haze. The man in the mask is on his knees now, one hand covering his face; blood drips between his fingers, runs across the hood of the car.

"*Now,* you goddamn freak," Harrod growls. "Now maybe you'll tell me what the fuck you want."

The man lowers his hand slowly and there's a neat hole in the mask, right between his eyes. Blood flows from the eyeholes of the mask like tears.

"For you to be waiting for me, Harrod," the man says, raising the shotgun again. "For you to be there waiting for me when I get back to hell."

The last thing John Henry Harrod sees is the barrel of the Remington 870P sliding in through the hole in the windshield, raindrops glistening on steel. He closes his eyes before the thunder.

Jared lies curled on the hood of the black car, his finger still wrapped tightly around the trigger of the shotgun. He never thought there could be pain like the pain behind his eyes, the hurt filling up his skull. The hit he took inside the cottage was nothing by comparison, an irrelevant, dull ache next to the pain in his head. He moves and the world spins. He is still again.

But the son of a bitch is dead. This is a small comfort, an aspirin for an amputation. Jared cranes to see the stump of Harrod's neck, a jagged few inches of spine jutting out between dead shoulders and then *nothing,* nothing but the gore dripping from the ceiling of the car. Everything inside the Oldsmobile seems to be covered in a fine crimson mist, a fog of blood and brains and vaporized bone. The only thing he can recognize as human is one ear stuck to the mangled headrest of the driver's seat.

Jared hears the crow before he sees her, the hoarse caw cutting through the whistling wind before she lights in front of him. She stares at him a moment, then stabs the hood of the car once with her ebony dagger beak.

"You have to get out of there," Lucrece says, and the crow pecks the metal again.

"He's dead, Lucrece. I killed him," he whispers to the crow. "He's dead."

"That doesn't matter now, Jared," Lucrece replies, her voice urgent, firm, frightened. "There will be cops coming soon. They can't find you there. Get up. Get moving . . ."

He closes his eyes. The afterimage left by the pistol is still there, waiting, an orange smudge in the pale dark. Lucrece doesn't say anything more. When he opens his eyes again, the crow is gone. Her insistent beak has left a small dent in the hood, a flake of paint missing and the gray primer showing through. Jared bites his tongue against the pain and drags himself off the car.

Lucrece is sitting alone at the kitchen table when she hears footsteps somewhere in the apartment. She's been clutching a single black feather for almost two hours now, a feather she found on the bedspread after she came back from the Eye of Horus. She's still surprised that it worked, that the bridge between the crow and Jared was strong enough, that she was strong enough to make an actual telepathic connection. If it even was anything as simple as telepathy. All Lucrece is really certain of right now is the terrible vertigo and disarming emptiness that the effort left coiled inside her. That, and her relief at hearing Jared's voice again.

"I'm in here," she calls out, pushing her chair back from the table. There are more footsteps and the flutter of wings, so she tries to stand, has to steady herself against one corner of the table.

Christ, maybe I broke something in my brain, she thinks, fighting back a sudden wave of nausea. From the bedroom, there's the sound of breaking glass and Jared cursing.

"C'mon, you pussy," she tells herself. This time she manages to make it all the way to the living room doorway before she has to stop and brace herself against a wall to keep from falling on her ass.

"We gotta get you a goddamn cell phone, Jared Poe," she says, and laughs, but it's a hollow, anxious sort of laugh. "I don't think I want to try that particular trick again."

Another ten feet and she's made it all the way into the bedroom. Jared is lying facedown on the canopy bed with the crow standing over him, faithful as a television watchdog. The bird glances up at Lucrece and caws once.

Jesus, so much fucking blood, she thinks, flashing back on the first time she walked into the room after Benny's death—it's not *that* bad, but it's bad enough. Bad enough to trigger a lingering déjà vu that leaves her feeling even more queasy and disoriented.

"I'm not dead," Jared croaks, the way someone with a really bad hangover whispers, as if he's afraid even his voice will break the world. "I'm still not dead."

"Shhh . . . don't talk, Jared." She tries not to sound as frightened as she is, tries not to look away. But there's a hole in the back of his head that she could put her fist into, a shattered rim of white bone matted with drying blood and hair and clinging bits of gray matter.

Lucrece sits down on the bed beside him. She reaches for his hand and he clutches hers, squeezes so hard that it hurts, but she doesn't say anything. She just squeezes back as hard as she can, and the crow looks at her approvingly.

"It's not as bad as it looks," Jared says, tries to laugh and starts coughing instead.

"You weren't supposed to go after them," Lucrece says. She only realizes that she's crying when she tastes a drop of salty water at one corner of her mouth. "The crow is here to protect you, Jared. But she can't, not if you—"

"But they're *dead,*" Jared says, interrupting her. Then he rolls slightly to one side so that Lucrece can see the carnival mask still strapped around his face and the place where the bullet went in—a small black hole, no bigger than a dime. The blood vessels in his eyes have hemorrhaged, the scleral whites turned red, and his pupils are huge and dilated. Those terrible, hurting eyes and the mask, but there's nothing left that she can recognize as Jared. Only his voice, and even that seems somehow changed, older and some of the anger drained away, and whatever's left behind is much darker. Much more dangerous.

"And I can't be sorry for that. I don't give a fuck *what* I was supposed to do . . . I can't be sorry for that."

"You don't have to be sorry, Jared," she says, wishes she weren't crying, wishes he didn't have to see her cry. "But the person who killed Benny is still *out* there, and *that's* why you've come back. Not to get your fool head blown off trying to settle all these old scores with the whole goddamn world."

"The bird hasn't exactly been much help with the main matter," he says, and closes his eyes, and she's glad not to have to look into them, ashamed of her relief but relieved anyway.

"It's not her fault," Lucrece says. "I think there's something *wrong* about the killer. Something that's getting in the way."

"You said that already," Jared mumbles. "Last night."

"The police found another one this morning. A body in the fountain in Audubon Park. The news didn't have a lot of details, but it's him, Jared. I know it's him."

"I'm not a goddamn detective, Lucrece. I don't know how to track down a serial killer. I was just a photographer . . ."

"Then you have to find someone who *is* a detective. The cop who's handling this new murder, maybe him . . ."

Jared's grip on her hand relaxes suddenly, unexpectedly, and his eyelids flutter.

"Jared? What's happening?"

"Maybe I'm dying," he says, so quietly that she barely catches his voice over the wind howling down Ursulines Street. "Maybe I screwed up, and that's the only chance I get."

The crow caws again and Lucrece moves closer to Jared. She brushes his hair back from his face, and when she begins to remove the mask he flinches, tenses, but doesn't stop her from doing it.

"I'm not going to hurt you, Jared."

Underneath the mask Jared's face is streaked with gore and dirt and there are livid bruises around both his eyes. His nose has been bleeding and there's a crust of dried blood caked around his nostrils.

"I'm going to clean you up a little, that's all." Lucrece looks past Jared to the crow. She can still hear its thoughts. She follows its instructions exactly, moving slowly, and Jared lets her. The cutting on her back tingles, the scars in the shape of a crow, as they did when they were fresh and just beginning to heal.

"We're going to help you, both of us. And you'll find the son of a bitch who killed Benny."

"One way or another," Jared whispers.

"One way or another," Lucrece replies, and drops the ruined mask to the bedroom floor.

8

The bad scene in Audubon Park was the perfectly shitty start to a perfectly shitty day. It's past three in the afternoon now and the hangover has found Frank again, even though he's already slipped into the bathroom twice for hits off the bottle of Jack Daniel's he always keeps tucked safe inside his locker. Otherwise he's just been sitting at his desk since he and Wallace got back from Metairie, pretending to make some sort of progress with the day's paperwork, the report on the murder in Audubon Park and stuff he should have finished days ago. His head feels like an overripe melon, ready to burst from its own weight.

"So you really gonna skip out on the party at the chamber of horrors this evening?" Wallace asks. Frank opens one eye, glares past his typewriter and the clutter of unfinished reports and carbon paper. By comparison, Wallace's desk is an exercise in obsessive neatness, more like some spinster librarian's desk than a cop's. Just the sight of those pathologically neat stacks and the freshly sharpened pencils in a souvenir Saints mug makes Frank want to punch his partner in the face.

"I think you and Tierney can probably handle the fucking autopsy without me," he says. Wallace shrugs.

"Shit, I don't even know what's left to autopsy, Frank. I mean, how's she gonna cut that mess up any more?"

Frank shakes three cherry Maalox tablets from a plastic bottle, four Bayer extra-strength from another, and pops all seven at once, chews them dry.

"That's disgusting, Frank," Wallace says, and starts typing again. Every time a key strikes paper Frank thinks that's the final straw and his head's going to pop.

"Jesus, Wally. Can't that wait?"

"I ain't gettin' behind with all this shit just 'cause you have a hangover, Frank."

"You're a damned considerate fuck, Wally," Frank says around the powdery mouthful of aspirin and antacid. He closes his eyes again and swallows the mess.

"Anyway," Wallace says, "if the evac orders come through, nobody'll be doing anything but wadin' outta here."

That morning the National Hurricane Center had posted a hurricane warning for most of southeastern Louisiana, from the coast as far inland as Baton Rouge. Michael was due to make landfall sometime between midnight and one A.M., unless they got lucky and the storm decided to kick the shit out of east Texas instead.

"One can always hope," Frank mutters. His mouth feels like he's just eaten a handful of bitter cherry-flavored chalk. He decides it's been long enough since the last drink for him to deserve another.

"I'm gonna go puke," he says, standing up, and Wallace just nods and keeps pecking away on his old Royal manual.

"Thanks for caring."

"Sure thing, Franklin," Wallace says and hits the return lever. The Royal's carriage pings and slams violently to the left.

"One day that piece of shit's gonna take off all your fingers, Wally," he says, and staggers toward the toilet.

The cloying smells of stale piss and bright green deodorant cakes burn Frank's sinuses. For a few precarious moments he thinks maybe he really will puke. He leans against the sink and stares at the face in the mirror. Frank hasn't shaved since the day before, and his skin is the color of raw oysters. There are little beads of sweat on his forehead and upper lip, bags under his eyes that could pass for bruises.

"You're not lookin' so great, Frankie," he says, and turns the hot-water knob. The faucet whistles and then makes an ugly coughing noise before it starts spitting icy, rust-stained water. Frank dips his hands into the sink, splashes his face with the stuff. It smells like mud but it feels good. When he looks back up at the mirror, though, he can't say that he looks any better—just wetter.

"You're a fucking slob," he tells himself. "*That's* what you are."

Frank takes the half-pint of bourbon from the inside pocket of his blazer and unscrews the cap. "Cheers," he says, offering a mercy toast to the sick-looking guy in the mirror. That's when he sees the bird perched on top of one of the stalls, watching him. A huge black crow like something from an old Hammer horror film. Frank almost drops the bottle.

"I need to talk to you, Frank Gray." For just a second Frank thinks the bird said that, the long second that it takes him to turn around and see the man in the black latex coat sitting beneath the room's single small window.

The man's wearing a leather hood, open zippers where the eyes and mouth should be, a slit for the nose. Frank thinks he saw something like it in a bondage magazine once.

"Who the fuck are you?" Frank reaches for his gun, stops halfway when the man pulls the shotgun out from under his coat and pumps it once.

"Please," the man says. "I've had enough of that shit today. All I want to do is talk to you. I swear."

"Jesus," Frank whispers, glancing at the door, at least five yards away. There's no way he could make it without getting his head blown off. "Someone else could walk through that door at any second. What are you gonna do then?"

"Deal with it when it happens," the man replies.

"I just don't want to get shot because somebody has to take a dump, you know?"

"Then we better get this over with quickly, Detective."

"Jesus," Frank says again. "Would you believe this is the second time in the past twenty-four hours someone's pulled a gun on me in the john?"

"You're investigating the murder in Audubon Park this morning, aren't you?" The man gets up slowly, keeping the barrel of the gun pointed at Frank's chest. The crow caws loudly and flaps its wings.

"I guess the bird's yours, huh?" Frank asks, sparing another glance at the crow.

"Something like that. Now answer the question."

"Yeah, me and my partner got that one. Sure. Now will you please point that fucking cannon somewhere else?"

The gun doesn't move an inch, and Frank tries to concentrate on being a cop, not just some scared asshole with a shotgun aimed at him. He notes the man isn't wearing a shirt under the jacket. No shoes either. He's wearing ragged black pants that might have been nice once. There's a pool of water at his feet, dripping off his body.

"You think it's the Bourbon Street Ripper, don't you?" the man says, but Frank's looking at the little window. Too small and too far off the ground for someone to climb through. And besides, it's locked from the inside. The rain beats on the dirty, fly-blown glass.

"What do you think?" Frank asks the man.

"I think you're stalling."

"No, I'm just trying to figure out how the fuck you got in here without someone seeing you. You and that bird aren't really what I'd call inconspicuous."

"It's a long story, and believe me, you wouldn't buy it if I did tell you. Now answer the question, Detective. Do you think the body in the park this morning was a victim of the Ripper or not?"

Frank nods slowly. "Maybe. I'm waiting to see what the autopsy turns up."

"So you think the Ripper's still out there? That Jared Poe wasn't the killer after all?" Frank catches a glint of anger in the man's voice now, like sunlight off the blade of a knife.

"That's not exactly what I said."

"But is it what you *think*?" the man growls, and the crow caws again.

Frank sighs and looks at the bottle of Jack Daniel's in his shaking left hand.

"You mind if I have a drink of this first?" he asks, and the man says no, so Frank takes a drink. Courage in a bottle. Right now that's precisely what he needs, because he's pretty goddamn sure there's no way this freak's just going to let him walk away no matter how many questions he answers.

Frank sets the bottle on the edge of the sink and wipes his mouth with the back of one hand.

"We thought it was just a copycat," he says. "It still might be a copycat. I didn't work the Poe case or any of the Ripper murders. So I'm a little new to this shit."

And then he notices the drops of blood that have started falling from underneath the man's long coat, a crimson trickle mixing with the rainwater on the filthy tile floor.

"You're bleeding." Frank points at the drops. "Why don't you just tell me who the hell you are and maybe I can help you."

"We're both looking for the same killer, Frank Gray," the man in the leather hood says. "And I don't really give a shit which of us finds him first. But I want you to know this—Jared Poe didn't kill *anyone.* Not Benjamin DuBois or anybody else."

"Is that a fact?" Frank replies, looking toward the door again, trying to think of some way to buy a little more time. "You need a doctor," he says.

"No, Detective. I need a goddamn undertaker."

The door to the rest room opens and the crow cries out, leaps into the air, and seems somehow to fill the whole room with the sound of its wings. Frank ducks for cover, dives for one of the stalls, reaching back for his pistol as he moves. The stall door slams wide open and he bangs his knee against the porcelain edge of the toilet bowl. He crouches, waiting for the freak in the mask to pull the trigger, waiting for the killing thunder of the shotgun.

"What the fuck are you doing in here, Frank?" Wallace asks, peering cautiously into the stall. "Who were you talking to?"

Frank's heart sounds like a kettledrum in his ears and every cell in his body is drowning in adrenaline. He feels more sober than he has in weeks. He shakes his head and returns his gun to his shoulder holster.

"If you didn't see him I think I'd better just keep my mouth shut, Wally," he says.

"You better not be gettin' the fuckin' DTs on me, Franklin. We got entirely too much crazy shit goin' down already without you seein' ghosts in the little boys' room." Wallace reaches down to help Frank up from the floor. "The orders just came in to evacuate the whole goddamn parish. *Everyone.*"

"Wonderful," Frank mutters. There's something greasy on his hands from the floor and he pulls a wad of toilet paper from the roll to wipe them.

"That ain't all. And you ain't gonna even believe this other shit. They just found the DA over on St. Ann, sittin' in his car with his head blown off. Somebody used both barrels on him."

Frank has to sit down fast or he knows that he's going to fall. So he just sits on the toilet, still holding the wadded paper, and stares up at his partner.

The shotgun, he thinks, and then, like tic-tac-toe: *Vince Norris and then Jim Unger. And now John Harrod . . .*

We're both looking for the same killer, the man in the black hood said, the man with a crow. The man who must have walked out through the fucking wall.

"It's gonna be a long night, Franklin," Wallace says. "You might want to get some coffee in you while there's time. I just made a fresh pot."

"Yeah," Frank says. He can still hear the sound of the crow's wings, the velvet flutter loud as the storm. "That sounds like a good idea, Wally."

Jared stands on the roof and stares toward the river, toward the place where the river hides behind cold and colorless sheets of rain. His body parts the hurricane like the bow of a ship; there's something inside him that's even bigger, wilder than the whirling demon of water and wind. He holds the crow close to his body, sheltering it from the gales.

"Nobody got killed," he says. Lucrece is there somewhere, approving, but he doesn't need an answer. There's nothing left to do now but wait and hope the detective eventually leads him to the man who killed Benny.

The wind screams. Jared strokes the bird's smooth feathers with his gauze-swaddled hands.

Frank is filling a Styrofoam cup from Wallace's scalding pot of coffee when the telephone on his desk rings. He lets it ring two more times, and a fourth, taking a tentative sip of the bitter brew, before he picks up the receiver.

"Yeah," he says. For a second there is nothing but silence from the other end.

"Hello?"

"Gray?" a voice asks. "Detective *Frank* Gray?" The voice is male—Frank's pretty sure of that—but high, soft, almost androgynous. He wonders if it's being electronically disguised. Frank sets the cup down on the edge of his desk. The coffee tastes almost as bad as he expected.

"Yeah," he says. "You got him. What can I do for you?"

Frank hears something dry, like paper being slowly crumbled between callused palms. The caller inhales loudly, draws a sharp, uneven breath.

"The homosexual police officer who was at the fountain this morning?"

The man drawls the word—"homo-*sex*-shul"—and Frank feels the sweat popping out all over his body, the cold, creeping sensation like icy spider feet up his spine.

"What do you *want,* buddy?"

"To talk." The dry crackling sound comes through the receiver again.

"Yeah, well, I'm real short of conversation right now, so unless you fuckin' get to the point in the next five seconds I'm hanging up."

"You wouldn't want to do that," the man says.

"Why is that, buddy?" Frank asks. The sweat is starting to make him cold.

Another pause, and then, " 'On the morrow *he* will leave me as my Hopes have flown before,' " the man says softly.

"Jesus," Frank whispers. "Who the fuck are you?"

There's the dry sound again, and the voice continues.

" 'Startled at the stillness broken by reply so aptly spoken, *Doubtless,* said I, "*What it utters is its only stock and store . . .*" ' "

"Look, freako. Tell me who you are or I'm hanging up right this fucking *minute.*"

"No," the man says, and Frank can hear him smiling. "No, you won't. Because I'm the man, aren't I, Frank Gray? Not poor Jared Poe. Me. *I'm* the *man.*"

"You're the fucker in the mask, aren't you?"

"I don't wear masks. Only They need masks. I have nothing left to conceal."

"I'm hanging up now," Frank says.

"I don't think so. I'd listen if I were you. Unless you want the photographs to go to the media."

"Excuse me?" Frank sits down in his chair. There's no sign of Wallace, who was going down the hall for an update on the storm.

"Don't make me get sordid, Detective. I don't like to have to talk like that. To *say* those things aloud. But there are pictures. There have been plenty of opportunities . . ."

"Listen, fucker—"

"My name is Lethe," the man says. "Joseph Lethe. The body you found this morning, that was my work, Frank Gray."

Frank holds the phone away from his face as if he's just discovered it's crawling with some contagion or filth, holds it a foot from his face and stares across the disorderly assembly of desks and typewriters. This phone isn't wired, even if there were time for a trace.

There have been plenty of opportunities, the man said.

"Jesus H. fucking," Frank whispers, and hesitantly puts the phone to his ear again. "What do you want?"

"Good boy," the man says. "You want to know the truth, don't you, Frank?"

"You're saying you put the body in the fountain?"

"Oh, I'm saying a lot more than that, Detective. But not yet. Not over the phone."

And then the man named Joseph Lethe gives Frank an address and a time, and Frank scribbles it quickly on an old deli napkin.

"I don't have to tell you to come alone, Frank. Or not to talk to anyone else about our little conversation."

"Yeah," Frank says. "There's a goddamn hurricane coming, you know?"

"It doesn't matter. I can't wait any longer," the man says. "But cheer up. You're going to be a hero. How many faggot cops get to be heroes? You should be happy."

"Why?" Frank asks. A fat drop of sweat falls from his forehead to the top of the desk.

"Because I'm tired. That's all. It's been a long time and I'm tired. I want to stop now. They know who I am anyway, don't They? So what's the point in going on?"

"But why me?"

"Because you're such a good boy, Frank. Because . . ." The voice trails off, is quiet for the time it takes Frank's heart to beat eight times and skip once.

"Mr. Lethe? Are you still there?"

"There was lightning here. Did you hear it?" The man sounds different now. The glee and smug self-assurance in his voice has been replaced by a distance, a sad uncertainty. "When I was a child, I was struck by lightning," he says. "I was struck . . ."

"I don't understand. Is that important?" Frank asks him. He sees Wallace coming back through the doorway from the hall, looking straight at Frank and shaking his head.

"Isn't it?" Joseph Lethe asks back, asks as though he really needs the answer. Then the line goes dead and Frank hangs up the telephone.

"You don't even want to know," Wallace says, sitting down at his own desk across from Frank. "If those eggheads at the weather bureau are right, we're gonna be lookin' for a new job soon, 'cause there might not even *be* a New Orleans when Michael gets done with us."

"Yeah, look," Frank says, standing up, not sure his legs will hold him, but he's standing up anyway. "That was my sister on the phone, Wally. There's a family emergency and I have to go. I'll meet you back here later."

Frank takes his raincoat off the coat rack near the radiator, where it's been drying since they got back from Metairie.

"You never told me you had a sister, Frank."

"We're not really very close," Frank replies, already halfway to the door.

"You don't tell me shit, Franklin. You don't tell me anything unless I ask . . ."

But then Frank's in the hallway and there are other voices, people getting ready for the storm, and he can't hear Wallace anymore. On his way to the car he remembers why the name Joseph Lethe sounded familiar. Something he had to read for high school, a book on Greek mythology, and it named the five rivers that divide the underworld from the world of the living. One of them was the River Lethe, the river of forgetfulness.

Joseph Lethe pulls off the tissue paper cover he put over the receiver to protect him from germs and nanites. He hangs up the pay phone, wads the paper, and lets it fall toward the wet asphalt of the parking lot. The wind grabs it and whisks it off before it can hit the ground. He watches it flying away, sailing high over the roofs of the few cars parked outside the K&B, into the low, uneasy sky.

"I was struck," he says again, wondering how long until there will be more lightning. "I was struck."

And it's true. When he was a boy, barely eight years old and living with his family in Houma. *Don't stand under a tree when it storms,* his grandfather had said. His grandfather had told him that lots of times. But once there had been a thunderstorm and he forgot and hid beneath an old oak for shelter. The white fire came down and split the tree in two, cleaved it open and flowed through the earth into him. He can still remember that instant when he was full of fire. He came to some time later, lying in the rain, and someone had been standing over him, asking him his name over and over. *Do you know your name, boy? Can you tell me your name?*

But the lightning had left something inside him, something small and hard inside his head, and he *couldn't* remember his name. He knew other things, though. New things the lightning had wanted him to know. But not his name. That was part of the cost, his name. And he could never wear a watch after that, and compass needles acted funny when he was around. He didn't tell his parents, made the man asking his name promise not to tell, because he was okay and there was no need to tell them, was there? But they knew he was different after that day. They looked at him differently and spoke to him differently.

An old black woman—Julianna, who sold his mother tomatoes—said he wasn't right after that. She told his mother there was something bad inside him and that she knew a voodoo man in the bayou who could make him right again. That was the last time his mother bought Julianna's big red tomatoes or green frying tomatoes. But his mother looked at him differently, like she knew that everything the old woman had said was true.

The faggot cop will come, he thinks. *Not because he really cares who I am, but because he's afraid of what I know and what I might do with that knowledge. The same reason They're all afraid of me. Because I'm the man . . .*

A red Volkswagen sputters noisily past the pay phone, spraying muddy water from the flooded parking lot all over Joseph Lethe's shoes. He watches it go, stands there expressionless, water soaking right through his socks to his feet. Then he wipes his hands on his raincoat, and, safe in his knowledge and resolve, safe from the black wings spread above the drowning city, he crosses Napoleon Avenue to his car.

* * *

Lucrece is sitting on the couch in the living room paging through one of Benny's old *Sandman* comic books. There's nothing else she can do and so she's been sitting here for almost an hour pretending to read her dead brother's comics. But she's having trouble making any sense of the story, something about the King of Dreams and his crazy little sister looking for their lost brother. And there's a raven named Matthew. But she's having trouble following the plot from one issue to the next, her head too full of Jared, too full of waiting.

The radio was on earlier but they weren't playing any music, just going on and on about the storm, so she finally turned it off. There's nothing she really needs to know about the hurricane that she can't hear through the plaster-and-stucco walls of the apartment. It's not as if she can run from it, can join the exodus that's already begun from the Quarter. So she'd rather not know the latest facts and figures, thank you very much, wind speed and expected landfall, tidal surge. She puts on a CD instead, Black Tape for a Blue Girl's *Remnants of a Deeper Purity.* The strings and keyboards haven't helped her relax as she hoped they might, but they are a better backdrop for the sound of the storm than the anxious voices on the radio. The music makes her drowsy and she thinks about trying to sleep. It's been almost two days now since she's slept or eaten or bathed.

But Jared's out there somewhere, so there's no way she can sleep. She has to stop herself from trying to send her mind out to find him every five minutes. Her nose has been bleeding off and on, and her head still hurts from the last time.

There's a hard knock at the door. Lucrece jumps, almost cries out. But it's probably just the cops, she thinks, or the Red Cross or someone like that, someone to tell her she has to leave, and she isn't sure how she's going to convince them that she can't. That she has to stay, has to be here for Jared, never mind the goddamn storm.

She lays the comic book on the coffee table and gets up off the couch, smooths the wrinkles from her black dress without thinking. Whoever's out there knocks again, impatient, and Lucrece shouts at the door, "Just a minute."

While I nodded, nearly napping, suddenly there came a tapping . . .

"Jesus, girl. Give that tired old shit a rest, okay?" she mutters to herself, and crosses the room to the door.

It takes Frank almost half an hour to reach the address on Tchoupitoulas Street that Joseph Lethe gave him. The streets are flooding and already there are fatigue-green National Guard trucks and soldiers at roadblocks. His badge gets him through, but the wind buffets his car like a toy. Driving against the storm is like running in a nightmare, racing something huge and terrible that's right behind you and gaining, and your feet weigh at *least* three hundred pounds each. Only in this dream there are fallen trees and downed power lines, stalled cars and accidents, that have to be circumnavigated.

So instead of the fifteen minutes the man on the phone gave him, it takes Frank half an hour. And then there's nothing at the address but a vacant, weedy lot with one withered chinaberry tree separating it from the street. Frank parks against the curb and sits staring out at the tree, cursing the fucking storm and his fucking luck. Then there's a brilliant flash of lightning and he sees something silvery nailed to the trunk of the tree, flapping furiously in the wind.

I was struck . . .

Frank gets out of the car. The storm drags at him, claws at his clothes and hair with invisible, windy fingers, as if it would rather he not see whatever's stuck to the tree. But it's only a deflated Mylar balloon; it was once shaped like a heart and he can still read FOREVER in big red letters. The balloon has been ripped open, flattened, and there's a plastic sandwich bag stapled to it.

Frank tears the bag free. The Mylar comes off too and is swallowed instantly by the storm. The hurricane tugs hungrily at the plastic bag in his hand as he heads back to the car, already drenched straight through his raincoat.

Inside his car the howling wind is muffled. *Muzzled,* Frank thinks, locking the door.

Inside the sandwich bag there's a folded page torn from a yellow legal pad. Frank removes it, unfolds it, smooths the page flat against the car seat. The paper is wet but the writing on it is in pencil, so that doesn't really matter. And it's only another address and another time, someplace on Millaudon Street on the other side of Audubon Park.

"Shit," he hisses and slaps his hand loudly against the sun-cracked dashboard. He remembers that day years ago in the Iberville projects when Linda Getty nearly bled to death while he shouted "Ten-thirteen!" repeatedly into the handset of his patrol car's radio. He remembers no one answering him, all because Linda was a dyke and they wanted her off the force. What if all of it, the phone call and that weirdo fucker in the crapper, *all* of it, is just a goddamn practical joke? Or worse. What if they *know*?

A branch comes off the chinaberry tree and crashes down onto the windshield, leaving a crack three or four inches long in the glass before the wind snatches it away again. Frank turns the key in the ignition, starts the car again, and pulls quickly away from the vacant lot before the storm brings the whole damn tree down on top of him.

You're gettin' paranoid, Frank.

"Maybe so," he says, and makes a wide U-turn on Tchoupitoulas, heading west toward the park. "And maybe not." His voice *sounds* brave, sounds certain, as confident as all the television cops of his childhood. But the fear filling up his belly and the prickling sensation on the back of his neck say otherwise. And a small but strident voice deep inside is telling him to get the hell out while the getting's good, that there's a fucking *hurricane* coming, for Christ's sake, and it's not like anyone would really blame him if he just let this one go for now.

Unless you want the photographs to go to the papers, the voice on the phone said. Frank doesn't think there *are* any pictures, but he can't be *sure.* He knows that he has no choice after all, that his apprehension is useless because it is irrelevant. That he's going to do whatever Joseph Lethe tells him because he has made secrets of his life, secrets that can maim, and now they're being held against his throat. He squints through the windshield as the useless wipers flail, and follows the unsteady beams of the headlights.

"Please tell me what you want," Lucrece whispers, hating that she sounds so scared. The hand in the latex glove slaps her again, slaps her so hard her mouth is full of blood. She lets it run down her chin rather than swallow it. The taste of her own blood has always made her sick.

"*I* ask *you* the questions," the man says. "That's the *rule.*" The man with eyes the color of stone is kneeling over her, checking the knots he's made with the white nylon rope, the knots that bind her wrists and ankles tight. He has a pistol pressed hard against the soft spot just below her breastbone.

"I know who you are," she says. He pauses and looks back at her from beneath the greasy, dangling hair that keeps falling across his face. He brushes his bangs out of the way again, exposing his thin, hatchet-sharp face. He looks excited and expectant, and his hands are shaking.

"You're the sick son of a bitch who killed my brother," Lucrece says.

"I'm so much more than that," the man replies, and a nervous, shy smile creeps slowly across his face. "But you already know that *too,* don't you? I'm sure They've told you everything about me."

"Jared died because of you," she whispers, flinching, expecting the hand again. But the man only smiles a little wider and hides his mouth with the latex-covered fingers of his free hand, as if he's suddenly realized that he's smiling and he doesn't want her to see, doesn't want her to know his excitement or the pleasure he's taking in this scene.

He moves his hand, slowly, and he isn't smiling anymore.

"Did They also tell you that it wasn't supposed to be your brother? Did They tell you it was *supposed* to be you and I sort of fucked things up?"

Lucrece shuts her eyes, not wanting to believe what he's saying, but she knows that he's telling her the truth. So many times she's wished that it could have been her instead of Benny, knows that if it had been her then at least Benny still would have had Jared. And now this crazy man is telling her that was his intention all along.

"But that's what we get second chances for, right, *Lucas*?" he asks her, and the way he says that name it's almost as good as another slap, almost as painful.

"You're already dead," she says. The words feel good coming out of her mouth, crossing her torn and swelling lips. "You have no idea what you've started or where it will end."

The man bends over her. She doesn't open her eyes but she can feel him just inches from her face, can smell his breath like mouthwash and bad teeth.

"Is that what They told you, Lucas DuBois? Did They tell you I was just some psycho serial killer with a hard-on for transsexuals and little boys in women's underwear?"

When she doesn't answer or even open her eyes, he slaps her again, hits her so hard that her ears ring.

"Answer me, you dickless bastard!"

"A dead man," she says, and he hits her.

"No, no, *no*!" He rages above her like the storm, as though all the wild fury of the hurricane has been distilled and poured into this skinny, insane man. She ignores the pain in her head and reaches into him, tries to reach into him the way she reached out to Jared and the crow.

When her mind brushes against his, she screams. There's something coiled deep inside his skull, a serpent made of living fire, a writhing bolt of pure white heat that strikes out at her and sears its way back across her thoughts. Lucrece's body goes taut as a board, seizing, and she bites a ragged slash across her tongue.

"I'm the place where it *all* stops, Lucas! I'm the foil that stands for order against Their chaos. Against *your* chaos, Lucas DuBois."

But now his words flow around and away from her, repelled by the charge from the white-hot crucible of his brain. The memory of a blazing power that can split trees like cordwood and incinerate bone, something more than a memory. Something hotter than a star that snakes its way inside her, between each and every cell in her body, that squeezes itself between her molecules, between the subatomic particles of her, until there's no telling what is Lucrece and what is the thing pouring out of the man's mind.

Her eyelids flutter open. He towers above her, fire and steam pouring from every orifice in his skull. It drips like molten slag from his lips, flows like lava from his ears, and falls sizzling to her skin. There's no pulling back, no breaking her link with this scalding mind. Her back arches and she can hear her vertebrae grinding against one another.

"I am the river," he says, and those fiery eyes are so terribly close now. But the last thought before Lucrece loses consciousness is not of this monster, this man infected by electricity and madness. Her last thought is of Jared, and she makes a tiny hole, a pinprick, in the fire and forces the thought away from herself, boosting it with the borrowed force of the lunatic's rage. Then there is nothing but the sound of static and merciful darkness.

Joseph Lethe backs quickly away from the thing that calls itself Lucrece DuBois, the thing that They've constructed so skillfully of male flesh to mimic a woman's. He's breathless and frightened; there's no denying that he felt it reach inside him, felt its unclean mind pressed squirming against his own before it screamed and began to buck about on the floor and foam at the mouth. It had been reading his very thoughts, his soul.

But there was something there it hadn't expected, something that shielded and protected him from its prying, alien attention. Something that struck back and left it helpless, unconscious, maybe even dead. He grips the stainless-steel butt of the gun tighter and jabs the snubby barrel between the thing's artificial breasts.

"You bit off more than you could chew, didn't you?" he says, gasping out the words. "You're not even *half* as fucking smart as you think you are."

It's gone now, that part of it that laid his mind open like a gray Gulf oyster, but he can still *feel* it. Like some sticky, sugary residue left to ferment inside his head, and he itches in places he knows he can never reach to scratch. Joseph Lethe feels something cold and undeniable that he hasn't felt in a long time, something he is only supposed to inflict, not suffer himself. He feels violated.

So he sheds the name Joseph Lethe and becomes Jordan again, hoping the change will leave him cleaner, but it doesn't. Cautiously Jordan touches the transsexual's throat, presses two reluctant fingers against its throat. There's a pulse, a very weak, erratic pulse, but it's still alive.

"What were you trying to do to me, fucker? You *touched* me," and his finger tightens the slightest bit on the trigger of the pistol. "You've contaminated me." He wants to empty the clip into its poisonous black heart. Maybe then he would feel even. Revenge isn't much, but he knows that he'll never be free of whatever wriggling, inhuman essence it has planted inside him, so maybe revenge will have to do.

"I am the river," he whispers, like a prayer, and the barrel of the gun moves slowly from the space between its breasts to a spot just beneath its chin. "I am the conduit for all that is pure, and you have polluted me."

But he can't kill it, not yet, not here. There's still too much it has to tell him about the nightmares and the black-winged creature chasing him across the sky. And it still has an important role to play in the trap he's set for the faggot police detective. It *will* die, but it has to die later, slowly, somewhere else. For the moment something else will have to do.

Something more subtle, he thinks. "Something more poetic," he says aloud.

Jordan uses the barrel of the gun to push aside its skirt. His gloved hands expose its clever, deceiving sex. His penis stirs awake inside his pants and he bites down on the tip of his tongue. He's never done this, not even once. He's never allowed himself to be fooled by Their masquerade and so there's never been any danger of that sort of contact, that sort of weakness. He's known from the very beginning that it was part of Their game, like the spiny jaws of a Venus flytrap spread wide, waiting for the flies.

But this is different, Jordan tells himself. It has nothing to do with desire, nothing to do with anything as base as lust. This will be a message to Them that he will not be violated again, that to violate him is to invite the rape of Their own. It's ingenious, really. And he will take proper precautions to protect himself from anything inside it that might be meant for him, from any viruses or nanites that might have been installed during the final stages of its reassignment.

"I am the river," he says again, and his trigger finger begins to relax.

Jordan unzips his pants and checks the clock on the mantle to be sure that there's time, that he won't miss the detective, and then he lays the gun on the floor of Jared Poe's apartment.

Jared and the crow are watching Frank Gray from the front porch of an abandoned house on Millaudon Street. Across the street from them the detective curses and rips a second patch of Mylar from the bole of a pecan tree. Then he struggles against the storm and climbs back inside his car.

"The killer's playing with him, isn't he?" Jared asks, and the crow answers him softly. Only her head is poking out of the front of Benny's frock coat.

"Keeping him busy. Baiting him . . ."

And then Jared hears Lucrece, hears her so loud and strong that the force of her knocks him backward a few steps until he collides with the boarded-up front door of the old house. A voice without sound that rushes straight through him; not even words, just a crippling flash of Lucrece, Lucrece hurting and afraid for him, *warning* him. Then she's gone again. Jared slumps, trembling, against the weathered boards at his back, shaken and sweating beneath the leather hood she placed over his bullet-shattered skull.

"Lucrece," he whispers. Then the crow caws loudly, shifts impatiently inside the rubber coat. Jared looks up and sees that Frank Gray's car is pulling away, heading north up Millaudon Street.

"If I lose him now, I might not get another chance," Jared says. The crow makes a sound that seems like confirmation. Already the detective's car is just a dim pair of taillights in rain.

"Jesus, Lucrece, be careful," he says. "And thanks." He steps off the porch into the waiting storm.

The second note has led Frank to a convenience store on a run-down stretch of Magazine Street. All the windows have been covered with fresh yellow-brown sheets of plywood and the place appears to be deserted, the owners and employees having long since fled the hurricane.

Smarter motherfuckers than me, he thinks, and spies a third patch of Mylar nailed to the plywood. He can see that there's a small brown paper bag stuck up there as well. The wind knocks him off his feet twice on his way to and back from the front of the store, sends him sprawling into the flooded street. There's almost a foot of frothy slate gray water flowing down Magazine Street now, and by the time he gets back into the car he's so wet he might as well have swum as tried to walk.

He sits behind the wheel holding another swatch of Mylar from another ruined balloon. This one says CONGRATS! in eager cursive. Frank tosses it into the backseat and takes a deep breath before he opens the paper bag.

This is the last one, he swears to himself. *Unless there's something really goddamn convincing in here, this is the last stop on this wild-goose chase.*

Inside there's another plastic bag, and this one doesn't have just a note. There's an index finger as well, severed cleanly at the knuckle, a smooth bit of white bone showing on one end and a nail painted black at the other.

"Shit on me," Frank groans as he opens the bag and fishes out the carefully folded note. There's dried and not-so-dried blood on the yellow legal paper, crimson still tacky to the touch, and it comes off on his hands as he unfolds the page. There's the next address in the same handwriting. "Just in case you're doubting me," it says at the top.

Frank refolds the letter and drops it back into the bag with the finger, puts them both back into the paper bag and shoves the bag under his seat.

Out of sight, out of mind.

"Yeah, right," he mumbles, shifting out of park into reverse and backing away from the convenience store. "Whoever said that wasn't sitting on top of a goddamn severed human finger."

Frank puts the car in drive and rolls back along the makeshift tributary of the Mississippi that Magazine Street has become.

Lucrece wakes up very slowly, drifts by almost imperceptible degrees from a dream about Aaron Marsh and the Eye of Horus, a dream about the stuffed dodo in its glass case. Only in the dream the dodo bird was the one from *Alice in Wonderland,* the one from John Tenniel's drawings, with hands and a walking stick. And it had been not inside the case but standing next to her and Aaron, watching the rain fall through the shop's display windows.

"The race is over," Aaron said, and Lucrece said, "As wet as ever. It doesn't seem to dry me at all."

And the dodo said very solemnly as it tapped its cane against the floor, "*Everybody* has won, and *all* must have prizes."

Lucrece is just about to ask the dodo if the thimble from the pocket of her dress will do, if it's a decent enough prize, when she smells ammonia and begins to cough herself awake.

She opens her eyes and there's a bright light somewhere close, so close that she can feel the warmth of its scalding bulb. The heat makes her remember what it was like to touch the man's mind, the man who forced his way inside the apartment, the man who killed Benny. She forgets the dream and remembers that sizzling flood of power from his mind, remembers his hands on her, the perfect *wrongness* of his soul. She coughs again, her throat dry and rough as sandpaper. Then a plastic straw is thrust between her lips.

"Drink," the man says. He's standing very close. The straw bumps insistently against her teeth, stabs at her gums. "Drink," he says again.

She sucks on the straw and her mouth fills with lukewarm water. She swallows and it helps a little, so she sucks another mouthful from the straw.

"That's enough," he says, and takes the straw away. It trails a string of thick saliva from her lips, down her chin.

Her wrists are still bound together, tied to something overhead, and she's hanging naked in the glare of the light. Both of her arms have gone completely numb from the weight of her body. She stretches her legs and the tips of her bare toes brush a hard, cold floor, like gritty concrete or sandstone.

"I was just saying it's a shame there's not time to do this properly," the man remarks. The light seems to move, plays across her body. "I was just saying that you're a prize."

The air smells like dust and distant rain, mildew and oily rags. The ammonia is still burning her sinuses. She can hear the storm outside, but now it sounds very far away.

"Where am I?" she asks him. Her voice sounds almost as bad as her throat feels.

"Where I need you to be, Lucas. At the nexus, at the heart of the snare."

"That isn't my name," she croaks, but he ignores her.

"I could learn things from you if there were more time. If I had time to do the whole procedure. But he'll be here soon and I've hardly even started."

It doesn't matter that she has no idea what he's talking about. Whatever it is, it means he's going to kill her. He's a predator and she is his chosen prey, stripped and hung up for the slaughter like a hog waiting for the blade across its throat. There's nothing else she needs to know.

"None of this is what you think," she says. "You don't have to do this again."

"Oh, it's *exactly* what I think," he says. She can almost see him standing in the shadows behind the light, a darker patch in the rough shape of a man. "It's much too late now for any more lies. I saw your back when I was . . . I saw your back. The scar."

"Nosy little fuck, aren't you?" Lucrece realizes that it's hard to get her breath, that she's slowly suffocating, as in a crucifixion. She might have been hanging here for hours.

"Tell me about the bird, Lucas. I *dream* about the black bird, and there's its mark on your back."

"You want to know about the black bird?" she replies, gasping for the air she needs to make the words, to remain conscious. "I can tell you about the black bird. Get me down from here and I'll tell you about the fucking black bird."

"I can't do that," he says sternly, reproachfully. "You know that, Lucas. I can't risk that. There's not time."

"Then I can't help you," she gasps. "Sorry. You'll just have to find out about the bird on your own." She sucks in another stinging breath and adds, "He's coming, very soon."

"I'm not afraid of you or any of Them," the man sneers, but she can tell that he is. That he's very much afraid. "You can't trick me into letting you go by trying to scare me."

She can taste his fear now. Because it is so fucking delicious, so sweet and ripe and maybe all she'll ever know of justice, Lucrece says simply, "The crow is *his* vengeance, motherfucker, and you're *her* victim."

She expects immediate retribution, swift punishment served in exchange for the truth he didn't really want to hear, a knife or a needle for her honesty. But the man just stands very still on the other side of the light. She can hear him breathing.

"Things fall from the sky," he says. "Shining, bleeding *things* fall from the sky and the fabric of humanity itself is altered. And They expect me to watch and do nothing? Did They really think that not a single man would stand against Them?"

"You're insane," Lucrece whispers, and knows that if he doesn't finish it soon, she'll begin to cry. There's simply too much pain and she's too scared of dying alone in this stinking dark place. And she doesn't want the son of a bitch who killed Benny to see her cry.

"Don't tell me about vengeance, Lucas DuBois. I am the whole world's vengeance against Their atrocities."

"No," she croaks, and swallows, shaking her head, wishing she had the strength to laugh, the strength to show him how ludicrous he is. "No. You're just a sad, crazy asshole who likes to kill people. And that's all you are. That's all you'll ever be."

And then there's the sound of metal against metal, the sound of small sharp things, and Lucrece closes her eyes because she doesn't want to see.

By the time Michael's outer rain bands have crossed the ribbonlike barrier of the Chandeleur Islands the storm has become a monster even by the monstrous standards of hurricanes. Its swirling cyclone bulk blankets the coast from the mouth of the Pascagoula River all the way across the southeastern corner of Louisiana. Born somewhere off the west coast of Africa, it has grown from an embryonic disturbance, a disorganized fetus of showers and thunderstorms, and has traveled the trade winds almost six thousand miles to the Gulf of Mexico.

Now it is ready to spend its fury against the Mississippi delta. By late afternoon there are maximum sustained winds of more than 195 miles an hour, and Michael is upgraded to a category-five hurricane.

At its calm, unblinking eye Michael has lifted a mound of seawater a foot and a half high and almost fifty miles across, a storm surge pulled up by its violently low pressure and aimed at the already rain-glutted bayous, at cypress swamps and small towns barely above sea level to begin with. And at New Orleans, the red bull's-eye at the end of its long odyssey across the Atlantic.

At 4:35 P.M. a tiny shrimp boat named *Eloise*, caught deep inside the storm, radios for assistance from its location somewhere in Breton Sound near Fort St. Philip. The captain reports that his ship's barometer is reading 26.10 inches; three days later he and his two-man crew will be found floating in the Gulf, but his report will be cautiously noted by meteorologists as the lowest pressure ever recorded in the Western Hemisphere.

At 4:57 P.M. a reconnaissance plane tracking the storm, dumping its load of instrument-laden dropsonde canisters into the eye of the hurricane, nervously reports a gigantic shadow, "like a huge black bird," falling across the relatively calm waters of the fifty-mile-wide center of the storm. The pilot and crew will later dismiss the incident as a mistake, as nothing more than the shadow of their own plane or a trick of the clouds.

At 5:03 P.M. a weather satellite in geostationary orbit twenty-two thousand miles above the Gulf sends back color images of another shadow, an India-ink-black smudge that will eventually be described in an internal NHC report as "the crow anomaly." Less than thirty seconds later the satellite's computer vomits a frantic, senseless stream of data and shuts itself down.

Michael turns, dispassionate as cancer, unstoppable as fate, its silver-white back turned to heaven and its bruise-dark belly laid across the face of an angry, impotent world. And a terrible, raging night comes to the living and the dead of the city of New Orleans.

9

The sixth note promised Frank that it would be the last. It has led him to this derelict hulk of a factory near the river, a towering edifice of stones laid before the turn of the century and abandoned now to rats and the homeless, to furry brown bats and the elements. He parks on a vast expanse of weed-fractured concrete, flooded now like everything else, a submerged forest of dandelions, thistles, and polk salad on the edge of the factory ruins.

Frank has to fight to get the door of the car open, wrestling against the zealous wind, and then he has to wrestle it closed again. For a moment the storm holds him at bay, pressed helplessly against the car, just another bit of debris at the mercy of the hurricane. He shades his eyes from the stinging rain and all the shit being hurled through the air and stares up at the corpse of industry sprawled out before him, its crumbling masonry and towering brick smokestacks silhouetted against the Erector-set framework of the Greater New Orleans Bridge and, farther on, the blue-black wall of the storm's turbulent heart. The sight of such a terrible majesty bearing down upon the city is almost enough to make him forget himself and whatever's waiting for him inside the old factory. Almost. A man could go mad, he thinks, staring into the faceless countenance of such a thing, forced to acknowledge such a power. Something sails through the air and grazes his left cheek, slices a deep furrow and is gone, and the wind is lapping greedily at Frank's bleeding face.

He pulls himself along the rain-slick side of the car. Tiny wavelets crash against his pants legs. A sheet of corrugated tin whirls past overhead, a rusty guillotine spinning end over razor-sharp end, and Frank gets the message: *Stay out here a little longer and you're a dead man.* So he grits his teeth like a good cop and keeps going.

It's less than twenty yards to the closest door into the factory, but the storm knocks him down again and again, and once he gashes the palm of his right hand on a broken wine bottle hiding like shark teeth just beneath the water. Finally he reaches the building, solid brick and mortar to support him. A peeling metal door hangs crooked on its hinges, ready to be torn loose at any moment and sucked into the maelstrom. Frank manages to pull it open a crack and immediately the wind rips the handle from his hands, slams the door back against the wall. He crosses the threshold and the storm lets him go, confident that the shelter of the factory can last only so long.

Frank stops just inside, faced with a darkness so absolute that the premature twilight framed in the doorway behind him seems brilliant by comparison. He's still standing in several inches of cold water, but at least he's protected from the wind and driving rain, and the noise of the storm is muffled by the thick walls to a dull and constant roar.

He reaches into his dripping jacket and draws his Beretta 92-F from its shoulder holster. The gash in his hand hurts bad and is bleeding like a son of a bitch, but there's nothing to be done for it now. Of course it *had* to be his fucking right hand, no way he could have fallen on his left. He takes a Kel-light flashlight from one back pocket, not expecting it to work, expecting it to be full of water and the batteries drowned. But when he switches it on, a weak beam shines across the vast dark puddle of the floor. He aims it a little higher and there's a brick archway only a few feet to one side where the floor slants upward to drier ground.

"You better be here somewhere, motherfucker," he says. His voice sounds very small in the vast tomb of the building.

He steps through the arch. There is more light on the other side, velvet-soft shades of gray only a few degrees from actual black, but it's an improvement. There are tall rows of windows along the southern side of the building, the side facing the river and the oncoming storm, the last dregs of daylight filtering down to the floor through air thickened by its time inside the factory. Frank shines the Kel-light along the wall near the arch and sees a rickety-looking iron staircase bolted into the brick, leading up into the gloom, toward the second story of the building.

"Hey!" he shouts. There is a sudden, riotous flutter of wings from high above him; only pigeons or maybe swallows nesting in the rafters, but he can't help remembering the big black crow the guy in the mask had with him. A couple of charcoal feathers spiral lazily down, passing through the beam of his flashlight on their way to the concrete floor.

When the birds are quiet again, Frank listens for any indication that he's not alone, that Joseph Lethe is waiting for him in the gloom.

"Listen, asshole! I'm tired of playing hide-and-go-seek with your dumb ass!"

But there's no response, no human response, only the incessant whistling drone of the storm outside and the subtler noises of the old factory.

"Jesus," he whispers. Keeping the flashlight aimed just in front of his feet and the Beretta's rubber grip squeezed tightly in his aching, bloody right hand, Frank Gray begins to climb the stairs.

There's a small landing at the top, a square platform of plate steel and cement that sags alarmingly to one side, and guardrails that have all but rusted away. As he steps onto it Frank realizes he is standing at least fifty or sixty feet above the factory floor. The tall windows waver on the opposite side of what seems like a bottomless void. Through the filthy, broken panes, he can see the roofs of lower buildings along the northern shore of the Mississippi and the swollen river itself like some impossibly giant cottonmouth moccasin, the rough white-capped water for scales. But he looks away; there's already enough shit to deal with without worrying about what's going to happen when the river comes across the levee.

There's a steel fire door set into the wall. When he pushes against it the door creaks loudly and swings open. What he sees through the doorway almost sends him screaming back down the precarious stairs: a floodlight clamped to a sawhorse, its glare revealing a mutilated body suspended by its wrists from a steel hook. The corpse's bloodless legs are spread out in a wide inverted V, each ankle bound with white nylon cord that has been tied securely through iron eyes in the floor. The body has been completely eviscerated, slit from the genitals all the way up to the chin, and the blood-drenched floor beneath it is scattered with discarded organs and entrails, bluish loops of intestine and darker, meaty lumps he can't identify. The abdominal cavity is empty, a hollowed-out shell of muscle and cartilage and bone. There are literally buckets of clotting blood on the floor, plastic mop pails filled almost to overflowing, and, behind the floodlight, a small table covered with surgical instruments and stray strips of skin and meat. Where the body isn't smeared with blood and gore, its skin is the powdery color of chalk dust. But at least he can't see the face. Its head has lolled back, away from him, and the dead eyes, if they've even been left in its skull, stare toward the ceiling somewhere high overhead. It's impossible for him to tell if the corpse is male or female.

Frank swallows hard and wipes his sweating forehead on the back of the hand holding his flashlight. He didn't puke at the mess in the fountain in Audubon Park and he sure as hell isn't going to puke now.

"Lethe?" he asks. When there's no reply, he says, "I know you're still here."

There's movement to his left, then something fast he only barely glimpses from the corner of one eye. Frank doesn't take time to check his target or aim. He's acting purely on fear and adrenaline as he squeezes off three rounds from the Beretta. The nine-millimeter shells hit nothing but solid brick and the gunshots leave his ears ringing.

"Fuck," he mutters, and there are footsteps coming up fast behind him and hard, cold metal pressed to his temple before he can turn around.

"It's over, Detective. I win." Frank recognizes the voice from the phone call. "Drop your gun and take one step backward."

"If I drop my gun I'm dead."

"You're already dead, Detective, just as soon I want you that way. Now drop your fucking gun *and* the flashlight and do exactly what I said. One step back."

Frank lets the Beretta slip from his bleeding hand and it clatters noisily to the floor, drops the Kel-light and its lens shatters. He takes one step backward. The pistol muzzle pressed to his skull moves with him.

"Now turn and look at it," the voice says.

"What is the fucking point of this?" Franks asks. "Do you just want to see me scared? Is that it? 'Cause if that's all you want, you already got it, okay?"

"I want to see you *dead,* faggot," the voice says, the purring, effeminate voice speaking directly into his ear now. "I want to see you dead and condemned for your crimes against your own masculinity. Turn and look at it, Frank Gray."

So Frank turns, slowly, to face the madman's butchery.

"This doesn't even make *sense,* Lethe," he says, trying not let the fear show in his voice. There might still be a chance to get out of this alive if he can stay calm, if he can stay cool.

"I'm Jordan now," the man says, and he steps around to stand in front of Frank but the barrel of his gun doesn't move an inch. There's nothing remarkable about him, a man younger than Frank expected and almost handsome in a gaunt, heroin-addled sort of way. Probably not the perfect match for an FBI serial-killer profile.

"But you are the same man I spoke with on the phone, the one who left the messages leading me here, right? The man who said he was tired and wanted this to stop?"

"Yes," the man says softly.

"So, what? Were you just lying to get me out here?"

"There's nothing here that you need to understand, Detective. Nothing at all. You are not an innocent."

And the man who has become Jordan pulls the trigger and for Frank Gray the world ends quickly in the cracking sound of thunder.

Jordan kneels beside the detective's still body and presses two gloved fingers to the throat, feeling for a pulse that he already knows isn't there. Then he examines the dark powder burns at the temple, lifts a loose flap of scalp and hair already matted with blood, and stares at the bullet hole a moment. He's never before killed anyone who didn't exhibit at least the behavioral symptoms of gender transgression.

And I still haven't, he thinks after a moment of quiet deliberation. *This man had sex with other men, and isn't that a violation of gender?*

Jordan nods, reassured. He places his gun in Frank Gray's right hand, folds the detective's palm around the butt of the pistol and carefully threads an index finger through the trigger guard. He uses the dead man's left hand to add a few additional fingerprints to the stainless steel barrel, and then he picks up the Beretta and steps away from the body. He glances from the gutted transsexual to the prostrate form of the cop like a sculptor admiring a finished piece. And it really isn't so different, he tells himself, the painstaking orchestration of matter into an arrangement that better suits his needs.

What the police will find here will suit his needs too, as perfectly as the body of Benjamin DuBois once did, as perfectly as the evidence he left in Jared Poe's apartment a year ago: a fingerprint lifted from a spoon with a strip of Scotch tape, a couple of pages of poetry. And this is so much more damning, so much more elaborate. He feels a staggering pride that he has actually managed to pull it off.

But it isn't truly finished, not yet. There's one small touch left to add for consistency's sake.

Jordan sits down in the space between the soles of the detective's shoes and the sticky, wet patch beneath the remains of the second DuBois twin and takes a black Sharpie marker from one shirt pocket. He's committed the whole poem to memory by now, all 108 lines of it, and that's something else to be proud of as he leans over the spot on the floor that he swept clean with a whiskbroom earlier in the day. He prints the lines as neatly as he can.

Stern Despair returned, instead of the sweet hope he dared abjure—
That sad answer, "Nevermore!"

When he's finished, Jordan goes back to Frank Gray's body and places the pen in his left hand, folds those fingers tightly closed around it.

Two birds with one stone, he thinks, and the thought makes him smile. It's good to be such a clever man. They'll all lose his trail now. Even if the cops believe that Jared Poe was guilty, he knows that they've begun looking for a second killer to explain the murders fitting the Ripper MO since Poe's one-way trip up to Angola. And a dead faggot cop is the perfect fall guy. Shortly before he reached the apartment on Ursulines, Jordan dropped a letter to the *Times-Picayune* into a mailbox, Frank Gray's confession to sodomy and the killings.

And the assassin bird sent into his dreams and visions by the others—it will lose him as well now that its link to this world has been severed. He saw the scar clearly enough on the transsexual's bare back. Without a living conduit the creature will lose his scent and be forced to return to Them empty-handed. But, just to be safe, he'll move on. There's a road map of the Southeast in his glove compartment, and he's circled Memphis and Dallas, Atlanta and Birmingham. All his calculations aren't complete, but at least one of these cities will be right for his work. By the time They realize what's happened, just how badly They've underestimated again, he'll be miles and miles away, hidden by the walls of a different city and the syllables of a different name.

Jordan looks back at the gutted corpse again and remembers what he told the thing before he killed it. It truly was a pity that he did not have more time. There was so much it might have revealed to him if only there had been the time to employ more subtle techniques. But then he thinks of those other cities again, those other cities on other rivers. He lets his eyes wander higher, up above the body and the white-hot nimbus of the floodlight. High above the abattoir this room has become, there are windows that have been painted over, windows painted black decades ago.

I have all the time I need, he thinks. *And the world, when I am done, will be as simple and solid as those panes, as perfectly, rationally opaque.*

But then the shadow of something immense and winged stretches itself across the row of windows, the shadow of something a hundred times darker than any shade of paint, darker than the eye of man can even see. *The color of absence,* Jordan thinks as the windows explode and the ebony shards rain down over him.

Even as he falls toward the floor and the cowering man caught in the single pool of light, Jared knows he's too late, that the storm and his injuries have slowed him down enough that some crucial chance has been missed, that something has gone horribly and completely wrong. And then he sees her face, Lucrece's pale face staring up at him through the razor torrent of falling glass, and her eyes are as dead as any eyes that ever looked out blindly from the head of a corpse. In the instant it takes him to reach the ground he sees the rest of it, exactly what has been done to her and the body of the dead detective and the words printed neatly across the floor.

He lands as smoothly as a cat, dropping to all fours as the last of the broken windows smashes to powder against the concrete around him. The skinny, frightened man has fallen, cut and bleeding from a hundred different wounds, and is scrambling frantically away from Jared across the factory floor. The crow flaps past Jared, a living missile of sleek black feathers, and dives for the fleeing killer.

"No!" the man screams as Jared stands. "No, I stopped you!" The crow has reached the man and is pecking viciously at arms and hands raised protectively over his head.

Jared looks back once at Lucrece and he knows that if anything but sour rage remained in him, even a faint speck of light, that the sight of her hanging there has burned it from him forever.

"I can't kill you slowly enough," he says, turning toward the man who murdered Benny, the man who killed Lucrece, the man he still has no name for. "Not to pay for half of what you've done to me and the people I loved."

The man swats wildly at the crow and scrambles another foot toward the open door.

"But I'm making you a promise, motherfucker. You can be sure that I'm going to try."

And then Jared sees the stainless-steel semiautomatic pistol clutched in the man's scratched and bleeding hands, sees the man's finger wrapped around the trigger. Before he can even shout a warning, the gun goes off and the crow falls in a heap of broken bones and blood-soaked feathers. She shudders once and the gun fires again, blowing off her head.

It is as if whatever life-substitute has animated Jared's cells, whatever dragged him from the grave and kept him moving for two days, is abruptly taken away, the strings on the marionette severed in one clean snip. Jared falls, breathless, to his knees.

"*No,* I said!" and now the man is screaming at the top of his lungs and there are flecks of spittle flying from his thin lips. "I *beat* you! I *beat* you," and then the pistol goes off a third time, splattering what's left of the crow in two or three different directions.

Jared's vision blurs and begins to fade out around the edges. He struggles desperately with the zipper on the back of the leather hood but it sticks. Finally the fabric rips, tears free open along a weak seam, and he pulls the mask off and collapses, curls himself into a fetal ball on the glass-littered concrete, a pathetic, hurting thing made of dead flesh unable to die.

The man with the gun is laughing, an awful, hysterical laugh that says everything there is to be said about insanity without using a single word. He turns away from the crow, apparently satisfied that she's truly, irretrievably dead, and he points the gun at Jared.

"What am I going to have to *do* before you start to take me seriously?" he yells. "Before you figure out that you can't win? That I'm never going to fucking stop?" Then he gets a look at Jared's ruined face and recognition washes slowly across his deranged features.

"Oh," he says, all the laughter draining out of his voice, and he takes a step away from Jared. "No. You're not him. He's dead."

Jared opens his mouth to tell the man to fuck off, to ram the gun up his ass, but all he manages is a dry, strangling sound.

"There are *rules,*" the man says incredulously, unbelieving. "There are rules that even They cannot violate, rules that bind even Their hands. Jared Poe is dead and the dead stay that way.

"I have no idea what kind of trick this is, my friend. But it isn't going to work. I know better," and he pulls the trigger and puts a bullet in Jared's chest. Ribs disintegrate, become shrapnel, puncturing his heart and lungs. Jared rolls over onto his back, coughing up gouts of arterial blood.

"I *know* the rules."

The next shot tears into Jared's belly and the bullet shatters his spine.

"No matter *how* much They twist and bend them, no matter how They try to cheat the natural order . . . I am pure of mind and body and I know the goddamn rules!"

Jared vomits another mouthful of blood and stares helplessly up at the thin and raving man. He opens his mouth and the words come slowly, slogging their way out of him in a sticky red trickle.

"Then kill me," he croaks. "If you . . . if you know the rules . . . then kill me."

The man chews uncertainly at his lower lip. Jared can see his Adam's apple bob up and down as he swallows. He leans over and puts the gun to Jared's forehead, presses its barrel an inch above the hole Harrod's pistol has already made in Jared's face.

"No," he says a moment later. "That's not why you're here. You're here to kill me, but you couldn't." The gun moves away as he stands up straight again. "Whatever you really are, I need to know the things you know. I need to know about the bird and the visions They've made me see."

The man's eyes almost seem to glimmer, like a child gazing deep into a bag filled with Halloween candy or someone poised on the brink of an abyss who has just grasped the concept of bottomlessness. He thumbs the safety switch on the gun and stuffs it into the band of his trousers.

And then there's the taut, staccato sound of ropes snapping and the man looks up, past Jared, and begins to scream.

Lucrece has no way of knowing how long she's been drifting in the gray places, minutes or weeks, floating weightless through mists the color of papier-mâché, cold mists that smell faintly of brine and pressed flowers. There is no up or down here, and only the vaguest sense of her body. Occasionally she remembers herself, or recalls the memory of herself, and hesitantly touches fingertips to her face to be sure that she's still there.

There's a faint tugging sensation at her feet, and that's all that might pass for direction. When she stares off that way, squints hard to try to see something through the insubstantial tendrils of the mist, she thinks that maybe there's a light there, far away. It seems warm, a soft, faintly pulsating point in a place where all other points are the same. And it would be so easy, she knows, to go to it, to fall through millennia and distances past perceiving, to let it swallow her the way it's meant to swallow everything in the end. To give up the pain and the weight of being in exchange for a brilliant, flickering moment of peace before oblivion.

Lucrece folds her arms about her chest, pulls her knees up close to her body, and looks away from it.

"This is a bunch of hippie bullshit," she says, and her voice seems to fill the entire universe, all the empty space eager to be filled, the sulking mist jealous of the light and its hoarding appetite.

For an instant or an hour the light flares, bathes her in a wash of its comfort, a gentle cascade of heat filled with promises. Lucrece closes her eyes, or only remembers what it's like to close her eyes, remembering Benny and Jared, remembering the man and his sharp and cutting tools, and she shakes her head.

"No," she says. "You can keep it. I don't want it now."

The warmth is taken away and there's a sudden rustling, like a rain of autumn leaves. Something rubs itself brusquely across her face, something musty and dry that tickles and makes her flinch, and when Lucrece opens her eyes again she's standing in a grove of dead and withered trees. The mist presses in close on every side, roils like alien storm clouds, as if this is only the most tenuous oasis and might be reclaimed at any moment. But at least there's solid ground beneath her feet, even if it's only cracked and barren earth that's never known rain. A breeze blows through the limbs and sets them to rattling, sweeps up an ashy dust that settles around Lucrece like a shroud.

And the trees are filled with crows.

A hundred or a thousand pairs of golden eyes, eyes like amber beads, watching her, patient as time.

"Send me back," she says, not asking, demanding, not caring if they can hear the anger in her voice, the acid contempt. "Send me back to help Jared."

They turn as one, releasing her from their glare, and look together into the highest branches of the tallest of the trees. Lucrece looks with them and sees the one they've turned to face, perched above them all: a crow so black, so impossibly enormous that he might have been the very first, the incarnation of age clothed in ragged black feathers. His eyes burn with a hundred million years of collected sunlight and starlight. And he knows her name.

"I have the right to ask," she says.

The great bird spreads his wings and a raucous cry rises up from the others, a cry that Lucrece understands is laughter, bitter, wicked laughter at her temerity, that she would dare to demand what is theirs alone to give. She looks away, unable to bear the sound or the glare of those ancient, piercing eyes. She glances down at her bare, dusty feet. Now there is something on the ground just in front of her, a barely recognizable smear of drying blood and feathers, and she knows that it's the corpse of Jared's crow.

The great bird folds his wings again, quieting the others, and she can hear him speaking inside her head.

One of us has already died for your brother, he says. *A single sacrifice is sufficient for his soul.*

She doesn't reply, can only stare at the dead crow at her feet, trying to recall what Aaron Marsh read from the old German manuscript, afraid to even wonder what has happened to Jared if his crow has been killed.

We will not give another.

"For those who have the symbol," Lucrece says, "the passage is easy." She forces herself to look up, to face those judging eyes and again the court of crows caws and croaks its scorn for her.

"For those who have the symbol, the passage is easy," she repeats, and turns to show them the scar across her back.

They're screaming now, furious, insulted bird voices raised in confusion and outrage, anger to match even her own. Lucrece knows better than to turn toward them again. She imagines them descending on her, their stabbing beaks and battering wings punishing her impudence. But she's been torn apart before and there are things she's more afraid of.

Then I'll take you myself, woman, and we'll be done with this. But if you fail . . .

"I *won't* fail," she says.

Without warning, this small wasted patch of ground is split silently apart. Lucrece is plunging, ferried on strong black wings that have made this trip too many times to count. They pass through fire and chilling cold places that have never known light, soar above nameless starving atrocities that snatch at them with claws of iron and ivory. And in the end Lucrece has no time to regret or be afraid for herself, only enough time to prepare for whatever's waiting at the end of the journey.

Lucrece raises her head and opens her eyes, and the man who calls himself by the names of rivers fills his lungs and screams again and again. The knots he tied so carefully are unraveling and the ropes are ripping loose, snapping like sewing thread. In another moment her hands and ankles are free and she drops to the floor.

Jared has managed to roll over and he too can see her and the crow, as big as a raven, bigger, big as a fucking vulture, perched on her shoulder. The man tries to move but his legs are paralyzed and useless and all he can do is watch as the organs heaped at her feet begin to twitch and slide toward Lucrece. The blood itself flows backward, pours over the rims of the buckets and flows like a retreating red tide across the floor. It all rises as if suspended on invisible wires, a puppet show for ghouls. Everything the man has taken from her, every bit of flesh and every drop of spilled blood, becomes a swirling, living cloud, rushing to refill the empty cavity of Lucrece's body.

She throws back her head and the sound that pours from her mouth makes the killer's screams seem as insignificant as a whisper. When the air is clean of her, when Lucrece is once again whole, the slash that his scalpels and bone saws have made closes itself up, knits itself shut with flesh that has become as fluid and impervious as water. She sinks to her knees, gasping, and the killer draws the Beretta and flips off the safety.

"Lucrece!" Jared shouts, but the gun goes off before she can move, blowing a hole in her left shoulder. The huge crow leaps into the air and flaps safely away into the shadows, and Jared watches as the bullet hole heals before his eyes.

Lucrece stands up then, and her lips are curled back from her white teeth in a terrible inhuman snarl, an animal smile for the man still pointing his useless gun at her.

"You're going to have to do better than that, Jordan," she says. "You're going to have to do a whole hell of a lot better than that."

He pulls the trigger again and the right side of her face dissolves in a spray of blood and splintered bone, a gaping wound that vanishes almost as quickly as it appeared. Lucrece shakes her head and takes a deep breath; the smile never leaves her lips.

"That's a pretty goddamn cool trick, isn't it, Jordan?" She takes a step toward the man.

"Stop!" he screams. "Stop right this fucking minute." Now he is pointing the gun at Jared.

"Oh, fuck this," Jared says. "Finish this tired bullshit, Lucrece. Get it over with."

"You can't kill him, Jordan. And you can't kill me." Before the man can move she takes the gun from his hand and flings it away into the darkness beyond the glare of the floodlight. "You're never going to kill anyone ever again."

Lucrece grips the man by the front of his shirt and lifts him into the air. She holds him almost a foot off the floor, his feet kicking uselessly at nothing.

"How does it feel?" she asks. "How does it feel to dangle with your life in someone else's hands?"

"I am the river . . ." he wheezes. She slaps him so hard that his upper lip splits and his front teeth snap off at the gum line.

"No, you're not, Jordan," she says. "But we've already been through all this once and I don't feel like saying it again. It really doesn't make any difference anymore what you think."

She drops him, but before the man can run she catches him by the back of his collar and shoves him to the floor next to Jared. He moans and tries to scramble away, but Lucrece holds him still.

"I think we have to do this together, Jared," she says. "Or one of us is screwed."

From somewhere in the shadows the crow caws a coarse affirmation. And all around them the storm howls and bellows. Cold rain is blowing in through the broken windows overhead and the walls of the old factory have begun to buckle and groan from the force of the wind.

"Thanks for coming back for me, Lucrece," Jared says as she begins to grind Jordan flat against the concrete. "You didn't have to . . ."

"Yes, I did, Jared," she replies. "Yes, I did."

As the factory that has stood for more than a hundred years beneath the baking delta sun begins to come apart around them, as the floor drops away beneath them and the walls are broken by the hurricane's fury, they crush the life from the man that has robbed each of them of the thing that they loved above all else. Satisfied, the crow rises into the storm-maddened night and the circle closes in the shriek of twisting metal and the crash of falling bricks.

10

Through the cyclops eye of the hurricane Lucrece carries Jared's body away from the ruin and rubble of the fallen factory. She follows the crow as it flies high above the devastated city, wades past overturned cars and the unclaimed corpses of the freshly drowned. When they reach Prytania Street, Benny is waiting for them just outside the gates of Lafayette No. 1. He smiles gently for them, the same gentle smile that Lucrece has kept inside her for so long, preserved in the imperfect scrapbook of her memories.

Benny bends and kisses Jared, presses his lips to his lover's. Jared's eyes flutter open and tears roll down his grateful cheeks.

"Is it over?" he asks.

Benny nods. "It's over."

And then Benjamin DuBois kisses his sister's cheek and the three of them walk together past the other monuments, all the other names engraved in weathered marble and granite, stone worn smooth by time and sorrow.

Outside the crumbling cemetery walls, as the backside of Michael's spinning eye wall reaches the city, the lull in the storm passes, and for the unfortunate living, the long night of rain and anguish begins.

Epilogue

Amsterdam, one year later

Aaron Marsh nibbles on a space cake as he leafs through an ornithological tome in Dutch, which he is teaching himself from the inside out. He has a little flat high above Prinsengracht with a nice view of the canal if he leans out and cranes his neck a little. The afternoon sky is like damp gray wool. An intermittent autumn rain spits against the thick glass of his window. He has come to love it here.

Aaron got out of New Orleans the night before Hurricane Michael hit, packing only the dodo in its oversized velvet traveling case and catching a Greyhound bus, the one form of transport that never seemed to stop running. At first he'd only gone as far as Birmingham, Alabama, where he stayed with friends and watched the destruction of his adopted home from afar. He felt very little emotion, even when he learned that the Eye of Horus was a total loss. The water had taken nearly everything and destroyed whatever it left behind. But he'd kept the place well insured, and the payoff might last him the rest of his life, provided he didn't live too long. The only things he really regretted losing were the books.

He found that he had no desire to return. This only intensified a week later, when he saw a news item from New Orleans about two bodies discovered in a warehouse near the river. They'd been on an upper floor and hadn't gotten washed away. Bodies were everywhere, of course, but these attracted media attention when one of them was identified as the cop who'd supposedly confessed to the new Ripper slayings.

There was some doubt about the cop's confession anyway. Several of his colleagues testified that he was a good solid detective, that they could alibi him for the dates of the murders, that the letter wasn't even in his handwriting. Suspicion fell on the other corpse, who turned out to own a Riverside mansion full of the flooded remains of some very sick shit. The cop was given a hero's funeral. The other fellow was still being looked into.

Thanks to a couple of persistent queer activist groups and a sympathetic reporter from the *Times-Picayune,* Jared Poe was finally and publically declared innocent of the Bourbon Street Ripper killings. When he heard of this, Aaron thought for a moment of beautiful, sad Lucrece DuBois and her strange predawn visit to his shop. He wondered what had become of her in the midst of all this hoopla. Mostly, though, he acted like the selfish old man he was, traveling where he liked, pleasing only himself, putting the pieces of his life in order. He has fetched up here in Amsterdam and believes he will stay.

Tap. Tap. Tap. The rain must be getting harder. Aaron glances at the window, and his hand freezes in the act of turning a page.

It is only a small crow, but it's peering in at him as if it has urgent business here—and perhaps it does. Even from this distance Aaron can see that it's carrying a tiny scroll of paper in its beak.

He stands up slowly, crosses to the window and hesitates only a moment before turning the latch. The window swings out and the bird hops in, glancing up at him almost apologetically, as if to say, *I know I'm dripping all over the place, I'll only stay a minute . . .*

"Make yourself at home," he says, holding out his hand. The crow drops the scroll into Aaron's wrinkled palm as if relieved to be done with it, stretches its wings and shakes out its feathers, glances around the room. It is just beginning to look comfortable when its eye lights upon the stuffed dodo in its gleaming glass case.

The crow gives a single strangled caw of horror, hops backward and disappears through the open window in a black fluster.

"Ah, well," says Aaron and unrolls the paper.

He recognizes the flowing hand at once; Lucrece DuBois came to him with plenty of shopping lists. There are five words only and room for no more, in ink the color of dried blood. But they are five words that will stay with him as long as he lives:

Sometimes fairy tales come true.

Clash by Night

by

Chet Williamson

To Mac and Robin—
Don't let the music and the dancing ever stop . . .

Acknowledgments

For their kind assistance in realizing the Crow's present incarnation in these pages, the author wishes to thank John Douglas, Rich Miller, Jimmy Vines, Jeff Conner, and Edward R. Pressman.

And we are here as on a darkling plain
Swept with confused alarms of struggle and flight,
Where ignorant armies clash by night.

—Matthew Arnold, "Dover Beach"

PART ONE

Ah, love, let us be true
To one another! . . .

—Matthew Arnold, "Dover Beach"

1

"It's payback time, friends. Time to make the wrong things right."

Everywhere you looked in the room there was trash and there were guns. The trash included empty pizza boxes, the sauce long dried into patches of a far brighter red than blood, the cheese hardened like burned and crusted flesh. Empty beer cans and throwaway bottles sat on tables, imparting a thick, yeasty smell to the room. The occupants viewed the scene through a haze of cigarette smoke, as though with eyes clouded by cataracts. The light of the two floor lamps, caparisoned with tattered shades, cast soft shadows into the crags and pockets of the men's faces, some gaunt, others full and doughy.

Cigarette ends glowed red like eyes in the jungle night, then dimmed as more smoke clouded the air and the ashtrays, already filled, mounded higher with the powdery fragments of dead breath.

"Payback for Waco . . ."

Piles of magazines with titles like *The Christian Patriot, White Pride, American Times,* and the quasi-Shakespearean *Arms Against Troubles* sat on two small tables.

"Payback for Ruby Ridge . . ."

There was a small bookcase with several dozen tired and tattered volumes, among them *The Turner Diaries, Mein Kampf,* and a number of books on guns and ammunition. On one shelf sat a collection of manuals from a small publisher on how to make bombs and perform assassinations, as well as a series entitled *How to Kill,* and another called *The Poor Man's James Bond.*

"Payback for Tim McVeigh . . ."

There was music playing in the background, just loud enough for a listener to make out the lyrics over the solid country-western beat:

The Jews'll be gone, and the black folk too—
We'll have an America for me and you.
Yeah, we'll get those mongrels on the run
When each American stands up pointin' his gun . . .

"And we're gonna start that payback with Senator Robert King."

But what caught the eye most readily in the smoky, warm room were the guns. The precision of their storage and presentation was in sharp contrast to the slovenliness of the rest of the room. Many were leaning neatly in racks, their dark metal shining, while others were secured to the expanse of pegboard fastened to the wall on either side of a large American flag. White outlines had been painted around each weapon as if to show their users where to replace them, leaving ghosts of themselves to whisper silently while their corporeal selves spoke aloud.

"That Jew-marrying, nigger-loving, patriot-hating, mother-poking sonovabitch liberal . . ."

Some of the weapons were legal, but many, capable of full automatic fire, were not. Among them were several AK–47s, two Finnish Jati-Matics, a pair of Ingrams, an obsolete but still functional Wilkinson Linda, a KG–9, and two MK Arms 70 submachine guns. All were cleaned and oiled, and loaded clips rested on small shelves or hung from hooks next to their prospective weapons. These were only the weapons for immediate use in the event of an incursion. The others were in the powder magazine in far greater numbers.

"And we'll get him when he comes to Hobie." Virgil Withers, known to his fellow Sons of a Free America as Rip, leaned back and smiled. His teeth shone whitely between thin lips. The rest of his face was far from thin. It was pouchy and wrinkled, lined with hate and fattened with a diet of beef and cheese and plenty of carbohydrates. But Rip stayed active and so was stocky rather than fat.

"King's coming here?" The words rushed from Junior Feeley's mouth on a carpet of cigarette smoke. Junior was what anyone would have called fat—but not to his face since he was also six feet, eight inches tall and an awful lot of his three hundred and twenty pounds was solid muscle. The Sons of a Free America had elected Junior Feeley treasurer since they figured that no one would ever dare to steal money from him, and he was too stupid to steal it himself.

"Damn right King's coming," Rip said. "Chip cracked into their website on the Internet . . ."

"It's hacked, not cracked, and I didn't have to hack into it," Chip Porter said, waving his bottle of beer in protest. "I just, hell, *found* it."

"Whatever. Anyway, we know he's gonna be in town, we know when, and we know where. Read them the itinerary, Chip."

Chip read from a printout. "Tuesday, April thirtieth, he arrives in Hobie at nine A.M., meets with the mayor at city hall. At ten, he tours the flood site . . ."

"That bastard gave our tax money away so those damn river rats could rebuild," said Sonny Armitage, "and now he's coming here to take the credit, get more damn votes for his damn presidential race."

"Your uncle's gonna rebuild his house with that money, Sonny," Ace Ludwig reminded him.

"Well, my uncle was a horse's ass to buy a house there in the first place, the damn senator was another horse's ass to give him money for being that stupid, and my uncle's a horse's ass three times over to take that money and build right in the same damn spot where it's gonna flood all over again in another year or two."

"Amen to that," said Junior Feeley. "Why you stickin' up for King, Ace?"

"I'm not sticking up for him, he's a damn traitor and I'd blow his brains out as fast as I'd blow out Reno's or Billary's or Teddy Kennedy's. I was just stating a *fact,* that Sonny's uncle got money from the prick and his damn senate bill."

"All *right,*" Rip said. "Now just shut up and let Chip read this thing. Go ahead."

"Okay, so the senator will do photo ops there for a couple of hours, then at noon they eat at Barney's Diner, he presses the flesh, meets the little people."

"Maybe we could get Barney to poison the prick," Ace Ludwig suggested, and the others laughed.

"After that he speaks to the chamber of commerce at one thirty, answers questions and bullshits till three thirty, then he starts visiting small businesses in the area."

"Five'll get you ten," Sonny Armitage said, "he doesn't go to Peters' Gun Shop. Hell, I bet we could get Jimmy Peters to give him a 'Death to the King' bumper sticker free."

They laughed again, even Chip, who continued reading with a smile. "Okay, now these visits aren't firmed up yet—we don't know what stores or offices he's gonna go to when, but we know what the last one's gonna be before he flies out of here at nine. It's the one closest to the airport, on the outskirts of Hobie."

"You gonna make us guess?" said Sonny Armitage, filling the pause.

"It's a day-care place," Chip said. "The Making Friends Child Care Center, it's called."

"Chip checked it out good," Rip Withers said. "Been open about six months, two women run it, got another one who helps. It's our best bet. The other places are like computer stores, electronics stores, and they got security systems up the ass or offices in buildings with even tighter security. But this place has nothing."

"Why not?" asked Will Standish.

" 'Cause they don't have anything worth stealing," Rip said. "Probably a couple VCRs, maybe a computer or two for the kids to play with. Other than that, toys, right? And best of all, it's in the suburbs, mostly houses around, on a nice quiet block with hardly any traffic after ten at night. Yessir, brothers, it's the perfect place to bomb a bastard."

Amy Carlisle hung up the telephone and looked around the room, almost dizzy from the news. Then to center herself, she pictured the room as it was just hours earlier and as it would be hours from now, filled with bright, happy children who she only wanted to make brighter and happier.

True, every one of the fifty-three children that she and Nancy and Judy watched over at different times during their six-day week may not have had genius IQs, but they all had something going for them, from the one year olds just starting to form their words to the first and second graders who were dropped off before school started or who spent an hour or two after school before their parents picked them up on their way home from work. Each of them had something different to offer and each of them was special.

Amy knew all of their names and all of their likes and dislikes. She knew, most importantly, what made them smile. When their little faces lit up, the younger ones at the sight of a brightly colored mobile or a noisy toy, the older children at a glimpse of art supplies or a well-loved book that Amy was about to read, she knew she was doing more than earning her money.

She had never wanted to be a mere baby-sitter but had wanted a true learning center, where the children would do more than just pass the time. They would learn new concepts and skills and how to interact with others and make friends. They would leave knowing more than when they came in. They were in her charge and she felt they had become *her* children, every single one.

What made them even more precious was that Amy would never have a child of her own. When she had turned twenty-seven, she and Rick had decided the time had come to have a baby, maybe more than one, and she stopped taking her pills. But after a year of trying, her gynecologist's examination proved that the problem was hers, not Rick's. They had looked into adoption, but the waiting list was long and they didn't want to be new parents at thirty-five or forty.

That was when the idea of a day-care center came into Amy's head. She had a degree in elementary education and had taught school the year after she and Rick had graduated from college. But although she loved her interactions with the children, she had quickly become frustrated by the inability of the system to deal with the problems she saw. When a child was having trouble, be it in hearing, speech, vision, or learning, it took months to schedule proper testing and longer still to get the student into a special program once the diagnosis was made.

There were other concerns as well. Amy had had several students who she was certain were victims of abuse, but drawing aside the bureaucratic curtain on such suspicions made the testing delays look insignificant. Children were sad and suffering and there was little she could do to change that. Though she tried to remain upbeat, she could not, and gradually grew depressed. This depression, along with the vast amounts of out-of-school time that she spent planning and preparing for class, drove her a few steps short of a breakdown, and she gave her notice at the end of the year, to Rick's great relief.

Through some contacts at the architectural firm where he worked, she found an administrative position at an educational supply company. There she learned about running a small business from the ground up and she remained for seven years. During that time she had mused about opening a day-care facility but it wasn't until she learned she couldn't have children of her own that she began to get serious.

She had the training but the money was slower in coming. She had been stockpiling her salary for several years, thinking that it would allow her to be a stay-at-home mom after their baby was born. When it became apparent that wasn't going to happen, it was another year before she could make a down payment on an abandoned health club a half mile from their house. A bank loan secured the rest, with enough left over to turn the ex-gym into a day-care center.

It had taken another six months to make the renovations and get the proper certification, but at last the Making Friends Child Care Center had opened. It had been in operation now for six months and was, by every standard except the financial, a huge success. But Amy was making enough to break even, and with the news she had just received, even that situation might improve.

"Last little mite gone?"

Amy turned and saw Nancy Fowler standing in the doorway to the infant and toddler area. "Yeah," she said. "Megan just left."

"And you're still standing here?"

"I was on the phone." Amy smiled, trying hard not to let the secret show, wanting to have some fun first. "Nancy, I was just thinking. You know what would be great for this place? If we were to appear on TV—really heavy local coverage and even some national coverage. Don't you think that would help get enrollment up to where we want it?"

"Uh, yeah," Nancy said. "What are you saying, you think we ought to take out a hundred thousand dollar loan and buy a few minutes of air-time on ABC?"

"All four networks, including Fox," Amy said, looking up at the ceiling as though plotting the strategy in her head. "Six thirty news shows would be perfect, I think . . . Parents back from work, watching before or after dinner . . . and saturation on the Hobie station, both at six and eleven o'clock, with coverage statewide, heavy in the Twin Cities . . ."

"Amy, what the hell—you'll forgive my language in these sacred halls—are you talking about?"

Amy grinned. "The phone call. You know any senators who are polishing up their presidential images for the next race?"

"King? Senator King?"

"None other. He's coming here to survey the flood damage from last month, *and* he's going to visit some small businesses in the area, probably to get some backing for his Business 2000 bill that's coming up for a vote . . . And guess what one of those new small businesses is?"

"Oh no . . . you're kidding?"

"One of his press people just asked me if I minded—can you believe that, if I *minded*—if he stopped here and they shot some footage!"

"Oh my God, oh my *God, when*?" Amy wasn't at all disappointed in Nancy's reaction. She did everything but jump up and down.

"Four days. Next Tuesday. It'll be around eight at night, they're going to get us on their way to the airport. Novak, the press guy, was real honest about it, said they wanted to get some shots of Senator King with kids *and* with small business owners, and that Making Friends was a perfect combination."

A frown creased Nancy's face. "Eight at night? The kids are all gone by seven."

"Maybe not," said Amy, the gears turning. "Not if we give the parents a free hour and a half, maybe to go out to dinner alone or to . . ." She wiggled her eyebrows up and down. "Well, do something else they can't when the kiddies are around."

"Ah, the old bribe of solitude, huh?"

"You got it. Oh, we'll tell them what it's for and everything, but I bet most of them would be happy to see their kids on TV with the senator. And we'd only need ten or a dozen. The parents could come around eight thirty for the kids, maybe even see the senator themselves."

"Sounds fantastic. But look," Nancy said, glancing at her watch, "I gotta pick up Karin at my mom's. Give me a call at home and we can talk about who can call which parents, okay?"

As Nancy swept out the door, Amy felt a little sorry for her. Nancy had her own daughter and there never was a sweeter third grader than Karin, but what she didn't have was a husband.

John Fowler had been, to all appearances, a friendly man, devoted to his wife and daughter. But the problem was, Nancy finally realized after denying it for several years, that John was a little *too* friendly, or as Nancy put it to Amy when she finally filed for divorce, "The son of a bitch would stick it in anything with a hole that moved." Nancy had never made clear whether she meant that the hole or its bearer moved, and Amy had never asked for details. But Nancy's lawyers had come up with so many corespondents that Amy realized Nancy was probably not exaggerating.

Her friend had gotten a good financial settlement and custody of Karin, with John only allowed visitation one weekend a month. But Nancy had been divorced for over a year now and still had not had one date. She had plenty of offers, including some from the few single fathers who brought their children to Making Friends. But she always politely declined and explained why to Amy.

"These guys are all divorced. The only guy I know who's divorced is John and I'm damned if I want to get involved with another John." The only way she'd go out with a divorced man, she said, was if she knew he had been cheated on by his wife rather than the other way around, and even then that wouldn't say much for his ability to keep a woman happy.

No, she had said more than once, the only good men were the happily married husbands, like Amy's Rick, and the only way to get one of those was to grab one out of the gate (for which it was too late), to steal one (which meant that he could then be stolen from you), or to catch one as a widower, and she wasn't about to start checking the obituary pages for prospective mates.

Maybe Amy wasn't lucky enough to have a child, but she considered herself very lucky indeed to have a husband like Rick. Through twelve years of marriage, they had never had a disagreement that wasn't cleared up by the time they went to bed. He had been faithful to her and she to him, and he had never given her any cause to doubt his love for her. It had been one of those love-at-first-sight things that had proven to be love now and forever.

So she was lucky after all, and maybe with this visit from Senator King, her luck would get even better. The exposure would mean more customers, and that meant that she could expand and hire more staff and maybe turn a healthy profit besides doing what she felt she had always been meant to do.

For the life of her, she couldn't see a downside to this visit no matter how hard she tried.

2

"Now wait a minute," said Will Standish, who was the official historian of Sons of a Free America. "Rip, are you saying that we're going to bomb a day-care center with kids in it? Because if you are, I've got to lodge a protest here. I'm not for that, no way. I mean, look at how killing all those kids made McVeigh look. That's not good, Rip, not good at all."

"Relax, Will," Rip Withers said. He considered Will Standish his pet in a way. Will was the oldest of the Sons and definitely the mildest of the council that made the decisions. He was the best spoken of them all and could write better than anyone else, which was why he was appointed historian, a title they preferred over secretary, which sounded too feminine for their tastes. "All the kids are out of the building by seven or so. The only people there are gonna be the ones who run the place, Senator Quisling and his ass kissers, and a bunch of lefty reporters and photographers."

Will shook his head. "Uh-uh. They'll have kids there, Rip, you know they will. What's the point in King going to a day-care center if he can't get a photo op with kids?"

"So what do you think, Will?" Sonny Armitage said. "They're gonna rent kids just for that night?"

"Besides, Will, what if a few kids *are* there?" Rip said. "There could be a few anywhere we try to hit him."

"I'll tell you *so what,* Rip. What's the one single image people remember most from Oklahoma City? And I don't mean us patriots, I mean most of the American public." No one answered and Will went on. "You're not saying because you know. It's that fireman holding that dead kid in his arms. You get one image like that, it sets our cause back twenty years. Hell, man, even if no kids get killed, we still bombed a day-care center, for pete's sake. What kind of image is that?"

"Maybe you're after images, Willie," Sonny said, "but I'm after results and the result of a dead Robert King would be one helluva coup to count. It'd be a warning of the highest caliber to every one of those sonsabitches. Look, there are civilian casualties in every single war that was ever fought, and when you're fighting a guerrilla war like we are, they're inevitable. And it's not just our side that kills innocents—remember a little boy up on Ruby Ridge?"

"Up to me," said Ace Ludwig, "I'd as soon take him out with a single bullet—and I could do it too."

"We've been through this, Ace," said Rip wearily, "and it's too big a risk. To give you a clean escape, you'd have to be at a greater distance than we'd have for an unobserved shot. Besides, you can't get him from the side. He's flanked too heavy. It'd have to be from above and there's no buildings higher than three stories around this day-care center."

"Let's take him in town then."

"Dammit, Ace, you got witnesses up the ass in town. Now I know you want to shoot and you'll get your chance soon enough, but not on this one. This one's Powder's."

Ace looked over at a thin, pale, dog-faced man sitting near the corner of the room and sneered. Ralph "Powder" Burns was leaning over, his scarred hands dangling between the bony knees revealed by his khaki shorts. "You mean fumble fingers there?" Ace said. "He's never blown up a damn thing but barrels."

Powder looked up at Ace through his wire-rimmed glasses, his face expressionless. "Never had to before. But you don't have to worry. I can take care of this just fine." His voice sounded like razor-legged spiders scuttling over glass.

"Oh yeah," Ace replied. "All them burns and scars show us just what good hands we're in."

"Explosives," Powder hissed, "is a learning process. It's like as if the first time you ever picked up a rifle, you had to experiment with making your own loads first. Wouldn't know you had too much powder in a casing till it blowed up on you. You think *you* wouldn't have a few scars and burns after a while?"

Ace made a disgusted noise. "So what you gonna do with your shit bomb, Powder? Rent a U-Haul van and park it outside the center? That ain't gonna look suspicious, hell, no . . ."

"Ain't gonna use no fertilizer bomb," Powder said. "You're right for once, Ace. Too big. Too unwieldly."

"Un*wieldy,*" Will Standish corrected, barely loud enough to be heard.

"So what the hell you gonna use then? Dynamite sticks take up a fair amount of room too, y'know."

"Let's let the master-at-arms explain that," Rip said, nodding toward Sonny Armitage.

"We've been stockpiling plastic for the past year," Sonny said. "Storing it inside the powder magazine."

"Plastic?" asked Ace. "Plastic explosives?"

"That's right. We've got a helluva stash now. More than enough for the two bombs."

"Two?" Junior Feeley said. "Who else we bombing?"

"Just King," said Sonny. "But there are two major units of the center, for different age groups. They're divided by a hallway down the middle of the building. We don't know where our target will be so we figure if we plant a device in each location, we can't go wrong."

"How big would these bombs be?" asked Will Standish.

Powder shrugged his knobby shoulders. "Small. Could look like a couple of wrapped books."

"And how would you detonate them?"

"Two timers, set to go simultaneous."

"What's that?" asked Junior Feeley.

"At the same time," said Powder.

"Could it be done remotely?" asked Will.

"Not as dependable."

"All right," Will went on, "for the sake of argument, couldn't you hook them up to a timer but have a remote that could stop the detonation if we learned the visit was canceled or something? You know, so if King doesn't get there for one reason or another, or shows up early or late, we could call it off? I mean, after all, our target's King, right? No point in blowing the place up if he doesn't show, right?"

Rip Withers nodded and looked at Powder. "Can you do that?"

"Yep. Have to be kinda close though. Two hundred yards, maybe, that's the range. But I don't wanna set it off with no remote. Might not work."

"Then," said Will, "a remote might not work to abort it."

"Might not," Powder agreed. "But my main concern is that it goes bang when it's supposed to, not that it doesn't. You can depend on a timer but not on a remote."

"Then you couldn't depend on a remote to stop it."

"Look, you want odds, your timer'll work ninety-nine times out of a hundred. A remote'll work nine times outta ten."

"Besides, Will," Rip said, "we're not gonna have to stop this thing. King'll be there. Now let's put your mind at rest. Powder'll hook up a remote, okay? Just in case. The bombs'll still be on timers, but ones that can be stopped by the remote, that make you happy?"

"Well, I just don't see any point in setting off bombs if our target's not there," said Will.

"And neither do the rest of us. Okay, Powder, you go ahead and set 'em up. I wanta get in there tomorrow night to plant 'em. Don't know how early they send in their secret service teams but the sooner we get 'em in the easier it'll be. Okay? That's it then. Powder, I wanta see you and Sonny in ten minutes in my cabin. And have somebody clean this shit up in here. This is supposed to be a meeting room, not a pigsty."

The men dispersed, leaving through the outside door. A dozen or so militiamen were leaning against trees or sitting on the white resin chairs around the heavy wooden picnic tables where mess was sometimes served. There were twenty men living full-time in the compound and another ten who still lived with their families but spent their weekends and many evenings at the compound. They could not be in the council, though they were sworn to secrecy just the same. The penalty for breaking their vow was instantaneous death.

There had been a few who had broken their vows in the past, and they had paid the price. But as Rip Withers walked past his current corps, he felt he could trust them all. They were one hundred percent dedicated to the freedom that their ancestors had bought for them with blood.

Rip considered himself a Jeffersonian, though he would have been hard pressed to explain exactly what that meant. The words he clung to, however, were the words of Jefferson that had been found on Timothy McVeigh's shirt, about the tree of liberty having to be watered from time to time with the blood of tyrants. Rip knew that was God's own truth.

But the problem was that it wasn't the tyrants' blood that was being shed, it was the people's. And it wasn't just Waco and Ruby Ridge. Hell, the normal guy was getting bled drop by drop, day by day in little ways they hardly noticed, until they were just zombies, doing whatever the government told them.

Yeah, the government was getting into every nook and cranny of people's lives. The schools taught your kids not just how to think but what to think with all their "values" training, teaching the kids how to be good little liberals and save the goddam rain forests while forgetting to teach them the basics of the three R's. TV and movies had become cesspools, with faggots and lesbians looking just like everybody else, but religious folks looking like backward idiots.

And as for just being able to make a decent wage so that you could feed and clothe and house your family, shit, forget that flat out—half your pisspot salary was going to feed niggers on crack or pump medicine into homos with AIDS who were gonna die anyway or get put back into the pockets of the rich sonsabitches who paid you in the first place.

Politics didn't mean jackshit. Every single politician in Washington was a buttboy for somebody. The Democrats wanted to take your money and give it to the junkies and wetbacks and welfare bitches, and the Republicans wanted to give your money to the rich bastards who paid you with one hand and snatched it back with the other. They were all pricks, and Rip Withers would've gladly put a gun to all their heads and splashed their brains all over until the Capitol dome looked like a big, bloody tit. Those assholes weren't Americans, none of them. They'd forgotten the meaning of the word.

But Rip Withers hadn't and neither had his brother, Ray, and neither would his son, Karl. Ray wasn't the brightest guy in the world but he was Rip's brother and Rip loved him and he knew damn well that Ray's heart was in the right place. Besides, he wasn't dumb the way Junior Feeley was dumb, with a kind of meanness that just dared you to laugh at him.

No, Ray was slow and he knew it, and it was okay if you knew it too. There wasn't a mean bone in his brother's body, and that was why he had made Ray vice president of the Sons. The vice president didn't really have to *do* anything, just take care of things if the president wasn't there, and Rip was always there and always would be. If he died or something, Ray wouldn't take over automatically. There would be an election and Rip felt sure that Sonny Armitage would win. That would be okay. Sonny was strong in a lot of ways and he wouldn't fuck up.

In a few more years, if they survived that long and weren't wiped out by Clinton's fire troops, Rip hoped that his son, Karl, would be fit for leadership. The boy had turned into a real good patriot once Rip had gotten him away from his mother, the bitch. She'd wanted him to go to one of those goddam liberal state colleges where he'd have been sure to become either a tree-hugging moron or, more likely, a young Republican Ralph Reed clone. And if he ever picked up a gun again, it would have been because some nigger burglarizing his house dropped it: *"Here you go, my black brother, you dropped this . . ."* Shit.

Not anymore though. Karl was eighteen and that bitch had no more hold over him, even if she *did* still have a hold on Rip's bank account after that divorce. No-good Jew lawyer made it real sweet for her, probably taking his share of more than the money too, with his little hebe circumcised pecker.

Well, he was welcome to her. All women were good for anyway was to procreate the race and dress up tool catalogs, and he pitied the poor dumbass who thought of them as anything more than wet holes in a dry bed.

No sir, there were no women in Sons of a Free America and no camp followers either. If somebody wanted a piece of ass, they went into Hobie or to the Twin Cities and got their nuts off, and they better damn well use a condom since anything worse than crabs meant they were dishonorably discharged, and that meant a discharge with extreme prejudice. The married or otherwise attached men who didn't live full-time in the compound got their nookie at home, but the longer they were in the Sons, the more likely it became that they'd break up with their women eventually. Patriotism, as Rip liked to say, was a jealous mistress.

Rip noted with pride that not one of the cadre standing outside asked any of the council what the meeting had been about. Sure, they were curious, but they were good soldiers who knew as much as they needed to know. When the time came they would be informed so that they could share in the joy of the strike. But until then loose lips sank ships, and things could come out accidentally, especially once you got talking in bed. That was another reason to stay the hell away from women.

Rip's cabin was just a ten-by-ten room with a cot, a couple of chairs, a foot locker, a stand with a basin, and a phone. He showered, shaved, and shat with his men in the community latrine. But the phone was there because he needed a private line, and there were times he had to talk to just a few of his comrades. That was what the folding chairs against the wall were for. He unfolded two of them now, then sat on his wooden, straight-backed chair and prayed.

He didn't do enough praying and that was ungrateful. It was Yahweh who had brought him to this point, same as he had brought Randy Weaver and his family to Ruby Ridge in Idaho. True, Vicki and their son, Samuel, had been shot by the damn government troops but Yahweh worked in mysterious ways. Those deaths had been the spark that ignited the patriot movement and Waco had been the flame that lit the fuse that blew up the federal building in Oklahoma City. It was all linked, all part of God's plan.

No, he thought, *Yahweh's* plan. The name God was nothing, *dog* spelled backwards. That's why they could say goddammit, but if anyone said Yahweh damn it, well, he just might lose his tongue. Of course, *Yahweh dammit* didn't roll right off the tongue either.

There was a knock on the cabin door and Rip called for the boys to come in. Sonny Armitage and Powder Burns sat in the folding chairs,

Sonny straddling his and crossing his arms on the back. "It's you two I want to do this work," said Rip without preamble. "Now we got three days till King shows and a day and a night before we plant them so you start building now, Powder, and I'll give you all the help you want."

"Don't want no help. People don't know what they're doin', make a crater outta this forest. I can get 'er done by tomorrow night."

"Okay. If the remotes are a problem, fuck 'em."

"I can do the remotes too. But like I said, no guarantees they'll work."

"Long as you guarantee the bombs'll work."

"Damn right."

"All right then, let's keep Will happy and give him his remotes. Now tomorrow night, the two of you go in and place them. You're gonna have to put them where they won't be found on a sweep but where they'll do maximum damage. And you've gotta get in and out without a trace."

"No problem," Sonny said with a confidence born of dozens of previously successful missions. It was Sonny's midnight visits to the Twin Cities that had a lot to do with keeping the Sons supplied with food and ammo. Sonny was ex-special services and could get inside a mom-and-pop or a corner drug store undetected, disarm an alarm system, pop a safe, and be off with several thousand dollars on a lucky night.

True, the Sons got most of their financing through labyrinthine channels from a pair of St. Paul businessmen, but it was Sonny's icing on their patrons' cake that enabled them to have an armory that would have been the envy of nearly every other militia group, had anyone outside of the Sons known about it. And that was damned unlikely since nobody outside the group even knew about the Sons at all.

"All right then. Set them to blow at eight ten. King prides himself on being punctual. No reason he ought to change now."

3

"Hey, monkey," said Rick Carlisle as his wife walked in the door. He was sitting at the breakfast nook, a half-full cup of coffee and the evening newspaper in front of him. Amy leaned over and gave him a kiss, which he returned in full, holding his cheek against her own before they broke the embrace.

"The monkey needs a banana," Amy said. "I'm starving."

"Well, there are three slices of pizza left—warming up in the oven."

"Three left . . . ? That means you ate five." Amy shook her head in mock exasperation. "Monkey and piggie."

"Why so late?" Rick asked, getting up and sliding the pizza out of the oven.

Taking a slice, she set him down in the chair, sat on his lap, and told him as calmly as possible about the phone call and the upcoming visit of Senator King.

"My God, honey," he responded, "that's *great*! Amazing publicity for the center—you couldn't *buy* stuff like that."

"I know . . . but I was thinking about it on the way home and I feel a little funny *staging* something and asking the parents to . . . well, *use* their kids, you know? It seems too commercial somehow."

"Hey, I know you get involved with the kids on a very pure level but this is a business first and foremost, right? And the parents love you. I'm sure they won't mind you commercializing their kiddies for an hour or so. I mean, how often does a chance like this come along? Once in a lifetime, maybe. And as hard as you've worked to get to this point, you deserve it . . ."

* * *

On Sunday Amy and Nancy made the telephone calls, asking for permission to keep certain children after eight the following Tuesday evening. When they were told why, every parent agreed, and by the end of the day Amy was getting calls from parents *asking* if their children could stay to be part of the senatorial visit. Amy happily agreed and by the day's end she realized that she was going to have ten children in preschool and another dozen in the kindergarten/primary section, with every parent promising to pick up their child by nine.

She didn't know how things could get much better.

"Shut the fuck *up,* for shit's sake!" Sonny Armitage hissed. He loved doing this kind of work on his own but he hated doing it with someone else, especially when that someone was as big a stumblebum as Powder Burns.

Christ, it was a wonder the guy hadn't blown up himself and the compound long ago. If there was anything on the floor, Powder's size-fourteen shoes would seek it out and trip over it. At least Sonny was carrying the bombs, both of them, each wrapped in brown paper. The weight of them made them feel like books of death in his knapsack. It had been years since he worked with plastique and that shit had been about as stable as a college boy draftee under fire for the first time.

But Powder was using the real stuff, as good as it got, and it had a solidity and heft that he somehow admired, though he found it hard to believe that such a small amount could do as much damage as Powder said. He hoped he was right.

Getting into the center had been as easy as talking a Vietnamese whore into a blow job. He had picked the lock so sweet and clean that he doubted he had left a scratch in the tumblers, let alone on the face. And all the blinds had been conveniently pulled down so they could have used standard flashlights instead of their infrared goggles. Still, the goggles gave them an unlimited range of vision and a guarantee that no stray beam would work its way around the edge of a blind to alert a passing cop, although this particular neighborhood seemed barren of life at this time of night. They had parked six blocks away and hadn't seen a single lit-up house, passing car, or living person anywhere. The peace and quiet of the suburbs.

A peace and quiet that would be loudly disturbed in forty-eight hours.

The center's front door opened into a building-wide lobby area ten feet deep. There were coat racks and benches as well as rest rooms on either side of the hall that went down the middle of the building.

To the left was obviously the preschool, infant, and toddler area.

There were a dozen mesh-sided cribs, beanbag furniture, and numerous small plastic chairs and tables. Toys were everywhere, as Powder's feet quickly learned. Pegboards with hooks showed where the kids hung their things. Sonny read the names: *Brendan Adams, Tyler Greer, Jacob Goldberg, Virginia Cash, Charlie Tran, MacKenzie Feldman, Luis Ruiz, Yolanda Jefferson* . . . The whole damn spectrum, he thought. Jews, spics, blacks, gooks.

On the other side of the building was the primary area, with toys and games oriented toward older children. Each area had its own pair of rest rooms and a kitchen area at the back with a refrigerator, double sink, and microwave oven. There was also a sink and a diaper changing counter in the preschool area. The names on the primary room pegboard showed the same kind of racial and religious intermixing.

"Any ideas?" Sonny asked Powder.

The bomb man scratched his scruffy chin, then walked back toward the sinks, opened the door to the storage area beneath, and stuck his hand up into the darkness. "How about under the sinks, in the space between the two. Tape 'em up in here."

"And somebody fills up the sink with hot water and the tape melts. Package goes clunk, kid says, 'Hey teacher, what's this?' I don't think so, Powder."

Powder turned back, looking for all the world in his goggles like some big bug trying to find a mate. "Well, how about under here," he said, slapping the side of the refrigerator. "Underneath at the back."

"Wouldn't the refrigerator sorta cut down on the impact? I mean, it's pretty heavy and—"

Sonny shut up. Even behind the thick goggles, Powder's face registered unmistakable amusement. "Sonny," he said, "that bomb goes off, that refrigerator might just as well not even be there."

They secured the first bomb packet high up within the coils but not touching them to avoid any tell-tale sound of vibration. The spot where it rested was warm but not hot.

"You gotta set it?" asked Sonny.

"Set it last night. Digital timer. Could set it for a month from now. Them 24-hour alarm clock days are long gone, man."

They set the second bomb in the other refrigerator with even more ease. "You got them synchronized?" Sonny asked.

"Close as I can. They may not be perfect, lose or gain a few seconds in forty-eight hours. But odds are the first one'll set off the other."

"Boom, boom," Sonny said.

"Yeah . . . the Boom-Boom Room." Powder chuckled at his weak joke. Sonny didn't.

As they walked down the hall to the front door Sonny asked Powder, "It bother you knowing you might be blowing up kids? I mean, even if it's an accident."

"Nope. Don't bother me a bit. You seen the names . . . Some of 'em probably niggers, some Jews, that Tran—that's gotta be Vietnamese. Got your other non-white, non-Christians too. Now I wouldn't bomb a Christian school or day-care, but this place . . . it's full of mongrels. And as for the white Christian kids, why aren't their mothers takin' care of them at home? Why they gotta bring their little babies here?"

"Because they don't know any better." By that time they had reached the front door and the conversation paused until they were safely out, the door locked behind them, and in Sonny's pickup on the way back to the compound.

"All the dumb shits know," Sonny continued, lighting a cigarette, "is that they gotta work harder and harder to pay the federal government's taxes so mom and dad both go to work and they dump the poor kids in some liberal day orphanage where they learn that the little colored boy and Jew boy and gook boy are their brothers and that being a Christian don't count for shit."

Sonny exhaled deeply, the yellow smoke adding another thin layer to the coating on the inside of the windshield. "Hell, Powder, now I think about it, blow up all those goddam places. Nothing but breedin' grounds for the enemy." He flicked on the radio and country-western came twanging out. "Find Wilson," he ordered Powder, who turned the dial until a soft but intense voice spoke from the twin speakers.

"But, friends, don't take my word for it," the voice said. "Listen to your neighbors, your friends, the people you work with, you go to church with. They're going to tell you, because they know firsthand, just like you and me, that this government is the most intrusive in our history.

"And if you don't do what they want you to, they'll arrange it so that they can *kill* you, my friends, kill you without fear of *legal* reprisal. Oh yes, they'll kill you the way they did Gordon Kahl and Vicki Weaver and Robert Mathews and the men, women, and children of Waco and all the other modern martyrs to freedom.

"But though the killers may not suffer a legal penalty . . . since they're the ones, my friends, who make the laws in the Jewish-run courtrooms, they can still suffer the penalties of the Lord and of those who act in his holy name. There are good Christian people out there—patriots each and every one—and the time is coming when the murderers and thieves of our freedom will pay, when Christian patriots will make the streets run red with unsanctified blood."

"Damn, you *tell* 'em, Wilson!" Powder muttered.

"I know you good people are listening and I'm not exhorting you to violence, make no mistake, you watchdogs of the FCC and the other government rabble who listen and watch our every move, desperate to take away our constitutional rights. And you know what Constitution I mean—the one our founding fathers set up, the Bill of Rights. Not all that junk that came later, once the Jews got their greedy hands into it. You're not going to get me on your sedition charges, oh no.

"But you can't stop me from making a prediction, just like your godless, New Age seers do. I predict a war in this country. A war of patriots against the Jew banker–controlled government, with their dark-skinned lapdogs and soldiers. It'll be a war of faith and a war of race, and when it's all over, the white Christians, *true* Christians, will lead this country once again.

"And then woe to the Jew, woe to the black man, woe to the Hispanic, to the homosexual, to the woman who disobeys the biblical injunction to be subservient to man, to . . ."

The list went on and Powder Burns sat back in the truck and smiled beatifically. "Man, is Hobie ever lucky to have Wilson Barnes on the radio . . ."

4

The night before Senator King's visit, Amy Carlisle had trouble sleeping, even long past midnight. She had gotten up quietly, trying not to wake Rick, and went to the kitchen to make a cup of herbal tea. She turned on the radio but the only station that came in clearly at that time of night was the small, twenty-four-hour "nut station," as Nancy always called it, that carried Wilson Barnes from midnight to six A.M. Even at a low volume the hate monger's voice seemed to fill the kitchen, and Amy made a face and turned it off.

She was barely a few sips into her tea when Rick appeared in the doorway, his bathrobe thrown crookedly over his nude body. "Whassa matter?" he said, then held up a hand. "No, don't tell me. Let me use my psychic abilities. You're, uh, concerned about something. I see a white-haired man in a dark suit, surrounded by other men in dark suits . . . This man looks vaguely, um, yes, *senatorial.*"

"Gee, is it that obvious?"

"Why don't you come back to bed?" Rick said, standing behind her and putting a hand under her pajama top to massage her shoulders. "I could relax you . . ."

"In that very special way you have?"

"Me and my little friend."

She felt something pressing against her back. "Your little friend's getting bigger."

"And promises to grow bigger yet, shown the proper appreciation and enthusiasm." Rick leaned down and kissed her at the soft place just in front of her ear lobe. "I love you, Amy. All kidding aside, I do love you. Don't worry about tomorrow. Come to bed, huh?"

She did and they made love, sweetly and gently at first, her desire increasing as her body relaxed, until she reached the point where the tension of the day had been forgotten, transformed into the tension of the night, the sensation of being pushed toward a vast cliff, teetering on the edge of the abyss, and then, finally, falling over the edge, the tension broken, surrendering to the moment, and letting the red blood rush into every part of you, filling your hips and belly and breasts, rolling up, up to your shoulders and into your face, across your arms until the burning blood sprouts from you, forming red wings that bear you up out of the abyss, up and up from the blackness of the chasm to the deep and blacker velvet of the sky, soaring into sleep . . .

And Amy Carlisle, sated by sex that, to her sorrow, planted only pleasure and not seed in the barren soil of her womb, slept and dreamed of flying, still flying, but as a bird. She could feel the wind as it whispered through her beating feathers and kissed her black eyes, eyes as shiny and unfeeling as onyx, open against the rush of air. Her wings were strong, bearing her at great speed through the night sky.

Above, pinpricks of stars glinted, fixed and constant lights, vast and eternal. Below, the artificial and puny illuminations of men, fleeting as their lives, blurred as she rushed past, vanishing as quickly as they were seen, born and dying in a moment, flaming into existence so fast, and darkening in a single breath of eternity.

And it was with eternity that she felt at one. She was a fixed and constant black star, moving in an orbit of her own around the world, seeing the sad and sullen lights shine below, watching for the ones that flared and sparked and were extinguished, but that continued to glow a dim but angry red. These were the ones to whom she could speak, to whom her raucous cry would tell volumes. These red souls, refusing to die, needed her wisdom, her power.

Yes . . . There was one, far below, like a cigarette tip winking in some dangerous alleyway. She folded her wings slightly and started to drop down, down toward that eye of redness.

But as she neared it, the air seemed to thicken, become dense and gray, as though she were sinking through airborne ash that clung to her feathers, weighing them down. The currents of air she had been riding vanished, and she fell now instead of drifting. She spread her wings wide, tried to flap them, tried to rise to seek the thermals once more, but the gray dust, the heavy ash on her feathers would not permit it.

And she fell.

She fell toward the red dot, still visible to her coal black eyes through the dead gray air. She fell, and as she neared the ground and the red soul that refused to die, the red blotch sharpened, became a figure whose face looked up at her, a dead face coated with pale ash, through which had cut tears of rage and hate and refusal to accept its fate, tears flowing out of the being's eyes and down its cheeks and over its lips so that it looked like a white mask, eyes and mouth rimmed with black.

And just before she fell directly into that face, just before she struck it with enough force and terror to end the dream and bring her, sweating and terrified, back to wakefulness, she saw that the face was her own.

By morning Amy had nearly forgotten the dream and would not remember it again until much later, both in terms of time and of events. There was too much to do today to think about dreams.

Amy worked with Nancy Fowler and Judy Croft in the preschool area for most of the day, occasionally sneaking over to the elementary room to supervise the cleaners there, making the center spick-and-span for the senator's visit. In the afternoon when the elementary kids started coming in and many of the working mothers picked up their infants and toddlers, the cleaners switched over to the preschool room while Judy fussed around, making sure that nothing the cleaners did endangered the remaining children in any way.

Judy was a gem and Amy had been lucky to find her. She was in her early sixties, had already raised four children of her own, and had been a registered nurse for twenty years. Though she claimed to be retired, she still put in as many hours at Making Friends as she ever did when she worked for Doc Garber, who had retired himself five years earlier. Though they had never had a medical emergency at the center, it was reassuring to know that there was someone to take care of things should any occur.

By four the majority of the remaining children were school age. Round, matronly Judy stayed with the younger children while Amy and Nancy took charge of the older ones. Amy was playing a game of Button Button with Ashley Corcoran, DeMarole White, Polly Phelps, and Pete Grissom while several of the boys were taking turns on the new Pocket Gameboy one of them had just gotten.

Brenda Tran was working on the computer, her younger brother Charlie looking over her shoulder, waiting his turn, his dark eyes staring intently at the screen. Such smart kids, Amy thought with a touch of pride. They owed their intelligence to the genes of their parents, native Vietnamese who had made a great success with a string of software stores that had started in Hobie and were now expanding into the Twin Cities area.

Still, Amy felt she had done a lot to expand the Tran children's world. Strangely enough, they didn't have a computer at home but they both took to Amy's old 386 like a duck to water. Brenda navigated both DOS and Windows with the ease of an MIT grad, and Charlie changed CONFIG.SYS files like hats. Amy was tempted to see if they could fix the constant crashes of the Pentium computer on which she kept the center's records but decided that she couldn't bear the feeling of computing inferiority if they were successful.

As she looked around the room she realized that she could find something special and wonderful about all her children. For an hour, or two, or six every day, she was a mother, raising, teaching, caring for her children, taking care of them, guarding them against harm. She was proud of them all. She loved them all.

At five thirty the pizzas came and the kids gathered for a party. All but a few were staying past their usual pickup time, yet none of them were impatient. On the contrary, it seemed special, even festive, and the pizza made it more so. Amy just hoped that tomato sauce and pepperoni didn't get thoroughly ground into the freshly cleaned rugs.

After they ate they played some more games, but at six the phone rang. It was an aide of Senator King. "Mrs. Carlisle," he said, "I'm terribly sorry to call you so late but something unforeseen has occurred."

Amy could feel her heart start to pound. She knew what the man was going to say as soon as he had identified himself. "Senator King won't be able to get out to your center tonight. A bill came up unexpectedly and he has to fly back to Washington immediately to vote on it. The vote's predicted to be close and it's one the senator's very concerned about, and . . . well, every vote counts. He asked me to please extend his regrets and he'll call you tomorrow personally to apologize."

"Oh, that's all right," Amy said. "I understand." And she did, but that didn't help ease the disappointment.

"I assure you," the aide said, "the next time the senator returns to the Hobie area—and I promise you he will—your center will be the first place he visits. I'm sorry to rush off now but I've got a dozen other calls to make. I do want you to know, though, that we've contacted all the media people so you won't have any mobile units or reporters banging on your door."

"Thank you. I appreciate that," Amy said, thinking that she had *wanted* reporters and TV crews banging down her door. "And I appreciate the call and the, what, the rain check?"

The aide chuckled. "Yes, consider it a rain check. Thanks for your understanding, Mrs. Carlisle. Sorry it didn't work out."

"That's quite all right. Well, good-bye."

"Till next time."

The children, with Nancy at the front of the room, knew there was something wrong when they saw Amy's vacant expression. "Amy . . . ?" Nancy said.

Amy brightened, forcing a smile. "Well," she said, "the good news is we won't have to share any of our dessert with reporters."

The kids' faces fell and they gave out with a heartfelt, "Awwwww . . ."

"The setter's not gonna come?" asked Mary Alice Shearer, a normally shy kindergartner who had gotten unaccountably excited about the visit.

"No, honey," Amy said, "the senator had to go back to Washington, D.C. He had to vote on a bill."

"Like a money?" Mary Alice asked.

"No, it's a different kind of bill."

"Like a law," Brenda Tran said. "They pass bills and then they're law." Brenda went on to explain the workings of the Congress while Amy went into the other area to tell Judy Croft about the cancellation.

"Well, I'm sorry," Judy said, "but I can't say I'm surprised. With politicians, I never believe *anything* until it happens. Are you going to call the parents?"

"I don't see how I can. I'm sure a lot of them made other plans."

"Maybe they'll hear about the senator going back early on the news," Judy said.

That was what happened with several of the parents, who heard the news on the sole Minneapolis station that ran it. The others apparently did not know. Neither did any of the members of Sons of a Free America.

5

At seven thirty that evening Powder Burns, Sonny Armitage, Will Standish, and Rip Withers drove into Hobie in Rip's 1989 dark green Plymouth Acclaim, a car that had been chosen for its nondescript quality. Under certain lights the dark green appeared deep blue, and in bright sunlight it looked black. The generic styling was indistinguishable from dozens of other models. And that suited Rip just fine.

Will had come along because he felt he should at least be nearby. "I agreed to this," he explained. "It's on my hands as well. And it'll be an event worth preserving in words." He made certain too that Powder had brought along the remote control in case the senator's visit was canceled.

When they arrived in Hobie they planned to park several blocks from the day-care center and wait for the explosion, but first Rip wanted to drive past to make sure that the visit was proceeding according to plan. When they did and saw only three cars and no limos or mobile television trucks, they knew that something was wrong.

"You got the right day?" Powder asked from the backseat as Rip pulled over and stopped against the curb.

"Of *course,* I got the right day," Rip said. "Don't be so fucking stupid."

"Well, *somebody* got their wires crossed," Will said, and Rip could hear his voice shake.

"Or somebody found the bombs," Will said, "and canceled the visit. My God, maybe they're watching us right now! Maybe they set a trap . . ."

"Godamighty," said Sonny, "if they'd set a trap, there'd be more cars there. There's nobody on the fucking street but us! No, they canceled," said Sonny. "I can't believe this . . . That *prick*, that goddam fuckin' homo shithead *coward*!"

"All right," said Will, "what are we going to do? Rip, we've got to stop this thing. Look at those cars—there are people in there, maybe kids."

"No sweat, Will," Rip said, trying to stay calm. It wasn't the prospect of the bombs still going off that upset him. It was the fact that they had missed their target and it could be months before King came back to the area, *years* before they had as sweet a shot at him. "Hell," he said, thinking aloud, "I should've let Ace take a shot at the bastard this afternoon."

"Rip," Will said, "forget about it—that's for the future, this is *now*. We've got to get those bombs shut off. Come on, Powder, get that remote out."

"Okay, okay, I got it here, no problem." From somewhere inside his coat he pulled out what looked like an old TV remote with a telescoping antenna.

"Are we close enough?" Will asked.

"Sure, sure . . ." Powder yanked the antenna open to its full four-foot length. "Just lemme stick it out the window. It'll shut off the contact points and we can come back and get them whenever the hell we want."

He pushed the button, then frowned. "Shit."

"What?" said Will. "What is it?"

"Well, that little red light, I think, is supposed to light up."

"Supposed to? Don't you *know*?"

"Yeah, I *know*—it's *supposed* to."

"Well, what's it mean if it *doesn't*?"

"Means it didn't work . . ." Powder shook his head in puzzlement, then pushed the antenna closed and turned the unit over. "Maybe the batteries are bad."

Will made an exasperated noise deep in his throat. "The batteries? Didn't you put in new batteries?"

"They were new, yeah, but I had 'em for a while."

"You—"

"I had 'em but I didn't ever use 'em. Batteries go bad on their own, y'know, Will."

"Oh, for God's sake . . . Well, can we get some new batteries?"

Rip pulled the car onto the street and turned around. "There was a SuperAmerica back a few blocks," he said wearily. "They'll have batteries. Now relax, Will. They're set for eight ten and that's twenty-five minutes from now, plenty of time to get batteries and a bunch of fuckin' Slushies to boot."

Powder bought four double A's, but no Slushies, and loaded two of them into the remote.

"Does it work now?" Will asked.

"I don't know," said Powder peevishly. "We're not in *range* now. Even if I pushed it and it worked, I wouldn't *know* that it worked."

"Well, let's go *back* then," said Will, gesturing to the road ahead. "Come *on*!"

Rip turned to Will and slowly set one arm on the steering wheel and the other on the back of the seat. "Will, let me tell you something. I don't enjoy being told what to do, not by you, not by any of my men. I am your superior officer and you will address me with the dignity befitting my rank."

Will swallowed and nodded several times. "Okay, I'm sorry, Rip, uh, Colonel, I'm sorry."

"Now I've told you that we are going to be back in plenty of time to successfully abort this mission, and as a soldier, you will obey your commanding officer, who now orders you to maintain silence except to respond to direct question with yessir or nosir until we are clear and away from Hobie." He raised an eyebrow. "Is that clear?"

"Yessir," Will said. Even the two syllables sounded upset and scared. Rip put his hands on the wheel and drove.

They stopped again near the school. "Okay," Rip said. "Ten minutes. Time to spare. Go ahead, Powder."

Powder once more slipped the antenna through the window, once more pushed the button, and once more muttered, "Shit . . ."

"Hell, now what?" said Sonny.

"Wasn't nothin' wrong with the batteries," Powder said. "I just figured it out."

"What?" Rip asked for Will, who looked like he was about to shit himself.

"The signal. It's gettin' through the windows okay, but it's the refrigerators that's the problem. We stuck 'em up in there and there's too much metal for the signal to get through."

"Oh Christ!" Will said, in spite of the silence imposed on him. Rip didn't reprimand him for the blasphemy, under the circumstances.

Rip looked through the window at the Making Friends Child Care Center and chewed on his lower lip. Eight minutes. And with Powder's imprecise timers, maybe less than that.

Then at the window, Rip saw a blind pulled aside and a face looking out. It was a woman, and behind her Rip could see small, moving figures, and he knew he was looking at a woman and children who were already dead.

Eight minutes. Just time enough to clear the area.

He looked away from the woman. Let her see him, he thought. Let her see them all. Let her see the car, get the license plate. In another eight minutes it wouldn't matter at all.

"What are you doing?" Will said, disobeying orders again. It didn't matter. In another eight minutes Rip would have enough on Will to make sure of his silence forever. They would all be bound by the shedding of blood. Like it or not, the Sons of a Free America was about to make its first strike.

Amy let the blind fall back against the glass as the car pulled away. She thought it might have been a parent coming to pick up a child, but instead it looked like four men who had gotten themselves lost.

She had become observant concerning cars around the center. There was always the possibility of kidnapping, if not for ransom, then for darker reasons that Amy didn't like to think about. But she kept the possibility in the back of her mind, as did Judy and Nancy. There were strict procedures to follow whenever anyone who wasn't a parent came to pick up a child.

Amy was startled from her reverie by a tap on the shoulder. "You want to keep an eye on things?" Nancy said. "I've got to run and pick up Karin from swimming practice."

Amy smiled and nodded. Hobie Community Center was only ten blocks away. Nancy would be there and back in as many minutes. "Be careful," Amy said. "There was a car outside with four men—probably just lost, and they took off pretty fast when they saw me—but keep an eye out anyway."

Nancy nodded and waved as she went out the door. Amy didn't worry too much about her friend. They had taken a self-defense course together and Nancy carried a can of pepper spray in her huge purse. But the training and the spray wouldn't be much use against four strong men. Still, she would probably be okay.

Amy turned her attention to the children. There were only six left in the room—Brenda and Charlie Tran, who had turned their attention back to the computer, Mary Alice Shearer, who was dozing in a beanbag chair, Pete Grissom and Ashley Corcoran, who were playing Chutes and Ladders, and DeMarole White, who was puttering around the toy kitchen, shoving pots and pans into the wooden oven and adjusting clickable dials with such panache that her plastic bracelets clattered. *I'm gonna be a chef—that's what my dad does,* she had told Amy innumerable times. Amy and Rick often ate at the hotel restaurant where Micah

White was the head chef and he never failed to present them with a special dessert at the meal's end.

"Whatcha making?" Amy asked DeMarole.

"Booly-baze," she replied, her bright teeth splitting her dark face in a grin. "Dad makes that a lot. I forget what all's in it, but it's neat to say. I *know* it's got fish heads."

"Okay, let me know when it's finished," Amy said. For a moment she thought about checking on Judy, but she didn't like to leave her charges alone and figured Judy was fine anyway.

She had four children there now. Two were babies, Mark Dreyfus and Shannon Pierce, who seemed struck from the same mold. They slept well and were a delight when awake. Frank Boone was a two-year-old who always nodded out promptly at six and remained sleeping until his mother picked him up at seven. Three-year-old Annabel Jorgensen, however, was a terror, or had been, until Judy got ahold of her.

Amy believed it was Judy's age that impressed Annabel, whose parents were in their early twenties. All it took was a look from Judy and Annabel would immediately cease running or screaming or flailing her arms or whatever combination of the three she was engaged in. The response amazed young Mrs. Jorgensen, who had only half-jokingly suggested that Judy become Annabel's live-in nanny.

Since all her own children seemed happily occupied, Amy decided to give Rick a call at his office. She seldom disturbed him but he had been working late on a project for several weeks and had told her that hearing her voice in his dismal office was an interruption he looked forward to. They were lucky, she thought once again, to still be so much in love after twelve years of marriage.

"Hey, it's me," she said when he answered.

"Ah, so how goes the media blitz?"

"The media blitz was a dud—you didn't hear?" She told him about the cancellation and he clucked sympathetically.

"I'm sorry, baby. Damn, that really would've lit a fuse under the business . . ."

"What are you doing?" Will Standish asked. "Rip, what are you *doing*?"

"I'm driving away. Believe me, you don't want to be around when those bombs go off."

"Amen and hallelujah to that," Powder said.

Will felt as if his heart was going to burst out of his chest. "We can't let this happen . . . There are *kids* in there!"

"Yeah," Rip said. "I saw them too. But it's too late now."

"It's not, it's *not*! Let's find a phone, call them . . . tell them to get out quick!"

"Will, when those babies go off, there are going to be cops and ambulances and fire trucks swarming through these streets. And if we're seen fleeing the area, we are going to be under suspicion. Now I'm prepared to be a martyr, like every last man here, but not if we don't accomplish something by our martyrdom. And blowing up that building isn't much of an accomplishment."

"A *building*?" Will said. "That isn't just a building—we're blowing up kids, little *kids*!"

"Little nigger kids," Powder said. "Little gook kids. Fuckin' place is a mini-UN."

"Pull over, Rip," said Will, trying not to sound as scared as he felt. "I want to call them."

"There's no phone booth around, Will. Now you just get a handle on yourself."

"I'm going to jump out of the goddamned car, Rip, if you don't stop." Will grabbed the door handle.

The rack of a slide jamming a shell into a chamber was deafeningly loud. Will winced at the sound and then felt a cold weight pressed against his neck under his right ear.

"You try it, Will," Sonny Armitage said, "and you'll hit the pavement a dead man."

Will knew Sonny well enough to know that he wasn't bullshitting. His voice was as flat and as dead as Will knew he would be if he pulled back on the door handle. He let it go and put his hands on his lap, wishing his fingers weren't shaking so much.

"All right," he said as gently as he could. "All right, I'm not going anywhere. Put the gun away, all right, Sonny?"

With relief he heard the sound of the hammer slowly coming to rest on the firing pin. "All right, Will," Sonny said.

"It's a done deal, Will," Rip told him. "I know you're upset but you're gonna have to live with it. We tried to stop it, we couldn't. Now we'll just deal with it."

They drove a few blocks before Rip spoke again. "There's one thing though. After this, they'll know that we're serious. They'll know we'll stop at nothing. No one's safe. No one."

A minute later they heard, far behind them, the explosion. Will's stomach cramped and he felt his bowels pushing down. Jesus Christ, *no,* he wasn't going to shit himself. He tightened his ass, held it back, tried to hold back the thoughts, tried not to see what was happening back there, tried to think about anything except what they had done.

But he failed. He saw it all in his mind, and wondered if the others did too, or if they had come so far on their dark path that they saw nothing and felt nothing but grim satisfaction.

The first explosion occurred in the infant and toddler care area. Amy was talking to Rick on the phone when there was a deafening blast and the wall separating her room from the hall shattered like glass, throwing large and small pieces of itself toward her and the children. It was, for an instant, like being in a tornado, with a wind so strong that nothing could stand against it.

Amy was hurled backward, toward the far wall, striking it hard enough to make her black out for a moment. Still, she felt the debris slamming into her. The pain brought her back to consciousness instantly.

She could barely see through the cloud of dust and smoke but as she looked toward the source of the blast she thought she saw a distant street light where the wall should have been. That meant that not only the wall between her and the hall was gone, but *all* the walls.

The entire preschool area was gone. Judy. The babies.

Amy looked around frantically for her own children and crawled over the wreckage, crying, *"Kids! Kids! Where are you!?"* over and over. She heard someone moaning, someone else crying and stumbled toward the sounds. Then she saw an arm sticking out of a pile of rubble, a dark arm with plastic bracelets around the wrist. DeMarole.

Amy grasped the hand, and the arm followed, too loosely. There was no weight attached to it. The bracelets rattled up the arm and fell into deeper darkness.

A cry ripped up through Amy's throat, a wordless, mindless keening sung for eons. *My children,* it said. *What has happened to my children . . .*

She hauled herself to her feet and stumbled toward the answering cries. There was Brenda Tran, bleeding badly in a dozen places but alive. She grasped the girl, trying to ignore her cries of pain. Amy didn't even think about the dangers of moving her. All she knew was that this was a bad place, a place that had harmed her children and she had to find them, find them all and get them out.

Now she followed the sobbing she heard near the back of the room. Half dragging, half carrying Brenda with her right arm, Amy held her left out before her, feeling for the boy amid the ruins of her dream. Finally her ringing ears heard the screams become words. *"Mommy . . . Mommy . . ."*

I'm coming, she thought. Mommy's coming . . .

She found him pinned under what had been part of the inner wall. She set down Brenda as gently as possible and pulled away the metal panels from over Pete Grissom's body with a strength born of desperation, rage, and motherly love. In Amy's shattered mind, these children were her children that never were, and nothing would take them away from her again.

Both Pete's legs were broken, and Amy positioned him over her shoulder as gently as she could, then raised up Brenda, and looked through the dust and the darkness. There at the back of the room was the emergency exit. The path was relatively clear and once there, all she had to do was push on the bar and they would be outside and away from this bad place. Then she could set the children down and go back to look for the others.

She staggered toward the door, carrying and dragging the children and paused for a moment, to gather strength for the final push to freedom. She paused just for a second, right next to the refrigerator.

At that instant the second bomb's timer, delayed through the imperfection of Powder Burns's skill and its own inexactness, reached 8:10:00 and triggered the cap.

The bomb exploded with more force than the first one. Amy never heard the sound of her own death, never had time to feel more pain than what she already felt. She died feeling only the pain of loss, the pain of love destroyed.

She, and the children she held, disintegrated, became a wet red cloud that dried to dust in the same instant. What had been left of the building after the first explosion was gone.

What had been left of Amy was gone.

6

Rick had not heard the first explosion over the telephone, which went dead. But he did hear the sound of it, five miles away.

In his office he could not tell the direction it had come from, but the fact that it *had* come at the instant he was talking to Amy stiffened him like a statue as he listened to the dead telephone. In a few seconds the busy signal started and he hung up and dialed again, only to receive a rising three-tone beep and a taped message telling him that the number he had dialed was out of order.

Then he heard the second explosion.

He grabbed his coat and bounded down the stairwell, ignoring the elevator, ran to his car in the parking lot, and headed for the center. The sirens started before he had gone a mile.

Officer David Levinson was the first policeman to arrive on the scene. He had been patrolling a half mile away when he heard the first explosion and saw the flash. He immediately turned the prowler around, hit his bubbletop and siren, and tore toward the area.

He was a block from the day-care center when he thought he was able to make out some moving figures in the dust of the shattered building. But then the second explosion occurred and its flash blinded him, the noise pounded at his ears, and debris clattered on his roof. He stopped his car dead on the street until his sight came back.

A mass of smoke and dust drifted skyward and Levinson got out of the car and walked toward the building. Irrationally, as he realized later, he had no fear of further explosions. There seemed nothing left to blow up. His first thought was of the people that he thought he had seen moving. But the closer he got to the site, the less of a possibility that seemed.

The building was leveled. Nothing remained but dust and rubble and a few smoldering fires, flickering weakly as if disappointed at not finding enough fuel to burn. This, he realized, had been the Making Friends Child Care Center, which he drove past three times a day. He lived in the same neighborhood as Amy Carlisle and her husband, had seen them at street fairs and in downtown Hobie. And here was Amy's place, destroyed, as close to vaporized as you could get. God, what had happened?

Levinson ran back to the prowler and started to call in an APB, but he already heard sirens and saw the lights of incoming emergency vehicles. They lit up the sky before they lit the ruined center, and when he looked at the rising cloud of dust and smoke, it seemed to shift oddly, thinning and thickening in places, spreading outward until it made a rough shape in the sky.

It was the shape of a bird, its wings spread.

For a moment, Levinson couldn't breathe. He could only watch the shadow of the huge black bird drifting higher into the sky, remembering the story his grandmother had told him, and fearfully wondering . . .

But then a gust of wind made the shadowy cloud shimmer and shiver and break apart, and Levinson was uncertain whether he had seen it at all. Maybe he had imagined it, the way people see animals in clouds against a blue sky. He hoped so.

The first fire truck pulled up then and the chief ran up to him, bulky in his rubber coat, and asked if anyone had been inside.

"I don't know," said Levinson. "I thought I saw something moving in that area there . . ." He pointed. "But then the second blast hit, and . . . and there *wasn't* any area there," he finished apologetically.

The chief turned to his men as more police cars came driving up, followed by an ambulance. "Crew One, search that area for survivors. Two and Three, get the hoses on those fires."

"You, uh, think it could've been a gas line or something?" Levinson asked the chief.

The man made a face. "You smell any gas?" Levinson shook his head. "Me neither. Uh-uh, this wasn't gas."

Levinson got out of the way while the firemen tramped into the rubble. Then he told the other officers everything he had seen except for the shadowy form rising above the site.

Dan Trotter, an older detective who had worked on the LAPD bomb squad before coming to Minnesota, shook his head. "This wasn't any accident. Two blasts, coming two minutes apart . . . and you know what was supposed to happen here tonight?"

Levinson knew, along with the rest of the force. "Senator King," he said. "But that got canceled."

"Too bad somebody didn't cancel this too," said Trotter. "Or maybe they just thought what the hell. This is your beat, isn't it, Dave?" Levinson nodded. "You know if people were usually in here this late?"

Levinson didn't think he remembered seeing cars in the small lot on his eight-thirty run. "Not usually, that I recall. But cars are here tonight." He pointed to the lot, where two vehicles lay, overturned and crushed by the force of the blast.

Suddenly a woman came running up to them. Her face was pale in the artificial lights, and her voice sounded like she was struggling to hold it under control. "Where's Amy?" she said. "And Judy . . . Where are the *kids*?"

"Amy . . ." Levinson said. "Amy Carlisle was in there?"

"Oh Jesus . . ." the woman said and then broke down, crying in soft, dangerous sobs that threatened to break into hysteria. "Oh my God, there were ten of them in there."

"Ten children?" asked the fire chief, who had come over as soon as he saw the woman. "Or ten altogether?"

"Ten *children.*" The word rasped out like a curse. "Babies . . . and Amy . . . and Judy."

"Ma'am," said the fire chief gently. "Who are you, please?"

Then things really became chaotic. Three cars pulled up, nearly at the same time, with parents who were picking up their children, followed by more just a few minutes later. Though the emergency medical technicians had no injury victims to care for, they were kept more than busy with the grief-stricken and, in some cases, hysterical parents who had to be physically restrained from running into the rubble and digging for their missing children.

"This was plastic explosive," Trotter remarked to David Levinson. "And a lot of it."

"What do you mean, a lot?" Levinson, who knew little of explosives, asked. "I mean, I don't even know how this stuff is packaged."

"Different ways," Trotter said. "Sometimes in canisters, so you can shape it—it's got the consistency of Play-Doh—or in small blocks of one pound each. But you'd need about twenty pounds of plastic to do this kind of damage, say ten pounds per bomb."

Levinson looked at the firemen picking through the ruins. "Are they going to find anything? Bodies . . . parts?"

"Maybe some but it's doubtful. Hell, you can see what it did to steel and wood and glass. Flesh and bone's a lot more vulnerable. Only chance is if somebody, or *pieces* of somebody, got thrown under a section of wall or something from the first explosion. In that case, they might not have been totally wasted. As far as surviving, though, forget it. And if their bodies didn't get buried by the first blast, they're gone. The power of that stuff is incredible. It goes off, a human being gets vaporized." Trotter shook his head. "One thing you can say for it is that it's fast. I doubt anyone suffered."

"So . . . we can't even recover the bodies?"

"Pick up a scoop of dust and put it in an urn," Trotter said in a voice that blended grief and anger into bitterness. "That's as close as you can get to—"

Trotter broke off and looked with concern over Levinson's shoulder. Levinson turned and saw a man getting out of a car behind him. His mouth was hanging partly open and his arms were dangling at his sides. He looked as if he had just been poleaxed. Levinson recognized him as Rick Carlisle.

"Rick," he said, moving toward the man. Rick started to shake his head and his arms came up as if pleading with Levinson to tell him that there was some mistake. Levinson didn't know what to say. The bare, blasted space before them was all too tragically eloquent.

"Rick . . ." said Levinson again. "I'm sorry. I'm so sorry."

Rick Carlisle scarcely heard the words the policeman said to him. The blood was roaring too loudly in his ears. Somewhere in the back of his mind was the realization that he knew this man but it wasn't important now. Nothing was important except absences. The absence of the building. The absence of Amy. Where was she? She could not, would not, be in the building because the building was not there, and if the building was gone, then Amy was gone and she couldn't be gone, that was not possible.

But then where was she?

He felt someone grip his arm and the sudden pain focused him. He looked at the face that was looking up at him and knew that it was Nancy, Nancy Fowler. Then he thought that everything would be all right after all because if Nancy was there, then Amy would be there as well.

He looked at Nancy and asked her, with the simplicity of a child, "Where's Amy?"

Nancy didn't say anything right away. Her face was wet with tears but maybe that was because of the building, Amy's dream that had vanished. But that was all right. Buildings could be rebuilt. And if Nancy was here, then Amy was too and Rick looked over her shoulder to see if Amy was behind her but she wasn't. "Nancy, where's Amy?" he asked again.

Nancy didn't respond in words. Her face seemed to shimmer, melt, almost fall apart, as huge, wracking sobs escaped her small frame and she shook her head, back and forth, back and forth. *No,* the movement said. *No.*

No Amy. No Amy ever again.

Then the heart and the spirit went out of him, and the knowledge crushed him, and his legs gave way and he fell to his knees on the asphalt, looking at the ruin in front of him—ruined building, ruined lives, absent forever.

7

At eleven David Levinson's workday was over. He had stayed at the site, helping as much as he could. There had been a lot to do. The grieving parents and relatives had been the biggest problem but the media had made things far worse.

By nine, mobile TV trucks and vans had descended on the formerly quiet Hobie suburb like crows on a piece of roadkill. While the cameramen's lights pinned the grieving, reporters shoved microphones into their faces and asked them how they felt. Uncertain of what to do, some waved them away while others actually tried to cooperate, attempting to put their loss and horror into words.

It sickened Levinson. He finally had enough when a testosterone-charged, lacquer-haired reporter kept pursuing an Asian woman who had made it clear she did not want to speak. The man still came after her, beckoning his cameraman and yammering at the woman, "Ma'am, please wait, we want to talk to you, won't you share your feelings with us . . . Hey, don't you speak English?"

He followed her beyond the plastic yellow police line, at last cornering her between three cars. "Please, ma'am, tell us how you feel."

The bastard was in Levinson's territory now and he walked up to the man, pressed his palm over the camera, and snatched the microphone away, yanking it from the power cord. "How the hell do you think she feels? Now you get your stupid ass on the other side of that line before I arrest you."

"Hey, pal, I'm just doing my job!"

"I'm not your pal and I'm just doing mine. Now *move.*"

He did, and Levinson sat the woman inside a police car and held her for a few minutes while she cried some more. "Both my children," she said and Levinson's stomach and throat turned to ice. What could you say, what could you do to respond to such pain, to loss that would always be felt, even in the midst of happiness. A fist had wrapped itself around this woman's heart and would squeeze until the day she died.

By ten thirty, federal investigators had arrived, since there was no doubt that the destruction had been caused by bombs. The small fires had long been extinguished and the firemen had searched diligently through the wreckage, but found no survivors. As Trotter had predicted, they found no body parts either.

In another half hour the relatives had either gone home or been taken to hospitals for the night, where they were kept under sedation. Levinson had heard that the husband of Judy Croft, one of the two missing adults, had suffered a heart attack and was in critical condition.

Now Levinson just watched as the investigators searched through the rubble, taking small samples of the debris and dust as they went, and using tape measures for what Levinson assumed was finding ground zero. Huge lights made the area as bright as a sunny day and hundreds of curious citizens crowded behind the police lines, looking at where a building had been and where twelve lives, by best reckoning, had been lost.

"Shift done?" asked Dan Trotter, coming up to him. Levinson nodded. "Any orders to stay?" He shook his head. "Why don't you go home then?"

"I don't know," Levinson said, although he did. The emptiness of his house would only make him think about the emptiness of this dreadful place.

"Want to get a cup of coffee? Maybe a roll or something?"

"Yeah. I'd like that."

They took Levinson's prowler and drove several miles to an all-night diner where the waitresses were friendly but never overly curious. Tonight would test their mettle, Levinson thought.

But they just smiled and nodded at the two policemen, took their orders, and asked no questions. Levinson sat back in the booth and took a long sip of coffee.

"Know why I left L.A.?" Trotter asked. "It was getting too violent. Every time I turned around some asshole was planting a bomb at some bank or some government office, hell, even schools. So I said to my wife, fuck it, let's get out of here before you're a widow. And I got two kids and it was getting to be a shitty place to bring them up in.

"So I came to Hobie, got a promotion, and ironically took a big cut in pay but the difference in cost of living made it a wash. I was a detective and I was happy and things were a lot less violent here than they were in La-La Land." He shrugged, spreading his fingers wide. "And now this." He pulled a note pad out of his pocket and looked at it. "Two women, four babies, six little kids. Gone in a flash. Worst thing I've ever experienced. Most hateful, sick, twisted, disgusting crime I've ever seen committed. And I don't know if we'll ever find the motherfuckers who did it." He closed his eyes and shook his head.

"I left Detroit for the same reason," Levinson said. "All the killing got to be too much after a while. That smell . . . it gets in your nose, you can't get rid of it. It's like a fisherman smelling fish or a farmer smelling shit all the time. I smelled the bodies, you know? Got to me, started affecting, well, my personal life."

He and his wife had started to pull apart as a result. Levinson had hated the gap that had started to come between them. He wanted a perfect relationship with Carol and it wasn't happening in Detroit. She seemed happy to go with him to Hobie and he hoped for the best, but by that time things were too far gone. She left him three months after they arrived and went back to Detroit, the same damned place whose crimes had torn them apart. But that wasn't something he wanted to tell Trotter about.

"So they tried to kill Senator King," Trotter said, looking out the window, "and they didn't care if they killed a bunch of kids in the process." He looked sharply at Levinson. "You know who they are?"

Now it was Levinson's turn to shrug. "Not specifically. But I know the mind-set. I know how they think." He smiled thinly. "I know who they hate."

"Who?"

"They hate me. They hate Jews. But they also hate blacks and Chicanos and Vietnamese and Japanese and anybody whose skin or religion isn't the same as theirs. They hate what's different."

The waitress came and Trotter took a bite of his coffee cake, chewed ruminatively, and swallowed before he asked the question. "You been getting any shit on the force?" Levinson didn't answer and Trotter went on. "Just between us. I heard a few things. Just want to know if they're true."

"There are a few fellow officers," Levinson said slowly, "who, I get the feeling, don't care for Jews very much."

Trotter snorted. "Don't know why they don't quit the force and join one of these damn militias." He grinned. "My wife's maiden name is Rachel Rabinowitz. She goes to synagogue, I don't. But I still catch it from some of the boys. So . . ." His tone grew more serious. "You think it's a militia thing?"

"The bombing? Probably. We've got enough of them around here."

"They do seem to love the north woods, don't they? Only thing is, they've been as quiet as church mice. I know of nearly a dozen different militia chapters within a hundred-mile radius of Hobie and all they do is train and recruit and stockpile arms. But the sons of bitches do it legally as far as we can tell."

"Even if they don't," said Levinson, "after Ruby Ridge and Waco all the authorities from locals to the feds are thinking twice before going into one of those armed camps and making arrests."

"You bet. The militia nuts *like* it when things escalate. Another damn chance to be martyrs to the cause of white Christian brotherhood. Hell, with all that training and all that propaganda bullshit they get fed, they'll jump at the chance to fight us storm troopers of the *guvmint.*"

"You think it was a militia did this then?"

"Well, I'll tell you—I don't know of any private citizen who would have access to the amount of plastic explosive you'd need to level a building like that. No, this thing was planted in that building early by somebody who knew about breaking and entering. And they knew that the secret service would do a sweep of the building before King went in so they had to hide it well. The whole operation shows some professionalism. All except the part where they miss their target and blow up a bunch of children instead. That was a little stupid."

"So do you think the feds will investigate the local militias then?"

"No, I don't. I don't think they'll have the guts to because they're not going to want another incident. If they had absolute proof that a militia was involved, then yeah, they'd go in. But to ask questions? Poke around? Examine armories? Uh-uh, it won't happen. In fact, unless something breaks our way, I'd be surprised if this bombing is ever attributed to anyone but 'person or persons unknown.' "

"I heard her die," Rick Carlisle said. "On the phone, when the line went dead, that's when she died."

He and Nancy Fowler were sitting in Nancy's living room. It was two in the morning. Once it had become clear to Rick that Amy had been killed in the explosion, he had grown more calm and had buried his pain and agony by cooperating in every way possible with the authorities.

He and Nancy had sat in the back of a police van and answered questions for a half hour, first with Hobie's chief of detectives and then with a federal investigator. Nancy had been able to give the names of the children who had been in the center when it had exploded and Rick had told about the final telephone call and the sound of the explosion that followed the line going dead.

That was all they could tell, that and the fact that Amy had seen a car with four men in it outside the building a few minutes before Nancy had left. No, they had no idea that anything had been placed in the building . . . No, they hadn't seen any sign of a break-in . . . No, there was nothing strange that occurred at all . . . No . . . no . . . no . . .

For a moment Rick felt that the federal investigator suspected Nancy herself of having planted the bombs and then leaving before they went off, but he was too weary to speak to the contrary. Let him think that if he liked. That was one theory that would quickly go up in smoke.

Up in smoke.

When the questions were finished and they were left alone, Nancy had said that she had to take Karin home. The little girl had been with a policewoman ever since Nancy had arrived. "Listen," she told Rick simply, "if you don't want to go back to your place tonight, why don't you stay in our guest room."

She didn't say that she wanted the company or suggest that Rick would find it unbearable to be in the house that he had shared with Amy, both of which he suspected were true. She just made the offer and Rick had nodded a weary acceptance.

And now they sat over cups of tea, the events of the night almost like a dream. How, Rick thought, can such a cataclysm occur in your life and hours later you're calmly drinking tea as though it never happened?

Still, it was all they could think about or talk about. They quickly came to the conclusion that the target had been Senator King. "They'll find who did it," Nancy said. "They found Timothy McVeigh, they'll find these guys." She closed her eyes, frowning. "Amy probably *saw* them," she said. "I wish I had asked her more about them—what they looked like, what they were driving. I just wish . . ."

She left it unfinished. There was so much, Rick thought, that he would have wished for. But wishing couldn't change things. It couldn't bring anything back.

"If they don't find her," he said softly, "it's almost like she didn't die but just went away somewhere, and maybe someday she'll be back." He looked at Nancy and saw surprise and pity on her face. "Oh, I know she won't. I'm not crazy, I know what happened. But this way, with no . . . body, it's like she's still out there somewhere, still . . . alive in a sense, though I know she's gone."

They were silent for a while and then he said, "You know what I hope? I just hope it was fast. I hope she didn't know anything. Because if she knew . . . if she knew about the children . . . I don't know how she could have died knowing that.

"I don't think she *could* have died. Knowing that."

* * *

I want . . . I want to come back . . .

Wait.

No . . . it wasn't right . . . I have to make it right again. They can't rest until I make it right.

Not yet. Wait.

I can't wait! It hurts too much to wait! It hurts me—hurts them . . . Oh God, the sound of their screams . . .

Wait, Amy, wait.

The crying . . . the crying for mommy . . .

Soon.

Soon.

8

"My friends, welcome back to the second hour of the Wilson Barnes Show. If you've been listening, you know what I've been talking about tonight. And that's the explosions that have rocked the home of the Wilson Barnes Show itself—beautiful Hobie, Minnesota. A day-care center, my friends. Yes, that's right, a day-care center has been destroyed. Two adults and ten little children have lost their lives, have been blown to *bits,* my friends, their bodies unrecoverable.

"Federal authorities are already on the scene—and I say *already* with a bit of irony, for in a very possible scenario, some clear-thinking folks might say that they were there *before.* Let's look at the facts . . .

"Senator Robert King, ultra-liberal god, was scheduled to appear at that day-care center at eight o'clock this evening. But the senator never arrived—instead he went back to his cesspool known as Washington, D.C. At ten minutes after eight, my friends, two bombs went off in that day-care center. Now what's the average person supposed to think? What does the media *want* you to think?

"They want you to think that some big bad right-wing, conservative kooks, maybe even one of those awful *militias,* my friends, was responsible. These people are so nefarious, so terrible that they'll blow up *babies* to assassinate one of their political enemies! Well, let's hunt these monsters down! And let's not rest until every one of these diabolical right-wing fanatical organizations is destroyed, their dangerous weapons and bombs taken away from them, and their leaders in prison where they belong!

"That's what they *want* you to believe, my friends. But we're Americans, we don't buy all that bull, do we? Now let's look at the facts . . .

"If this was a plot to kill Senator King, it sure was a lousy one. There were dozens of opportunities to do so today. The quisling senator was out in the open in half a dozen neighborhoods. Bombs could have been planted anywhere or a sniper could have easily executed the senator—not that I'm saying that would have been a good thing now.

"But where do these terrible right-wing kooks put a bomb? In a day-care center with little children, on the very last stop of the day, the stop that is *most likely* to be canceled! And when the bomb goes off, King isn't even there! They say it's because he had to go back for a vote, but is that true, my friends?

"Or did he know all along that there was a bomb planted there?

"Did he know who did the planting?

"Was he even part of a conspiracy to smear the right-wing, conservative, and militia movements in this country so badly that they could never hope to rise from the dust of the Making Friends Child Care Center?

"Did he aid in the *staging* of an assassination attempt by the government purely intended to discredit the right, sacrificing ten innocent children in the process? Is the government capable of doing such a thing?

"Well, they were capable of shooting Vicki Weaver in the face while the only thing she held in her arms was her baby . . . They were capable of creating a firestorm at Waco in which over *twenty* children died, children they claimed they were acting in the best interests of . . . Hell, what's ten more?

"You tell me what Bill Clinton and Teddy Kennedy and Janet Reno and Robert King *aren't* capable of, my friends!

"And add to all this the fact that this wasn't any homemade fertilizer bomb, oh no. This bomb, claim experts who have seen the destruction, was plastic explosive. The *same* kind of plastic explosive, I might add, that the United States military has in abundance.

"And the children? It was a rainbow coalition, my friends. Jews, gentiles, Orientals, Negroes—almost as if it was *planned* that way, as if these children were sacrificed so the liberal Jew media would be certain of having everybody in the United States hating the people responsible for this dreadful act.

"It was a dreadful act indeed, and in deeper ways than just the killing of innocent children. Am I making accusations, my friends? No, I'm asking questions. You're going to see *plenty* of accusations from the government and the Jew liberal media in the next few weeks. And when you do, don't forget the very real possibility of government involvement, of people so hungry for power that they will sacrifice anything, even the lives of little babies, to achieve their nefarious ends . . ."

* * *

At six that morning, after Wilson Barnes left the radio station, he went back to the downtown apartment house that he owned, and rode the elevator to the penthouse where he lived alone. He poured himself three fingers of Tennessee whiskey and sipped it as he dialed a familiar number.

"Yeah?" said a sleepy voice.

"It's me," said Barnes. "You were sleeping. You heard earlier?"

"I heard."

"Worth something?"

"Yeah."

"You bet it was. I'll keep on it, too—pass the line to the brethren on the air. And I'll expect a show of appreciation?"

"The usual place."

"Pleasure doing business," Wilson Barnes said, and hung up before Rip Withers could say anymore.

9

The following day was one for more speeches and rhetoric. News of the explosion led every national TV broadcast, and by the time the morning anchors were ready to tell the public what had happened to the Making Friends Child Care Center, federal investigators reported finding traces of cyclonite, the active ingredient in C–4 plastic explosive.

This seemed to indicate, according to the carefully worded report, that one or more explosive devices had been planted in the building. The fact that Senator Robert King had been scheduled to visit there only added more fuel to the conspiratorial fire.

The mainstream media and press quickly came to the conclusion that the explosion had been a tragically botched assassination attempt by a right-wing extremist individual or group. In a midmorning statement, the President promised to use the full force of every federal law enforcement agency to find the perpetrators of "this heartless and terrible attack." Media pundits, however, were not as certain, echoing Dan Trotter's remarks to David Levinson concerning the reluctance of the government to enter the armed camps that comprised most militia groups.

The ultra-conservative media took another tack, the same one suggested by Wilson Barnes. The less extreme radio show hosts with the largest audiences urged their listeners not to jump to conclusions, that this might indeed have been a conspiracy, but a conspiracy of the left. That the government itself was involved *seemed,* they said, unlikely but possible. But there were "left-wing wackos" as well as so-called "right-wing kooks" out there, and the left-wingers were more dangerous because they worked alone. Theodore Kaczynski's name was frequently mentioned in that regard. It was altogether possible that one of these "lone wolf lefties," with advance information of Senator King's agenda, might try to discredit the right by staging such an assassination attempt.

The more extreme commentators went with Wilson Barnes the whole way, suggesting in no uncertain terms that Hobie was just another Oklahoma City, a terrorist act staged by the government in their efforts to destroy their strongest enemy, the patriots of the white Christian militias. This theory was bolstered later that afternoon when the news came out that one of the victims had claimed to see a car with four men inside, who were immediately transformed by the radical commentators into the federal government's dreaded "men in black."

But in all the United States it was only inside the compound of the Sons of a Free America that one could hear the truth.

At one o'clock, just after noon mess had been finished, Rip Withers had all the members of the Sons come to the indoor drill building, in which training sessions were held, mock combats were fought for prizes, and speeches were given. It was this last activity that Rip engaged in now.

"By now you've heard the news on the radio. For all I know, you might have heard more. But I'm here to tell you the truth." He looked at his men, hard and faithful soldiers all, who were sitting on the backless wooden benches, listening intently.

"The truth is what makes us different from them," Rip went on. "They lie to the people, they lie to each other—they lie *with* each other too but that's something else entirely." He was rewarded with a knowing chuckle from the men.

"I'm not going to lie to you. I'm going to tell you the truth. Your council of commanders made the decision to terminate with extreme prejudice the life of an un-American traitor, Robert King. Our intelligence told us that there was little chance any children would be harmed in the attack. But as you all know, intelligence is not always correct. There were children present and, what was equally harmful to our cause, our primary target was not."

The reaction was what he had expected but not what he hoped. While most of the men listened without emotion, some of them seemed disturbed, a few even shocked.

"It was tragic, yes, but it sent a message. No one is safe. In our struggle, we have to be as ruthless as the government that gunned down and firebombed innocent children. And if the only way to show that we are is by something like what happened last night, then so be it.

"I wish it hadn't happened. I wish we could take it back but we can't. It's finished, it's over and now we not only live with it but we must figure out how to use it to our advantage. If you heard Wilson Barnes last night, he showed us one way.

"Now if there are any men here who can't live with what happened, you let me know right now, and . . . we'll work something out." Rip looked at Will Standish, who sat near the back, his head down, eyes fixed on the dusty ground. Then Rip looked at the other men who had been uncomfortable with the news, but they too seemed reluctant to speak.

"All right then," he said. "You know the regulations. If any man betrays his brothers by word or deed, death is the only penalty. We have another secret now that we have to share the way we share our convictions and our commitment. Be true. Be loyal. And our day of victory will come, praise Yahweh."

There were a few shouts of Amen, then a few more, and soon they all were standing and giving the salute of white Christian patriots. Even Will Standish was standing and saluting, though Rip saw little enthusiasm in the gesture. At least there would be no protest, no breach in their carefully constructed bulwark of command and obedience.

Finally Rip Withers smiled and saluted them back with pride.

When Rip gathered the council later that day, he did not hesitate to invite the historian, Will Standish, as usual. Before the meeting, however, he drew Sonny Armitage aside privately and told him to keep a watch on Will. Sonny nodded, and Rip knew that was all he had to say. If Will had second thoughts about his loyalty to the Sons, he would be quickly taken care of.

At the meeting he told the others that they would be lying low for a time, taking no risks, until they were able to gauge the government's reaction. In the meantime they would continue to drill, train, and stockpile for the inevitable confrontation.

This they did and as the days became weeks, no government troops invaded their territory, and no investigators came with warrants to search the "White Oak Hunting Camp," the cover name for the Sons' compound. Had that occurred, the Sons would not have allowed it. They would have resisted, whatever it took, at the last blowing up the powder magazine and the compound itself before they would allow themselves to be captured.

The government knew this all too well, Rip exhorted his troops. They were not willing, not *yet,* to have another bloodbath. That was why they had not bothered *any* of the known militia in the area. And even if they had, the Sons were a covert militia, known only to its members.

Still another reason, however, was that the federal investigators had no physical evidence, aside from quantities of C–4 residue. The explosion had been so violent, the destruction so complete, that the only remaining traces of the bomb were microscopic. As for the sighting of men in a car, no witnesses had noticed any strange vehicle leaving the area just before the explosions. This added fuel to the "men in black" theory since once these contemporary phantoms were sighted, they did not appear again.

There had been a number of crank calls taking credit for the bombing, but since the primary victims had been children, there were not as many as usual for a terrorist act. None of these calls produced any tangible results.

In short, the investigators had no leads whatsoever, short of searching for an unaccounted-for supply of plastic explosive in government facilities, a search that continued and was made nightmarish by the reluctance of each agency to fully open its operations to another. The media was all too aware of the investigation's impotence and, naturally, so was every militia group in the country, including the Sons of a Free America.

As the weeks and months passed and absolutely nothing happened, the Sons' apparent success in the bombing of the Making Friends Child Care Center led Rip Withers to believe that Yahweh was truly with them, and that their continuing freedom was a sign from Him that the time had come for something else.

The time had come for another explosion, one that would shake this godless, traitorous government to its core.

PART TWO

Ah, love, let us be true
To one another! for the world, which seems
To lie before us like a land of dreams,
So various, so beautiful, so new,
Hath really neither joy, nor love, nor light,
Nor certitude, nor peace, nor help for pain; . . .

—Matthew Arnold, "Dover Beach"

10

All the while, the dust remained.

When the investigators had taken their last samples, when the searchers had finished gathering the few bits of human remains that were larger than the particles in which they lay, when the media had taken their photographs and videotapes of what had been a child care center, the dust remained, a variegated relief map of a village lost.

In some places it lay gray as ash, in others the ivory pallor of bone, and in still others brown as rust or long-dried blood. Fine as powder, coarse as gravel, the place and the people had intermingled, become one, in a thick sheet of dead lives and dead dreams. The plastic ribbons that marked the police lines still remained. Where once they had been a yellow as bright as the balls and toys the children had played with, now they were tattered and rotting, bleached by sunlight into the shade of jaundiced flesh.

At once cemetery, memorial, and place of execution, the site seemed to call out to people. Even after nearly six months had passed, they still brought flowers and teddy bears. They prayed, they cried, they stood and looked at the dust.

Some knelt and picked up a handful, letting fall between their fingers what had been both a place of love and the beloved ones who had occupied it. The voices that had laughed, the legs that had run, the faces that had smiled, the hands that had cared were now all dust, dust that clung like memories to the fingers and made its way thoughtfully to the lips, entering the worshipper like an unblessed host.

But for all the dust that departed on fingers and lips and soles of shoes, for all that the wind blew away, mingling with the dust of the playgrounds and yards where the children once played, an infinity of that dust remained and would remain for as long as anyone could guess. The property, still in the names of Richard and Amy Carlisle, had gone into receivership until the class action suit of the victims' parents against the Making Friends Child Care Center had been resolved, which would not occur until the government investigation into the cause of the explosions was complete.

It seemed unlikely that such a day would ever come. But when and if it did, the dust would still remain.

No one remembered, except for Rick Carlisle, that that particular night in late October was the anniversary of the founding of the center. The memory came to Rick in spite of himself, for he had been trying to forget about the center, about the explosion.

He had been trying, with all his heart, to forget about Amy. But his heart was where he held her.

On that Halloween night the children were trick-or-treating. But those who lived near where the Making Friends Center had once stood stayed away from the site and traveled several blocks to avoid passing it. Every child knew that it was haunted by the ghosts of those who had died there, and the hauntings would be far worse around Halloween.

Police patrols had been doubled during the two nights of trick-or-treating and David Levinson had volunteered for double shifts on those nights. He didn't mind the extra pay and it gave some of the second-shift officers a chance to go out with their kids.

He had finished the evening shift, feeling like a good spirit watching over all the little kids dressed up like vampires and clowns and whatever cartoon and adventure characters were hot that year. But by ten they were all off the street and safe at home, probably in their bedrooms surreptitiously stuffing their faces.

God, he thought as he cruised toward the diner for his break, what a difference from Detroit. Devil's Night was a whole lot more active than a Hobie Halloween. The toughest thing he had had to do tonight was to warn an older kid who was swiping some of the younger kids' stashes. Not a single burning car, rape victim, or homicide.

But there was darkness and evil everywhere, he thought as he drove slowly past what he had begun to think of as the Blasted Heath. He wished that damn lot full of dust and debris would get paved over as soon as possible. Or a couple of houses would be dandy, with happy, shouting kids and a couple of big, dopey, friendly dogs. Anything but that block-wide Death Valley. Halloween was creepy enough without having that hellhole around.

This was far from Levinson's favorite time of year anyway. When he was a kid he had always hated Halloween. It usually coincided with his father's biggest trade show, which was held in Florida. His mother went along for a vacation and that meant that David and his brother had to spend five days and four nights with Grandfather and Grandmother Levensohn.

Grandfather had refused to change the spelling of his name from the traditional Russian, claiming a family tie to the Russian Hebrew writer Michal Levensohn. He and Grandmother had both come over from Russia and spoke Yiddish to each other, a habit David had found weird and creepy. He hadn't liked not understanding what someone else was saying while knowing that they could understand you. It seemed an unfair and selfishly adult thing to do.

But what creeped him out most about his grandparents were the stories they would tell of the old country. It wasn't so much the anti-Semitism of the czar's troops and the cossacks that frightened him. After all, he was used to that in his own life, even if the Jew haters at his school and in his neighborhood didn't come at him with sabers. It was the tale of Abraham Levensohn, his grandfather's uncle, and the crow that guided him.

Even now Levinson shuddered at the memory of it. There were things that should not happen in life. Some, like prejudice, were wrong, but you lived with them and tried to change them. Others, like the recent bombing, were abominations, atrocious and dreadful. These things you fought with all your might.

But others were unthinkable, like a dead man coming back to life, no matter what the reason.

Or was that really true? Were there some abominations even more unthinkable than the dead rising to life again to kill? And what if the dead rose to avenge those abominations, the way Uncle Abraham had?

Levinson hissed air out hard through his teeth and shook his head jerkily. Forget about that, he told himself. That damned story came back to him every Halloween, and it was probably no more true than the other tales Grandmother Levensohn had told, the ones that he had found later in books of Jewish folklore.

But he had never found the one about the crow, and it was that one that she had told more convincingly than all of the rest.

He saw the lights of the diner ahead. For the fifteen minutes he was allowed to sit on his ass without a steering wheel in his gut, maybe a good cup of coffee and a nice piece of pie would get rid of Grandmother's old stories. He didn't have to be on his way again until midnight.

And still the dust remained.

It waited, the street lamps turning all its undulations a uniform gray, like a sea on a cloudy, windless day. But as the clocks of men tolled and told that it was midnight, that the night was at the center of its darkness, the pendulum between the extremes of dusk and dawn hanging straight down, something black fell from the blackness of the sky, drifting and turning as it neared the earth, neared the dust that remained, waiting for its coming.

It slowed its descent, seeming to hang for a moment in the air, and from beneath its dark body, its feathers shining as if lacquered or sculpted in jet, two feet emerged, seeking a perch. They found one on a wooden stake holding the tattered police line ribbon, and the obsidian daggers of its fore claws dug into the wood while the hind claws of each foot gripped and balanced.

The crow sat unmoving, a gentle wind that stirred the ragged ribbon having no effect upon its feathers. The crow watched with eyes of glittering coal, watched that same wind dance in the gray dust, whirling and eddying, making the waves of that dry sea roll and shift as if creatures swam darkly beneath its surface.

Then the wind passed over the sea of waiting dust and left it, moving on to shake dead leaves, rattle loose windowpanes. Over the dust, the air stopped, died.

But the dust continued to move.

It was as if the wind, though none could be felt, continued to blow, but from all sides, in toward the center of the ocean of dust. And that dust began to mound, to grow in a shape that first suggested, and then reflected, humanity. A head, arms, a trunk, legs, all rose slowly from the dust as if they had been there all along, just waiting for the moment to rise and be recognized by the creature that sat above it, watching the recumbent woman being shaped by its dark will, or by the will of the soul that still occupied it. The shape formed as, in the old tale, God may have formed Adam from the dust of the ground.

But this was no Adam, and no creator-god blew the breath of life into its nostrils. Instead, breath burst from it in a scream of birth or rebirth, as its dust became flesh and muscle. Ash became bone and blood that surged like fire, bringing the being to life with a jolt of pain, a burst of agony, and memory of how it had died, and why it now returned.

11

And while the body of Amy Carlisle reintegrated itself from its own particles and its own desire, Rick Carlisle dreamed of that reformation, his soul, still one with hers, witnessing her bursting from her womb of dust.

He saw her face coming up out of the debris of the empty lot like a woman rising from being buried in the sand. He saw her mouth filled with dust, and saw that dust explode from between her lips in an ashy cloud, saw her eyes open wide in pain and terror, and thought that he was seeing her in the instant before her own life ended, in the moment of realization that she and, most importantly, all her children would die.

Rick's eyes opened and he sat bolt upright in his bed, still seeing Amy in the darkness of the walls and ceiling. He was awake, he *knew* he was awake but Amy was still there in front of him, the dust and the ashes falling away from her, showing unmarked flesh, pink, bare skin, her shoulders and breasts untouched by the blast that had torn her apart.

She was whole, though her face was still alive with the anguish she must have felt in her last moments. *How could this happen?* it seemed to say. *How could I have* let *this happen?*

And then he saw her turn, put her hands on the dust that remained, and push herself up, up from the dust like a new creation. She stood naked against the wall of his bedroom, looking down at her body, as sweet and full and strong as he had ever seen it, then all around her, and finally at him.

She stopped and looked directly at him, her violet eyes, those eyes that had seared and crisped and vanished, staring into his own . . .

"No . . ." he whispered, then said again more strongly, *"no!"*

This was a dream, a vision, a torture of the mind born from his desire to have her alive again. There was nothing of reality in this. It was merely a dream child of his wish, and he closed his eyes, pressing them shut tightly, and opened them again.

But she was not gone. She was still there, only fainter, farther, receding as he watched until, in a few more seconds, her form was gone and only darkness remained.

If he had seen her body, he thought, it would have been better. If there had been something to prove that she was dead, he could have believed it fully. As cruel as it would have been to see her crushed and shattered body, it would not have been this cruel.

But never having seen evidence of her passing beyond the flattened building she had loved, he could never be sure. Though his conscious mind told him that she was dead, he would never *truly* believe it without proof.

And even then, perhaps not. Love never died. And if his love for her never would, then why should hers for him?

But why would her love torment him this way, with visions of her rising from the dust with which her body was mingled? It was a cruel and cunning torment, which gave hope where there was none.

No. She was gone. He would always love her, but she was gone, and he knew that she would have wanted him to try to love again. He would. He would do what she wanted, whatever she wanted.

But he would not go to where she had died in the feeble misapprehension that she had somehow returned. He was not a fool. Life, and the "person or persons unknown" who had planted their packages of hate in Amy's heart, had taught him that. There was no coming back in a world that murdered love.

Something moved in the bed next to him.

He lay back down slowly on his side and put his arm around his wife, pressing against her so that they were lying like a pair of spoons. "Are you all right?" she asked sleepily.

"Yes . . . a dream," he whispered into her fragrant hair.

"Mmm." She took his hand in her own, tucking it warmly against her breast. "It's all right . . . Go back to sleep. I love you."

He closed his eyes, trying not to cry, trying to make the words the truth. ". . . I love you, Nancy . . ."

For a moment she had seen him, Rick, looking into her eyes, and then he was gone and she was alone, feeling more pain than she ever had in her life, more pain than when she had died.

For then the physical pain had been nothing. A flare of light, a moment of severance from the earth, from life, from thought, from her body itself.

But not from pain, not from the pain of knowing what had happened, what she had lost. That pain alone survived, and maybe something deeper was mixed in. Maybe love was there.

But now, standing there in the dust, she felt not only the agony of knowledge, the torture of loss, but the greatest physical pain that she had ever experienced. Every atom of her body wrenched and twisted and jerked. She had pushed herself to her feet, thinking that the cool night air might prove a soothing balm. She could not believe her flesh appeared unmarked, while her senses screamed that her skin was torn from her, her body an open sore, oozing pus like a burst blister.

Yet as she stood and trembled and endured, having no other choice, the pain slowly began to pass, as if evaporating in the night air. And at last she breathed and there was no pain. She moved, touched herself, and it was gone.

But what remained? She was alive, but how had that happened? There had been a bomb . . . Had the blast blown off her clothing and left her otherwise untouched? But then where had the pain come from? And the children, they had died . . .

The thought stabbed a blade of anguish through her soul. Oh God, if God there were, all of them were dead, dead and gone. Had they been taken away or were they mixed with this dust?

She looked around, saw all her dreams, the things she had loved, reduced to dust and ash. Yet here she stood, naked and alive. Why? What had happened? Who had done this?

Then she saw the bird, huge and black, sitting on the post. The beads of its eyes were fixed on her, and its head cocked first to one side then to the other, as if it were waiting for her to speak, to ask a question, to cry, to rage, to wonder aloud if she were in heaven or hell.

And she stood and watched the crow, not understanding, lost in the ruins of her first life, and in the madness of her second.

It was shortly after midnight when David Levinson received the radio message. He had just fortified himself with several cups of black coffee and a slice of blueberry pie when the report came to him of a naked woman seen in the vicinity of North Spruce and Oak Streets. An elderly woman who had been walking her dog called it in, and Levinson was the closest officer to the vicinity.

North Spruce and Oak. God, he thought. That was the site of the Making Friends Child Care Center. All he needed to make his night was some mother pushed over the edge by grief, returning to the scene of her child's death—a naked woman rending her garments and searching among the ashes. The image made Levinson think of the passage from the book of Jeremiah, of Rachel weeping for her children because they were no more. Ah well, he had a blanket in the trunk, and handcuffs if they became necessary.

If only something had been done, if the feds had caught the unspeakable bastards who had bombed a dozen people to ashes, maybe the town could have put it to rest, and the wounds could have begun to heal. But this way, with the gutless government, his own local branch included, afraid to investigate for fear of stirring up a hornet's nest of self-proclaimed patriots, hell, it was no wonder the relatives might go crazy. The most frustrating thing in the world had to be knowing what kind of group was responsible for the death of your child, but knowing too that no one was even investigating. A sure recipe for madness.

"Shit . . ." he whispered to himself as he crossed North Spruce Street. The report hadn't been a Halloween trick. He saw the woman all right, standing smack-dab in the middle of the Blasted Heath. He couldn't see her face but she was standing, legs slightly apart, arms at her side.

There seemed an electric tension in the slim, supple body. At least she wasn't carrying a gun or knife, and a concealed weapon was out of the question.

He pulled the prowler over to the curb, deciding to approach her on foot. If she saw the police car, she might run, and he didn't want to chase a naked woman through the sleepy streets of Hobie. Levinson got out of the car and took a heavy brown blanket from the trunk. Then he started walking toward the woman from behind, treading softly in the dust.

When he was a few yards behind her, he saw the crow. The bird was sitting on a post, twenty yards from the woman. Yet in spite of the distance between her and the crow, it appeared to Levinson that they were somehow communicating, as absurd as that seemed. The woman's long dark hair hid her face from Levinson's view, and for a moment he wondered what he would do if she turned around and showed him a Halloween face of a skull, obscene in her nudity.

Then he dismissed the fancy and, stopping a few feet from her, said softly, "Ma'am?" and held out the blanket toward her.

What warily turned and looked at him was worse than a skull face. It was the face of Amy Carlisle. Gray dust lightly coated her face and body, but her violet eyes were clear.

Suddenly the blanket felt so heavy in his hands that he could hardly hold it. But he feared that if it dropped, the delicate balance of stillness between himself and Amy Carlisle and the crow sitting on the post would dissolve. It was as if they made a tableau formed in a dream. This can't be real, he told himself, and if the composition wavered, if the line joining the three of them broke, he did not know what stranger, more terrible dream might replace this one.

But then Amy Carlisle opened her mouth and spoke to him in Amy Carlisle's voice. "What . . . is this?"

She sounded frightened and helpless and lost, and he became a policeman again instead of a scared child dreaming, and went to her and wrapped the blanket gently around her. Then he looked at the crow again, sitting quietly, but watching with an intensity that bespoke more than mere sentience, and he thought he realized what had happened and what would happen still.

He recalled all too well Grandmother Levensohn's story about old Uncle Abraham and the crow.

12

"What's happening to me?" Amy Carlisle asked. "I don't . . . I don't understand."

"Tell me your name," said the policeman who was holding her. She thought she recognized him, but her mind . . . everything was so confused that she didn't know if she could remember her *own* name.

"I'm . . ." She looked at the man's searching face, then at the crow sitting on the post and held its gaze as she answered. "I'm Amy Carlisle." Then she looked back at the policeman. "And this place is mine—or was." She shook her head, remembering. "They killed my children. And they tried to kill me. But they didn't . . . I don't know how . . ."

"Amy," said the policeman, "tell me something. Tell me the last thing that you recall."

She looked into the darkness and tried to remember. "It was—just tonight. There was a terrible explosion . . . The wall caved in and the lights went off and the children were crying." She remembered DeMarole's arm then, that little arm attached to nothing else, and bit into her lip, biting back the memory, hard enough to draw blood though she could not taste it.

"I found two of them. And I was trying to get them out and I saw some lights, far away, and then . . . I don't remember."

"Amy, my name is David Levinson. I've met you before. I'm a policeman. Will you come with me? We'll go somewhere, get you some clothing, something to eat."

"All right." She nodded her head although she didn't want anything to eat. She wasn't hungry. "And then you'll help me find them, won't you?"

David Levinson's face looked even sadder than before. "Come on," he said, and with his arm still around her, he guided her to the police car. She sat in the front seat and he got in the driver's side and started the car. "I want to take you to my house," he said. "Away from here."

"You'll help me find them?" she said again.

"Amy, I can't. The children are gone . . . They're dead. All of them."

"I know that. I mean, find *them.* I survived, you see. I was the only one, the *only* one. So I have to . . . make things right."

She looked in the rearview mirror and saw the crow following them, flapping its wings slowly, yet easily keeping up with the speeding car. "I think I should go home," Amy said. "I think I need to . . . My husband, Rick, needs to know I'm . . . okay."

"We'll take care of that later."

They drove for a few blocks and Levinson turned on his radio. "Jean, on that report," he said, "it was just a prank. Some kids with an inflatable doll. I chased them off." Someone at the other end said something Amy didn't understand and Levinson spoke again.

"Jean, there's another problem. I've got some real—gastric distress. Been stopping every ten minutes or so and it's really wasting me. Is there another car could double for me till six? I'll make it up to them." Jean said something again and Levinson said, "Great, thanks. I'm heading home then."

He put the unit back in place and kept driving until he came to a row of houses in a cul-de-sac in a quiet neighborhood.

He pulled into a driveway, pressed a button on a remote, and a garage door opened up. Amy turned and saw the crow settle down to perch on a darkened wrought iron lamppost. Then the garage doors closed and she saw it no more.

Levinson led the way out of the garage, across a screened porch, and then into a kitchen, where he pulled down the shades before turning on lights. "Let's find you some clothes," he said, and led her down a short hall to a bedroom, where he once more pulled the shades before he dug into the back of a closet.

"These were my wife's," he said, taking out a blouse, a sweater, and a pair of jeans. "They should fit you. There's a bathroom through there if you want to wash off the dust first. Take your time, get changed, and then come out. We have to talk."

After he left, Amy dropped the blanket and stepped into the small bathroom, where she took a shower. The water didn't feel hot or cold. It barely felt wet, but she could see the dust washing away, swirling down the drain. Then she dried herself and slipped on the clothes.

She couldn't say whether they were comfortable or not. She could scarcely feel the weight on her skin, which almost seemed to belong to someone else, just the way the clothes did. In the mirror, however, they seemed to fit.

Then Amy looked more closely at herself, studying her face and her hair. If she looked hard, she thought she could make out a thin, pale network of lines in her face, even on her cheeks and forehead, which had never before had a wrinkle. Her skin looked like the underside of leaves, a patchwork of small cells stitched together so delicately that it appeared smooth until viewed at extremely close range.

Then she noticed that the surfaces of her eyes possessed the pattern as well, and when she examined the other parts of her body, so did her nails and the smooth skin of her inner arms and thighs. The nearly invisible markings were everywhere.

When she joined David Levinson in the living room, he had a tray of sandwiches, cookies, and fresh fruit and a pot of tea. "Something to eat?" he offered, but she shook her head.

"No, thank you. I'm not really hungry. Not for food, anyway. But for answers, yes." She sat next to him on the sofa, folded her hands so tightly together that her fingers whitened, and leaned toward him so demandingly that he drew back. "What happened? How did I survive? Why did they all die and why am I alive? Can you tell me that, David Levinson?"

He looked for a moment as though he didn't know what to say. Then he shook his head uncomfortably and looked away, closing his eyes. When he looked back at her, his eyes were colder, his mouth a stern line. "I can tell you some things, Amy Carlisle. I can tell you things that aren't going to make matters any clearer, that may puzzle us more than we already are. But as to why you're alive? Amy . . . I'm sorry . . . but you're *not* alive. You've been dead for six months."

What in God's name was he saying. "Six . . . *months*?"

"Yes. And you're dead now. Moving, thinking, yes, but not . . . not truly alive. You've been brought back for a purpose."

She wanted to argue with him, to hit him, to tell him that he was a fool, but instead it seemed that she was hearing a confirmation of knowledge buried deep within her, knowledge that had been given to her in silence and in secret, by something dark and hidden.

The crow. The crow had something to do with this.

"I know you're anxious," Levinson said. "I know that you want to know what happened and who was responsible and all the rest. But first,

I beg you, sit here and listen, and let me tell you a story that my grandmother told to me. And after it's finished I think it might help you to know who you are.

"And what you have to do."

13

"My family, the Levensohns," David Levinson began, "lived in Kishinev in Moldavia, under Russian rule. The beginning of this century was a terrible time for Russian Jews. We had few rights compared to non-Jews, and though there was no sanctioned government program against us, the officials did little, if anything, to prevent the pogroms from taking place.

"These pogroms were attacks on Jews by angry mobs. Everybody hated us. Since a lot of Jews were in business, the lower classes thought we were all capitalists, and since some Jews were political radicals, the bureaucrats thought we were all socialists. If there was a reason to hate, they found it.

"My grandfather was a boy at the time of the Kishinev pogrom in 1903. A mob attacked the Jewish community and savaged it for two whole days. It was the local leaders who egged on the mob, and the czar's soldiers did nothing to stop it. Many Jews were killed, many more wounded. The Levensohn family was one of the unlucky ones, and my grandfather's Uncle Abraham perhaps the most unlucky of all.

"He lost his wife and three of his children, my grandfather's cousins. My grandfather wasn't harmed—his mother hid him in a latrine for two days. He'd climb up and look through the cracks in the walls from time to time, so he saw everything and lived to tell about it.

"Uncle Abraham was a big man in his early fifties, who had started working as a tallow melter and had worked his way up until he owned a successful tallow business. He was a fierce competitor, energetic and tireless. He also had a dissident streak in him. When the riots began, his non-Jewish competitors saw it as a chance to end his success—and his life.

"They beat him and stabbed him, but Abraham survived, though badly wounded. At last the soldiers and police came out to disperse the rioters, and at last my grandfather came out of the latrine and saw what happened next. Uncle Abraham was probably dying already, but was perceptive enough to see the truth about what had happened. He grabbed the bridle of a cossack captain and accused him and his men of collusion with the rioters by their inaction. 'You killed my family as much as these stupid and greedy bastards,' he said. 'Yours is the greater guilt.'

"Well, it was the truth, but the cossack didn't want to hear it, especially not from a bruised and bleeding Jew. So he drew his saber and brought it down at the side of Uncle Abraham's neck, nearly severing his head. Uncle Abraham fell dead to the ground. The cossack said to all those watching that they had seen the crazy Jew attacking him—he had no choice but to defend himself. And no one said or did anything about it. Who wanted still another pogrom?

"So they buried Uncle Abraham and his family in the Jewish cemetery in the lower town, on the banks of the Byk River. His competitors took control of the tallow trade, and the soldiers and police and cossacks waited for the next pogrom when they would turn their faces away and let more Jews die. But that was not what happened.

"The cemetery was a very busy place for the weeks after the pogrom. People came to pay their respect to their loved ones, but after a while the mourners were content saying Kaddish in the synagogue. My grandfather, however, continued to visit the cemetery frequently, often at night, which was the only opportunity he had after his work was done. His mother, who had hidden him so safely, had been killed in the riots, and he sat next to her grave almost every night, until he grew sleepy and returned home to his father.

"One evening he was sitting by his mother's grave when he heard a loud cry from overhead and looked up to see a giant crow drifting down toward him. It landed on his Uncle Abraham's grave marker, a few plots away. Then my grandfather saw the earth over Uncle Abraham's grave start to shake and break apart, and Uncle Abraham rose up through the ground, dressed in his grave clothes, which were partially torn from him as he arose. My grandfather could see the wound that had killed him, but it seemed to be healed, with just a white scar showing where the saber had cut.

"Naturally my grandfather was terrified, but he remained frozen to the spot, unable to run. Uncle Abraham looked at the crow, and the crow looked at him for a long time. Then the resurrected man saw my grandfather and smiled. My grandfather said that he was sure the purpose of the smile was to reassure him, but it was so terrible that my grandfather admitted to having peed his pants instantly.

"Then the crow rose and flapped slowly away toward the upper town, on crags high above the river, where the Russians lived and where the soldiers' and policemen's barracks were. Uncle Abraham followed, his grave clothes trailing behind him. My grandfather had to see what was going to happen, so he followed them.

"As Uncle Abraham walked through the streets, plenty of people saw him. After all, Kishinev had more than a hundred thousand people in it. All the Jews ran screaming, shutting themselves inside their houses and praying until dawn. But they had nothing to fear from Uncle Abraham or from the crow.

"The bird led the dead man and the boy to the house of the tallow merchant who, along with his sons, had beaten and stabbed my uncle and helped to kill his family. There my grandfather watched as the crow sat on the edge of the roof while Uncle Abraham kicked in the door and went inside. There were screams and the sound of a pistol firing, and other sounds that my grandfather only described as *wet.*

"After a while the police arrived and went inside, and there were more cries and sounds of struggle. Several of the police ran outside and kept running. One man, my grandfather saw, had part of his face ripped away.

"Then all was silent inside, and Uncle Abraham came out, his grave clothes sodden with blood and gray pieces of flesh that clung to them, his face terrible. Some policemen who had been stationed outside fired at him with rifles. The bullets struck him but he did not fall, and was scarcely slowed by them.

"One young soldier attacked him with a saber, and although the blade struck nearly the same spot where the cossack captain's killing blow had gone, Uncle Abraham did not fall. He wrenched the saber away, and in a single backswing severed the young policeman's head from his body. Then the crow took to the air again, toward the soldiers' barracks, and Uncle Abraham followed.

"Someone must have warned the soldiers for they were all out in force, with a line of riflemen. The cossack captain was on horseback commanding them, and when Uncle Abraham walked toward them, holding the saber ahead of him, the cossack waited until he was scarcely twenty feet away and then ordered the men to fire.

"Two dozen bullets tore into Uncle Abraham, and he staggered for a moment but did not fall. Then the riflemen threw down their guns and ran, and although he could not see Uncle Abraham's face, my grandfather said he thought it was because Uncle Abraham smiled at them.

"The cossack captain had not run, though, and neither had his horsemen. They all drew their sabers now, and the cossack captain galloped down on Uncle Abraham, his saber raised. But when he brought it down, the dead man grabbed the blade and yanked the captain from his saddle. Then he stamped a foot on the cossack to hold him on the ground, and with the two sabers he now held, he plunged the points into both the man's eyes, killing him.

"The horsemen attacked then, and Uncle Abraham turned into a mad dervish of destruction, slashing the horses' legs so that they fell crippled, then hacking at the riders, lopping off heads and arms and legs with every swing of his sword, taking many wounds, but never a one that made him pause in his slaughter.

"In only minutes the horsemen were all dead, the street was empty. No one else dared to challenge this dead man in grave clothes. Uncle Abraham then severed the cossack captain's head, stuck it on the end of the soldier's own saber, and walked through the wide and empty streets to the cathedral, the seat of the archbishop of Bessarabia. There Uncle Abraham plunged the saber, the cossack's head still adorning it, into the wooden door of the cathedral, leaving an unmistakable message for the archbishop and the czar.

"The crow flew back toward the old town again and Uncle Abraham—and my amazed grandfather—turned and walked back to the cemetery on the river bank. And there the dead man lay down on his grave. My grandfather saw the ground part, and his uncle sink into the earth out of sight. Then the crow cried once, and flew away across the river."

14

"My grandfather told that story to my grandmother," David Levinson said. "He never would tell it to us himself but my grandmother told it plenty of times, maybe at first with pride, but finally, I think, to scare us."

"It's . . . just a story," said Amy Carlisle, hoping she spoke the truth.

"That's what I thought too, at first. But whenever my brother or I would ask our grandfather about it, he became . . . different. Unlike himself. As if he had stared into an abyss and didn't want to be forced to think about it again. That was when I knew it was true."

"And you think what? That the crow we saw brought me back from the dead? That's ridiculous. It couldn't happen."

"Then why are you here?"

"Because I'm alive!" she flared. "I never died to begin with. I . . . I lost consciousness, didn't know who I was, wandered away from the explosion . . ."

"Wandered away for six months and nobody noticed you when your picture was all over the newspapers and TV. And then you wandered back stark naked, covered in the dust of the child care center. With a crow who just happens to accompany you everywhere you go . . ."

Levinson yanked the cord so that the front drapes flew open, revealing the black bird still sitting on the lamppost. He flicked a light switch and the outside lamp went on, illuminating the bird's feathers, turning the black to a deep violet tinged with blue.

Levinson sat down next to her again, took her hand and turned it palm up so that he could see the skin of her arm. "Look at yourself," he said. "You see these?" He pointed to the tiny new lines in her flesh, the thousands of individual bits that made up the expanse of her skin. "They're *pieces,* Amy. They're the pieces of you that came apart and then came back together again. The pieces that came together tonight, from out of the dust, when that crow appeared."

Amy pushed Levinson away with such strength that his back hit the arm of the sofa and he grunted with the pain. "No!" she said. "No, it's not true . . ."

"How strong are you, Amy?" Levinson said, rubbing his back. "You were fit but never really buffed, were you? Couldn't hope to fight off a guy as big and strong as me, could you? A guy who saw you naked and got turned on and maybe wanted to get some cheap action . . ."

He went for her then, his arms coming around her, burying his face in her neck. And without thinking she reacted, using not leverage but pure force, tossing him away from her, over the coffee table and onto the floor. The force of the impact knocked the wind from him. Then before she knew it she was on top of him, her left forearm crushing his neck, her right fist raised to strike. Only the panic in his eyes stopped her from slamming his nose flat against his face.

Amy sat back then, lowering her arms while Levinson coughed and choked, then waved a hand as if in surrender. "I'm sorry . . . sorry," he said tightly. "That wasn't very gentlemanly but I wanted to prove my point. You're strong, stronger than you've ever been before. And you said you weren't hungry. Why would you be? You're dead."

"I'm not dead," said Amy, her head swimming.

"No, Amy, I'm sure you are," he said, walking to the other end of the room. "In fact, I'm so sure that I'm going to do something that will destroy my life if I'm wrong. That's how sure I am. And then there won't be any more arguments about it."

In one movement he whirled around toward her, jerked the pistol from his holster, cocked the hammer, and pulled the trigger.

Amy started to move toward Levinson and had actually halved the gap between them when she felt the bullet hit her in the chest. Its impact slowed her only for a moment and then she was on him, yanking the gun from his hand and pushing him back. His head struck the wall, the pupils of his eyes rolled up, and he slid to the floor unconscious, his back against the wall.

She looked at the smoking gun in her hand, then dropped it noiselessly on the carpet as she brought both hands to her chest to touch the place where she had been shot. It had felt hot for an instant, and then cold, and then she felt nothing at all and wondered if she was in shock. She saw the hole in the flannel shirt she wore, blackened around the edges. As she unbuttoned it, she felt as though she were dreaming. She had been shot in the chest and felt no pain. Then she drew back the front of her shirt.

The wound was still closing, a circle becoming smaller until it vanished altogether, leaving only a pale circle, a slight indentation, like the imprint of a lover's fingers, which faded even as she watched. She had been shot, shot over the heart, and she was still alive.

Or dead.

Then the truth overwhelmed her, the truth that she had suspected, but now knew for certain. It built up within her as thickly as the dust that had burst from her reborn lungs, until she felt that she would burst again, that the millions of fragments that had coalesced would once again disperse in a silent explosion born of her own terrible self-knowledge.

The sensation took what seemed an eon to pass, but then she regained control. Her eyes were open: it wasn't a question of *what* she was, but a new understanding of *why* she was.

She was a child of death come back to give birth, not to life through her still dead womb, but to *more* death through the strength of her hands. She had never been able to be a mother before but she would be one now—the Mother of Vengeance.

The only children she could ever think of as her own had died, and she had died with them. But her heart had survived, her savage mother's heart, a heart that knew that the deepest grief, the saddest story ever told, is that of parents outliving their children. A story sad and unnatural. An act too foul for breath to tell.

Who would do such a thing? Who could be so heartless as to bring it to pass? She would find out and she would visit a mother's vengeance upon them. The story of the old Jew had shown her the way. The Crow had brought him back for vengeance.

No. For *justice.* To put the wrong things right. And was there ever a deed more wrong than this?

But the old Jew had known the killers of his children, his wife, himself. That was an advantage she did not have. He could stalk through the streets, knowing where to go, whom to seek, but she could not. First she would have to learn the names of the monsters who had killed her babies. Maybe this policeman could help her.

She knelt next to Levinson and heard his regular breathing. There was a lump on the back of his head, but no blood ran from it, and his face looked peaceful.

It reminded her of Rick's face as he lay in bed next to her in the early morning when it was just bright enough to make out his features. Rick. Oh God, what could she do about Rick, with Rick, for Rick? If she was truly dead, there could be no place for her in his life, or for him in hers. Still, she loved him as she always had, and would, beyond death, forever.

But Rick was not why she had returned. She had returned for her children—and the people who had killed them.

"Wake up," she said, gently shaking Levinson's shoulder. He stirred and mumbled something, and then his eyes opened and he looked at her.

"Wow," he whispered. "You are *fast* . . ." He looked down at her half-open shirt, at the bullet hole in the cloth. "And alive." A smile creased his features. "Which proves that . . . ." He raised his eyebrows as though wanting her to finish it, and she did.

"I'm dead. Yes, you're right, I know that now. The Crow brought me back, out of the ashes. Because there's payment to be made. Justice for my children."

Levinson nodded, then winced and rubbed the back of his head. "And I have no doubt you'll get it. As fast and as strong as you are . . . impervious to bullets, a militia's nightmare."

"Militia?" she asked. "What do you mean?"

"I mean that it looks like a militia—or somebody involved with one—planted two bombs as an attempted hit on Senator King. He never made it, but you were there. You and the other woman and all the children." Levinson kept talking as he got slowly to his feet. "I think I saw you that night after the first bomb had gone off. I was driving up and I saw several people moving inside. I think it was you trying to get the children out. Then the second one went off." He looked down and chewed on his upper lip.

"And I died."

"Yeah. You died."

"Will you help me to find them? The ones who did it?"

"I don't know how I can. I mean, I'm a cop, I can't go outside the law, can't bend it to fit my view of justice."

"But I can." She tried a smile. It didn't feel natural to her. She felt strange and scary smiling, and imagined she knew what those Russian riflemen had seen. "I'll need a place to stay." She touched the bullet hole. "And some more clothes."

"And a way to get around too. There's a lot you need."

Her anger broke through then. "You say it's been six months and they still don't have these bastards? Don't you want to see them pay for what they did? I can make that happen, Levinson! But you've got to help me!"

He thought for a moment, then nodded. "All right, I will. But you don't say anything to anybody about me. And I want it understood that if I, or any other law enforcement official, get to these fuckers first, they're mine. The law and the courts take your vengeance then. I won't give that up—that's the code *I* live by."

She pursed her lips and nodded slowly. "It's a race then."

"If that's how you want to look at it."

"I do."

"Okay. This place has a spare bedroom, I'll hole up there—do you sleep?"

She thought for a moment, trying to assess her body and its needs. "I don't know. I'm not tired now."

"Well, you can take my bedroom anyway. All the clothes that my ex-wife left behind are in that closet."

"What about transportation?" Amy asked. "The Crow may fly but I don't think I can."

"Let me show you." He led her back to the garage. Before, in the darkness, Amy hadn't noticed the long, low covered shape in the second bay. But now Levinson turned on the hanging light and whipped off the cover, revealing the sleek black lines of a hardtop sports car. The styling made the hood appear twice as long as the passenger area. A single pair of headlights stared from a solid, grill-less front like a pair of owl's eyes.

"This," he intoned, "is a Studebaker Avanti, circa 1964. I've worked on this baby for several years and just finished it a week ago. I don't even have it registered yet. It's a phantom car. Now if you were to steal an old set of plates somewhere, you'd be riding high." He gestured to several old Minnesota license plates that had been nailed to the garage wall. "Well, well, look what the previous owner left."

"God," said Amy, still looking at the car. "It's beautiful. Thank—"

"It *also,*" he interrupted her, as he took a three-year-old plate from the wall and affixed it to the Avanti's holder with a screwdriver, "is a classic car. It is a gem, my baby, pretty much all *I* have to live for and if you let anything bad happen to it, I will . . ." He paused.

"You were going to say 'kill you,' weren't you?" He looked embarrassed. "Well, that would be redundant. Don't worry. I won't let it get hurt."

Levinson shook his head. "Do with it what you need to do. Maybe this is why I've spent all those years on it—so it would be here for you when you needed it."

"You believe in synchronicity?" she asked with as friendly a smile as she knew how to give.

"Lady, after tonight I believe in a whole lot more than I used to. Come back inside. There's something else I need to show you."

Levinson led the way to a large, semi-finished basement room lined with shelves. Labeled boxes sat on the floor and three four-drawer filing cabinets stood at one end. "My own little fortress of solitude," he said. "One of my hobbies is tracking these anti-Semitic groups and that includes a lot of militia groups." He chuckled. "Maybe I'll write a book someday. There's tons of raw data here, but it's stuff that I haven't had much time to correlate or do much with except collect."

He lovingly patted a computer that sat on a big desk near the filing cabinets. "This is a 300-megahertz Pentium 2. Top of the line when I bought it and still pretty damn powerful. Got a 57.6 modem in it and access to a number of sites that I really shouldn't have at home." He grinned. "Don't tell anyone. But you might find it useful. You know your way around computers?"

"To a degree. I always caught on pretty fast."

"Well, don't let the speed and power bother you. Works the same as the slow and clunky ones—just better and faster."

"Frankly," Amy said, "I don't think I want to spend my time sitting at a computer. For one thing, I don't know how long I have. And for another . . . I feel like I have to move. So tell me, if you were me, where would you start?"

Levinson had barely opened his mouth to speak when a tap sounded at the painted-over basement window. The tap sounded again. "I think there's someone else who can answer that question," Levinson said. "Maybe you won't need my files after all." He reached in his pocket and took out a pair of keys. "Maybe you'd better change before you hit the road," he said. "That bullet hole's a little suspicious looking."

Alone in Levinson's bedroom, Amy looked through the clothes in the closet, searching for something dark and unobtrusive that would let her move in and out of the shadows unseen. Near the back she found an outfit that would be perfect. Levinson's wife must have gone through a bleak period before the divorce, Amy thought. A plastic bag covered a pair of black denim slacks and a black long-sleeved top made of some stretchable synthetic material with not a trace of sheen.

Amy threw off the bullet-riddled shirt and blue jeans and pulled on the black top. It felt like a second skin, holding her small, high breasts comfortably, but giving her plenty of room to move. Then she slipped on the black slacks, which fit perfectly.

A pair of low black boots finished the ensemble, and she left the bedroom and went back to the living room. Levinson's eyes widened when he saw her and he glanced at her chest once, then looked quickly back at her face. "I think you need . . . a jacket or something."

He went to the front closet and removed a black leather jacket. "This'll . . . keep you warmer," he said lamely, handing it to her.

"Thanks," she said, feeling oddly pleased that she was still able to arouse a man, if arousal was what Levinson was feeling, but thinking at the same time that her pride was perverse. She was, after all, dead. Wasn't she just dressing up a corpse? And wasn't what Levinson feeling an unprecedented form of necrophilia?

She put on the jacket but didn't zip it up.

"Now what?" Levinson asked.

"Now I go."

"You'll need something, something to . . . defend yourself with. I can't give you a gun but maybe you can use this." He handed her a knife in an ankle sheath. She withdrew it to reveal a six-inch slightly curved blade. The handle had separate finger holes, like brass knuckles. "A survival knife," Levinson said. "Though I don't have much doubt of *your* survival."

"Thank you," she said, strapping it to her leg and fitting her pants leg down over it. Then she turned and went through the kitchen and into the garage, where she lifted the garage door and got into the Avanti. She started it and backed out.

She had expected the engine to roar, but it purred gently and she wondered if one could hear it ten yards away. That was good. Stealth would have to be one of her tools.

The Crow still sat on the lamppost, but now it faced her and stretched its wings, lifted one leg, then another, as though it were ready and anxious to fly. Amy sat there in the softly idling car, watching it. "Go ahead," she said. "I'm ready too."

The great bird spread its wings then and took to the night sky, flying above the street out of the cul-de-sac. Amy followed.

Jesus, Levinson thought, mentally swearing by the name of the non-divine prophet, what the hell have I done? What have I let loose on the world?

He was terribly frightened but also relieved, relieved that he had been right and that the returned Amy Carlisle was indeed what he had thought she was, a supernatural creature brought back to life by still another such creature. If she hadn't been, Levinson would have been sitting in his living room with a dead woman and either an awful lot of explaining or an awful lot of digging to do.

It had been a lot to wager on an old wives' tale and if he had been using pure logic, he might not have taken the risk. But there was something about the situation with Amy Carlisle that went beyond rational thought. After all, if he had been thinking rationally, he never would have entrusted this woman with a weapon, his car, and his home as a base of operations.

But what if he had done the rational thing and assumed she was a living woman, taken her to the hospital, had the doctors examine her, and say, *Sorry, no pulse, no lung function, no nuthin', nada, she's dead.* Amy Carlisle would have wound up in some secret government lab for the rest of her un-life, which could be immortal, for all Levinson knew. And if Amy chose *not* to be imprisoned, well, there could have been a lot of messed-up doctors before she got free.

The question was, what would she do now? If she followed old Uncle Abraham's game plan, she'd kick major ass and then go back to the arms of Mother Death. He just hoped she wouldn't leave too obvious a trail of destruction along the way. Or anything that anyone could trace to him.

And of course there was always the possibility that Levinson would get there first. That was unlikely though. With all the goddamned militia groups in this area, it was like looking for a needle in a haystack when all the haystacks were behind rows of armed guards. That frustration was why he had turned her loose. If the cops wouldn't do it and the government didn't have the guts, then maybe Amy Carlisle and the Crow could take care of the job.

He hoped so, and though his Jewish faith had lapsed, he had seen enough tonight to almost make him pray for it.

15

The Crow soared over the flatness of Hobie, ignoring the houses below, its black eyes fixed on a red light before it, like the red glow that had been the spirit of the woman mingled with the dust, the red glow that had caught the eye of the Crow. Flying high over the earth, the Crow was searching, always searching for the burning souls that could not rest, for the ones who needed justice before they could move on, into the country of Death.

But the glow the Crow sought now was not the radiance of a soul in torment, but a manmade glow, the topmost red light in a series of lights that climbed a radio tower, ascending like the words of hate that crept up the webwork of metal and then exploded outward, like lava from a volcano, spewing hot venom into the air that spread to wherever machines could catch the waves and translate them back into words.

The wings beat on, slowly, steadily, ever approaching the building that housed the station and the transmitter that brought Wilson Barnes's message to a hateful nation, to minds ready for hate.

". . . the time has come to rise, to speak out, speak up, and if words won't do the trick, won't convince those who need to be convinced, then there are other ways of speaking, my friends, other ways of making yourself heard, of shouting in a voice of *thunder* at this evil, oppressive, Jew-controlled, liberal-minded, godless government and the men who run it, both the puppets in the White House and the Congress and the shadow rulers who pull the strings behind the scenes.

"But do they pull these strings for white Christian Americans? Goodness no! You're the forgotten men, the ones they tax and tax and tax so that they can take your money away and give it to the black junkies and welfare mothers and the Mexicans who sneak across the border to take your jobs and the Vietnamese who ruined their own country and now want to ruin ours! Well, it's time to stop these traitors to America, these traitors to Christianity, and I believe you know how to do it!

"I've *seen* you do it! I know who you are and I know what you believe and it's what we *all* should believe in. Jefferson himself said it—you have to water the tree of liberty with the blood of tyrants. And you have to be merciless when you do it.

"Now, my friends, when you care for your gardens—and I know an awful lot of my listeners have their own gardens, live off their own land, keep the government out of it—you try to root out the bad influences on your crop. And sometimes when you spray to kill the pests, you can kill good insects too that do no harm. But if your vegetables are infiltrated with cutworms, do you say, 'Oh, I'd better let them live because I might accidentally spray a beautiful butterfly or an innocent ladybug or the earthworms that till the soil?'

"Of course not—you kill the interlopers, you root out what has to be destroyed, and if you kill a few innocents, that's the price you have to pay to ensure a good crop! Now you can read into this what you want, my friends—I'm sure you see what I mean, what I'm *really* talking about—and I know you're willing to make that sacrifice, because I know your hearts and souls . . . I know who you are, you true patriots, and you have my support and my prayers . . ."

I know who you are . . .

Amy Carlisle listened to the voice of Wilson Barnes and watched the Crow fly. Above the rising buildings she saw the red lights of the radio tower and she knew where the Crow was taking her. She felt the pressure of the knife sheath against her ankle and hoped that its metallic shine would soon be replaced by a darker shine, a red, wet luster.

The hands of the dashboard clock read two forty-five. Wilson Barnes was halfway through his show. He had found his groove and was riffing on his listeners' favorite themes. Well, Amy thought, there would be a new theme tonight. If the audience wanted blood, they would get it.

Of course, Wilson Barnes would know about the militias and might even know which one was responsible for the bombing. He was their hero. It would be natural for one or more of them to brag to him, to let him know how his words had inspired these patriots to action.

Against children. Babies. Her babies.

The Crow alighted atop a marquee over the building's front door. On it were the station's call letters and the words *Home of the Wilson*

Barnes Show. Amy drove past the door and parked her car a block away, then walked back on the deserted street.

She looked through the glass doors and saw, twenty feet inside, a U-shaped security station and a beefy armed guard sitting behind it, reading a newspaper. Amy pressed the buzzer and the guard looked up, wary at first. But when he saw her he smiled, nodded, and pressed a button on his console. There was a buzz and she pushed the door open and walked in.

"Howya doin'?" the guard, whose name tag identified him as Donald, asked. "A little early, huh?"

She looked at him curiously.

"You know," Donald went on, leering at her with his fleshy face. "Wanna warm up with me first? The boss got another ten minutes before the network feed kicks in with the news." He gestured to the portable radio beside him, from which the voice of Wilson Barnes continued to spout invective.

Now she got it. He had thought she was one of Barnes's whores. Apparently the man of the people gave little Wilson some exercise midway through the night. "Sure," Amy said, "I'll be happy to warm up with you."

As she came around behind the desk, Donald's eyes widened. "Holy shit," he said. "One of you finally said yes. Hell, I can't believe it. Thank God for the new girl." He laughed and wiggled in his chair, fumbling with his zipper. "Don't tell Mr. Barnes though, huh?"

"My lips are sealed . . . or will be. Hey, let me take care of that," she went on, kneeling in front of him.

Her hand snaked to her ankle, found the grip of the survival knife, and brought it up quickly across the fat man's face. The heavy brass knuckles collided with his temple and Amy heard a crack. He collapsed like a dead fish, sliding out of the chair onto Amy, who easily disentangled herself from the layers of flesh.

She slipped the knife back into the sheath and hauled Donald back to a sitting position as easily as if he had been a willowy girl. Not yet used to her strength, she had hit him a lot harder than she had thought, but whether he was unconscious or dying she neither knew nor cared. She arranged him so that he looked like he was sleeping and then consulted the floor directory posted near the elevators.

Meeting rooms were on the first floor, offices on the second, and the studio was on the third. She took the stairs, not wanting to let them know she was coming.

The stairs opened onto a long hall dimly lit by recessed ceiling bulbs.

Bright light spilled from windows set into the wall on the left. Amy stepped slowly toward the nearest one until she could see Wilson Barnes.

He was sitting in front of a table covered in black velvet. A single standing floor lamp strongly illuminated his work area. Another table, loaded with newspapers, magazines, and books, was to his left. A microphone hung from a boom directly in front of his face and a thick pair of headphones covered his ears. His back was partially toward her and he was facing another, higher window with a row of colored lights visible through it. She assumed it was the engineer's room.

Amy had never seen Wilson Barnes or even his picture, so his appearance startled her. She had expected a robust, Limbaughesque figure in his midforties, but instead Barnes was thin and wiry, almost emaciated, and he might have been anywhere from forty to sixty. It seemed a freak of nature that such a round, full voice could come out of so spindly a frame. Maybe hate had eaten him away, Amy thought. He seemed well dressed, however, with a white collar peeking up from beneath a tailored gray suit coat.

His voice droned on from the inset speakers in the hall. There was no escaping from Wilson Barnes here. And there would be no escape *for* Barnes either.

Amy waited until the large analog clock above the engineer's window read two fifty-nine and Barnes was only a minute away from the news. Fat Donald downstairs had called it a network feed. That meant it would be coming in from outside the station, so Barnes and whoever was in the control room were probably the only ones here tonight.

Amy crouched and duck-walked past the window below Barnes's field of vision. The next window showed her the control room and had probably been placed there so that people touring the station could see the activity without disturbing the bigots at work. She wondered how many ignorant, easily misled, poor white assholes had come through here, wearing their mesh baseball caps and their faded T-shirts with "Where's Lee Harvey Oswald When You Need Him?" imprinted on them. Like a tour of the Reichstag, only jollier.

Only one man sat behind the controls. He was somewhere between Barnes and Donald in size but Amy didn't care. She felt invincible. When Barnes finished talking and the engineer switched to the network feed, she pushed open the door and stepped into the control room.

The engineer turned and looked at her in surprise. "New girl? Where the hell is Marie?" he asked angrily. "Look, you're *supposed* to be down *there,* bitch, so haul it. You got five minutes so do it fast and sweet, okay?"

Ignoring him, Amy leaned over the console and looked through the glass into the studio. Wilson Barnes was looking up at her. At first, he seemed unsure of what he was looking at but then something happened to his face that hideously split it in two. Amy thought it was his idea of a smile. He turned off his microphone, took off his headphones, and stood up from behind the table.

Amy was shocked, then immediately amused, to see that he was wearing no pants or underwear. A small penis was standing at attention, though feebly. He grabbed it with his right hand, and with his left gestured at her to come down.

She wouldn't disappoint him.

Amy turned back to the engineer. "Would he mind if you went first?" she said. Without waiting for an answer, she grabbed the hair at the back of his head and slammed his face down onto the console, once, twice, three times, until his body went limp and slid into the darkness beneath.

When she looked back at Barnes, he was staring at her slack-jawed, his poor excuse for a cock drooping to half-mast as if in honor of his fallen comrade. In one swift move, Amy reached down for her knife, brought it up, and with a fist of brass she smashed through the double-paned glass that separated her from the man.

Barnes gave a startled cry but hesitated only a moment as Amy climbed through the opening, pushing the jagged edges of glass aside with her bare hands. He leaped to the table at his left, swept aside some papers, and jerked up a .357 magnum, which he grasped in both hands and began to fire at her.

She had to give him credit. He held that pistol steady as a rock as it exploded in his spidery hands. She felt the bullets slam into her, one after another, hitting her in the chest and pushing her back.

But she took two steps forward for every backward step that a magnum load cost her, and now she grabbed the gun by the barrel and ripped it from Barnes's fists. For a moment they stood there staring at each other and then Amy jabbed the barrel into her waistband. "You got any more bullets?" she asked. "I'm going to need them."

His mouth dropped open even further and he turned to run toward the door, but she grabbed his neck like a fleeing chicken's, grimacing at the way her fingers sank into the stringy wattles of his throat. With one arm, she turned him toward her and dragged him kicking and choking, his little cock flapping like a popped balloon, back to the velvet-covered table.

There she slammed him down on his back, still holding him by the throat, her other hand brandishing the shining blade of the knife, turning it slowly in front of his eyes. "You see this?" she said. "It could be the last thing you see, Wilson Barnes. But not because I'm going to kill you. No. Because if you don't tell me what I think you know, I'll take your eyes.

"I'll ask you one time. And if you don't answer me, I'm going to cut you, just cut you once." She moved the knife down to Barnes's testicles and pressed the point against them. He gasped and froze.

"That's right. There. Not badly. Just enough to hurt. And if you don't tell me the second time, I'll cut out your tongue, Wilson Barnes, so that you'll never speak those words again, those lying words that make people kill."

Barnes gave a little yelp of fright and humiliation, and when she looked down she saw urine trickling from his cock. "The third time, I'll take your fingers, all of them, so that you can't write your lies. The fourth your eyes, so that you can't see words and letters to respond to anyone. And finally your eardrums so that no one can tell you, thump once with your stump for yes, twice for no.

"I'll cut you off for good, Wilson Barnes. I won't kill you but I'll banish you from the land of the living so that you'll never communicate again. But if you position yourself just right, maybe you can rub your dick against something. At least you'll have that much."

She put her face so close to his that their lips nearly met. His breath smelled like shit covered with mint. "That's more than my children ever got, Wilson Barnes. Remember them? *Remember?*"

"Wh . . . who?" Barnes husked out, his oratorical voice dried up by fear.

"My children. Remember the innocent ones? The ones that sometimes just have to die if you're going to purge the garden of pests? I want to know who did the purging, Wilson Barnes. I want to know who killed the children with those bombs."

"I . . . I don't know, really I don't, I swear on the Bible, I swear by Jesus Christ almighty . . ."

Amy felt her face grow as hard as her resolve, and she pressed the flat of the blade against Barnes's scrotum until he squealed. Then she turned it so that the sharp blade just barely sliced into the puckered flesh.

The squeal turned into a scream that drowned out the faraway sound of the network news on the speaker in the control room. Barnes's body writhed and trembled, but he did not jerk about for fear that the knife would do worse than it already had.

As the scream died away, a cheery voice over the speaker intoned, "And that's the news . . ." A musical theme played briefly and then there was nothing but dead air and the labored breathing of Wilson Barnes.

"What's it going to be?" Amy asked. "If I have to cut apart an innocent man to get what I want, I'll do it." She held the knife, bright with his blood, in front of his eyes and he pressed them shut and clenched his teeth. Amy reached up with the point of the knife and quietly turned on the microphone.

"Who was it, Wilson Barnes?" she asked. "Your tongue. I promise you."

The skinny man moaned and whimpered, his eyes still tightly shut. Then Amy touched his lips with the point of the knife, pushing it slowly and gently into his mouth, so that he could taste his own blood.

Wilson Barnes's eyes shot open and he nearly shouted his reply. "The *Sons*!" he said. "Sons of a Free America! Please . . . please don't hurt me . . . It's the truth!"

Amy had heard the faint echoes of his voice from the control room. She held the knife in front of his eyes again, bringing it toward them, and he pressed them shut once more. Then she moved the microphone so that it was directly over Wilson Barnes's cringing face, and rested the flat of the blade over the man's closed eyes.

"Who? Tell me again. Tell me who the bastards are."

"The Sons . . . of a Free . . . America," he panted. "It's the truth. They're the ones, they're the ones, I swear . . . It was them, it was them . . ."

He continued to babble as she took the knife away from his eyes and released his throat. At last he stopped talking and began breathing more deeply. And then he opened his eyes and saw the microphone less than six inches from his lips, the switch in the *ON* position.

"This confession brought to you by Wilson Barnes," Amy said formally.

Barnes grabbed the mike and switched it off. He looked about panicked, too scared to be concerned about his half nakedness or the piss running down his skinny thighs. "You . . . you turned it *on,*" he said accusingly, some of the old fire back.

"Yes. And you'd better not leave it off for long. If there's anything listeners hate, it's dead air. That and an informer. I have a hunch, Mr. Barnes, that you'll be hearing a lot more dead air soon." She rummaged through the items on the desk and came up with a box of .357 cartridges. "I knew a man like you would be properly equipped," she said with a smile, glancing at his groin, which he embarrassedly covered with his hands.

"Thanks for the information, Mr. Barnes. Now if I were you, I think I'd try and mend some bridges . . . with *your friends.*"

She turned and walked out of the studio, down the hall, down the stairs, and out of the building past the still unconscious Donald. All the way, she heard Wilson Barnes's shaky but persuasive voice over the speakers that pocked the building's walls:

"And that's what could happen, my friends, if this government continues on its ruthless path. As this dramatization shows, government agents—even female ones, inspired by pro-abortion feminists—could burst into a radio studio—or even your very own *homes!*—and torture you into giving up . . . into telling things that you didn't want revealed, such as the names of any groups that you were associated with, like this, uh, fictitious organization that the character I was portraying was forced into telling the name of . . . It could happen here, my friends, so be sure to preserve your freedoms, and . . ."

Amy had to hand it to him, the man sure had a way of covering his skanky ass. But she didn't think the bullshit would do much to soothe the ruffled feathers of the Sons of a Free America, whoever they were.

As she opened the outside door a skinny redhead with large breasts tried to push her way in. Amy grabbed a handful of red vinyl coat and forced the woman back outside with her, pressing the door shut until it clicked. "Forget it," she told the woman. "Believe me, you're the last person in the world Wilson Barnes wants to see right now." Then she thought about the Sons of a Free America and smiled a smile that made the hooker back up several steps.

"Okay," Amy corrected herself, "maybe the *next* to last person."

The Crow was perched on the parking meter next to the Avanti and Amy nodded at it. "Got a name," she said. "Now I just need the people to go with it . . ."

16

It had been Junior Feeley's turn to pull night guard duty. He hated night guard. There were a thousand and one weird noises in the woods that surrounded the compound, not to mention an assortment of land mines positioned just inside the perimeter. If anyone was able to get over the ten-foot-high chain link fence topped with razor wire, they'd have to cope with Powder Burns's little surprises.

Junior didn't know how many of them there were, though he figured near a hundred. However, he wasn't about to go and count, since he had seen what had happened to a deer that had stepped on one. At least, they *thought* it was a deer. It looked more like deer jelly afterward.

Still, several deer remained within the compound, which encompassed thirty acres. The Sons, under a dummy corporation, also owned, or used at the pleasure of the businessmen who financed them, a surrounding four square miles of woodland. Junior didn't have to pace the whole perimeter of the compound and would not have if ordered, for fear of the mines. But because of the thickness of the woods, the only place that Rip Withers was constantly concerned with was the main entrance, reached by a narrow dirt road that was in turn accessed only from a little-used state road known primarily to hunters.

So now Junior stood by the gate and watched the dirt road, guarding the compound that no one had ever attempted to infiltrate. So that he had something else to listen to besides the sounds that alarmed him, he carried a small transistor radio in his pocket and listened at low volume. He had been listening to Wilson Barnes when something really weird happened. The news ended and then there was just silence and Junior thought maybe the batteries had gone dead. But then he heard a woman say something about a tongue and that made him perk up.

But then all of a sudden Barnes yelled out the name of the Sons of a Free America and Junior had nearly shit himself. That name was a *secret,* goddammit, *nobody* was supposed to hear that name except the ones that the council approved of. Hell, they were the White Oak Hunting Camp—that was what the sign said if anybody drove in far enough to see it. And here was Wilson Barnes, with thousands and thousands of listeners, *yelling* about them, the asshole.

Then the woman said something about bastards, and be damned if Wilson Barnes didn't say the name again and say how it was them, it was them that did something or other. And then the woman says it's a *confession.* Junior Feeley didn't know what the hell was going on here but he knew damn well that Rip and the others needed to know about it, even if they did give him shit for listening to the radio on duty.

So he abandoned his post long enough to run to Rip's cabin and knock on the door. But Rip didn't open it, his brother, Ray, did. And inside were Rip and Will and Sonny Armitage all gathered around Rip's radio, listening to Wilson Barnes's show. Ray raised a finger to silence Junior.

Shit, this was great. They were already listening, so now he was going to get into trouble for nothing. Unless he could come up with something else. The thing was, they didn't seem all that interested in what he had to tell them. They were staring at the radio and every now and then at each other.

Wilson Barnes was still talking but now he sounded like his usual self. It didn't look like Rip and Will and Sonny were all that pleased with what they were hearing though. Rip and Sonny looked madder than hell and Will looked kind of scared. Ray just looked like Ray always looked. Then there was a pause and a commercial came on and they started talking.

"That chicken fucker," Sonny said. "Goddam him, Rip, he ratted on us."

"He sure did," Rip said. "That lousy little shit."

"But who *was* that?" asked Will. "Who was that woman?"

"I don't know—we'll find that bitch soon enough. But we're gonna take care of Barnes right now."

"What are you talking about, Rip?" Will sounded scared again. "You mean—?"

"You bet I do." Rip shook his head, gritting his teeth. "And then trying to cover it up like that—fictitious organization, my ass! Ray, you go get Ace. Tell him we got a job for him. That oughta brighten him up considerably." Then Rip finally seemed to notice Junior Feeley. "What the hell's with you, Junior?"

"I, uh . . ." Junior thought quickly. "I heard something, thought I oughta report it."

"Heard what?"

"Uh, somebody walkin' around . . . outside the fence."

"What!" Rip leaped to his feet. "Jesus, man, why didn't you fire your gun?"

"Well, I . . . I didn't want to scare 'em away, so I came to get somebody."

"Let's go!" Rip said, grabbing a weapon from the wall, and the others followed him. Shit, Junior thought. Here they were going out to look for nothing, just because he was too afraid to tell them he was listening to the radio during his watch. Hell, he was the fucking *treasurer,* he ought to be able to listen to the radio whenever he wanted to. And on top of that, he would have been able to pound any three of these guys into horse meat.

The fact of the matter was that Junior Feeley was a coward. Though he had been in a lot of fights, beaten up a multitude of men, and even killed a couple with his hands, he didn't like the possibility of getting hurt. He was big and he was strong, and because of that size and that strength there were always people who would challenge him. But he hated pain, although he liked inflicting it.

That was why he liked hurting women, because he wasn't afraid of them. It was the only time he could get rough with somebody and not have to worry about being hurt in return. Only thing was, there were no women in the Sons. *Hell,* Rip had laughed lots of times, *then we'd be the Sons and Daughters, and that sounds like shit.* He knew Rip was right, but that didn't stop him from getting horny as a hoot owl in heat.

He'd have a chance in a few weeks. He and Sonny were going to man a table at a gun show, and there was always a lot of hot pussy either cruising the tables or demonstrating the weapons, holding them up and rubbing them like they'd like to stick them somewhere where the sun don't shine.

But now he had to worry about Rip getting mad at him and it didn't seem far away. All the search lights were on, covering the small open area in front of their gate, and Rip was up in the guard tower holding his AK and glaring into the brush. "Open the gate and send out a search team!" he yelled down.

Junior opened the gate while Sonny went to the barracks and

rousted half a dozen men, who ran out through the gate with their weapons and scattered as they had been trained to do. But after ten minutes they returned, shaking their heads and looking dubiously at Junior.

"There's nobody out there, Junior," Sonny said. "You hearing things again?"

"I heard *something,*" Junior insisted. "Must've been a deer."

"Shit," said Rip, "as if we don't have enough to be concerned about with that weasel Barnes. Use your fucking head next time, Junior—shine a fucking flashlight, okay?"

Damn Junior anyway, Rip thought. For such a big boy, he sure was jumpy. And now he had woken up the whole camp. The lights and noise had brought most of the men out of their cabins and barracks and they stood around shivering in the cold night air, wondering what was happening. They didn't look as if they had been sleeping and Rip suspected that a few may have been listening to Barnes and then spread the word.

"False alarm," Rip told them. "Unless you've been listening to Wilson Barnes." From the looks on the men's faces, he knew they had been. They seemed angry and concerned. "We heard it all," he told them. "And we're going to do something about it. You don't betray the Sons of a Free America and get away with it. Now you all just go back to bed and don't worry about it. Though you might want to listen to Wilson Barnes finish his show. It's his last."

Most of the men nodded and smiled as they went back to their cabins. But none smiled more broadly than Ace Ludwig, who walked up to Rip. "Ray said you wanted me."

"You know what for?" said Rip.

"I'd guess a little rat extermination. A skinny little rat who talks too much. Even has his own rat show."

Rip nodded. "If you want to make him hurt, feel free."

Wilson Barnes wondered if he would be able to make it to his car. It wasn't the pain in his testicles that bothered him, although they still ached and the small cut stung. But his legs were shaking so hard that he wondered if he'd be able to walk the whole way.

Christ, tonight had been a nightmare. That crazy woman had been bad enough, but talking for another three hours until the show was over was a nightmare. Thank God Phil, his engineer, had come to. He had a broken nose and possibly a concussion but he had finished the show along with Barnes, jamming his nose with cotton until it stopped bleeding. Barnes had packed his own crotch with cotton but the slight cut hardly bled at all.

Donald, the apparently inept security guard, had come up to the studio at five o'clock with a bruise and contusions on his fat face and Barnes fired him during the news. The man threatened to tell people about the female visitors to the studio, but Barnes told him that would be a bad idea and that Barnes had many friends of a violent nature who would not take kindly to an insider making false accusations. Donald, not surprisingly, changed his mind. Barnes didn't, and Donald remained fired.

After the show was over Barnes stressed to Phil the importance of remaining silent and Phil, happy with his job and salary, agreed to do so. His doctor would be told that he had been mugged by an unseen assailant.

So now Wilson Barnes walked on unsteady legs toward the front door of the building, past the unmanned security desk, wondering who in hell that woman was. Not a cop but maybe a government agent, just like he had said. Who else would have been so well trained in interrogation techniques? He would have to talk to Withers, of course, convince him that no harm was done, that merely knowing the name of an organization doesn't mean that anything bad would—

And in the middle of that thought, just as he was about to open his car door, the first round caught him, punching him in the back, straight through his right kidney and out a hole in the front, spraying a shower of blood and piss onto Wilson Barnes's shiny Buick. He stood there for a minute, uncertain of what was happening, and then he felt the second bullet hit him in the shoulder and spin him around so that he slammed against the car door and slid down it until he was sitting on the blacktop of the parking lot.

He saw the man then, leaning out the passenger side of the window of a dark green van a hundred yards away. He was holding a rifle, aiming it at Wilson Barnes, who could do absolutely nothing about it except shake his head and whisper words that the man could never hear.

The man shot again and Barnes felt his stomach explode. The pain the woman had caused him was now totally forgotten, as Barnes feebly moved his fingers, trying to keep looking at the man, to tell him with his eyes that he shouldn't be doing this.

But then the man raised his head from the rifle's telescopic sight and smiled at him. He spoke one word, but loudly enough for Barnes to hear:

"Bigmouth . . ."

In between the moment when Barnes processed that word and the rifleman aimed again, Barnes concluded that he would not be able to explain anything to Rip Withers, that Withers had already made his decision.

Wilson Barnes did not hear the shot that killed him, nor see the bullet that hit him right between the eyes.

17

Amy Carlisle had not yet returned to David Levinson's home. After she left the radio studio she had driven to the site where the Making Friends Child Care Center had once stood, and watched there until dawn lit the sky and the dust and ashes turned from black to gray.

She never got out of the car. She felt that if she did, she might somehow be taken back again, made one with the dust before her work was done, and that could not happen. Surely whatever force had birthed her from the rubble in agony and love would not take her back so soon.

Still, she did not open the door or even the window, until a wind began to blow from the east, as though carried on the rays of the rising sun, and stirred the dust, carrying it up and into the air. Though Amy could see no dust blowing to where she sat across the street, she knew that the breeze contained fragments of it, and she opened the window and breathed it in, thinking that she breathed in the atoms and the essence of her children.

Fill me. Be with me. Come deep inside me and never leave. Make me strong.

They were within her now, one with her, the children she had never had, the children who could never grow up. On her tongue was the bitter taste of their pain and their love and their loss, the husbands and wives and fathers and mothers who would never be, the lives that would never be lived.

Because of them. Because of the Sons of a Free America, who proclaimed their freedom by killing children, by stealing not only years but generations to come.

She lowered her head and cried, but no tears came. Maybe, she thought, she was made too much of the dust. And maybe whatever had made her knew that it was not tears that were needed now, but blood.

She had shed it and she would shed far more before she could finally rest. But before she started to track them down, there was one thing she had to do first. She knew she should not, but she could no more stop herself than she could make the bright yellow ball of the sun sink back down in the east.

Rick Carlisle loved the house that he had built with Amy.

Nestled in a half acre of trees, it was only minutes from the heart of town but seemed isolated, so that you could leave the curtains open and walk around naked and no one would see except the water meter reader. Its single story sprawled under the trees and when they had sat together on the small deck out back, it was like they were living in the middle of a forest.

But although Rick had built the house with Amy, he didn't live in it with her anymore. He lived with his second wife now, with Nancy, who had been Amy's friend, and her daughter, Karin.

Sometimes it felt strange, as though he were cheating on Amy, but both he and Nancy had needed someone after the loss, and it had been only natural that they had comforted each other.

At first Rick wanted to sell the house and move. Everywhere he looked he thought of Amy. Her belongings, her influence, her *presence* was everywhere. But Nancy had talked him out of it. "It's not the physical things," she had said, "as much as the mental. You have to face it, Rick, Amy will be with you always. The loss is always going to be there—it just won't hurt as much with time."

He knew she was right and decided to try and stay in the house. But he did, on one painful night, purge it of Amy's things. Those that they had gotten together, some paintings and prints, knickknacks and books, stayed in their places. But he removed the things that he closely identified with her, such as those books he had bought as presents for her with no intention of reading himself; the photographs of her parents, who had died five years before in a plane crash; and the original half-sheet poster of one of her favorite movies, *An Affair to Remember,* that hung framed in the basement rec room.

So Anne Tyler and Louise Erdrich fled his shelves and Deborah Kerr his walls. But Amy remained nonetheless in the closets and on top of the dressers and in dozens more places. These Rick tried to make vanish as well, giving her clothing to charity and sending her jewelry to Amy's sister, Fran.

He kept all their photographs and the videos that they had taken of each other, though he put these away in a box and stored them in the back of the bedroom closet. However, he ceremoniously placed one photograph of Amy on a bookcase in the living room, around a partition where it was not easily seen from the rest of the room. There, he decided, it would stay, no matter what happened.

After his marriage to Nancy, she had said nothing about the picture, except for the fact that she had always liked that particular portrait of her friend. Rick was glad she hadn't protested. He needed a piece of Amy to remember. He had placed a small stone in a nicely kept memorial park outside of town, but he knew that there was nothing of Amy beneath it. It read "Amy Carlisle—Beloved Wife," along with the years of her birth and death, but he knew she was not there.

In a way, the disposal of her remains was what Amy would have wanted. Though they had never made arrangements, they had discussed it and both of them wanted cremation, finding the thought of their bodies rotting in the ground unpleasant to the point of being horrifying. Interment of ashes in a columbarium or grave was what they had preferred. It allowed the grieving to come and stand in a place that held the departed's remains in a form that bore thinking about.

But that wasn't possible now. Rick had thought about taking an urn full of the dust and ashes from the site, but odds were that there would be nothing of Amy within. So he settled for the stone, which he had visited only once. His heart would be her memorial.

At last the alarm went off, sparing him more memories of her. He kissed Nancy as she awoke and together they prepared for the day, getting Karin ready for school. Rick was planning to work at home that day, but he made coffee and cooked oatmeal and got what had become his family off to school and work with warm bellies and a kiss.

Left alone in the house, he sat back in the breakfast nook with his coffee and thought about the last time he had sat there with Amy. They had both been so excited about the visit of the senator, but a day hadn't gone by since when Rick hadn't cursed the man. If only he hadn't canceled, the security people might have gone in first and found the bombs. But his cancellation, no matter how valid the reason, had broken Amy's heart and ended her life.

He knew he should blame the people who had set the bombs, but how could you hate people with no names and no faces? Rick tried to keep the thoughts of those men, the four Amy had seen in the car, far away. When he thought about them, anger and frustration built up inside him like tons of water behind the wall of a cracked dam. He shoved the thought away, letting Amy's face come back into his mind.

Then he thought about her gentleness, her kindness, and how much she had loved him. And as so often happened when his thoughts went to her, he found himself crying softly, not sobbing, but feeling tears run down over his cheeks and into the corners of his mouth so that he could taste them.

He had to see her then, had to look at and hold what remained of her in this house, and he got up and walked into the living room, around the partition, and picked up the framed picture. Amy, standing in the sunlight, her dark brown hair glowing like strands of gold, her violet eyes half closed from the sun, her smile just for him.

His tears blurred his vision and he looked away from the picture toward the window.

The image remained. Amy's face, no longer in sunlight but in shadow, looked in at him through the glass.

A chill gripped his heart and he blinked savagely to clear his vision. His eyes caught movement but whatever had stood gazing in was no longer there. He dashed to the window and looked out, but saw nothing except perhaps a hint of motion in the green of the deep brush that hid his house from the road.

Rick ran to the front door, yanked it open, and ran outside, but he saw only a large, black crow riding the wind between the trees, drifting toward the road. Rick opened his mouth to call Amy's name, then hesitated and closed it again.

Amy was dead. What he had seen had only been a negative afterimage of the photograph on the light source of the window. Of course. That had to be it. The face that had been in sunlight was in shadow, and the white clothes in the portrait had turned to black.

But he had seen her eyes. Even through the tears that veiled his own, her deep violet eyes had fixed him with love and longing and something else. No, it had not been an afterimage, no optical trick. He had seen Amy standing outside his window. Or her ghost.

Maybe that was the explanation, for he could think of no other that made sense. What had her look asked of him? There was something deeper there, some emotion other than sadness.

Then he knew. What did ghosts come back for? Because of an unhappiness that would not let them rest. Because of injustice unavenged. Because of a murder that had not been solved. He had seen *Hamlet* innumerable times, he had read ghost stories, he knew how these things worked. He just hadn't believed them before.

Now he did.

The police and the government had been totally ineffective in finding the crew who had blown up the center and killed Rick's wife and her children. And Amy's ghost had returned to tell him that it had to be done for her to rest. If the police couldn't do it, then he would have to.

He would have to, for Amy.

She drove away too fast but she couldn't help herself, just as she couldn't help going to the house and seeing Rick again.

Now Amy wished she hadn't. She wished that she didn't know he had gotten remarried to Nancy and had a family again and this time a child to love.

It wasn't that she didn't wish Rick happiness. She loved him and always would, and wanted only the best life for him. But there was still enough selfishness alive in her to feel hurt, more hurt on top of the pain that she already carried like a heavy sack, the pain that she had come back to assuage.

But slowly as she looked in window after window of the house, the truths had come to her. First was the shock at seeing Rick in bed with Nancy, then the deeper yet ironically reassuring shock of the rings on their fingers, Rick's narrow gold one replacing the broad one she had slipped on his hand a lifetime ago. Amy should have left then but trapped, helpless, she could not look away.

She watched with a dull numbness as they got up, a family, and had breakfast together, Karin hugging Rick as she left for school, Nancy kissing him warmly, lovingly when she went out the door. She watched Rick alone with his coffee and wished that she could knock on the door and put her arms around him when he opened it.

But then she watched as he started to cry and she knew what the tears were for. She followed him around the side of the house and watched as he picked up her picture, and then she knew what she had always known, that he still loved her and would love her always. This one truth, the joy and the sorrow that she felt, held her, even when he looked up and saw her standing there.

She had frozen for a moment and then run, hoping against hope that he hadn't seen her face. The thick brush tore at her as she ran through it, but she felt no pain from the slapping twigs or the buffeting branches. All was eclipsed by the hole in her heart.

Now as she drove swiftly through the streets, she knew that she had to put Rick out of her mind. He was not her husband, he was her widower, and now the widower had gotten married again and to a woman Amy had loved as a sister. Over time his hurts would heal. He had a family that loved him and he would be all right.

She headed back toward David Levinson's house in the black Avanti and saw no cars coming out of the cul-de-sac as she drove in. She parked the car in the garage and went into the kitchen. Levinson was sitting there in a bathrobe, holding a mug of coffee. "Give me your hands," he said.

She held them out and he sniffed her fingers. "Good. No cordite. I take it then that you're not the one who shot Wilson Barnes."

She tried to show no surprise. "Who's Wilson Barnes?" she asked coolly.

"That's what I like to hear," Levinson said. "I see nothing, I know nothing. I harbor . . . what, a fugitive?"

She nodded. "From death. I need to use your computer."

Levinson pointed toward the basement door.

Within a half hour of searching, she had found a lead. *Sons of a Free America* had drawn no hits, but *Free America* had taken her to a Usenet message from alt.militia.freedomfight, posted by a W. J. Standish. It read in part:

> Too many times our freedoms and, in some cases, our precious lives have been taken away by this present government. We should all pledge ourselves to a Free America once again, and be Sons of that Free America, even if the payment is in our own blood.

Standish's address was wstandish@rangenet.com. After some more searching, Amy discovered that Rangenet was a Grand Rapids–based Internet carrier that served north and central Minnesota. Now it was time to locate Standish.

She sent an e-mail disguised as a spam, concerning a Chevrolet truck sale in St. Cloud, to see if the address was current. It was not, as a "Mail undeliverable" message informed her a minute later. Then she made a phone book search and found a William J. Standish in Hobie. But when she dialed the number she received a recorded message telling her that the number was not in service.

There was one other Standish listed in the Hobie area, a Dorothy J. in Kilton, a small town five miles north of Hobie. Amy called the number but there was no answer. She decided to go to Kilton that evening.

For the rest of the day she busied herself among Levinson's files. Though his holdings on militias and their members were extensive, she came across no other mention of William Standish, except for a few letters to the editor that he had written to several "patriot" magazines.

The contents were similar to what he had posted on the Internet, but different from the other published letters in that they were far more eloquent and not nearly as rabid. The address on each of them was simply Hobie, MN, and the most recent letter had been published over a year before.

It was nearly dark by five o'clock and Amy left for Kilton without seeing Levinson, who she assumed had gone out on patrol. He had not bothered her the whole day except to ask her if she wanted any lunch. She had declined.

As Amy drove the Crow flew ahead of her as though guiding her. Although she knew where she was headed, she found its presence reassuring. The tie between them was something that she didn't begin to understand but she knew it was there for her, that somehow it was the avatar of whatever power had brought her back to life. She felt the same comfort in its presence that as a Christian she had felt in the cross.

Dorothy Standish lived in a mobile home set on a small corner lot. The back of the trailer faced thick woods and there was a small stone driveway into which Amy pulled the Avanti. As she walked to the door at the end of the structure, she saw that the pale green and white metal was rusting in dozens of places. The corrugated metal skirt that covered the bottom of the trailer was actually rusted through in spots.

Even before she knocked on the door, she saw the old woman looking at her through its opaque glass window. The crazed surface made her face look fragmented and monstrous, until Amy remembered that *she* was the monster. The door opened a crack and Amy stared into a room hazy with cigarette smoke. In a low, grating voice, the woman asked Amy who she was.

"I'm Margaret Evans from Publishers' Clearance," she said. "I'm looking for William Standish. Is he related to you?"

"What do you want him for?" she asked, her thin lips barely moving, more interested in retaining the cigarette clenched between them than in being understood.

"He won a prize in one of our sweepstakes, but we haven't been able to find him at the address we have."

The old woman's face brightened just a bit. "What'd he win?"

"Well," Amy said hesitantly, "in order to reveal that, I'd have to either talk with Mr. Standish or his appointed representative."

"I'm his mother," Dorothy Standish said, finally removing the cigarette from her mouth. "Isn't that good enough?"

"I'm sorry, Mrs. Standish, but I can only deal with a third party if Mr. Standish presents us with a written authorization. Now do you know where I might be able to find him?"

"He's not around right now. You can't reach him. What'd he win?"

Amy smiled in spite of the woman's countenance. Her chin was wreathed with thin white whiskers and her teeth, or dentures, were uniformly brown. Her breath reeked of tobacco and garlic and decay.

"As I said, I can't reveal that. Perhaps he could contact us. Do you expect to see him soon?"

She nodded. "Tomorrow. He's coming to see me tomorrow."

"Well then, if I gave you my phone number, maybe he could give me a call and we could make the arrangements for him to claim his prize."

"Look, you tell me what it is first. How do I know this isn't one of them things where you win a condo in Florida or something, but then you got to pay for it, one of them tricks or something?" She moved her right hand in circles as she talked, so that the ash from her cigarette jerked in every direction like tiny bugs.

Amy nodded and smiled as if she'd been bested. "I see there's no getting around you, Mrs. Standish. All right, your son has won five hundred dollars."

"Five hundred?" Her face was a mixture of greed and annoyance. "I thought you people gave away ten million dollars. That's what your ads say."

"Oh, that's the one Ed McMahon's with. We're a much smaller company. But our grand prize was fifty thousand—a woman in St. Paul won that."

"Wait here," Mrs. Standish said, closing the door on Amy. When she came back she had a pencil and paper and a new cigarette and wrote down the name and number Amy gave her. Then without another word, she shut the door again, this time, Amy suspected, for good.

Amy had made the number up, along with the name. If Standish called it, he would assume that his mother had gotten the number wrong. But by that time Amy would have him. And then she would get the information she wanted, the names and location of the rest of the killers, these Sons of a Free America. And then she would see to it that the only freedom they had was deciding whether or not to scream when they died.

18

The next morning Amy Carlisle drove back to Kilton at eight o'clock and parked her car four blocks from Mrs. Standish's trailer. She went through a vacant lot and into the woods, coming around behind the old woman's trailer until she could see the stone driveway and the door from the cover of the trees. Then she waited.

Amy had never been very good at waiting but now she seemed one with patience, made of black stone. She sat on a fallen tree several yards within the relative darkness of the woods and the Crow sat next to her, stolid and unmoving, on a branch that bent and twisted like the arm of a drowning man. Its concentration fueled her own and she tried to emulate its stillness and implacability, to conserve the energy for when it was truly needed.

Now was the time to rest, though she didn't know if she even needed rest. She had no idea what her body was capable of, but since she had not had a bite to eat nor a second of sleep since her resurrection, she suspected that her powers were formidable. And if her seeming invulnerability, as terrifyingly demonstrated by Levinson, and the ease with which she had taken control of the radio studio were further indications, there would be few situations with which she could not cope.

She sat there as the day brightened and the sun reached its zenith and then fell into darkness again. It was not until six that evening that a car pulled into the driveway and someone got out. Amy saw him clearly, a tall, thin, almost cadaverous man, who walked with his head bowed down, as though he carried a great sin upon his soul. Oh yes, thought Amy. If he was who she suspected, he did indeed.

She moved across the grass with the lightness of wind and crouched beneath the picture window. The murmur of voices inside was indistinguishable at first but as she attuned her ears to the rhythms, she found that she could easily make out what the son and the mother were saying.

When she raised her head above the window she saw them sitting in a smoky room filled with clutter. Antimacassars covered every arm of every piece of furniture, piles of magazines and romance paperbacks were scattered across the floor, and cheap china figurines littered every tabletop and the huge console television. Ashtrays were everywhere, most of them filled, and several opened packs of Pall Malls were scattered about so that a smoke was never more than an arm's length away.

Mrs. Standish was sitting in an overstuffed chair that faced the TV. Her eyes were on a strand of faux pearls being sold on a home shopping channel, though the sound was turned down. Her son, who Amy guessed was in his midforties, was pacing back and forth, quite a trick in the crowded room, and talking quickly, like a teacher with an urgent need to stuff his students' heads before the bell rang.

"I can't stay, not after this," William Standish was saying to his mother. "I mean, the bombs were bad enough but then they go out and shoot Barnes in broad daylight? And that's nothing compared to what they're planning next. I just can't be a part of it, Mother, I just *can't.*"

William Standish sounded close to tears but the old lady kept her eyes fixed on the screen. It was as if she didn't hear her son's words at all.

"I mean, I believe in what I've said and written in the past, but this way . . . I hadn't imagined how it would be, all those children dead, and for nothing . . ."

If Amy's dead blood had ever run hot since her return, it ran ice cold now. This was one of the men, these Sons of a Free America, who had killed her children. His own words condemned him. Amy felt triumph and rage and hate. She wanted to burst through the window and break the man's neck. But she would wait. It wasn't revenge she needed now, but knowledge.

"I've got to get out. I know the Sons will try and kill me but maybe I can get away. If I tell what I know, they'll protect me."

"*Who'll* protect you?" Mrs. Standish finally asked.

"The . . . the government," said William Standish in a voice so low that Amy barely heard it. "Or the press—I could tell what I know and they'll turn me over to the government. That way the whole truth will get out and they won't go back there . . . do what they did at Ruby Ridge and Waco . . . A lot of good boys back there in the compound, can't help what their leaders do . . . Oh *God,* Mother, I don't know, I just don't know . . ."

The man started crying then but his mother said nothing to comfort him. Instead she looked away from the TV screen at her sobbing son. "Do you know what it means to be a Standish? To have the blood of patriots run in your veins?"

He rubbed tears from his eyes and looked at her. "I know, Mother. I know . . ." Then he ran to the door and flung it open. Amy started toward him but it was too late. As she rounded the corner of the trailer, she saw that he was already in his car, backing out of the stone drive. The only way to follow would be in the Avanti.

She did not return to her car through the woods. The darkness of night provided enough cover and she ran through the streets, amazed at how fast she could go and how tireless she was. She was not even panting when she reached the Avanti. She threw the car into gear and headed in the direction Standish had driven.

There were several ways out of town but she didn't have to guess Standish's route. The Crow flew above, always in sight, the flat plane of its wings tilting on the turns. It seemed to fly without effort, as Amy had run, and she thought dreamily that there was ease in death.

She picked up Standish's car, a dusty white Ford Tempo, within a few blocks. There was a pickup truck behind the Tempo but she made no attempt to pass, thinking the truck would provide cover for her.

Amy decided not to try cutting Standish off. After all, she couldn't lose anything by following him. For all she knew, he might be returning to the compound, and then she could confront the killers all at once. On the other hand, if he decided to carry out his threat and go to the press, she would have to stop him. This was to be her vengeance, not that of the police. Her law, not the state's.

They headed back toward Hobie and Amy kept the pickup between her and Standish. As they got on the four-lane that would take them into town, she noticed that the truck followed Standish whenever he passed a car, then fell back into line behind him. After this happened several times she concluded that the driver of the truck was following Standish too.

Who was it, she wondered. A cop? Or could the Sons of a Free America mistrust one of their own enough to put a tail on him? That seemed more likely. The bumper bore an "Impeach Clinton" sticker, and NRA and American flag decals were stuck on the back window. Maybe William Standish had his own personal tail. She would find out soon enough.

Once off the four-lane they headed into the heart of town. The city was sleeping now. At six o'clock most of the stores and offices closed and the streets were nearly deserted. Even the parking garages used an honor system after eight.

A green light changed to yellow and Amy got ready to floor the Avanti if Standish tried to slip through. But he stopped, as did the truck behind him, and the glare of the halogen street light shone directly down into the cab of the pickup so that Amy could see the top half of the driver's face in his rearview mirror.

He was looking straight ahead but she recognized the face anyway and felt her own face harden, her teeth clench, her lips draw back in a snarl. It was one of the faces that had looked at her from the windows of the dark car outside the center, one of the four men who had been there that fatal night.

Amy fought back the urge to plow the Avanti right into the back of the truck and watch the man's head snap. There was no rush, she told herself. She had two of them now. One of them would talk and then both of them would die.

The light changed and they started moving again. The *Hobie Sentinel* building towered ahead, an eleven-story structure that was the downtown's tallest building. The newspaper's business was conducted on the fourth through eighth floors while the presses occupied the first three. Amy had taken the older children there on a field trip the year before.

A parking garage adjoined the building and William Standish pulled his car into its narrow entrance. That meant only one thing, that he was going to make good on his threat to tell the newspapers everything. And that meant that Amy had to get to him first.

The pickup truck slowed at the entrance to the garage, as if the driver didn't want Standish to see him come in on his tail. Amy waited impatiently for the man, who finally drove into the entrance, through what Amy had always thought of as the cattle chute, with high concrete walls on either side.

But instead of driving straight through, the pickup truck stopped dead just as it was about to come out into the garage area itself. The passenger door opened, and the driver jumped out and ran around the corner out of sight.

The son of a bitch had boxed her in. The sides were so close to the Avanti that she couldn't even open the door far enough to slip through. Quickly, with fury building inside her, she lowered the window and began to crawl out.

That got her, Sonny Armitage thought as he trotted toward the elevator. He didn't know who the hell the bitch was who had tailed him ever since he came into the city. Maybe just some broad on the night shift at the paper. But with what he was going to do now, he didn't want a witness, and the truck was expendable, stolen earlier that night. He had hated to rip off a fellow NRA member, and a Clinton hater to boot, but he had to take what was available.

He heard the rumble of Will Standish's old Tempo as it pulled into a space somewhere up out of sight, and he ran down the incline to the elevator. Will would get on at floor three and come down to the main entrance on one. But someone else would get on at two with a big surprise for Will Standish, Traitor.

As Sonny pushed the down button, he thought that Rip had been right to mistrust the prick, especially after the way he'd gone belly up that night they blew up the center. They should have killed him then and saved themselves a lot of hassle. Once a man showed signs of weakness, you had to cut him loose and the only way to cut loose a man who knew as much as Will Standish did was with extreme prejudice.

Sonny Armitage loved those words. That was what it was all about, wasn't it? Extreme prejudice, toward Jews, niggers, beaners, gooks, and all the liberal lowlifes who thought they were all brothers under the fucking sun. No, Sonny had had enough of *that* crap, fuck you very much.

He had fought in Vietnam alongside those "black brothers," goddam street punks more interested in where their next jays were coming from than in killing the enemy. They were animals, subhumans, and so were the gooks. If the niggers were apes, the gooks were monkeys, little slanty-eyed monkeys that darted through the jungle like ghosts. Sonny never admitted it but they had scared the shit out of him. If they had fought like men, out in the open, instead of hiding in the leaves or in their narrow rat tunnels, he might have had a little respect for them.

Then when he finally came home, the little bastards *followed* him. It seemed like the gooks loved killing Americans so much that they thought they'd just come over and kill their economy too. So they worked hours you wouldn't expect a dog to work, took just enough salary to buy rice for their little gook litters, killed rats and dogs to add some meat, and put the vets out of work, like with those shrimp boats down in Galveston.

And what little money you *were* able to make, the government took most of it to give to the nigger junkies or the AIDS faggots or the schools to teach the wetback kids who weren't even here legally. The rest of it went to the Jews, who ran the whole damn thing. Then they had the guts to accuse the real patriots of conspiracy.

The whole thing stunk to high heaven and Sonny thanked Yahweh every day that he had been able to find other people who thought the way he did, who saw what needed to be done, and weren't afraid to do it, the way this pussy Will Standish was. Probably a faggot on top of it.

Finally Sonny heard a ding and the elevator doors slid open. There was Will Standish in all his gutless glory, looking up at Sonny as if he'd taken a wrong turn somewhere and didn't know where in the hell he was, like the whole world had gone butt-side-up on him, and it had. Boy, how it had.

"Hey, Will," said Sonny, both his teeth and his knife smiling brightly, "goin' to buy a newspaper?"

Will tried to get past him but Sonny easily shoved him back against the wall of the car. The doors slid shut and Sonny pulled the lock knob. Then he slid the blade of the long knife smoothly between Will Standish's ribs.

"You fuckin' chickenshit quisling liberal pinko faggot traitor pussy," Sonny said softly into Will's ear, holding him up so that he would not fall to the floor, and drawing the knife across until it clicked against Will's rib cage, then sliding it out again. He felt blood fall warmly across his knuckles and thought that it felt good. It was a traitor's blood, a traitor who kissed the ass and sucked the cocks of tyrants and it made Sonny feel strong to have it pouring across his hand.

"Traitors shouldn't die easy," he told Will and then stuck the knife in again, right into Will's guts, and moved it around in small circles. Will was too shocked to scream, although his mouth worked at something. Sonny smelled Will's piss and shit escaping him and laughed. "Mama's gonna have to wash your panties, Will," he said, then pushed the lock knob in and hit the button for six, the top floor of the garage. He would leave Will there. No one would find him until morning.

Sonny chuckled softly as the elevator climbed. "Slow ride, Will," he said, "but getting there's half the fun, huh?" He twisted the knife again, joying in Will's unbelieving grimace, and pulled it out just as the door opened on the sixth floor.

"Does not play well with others."

The soft, feminine voice spun Sonny around and he found himself staring through the door at a woman, the sports car driver he thought he had boxed in. She was dressed all in black and her violet eyes were narrowed ferally, but she was smiling with white, even teeth. Her pale, long-fingered hands hung empty at her side.

Sonny didn't know what the hell she was smiling about. He was the one with the knife. He held it up, blood dripping from the end, uncertain what to do next.

The woman looked at it and shook her head. "Runs with scissors," she said, and the smile winked out like a candle flame. "And kills babies. That's three infractions. You need to be punished."

"Fuck you too," Sonny snarled and lunged at her with the knife, but she was fast, faster than he could have imagined, and sidestepped him so that the force of his blow made him stumble and fall onto the concrete.

The air went out of him as she kicked him in the side. It hurt bad, far worse than he had ever been kicked in any fight before, and he had been in a lot of them. Enough of this shit, he thought, as he winced in pain and rolled over, reaching behind him for the pistol he kept at the small of his back, thinking no bullshit, she's too fucking fast, just shoot, shoot quick, shoot now.

He fired from the ground, three shots in rapid succession, moving his shooting hand up as he fired, and was rewarded with the sight of them slamming into her, pushing her back—one in the gut, one in the chest, and one in the soft spot under her chin.

But she didn't fall. She kept standing, looking dazed for a moment. The bullet holes were in her clothes, so Sonny knew that he had hit her, but the spot where the bullet had gone in under her chin—and he had *seen* it, goddammit!—was no longer there. It had closed up like a finger hole in pudding.

The second of shock at the sight was long enough for her to pluck the gun from his hand as if he were a baby. She threw it into the darkness and it skittered for a long time across the concrete. Then she took the survival knife from its ankle sheath, slipped the brass knuckles over her fingers, and crouched down next to Sonny.

"Look at me," she said. "Do you know who I am?"

"Yeah," Sonny said, scared as hell but more scared to show it. "You're a fucking whore."

She raised her fist and hit him in the stomach so hard that he heard a rib snap and he gagged at the pain. "No." She shook her head. "Look close. Remember me? You've probably seen my picture in the newspaper."

Then Sonny Armitage got even more scared as he recalled the newspaper stories he had devoured after the explosion and the photos of the victims. Jesus fucking Christ, it couldn't be. But it was.

"You're . . . her," he said. "The one we . . ."

"The one you killed," she finished. "But not the only one you killed. You killed my children too. I was supposed to take care of them and you killed them. You and the others." She spat the words in his face. "The Sons of a Free America. Now I want to know who the rest of them are and *where* they are."

"I don't believe this," Sonny said, his mind swimming. "This ain't true, it ain't happening. I'm dreaming or something or it's a trick."

"Well, if it's not happening," the woman said, "if you're dreaming, then it won't matter if you tell me or not and . . ." She hit him again, this time across the jaw, so that his teeth snapped together. After the first flash of pain subsided, he could feel that several teeth had been loosened in their sockets. ". . . And you'll save your dream self a lot of pain."

"If it's a dream," Sonny said, swallowing blood, "then fuck you. You might as well kill me. Then I'll wake up. And you know what I'll do then? I'll find me some more nigger kids and gook kids and Jew kids and I'll shoot out their little pig eyes and fuck the—"

He didn't finish the sentence. The survival knife came down, not the knuckles but the blade, straight into his open, bleeding, cursing mouth.

19

"Wake up then," Amy whispered. "Wake up in hell."

In her rage, she had slammed down the blade so hard that it had driven through the man's neck bones and into the concrete beneath. She wrenched it out and stood up.

William Standish was still breathing, his eyes wide, his hands, wet with his blood, clamped over his dreadful wounds. Amy went back into the elevator and pulled out the lock knob so the car would not descend, then looked hard into his eyes. "You're dying," she said. "But you have a chance to help put things right. I know you want to do that. So tell me—where are they?"

He couldn't tell her although he wanted to. To list the route numbers, tell where the county road was, describe the place where the dirt road left the county road, all these things were far beyond Will Standish's ability. He tried to show her with his eyes how much he wanted to help and hoped that she read them correctly.

She said something else now and he could barely hear her for the rushing of the blood in his ears. It was as though he were hearing his life running out of him. Then the woman positioned herself directly in front of his gaze and her lips formed an O. And though he could not hear her, he knew she was saying *Who?* Maybe he could get that much out. Maybe he could tell the names.

He tried to remember who was in the car with him that night, then performed the mental gymnastics necessary to form the words. He barely had any air, for his lungs had been punctured, but he breathed out the first name that came to his dying mind: "Ruh . . . Ruhp . . . Withuhs."

"Withers? Rip Withers?" she repeated, and he tried to nod, then went on. In all, he was able to communicate only three more names and she repeated every one to make sure that she had heard them correctly. He couldn't remember who was in the car that night so he told her all the names he could think of. Junior Feeley. Powder Burns. Yes, he knew that Powder had been there but he wasn't sure about Junior. The only other name he could think of was Chip Porter and he managed to get that out as well before the cells that held that part of his memory were turned off by the lack of blood.

There was only one more thing that he wanted to tell this woman and he was able to reach out his left hand to her to make her know how important it was. Though it took several minutes Will Standish was finally able to say the words "Forgive me" and "Tell Mother I tried."

To which Amy Carlisle replied, "Yes . . . I forgive you" and "I will." She held William Standish's bloody hand for another minute until his breathing stopped and his eyes no longer moved. Then she dragged him off the elevator onto the dirty concrete floor and lay him on his back, his hands at his side.

She walked over to the other dead man, took the money from his wallet, and spat into his upturned face. Then she ran down the stairs to the street.

The Avanti was still there and she slipped in through the window, started the car, and backed it down the chute. It was indicative of the somnolence of nighttime Hobie that no one had even noticed that the parking garage entrance was blocked. Amy headed the car back to Kilton to fulfill William Standish's last wish.

It was near midnight when she parked the car several blocks away from Mrs. Standish's trailer. She covered the remaining distance quickly and was glad to see that the flickering light of the television set was still on. She went to the door and knocked gently. Then the television went silent, as though the old woman had hit the mute button, and Amy knocked again.

She heard slippered feet shuffling toward the door and the porch light over her head went on. Mrs. Standish's face appeared behind the glass, cracked and aged even further by its textures. Then the door opened a few inches and Amy smelled the reek of the smoke and the woman's breath.

"You again? What you comin' so late for? I told him about your money and he didn't care, had other things on his mind."

"I know," Amy said.

Mrs. Standish eyed her warily. "You *know*?"

"I think you'd better let me in, Mrs. Standish. Your son is dead."

The woman's face went soft for a moment and Amy thought that at last she glimpsed motherly concern. She pushed past Mrs. Standish and walked inside, pulling the door closed behind her. The only lights were from a small table lamp, the TV set, and the red glow of an electric space heater, whose grill guard had long since fallen off.

"Sit down, ma'am," Amy said, and stood waiting until Mrs. Standish sat in a small easy chair and fumbled for a cigarette, lighting it and taking in deep breaths of smoke. "William died bravely," Amy said. "Honorably. He wanted me to tell you that he tried."

"You ain't from no Publishers' Clearing."

"No."

"How'd he get killed?"

"He was going to tell the truth. To the papers. But a man stopped him. Killed him. Before he died, he told me where to find the other killers, the ones who . . . who blew up that child care center."

For a long while the old woman said nothing. Then her face twisted slowly into an expression of profound disgust and she shook her head angrily. "That little homo," she said in tones so bitter that they burned Amy's brain. "That damned little nancy boy, I should've killed him in the womb. I knew, I *knew* that he'd mess up whatever he got involved with. Little *coward* . . ."

Amy's mouth tasted of blood and metal. "He died trying to tell the truth," she said dully.

"He died betraying *patriots,*" she said. "He was gonna turn 'em all in, wasn't he? All those good boys! His own father, God rest his soul, woulda killed him, he'da known that!"

"You're with them . . ." Amy said. "You *support* them . . ."

"Well, where the hell you think Will got it from in the first place, the TV? You're damn right—his daddy got him into the Sons. His daddy was a Klansman and his daddy before him and there wasn't a one of us wasn't proud of that." The old woman jammed her cigarette in an ashtray and pushed herself to her feet. "And you think you're gonna tell what he told you? Hell you are, not while there's a breath in *my* body . . ."

Mrs. Standish reached to her right side, down between the cushion and the chair, and came up holding a small revolver with a large bore. But just as she pulled the trigger, Amy cupped the pistol in her hands.

The sound of the shot was loud and it felt as if someone had pounded Amy's hands with a sledgehammer, but she took the pistol away and dropped it on the floor. Then she held out her hands so the woman could see them.

There was a hole and a black powder burn in her left palm, but in a matter of seconds it had closed up before Mrs. Standish's eyes and the burn had faded into white flesh. Mrs. Standish looked at Amy's hand in awe, then up at her face. "You're the *devil,*" she whispered.

Amy took her hands and put them on either side of Mrs. Standish's face, cupping her gaunt and stubbly cheeks. "Yes," Amy said. "I'm a devil. And an angel. I came back from the dead for my children—now you go *to* the dead to beg mercy from your own."

And with her hands she snapped the old woman's head backward until the brain stem kinked and the neck bones cracked and her eyes rolled up in their sockets. Her face became as empty and hollow as her heart and Amy knew she was in the country to which her son had preceded her, the dark country from which Amy had returned to bring death to such as she.

Amy spread her arms apart, letting the lifeless head fall to the side and carry the body to the floor, where it struck with a heavy thud, echoing in the blackness under the trailer. Amy stood still for a moment, listening to hear if there was any response to the shot. But there was none and she ransacked the trailer, opening drawers, reading letters and papers to see if there was anything that would help her find the Sons of a Free America.

After a twenty-minute search Amy came to the conclusion that this supporter of the Sons covered her tracks carefully. There was not a single mention of any of the names that Will Standish had given her, not even in the small second bedroom that housed a chilling collection of Klan memorabilia and a small library of racist books and pamphlets. In the back of the closet were two boxes of boys' books, among them the Hardy Boys and Tom Swift, which proved to her that the Standish family had lived here for many years.

This trailer, Amy thought, had been a breeding ground that had taken a young boy who liked adventure books and turned him into a man trained to hate, and who had only stopped when he saw what that hatred had done. Will Standish, Amy thought, might have been an intelligent man. The skill of his writings proved that. But he had not been wise enough to see the lies through the veils of revelation. Maybe he joined the militia to prove his own manhood, to deny to himself and the world that he was gay, if indeed he was, as his mother had suggested.

To this sick and twisted slice of humanity that used the lying label of patriots, anyone who believed other than they did was a queer, a liberal, a nigger lover, gook lover, Jew lover. Amy would be all of those and more. They hated these things because they feared them, and Amy would give them one more thing to fear. Death.

Already two of them were dead, along with the old woman. That would make them afraid. And soon she would destroy them all, would burn out this viper's brood.

The thought of fire reminded her of the space heater she had seen. It would be a good way to start the purge. This den, at least, would breed no more monsters.

She moved the heater over to the side of the couch, on whose arm hung an assortment of afghans and antimacassars. Then she tipped it over and watched as the glowing red coils met the filaments of cloth. In a few seconds the arm of the couch was smoldering. In a few minutes it would be ablaze.

Amy walked out of the trailer, closing the door securely behind her. Let it become a furnace, she thought. Let it punch out the windows and fling wide the doors. Let the reign of fire and death begin.

Let the fire devour. And let the fear come down.

20

A few minutes after Amy returned to David Levinson's house at three A.M., he came out of the guest bedroom in a bathrobe. "Well, at least I got a few hours sleep this time," he said, then glanced down at her hands. "There's blood on your hands. Care to tell me where it came from?"

"Not really. What would be the point?"

"If I find that there have been any unsolved murders committed tonight, I'm going to be very suspicious."

"And if you are," she said, "what can you do about it? Are you going to arrest a dead woman? Tell your superiors that Amy Carlisle, who was blown to bits, committed these crimes?"

"Amy Carlisle exists. Therefore she wasn't blown up. She escaped the blast and now she's getting her revenge. *That's* what I tell them."

"You don't believe that. You could have believed that at the start, when you first saw me, but you didn't."

"No. Because of the Crow and because of, well, I just knew. And I was right. But what if you're traced here?"

"I won't be. Except for you, not a living soul knows I exist."

"A *living* soul, huh? I can't wait to read the police reports tomorrow."

"Levinson," said Amy, "either you're with me or you're against me. If you're against me, then tell me right now and I'll leave and you'll never see me again. I'll find somewhere else to go. But if you're for me, then leave me be. Let me do what I came back to do, what you *know* I must do. You know that I came back for blood, for vengeance. That's my job. Are you going to let me do it?"

Levinson was silent for a moment, then he nodded his head. "Just try to see to it that it's only the bad guys that get hurt."

"It will be. And it *has* been."

"That's what I was afraid of. By the way, maybe not a living soul knows you exist but there are a hell of a lot of people who've heard your voice today."

"What do you mean?"

"I mean the Wilson Barnes show. The news media has been playing the tape every half hour. I have it memorized: 'Who was it, Wilson Barnes? Your tongue, I promise you.' And then she says, 'Tell me who the bastards are,' and finally, 'This confession brought to you by Wilson Barnes.' Barnes tried to bluff it out but apparently the Sons of a Free America didn't take it lightly. I—and the world—suspect that they're the ones who popped him."

"Who are the Sons of a Free America?" Amy asked, not letting any emotion show. She had known something like this would happen.

"That's what nobody knows. There isn't a trace or a whisper of this group anywhere. They sound like a militia but who knows? This state's got so many woods on private land that you could train an army and nobody'd be the wiser. And even if the police or the FBI could find out where they were, so what? They're not tied to anything in particular—except maybe the death of Wilson Barnes. No, only somebody with no official attachments could actually *do* anything about these people." Levinson cocked his head. "Sound like anyone we know?"

Amy didn't answer. "I'll be in the basement," she said.

She was scary as hell, thought David Levinson. Her eyes were cold when she spoke to him and it was easy to believe that there was actually no life in them.

But while he was afraid of her, he reveled in knowing that there was an avenger out there, resolute and invulnerable. And as he watched Amy go through the basement door, down into her lair, he was glad that she was there, glad that someone could treat this anti-Semitic garbage the way they treated his people when they got the chance.

He would have liked to have found them, have given Amy Carlisle the run for her money that she, and justice, deserved. But she had the passion and the motive and the power to try these men outside of the courts and execute them without going through the process of appeals. Appeals to Amy Carlisle would have been futile.

And what if the worst scenario happened and Amy got linked to him? He didn't think that she would let that happen, but if she did? Well, fuck it. He just didn't know and he didn't really care. He had had enough in Detroit of seeing scum walk free to kill again and he had tried to escape it. But sometimes you just had to stop and make a stand.

Sheltering Amy Carlisle wasn't especially proactive; in fact, it was downright passive. But it was the best he could do for now and he would keep on doing it until all the scumbags were dead or somebody stopped him.

Amy's first attempt at finding one of the names Will Standish had given her was a huge success. Chip Porter had his own website and by the time Amy finished examining its contents, she knew she had the right man.

Chip's Internet carrier was Rangenet and his site included a photo of Porter that showed a young man with close-cropped hair and a long, thin face. There were several strange pale spots on the jpeg's skin tone and Amy thought Porter might have digitally removed his pimples. If every one of the spots was a blemish, this guy was a real pus-face.

It made sense, though, considering that his brain was probably a mass of pus as well. The website's contents were hateful in every way, with short essays written by Porter about the virtues of white supremacy, the usual bullshit about Jews controlling the government, and dozens of links to other anti-Semitic and white supremacist sites.

But Porter, she discovered, wasn't just a bigot, he was a cyberbigot. Apparently he knew his computers and had devoted one area of his site to pranks to play on your on-line enemies, be they government sites or people whose names ended with "stein." Spamming, sending endless faxes, e-mailing false messages, locking up networks of liberal, Jewish, or black organizations—the list went on and on, always with a disclaimer that you *could* do these things but the webmaster wasn't *promoting* them.

Porter's passion for trickery was matched only by his love of skinhead music. There was a large section with profiles of skinhead "artists," and reviews of CDs apparently available only by mail or at special shows. It was doubtful, Amy thought, that Sam Goody was going to stock *Burn 'Em Up* by the Yidkickers or the Krazy Klanboyz's *Black Ain't Beautiful.*

Then she got a real surprise. Though she had as yet come across little information of a personal nature about Chip Porter, she discovered that he was in a white power band called Shoktrupz, pronounced *shock troops*, she assumed. She found it amusing how many of these anti-black groups used the "z" plural made popular by the "niggaz" and "homeboyz" they hated so much.

Though Porter's band had no album out, he had posted the lyrics of their best-known song, "White the Power," and they were as inept and ignorant as Amy had thought they might be. There was also a picture of

Shoktrupz, good little leather-clad, skinheaded Aryans all, and the band's itinerary, such as it was, was listed. There was only one gig in November, none in December, and another in January.

The November date, however, was the following Sunday, a "White Christian Brotherhood" festival held at a fairground just north of Eau Claire, Wisconsin, a short drive southeast of the Twin Cities. There would be nationally known speakers, bands on two stages, vendors, and food in two different buildings. Everyone who "hates Jews, mongrels, and all anti-Christians is invited."

How, Amy thought, could she refuse an invitation like that? But that was two days away. Amy couldn't just sit on her hands so she searched for the next name on her mental list, Junior Feeley. That one sounded like an intellectual giant.

She searched for "Feeley, Jr." and hit pay dirt, finding the name, Clarence Feeley, Jr., on a list of registered arms traffickers. A little more searching and she came up with a gun show that would be held Saturday at the Holiday Inn in Hobie.

The show was held every three months and there was a contact address posted. Amy decided to wait until morning, only a few hours away, to call the number.

In the meantime, she searched for Rip Withers and Powder Burns, both of whose first names she assumed were nicknames. Her search turned up nothing. Burns was a common name and there were dozens of Witherses in a hundred square mile area.

When she was finished, she called the contact number for the gun show. "My husband asked me to call," she said to the man who answered. She spoke quickly, trying to sound like a mother in a hurry, sloppy in her speech. "He wondered if Junior was gonna have a stand at the show tomorrow?"

"Junior," the man said thoughtfully.

"Yeah, Junior something? He told me the last name, but I just remember Junior. Is there a Junior sells guns?"

"Maybe Junior Feeley?"

"*That's* it! Oh yes, thank you, that was the name. Yeah, is he gonna be there, my husband wanted to know?"

"Yeah, I think Junior has a table. He usually does."

"Oh thank you, I mean it, thank you very much. I just *couldn't* remember his name and my husband woulda been so mad 'cause he was gonna take off work to get over there if this Junior was there, and if you wouldn'ta known, well, he woulda been fit to be tied at me. He says I can't remember nothin' and I guess he's right."

"Okay, was there anything else?" the man said impatiently.

"Oh no, no, thank you, that's all."

The man hung up without saying good-bye, probably thinking that he just saved some stupid bitch from getting smacked around by her husband. Dandy. Let him feel good while he could because his little gun show was going to make quite a bang tomorrow.

It was a date between her and Junior Feeley. She had the place and the time. Now she just had to figure out what to wear.

21

He had to look the part if he wanted to be accepted. Or was "accepted" the word? Maybe tolerated could be the most he could hope for at the beginning.

Rick felt certain that these people would be among the most distrustful he had ever met, and with good reason. The books he had read in his crash course on the militia movement indicated that government agents were quietly infiltrating many militia to gather information and evidence that could be used against them. So his cover had to be solid and unbreakable. And he might have to prove himself in some way that he would find distasteful. But he would do what he had to, short of killing.

Rick had told his partners in the firm that he wanted to take a couple of weeks off and they readily agreed. He had continued to work after Amy's death to keep his mind occupied and had only taken a weekend for a cursory honeymoon after he had married Nancy.

Nancy was not as agreeable. She was his wife now and he felt that he had to be honest with her. So he told her what he had not told his partners, that he wanted to take some time to see what he could learn about the bombing. But he did not tell her about seeing Amy at the window. That he kept to himself.

"You can't be serious," Nancy had said in disbelief. "Rick, these monsters took my best friend and the children we both loved. I don't want them to take you too. God, please don't do this."

"It's not . . . much," he said. "I'm just going to some of these meetings, places and functions where they might gather, just to see if I can hear anything. If I do, I'll go straight to the police."

"Why not let them handle the whole thing? The only good that came out of all this was *us*. We picked up the pieces together. Don't throw that away."

"I'm not throwing anything away. I'm not throwing *us* away, Nancy, don't worry. I'm not going to be in any danger."

"Why are you doing this?"

"I'm doing it for Amy."

"But Amy's gone, you can't help her."

"I think I can. And I have to help myself too. I'm doing it for me."

Nancy got angry then and walked out of the room but Rick didn't go after her, although he wanted to. He knew that if he did, if he weakened for a moment, he might allow her to talk him out of this and he didn't want her to.

He knew he had made the right decision an hour later when he was coming back from buying clothes at a local thrift shop and heard Amy's voice on the radio. It had been recorded in the studio the morning that Wilson Barnes had been killed and when he heard it, he became one of only a few people who knew what it was all about. The Sons of a Free America knew it was about the bombing, but only he and Amy and David Levinson knew who the mysterious woman really was.

The sound of her voice shocked him so much that he pulled the car off the road and sat there trembling while he listened to the rest of the story. What the hell did it mean?

It was Amy's voice all right, there was no doubt of it. Had she appeared somewhere else—in that radio studio—in the flesh? But why? So that he would know, that the *world* would know, who was responsible for the bombing?

But the world didn't know, did they? They didn't know what the hell Wilson Barnes was confessing to. Only he knew because only he recognized Amy's voice and made the association. Only he had seen her and knew why her spirit had returned.

The realization put steel into him and he got back into the car and drove on, preparing to disguise himself, to change his looks, his attitude, his desires, to hate this oppressive government and anyone who worked for it. He would become one of them, and then he would find the ones who killed her.

"They killed Sonny," Junior Feeley said. He sounded close to tears.

Rip Withers looked up from his lunch. "What?"

"Sonny's dead," said Junior in a loud, upset voice that made the rest of the men in the mess hall put up their heads and listen.

Rip's belly went hot and he felt blood surge to his face. "The cops?" he asked.

"No . . . they don't know. I heard it on the radio, they . . ."

The mess hall door slammed open and Chip Porter walked in with a sheet of paper in his hand. "Off the local news service," he said and handed it to Rip, who quickly read it, then read it again more slowly before he spoke again, addressing the two dozen men who sat at the tables.

"Weird . . . shit went down last night, men. Let me tell you first of all that there was a traitor in our midst. Our brother Will Standish wasn't our brother at all. He turned on us. He went to the newspapers." There was a sudden uproar and Rip raised his hand for silence.

"No need to worry," he continued. "He never made it. We saw what was happening and Sonny Armitage was assigned to follow him. If Standish showed any signs of capitulation to the enemy, Sonny had orders to terminate him immediately. And when Standish drove to the *Sentinel* building, that's what Sonny did.

"But then something went wrong. Sonny was killed, stabbed to death. They don't say by who. But both Standish and Sonny are dead. I think we can safely assume that Sonny sacrificed his life for the Sons of a Free America." He looked every man there in the face. "Let's not forget him and let's not forget that any one of us may have to make that same sacrifice for our freedoms. This is a dangerous time and now that our activities are increasing, now that our attempts to bring down this godless, evil government are touching these villains so close to home, we need Yahweh's help more than ever to keep our courage up and our hearts on fire for Him. Let's all pray."

Rip Withers prayed aloud for Sonny Armitage's soul and when he was finished, everyone said amen and put their right fists over their hearts. Then Rip called Ray and Junior and Powder Burns and Chip Porter together and they went to Rip's cabin.

"All right," Rip said. "One thing that I didn't say because it wouldn't mean a lot to the men, and frankly, I'm not sure what it means myself, is that old Mrs. Standish is dead too." The men's faces registered surprise and Rip nodded. "I know," he said. "She was one helluva good old woman. Sent us twenty dollars a month for the cause. I met her a couple of times and I never knew how a woman that feisty could have given birth to a mama's boy like Will Standish."

"He was a good writer," said Ray.

It wasn't worth a reply, Rip thought. "They found Mrs. Standish in her trailer. It had burned up, pretty much destroyed everything inside, but there was enough of her left that the papers reported her neck was broken. That doesn't happen in a fire. The papers didn't have any theory yet about how it all happened—probably they want to get their stories cooked up so it looks as bad for the patriot movement as possible. But as far as I can see it, there are a couple different possibilities. The first is that Sonny stabbed Will and then Will stabbed him."

"That's a crock," Junior Feeley said. "Sonny'd never let Will get the drop on him that way, especially after Sonny stuck him. Hell, you know Will, he got hurt, he'd whimper like a goddam puppy and wait to die."

"You're right, Junior," Rip said. "And that's why I don't think that scenario's any too likely. I think probably what happened is that there was somebody else there. Sonny kills Will and this other guy kills Sonny."

"But then," said Ray slowly, "who killed Will's mama? Sonny?"

"Hell no," said Powder. "He was followin' Will, right? So why would he take the time to kill the old lady and then go after Will? Especially if he had orders to keep on Will's ass? And why the hell would he kill Will's mama anyway? She was a fine old lady, even if her boy was a shit."

"What if," Chip Porter said, "that third person you're talking about, Rip—what if *he* went out and killed Will's mama?"

"Why?" Junior said, struggling to follow the logic. "If he killed Sonny, it was because Sonny killed Will. So that means this guy *liked* Will. If he liked him, why would he kill his mama?" He shook his head, "Shit, this is confusing."

"Unless," Rip said, thinking it through, "this guy liked Will betraying us and knew that his mama was *for* us." Then Rip remembered the voice of the woman from Wilson Barnes's final show. "Or maybe not this guy—maybe this *girl.*"

"What?" several of the men said.

"Look, what about that woman who was on with Barnes the other night—who got him to say our name?"

"You sayin' some *woman* stuck Sonny Armitage?" Powder asked in disbelief.

"I'm just saying it's a possibility," Rip answered. "You don't rule anything out if you wanta stay alive."

Junior snickered. "Day you catch me lookin' over my shoulder 'cause I'm afraid of a woman—"

"—Will be the day you're a whole lot smarter than you are, Junior," Rip finished. "Makes more sense to be scared of a crazy woman than it does a little deer trotting through the woods. I'm just saying let's be on our toes. This could be anybody, we don't know. Maybe some mother went ballistic and decides to start hunting down people she thinks had something to do with the bombing."

"Wait a minute, Rip," said Powder. "A *mommy* goes wacko, breaks into Wilson Barnes's studio, past his guard, gets him to give our name over the air, then knifes Sonny, breaks Will's mother's neck, and torches her place. We talkin' Wonder Woman here?"

"All *right,* you assholes!" Rip shouted. There was too much bullshit smartmouthing here. It was time to retake command. "I'm saying don't take a fucking *thing* for granted, okay? It could be a man, a woman, a bunch of kids, your fucking *grandmother,* all right? It could be the last man you drank with, the last woman you fucked, the last Salvation Army lady you gave a nickel to, that's what I'm saying and that's *all* I'm saying! So don't give me any shit about it unless you know exactly who it is! Do I make myself *clear,* gentlemen?"

Muttered yeahs and a yessir from Junior Feeley filled the room for a few seconds and then they were all quiet again.

"This isn't going to change a thing," Rip said. "When it comes to the big strike, we're going to do exactly what we've been planning, and on our schedule. As far as everything else . . . Junior, you're still going to the gun show tomorrow."

"I need somebody else to help me," Junior whined. "I can't carry in all that stuff alone."

"And you'll have somebody. I'm sending Karl along with you."

"Karl? Jeez, Rip, I know he's your boy and all but can he handle—"

"He can damn well handle anything you can, Junior. He'll tote those gun cases just fine. And I'll look on it as a personal favor if you take good care of him."

Junior Feeley nodded and tried to smile but it didn't work too well. Damn, he was going to miss Sonny Armitage. He and Sonny were buds. And Sonny was so great at getting the customers talking real easy, and about more than just guns.

Sonny would find out what they thought of the government's gun control laws and then he'd lead that into other directions and find out about them personally, if they hated Clinton, hated Jews, hated niggers, and if they were willing to do anything about it; in short, if they were prospective members of the Sons.

Hell, it didn't make much difference whether they sold any guns or not, though Junior personally got a cut of the profits when they did. The main reason they had a table was to recruit members. They did it slow and carefully, maybe talking to a guy three or four times before finally inviting him to a private meeting with Rip. Sometimes it worked out, sometimes it didn't. But they never told so much that anybody they had read wrong would go running to the cops and the feds. When they got turndowns, most of the time it was along the lines of: *Well, this sounds like a great organization, but I'm afraid it's just not for me. More time than I could manage, with my job and the wife and kids—I'd just miss that too much. But hey, I think it's really great what you're doing and I'd like to make a contribution, you know? I'll pray for you too, I promise you that.*

No, by the time they got to that point, they knew they were good people. Not once had anybody even tried to rat on them. And maybe one time out of four you'd get a new member, someone who *was* willing to give up more than some money, someone dedicated to the work and to God and the White Race. And Sonny had been an expert at landing those big fish.

Another reason Junior was going to miss Sonny was that Sonny understood Junior's little quirks, the things he liked to do with the bimbos at the gun shows when he and Sonny could talk them into going out with them after the show closed.

He had let Sonny do the smooth stuff, telling them come on, it'll be fun, a few drinks, a few laughs, because Sonny was a pretty good-looking guy, and really well built. Junior was husky, and even though a lot of it was muscle, he looked fat, there was no use denying it.

And he farted a lot too, especially when he got excited, and the bimbos didn't like *that* at *all.* But generally by the time Junior got excited and started farting, he didn't give much of a shit what they liked or didn't like. One time when one of the bitches had started calling him names, he had done a whole lot worse than fart in her face. Call him a fucking pig and he'd damn well live up to it.

But now here he was stuck with Rip's kid, a skinny, eighteen year old who looked like he'd piss himself if you so much as yelled boo, let alone *"federal troops outside the compound!"* Well, Junior would just have to make of it what he could. Maybe he could dump the kid somewhere after the show, stick him in the game room or something, and go to one of the bimbo's rooms. He might have to pay one this time and the thought of it pissed him off since he never had to pay with Sonny. Dammit, he *missed* Sonny.

Of course, there was always the chance the kid might be ready for some action. Still waters ran deep and a man had to be a man, that was something that everybody in the Sons agreed on. Women were men's helpmeets, just like the Bible said, and they were supposed to be subservient to men, and as far as Junior was concerned, that meant they fucked when you wanted to fuck and if they gave you any shit, then they deserved it if things got rough.

The more he thought about it, Junior kind of liked the idea of holding one of those little gun-honeys down for the kid. In fact, he got a big ticket to Bonerville as he imagined it in more detail. Sure, let Rip's kid have first crack at it, get the bitch wet and warmed up for him and then Junior would have his fun. It might be a pretty damn good gun show after all.

Of course, he'd still miss Sonny. He was his bud.

22

"Arnie, I got a favor to ask."

Arnie Bailey made his *Christ, what now?* face and looked at Cyndi with his head cocked over almost onto his shoulder. "What?"

"I'm not feelin' so good," Cyndi said. "I think I swallowed some bad fish last night at dinner."

You swallowed some bad something after dinner was what Arnie wanted to say but he didn't. Instead he abruptly beckoned Cyndi into his room. "So what are you saying, we come all the way up from St. Paul and now you don't wanta do what you came to do? I already paid you half your money, Cyndi, *and* your hotel room and the per diem. So now I'm supposed to have only one girl holding up the guns?"

"Hell, no, I wouldn't do that to Tracy. I got another girl."

"What, come up from the agency? This morning already?"

"No, she's from here in Hobie. Name's Arlene. I met her last night, she was saying that she'd like to model sometime, and she was pretty good-looking, maybe a little older, like thirty or so. But a really good body, Arnie, honest. Flat stomach, never had a baby, y'know? So I gave her a call this morning and she said she'd *love* to do it. I can pay her out of my own pocket, from what you pay me."

"Yeah, well, that's between you two. What *I* want is a woman looks good in a two-piece, nice tits, nice ass."

"Oh, she's got good breasts, not *huge,* but good. Good butt too."

"You let me be the judge of that. Where is this Arlene?"

"Down in my room."

"Get her up here. Christ, the show starts in a half hour."

* * *

Amy Carlisle was looking at herself in the mirror in Cyndi Rose's room when Cyndi called her from Arnie's. Amy didn't particularly like what she was seeing.

In the high-rise red shorts and the silver halter top that covered the tips of her breasts, more of Amy's flesh was exposed than had ever been seen in public. But it wasn't the exposure that bothered Amy as much as the flesh itself.

The tiny, veined lines were there if one looked closely enough and although they were not nearly as deep as the wrinkles of age, Amy felt they gave her away, told everyone with a probing eye that she had been sewn together in a Frankensteinian experiment that had succeeded all too well.

Perhaps she was too rough on herself, she thought. If you didn't use a magnifying glass, her body looked good in the tiny outfit. Yet that thought made her uncomfortable as well.

She would be an object of desire but her flesh was dead, blasted into fragments and reassembled. To parade herself in front of men seemed an act of reverse necrophilia, a dead woman craving sexual attention. And the men who desired her would have no idea what she actually was, a revenant, a body that existed for the purpose of revenge, of making the wrong things right.

She tried to put the thought from her mind. She had to be what she appeared to be, a seductress with a gun. The red-haired wig helped, as did the extra layer of makeup she had put on. She doubted if anyone would have recognized her, even the Crow.

But as quickly as that thought came, she dismissed it. The Crow had known her even as dust. This tawdry disguise would not fool it for a second.

When the phone rang, Amy picked it up. As she had guessed, it was Cyndi calling from Arnie's room. Amy said she would be right up.

Cyndi seemed like a nice girl. It was a shame she had to flaunt her body (and more, Amy suspected) for a bunch of gun nuts. For all her hard-boiled surface, though, the girl seemed naive, immediately accepting Amy's story the night before after Amy found out that she worked as a gun show "model" for a dealer with a string of stores in the Twin Cities area.

Listen, hon, you could do me such a favor . . . See, my boyfriend is flying in tomorrow and we were gonna meet at the gun show, because that's what he's comin' in for mostly, oh, to see me, sure, but that boy's just crazy about guns, so much so that he just ignores me times like this. And I was thinkin' that if he was to see me in a cute little outfit, you know, showin' a lot of skin and all, and holdin' a big old rifle, well, I think that would make him so hot that he'd not only forget about all those guns, but he'd pop the question . . . Oh no, I don't want your boss to hire me or anything like that, I'm just talkin' about takin' your place for a little while, y'know, in the morning? I could make it worth your while too, pay you for the fun of it instead of takin' your money. That way, you get paid twice and don't hafta do anything. Whaddya think?

Cyndi had taken her back to her room and had her strip down, and Amy hadn't had to feign embarrassment. *Oh sure, I'll be okay tomorrow, I won't be shy at all, why, you should see what I wear at the beach. But I guess I feel a little funny lettin' another woman see what I got, I mean, I'm a man's woman, you know what I mean?*

Cyndi had assured her that she was a man's woman too and only wanted to see her "credentials" because as sure as God made little green apples, Arnie would want to see them before Amy (or Arlene, as she called herself) hit the show floor in the morning. Cyndi accepted the hundred dollar offer to play sick so quickly that Amy wished she had offered less but then thought what the hell, it was right out of dead Sonny Armitage's wallet and it still left her with three hundred more.

So now she pulled on her denim slacks and her leather jacket and trotted upstairs to see Arnie. He was about what she had expected, in his late forties, a little paunchy, and with dyed hair that he had carefully spread out to make it look fuller. His face, however, was almost handsome and she bet that he had been a lady-killer in his younger days.

He didn't smile when he saw her, however, and there wasn't the trace of a come-on. He just said, "Okay, let's see what you got," and gestured to the jacket. She was glad that Cyndi was still in the room, encouraging her with a close-mouthed smile.

Amy unzipped the jacket and shrugged it off, then stepped out of her pants. Arnie looked her up and down, then spun his right hand, index finger downward, as though he were stirring batter. "Turn," he said. She did, slowly, until she was facing him again. He gave a businesslike nod. "Okay, you'll be fine. Cyndi, fill her in on the do's and don'ts, then go back to bed. You look like shit."

Cyndi lost her smile after that but she demonstrated with several rifles that Arnie had in his room, showing Amy how to hold them up and turn, how to work the bolt-actions, and how to snap in the magazines of the semiautomatics.

"Do it as loud as you can," Cyndi said. "It gets the guys' attention and they love to see a girl work the guns, it's like phallic or something."

"You mean like we're handling their . . ."

"Yeah," Cyndi said, and giggled. "That's it. Now don't worry about questions. Arnie answers all the questions and makes all the sales."

"Do we ever really load the guns?"

"Uh-uh. That's like against the law or something. But we sell the bullets and stuff from under the table. Look, you got any other questions, Tracy will help you out, she's the other girl, okay?"

Tracy wasn't nearly as friendly as Cyndi. Amy suspected it was because she was older and looked on Amy as more of a rival than Cyndi did. As far as Amy was concerned, Tracy didn't have to worry about a thing. She was a knockout. An inch or two taller than Amy, who was five foot eight in flats, she had a pair of large, high breasts which Amy suspected were surgically enhanced. Her shining black hair was perfect for her dark complexion and her slim waist led down to tight and muscular buttocks and perfect thighs. Her face was thin and exotic and Amy felt pedestrian next to her.

Fine. Let Tracy get the attention, Amy thought. That way she would be free to do what she had to do.

"Whoa," said Junior Feeley softly, "whadda we got here?"

Junior had left Karl back at their booth while he made a little tour of the gun-honeys. With well over two hundred displays in the large meeting room, there had to be a nice selection of pussy.

But as he cruised down the aisles, he realized that he had seen most of them before and when they saw him, they looked away. There wasn't any point in trying any lines with them. They either had experienced Junior's peccadilloes personally or had heard about them in no uncertain terms. It was fresh meat he was looking for. Fresh and dumb.

And he thought he found it over at Arnie Bailey's booth, all the way at the end of the big room. There were two girls working there, wearing tight little shorts and even littler halter tops that turned the place into Titty City. One was a brunette Junior had seen before. Bitch's name was Stacy or Tracy or something, and she had actually pulled a blade on him in a hallway when he had tried to press her up against the wall for a little dryhump. Mean woman, not worth messing with.

It was the redhead that caught his eye and promised possibilities. She was a little older than most of the models but had a nice build, long and tall, the way Junior liked them, and he thought his fat ass would look pretty good sitting on those tits. Besides, he *loved* redheads, especially if they were natural. This one's hair kind of looked like a wig, but hell, that was okay. In Junior's experience, natural redheads were scarcer than honest Jews or smart niggers.

He decided not to say anything to her right away but to come back and talk to her later. It was almost nine and the doors would open soon, spilling hundreds of gun nuts and potential militiamen into the aisles.

Junior knew there was no way that young Karl was going to be able to handle the rush. Big Red would have to wait until later.

Rick Carlisle tried to make himself feel at home in the throng waiting to go into the gun show. He was dressed correctly, anyway, in a worn red wool shirt, green duck pants that were thin at the knees, and low, thick-soled boots with heavy laces. It seemed to be a variation of what every other person there was wearing.

Some of the men waiting outside with him were talking to each other but many stood silently, watching the doors. Older, white-haired hunters gathered in small groups. Some wore jackets with state wildlife patches that dated back decades. They seemed serious and professional, as though expecting to find something to help them retain the aim that aging and shaking hands were spoiling. They reminded Rick of his father's hunting companions.

Rick had nothing against guns. His father had hunted and Rick had too when he was a boy. But he had lost interest as he grew older. He recalled a lot of his dad's gun-toting friends as good, decent men who obeyed the game laws and mostly ate what they killed. He assumed the older hunters here followed that pattern. But he wasn't so sure about the younger ones.

There were a lot of loud young men with shaven heads, Doc Martens, and military surplus coats who, if they had ever taken aim, had probably had humans in their sights rather than deer. More than a few of these skinheads were wearing white power buttons and Rick saw one with an SS patch sewn on his sleeve. The older hunters' conversations seemed genteel compared to the skinheads', which were sprinkled with swear words that brought them several hard looks from their elders.

There was also a contingent of men in their thirties and forties that seemed more political in nature. Most of these men wore full beards or mustaches and had on camouflage clothing and campaign hats. A few wore shoulder patches or caps that identified them as belonging to a militia, and Rick glimpsed a T-shirt beneath a camouflage vest that read *Just Say No to ZOG.* One of the older hunters noticed it too and asked its wearer, a bearded man with a ruddy tan, who ZOG was.

"Zionist occupied government," the man replied in an angry tone.

Jesus, what a crew, Rick thought. Firearms made strange bedfellows, everybody from legal hunters to neo-Nazis to militia nuts, all looking for something that goes bang.

Then the double doors rattled as though someone were unlocking them and at the same time a black shape shot from above the roof, casting a shadow on the men below. Rick, like most of those waiting, jumped at the sudden movement, then saw that it was only a crow, large as a hawk and black as night, that must have been sitting on the roof and been startled from its perch by the rattling of the doors.

A few of the men laughed and aimed imaginary shotguns and pistols at the bird, which was placidly drifting toward the trees across the parking lot. They yelled, "Pow!" and "Blammo!" as their fingers pulled the air triggers and they laughed again.

Then the crow circled and came back toward them, flapping its wings with an easy and enviable economy of movement until it was directly above them, its wings outspread, riding the wind, moving neither forward nor back. It hung magically suspended in space as the sun suddenly vanished behind dark clouds.

The sight was eerie, uncanny, and a silence fell over the crowd. Then a few men laughed uneasily and a young skinhead raised his arms to mimic shooting once more, opening his mouth to imitate a gun's roar. But something in the mien of the crow hovering above them, wings outstretched like arms giving a blessing or a curse, stopped him and he lowered his hands with another edgy laugh.

Then suddenly the doors screeched open and latched into place and the crow swept away out of sight. The crowd, forgetting the crow in their excitement, surged into the building like an amoeba, splitting in a hundred different directions when they got inside the large room.

Rick found a spot from which he could observe a large part of the chaos and decided to home in on the booths that catered to the paramilitary crowd. He had worked up his cover story but he didn't know whether he would have the chance to use it. Maybe everybody here was just interested in selling and buying guns.

As he strolled throughout the room, he was amazed at the number of different ways there were to deal death. There were booths that catered to hunters but he wondered what kind of hunters would go after wildlife with the semiautomatic assault weapons that many of the vendors displayed.

Most of them were obviously designed to kill men, to allow the shooter to fire just as fast as he could pull the trigger. There were stands that sold sniper rifles, assault rifles, short-barrel military shotguns (some with bayonets), and even assault shotguns with round magazines that looked to Rick like pregnant tommy guns.

Rick was also surprised to see a number of scantily clad women behind the tables holding up rifles and pistols and shotguns and parading back and forth with them in the few square feet they had to move. It was one hell of a draw, as the tables with the models had the lion's share of customers. Most of the women were playing their roles to the hilt, giving lascivious looks to all the passersby and bending over to deepen their cleavage whenever a man looked their way. Rick, embarrassed, avoided their glances, keeping his attention focused on the arms sold at the tables and searching for other signs that would, against all odds, lead him to his quarry.

When Amy saw Rick, she froze for a moment. Then knowing that the sudden stillness would only draw attention to her, she continued to do her assigned work, snapping in magazines and detaching them from the weapons she held.

Still, her thoughts fragmented as she performed the automatic actions. What was Rick doing here? He wasn't a hunter. Could he be looking for a pistol to defend the home that he now shared with Nancy, to protect his new family? If so, why didn't he go to a sporting goods store or a gun shop?

And why was he wearing those clothes? They weren't like Rick at all. It almost seemed as though he were in disguise . . .

Then she realized that was exactly the situation. He *was* disguised—just as she was. They were both hunting, acting as bait for the predators that they wanted to make their prey. He also had come here to find those responsible for the bombing.

But things were different with Rick, she thought. He wasn't a hunter, he wasn't up to this. He had never wet his hands with human blood. She had. It was why she was here, why the Crow had brought her back, and no harm could come to her.

It wasn't the same for Rick. Amy knew what these people were capable of. They had shot Wilson Barnes, and the man she had killed in the garage had gutted William Standish like a pig. Even the old woman had been potentially deadly. They wouldn't hesitate to kill Rick in a minute if they thought that he endangered them.

And her shock at seeing him was further intensified by their confrontation through the window the other morning. What would he think if he saw her now?

But he wasn't looking in her direction or at any of the half-clad women scattered here and there in the booths. That was like him, she thought, and smiled. He had always had an embarrassingly puritanical streak. He passed Arnie's booth without a glance at her, his eyes remaining on the guns on the table, and moved down the aisle, toward the front of the room.

"Like lockin' and loadin', sweetie?" said a tall, rangy man who was staring at her chest. "Or was that smile for me?"

"That smile," she said, "is for anyone who purchases a new weapon from Arnie's Arms, sir."

"Fat chance," said the man. "Got my own stand down there. But I don't have any pussy to look at." He laughed and smacked his buddy on the shoulder. Then with one more appraising look at Amy, who felt naked under his eyes, he headed back toward his stand.

It was an oppressive morning of being eyed and ogled. Never before had she felt like such a piece of meat, hung up for all the wolves to admire. The feminine draw worked, however, for Arnie was doing a good business, steadily selling ammo and guns and filling out the endless array of government forms that were required with each purchase.

And while she was examined by the passing crowd, Amy examined them as well, looking at the name tags the dealers wore, reading each one to find a name that she recognized—Rip Withers, Chip Porter, Powder Burns, whoever those bastards were, and especially Junior Feeley. And then after she had swatted them all, she had to find the nest those creatures had crawled out of.

During her five-minute breaks she got ready for them. Arnie had thoughtfully arranged a curtain at the back of the booth that gave one girl a four-by-eight-foot area to sit and relax in while the other drew all the stares. He had stored arms and ammo back there too and Amy had been "lockin' and loadin' " on every break, then replacing the fully loaded weapons back in their small crates.

She had already loaded a 9 mm Weaver Nighthawk and four magazines, giving her a hundred and twenty-five rounds, and a Cobray M11/Nine, a semiautomatic machine pistol that she intended to fire while changing magazines on the Night-hawk. As an afterthought, she loaded an old Army .45 to stick in her belt as backup if one of the others jammed.

All she needed now was Junior Feeley to wander by, and the gun nuts would see some real action.

23

Rick slowed at one of the stands halfway to the door. There were a number of weapons and boxes of ammo on the table but what drew his attention was a small stack of red-covered paperbacks. On the cover a man and a woman were firing guns at an unseen target. It was *The Turner Diaries,* the book that had supposedly helped to inspire Timothy McVeigh and was considered a second Bible to the militia movement.

He picked it up and started to flip through the pages, careful not to look too interested or to look at the people behind the table. "Y'ever read that?" one of the people asked and Rick looked up at him. He was built like a six-and-a-half-foot fireplug, tall and heavy, and wearing a camouflage vest over a green flannel shirt. His name tag read "Clarence Feeley, Jr." with "Dealer" underneath.

"Yes, I did. Some years ago."

"Yeah? How'd you like it?"

Rick smiled. "It is one helluva book. Oh, it's a great story but I liked it more for what it said, you know? About . . . the way things are."

"Changed my life," said Feeley. "How 'bout you, Karl?" he asked the boy sitting next to him. His face was spotless and Rick wondered if he even shaved. His eyes were blue and fringed with long lashes. His nose and mouth were small, almost petite, and he had a little smile in which Rick could see no trace of guile. He looked like a Norman Rockwell teenager crossed with a Giotto angel and he was wearing a small button with a picture of Bill Clinton and the words "Wanted for Treason."

"I liked it a lot," the boy said in a soft, shy voice. His smile widened, just a little.

"Well, I lost my copy a long time ago," Rick said. "I'll take one." He handed Feeley a twenty and accepted the change.

"You a shooter?" Feeley asked him.

"Aw, a little. Don't hunt, though. Mostly interested in self-defense. I really didn't come to the show for the guns, but for stuff like this." He held up the book. "You're the only one selling anything like it though." He started to move away, hoping that Feeley would call him back, and he wasn't disappointed.

"Whaddya mean, stuff like this?" Feeley said.

"Oh, you know," Rick said, turning back, "stuff a little more political. I heard some groups have stands at shows like this, militia and such. Little disappointing, though."

"Well," said Feeley with a smile, "you gotta know where to look. There are sympathetic folks around but you don't wanta be too obvious about it."

"Why?" Rick said. "Because of the goddam government?"

"Part of it."

"Shit, they got their fingers in everything. Every time you turn around, they're telling you what to do and how to do it. Fuckers." He glanced at the boy. "Excuse me, son." The boy shrugged, as though he had heard worse. "They took an awful lot from me," he added softly.

"Yeah?" said Feeley? "Like what?"

Rick fixed him with a hard look. "Why should I tell you?"

"You don't have to tell me *shit,*" Feeley flared. "Just making conversation. What, you think I'm a fucking fed or something? Hey, asshole, you don't have to talk to me."

Rick shook his head apologetically. "Sorry. It's just that I gotta be careful." Feeley eyed him suspiciously and Rick snorted a laugh. "There are people'd like to find me."

"You telling me you're wanted?" Feeley said with a smirk of disbelief.

Rick looked around uncomfortably. "Well, I ain't public enemy number one, but, uh, yeah, I'm what you might call a felon, if believing that you got a right to be free in your own country is a crime. I guess it is."

Feeley gestured him closer. "What'd you do?" he asked softly.

"Look, I don't wanta talk about it, not with all these people around. You never know who's who, know what I mean?"

"You wanta grab a beer?" Feeley asked. "Trade you a beer for your story."

Rick smiled as though he had found a comrade. "A fed wouldn't make an offer like that—you're on."

"Watch the place, Karl," Feeley told the boy, then ducked under the table and together they made their way to the bar.

They sat at a back table. There was only a glimpse of the outside but Rick could see that the dark clouds, the ones that had begun to gather when the crow had flown overhead, were now pouring down rain. Feeley ordered a pitcher of beer and Rick began to improvise the way he had planned, using the details from the books he had read on militias and the patriot movement.

"I just wanted to get off the grid, you know? Lost my job to a nigger, you believe that, after six years? And this is when my wife's dying of cancer so we lost the medical coverage too. Just made her go faster. When she died, wasn't any reason for me to hang around anymore so I figured why not start fresh? I was pissed as hell at the way things had happened. It made me see the only thing a body can depend on is himself. But not enough people believe that, they're too busy sucking at the government tit, everybody without the guts to stand up on their own.

"So I said fuck that, tore up my social security card, driver's license, every damn thing I had that connected me to that nigger-loving Jew government. But though I let *them* alone, they wouldn't let *me* alone. Arrested me for driving without an inspection sticker or registration, but by that time I'd read a lot, you know? And I knew how full of bullshit this government was and I said fuck you, you don't have any jurisdiction over me, and I didn't show up in court. After that, things got nuts . . ."

Rick spun his tale of a man against the system, of how he coldcocked the constable who came to arrest him and stole his car, abandoned it three states away, and made his way to Minnesota because he had heard there were a lot of militias there, places with people who thought the same way he did and into which he could disappear.

"Like a hole in the wall. You know Butch Cassidy and the Sundance Kid? They had their Hole-in-the-Wall Gang and I guess that's what I'm looking for." He looked at Feeley strangely for a moment, then shook his head. "But hell, why am I telling you all this? Just because you're selling this book," he slapped it with his palm, "doesn't mean I can trust you."

"Well, fuck you," said Feeley. "You think I'm a traitor to my race? You think I'm gonna kiss ZOG's sorry ass by turnin' you in? Fuck that . . . fuck that, uh-uh. You wanta meet people, you can maybe meet people, but it isn't as simple as all that, oh no. Now what's your name anyway?"

"I've got no name anymore. I'm just a guy, you know? So I call myself Guy. Guy Adams, since Adam was the first man and Yahweh made him. Yahweh made me what I am too. So that's in honor of Yahweh."

"Okay, Guy Adams, you hang around after the show and maybe I'll introduce you to some people can help you, okay?"

"Why?"

"Huh?"

"Why would you do that for me? For a stranger?"

"Hey, remember what Jesus said? I was a stranger and you took me in, right? Besides, you seem like a really pissed-off guy—hey, *Guy,* get it?—and pissed-off guys make good soldiers."

"You connected?" Rick asked dubiously.

"Am I connected?" Feeley chuckled. "You wait, pal. You wait and see."

They finished the pitcher, mostly talking about who they hated most, but Feeley said nothing more about his "connections." That was all right. Rick could wait. He had gotten his foot in a door. Whether or not it was the right door remained to be seen.

It had been one helluva morning so far, thought Junior Feeley as he rejoined Karl Withers at the table. True, they had hardly sold a damn thing—one secondhand deer rifle, a few boxes of shells, and two books—and it was raining like a sonovabitch outside, but Junior had found one helluva good-looking redhead *and* had turned up a prime candidate for the Sons.

This Guy Adams had new recruit written all over him in the blood of the ZOG oppressors. Junior knew he was going to be just fine and once old Guy got out there to the compound, he wouldn't have to worry about being nailed by ZOG again.

Junior was so delighted at his find that he told Karl all about "Guy Adams" and the kid seemed to be happy at the news, though you could hardly ever tell what he was thinking. Junior couldn't wait to get Karl laid just to see an emotion cross that blandly smiling face of his. It wasn't that the boy was stupid like his Uncle Ray but he just seemed detached somehow, floating above everything in some dream world. Junior hoped that breeding would tell when the war against ZOG began. The kid was a damn good shot if he could ever be bothered to shoot the federals and the niggers and the other mongrel troops that the Jews would send against them some fine day.

Then Junior realized that although his capacious belly was now full of beer, he hadn't eaten since breakfast. "Stay put," he said to Karl. "I'll get us some chow."

Junior walked to the snack bar at the front of the room and bought two orders of fries, two cans of Coke, two hamburgers for himself and two for Karl. If the kid only wanted one, Junior would eat the other one.

On the way back he decided to sidetrack to the booth where he had seen the redhead this morning. Might as well make the little lady's acquaintance. It would be rough without old Sonny along but a lot of girls liked the big and burly type.

There were only a few people in front of the girl's stand. Arnie was filling out a form for some skinhead kid who was holding a fat roll of bills, probably trying to pay cash and give a phony ID so that nothing could be traced to him. The brunette, Tracy or Stacy, was nowhere in sight, but Big Red was strutting her stuff nicely for two lamers standing there watching.

Junior could have picked them up and knocked their heads together, they were so damn thin and skanky. But he only stepped between them, pushing them to either side as he held the cardboard tray with his food in his hammy fists. "Hey, you're new here," he said to the redhead. "I never seen you before. And I'm real, real sorry about that."

The redhead kept smiling as she looked at him and his name tag. She was holding a pump shotgun and she racked it and pointed it at him, widening her eyes innocently. All right, he thought, a playful one, though he felt a little stir in his balls as he looked into the shotgun's mouth.

"Whoa," he said. "Be careful there, red." He glanced down at her tight shorts. "If you *are* a redhead."

"Don't worry . . . Junior," she said in a husky voice that sounded somehow familiar. Then she pointed the muzzle toward the ceiling and pulled the trigger, dry-firing it with a sharp click.

"Hey, hey, Arlene," Arnie said, looking up annoyed from his paperwork, "don't fuck around like that, huh? Don't go pointin' shit at the customers, for crissake."

"It's okay, man," said Junior. "It's empty."

"Yeah, well, dry-firin' ain't good for the guns, Junior, you know that."

"Dry-firin' ain't good for *nothin'*," Junior said suggestively, then lowered his voice so only Arlene could hear, while Arnie turned back to his work. "When I shoot, I always shoot with a full load." He grinned. "So whaddya say, are you really a redhead all the way?"

Arlene held up a finger and set the shotgun on the table, then turned and went toward the back curtain of the booth. Just before she disappeared behind it, she turned and said in a voice that gave Junior a quick ride to Woodville, "You wanta see red, you just wait one minute, Junior."

Shit, Junior thought, what was she gonna do, come out in open crotch panties or something? Or maybe just give him a quick flash of red-haired pussy from behind the curtain? Man, this chick was hot. And she really seemed to dig him too. It almost made him suspicious.

But then she came back out and she wasn't wearing less, she was wearing more, a black leather jacket, and she was holding a gun in each hand, with another one jammed into her shorts.

And she wasn't smiling anymore.

24

When Amy saw the man's name tag, she felt her teeth clench. She had noticed him before, when he blatantly checked her out before the place had opened to the public, but he hadn't been wearing his name tag then.

And now here he was, delivered into her hands. Clarence Feeley, Junior. Her jaws ached as she held the smile on her face and played with him, making sure that he would stay. And now here *she* was, ready for him.

He lost his grin, not understanding what she was doing, and she leaned across the table and put her face close to his and said, "I always wanted to meet a Son of a Free America."

His look of shocked surprise told her beyond doubt that she had the right man and she brought up the Nighthawk and fired several shots as quickly as she could pull the trigger. The explosions sounded as one and the tray of food he was holding turned into a thick paste that instantly became one with his flesh.

His stomach split apart under the fusillade and he staggered backwards, arms waving, head jerking. Gouts of blood flew from him like demons escaping hell. His fat ass bumped against the table across the aisle and he flopped down onto the floor in a sitting position. His eyes, still miraculously alive, were looking at her and she knew that he saw her, the bringer of his death.

"You wanted to see red," she said and shot him in the face with seven rounds so that his eyes pulped and his brains painted everything around him.

"Get her!" somebody yelled, and the roar of another shot punched

the air. Something tore into her shoulder and when she looked to her right, she saw the thin dealer who had talked to her earlier. He was standing behind his table several stands away, racking another round into a pump shotgun. He lifted it and fired at her again, catching her full in the chest and knocking her backward so that she toppled into the skinhead behind her.

The kid squealed and rolled away, his hands over his head as if expecting to get kicked. Amy sat back up and glanced at her chest. The halter beneath the open jacket had been shredded by the tightly choked wad of shot, but as she watched, the gaping hole in her chest closed up and she leaped to her feet, firing at the shooter before he could rack another shell. A ribbon of blood streaked from his neck and he fell.

Then all hell broke loose.

Rick Carlisle was standing by Junior Feeley's booth when the shooting started. He had seen that Feeley wasn't there and thought he would use the opportunity to try and make friends with the kid. He had scarcely said three words when the gunfire started.

He jerked his head around but could see only the people between himself and the noise. Many of them tried to scatter but because of the crowded aisles found nowhere to run. Most dropped to the floor, some crouching, some lying prone, heads down.

As the bodies dropped, Rick saw the glow of muzzle flash and then heard a single, louder boom quickly followed by another. Somebody was unloading a shotgun.

Then there was another blast of fire and as more spectators dropped out of harm's way, Rick saw a flash of red hair and a ripped leather jacket. It was a woman, and she had just hit the man with the shotgun, who was falling in a cloud of blood.

Then half a dozen more weapons sounded at once, spraying the woman with bullets. Many of them got past her and Rick saw bystanders fall, some hit in the head, some in the chest, thrashing about where they stood or toppling like trees. Suddenly a string of automatic rifle fire snaked behind him, pocking the walls.

Rick dove over the table for the kid, who was just standing there as if stunned, and hauled him to the floor a fraction of a second before another string of wildfire traced its way across the wall where he had stood. He raised his head from the floor and looked at the surprised boy lying next to him. "Let's stay down," he said, and Karl breathlessly nodded agreement.

* * *

It seemed to Amy as if every son of a bitch with a weapon had ripped open cartridge boxes, loaded, and was firing at her. The bullets hurt when they hit but she was able to stay on her feet as shots from one side would push her one way and those from the other side back again.

With the press of panicked bodies moving slowly away from her and the people lying facedown on the floor, she didn't know how the hell she was going to work her way out before her clothes were chewed to bits, and she wondered if there were a point at which her torn flesh would stop healing itself. So far there didn't seem to be.

Then she saw her escape route, as well as a way to better target her fire. The tables ran the entire length of the room and they were empty except for guns, a few cardboard stand-ups, and the bodies of those who had been hit by her attackers' stray gunfire.

She leaped up onto the closest table and ran down the white-tableclothed runway, firing at the bursts of muzzle flash or whenever she saw anyone aiming at her. She was hit frequently but made the shooters pay, firing with pinpoint accuracy and holding her fire whenever unarmed men were in the way.

The shooters weren't as particular and Amy saw more than a few people go down because they happened to come between her and a bunch of trigger-happy assholes. She would have been content just to blast Junior Feeley and walk out but they had taken that option away from her.

At last she had battled her way to the doors and now she leaped off the end table while the onlookers who hadn't already run out screamed and scattered at the sight of her flying through the air toward them, her tattered black leather fanning out behind her like the feathers of a giant black bird descending to feed upon their souls.

She ran unimpeded out into the parking lot, which had become almost as chaotic as the show inside. A cold and heavy rain was falling and cars, RVs, and pickup trucks were skidding in the water, smashing into each other in their haste to get away from the carnage or to take the wounded to hospitals. Amy darted through the mess, her feet slapping the puddles as she ran toward the back of the building where she had parked the Avanti.

But just as she was about to round the building, she heard someone yell *"Bitch!"* and turned to look.

Only a few yards away a man was standing in the back of a pickup truck aiming a double-barreled shotgun directly at her. She started to bring up the Nighthawk but he fired and both barrels discharged, sending two wads of shot right into her face.

The pain was shocking, beyond life's ability to bear. She felt her eyes implode, her teeth splinter, her mouth and nose and forehead cave in. And in that moment she remembered the pain of the explosion, *all* the pain, the psychic as well as the physical, and she fell back into darkness, hearing the triumphant cry of the shooter, hearing his words like sharp pellets of rain: *Yes! Goddammit yes, I nailed her! Shit if I didn't, fucked her right in the face, right in the goddam—*

And then she opened her eyes, newly made. She raised her reshaped head from the ground and let the rain reannoint it. She thought with her mind, reborn, that this man must die. And she stood up.

The man, his shotgun empty in his hands, only stared, his mouth open, his face trembling, rain running off of it like copious tears. His fingers unclenched and the shotgun fell at his feet, hitting the truck bed with the sound of a deep bell tolling, then instantly dying away.

Amy bounded up onto the truck bed and grabbed the man by his neck with her left hand. With the right, she grasped his face with fingers as strong and wiry as a metal claw, and dug in.

Her index and middle fingers pierced his eyes, her thumb and other two fingers popped through either side of his cheeks like a screwdriver through paper, and she ripped away the flesh—lips, cheeks, nose, and chin—pulling it right off the bone the way the explosion had ripped away her own flesh and that of the children.

And Amy screamed. She screamed for the man she killed, for the memory of her children and her own pain, and she screamed for what she had become.

The raindrops were her tears and they soaked the earth.

25

No one saw where the woman went after she killed the man in the truck. If they had been panicked before, the sight of her getting up after taking a shotgun blast in the face and then tearing the man's flesh off had driven them over the edge.

A few who had witnessed it remained, however, to tell the police what they had seen, and one man, a grizzled old hunter who had come to the show to get a bargain in .30–06 shells, was apparently the last to see the woman.

"She ran around the back of the building there and that was the last I seen of her."

"Didn't you look to see where she went?" asked an officer.

"Mister, I don't care *where* the hell she went as long as it wasn't around me. And it's gonna be a long time before I come to one of *these* shows again, lemme tell you."

The police interviewed Arnie Bailey, who couldn't tell them a thing about his temporary model except her description, her first name, and the fact that "that's the last fucking time I ever let that bitch Cyndi get her own fucking replacement."

The story made all the network news programs that evening, although the only footage had been that taken after the incident. The show's promoter examined a video that he had shot earlier but the only glimpse of the alleged assailant was from the back and twenty yards away. The only thing anyone could tell was her approximate height and the fact that the red hair was in all likelihood a wig, something that Cyndi attested to later on *Hard Copy.*

The final toll was ten dead and fifteen wounded. The bullets in the wounded were not from the guns that Arnie Bailey claimed were missing from his stock. "I was there," he told the news people, "and believe you me, when she aimed at something, she hit it."

Besides Clarence Feeley, Jr., and Barton Douglas, the man in the parking lot, four other people had been killed with bullets from the Nighthawk and the Cobray. All of them had been shooting at the woman. The other four dead, as well as all the wounded, had been hit by "friendly fire," shooters who were trying to bring down the woman.

The conclusion was that it was a planned killing. The first victim, and the only one the woman had shot without being fired on, was Clarence Feeley, Jr., a thirty-two-year-old unemployed bricklayer who had a series of arrests for sexual offenses, none of which had ever resulted in a conviction. Theorists guessed that the execution had been carried out in retaliation for a sexual attack, either on the woman herself or on a friend, and police were questioning all the women who had ever made complaints against Feeley.

What no one could explain was the impression given by witnesses that the woman had been hit by gunfire innumerable times, including a double-barreled shotgun blast full in the face, and had fled seemingly unharmed. Those who had not been there suspected body armor. Those who saw knew better.

Rick Carlisle had seen. Against all common sense, he had raised his head over the table where he was sheltering with Karl and amid the barrage of bullets that flew over his head saw the woman near the other end of the room, running down the tables, firing as she went. He saw the bullets hit her bare legs, smack into her back, and at one point strike her in the head. Her head had rocked but she had paused for only a heartbeat, then continued to run as if nothing had happened, firing again.

There was something too familiar about the woman and he knew as soon as he saw her what it was. She looked like Amy, moved like Amy. She *was* Amy.

The vision in the window, the voice on the radio, and now this. If he had not seen her shot, he might have thought that she had never died, that she had somehow survived and had remained hidden for six months and come back to wreak vengeance on those who had destroyed her dream.

But he *had* seen her shot. She had taken rounds that should have killed her and she kept going, "like that fuckin' pink bunny with the batteries," as one witness told a news team. They had not used the quote.

Rick believed implicitly the story of the shotgun blast in the face. He had seen, and he knew that she was not human. She was something strange and alien and unknown, and she was finding her way to them.

Rick was finding his way too, and he would continue to try and infiltrate them. And now Amy's slaughter had dropped the perfect opportunity right into his lap.

He had saved young Karl's life and the boy knew it. He had seen those bullet holes in the wall right where he had been standing before Rick had pulled him down. And when the shooting was all over and they had seen Clarence Feeley's bloody corpse, Karl turned to Rick and said, "We gotta get out of here. Can't be here when the police come, right? I mean, Junior told me about you, and . . . well, I shouldn't be here either."

Rick nodded. He was a fugitive from justice as far as this kid was concerned, and it seemed there was more to the boy than met the eye. They easily got outside in the melee and Karl led the way to a dark, dusty sedan. "Get in," he said, unlocking it.

"You're going to leave the guns?" Rick asked.

"No time to get them."

They got into the car and Karl drove slowly away, as if trying to avoid attention. In truth, his studied driving was in sharp contrast to the vehicles around them, tearing out of the lot as if trying to get away from hell.

"Thanks," said Karl. "You saved my life. Man, I thought I was done for. I couldn't even move."

"That's all right," said Rick. "My name's Guy. Guy Adams."

He held out his hand and Karl shook it. "I know. Junior told me. I'm Karl Withers."

"Good to meet you, Karl. So . . ." He felt as though he had to make some comment about Feeley. "So Junior? Is that what you call him? So were you related to him?"

Karl shook his head. "He was a friend, that's all, and one of the . . . well, a friend of my dad's. So you want me to take you somewhere?"

"Well, I'd been hoping that maybe Junior was going to hook me up with some people."

"Yeah, he told me."

"Sounds like he told you a lot."

"Yeah, he did." Karl seemed to think for a minute, then he flicked the car's turn signal and pulled into a gas station, parking next to the phone booth that sat in the corner of the lot. "I want to make a call," he said. "You wait here."

Karl talked for a long time but Rick wasn't able to hear anything. When the boy got back in the car, he was smiling. "I got some people for you to meet," he said and pulled back onto the road.

* * *

She had done it. She had killed the fat bastard. She hadn't known if she was going to be able to just shoot down a man in cold blood, but she had. It was as if something had taken over her body, turning her pain and loss into red rage. And while she was shooting him, *killing* him, it was the most liberating feeling that her spirit had ever known, as if loosing him from life loosed weights from her own aggrieved soul.

But after he was dead, then she had to kill more. Her response was automatic, animalistic. These men firing their weapons caused her pain and she had to stop them, to get through and away from them, and the simplest way to do that was to kill them.

And that had been the easiest thing in the world, to target their chests with her guns and fire, dropping one after another until she had reached the end of the room. If the stupid fools' bullets had hit others, that was no fault of hers.

But then she had come outside and the man had fired his shotgun at her and the pain had maddened her and she had made him pay. She saw in his face the faces of the men in the car, and something told her that by destroying that face she would be destroying all those faces that had caused the pain of the past. And she had done it.

Standing there in the rain with the dying man's flesh in her hands, she had for a horrifying instant felt as though she had become a monster, felt like old Uncle Abraham stalking the streets of Kishinev for his victims.

And then she had run. And now she was back in David Levinson's garage, sitting in the welcome darkness, the door closed behind her. She tried to focus on her next step, the festival tomorrow, Chip Porter.

The door to the kitchen opened and David Levinson stood framed in the light. He was wearing his uniform and his service revolver hung at his hip. She couldn't see his face but she could hear his voice.

"Ten bodies. You left ten bodies behind you." He turned and walked back into the kitchen, closing the door behind him, leaving her in darkness again.

She could stay there, she thought, or she could go inside, into the light, and face the truth. She got out of the car and went into the kitchen.

Levinson was sitting in the breakfast nook, a cup of coffee in his hand. He was freshly shaven and his hair was neatly styled and she knew he was ready to go out on his shift. His face was expressionless as he looked at her, eyeing the tattered leather and the ripped shorts. "You weren't hurt at all, were you?"

"I was hurt," she said softly. "I was hurt, David."

"And a lot of other people got hurt too, didn't they? I mean, at least if what I just heard from my friend Trotter on the force is true. This

Feeley, he was your target, right?" She nodded slightly. "And you killed him."

"Yes."

"And then what happened? You decided you liked it?"

"No! That's not it at all. They started shooting at me."

"Oh really? Just because you blew away an unarmed man, and one of their fellow dealers to boot, in the middle of the show floor? God, that was shallow of them, wasn't it."

"I had to defend myself."

"Against what? Getting temporarily perforated?"

"If I hadn't kept shooting, they would have grabbed me."

"And you could have tossed them off like a bull tossing kittens. But okay, even assuming that you were justified in shooting the people who were shooting at you, innocent bystanders got hurt too, Amy."

"Innocent bystanders," she repeated. "You mean like my kids? Like me? Like my friend Judy?" She sat across from him and looked him hard in the eyes. "I've come back to fight a war, David. And there are no innocent bystanders in a war. I killed the ones trying to kill me, that's all. If their bullets hit *innocent bystanders,* well, the ones who killed those bystanders are dead now at my hands, so I've already avenged their deaths. And if I'm wrong, if it's all my fault, then let the Crow bring them back to avenge themselves on me. So help me God or the devil, I'll fight the living *and* the dead if I have to, to set things right again."

Levinson looked at her for a moment as if trying to fathom her depths. "Do you remember how this all started?" he asked her. "With the shedding of innocent blood. Now I know what Junior Feeley was. He was a turd with legs. I think he must have hated women, he did things so nasty to them. And when they made complaints and brought charges against him, by the time the court dates rolled around they always changed their minds, like somebody had convinced them not to testify, and the charges were dropped, the complaints withdrawn. He's been involved with white supremacists and racists ever since he was a punk kid. He's beaten up gays and blacks and Jews and it was always the same story as with the women.

"Amy, you could have killed that fucking slug ten times over, while he was feeding a puppy or making confession or saying his bedtime prayers, and I wouldn't have made a peep. I'd have said great, kill the prick a few more times while you're at it. But your target was him, nobody else, and as far as I'm concerned, nine other people died for nothing."

"So what are you going to do about it, take me in, officer?"

"I don't think I could, could I?"

"You're damn right you couldn't. If you tried it, David, if you tried to stop me from what I have to do, I'd kill you."

He shook his head slowly. "I don't believe that, Amy."

"All right then, maybe I wouldn't kill you. But the Crow would. The Crow knows what needs to be done." She held out her hands. Just like the last time Levinson had seen them, they were rusty with dried blood. "But the Crow would do it with my hands."

Levinson looked at her hands for a very long time. Then he reached across the table and held them, his fingers curling slowly around hers. "Do what you have to do," he said. "But don't let them make you what they are."

Amy looked down at the pair of strong, heavy hands, knowing that she could easily have crushed them with a grip. "It's too late, David," she said, pulling her hands away from his. "I think I'm already far worse."

26

Rick Carlisle had never before been to the Dallas Diner. He had never even been on this road, fifteen miles northwest of Hobie near Petersburg, a one-store, one-street village. He couldn't figure out why it was called the Dallas Diner, since neither Texan decor nor cuisine was evident. It looked just like a hundred other aluminum diners that had survived from the forties and fifties, only in worse shape than most.

He was having a piece of blueberry pie to finish the meal that Karl had bought for him. "Least I can do for saving my life," the boy had told him. "Besides, we're gonna wait here for my dad."

That had been an hour ago. Karl hadn't said much and they had eaten mostly in silence. Rick figured that the boy wasn't too broken up about Junior Feeley's death. His expression seldom changed from the look of benign disinterest he had worn since Rick had first seen him.

His face did not even brighten perceptibly when a dark blue pickup truck pulled into the parking lot. Karl just pointed at the window and said, "There's my dad."

Karl's father came into the diner alone although Rick could see another man waiting in the truck. "Rip Withers," the man said, coming up to the table and shaking Rick's hand, then sliding into the booth next to his son. "My boy tells me you saved his ass," Withers said, peering at Rick from beneath frowning brows. He was a stocky man about six feet tall and was wearing a brown field jacket and a red wool cap with a tan canvas bill. His cheeks were ruddy above a well-trimmed beard.

"I just pushed him down when the shooting started," Rick said.

"He jumped over the table and everything," Karl said with as much animation as Rick guessed he was capable of. "I'da been shot sure."

"I owe you my thanks then," Withers said. "Karl's my only child."

"Well, you're welcome," Rick said, looking away in what he hoped came off as embarrassment.

"Karl tells me you need a little help. You and the government don't exactly see eye to eye, huh?"

"On some things, that's right. There are some people who'd, well, like to talk to me, to put it mildly."

"You're wanted."

"I am. I was telling Junior that I was looking for a group of people who . . . thought the way I do. Place to get away from the ones looking for me, maybe I could help do things that had to be done. Help in the struggle, you know?"

"And your name is . . ."

"Guy Adams. That's my name now."

"What was your name *then*?"

Rick shook his head. "Nope, sorry. I swore before Yahweh I'd never speak that name again nor use it in any way. That was ZOG's name for me. That name is dead and that man is dead. I'm Guy Adams and that's all anybody has to know."

"Well, I'll tell you something, Guy Adams," said Withers. "Somebody that does what you did when that shooting started, somebody that's got that much discipline is either one of two things. First, he's a good, brave, trained soldier who saw a boy in trouble and helped without thought of his own safety. Second, he's a fed. A cop or an FBI man or a company spook or somebody trained in situations like that. Now which one are you, Mr. Adams?"

Rick made his face look as stern as he could, trying to be Henry Fonda in *The Grapes of Wrath.* Then he stood up. "I'll tell you what I am, Mr. Withers—I'm gone. Thanks for the meal, son. Glad I could help you."

He was out in the parking lot, walking purposefully toward the road back to Hobie before Withers caught up to him. "Hey," Withers said. "Hey, come on, just a minute."

"I don't need this shit," Rick said. "I've eaten this shit since I was old enough to crawl and I don't need any more of it from you, not from somebody who's supposed to know about how I feel . . ."

"Goddam it, all *right*!" He grabbed Rick and spun him around. "Now you listen to me a minute, *Adams*! Do you know what it's like to have several dozen men that I'm responsible for? Do you know how confident I have to be of a person before I take them into our group, show them where we live and work, tell them our plans? I have to believe that person is a *brother,* man! I have to believe beyond the shadow of a doubt that that man is a true patriot, a real son of what will one day be a free America! So don't you give me your 'I'm all insulted' shit when I'm trying to preserve my men's lives!"

By the end of his speech, Withers was breathing hard and Rick found it surprisingly easy to feign sympathy and admiration for the man. Rick was playing a role, yet Withers's passion made it easier for him to make himself believe in the part. He could see how driven the man was and as a result Rick's mumbled apology came out easily and almost sincerely.

"All right then," Withers said, more calmly. "I truly appreciate what you did for my son. And I want to make it up to you. I believe you're a good man and that you're telling me the truth but it's not my decision alone. There are other people I have to talk to. That is, if you're still interested."

Rick nodded. "I am."

"Karl will take you back to Hobie now. Tomorrow over in Eau Claire they've got a White Christian Brotherhood festival. Be there. There'll be a band playing called Shock Troops, though they spell it some weird, dumbass way. The bass guitar player is one of our men. You go up to him and tell him who you are. And he'll either nod his head yes or shake it no, depending on what we decide. If it's no, we don't see you again. If it's yes, he'll take you in the van after the festival's over and bring you to us. But if it is yes, then you're one of us. You don't leave the compound. You're a soldier. You got any problem with that?"

"Nope. Got a problem with getting to Eau Claire though. That's about a hundred and fifty miles from here and I've got no car."

"Then I guess we'll see just how resourceful you are, won't we? You got any money?"

Rick shrugged. "About twenty bucks left. I'll manage."

"I'm sure you will. The only thing you can depend on in this country is yourself, my friend."

Rick smiled cynically. "Unless your skin's not white."

"Amen to that. Yahweh watch over you."

"He will. Same to you and your boy."

Withers walked back to Karl, who had been standing a few yards behind his father listening to the conversation, and said a few words to the boy that Rick couldn't hear. Then Withers got into his truck and drove away. Karl smiled and nodded toward the dark sedan.

They drove back to Hobie and Karl asked him where he wanted to be dropped off. "Doesn't matter," Rick said. "Downtown, I guess."

"I really want to thank you again, Guy," Karl said as Rick got out. "You really did risk your life for me and I really appreciate it. If there's ever anything I can do for you, you let me know."

Rick smiled. "You could put in a good word for me with your dad."

"I'll do that. I hope to see you again. Yahweh bless you." He drove away, leaving Rick on the street.

The first thing Rick did was go sit on a bench and think about what to do next. The best thing would be to get a cab to take him back to the Holiday Inn parking lot where he had left his car and go home, get a good night's sleep. He'd leave for Eau Claire early in the morning, parking his car far from the festival and hitching a ride in.

But when he stood up, he noticed a familiar form in the reflection of a shop window. It was Karl Withers standing across the street a dozen storefronts down. He was walking stealthily and Rick could only assume that he didn't want to be seen. To test his theory, Rick slowly turned toward where Karl stood and from the corner of his eye he saw the boy crouch down behind a parked car.

It was only too obvious to Rick what Rip Withers had told his son: *Follow him. See where he goes. Don't let him see you.* So the kid had pulled around the corner and come back on foot.

Rick thanked God, or Yahweh, he thought sourly, that he had noticed the kid. If he hadn't, in another minute Karl would have seen him get a cab, a strange move for a near penniless drifter. And if the kid had followed him, he would have seen right through Rick's pack of lies as he took him first to his car and then to his wooded, suburban home. Rick would have been lucky if there hadn't been a kill team sent to dispatch him, another lying agent of ZOG.

So instead, he had to do what Guy Adams would have done. Rick started walking slowly toward the seedier side of town, looking for the cleanest cheap hotel he could find. He stopped before each one, just the way anyone, even Guy Adams, would have done, thinking about its appearance, and finally settled on the Excelsior, a hotel that consisted of three shabby rowhouses.

Rick signed the register as Guy Adams, writing down an address in St. Paul, though he doubted the clerk, who didn't ask for identification, cared. The room was eighteen dollars and Rick paid in cash. When he asked for a room that fronted the street, the clerk looked at him oddly but complied.

The room was exactly what Rick had expected. There was a slightly musty bed with clean but gray sheets, an old chest of drawers with a washstand on it, and an open closet with no hangers. A thin white towel and a washcloth whose nap was nearly rubbed off were folded at the foot of the bed. The shared bathroom was down the hall.

But Rick was more interested in what was outside the room than inside. He turned off the light, crossed to the window, and looked down at the darkening street.

Karl Withers was there all right, standing across the street and looking at the Excelsior Hotel uncertainly. He paced back and forth for a while, then seemed to make up his mind, and headed back down the street the way that Rick had come.

Rick smiled. He hoped he had passed the test. But now he had to let Nancy know where he was and where he was going, at least as far as he knew. He walked downstairs and went outside. Karl Withers was nowhere to be seen but Rick walked several blocks just to make sure he was not being followed.

Then he found a pay phone and called Nancy.

27

Nancy grabbed the phone when it rang and when she heard Rick's voice she nearly cried with relief. She had tried to talk him out of going to the gun show but he had refused to listen, and when she heard the news stories about the shootings, she had called the police but was told that she would be informed if her husband was among the injured.

She had left Karin with a neighbor and driven to the Holiday Inn but the place was surrounded by police lines and they would let no one in. So she had gone home and waited for the call to tell her that her husband was dead.

And now here he was, alive, and she was so happy to hear him that she couldn't get out a sensible word for several seconds. He assured her, however, that he was all right, although he had been there when the shooting occurred.

"Oh God," she said, "I'm so glad you're okay, so glad. Oh Rick, when are you coming home?"

"I can't for a while."

"What?"

"That's why I called, to let you know. And to tell you not to worry. I think I'm getting close to them—the ones that planted the bomb. The first man who was killed? This Feeley? I think he was in on it. It's this Sons of a Free America that Wilson Barnes mentioned on the radio."

"But how do you know?" Nancy pleaded. "How do you know it was them with the bomb?"

"I . . . just know," he said, and she could tell from his voice that he was holding something back. "Believe me."

"And you're . . . *meeting* with these people? Why can't you call the police, just call the police and tell *them*, let *them* handle it!"

"I can't do that. I'm not close enough yet. But I will be and then I'll know everything and *then* I'll turn them in—all of them."

"Oh Rick, God, please don't do this, it isn't safe."

"I have to. It'll be all right. I'm being careful."

"How can you be careful with these people!" she shouted into the phone. "They're *killers*! They kill children! Why would they hesitate to kill you?"

"I'm sorry, Nancy. I've got to go. I'll be in touch with you when I can but don't be alarmed if you don't hear from me for a couple of days."

"A couple of *days*? Rick, you can't—"

"Good-bye. Give Karin a hug for me." There was a click on the other end, then silence as deep as a cave, as black as death.

Then she cried. She cried so loudly that Karin came out of the rec room in the basement and asked her what was wrong, if she had heard from Daddy yet. The name came hard to the little girl, who had always called him Uncle Rick during their friendship.

"He's all right, honey," Nancy told her, taking her into her arms. "I just talked to him and he's fine and he wanted me to give you a big hug." She wiped away her tears and looked into Karin's face. "He's going to be gone a few more days though. On business."

"Why are you crying, Mom?"

"I just . . . miss him a lot, that's all. I worry when he's gone."

"Don't worry," the girl said, hugging her mother again. "He's okay."

Nancy nodded and smiled. "Sure. Sure he is." Karin went back to her TV show in the basement and Nancy sat for a minute and then put on her coat and went outside into the cold November evening. She ached inside, both from the fear for what would happen to Rick and for the suspicion that he didn't really love her. What hurt most was when he hadn't told her on the phone.

She knew that it was going to be an uphill battle when the thought of marrying Rick first came into her mind. He was a one-woman man, always had been, and that woman had been Amy. During Nancy's own bushfire of a marriage, it had been Amy's marriage and Amy's husband that she had envied—not coveted, never that, but envied.

And when Amy had died, when Rick was free, it had been only natural that the thought of the two of them getting together had crossed her mind. He seemed so sad, so alone, and she shared in his grief since Amy had been her best friend. And the more time they spent together, the more Nancy realized that she had loved Rick for years, loved him for his thousand kindnesses to her and Karin, for the countless attentions he had paid to Amy, for the fact that he had been a good husband and a good man.

And to see such a man in so much pain made her discard her reservations about propriety and the proper amount of time to mourn a friend and a wife, if anyone still followed such conventions. They drifted toward each other like two boats and when they came together, each made the other stronger.

But her mistake had been to think that they had so much in common when what they had most in common was Amy, whose memory they both loved and whose loss had brought them together; Amy, who Rick still loved and would not give up.

Why else would he endanger himself and their marriage in this way? Didn't it mean anything to him that he had a wife and a daughter now, the child that he had always wanted? Nancy had given him that and could still give him children of his own. But he was willing to throw that away, along with his life, to seek the kind of vengeance that was best left to the law.

He was going to die. Nancy knew it. He was going to die and leave her and Karin alone again. He didn't care. He didn't love her. He loved Amy, a dead woman, and the only thing that would make him happy would be to die too.

Nancy wept, and her tears were cold in the night air.

"Somebody is fucking after us. Somebody has our number." Rip Withers looked at the other men in the room. The council was growing smaller. First Will Standish had turned traitor and had to be disposed of, but Sonny had gotten himself killed in the process. And now some crazy bitch had blown away Junior and nearly taken out Rip's own son.

And who was left? Ray, Yahweh love his poor dumb soul, Powder Burns, Chip Porter, and Ace Ludwig, who had become master-of-arms after Sonny's death.

"It started with that bastard Wilson Barnes," Rip said. "All he did was say our name on the air and now we're dropping like flies."

"And he said it to a fucking woman," Powder said. "Some *chick* made him give us up."

"And some chick shot Junior down too," said Rip. "Weren't you the one, Powder, who said he didn't believe in Wonder Woman? Well, maybe you better start believing. It wouldn't surprise me one bit if this is the same cunt who killed Sonny and Will's mama too."

"You believe that stuff about her getting shot and not getting hurt by it?" Powder asked, less cocky than usual.

"No. I believe there were a bunch of half-assed, panicky shooters in there who were firing at anything that moved, which is why so many damn people got hit. Karl said it was a fucking nuthouse and he never saw her get hit. Assholes just missed her, that's all. You know how people get when they panic. That's why we stress discipline.

"But she was after Junior, there's no doubt about that. He was the first she shot and she killed him hard." The phone rang and Rip snatched it up. "Yeah? He didn't come out . . . How long you wait? . . . Okay, come on back then."

Rip hung up and looked at the others. "Maybe one good thing came out of this—a guy saved Karl's life." Rip told the others about Guy Adams and his shadowy past and how he had Karl follow the man. "He seems on the level. I told him to go to the festival over in Eau Claire tomorrow. Chip, end of the day, he'll come up to you. You just nod yes and bring him on back. But don't talk about anything important, not about the Sons at all. And make sure you're not being followed—check him for sensors and all that shit, go up his ass if you have to. I trust this guy enough to bring him here and once he's here we'll see how sincere he is. We can use another soldier. So, all agreed on bringing him in?"

The men nodded. "Sure, sure," Powder said. "But what about this bitch? How the hell does she know who we are? Barnes didn't know anybody but you, Rip."

"That's right. And he didn't even know my name. No, I suspect that she got her information from either Will or Sonny."

"Sonny would *never* turn us," Powder said. "He was a straight guy. But Will was a cocksuckin' traitor all the way. It *hadda* be him."

Rip nodded. "He probably gave her a few names before he died. Junior's anyway."

"But who the hell *is* she?" Chip Porter asked. "Some crazy mother, like you said, Rip? Out for revenge or something?"

"No way. No little mother could take Sonny with a knife or shoot Junior and then blast her way out of that show today. This slut's a professional—a one-woman government hit squad. I'm betting she'll have no identity if she's captured or killed. Goddam killing machine, that's all she is. One of Clinton's cunts."

"Hillary herself!" laughed Powder, but no one else joined in. "So what do we do about her?"

"Watch our backs, that's about it. One person working on their own—how *can* we do anything except wait until she comes after one of us again? But if I were you boys, I wouldn't go picking up any strange pussy.

"But I'll tell you what we *can* do—and what I *want* to do." Rip took a dramatic pause while he looked at each man in turn. "We can move the schedule up for the big bang. To next week."

The men looked at each other and some took deep breaths. "Are we ready for that?" Chip asked.

"We can be. Right, Powder?" Powder Burns nodded. "Way I see it," Rip went on, "if they think they're getting to us, they'll expect us to lay low, keep our heads down, not do anything except be concerned over the state of our own hides. And that's the perfect time to strike. We do that fast and hard and it's retaliation for their assassinations and the loss of our men."

"I get you," Ace Ludwig said, and Rip could see the battle lust in his eyes. "They've thrown down the fucking gauntlet so we pick it up and smash them right in the face with it, right?"

"Right."

"When are we looking at?" asked Chip.

Rip looked at Powder. "When can you be ready?"

"Well, this is Saturday . . ." Powder thought for a moment, then nodded his head slowly. "Tuesday."

"Shit, *this* Tuesday?" Chip said.

"Yeah. This Tuesday. I got enough shit, all I gotta do is put it together, but do it right, y'know? Need time to do it right."

"The bird shoot's scheduled for Monday," Ace said. "You wanta cancel it?"

"No, we'll still have it," Rip said. "The men need their fun. We'll tell them about it after the shoot."

Rip had no doubt that they would all be glad to hear it. They all knew the plan, but now at last the day was almost here. It was an ideal target, occupied by most of the major villains that threatened the principles of the Sons of a Free America: an FBI field office, a regional Office for Civil Rights, a Minority Business Development Office, and an Office of Criminal Enforcement for the Bureau of Alcohol, Tobacco, and Firearms.

All in all, Hobie, Minnesota's Floyd B. Olson Federal Building, with its four hundred and fifty government workers, was more than a worthwhile target.

28

The next morning the Frontier Fairgrounds parking lot was packed to its four hundred car capacity. People were parking in the adjoining fields and all along the road out front, and Rita and Billy Joe White, organizers of the White Christian Brotherhood festival ("Whites for the Whites" was on their letterhead) were praising their white Christian Lord for the fine turnout.

They had worked long and hard to find a place that would allow them and those like them to gather and share in their beliefs, and the Frontier Fairgrounds had the advantage of being privately owned, so there was no town council or board of supervisors to deny them their God-given rights. The man who owned Frontier just told Billy Joe and Rita that if they paid him the money and promised not to kill anybody, the place was theirs for two days and two nights.

Although it wasn't what Rita would have chosen, the fairground buildings were functional enough, with electric heat, corrugated tin sides and roofs, and good concrete floors. The tin, however, was rusty in spots and must have rusted through in a number of places on the roof, for there were puddles and streams all over the concrete floor. But praise the Lord, the sky had stopped spitting down that cold, devil's rain and it promised to be bright and sunny all day. Folks would just have to step around the puddles, that was all.

Some of the vendors had arrived the night before and some between four and eight the next morning. Most of the early birds brought RVs and slept in them on the grounds, as did many of the attendees.

The first and largest building was the meeting hall. This was where the speakers would give their addresses and where the featured musicians would play in the evening. It seated well over a thousand, and Rita and Billy Joe expected it to be filled much of the day.

The second building was the exhibition room, with all the vendors' displays. Anything could be sold except guns, for which the Whites couldn't get a license. It was just as well, since that big gun show the day before over in Hobie had surely been visited by the devil, and the devil in this case had been a woman.

Rita wasn't surprised though. She had always said that guns and half-naked women were Satan's mix, and that was why whenever Billy Joe went to a gun show, Rita always went with him, to keep him company and out of the hands of those whores who worked in some of the booths. In the hands of the Lord's servants, guns could be a real blessing, but Rita didn't for the life of her understand why they had to have harlots showing them off along with their boobies.

But though there were no guns at the festival, there were plenty of books on them, along with lots of books on pure Christianity (none of that liberal, Billy Graham stuff, as Rita said), the dangers of race mixing and faggotry, the *Protocols of the Elders of Zion,* and plenty of tables selling *The Turner Diaries,* Billy Joe's favorite book next to the Bible. Rita had tried to read it but hadn't liked all the violence.

At eight A.M. Rita and Billy Joe were strolling up and down the aisles of the exhibit room, greeting all their friends and a lot of good folks they didn't know but welcomed as brothers and sisters in White Christian Brotherhood. Billy Joe, in keeping with the occasion, had foregone his usual camouflage and was wearing a freshly pressed dark green suit, his only concession to the private militia he headed an olive beret and a necktie with a cross and American flag design. Rita had seen to it that his gray-white beard had been carefully trimmed, along with his nose hairs.

Rita had on a dirndl dress with puffed sleeves, lace trim, and a bodice that she thought was a wee bit too tight but which Billy Joe and every other red-blooded American male never failed to compliment her on. Her hair was the crowning touch, a bouffant that both invited and forbade touching, like a beautiful soufflé so dainty a breath would destroy it. Still, Rita wasn't worried. She had used plenty of hair spray.

Before too long Billy Joe got into a nice conversation with a man selling Nazi memorabilia and books debunking the so-called Holocaust while Rita "just rattled away," as she put it, to a woman and her husband staffing a Ku Klux Klan recruitment booth. The place was full of booths for various militias, church denominations, and white supremacist groups, but there was much more available.

T-shirts, bumper stickers, and mesh caps were in abundance, all of them with anti-government or anti-mongrel sayings and logos. A lot of them had been around forever and had lost their humor for Rita, but one that she hadn't seen before was a T-shirt with a hook-nosed man hanging by his neck from the Nike swoosh. It read, "Just Do It," but NIKE had been replaced by KIKE. Rita had to chuckle. Billy Joe bought one of the shirts but the message wasn't quite subtle enough for Rita's tastes. She wasn't much of a T-shirt wearer anyway. She liked buttons.

There were computer-oriented booths showing how to set up your own website (Rita's nephew ran the site they had—she didn't know a thing about those computers) and a lot of CD and tape booths, selling everything from old-fashioned gospel to white power country to this new skinhead music.

Rita was surprised to see a lot more skinheads than usual, even as early as it was. She didn't like the way they dressed and their music was just awful to listen to, but they were always nice and polite to her and Billy Joe, and an awful lot of full-fledged patriots started out as skinheads. They did get into their fights but it was always with each other or the niggers or the sodomites, so that was all right. Boys would be boys.

A short whoop of feedback made Rita cover her ears and look up at the raised stage at the end of the exhibit building. That was where the lesser-known bands would play throughout the day to entertain the vendors and their customers. Everybody got a ballot with the bands' names so they could vote for who they thought was best, and the winner would get to play a set on the main stage before Wild White West, the nationally known country rock band that would close out the day's festivities.

The first competitor was setting up. Rita saw a banjo and a mandolin and was sorry she'd have to miss it, but it was already eight forty-five and the Sunday morning service next door started in fifteen minutes. Then all of a sudden the whole room seemed to get a little quieter and Rita looked up toward the main entrance to see who had come in.

Most of the women attending were with their husbands or boyfriends, but there were a few unescorted females. They were mostly tough, no-sass country girls, not that there was anything *funny* about them, like that horrible Ellen person on the godless television networks. They would find menfolk to take care of them soon enough, just like the Bible said, while those homos would go to hell sooner or later where they would burn forever with the Jews and the Clintons.

Still, Rita White didn't think she had ever seen a woman like the one who was now walking in alone through the main entrance. She was dressed all in black, almost like a motorcycle rider, and had on glasses that were tinted just enough to hide her eyes. She wasn't a skinhead—she looked a little too old for that—yet she had that swagger that so many of them had.

A lot of eyes turned to follow her as she came in, but she didn't seem to notice. One skinhead, probably ten years younger than the woman, walked up to her and though Rita couldn't hear what they were saying, she got the general idea from the way the boy's smile changed to a frown and his cheeks reddened as he walked away. "Whatever he's sellin'," she told Billy Joe, who had also noticed, "she ain't buyin'."

Well, Rita didn't have the time to watch any more young pups try to impress the mystery lady. It was getting on nine and the Reverend Johnny Harkins's keynote address was something she didn't want to miss. Now there was a man who knew his Bible.

Amy thought that if Dorothy Standish's trailer had been a den where monsters were bred, this was the college where they were trained. What appalled her most was the seeming normality of the people who walked through the narrow aisles and sat behind the tables selling hate. It seemed to her as though she could as easily have been at a craft fair or the Arts on the Square that was held every June in Hobie.

These people were smiling and happy, laughing and waving to each other and hugging when they met and shaking hands like an insurance salesman trying to double your coverage. Some even had their children with them. Boys and girls as young as five or six were wearing T-shirts with stomach-turning words of hate on them, and little caps with white supremacist symbols. A few were even sporting swastikas.

For the most part the children seemed well-behaved, although Amy saw one incident that made her flesh crawl. A mother and father were moving through an aisle but their kindergarten age daughter was lagging behind. The mother took a swipe at the girl, slapping her on the side of the head and knocking her to her knees in one of the puddles of water that dotted the floor.

The girl immediately jumped up and hit her mother in the chest as hard as she could. With that, the mother grabbed the child by her long hair and dragged her toward the father, who seemed embarrassed by the whole thing. The girl burst into tears, her mother released her, and she ran toward the door, the father following, then the mother, shaking her head.

"That's the way," a man called after the mother. "Don't take that from them. Bring them up right." Then he chuckled and turned back to the grinning salesman of survival foods to whom he had been talking.

Jesus. It was no wonder the kid hit back when she had been taught that hitting was what you did when you got mad. Amy wanted to run outside and show the woman what hitting was really all about, wanted to hit her and her dumb redneck husband so hard that both their necks snapped and their stupid brains smashed open against the pavement.

But she kept her temper. She was here for *her* children, not for these poor little creatures who were destined to grow up and become the beasts their parents were making them. And those like Amy would have to fight their own battles against the hate-filled brutes that were being created. These *parents* weren't fit to bear the name, she thought. They were only monsters that bred more of their own kind.

In Thailand, Amy had read, parents sometimes prostituted their own children, and the government, which seemed to profit from the child-sex tourism trade, tacitly approved. Amy had joined a boycott, vowing not to purchase Thai goods until the government did everything within its power to stop the horrible practice.

But it seemed that Thailand was not the only country where parents turned their children into something unspeakable. If Amy had had anything in her stomach, she could have brought it up then and there.

But she did not. She had neither eaten nor slept since her advent back into the world. She hungered solely for revenge and the only sleep she longed for was that unending rest that would be hers when she had satisfied not only her own soul, but the souls of the children, with the deaths of their killers.

Today she had a chance to feed the fire of vengeance that burned within her until she could finally enter the den itself and find those responsible—Powder Burns, Rip Withers, and whoever else had helped them, supported them, been a son of a warped and twisted "free" America. And then she would let that flame grow until it devoured them and her in one white burst of light.

But today it was Chip Porter's turn. Chip Porter of Shoktrupz. And when she found him, it would be time to rock and roll.

First, however, it was time to pay and pray as Amy learned when she went to the building where the Sunday service was just starting. She doubted if she would get any leads on the Sons of a Free America from the speakers, but she couldn't cruise the booths all day. Besides, after the gun show, she was damn sick of dealers' booths, and if anyone had been at the fracas yesterday, she didn't want them to see her, even with a different look, in an environment that could jar their memory.

Of course, there was a big difference between a redhead in black leather, shorts, and a halter, and a brunette in denim, even if it was so dark a blue as to appear almost black. Levinson's wife must have outgrown her denim phase too, which was lucky for Amy, who needed to replace her shredded black clothes. She had found a brown blouse to wear under the jacket and felt fairly confident that this outfit would not be chewed to pieces by bullets, not today.

Taking to heart what Levinson had said, Amy had determined that there would be no gunplay here, at least not on her part. Her knife was strapped to her ankle, and she would use it to kill Chip Porter unless she could find a better way.

Then the Reverend Johnny Harkins of the Church of White Christian Brotherhood was introduced by Rita White, the founder of this hate feast. Harkins fit the mold perfectly, with a gravity-defying pompadour whose dark and solid color had come out of a bottle. Amy thought it didn't look as much like hair as it did a shellacked armadillo.

Harkins offered a prayer calling for universal peace, which seemed holy enough, until he added that he would prefer to see that peace achieved by the destruction of all races but the white one and all faiths but the true faith of the Lord. He also prayed for the rapid destruction of homosexuals, fornicators, race traitors, tyrants, which he quickly defined as liberals, and those leaders who would impose any laws other than the biblical laws of Moses.

Then he called for an offering. Needless to say, Amy was not in a giving mood. But not wanting to tip her hand, she dropped a dollar into the plate.

After the good reverend had finished his prayer, he preached a sermon even more spiteful, always being careful, however, not to inspire his listeners to any actual violence, "lest there be persons among us who belong to Satan and not the Lord and who would go to the authorities in the cowardly and Jew-like spirit in which those who hated Jesus bore false witness against him to the authorities of their own time."

Yeah, Amy thought. When it comes to you, pal, put me on the side of Satan. But don't worry, I wouldn't turn you in—I'd hate to miss the pleasure of killing you myself.

The sermon finally ended and the congregation sang a hymn that everyone seemed to know, but which Amy had never heard. The last few lines were:

With thy help we'll take our stand
To make our home a white man's land.
So preserve us in our fight
For all that's holy, true, and white.

Amy could not shake off her feeling of amazement that there were people in the world who could believe these things, who could hate this way, who could use a vital and uplifting concept like faith to drag people down to such a brute level. Amy had been raised a Lutheran and she and Rick had always attended church regularly. But never had she heard the gospel of love used to rationalize hate, and try as she would, Amy could imagine no deeper sin.

It was that certainty of right, she thought, absolute right, that had driven the killers of herself and her children. This was where it started, where it was nourished, and where today it was going to stop for Chip Porter. If the wages of sin were death, today was payday.

After Harkins's rant was finished, a gospel quartet came up. The two men wore white jackets and the two women white dresses, and they sang very white songs that danced completely around the black gospel tradition. The lyrics were in keeping with the occasion, about how we would all stand around the great white throne and give praise to the great white lord. There was another real crowd pleaser whose refrain included the words:

Watching them burn (oh, yes Lord!)
Watching them writhe and twist and turn (oh Lord!)
From our home up in the sky,
We will watch those sinners fry.
As the fires of hell leap high,
We're watching them burn! (Praise the Lord!)

As Amy sat and listened to the songs, the words, the laughter and the praise of some hideous, spiteful god that had never been hers, she began to hate these people. The lessons she had learned about love were forgotten and David Levinson's cautionary words along with them. She had intended to creep up on Chip Porter in some hidden place, behind his van or at the back of the makeshift stage, and tell him who she was and then cut his throat.

But no longer. Now she wanted everyone there to see how these dark wages were paid.

Watching them burn . . . Maybe it was possible.

29

It was early afternoon when Rick Carlisle arrived in Eau Claire. He had left the Excelsior Hotel at six in the morning, unable to sleep for more than a few hours on the lumpy and odoriferous bed, and had walked to the outskirts of Hobie, where he started trying to hitch a ride, something he hadn't done since his college days. He didn't think he was being observed but he wasn't about to take a chance on retrieving his car.

Hitching seemed harder than it had been when he was younger. He had to walk several miles before a trucker finally picked him up who would take him as far as St. Paul. He made Eau Claire in a series of short hops and every time it took a little longer to get a ride.

But finally he saw the sign for the Frontier Fairgrounds and asked his driver, an Eau Claire businessman who was coming back from a visit to Minneapolis, to let him off. The man's jovial personality changed instantly, dropping several degrees toward chilliness. "You going to that thing? That festival?"

"Yes, sir."

"You don't seem like the type."

"Well, I just have to meet someone there."

The man nodded as if he thought Rick was lying, and the sour expression stayed on his face as he drove straight away. They had had a nice conversation up until then.

Rick paid the five-dollar admission fee at the door and was handed a White Christian Brotherhood button which he was told to wear at all times. "It lets you in this building here and the one next door where all the speeches are," said a gaunt and raw-boned cashier, who Rick thought looked like a misplaced Okie. "And that ballot there lets you vote for the best band that plays in here. Mind the puddles now."

The place made him sick. The ignorance and the hate was palpable in the huge metal barn of a room. Nevertheless, he bought a hot dog, his only meal of the day so far, and sat alone at one of the picnic tables by the snack bar.

At the other end of the room on a raised stage made of wooden and metal risers, a country band was playing and a dozen people were standing around listening. The lyrics were hard to make out over the twangy guitars and when he was able to comprehend a few of them, Rick was glad he couldn't hear more. Christ, he ought to just turn this whole damn bunch in to the police—or to some mental institution.

He read the ballot while he chewed his rubbery hot dog and saw *Shoktrupz* among the alphabetically listed band names. When he finished his rough meal, he returned to the ghost of Tom Joad and asked him if he knew when Shoktrupz was going to play. The man pointed to a handwritten poster on the wall.

Shoktrupz wasn't scheduled to hit the makeshift stage until four o'clock. Shit, that meant three more hours of listening to this crap or going next door for the speeches. Rick sighed and started drifting down the aisles between the tables, trying not to look too closely at what was being sold.

Amy sat patiently listening to everything, letting the music and the prayers and the speeches and the sermons brand her already burned soul, letting their hate feed her own. But at last she could bear no more and had to get a breath of fresh air.

She walked outside and around the back of the building. Behind the fairgrounds were acres of farmland. There under the cloudy sky on the wooden rail fence that divided a field of dry corn stalks from the buildings sat the Crow.

Amy knew it was her Crow. Its feathers were unruffled by the slight breeze that blew coldly through the dead corn, making a sound like whispering children. It watched her dead-on and she walked slowly toward it, afraid that her approach might make it fly away. She did not think that she would scare it, for it did not seem capable of fear.

It seemed, rather, like some divine mystery that would not deign to let mortals, even resurrected ones, approach too closely for fear of letting them see too far beyond the veil, into the mind of . . . what? God? Or something else?

Yet the bird did not fly as she approached and soon only a few feet separated them. "*Is* it God?" she asked softly, but the Crow did not move. "Or is it the devil? What are you? Who sent you? Who gave you the power to give to *me*?"

There was still no response. Amy smiled and said, " 'Prophet still, if bird or devil.' But that was Poe's *raven,* wasn't it? Not a crow." She thought for a moment, looking into the deep black beads of the Crow's eyes. "Bird or devil," she repeated. "Or bird . . . *and* devil." She touched her breast and said to the Crow what she had once said to God in prayers: "Use me as you will."

The Crow's beak slowly opened, and Amy could almost hear a word or the beginning of a thought in her head, when suddenly something flew from over her shoulder and brushed the right wing of the Crow. It rose into the air in a rush of black feathers, then whirled and vanished amidst the corn.

Amy jerked her head around and saw, ten yards away, a hatless skinhead in a long military coat. He was tossing a second rock up and down in his hand. "Thought it was gonna peck you," he said with a broken-toothed grin. "And I didn't think that was the kind of pecker a woman like you would want."

She didn't reply but held her face expressionless, with just the hint of a smile for the fool who approached her.

"I saw you leave," the skinhead said, chucking the rock over his shoulder. "Looked like you were gonna take a little walk and I thought maybe you wanted a good strong Aryan man to accompany you." He nodded toward the cornfield where the Crow had disappeared. "Some of the wildlife can get pretty dangerous."

"I like . . . the wild life," Amy said.

"I thought you might. You don't look like a lot of those other chicks in there, into the whole God thing, keeping it until you're married and all. You look like you're into this whole scene more for the fun of it."

"What kind of fun?" she asked, leaning back on the fence in as sluttish a pose as she could imagine, and tossing her head so that her hair shimmered in the pale light.

"Well, of course there's kicking the shit out of niggers and faggots, which is fun." He laughed almost self-consciously, which puzzled Amy. "But there's also Adam-and-Eve fun. That's in the Bible too. And the Song of Solomon. Like, sex?"

Amy nodded. "I like sex. But boy, you're not gonna find it in there with all those holy rollers, those women wearing white, buttoned up to their necks."

"Yeah, pretty tight-assed. But when I saw you, I thought now there's a woman looks like she accepts her God-given body and knows how to have fun with it, am I right?"

Amy had had enough of this shit. She knew what she was after and how to get it. "So do you wanta talk all day or do you wanta fuck?"

The skinhead's jaw dropped for a moment and then he smiled what he must have thought was his studly smile. "Fucking sounds real good."

Amy nodded toward the field. "I want to do it out there."

"Huh?" He looked surprised. "It's pretty damn wet . . . and *cold.*"

"I'll warm you up. And my nipples get *real* hard in the cold. Besides, the corn stalks have dried out, and we can bend them down. Make our own cozy bed." She licked her lips. "I want to hear them rustle and crackle as we do it . . . if you're not afraid of the wildlife."

He snorted a laugh. "Shit, no." Then he looked back toward the building. "But you know, I got a pickup with a cap . . ."

"Forget it," Amy said, starting to walk past him toward the buildings. "If you're not man enough . . ."

He grabbed her arm and whipped her around to face him, and she almost lost it then. But here out in the open wouldn't be good, even if no one was watching. You never knew who'd come through the door. And this asshole was just an appetizer for the main event, just a way for her to vent some of the hatred she felt for these holy monsters and the frustration at not being able to do anything about them.

"I'll show you who's man enough, missy," he said sneering down at her, trying the ape-man thing. *Missy?* Jesus. "Come on."

Keeping hold of her arm, he led her to the fence and helped her climb over into the rows of corn stalks taller than their heads. Before long they had passed from the sight of anyone watching from the buildings.

The ground was muddy but the cold had hardened and dried it in spots. After about fifty yards the skinhead came to a dead stop. "Fuck this corn stuff," he said, "and fuck you." He pulled back the front of his coat and unzipped his fly, taking out his penis. "Now get on your knees and get to work."

Amy looked at the small and shriveled penis peeking through his fingers, then back up at the man's face. "Is it the cold," she asked, "or is that just the way it normally is?"

The skinhead drew back his hand to slap her, but when he swung his arm she grasped the hand as if in a steel vise and squeezed. She was rewarded with the sound of cracking finger bones and a high-pitched squeal.

Instantly she let go and smashed both her palms against the skinhead's mouth. The blow knocked him backward and he fell, Amy riding him to the ground. He struck hard so that thick gobbets of mud flew up on either side of him, missing Amy. She crouched on his stomach, her hands still over his mouth, and pressed down, pushing his shaven head downward into the thick, sodden earth.

His eyes rolled at her but she continued to push, and slowly the mud covered the back of his head, his ears, and was up to his temples when there was a noise over her shoulder of crackling and rustling cornstalks. She looked and there behind her was the Crow, its claws clinging to a cornstalk, swaying in the breeze. But its feathers never moved.

Amy looked back at the prone man and saw that his eyes were staring in horror at the Crow. "It all started," Amy said, "when you threw stones at the birds when you were a little boy. And you've been throwing them ever since."

Then she pushed one final time and the head went slowly under the earth, so that mud filled the hollows of his eyes and seeped into his nostrils, and only Amy's wrists remained above the surface of the ground.

The skinhead's body kicked and spasmed beneath her, but was soon still. And when she pulled her hands out of the mud and stood up, she saw that urine was dribbling pitifully from the man's still-exposed penis. That too soon stopped and the man lay there, his head buried, his body sprawled in the mud.

"A time to sow and a time to reap," said Amy, looking at the Crow. It cawed once, but Amy heard no sense in the sound other than perhaps a cry of triumph colored with a note of regret.

And why regret, she wondered. Regret for what this dead man might once have been? Or regret for Amy, for one who was once so full of love and now lived for vengeance?

"It doesn't matter, does it?" Amy asked the Crow, and the bird rose again, flying back toward the fairgrounds. Yes, it was time to go back there where there was more work to be done. She felt tired, but it was not a physical tiredness as much as a weariness of the spirit. More work to be done. Many to die. Miles to go before she slept the good sleep.

30

Amy used the end of the skinhead's long coat to wipe off what little dirt had gotten on her clothing; then she walked back through the corn. There was a faucet outside and she washed the dirt off her hands and wrists. No one came around to the back of the building while she washed and she thought that maybe God was on her side after all. Something was. Maybe it was just the Crow.

She decided not to listen to more speeches. Her ears already felt as though they had been syringed with strychnine. According to the schedule, it would be another half hour before Shoktrupz, Chip Porter's band, would play. She decided to go and watch them set up.

Amy saw Rick within seconds of coming in the door. His back was partially to her but she could see the side of his face. Her immediate response was exaltation and in that instant she knew that it was no use denying that she still loved him.

But a second later she stepped back around a pegboard that one of the vendors had set up to hang his caps and sweatshirts. From that safer viewpoint she suppressed the urge to go to him, and let the logic of the predator take over, asking herself the obvious questions.

Why was he there? It almost seemed as though he were following her. Had he somehow gotten a lead on Porter? Or was he just fishing, sniffing for clues, as she had assumed he was yesterday?

But Eau Claire was pretty damned far afield to be searching at random. She had spoken to Levinson of synchronicity and maybe that was the cause here. Maybe something *wanted* them together.

But she dismissed that thought as quickly as it came. No one would want the dead and the living together for any longer than it took to . . .

well, to do what she was doing, to put the wrong things right. Maybe he had been brought here for another reason, to help Amy somehow.

She nearly laughed at her own fancies. It was remarkable how she had changed, seeing cosmic significance in what before she would have accepted as coincidence, no matter how bizarre. But that, of course, was before she had been brought back to life from sundered pieces of herself by a large black bird. After such an occurrence, what was impossible?

Amy remained sheltered behind the pegboard, pretending to be interested in the religious books on display in the next stand, until she saw Rick get up and move toward the stage. She stepped into the aisle to watch him and saw that he was greeting a man with hair just a quarter inch away from being a pure skinhead. He had an electric bass strapped around his neck and Amy recognized him as Chip Porter from the picture on his website.

Rick didn't shake hands with him but just went up and said something. Porter nodded his head up and down and smiled, then said a few words to Rick, and gestured toward the wall beyond which was the parking lot. Then Rick said something else and turned to walk back down the aisle toward her.

Amy ducked behind the pegboard, crossed over to the other aisle, and waited until Rick passed. When he did, she followed him until he went outside. Then she counted to a hundred and went through the door.

He was already far down the road, walking toward Eau Claire. Amy could make out an assortment of buildings and lights a mile or so away, maybe a strip mall. That was good. She was glad he was going. She wanted to do this on her own.

Still, she couldn't help wonder what Rick had talked to Porter about. At least it seemed to indicate that he wasn't just fishing. He had somehow contacted one or more of the Sons of a Free America and was closing in just the way she was. She only hoped she could get there first and keep him out of danger.

Now she went back inside and stood at the back of several rows of metal folding chairs that had been set up for people to relax and watch the bands. Most of the skinhead contingent seemed to have gathered for Shoktrupz's set. There were about fifty of the breed, posturing and preening for each other. Amy was the only woman around.

One of them eyed her and came over. She got ready to make a ball-busting crack but the young man only said, "Hey, you seen my buddy Pete around?"

"Pete?"

"Yeah. He said he was gonna go outside and talk to you a while ago."

She chuckled. "Oh, he came outside all right, but I think I kind of put him down. He can't take much teasing, can he?"

Dead Pete's friend looked confused. "Well, uh, no, I guess not. Did he say where he was goin'?"

"Just something about a corn roast. That make any sense?"

The skinhead shook his head again. "Okay, well, thanks. Um, you doin' anything later?"

Amy smiled. "Sorry. I have plans."

The young man nodded, rather politely in contrast to his friend Pete's brusqueness, and went back to the safety of the other skinheads. Amy wondered how long he would look for Pete. She was damn sure they wouldn't go into the muddy cornfield in search of him. No, the first time old Pete would come to light would probably be next spring when a plow turned him over.

Amy turned her attention to the stage. The band was nearly finished setting up. In addition to Porter on bass, there was a lead guitarist, a rhythm guitarist, and a drummer, who had painted the band's name on his bass drum with a lighting bolt providing the final Z. So original, Amy thought.

They all had shades on, even though the fluorescent strip lights hanging from the ceiling were far from blinding, and wore metal bands with studs on their wrists. Porter and the lead guitarist had added what looked to Amy like spiked metal dog collars around their necks.

The drummer wore black leather pants and a ripped T-shirt with *White the Power* scrawled across the chest in laundry pen. The lead guitarist's scalp was painted in alternating red and black stripes from front to back like a multitude of Mohawks, and he wore a black leather vest with no shirt underneath, despite the November weather. Maybe his tattoos were insulated, Amy thought.

The rhythm guitarist sported pegged jeans and a sleeveless gray sweatshirt that displayed a massive set of biceps, and Porter had on a denim work shirt heavy with slogan buttons, and a pair of black jeans. The overall look seemed to strike the right chord for their sympathetic audience, who stood or sat, ready to comment favorably on each bit of instrument tuning or thrown away drum riff.

At last the rhythm guitarist stepped to the microphone and said, "We're Shoktrupz, spelled S-H-O-K-T-R-U-P-Z!" The skinheads yelled, applauded, and spelled along. "And we hope you like what you hear. If ya do, vote for us to play in the main room tonight. If ya don't . . ." He took a brief pause. "Then yer a Jew nigger faggot. Hit it!"

There followed twenty minutes of the most cretinous music Amy had ever heard, a combination of garage band, punk, and metal, with the worst qualities of each. Surprisingly, though, the language was fairly circumspect. There were no coarse sexual words used, no *goddams* or *shits* or *Christs* or *asses.*

But there were numerous references to Jews and niggers and faggots, as might have been expected by the spokesman's opening remarks. There was a power ballad about the white man being the

One against the many,
Light against the darkness,
Fire against the icy grip of night . . .

Amy thought she counted night-white-light-fight rhymes ten times in as many minutes.

But the real mind twister was when goon-boy said, "Here's our theme song—'White the Power!' " Then to the screams and cheers of their devotees, they launched into a *rap,* an out-and-out rip-off of Public Enemy's "Fight the Power," in which they chanted, "White's the power . . . white's the power, be free!"

That people who hated blacks so much would use a decade-old black power anthem and art form to express that hate only proved incontrovertibly to Amy that they had shit where their brains ought to be. The idiots would have been more racially pure if they had written an oratorio.

Still, their intended audience ate it up, chanting along, shaking their fists in the air, and pogo-ing up and down, at first disregarding the fact that three times out of four they came down in puddles of standing rainwater and then delighting in the fact. In the midst of this action Amy made her way to the side of the stage and gave a once-over to the band's setup and equipment. She liked what she saw and she hoped the current popularity would bring Shoktrupz to the main stage.

She didn't have much to worry about. After the song was over and the set was done, the skinheads passed around pens and pencils, filling out the ballots and dropping them into the box at the front of the room. "You're gonna *win,* man!" dozens of skinheads assured them.

"Hardly nobody's been votin'," said one skinhead, "and when they do it's in like twos and threes for the ones they just seen. But you guys got a *block,* man!"

By the time Shoktrupz had packed their gear and taken it to their van, only three people were left in the stage area: a teenage brother and sister who sang gospel duets to the accompaniment of the boy's acoustic guitar, and their mother. Amy figured they were no competition.

The ballots would be counted at six. That meant that she had an hour and a half to check out the main stage and go and get what she needed to make Shoktrupz's appearance something to remember.

Rick Carlisle was sitting in a booth in the Neptune Diner, looking out the window at the road. In front of him was a plate of meat loaf, mashed potatoes, and corn that had cost him $5.95 and that he was devouring hungrily. He was keeping an eye on the road on the off chance that he'd spot either Rip Withers's pickup or the sedan young Karl was driving, though he still hadn't seen anyone tailing him by car or on foot.

Nevertheless, if one of those two vehicles pulled into the Neptune's parking lot, Rick intended to get up, drop a ten on the table, and walk out. If anybody asked, he had had a cup of coffee, all he could afford.

But nobody came or asked and he relaxed, enjoying his meal, watching the occasional car pass by. Once he saw a low, slightly boxy black car flash by, a model that he couldn't recall seeing in years. A professor had used it as an example in one of Rick's design courses. He tried to remember the name and finally came up with it—an Avanti. He was surprised there were any still on the road. That style had to date from the sixties.

So when he saw it returning, traveling in the opposite direction fifteen minutes later, he looked more closely. Though he had only a split second to see the driver of the fast car, a shock went through him as he saw Amy's face in profile.

At first he didn't believe it, then he *knew* it was her, and then he didn't believe it again. By a stretch of the imagination, he could imagine her, if she really had somehow come back, tracing the Sons of a Free America to the White Christian Brotherhood festival, but driving a classic sports car? Couldn't she just *fly* or transport herself somehow?

God, no. This was ridiculous, just ridiculous. It wasn't Amy at all, it *couldn't* be. The voice on the radio, the figure at the window, the woman at the gun show—all these things had to have some rational explanation short of his wife returning from the dead. He had just projected Amy into and onto all of these occurrences because he so much *wanted* her to be alive.

That had to be it. It was easier to think that he was going a little bit insane than it was to really accept the fact that she had somehow been resurrected. He smiled bitterly at his reflection in the window. He had to be careful and keep his sanity intact.

Otherwise he'd be seeing Amy everywhere.

31

As people got settled for Dr. Gary Skelton's speech and the evening concert, Rita White felt as if she was walking with the Lord. That was what she called it when everything was going right and that was certainly the case today.

Attendance had been grand, the response had been overwhelmingly positive, and all the people were so nice, even those skinhead boys. Rita was mildly disappointed, however, that their band had won the contest and would be playing here in the main building following Dr. Skelton's speech and before the Wild White West's concert. But they had won fair and square. Next festival, she thought, maybe they'd have a panel of judges instead.

"I hope that you and Dr. Skelton won't be too put off by the rock and roll," Rita told Mrs. Skelton, who was sitting next to her in their reserved metal folding chairs in the front row. Dr. Gary Skelton was the most eloquent and persuasive speaker Rita had ever met in the movement. In fact, tonight Billy Joe was going to introduce him by saying that if you gave him an hour, he could have talked Martin Luther Coon into lynching himself.

But Dr. Skelton was also gentlemanly, and Rita didn't know how he was going to like these Storm Troopers, or whatever their name was, with their loud drums and guitars and their yelling their rhymes. It could be a long half hour.

"I only wish," Rita went on, "that one of those nice gospel or country groups would have won."

Mrs. Skelton shook her head to dismiss Rita's concerns. "No, it's quite all right. Like Gary always says, times change, and if you don't get the young people involved, in twenty years we'll all just be a bunch of old dinosaurs everybody will laugh at. That's why I'm glad to see these young men play." Mrs. Skelton looked back at the crowd. "And I'm glad too that so many good parents have brought their children along. It's never too early to learn the truth about the direction the Lord wants us to take."

Suddenly the song "You've Got to Be Carefully Taught" started playing on the P.A. system. "Well," said Mrs. Skelton, "a sign from heaven!" Both women laughed. "That's from a show, isn't it?"

"*South Pacific*," said Rita. "You know, that would have been really good if it hadn't been for that part about that Navy man falling in love with that South Seas girl."

"Mmm." Mrs. Skelton nodded. "Yellow or brown, a nigger *is* still a nigger and has no business being with a white man." She chuckled. "The ironic thing is that that song was written to criticize people with our views, and I think Rodgers and that Jew Hammerstein would roll over in their graves if they knew that we can take it quite *seriously*."

"You're right," Rita agreed. "You are so right, it's all true—kids *do* have to be carefully taught while they're still little."

"Mmm, before the system of ZOG gets ahold of them and teaches them the opposite of everything that's right."

"And that's why I say thank the Lord," Rita rattled on, "that nearly all of the parents here home school or send their children to those good little private schools that teach the principles of White Christian Brotherhood."

"They'll be the leaders of tomorrow," Mrs. Skelton said so proudly that it made Rita proud too.

She smiled and looked up at the stage where Billy Joe was fiddling with the lectern, trying to get it to the right height for his introduction. At least he and Dr. Skelton were the same height, tall, fine-looking men.

Behind Billy Joe the skinhead band was getting themselves ready for their part of the concert. They seemed really excited and happy and Rita thought they would probably be just fine after all since their hearts were in the right place and since Mrs. Skelton thought they were okay.

She looked back over the crowd and was delighted to see that the room was filling up so fast. The seats were all taken or saved with coats, and folks were starting to stand along the sides and in the back. It was going to be a real party, a true celebration of white brotherhood and superiority.

After a few more minutes Billy Joe tapped the mike and called for attention. He thanked everyone for coming and said that since it was so successful they'd have another festival real soon, and everyone cheered.

Then he apologized for all the water on the floor and made a little joke about the festival scaring the pee out of all the niggers so watch your step. Rita thought it wasn't in very good taste but the crowd laughed and moaned at the thought of stepping in nigger pee.

Then Billy Joe introduced Dr. Skelton, and to his joke about Martin Luther Coon, he added "or he could talk Bill Clinton into being faithful to Hillary" and that got a good laugh too. No doubt about it, Rita thought proudly, her man knew how to work a crowd.

Then Dr. Skelton came to the microphone and gave a masterful speech that had everyone clapping and shouting *amen!* after nearly every sentence. Rita would have entrusted her sacred soul to that man.

He talked about the shining city on the hill, a pure white Christian America where all men were brothers, a paradise on earth to prepare us for that paradise in heaven, a country governed by the Mosaic laws given by the Lord, where adulterers and homosexuals and witches would be stoned to death, "and that pretty much takes care of the current administration," he added in one of his few jokes.

When he was finished, after calling for all of them to keep their faith strong and fight for what was right by whatever means necessary, he sat down beside his wife to thunderous applause and a standing ovation that lasted five minutes, during which he got up and bowed several times.

At last Billy Joe got back up on the stage and quieted down the crowd. "And now," he said, "we get into the musical portion of our evening's festivities! A little later we've got the greatest country band anywhere on the face of the earth, Wild White West!" The crowd went crazy and Billy Joe waited them out. "But first we've got a real treat for you youngsters, the winner of our band contest today, a young white power group from, well, these boys don't like to say where they're from, for fear that the forces of ZOG will hunt 'em down and steal their *git*-tar strings! But they're here for us tonight. Are you ready to rock and roll?"

The crowd, even the older members, roared and Billy Joe shouted into the mike, "Then give a loud White Christian Brotherhood welcome to Shock Troopers!"

The band hit the stage like Hitler taking Poland. They slammed out a series of power chords that rattled the tin walls and roof, and Chip Porter felt his dick grow hard with the thrill of playing to so many people. There had to be nearly fifteen hundred in here tonight.

With the first notes, their fellow skinheads mobbed the area directly beneath the stage, some of them dragging along girls they had met during the day, turning the eight feet between the first row of chairs and the stage into a mosh pit. Some leaned on the front of the stage, moving their shaven heads up and down in rhythm while others stood bouncing, grinning, and laughing. Chip had to laugh too. From where he stood the rhythmically moving bald heads looked like a bunch of bobbing ass cheeks.

Billy started singing then, launching into "Sailors on a Sea of Blood" with more raw guts than Chip had ever heard before. The amps sounded diamond sharp, with none of those shrieking highs or gutbucket lows that you got from cheap, modern solid-state crap. Uh-uh, these were *tube* amps, man, old-fashioned shitkickers from the days of yore. Shoktrupz's music was today all the way, but the sound technology was motherfucking *roots.*

And also motherfucking cheap. Billy's dad had used these amps back in the sixties when they were the only Ku Klux Klan–associated country-western band north of Tennessee. Chip had played with the amps and tweaked them into near perfection so that they could afford their axes, and it was damn well worth every hour he had sweated and slaved over them. If there was one thing their fans loved, it was their *sound.* And now, tonight, they were the big deal, with no keeping the volume down for the dainty-eared shits in the vendors building. Now they could let it rip, and they did.

We ain't gonna rest till we smash 'em in the mud,
We're sailors on a sea of blood! . . .
We'll stand alone against the flood! . . .
We'll buy our freedom with our blood!

The first number finished with a flourish of faux gunfire from Kurt's tom-tom and the others went down on their knees, White Christian soldiers sacrificing their lives for the cause.

Then, with a huge four count—POW! POW! POW! POW!—they rose with each beat until they were on their feet again and slashed their way into "White Blood, Black Blood," snarling out the lyrics:

White blood, black blood, they ain't the same!
To us it's a crusade, to them it's a game!
True blood, Jew blood, they ain't the same.
We're true believers—they'll die in our flames!

Chip didn't think they had ever sounded so good. Billy's voice was like an angel's coming down from heaven, totally pissed off, sword in hand, ready to kill. Kurt's drums were pounding and sizzling at the same time, fire and cannons, and Sandy's lead guitar was saying everything that they couldn't get into their lyrics.

Chip felt newborn. He had seen good crowds before but nothing where it had all come together like this. Even the old farts seemed to be digging them. Hell, most of them were standing up—the whole damn house on its feet. Little kids were scooting down the side aisles and pressing forward and the skinheads were letting them in, even putting some of them up on their shoulders to grab their shiny domes and get the best seats in the house.

The babes were loving it too and Chip figured he could pretty well have his pick. He really had his eye on that more mature-looking chick in black or dark blue who had checked out their first gig at four. She was working her way through the crowd, sliding around toward the side of the stage, probably wanted to be there when they finished. Helluva good-looking woman, and that dark getup she had on looked cool, a little dangerous.

He looked away from her, getting his attention back to the music. It was such a trip, maybe the start of a whole new thing for him and the guys. Yeah, maybe the Sons would have to take a back seat to Shoktrupz. He'd hang in on this big bang coming up, but after that, well, maybe he'd just hit the trail with Kurt, Billy, and Sandy, head on out to L.A., and see what happened.

Hell, you worked for the cause in the best way you could, and why should he tinker around with computers for Rip Withers when he could be tearing up the halls and bringing hundreds, thousands, maybe someday even *millions* of kids into the camp of white power?

Chip closed his eyes and let the music take him, whirling him into his dreams.

Oh my, Rita White thought, standing and trying to look over the heads of the young people. They were getting rowdy now, jumping up and down in the puddles near the front of the stage so that the water splashed onto her stockings and, worst of all, onto Dr. and Mrs. Skelton too.

Rita looked at Mrs. Skelton apologetically but she only gave a long-suffering smile and rolled her eyes slightly as if to say these are the things we just have to put up with. Dr. Skelton was graciously watching the stage and nodding his head in time to the music. Billy Joe, next to Rita, leaned over to her and shouted above the racket, "These boys are all right . . . Good words, *good* words . . ."

The group must have been on their fourth or fifth song now and Rita glanced at her watch to see how much longer they had to play. She hoped that all these young people in front would sit down when Wild White

West started since they were scheduled to play for an hour and Rita knew she couldn't stay on her feet all that time, especially with these sweaty teenagers all around her.

The band finished their number and Rita thought that maybe they would stop now, but they started another. The boy playing bass and the lead singer stepped up to their microphones again and started singing in what Rita thought was supposed to be harmony. It was some song about fire in the hole, whatever that meant, and two of the boys kept chanting *Fire, fire, fire* over and over while the singer sang the verse. Rita thought it was about hell but she wasn't sure.

Then suddenly something sparked behind the stage, ten times as bright as someone taking a flash picture, and the speakers screeched for a second and then, with what sounded like a huge pop, died.

So did Shoktrupz.

There was a smell of ozone, and the three boys at the front of the stage started to tremble. Their eyes rolled up in their heads and the guitars dropped from their hands, but still hung around their necks.

Then smoke started to come from their clothing, and the guitar player's long hair began to smolder, then quickly burst into flame. Rita tried to scream but realized she could not, that a feeling of intense vibration, which prevented it, was rolling up her body.

She could feel the vibration in her heart as though it were beating faster than it ever had before, as though it were *humming* and she could do nothing to slow it down, could do nothing at all except stand there and feel sweat burst out all over her. And then Rita's heart muscles fibrillated and before she even realized that she was being electrocuted, she was dead.

When her body fell to the floor the current continued to run through it, more strongly now that Rita's flesh was in direct contact with the water on the floor. Billy Joe stood beside her for a while longer, but then he too fell right on top of Rita without even knowing it. The Skeltons joined them, as did nearly everyone standing in front of the stage and sitting in the first couple of rows.

Others further back felt the tremors of the shock but were far enough away that they could react and flee. Chairs were overturned, the slow and the weak were pushed out of the way and trampled by the strong.

But the skinheads, the children on their shoulders, the girls who had been dancing and laughing, the older people standing up to see over the heads of the revelers, those still sitting on their metal chairs, the hearts of all trip-hammered, staggered, stopped.

* * *

What have I done? thought Amy. What the hell have I done?

She had wanted to kill Chip Porter, of course, and figured it would be no great loss if the other members of the band from hell died too. So she had gone into a Wal-Mart a few miles up the road and bought a roll of copper wire and a small wire cutter.

Then while everyone else was watching Shoktrupz play, Amy had gone behind the stage and connected lengths of wire to the legs of the metal risers on which the band was standing, twisting them all together with still more wire. Then she disconnected the grounds from the amplifiers and used the wire cutters to scrape away the insulation from the amps' power lines.

She wrapped an end of the copper wire around a cold water tap in a janitor's sink, then took two more strands of the wiry Gordian knot and hooked them around the exposed hot wires of the amps, twisted them, and finally let them make contact.

The shock nearly knocked her on her ass. She staggered back into the wall and immediately felt the concrete floor vibrating with electricity. The sound from the stage died and was replaced by screams and the sound of metal chairs clattering to the floor.

Then Amy realized with a start of horror that the electricity had not been limited to the stage alone. The concrete floor, damp everywhere and dotted with puddles, was acting like the wet sponge the executioner placed on the shaved head of the condemned as he sat in the electric chair. The current was flashing down the risers' metal legs onto the wet floor, a grid of death.

From behind the risers Amy could see the band members lying where they had fallen, still twitching with the electrical current. Smoke was rising from their bodies and little flames still licked at the few locks of hair that remained on the lead guitarist's scalp.

And beyond them in the packed audience were mounds of bodies and some people still standing, shivering with the shock that was still climbing up and passing through their flesh.

Amy turned, ran to the wires, and grasped them, ignoring the amperage flowing through her as it attempted in vain to fibrillate her already dead heart. It fought her but she clung to it, her muscles trembling as she untwisted the copper wires and jerked them away from the hot wires connecting the amps to the outlet. The electricity that had literally filled the room ceased so that only its ozone ghost remained to welcome into the beyond those ghosts newly made.

Then she walked around the side of the stage and looked at what she had done.

* * *

Returning from his meal, Rick Carlisle saw dozens of people running out the door of the main fairgrounds building. Some were shouting angrily while others were screaming. The street lights brightened and darkened in cycles and he ran until he reached the door, hoping that whatever happened had not happened to the bass player who was supposed to take him to the Sons of a Free America.

He quickly found out from the people fleeing the building that his contact was dead. Still, he pressed against the throng until he managed to get inside, where he found panic and confusion. But whatever the danger had been, it was now past.

People were dead, dozens of them lying over toppled chairs, their faces in puddles of water. He saw the members of Shoktrupz sprawled on the stage, their faces frozen in a death rictus, eyes wide, lips pulled back from their grimacing teeth. The sickness he felt increased as he made out the smaller forms of some children, but he went down the aisle toward them in the dim hope that he could be of some help.

A woman was holding a little girl in her arms, her head bowed, pressing against the girl's chest as if trying to breathe life back into her. The woman seemed to be crying, and even before she looked up at him with tearless eyes, he knew who it was.

"Amy," he said.

If she could do so much, if she was so strong, so powerful, so invulnerable, then why couldn't she bring this little thing back to life? She could feel the tears start to form but they wouldn't come, and then she heard someone call her name, and she looked up and saw Rick.

He looked surprised to see her but not amazed or stunned or terrified. And most incredibly of all to her, he didn't ask her what she was doing there or why was she alive. He asked, very simply and almost numbly, "What happened?"

But before Amy could answer, a young woman pushed her way through the people who were still congregating inside. She looked as though she were in shock, and she stared at Amy and the little girl, then knelt down and held out her arms. Amy put the girl into them, and the mother, tears streaming down her face, embraced her daughter while Rick and Amy watched. Then she stood up and staggered up the aisle to her dark future.

Amy looked back at Rick, who was again staring at her. He took a step closer and his arms started to come up toward her but she stepped back. "No," she said. "Don't."

"What is it?" Rick spoke as if he were in a dream. "What is happening?"

"I'm killing children," she said softly, even before she knew the words were coming. "Oh, Rick . . ." Her words drifted out like prayers. "I'm killing children."

32

They heard the sirens as they went outside together. Ambulances, fire trucks, police cars descended on the fairgrounds like flies streaming to a roadkill rabbit. The firemen went inside first, then quickly beckoned the medics, who ran inside with their stretchers. Someone detached the power from the entire building, and from the doorways the glow of emergency lights appeared, making the figures coming out with their burdens appear white and ghostly.

Rick and Amy walked away from the building and into the parking lot, where they sat in the Avanti. "I saw you in this car earlier," Rick said. "And I saw you at the gun show. And it was you outside my window, wasn't it?"

"Yes, it was me," Amy said, looking through the windshield.

"How did you . . . survive?"

She paused before answering. "I didn't."

For some reason, the answer didn't surprise him. He supposed he already knew.

Then Amy told him everything, how the Crow had brought her back from the dead, how David Levinson had discovered her and told her the story of his Uncle Abraham. She told Rick about questioning Wilson Barnes, about following Will Standish and killing Sonny Armitage and Standish's mother, and about finding Junior Feeley and shooting him down.

"I saw you yesterday," Rick said. "I was there looking for these people too. You got shot but you weren't hurt."

"No." She still refused to look at him. "And I just got God knows how much electricity through my body—enough to . . . kill all those people in there—and I just walked away from it." She shook her head. "I didn't mean for that to happen. I just wanted to get him and his band."

"Chip Porter," Rick said, and was rewarded with her turning to look at him at last. Her eyes seemed haunted, but there was an intensity in them that bored into him.

"How do you know him?" she asked.

"I was supposed to meet him. He was going to take me to the Sons of a Free America. They think I'm one of them, that I believe like they do and I'll join them."

She looked at him in disbelief, then pounded the steering wheel in frustration. "*Jesus,* I can't believe this—I've been tracking these bastards down and you just stumble right into them."

He nodded. "Yeah, a lot of it was luck. I happened to save a kid's life yesterday during the shoot-out. I think he's their leader's son."

"What's his name?" Amy demanded. "Burns? Withers?"

"Withers. I don't know any Burns. The father of the kid is Rip Withers."

"Do you know where they are?"

Rick felt as though he were being pushed against the door by the force of her questions, and had the uncomfortable feeling that she would go right through him to get to the people she sought. "No. Porter was going to take me."

"God *damn* it! Goddammit! If I'd only have known . . ." The breath hissed out of her and the sound somehow relieved Rick. At least, he thought, she breathed.

Then silence sat with them in the car, while outside people scurried and ran and wept and screamed. It all seemed unreal to Rick, as though they were on a calm island in the midst of a terrible storm. "Amy," he said at last, "I don't know what to say . . . I never expected to see you again. I got . . . Nancy and I, we—"

"I know. It's all right. I'm glad. I didn't want you to be alone."

"But you're *here* now . . . You're *back* and I—"

"*No.* I'm not back, Rick, not for good. I'm here to do what I came back to do."

"Which is?"

"To make them pay for what they did . . . To put the wrong things right . . . But I don't know, I don't know . . ."

He knew what she meant. What had happened tonight seemed wrong, very wrong. "I'm sorry, Amy. I'm sorry for . . . everything. What happened to you, and the children, and tonight . . ."

Rick just shook his head. Words couldn't begin to contain what he felt, what he wanted to say, so he tried to turn to the task. "They have a place somewhere, I'm sure of it—a camp, a headquarters, something. And there are a lot of them. Porter was going to take me there, but maybe I can still get there. And you can follow."

"How?"

"They know I'm here and they'll soon hear about this . . . accident. Maybe they'll send someone else for me. Now Withers said that Porter had a van here that he'd take me back in, probably what they hauled their equipment in, so somebody should be by to pick that up. I could just . . . wait, hang around the parking lot. And when they come for me, you can follow."

She looked at him for a long time, then said, "Why do you want to do this? Why did you start this in the first place, tracking them down?"

"The same reason you did, I guess. So I could rest. And now I have more of a reason—because I want you to be able to rest too, Amy." He felt his face begin to quiver, and tears filled his eyes. "Oh God, I love you. I never stopped loving you. And if you can't be back with me, if you can't stay, then I want you to be happy and at peace."

"I don't know if I ever will be, Rick, or if I'll just . . . snuff out like a candle when this is all over. But know that I love you too. I always will, no matter what happens to me, because I don't think that love can ever really die."

He took her hand then and she didn't pull away. But it felt cold, as though no blood warmed it, and she squeezed his hand gently and then withdrew hers. "Let's find that van," she said.

It was parked close to the building, a dark gray panel van with Minnesota plates. A cheaply produced Shoktrupz bumper sticker adorned it, and on the other side of the bumper were three small Day-Glo letters, *SFA*.

"Convenient," said Rick.

"Stupid," said Amy. "A secret militia that this idiot couldn't resist bragging about. It's a wonder they haven't accidentally blown themselves up a long time ago. You wait here and I'll watch from the car. It could be a long time. What if the police question you?"

"I'll just tell them the truth. I'm waiting for my ride. Besides, I think they've got enough on their hands right now."

It was true. Bystanders and news crews had appeared, as they always could be counted on to do at a disaster. Along with clearing out the bodies and directing the traffic of medics, firemen, reporters, and survivors, the cops were going to have plenty to do.

"All right then," said Amy. "But I want you to promise me something. After you lead me there, I may not come in right away. I don't know what I'll need. After all, I can't fly. And if it's too close to dawn, I won't come in until the next night. I want to do this in darkness. But when . . . *something* happens that makes you know I've arrived, I want you to stay out of it. Hide somewhere, keep yourself safe, don't try to help me anymore. Remember, Rick, they can't hurt me. They've already hurt me enough. And when it's over, get away. Don't tell anyone what happened. No one will believe you, not even Nancy.

"And finally, take good care of her and of Karin. Will you promise me that?"

Rick nodded. "Yes. I promise."

She looked at him for a moment longer and then turned and walked back toward her car. He watched her go, wanting to run after her, embrace her, take her away from there, go somewhere together where there was sunshine and warmth and *make* her live, will her with his love to be fully alive again. In a world where the dead could return, how could such a simple thing be impossible?

But it was. He knew it as surely as he knew that this would all end in more blood.

Ace Ludwig steered his black Chevy east on Route 94 heading for Eau Claire while Ray Withers kept hitting the scan button on the radio. They listened to station after station, trying to catch more news about the accident at the White Christian Brotherhood festival. When the first stories came on the air, Ace had thought Rip was going to go ballistic.

"It's that fucking bitch again!" he had roared. "That fucking government hit squad! They were after Chip this time—*shit!* Those *bastards*!"

Ace thought it was a hell of a conclusion to draw on the basis of the news story, which was simply that during a rock concert at a "white supremacist gathering" near Eau Claire, what was apparently an electrical malfunction had caused serious injury to both the band that had been performing and audience members, though the extent of the injuries was not yet known.

But that had been enough for Rip. He had ordered Ace and Ray to get down to the Frontier Fairgrounds right away and see if Chip was still alive. If he wasn't, they were supposed to bring back the van and try and find this Guy Adams that Rip had such a hard-on for. "And you make fucking well sure that nobody follows you. Anybody tries, lose 'em, and let me know. And once you pick up Adams, don't let him out of your sight."

"You don't trust him?"

"It's not him I'm necessarily worried about. Just do what I say."

So he and Ray had hit the road. The radio reports had come in in bits and pieces, but by the time they reached the fairgrounds they had learned that a group named Shoktrupz had been performing when the electrical mishap had sent power from the stage onto the floor. Dozens of people had been electrocuted, some fatally, particularly those in the immediate vicinity of the stage. The last report stated that all the band members had been killed.

"So long, Chip," said Ray as the announcer finished the story, but Ace was damned if he could hear anything but sincerity in Ray's tone. The guy wasn't smart enough to joke.

The area of the fairgrounds was a real zoo all right. It looked like the Martians had landed, what with all the remote TV trucks and their antennas and blinking red lights along with the blinking red lights of a fire engine, several emergency medical vehicles, and more police cars than Ace had ever seen in one place or ever wanted to see again.

He parked the car along the side of the road, and he and Ray walked into the parking lot near the back of the main building. There was already a police line around the building itself, but Ace quickly found the van parked nearby. Sitting on the asphalt, leaning against the driver's door, a man in his thirties was sleeping, head to one side. He looked like the Adams guy that Rip had described.

"Hey," Ace said, touching the man's leg with his shoe. The man opened his eyes drowsily and licked his lips. "What's your name?"

"Guy . . ." he started but his voice cracked and he cleared his throat. "Guy Adams. Who're you?"

"We're here instead of the man you were supposed to meet. You know who that was?"

"Yeah, Chip Porter." Adams got to his feet. "He one of the dead ones?" he asked, nodding toward the building.

"Appears so."

"So . . . you gonna take me to Mr. Withers?"

"*Colonel* Withers," Ray said.

Ace waved a hand, telling Ray to be quiet. He got the message and looked down at the ground. "Maybe. You see what happened in there?"

Adams shook his head. "I was outside getting some air. Pretty loud band."

"Not anymore." Ace tossed a pair of keys to Ray. "Ray, you drive the van back. Go ahead, you can leave now." Ray got in the van and pulled it out of the lot onto the road, heading for 94. Ace gestured for Adams to follow him and together they walked out of the lot and down the road to Ace's Chevy.

God, at last. Amy turned the key in the Avanti's ignition but didn't turn on the lights. She wouldn't do that until she got out on the road. Now she let out the clutch and the car slipped forward out of the parking space toward the road. The Crow, which had been standing on the hood of her car all that time, rose and flew slowly ahead of her. When she reached the road, Rick and the other man were a hundred yards away, their backs to her.

She had seen the van pull away and had nearly followed it, but made herself be patient and wait for Rick's contact. She had no idea where the van would go, but from what Rick had said, she felt certain that whoever met him would take him to the Sons of a Free America.

They had been waiting for six hours until the two men came, and in that time, sitting alone in the dark car, her only companion the silent and inscrutable black bird, Amy had battled with her guilt. Part of her said that it didn't matter, that the Crow had brought her back for one purpose alone, and what was imperative was that she accomplish that purpose no matter how many people died in the process.

But the part of Amy that had held the dead girl could not accept that. She had killed in cold blood, and though she had not intended harm to anyone other than the killer she sought and his blood brothers in hate, many were dead nonetheless.

The two sides of her had struggled for hours as she tried to rationalize her actions, then spat in the face of those rationalizations. By the time the vigil and the debate were over neither side had won, and she doubted if a victory would be forthcoming.

But now she had action to occupy her thoughts, again playing the game of follow the leader without letting the leader know he was followed. Down the road she saw Rick and the stranger climb into a dark Chevy and watched as it drove onto the road and moved quickly away. Still, she bided her time before she turned on her lights and slipped into its wake. The two red tail lights were far ahead, but she expected the car to head back toward Minnesota and was not disappointed when it got on 94 West.

She followed it for two and a half hours, hanging back as far as she could. Although she had been concerned about keeping it in sight through the Twin Cities area, she had no problem since they passed through at three in the morning. The problem came when they got off the four-lane.

If the driver was heading for Hobie or beyond, she figured she had been spotted. He could have stayed on that road nearly all the way to Hobie, but instead he got off on a two-lane state road. She followed, trying to hang back even further than before. Still, it was difficult. She couldn't drive without headlights.

The road became more twisting, and for minutes at a time she saw no lights ahead of her. Finally, after several miles she came out onto a length of straight road to discover that the Chevy had vanished. It had either put on a tremendous burst of speed or it had taken a smaller side road or pulled into a driveway and backtracked once she had gone past.

She whipped the car around and headed back the way she had come, but realized that the Chevy could have been miles ahead of her by now. She slapped the wheel in frustration but was startled by a sudden streak of darkness that appeared at the top of her windshield and shot out ahead of her.

It was the Crow and it hung just beneath the top of her headlights' beam, its pounding wings an invitation to follow.

Of course, Amy thought with a burst of relief as she stepped on the gas pedal. The bird, high above the trees, had seen where the Chevy had gone and could keep it within eyesight, flying high overhead and returning to Amy before she reached the places where the roads met and split. The Crow would be her guide.

And it happened as she had hoped. The bird would soar out of sight for a minute or two while she continued to drive straight ahead. Then it would drop back into her headlights' beams, banking to show her where to turn. The dark cicerone who had guided her from the land of the dead now led her to the place and the goal through which she would return to that shadowed land.

The Crow led. She trusted and followed.

The trail brought her back to the four-lane road, back toward Hobie, and past it, northwest, toward the heavy forests and the hills. She never saw the car again, but she saw the Crow, and it was all that she needed.

33

Just as dawn was starting to touch the rim of the eastern sky, the Crow alighted. They were in back roads passing through thick woods, and had just come up a hill when the bird stopped, perching on a dead branch of an oak tree whose leaves autumn had nearly denuded. To Amy's right a dirt road led back into the forest, wide enough for only one car at a time.

Amy wondered if she should drive in on it, but decided that if the Crow had intended for her to do that, it would have flown in, leading the way. No, this was where she was supposed to stop.

She pulled the car off the road in among some trees where it would not be seen and climbed out. It was growing lighter every minute and she had nothing with her, so this would be a reconnaissance trip, to make sure she had found the right place, to gauge the strength of whoever and whatever was at the end of the dirt road, and to see what she would need to combat it.

Tirelessly she jogged along the lane, the Crow flying just ahead of her. After fifteen minutes along a fairly straight road, she came upon a sign that read:

WHITE OAK HUNTING CAMP

MEMBERS ONLY

TRESPASSERS WILL BE PROSECUTED

Prosecute away, thought Amy as she continued running. The road began to twist now and she thought what an ideal location this would be for a militia group. A long, straight, narrow road that prohibited access and allowed the defenders to fire at any invaders, including the government, then a series of twists and turns that made it easy to set ambushes. As far as tanks went, the road was too narrow, and the trees were old growth, perfect guardians against military encroachment. What was next?

She found out when she rounded a curve and saw the glint of metal ahead. She got off the path and ran through the brush instead. It was slower but it assured that no guard or watcher would see her approach.

Finally she saw a chain link fence several yards in front of her. It was ten feet high and topped with razor wire. Whatever this place was, it wasn't a hunting camp. Staying in the cover of the brush, Amy started to circumnavigate the compound, heading to her left.

The place was huge, she quickly discovered from the nearly flat arc of the fence surrounding it. It must have taken up a couple dozen acres, and to put a chain link fence, not to mention razor wire, around it all must have cost in the tens of thousands.

Finding no gate, she went back the way she had come and finally discovered the gate at the end of the dirt road. It too was narrow and fringed with heavy trees on either side. She could see the buildings from where she stood and was relieved to find among several other parked vehicles the dark Chevy in which Rick had been driven away, as well as the van the other man had taken. Rick was here then. The Crow had guided her well.

The buildings sat in a large open area and were utilitarian, barracks-style structures painted a gray-green that blended into the trees. The roof shingles were dark green.

There were three large buildings and several smaller cabins. Beyond the back of the open area, tucked among the trees, was a round-roofed building partly dug into the earth like a bunker.

A shooting range was on the right, with targets at one end and benches at the other where guns could be sighted in. Next to the gate was a twenty-foot-high tower reached by a ladder. Its height was far less than the trees around it, but it would provide an effective platform for firing on any people or vehicles that came near the gate.

Amy could see a man standing in the guard tower. He was looking through the trees but she knew he could not pick out her dark form in the heavy brush. Even though most of the leaves had fallen, the trees grew so thickly together that they provided plenty of cover. The greater danger was that he might hear her footfalls in the dead leaves, so she trod carefully, looking for bare ground or patches of moss.

No one was stirring in the camp, and Amy decided to exercise her patience and wait until they rose, to try and see how many of them there were. An hour after dawn they began to come out of one of the larger buildings and head toward another one, probably for breakfast, Amy thought. She counted twenty-three before she saw Rick appear with the man who had driven him there that morning. Two others were with them, a boy in his late teens and a man in his forties who carried himself with a bearing that told Amy he was a leader, if not the leader.

These were the men, then, the ones who had killed her, Judy, and the children, this *militia,* a group of cowards who hid from the world and showed how tough they were by blowing up babies. Amy wanted to storm the fence and attack them with her bare hands. But she didn't know how great her physical strength really was. She would have taken on any three of them, but two dozen was a different story. They might be able to overcome her by sheer numbers.

And if she were captured, what then? They wouldn't be able to kill her but they could imprison her, maybe forever. She wasn't Superman, she couldn't smash her way through walls, but she didn't think she would ever starve or die of illness or exposure. She wasn't sure just *what* the hell would happen but she couldn't afford to take the chance.

No, she would return by night and take them in the darkness, the same darkness that had hidden them and their crimes. She would come equipped with enough firepower to end it all. No innocent bystanders would be harmed, not out here. And when it was over, she could rest. They all could rest.

For Amy knew that somehow the spirits of the children were with her. From the moment she had arisen from the dust, from the time she had asked them to be with her and inspire her, they had never left. Their souls were in just as much torment as her own, if not more, for they were helpless to do anything but suffer while she at least could take action.

And it was time to act and stop thinking about it. She trod carefully away from the fence until she could no longer be seen or heard by anyone in the compound, and then she ran back toward her car, paralleling the dirt road.

She arrived back at David Levinson's house in Hobie at nine in the morning. Levinson was sitting on the couch in the living room, wearing a warm pile bathrobe over his pajamas. A nearly empty bottle of single-malt scotch sat on the coffee table. He was holding a rocks glass with ice cubes that had melted to pale beads. He looked at her with heavy-lidded eyes and poured himself another drink.

"Nice work," he said. Though his voice was soft, it held an edge. "That was you, wasn't it? That thing in Eau Claire?"

She held his gaze and nodded. "That was me."

"Well." He took a deep breath and sat back, resting his arms on the back of the couch, still holding the drink in his right hand. He nodded toward the coffee table. "Have a drink. You earned it." Levinson took a sip of the scotch and smiled. "Nineteen people dead, Amy. Four of them were children. That's a higher body count than the gun show, and the best part is they were all your kills, no friendly fire necessary."

She didn't say anything, but kept watching him. She was damned if she was going to look away.

"And I have to tell you . . . that I'm so proud to be a part of this. To give aid and comfort to . . . what do you call a child killer anyway? I'm a cop, I ought to know that. There's fratricide—that's killing your fraternity brother, matricide, which is smothering somebody with a mattress. There's patricide . . . So what is this? Kidicide?"

"You're drunk."

"Yes ma'am, I'm afraid I am," he said, shaking his head loosely, as if it were on a spring. "But not enough, because I'm still pissed. If I was drunk enough, I wouldn't still feel this pissed. And you know who I'm pissed at?"

"Me."

"Yeah." He half smiled, half leered at her. "Because you didn't give a damn who you hurt, didja? You didn't hear a fuckin' thing I said after the gun show fiasco, didja?"

"Go to hell, David. You didn't see these people, I did." All her practice at rationalizing paid off now. "They were monsters, every single one of them. And they were turning their kids into monsters too! Another ten years and they'd be ready to burn you because you're a Jew!"

"And who the hell let *you* predict the future!" Levinson roared, springing to his feet, staggering and bumping the coffee table so that the scotch bottle tipped over and spilled. "Yeah, maybe they would have—but maybe they *wouldn't*! Maybe they'd have met some teacher or some preacher or even some *Jew* who'da straightened them out! Jesus Christ, Amy, they weren't doomed! They were only seven, eight years old, for crissake! You got your own fuckin' battles to fight, not ones that won't take place for another decade . . ."

"I'm telling you, everyone there was mad, insane. Those children were . . . *preconditioned,* David. They would have become just like the adults there."

"And *so fucking what*?" Levinson said heavily. "What if they had, Amy? This is America, you have the *right* to grow up to be a total racist idiot."

"What about the old Hitler question, David?" Amy said. "You go back in time with a gun in your hand and see Hitler as an eight year old, are you going to pull that trigger? Or are you going to give me that bullshit about talking to him and making him see what was right to do with his life?"

"No, I wouldn't do that, I wouldn't talk to him, and I wouldn't shoot him either. I wouldn't do a goddam thing, Amy, because people like that aren't unique—the devil doesn't make one in a century. They're made in *mass,* and they're made by *history.*

"You wanta know what would happen if somebody had plugged Hitler when he was cute little Adolf?" Levinson went on, his words slurred. "There wouldn'ta been any Hitler, no. But sure as shit there woulda been somebody *else*—maybe Kurt Von Fuckmeister—who woulda come along and made the Jews the villains anyway, and maybe old Fuckmeister was even *smarter* than Adolf, maybe so much smarter that he went slower and cagier, built a war machine five times better than Hitler's, put his boys to work on an A-bomb earlier than we did, invaded Poland in 1945, and then dropped the big one on London. Roosevelt surrenders. Fuckmeister conquers the world. Heil Fuckmeister!

"Six million dead? Shit. Chicken feed. *Sixty* million . . . six *hundred* million—those are Fuckmeister numbers! And that's all your fault, Amy. It's all your fault for blowin' that eight-year-old kid's brains out." Levinson fell back onto the couch and the air went out of him.

"Lady, you got your own battle to fight. Don't you pretend to fight anybody else's but yours. People hurt you, they hurt your children, so go hurt them. Kill 'em, make 'em pay. *But you can't kill everybody who agrees with them.* And don't you *dare* brush away your crimes by saying that because of what you've done that's one less battle that'll have to be fought someday."

He smiled grimly and went on. "Way I look at it, you've given every fuckin' wacko right-wing extremist in this country a whole stellar pantheon of martyrs. Look how much mileage they got out of the old lie that medieval Jews killed Christian children and threw their bodies in latrines. They'll be painting *these* people on their chapel ceilings."

34

Amy couldn't look at Levinson anymore. She had looked away a long time ago. "I didn't mean for it to happen," she said softly in the brooding silence. "I tried to kill the ones on stage, but not anyone else."

"That makes *me* feel better," said Levinson. "Not a whole lot, Amy, just a little. But I don't think it's gonna do much for the survivors." He shook his head as though he were trying to clear it.

"See," he went on more slowly, "the sorrow and the pity of all this is that you came back because they killed your children and now you wind up killing theirs. Strikes me that the kids themselves didn't have a whole lot to say about any of it." He gave a bitter laugh. "You know that old chestnut from Nietzsche? I used to read a lotta horror novels, and for a while there every other one you picked up had that quote that if you fought monsters—"

"You had to be careful not to become a monster yourself."

"You read 'em too, huh?" Levinson continued dreamily. "And if you look too long into an abyss . . ."

"The abyss will look back into you," Amy finished.

"When I was in Detroit," he said, "I looked into the abyss too long. That was why I came here. I wanted things to be better. I wanted to live in a perfect town with a perfect wife in a perfect marriage." He closed his eyes. "And now that old abyss seems to be yawning again. Close it, Amy. Do what you have to do and close it for good. No more innocents dead, no more angels taken from earth to heaven too soon." He opened his eyes and looked up at her. "Swear to me. Swear on their souls."

Amy knelt next to where he sat and put her hand over his, trying to ignore the small shudder that went through him at the touch. "I swear to you. On their souls. No more innocents will die. *On their souls.*" Then she stood up, paced to the far wall, and turned. "I have them now, David. I know where they are. All together. I'm going back and I'm going to end it."

"No innocents."

She shook her head. "No children, no women. Soldiers. At least that's what they'd call themselves."

"I don't suppose you'd consider turning this information over to the police and let them deal with it."

"No, I wouldn't. I wouldn't even consider it," she said without a trace of a smile. She wanted him to know there was no joking about this, no compromise.

"What if I wouldn't give you the Avanti?"

"I'd take it. Or I'd steal another. You know that nothing is going to stop me. So why don't you help me?"

Levinson sighed. "Before I make my decision, I think I'd better have some coffee."

He ground beans and put them in the coffee maker while she sat at the breakfast table. After he turned the machine on, he walked to the door to the garage, opened it, and turned on the light. "You got some mud on it," he said.

"It was raining."

He walked around the car and came back into the kitchen. "No scratches. Thank you."

"You're welcome. I'll try and take as good care of it on this last trip."

"Wouldn't want me to take you there, then I could bring it back safe and sound."

She smiled. "No, I don't think so. I'll put a letter in the mail, let you know where to find it."

He took a pad of paper and a pen out of a drawer and handed them to her. Then he got an envelope and put a stamp on it. "Mail it today, I'll get it tomorrow. Will that be time enough?"

"By tomorrow," she said, "everything will be finished." She tore off the top few sheets of paper and put them on the hard surface of the table. "I wasn't born yesterday, David. I know the old impression trick."

He got a cup of coffee while she wrote. She described how to get to the road leading into the compound and told about the thick grove of trees where she would leave the car:

> *Even if the authorities descend on the place afterward, no one should find it. I'll cover it with brush, so you might have a problem yourself. But look hard. Remember, you're a cop.*

Thank you, David, for everything, and for knowing about what I am and how I came here. I'm sorry things worked out so badly for so many people. I didn't want these things to happen, but they did. I didn't want any of it to happen, from the very beginning, but it did. Sometimes I think no one gives a damn what we want, but then I remember how I returned. Someone, something was listening, and that knowledge makes me feel not quite so alone.

She signed her first name, then folded the paper in thirds, slipped it in the envelope, addressed it, and put it in her pocket.

"If you want to help me," she said, "and get this over fast, there are a few things I'm going to need."

"Such as?"

"Ammo. I put the guns in your basement. I've got a Weaver Nighthawk, nine millimeter, and a Cobray M11/Nine. A couple hundred rounds for each should do it."

Levinson nodded. "Enough for a small army, huh?"

"Exactly. Also, I want some camouflage clothing. Dark. And tight—I don't want to get caught on the vegetation. Doesn't have to be warm. I don't feel the cold anyway. And camouflage paint too, for my skin." She thought for a moment. "Bring me white too, just a small tin of white."

"Jesus, I ought to write this down," Levinson said, reaching for the pad and pen. "Getting to be quite a list." He listed the items she had asked for. "Anything else?"

"Yes. Wire cutters, heavy gauge."

"I've got some. This other stuff I'll have to go out for. Some reason you can't do your own shopping?"

She shrugged. "You're a cop, you can get the ammo easy. Besides, for all I know, they might be seeking a woman of my description not only for the gun show, but for the Eau Claire . . ." She searched for a word.

"Fuckup," Levinson said.

She nodded. "So I'd prefer not to go out again until . . . it's time."

"I don't think you have to worry about the gun club thing. No one reported seeing the Avanti. As for Eau Claire, I don't know. That's another state and we don't have access to their records—or their thoughts—without a good reason. But odds are they're not going to be looking seriously around here, no reason to. Still, I'll do the shopping. You save your strength." Then he winced. "You know what I mean."

"Yeah, I know."

She went down into the basement then, not because she needed to learn any more from Levinson's files or computer, but because she sought the darkness. It seemed the right place for her now. It would happen in darkness tonight, at the very end, with the guns and the knife and whatever else she found to kill them with.

She sat in the darkness for a long time, seeking a calm, a peace, something on which to center and something to drive her, a core of iron that would sustain and strengthen her when the dark came down. She thought about the children first of all, about their smiling faces that would never smile again, the laughter that would never be heard, lives that would never be lived, generations vanished in a heartbeat.

She thought about Judy Croft, her joy in the presence of the children, her patience and humor and understanding blotted out in an instant.

She thought about her own life, her own love, Rick, and how he was risking everything to lead her to the killers and bring them to the dark justice only she and the Crow could mete out. She prayed that he would survive and return to the family he had wanted for so long.

The thought of Rick in Nancy's arms pained her for a moment, but she pushed that pain down, made it part of the greater pain that drove her, rendered it faceless. She knew that he had to love again, and prayed to whatever was there that he would live so that he could.

When that first prayer came, she tried to focus on the deity in which she had always believed. But when she tried to picture him, the kindly, white-robed, white-bearded Judeo-Christian God to whom she had prayed for all her brief life seemed to move and shift in her mind, darkening, its robes and hair and beard fading to black, their textures blending until she saw the Crow sitting like an ancient statue, many times larger than its present form, its ebony eyes looking down at her.

And in them she read a vast indifference. They were black, devoid of emotion, glistening with reflected light and nothing more.

But how could that be? The creature, be it god, demon, or avatar, had brought her back from the dead. Why would it do that if cosmic indifference was its raison d'être?

No, it had brought her back out of some other emotion. If not out of love for her, as she had always expected from God, then perhaps it was out of respect for *her* own love and how that love had been betrayed by those who had killed her and the children. And it had brought her back so that she could put the wrong things right.

But how did it expect her to do that? Expectations, yes—perhaps she could find its motive in its expectations . . .

She realized, with a chill even colder than her flesh, what she had always known:

It expected death.

It expected lives.

Would God have done that? Would her gentle Christ have brought her back to kill, to put her in a position where she would take the lives of children, no matter how predestined toward evil?

No, surely not. But then, if not an agent of God, what was the Crow? Though Amy had believed in God, she had never believed in the devil or demons or any other manifestation of evil other than what dwelled in the hearts and minds of men and women. But now she wasn't so sure.

Still, if the Crow were evil, wouldn't it have wanted evil men, such as the Sons of a Free America, to live and thrive? Why would it have brought her back to kill them?

Perhaps then it was something between good and evil, a more primitive deity from an earlier time, surviving through the eons, a force that demanded justice and used the unjustly killed to achieve its ends, not a devil, but a dark and angry god in its own right.

And a hungry one.

Though she would never truly know, she would let that be her answer then. It was as good as any other. And if Amy was somehow damned for what she had done so far, then so be it. She would go ahead. She could not be damned twice.

She would feed the dark creature that was the Crow, feed it the justice it demanded and that she desired more than love, more than life, more than the eternal rest she hoped would be her reward.

PART THREE

Ah, love let us be true
To one another! for the world, which seems
To lie before us like a land of dreams,
So various, so beautiful, so new,
Hath really neither joy, nor love, nor light,
Nor certitude, nor peace, nor help for pain;
And we are here as on a darkling plain
Swept with confused alarms of struggle and flight,
Where ignorant armies clash by night.

—Matthew Arnold, "Dover Beach"

35

"As soon as you step on it, you hear a click and then if you know what that click means, you just stand there, not knowing what the hell to do. If you *don't* know what it means, or what's more likely, you don't even hear it, you just keep walking. And as soon as you lift up your foot, boom. Your legs disappear into a big red cloud, your dick and your balls get slammed up inside your guts, and you die pretty fucking fast. If you're lucky. Most of the men know where they are by now, but there are some that can't remember, like Ray. He's my brother and a sweet guy and I love him, but he doesn't have a lot upstairs. So if you can't remember where they are, avoid the perimeter. Not much reason to walk around there anyway."

Rip Withers was giving Rick Carlisle the grand tour of the compound of the Sons of a Free America, of which he would become a member that night. When they had arrived early in the morning, Withers had been there to greet him. He had not been a happy man because of the loss of Chip Porter, his computer and electronics expert, but he had been genial enough to Rick.

Withers had shown him to the barracks building where the men lived and slept, given him a towel, washcloth, and toilet articles, and shown him a bunk. Rick was able to get two hours sleep before the rest of the men started getting up, and when he joined them, Withers took him under his wing for the tour, starting with the gate, the fence, and the land mines.

Then he showed Rick the various rooms in the barracks, including the activity room, with a television, a VCR, and an assortment of videos. There were also several hundred books on shelves, most of them concerning American history, military arms, and politics. Rick recognized none of the authors or the publishers. There was also a pool table, a ping-pong table, and several card tables.

The mess hall, where they had breakfast and where Rick was introduced to the men as a new recruit named Guy Adams, was large enough to seat a hundred, although Withers told Rick they had twenty people living there full-time, which increased to thirty on weekends. "Some of the men still hold down jobs, have families. But everybody's here today, staying over for the shoot, and . . . something else."

"The shoot?"

Withers led the way to a large storeroom at the back of the mess building. When he opened the door, Rick heard the sounds of birds, some singing, some making more raucous sounds. Several large cages held an assortment of wild birds, everything from pigeons to crows to small sparrows.

"We do this every few months," Withers said. "Got the idea from that pigeon shoot in Pennsylvania. But we're equal opportunity shooters. We put up nets and traps for a week beforehand and put whatever we catch in here. Then tonight we let them go and take turns bringing them down. Some of them get away to fly another day, especially the little ones—they dart around a lot, make harder targets. But the doves and the crows, they don't have much of a chance with our shooters. These men are good. How are you, Guy?"

"I hate to say it," said Rick, "but I haven't held a gun since I hunted as a boy."

"No service time?"

"I tried to enlist in the Marines but they wouldn't take me. Look." Rick kicked off his right shoe and peeled off his sock. "Little toe turns under. They saw that and said good-bye fast."

"Well, don't worry about it. You'll learn to shoot here."

The third large building was an indoor drill area and pistol range. There were also thick mats on the floor. "This is where we practice hand-to-hand. A lot of the men are skilled in martial arts. Any background?"

Rick shook his head. "The spirit's willing but the flesh needs some training."

"You'll get it. Now let me show you something *really* interesting."

Withers led the way toward the back of the open area, where a structure sat half buried in the earth. It had an arching roof of corrugated metal and the end was brick. Cement steps led down to a door.

"This is what we call the powder magazine," Withers said. "A little old-fashioned name. You might just as soon call it the armory, I guess, but the older name gives us a sense of tradition. This is where we store our weapons, ammo, explosives . . ."

"Explosives?" Rick said.

Withers smiled. "You bet. And here comes the master now."

Rick turned and saw a loose-limbed man with greasy black hair and a dirty pea coat coming toward them. His face was crisscrossed with scars, some pale, others red. "Hey, new guy," the man said, and nodded to Withers.

"This is Ronald Burns," Withers said, "but we all call him Powder. You can see why."

"I put a lot of myself in my work," Burns said with a smirk, holding up his left hand, which was missing the ends of his little and ring fingers.

"How's it cooking?" Withers asked.

Burns nodded happily. "I'll be done another couple hours. We can load it up tonight after the shoot, take it in by dawn's early light." He looked at Rick and frowned. "This guy isn't with *Sixty Minutes,* is he?" Withers laughed and so did Rick. In another few seconds so did Burns. "Well, you came at just the right time for fireworks, man. You told him yet?" he asked Withers, who shook his head no. "Your party," Burns said, and walked down the stairs to the powder magazine, opened the door, and went inside.

"You don't lock that?" Rick asked.

"We don't need any locks here. We're all brothers. If we start thinking we can't trust a brother, well, he doesn't last very long. See, once you come in here, you don't go out for two months. By then we can pretty well tell who's a true Son and who isn't."

"And what if you decide somebody isn't?"

Withers pointed beyond the powder magazine to another stairway leading down that Rick hadn't noticed before. The earth was slightly humped above it. "That is the only cell we have here in the camp. If someone proves to be a traitor, we imprison him there. Then we have a trial. And then we have an execution."

"That ever happened?"

"Guy, way back in those trees . . ." he pointed, "there's a real mossy spot. And under that moss is real soft dirt. And four feet down in that dirt there are three men. Now we thought they were good, white Christian warriors like yourself. But they weren't. They were Judases. They would have sold us out as quickly as Judas sold out Jesus. Two came in together and one came in alone. I don't know whether the two knew the other one. I don't care much. They disappeared and nothing ever happened as a result. No sheriffs or feds or anybody ever came looking for them."

"So . . . what did they do?" Rick's balls were crawling and he hoped his anxiety didn't show.

"Not much, really. Maybe another militia would have let it slide. But we couldn't. We're more *serious* than most other militias. Now I don't want to tell you what it was because I don't want you to constantly be on your guard." He grinned. "There's no point in getting paranoid after all. Besides, I don't think you'll be doing anything like those other men. I really feel that I can trust you, Guy. Or at least I'll be able to after we talk about something."

Oh shit, Rick thought. "What's that?"

"Last night, Ace said that you had a little visitor on the way here. Somebody was following you."

"That's right. But Ace lost him. I don't know why anybody would be following me. Maybe they were following Ace."

"Maybe they were. So you don't know who it was?"

"No, I don't. If I did, I'd tell you."

Rip was quiet for a moment and then he nodded. "Okay. Okay. Well, let me hook you up with some of the men right now—give you some firearms instruction, whaddya say?"

"How do you know he isn't the guy who's been knocking us off, Rip?"

"It was a woman, Ace," said Rip Withers. They were sitting in Rip's cabin, along with Ray and Powder, who had been called from the powder magazine for the meeting to discuss Chip's demise and the advent of Guy Adams. "A woman killed Junior and definitely had something to do with Wilson Barnes spilling the beans."

"What if it was two of them?" Ace went on. "What if they're government people working together? I mean, ain't it a real coincidence that he was at the gun show where Junior bought it *and* at the White Christian Brotherhood thing?"

"Hell, no—*I* told him to go there, Ace. I wanted to see if he could get there and I wanted some time so Karl could tail him, see if his story was straight, see if he met anybody—and he didn't. He said he was dirt poor and he went to a flophouse. He didn't know anybody was watching him."

"I still don't like him. I drove nearly three hours with him last night, Rip—you didn't. You spend three hours alone in the dark with a guy, you get a feel for him and this guy don't feel right. Besides, I swear I seen him somewhere before."

"Well, when you figure out where, you tell me."

"Dammit, Rip, I just don't think this is the time to bring somebody in, with what's going down tomorrow and—"

"He saved my son's life!" Rip exploded. "Why the fuck would he risk his own neck to do that if he was out to kill us? I owe him, Ace! Now we'll keep an eye on him, we won't let him alone." A thought hit him. "Tell you what. We'll let him in on what's happening tomorrow. If he's really with us, he won't do a thing. But if he's not, he'll either try to get out and warn people or he'll try and fuck it up by messing with the bomb. We'll just watch him, stop him if he tries anything, and the next twenty-four hours will tell the tale. Agreed?"

It made sense to everyone there, and Rip sent Ace to assign two men to watching Guy Adams around the clock. When he got back, it was time to talk about what had happened to Chip Porter.

"The main thing is, whether Adams had anything to do with it or not, someone is carrying out a vendetta against us. We know it was a woman who got Barnes to squeal on the air. Then somebody killed Sonny, then Junior, and now Chip's dead. You know how Chip was, he never would've let an electrical fuckup like that happen. Would he, Powder?"

Powder shook his head. "Definitely not the Chipman. He knew his wiring front and assbackwards. His stuff was old, so he had to take more care with it, but he always did. Whatever went down wasn't his fault."

"And if you noticed," Rip said, "they're not calling it an accident. Nobody's said yet that it was an act of sabotage but that sure sounds like that's what they're setting us up for."

"Well, why would they tell us that?" asked Ray.

"What?"

Ray spoke slowly as if trying to choose every word. "Why would they . . . the liberal press . . . say it was sabotage? I mean, if these government people did it, wouldn't the government want it to look like an accident? So why won't they *say* it's an accident?"

"I don't know, Ray," Rip said impatiently. His brother seldom spoke but when he did Rip always hated it. When it was just the two of them, fine, but these meetings were official and he didn't need Ray's thoughts wandering. "But that doesn't matter. What matters is finding out who's responsible and how they've been tracking down and fucking *eliminating* us. They got three of us so far and damn near got Karl.

"Now we're going to strike back *big* with this bomb but that's not going to stop this. We've got to find this bitch and whoever's working with her and terminate their asses for good."

"So how, Rip?" asked Powder. "I mean, it ain't like we got a surveillance or intelligence section or anything."

"No, but maybe this piece of shit will come to us. I think that whoever was following Ace and Guy Adams last night was the same person who wired up Chip to die. It'd be too big a coincidence otherwise. And if they were smart enough to track us down one by one, they'll eventually be smart enough to find this place."

"And bring the feds," said Ace.

"Not necessarily. If this was the feds they'd have taken one of the men for questioning before they killed them."

"That's right," said Powder. "But with Sonny and Junior and Chip, it was out-and-out assassination—they didn't try to interrogate them before they snuffed them."

"And that's what I don't quite get," said Rip. "It's like they're not out to arrest us but to pick us off one by one. Well, lots of fucking luck, sweetheart. Next time we leave this place, it'll be tomorrow with the bomb, and we'll be leaving in a van and two cars with four soldiers in each, and all of us will be armed to the teeth. So if this cunt and whoever else is with her want to get us, it's going to have to be today. She's going to have to bring Mohammed to the mountain. I want double guards tonight and nobody better fuck around. We've come too far to blow it now, especially when we're really going to *blow* it tomorrow. Got me?"

Rick hoped that Amy would come tonight and end it all. He felt unclean among these men, as though their madness had rubbed off on him in the hours in which he shared their lives and their twisted dreams.

Some of them had actually talked about what they had done so far—the executions, as they termed it, of Wilson Barnes and William Standish and, far worse to hear about, the explosion at the day-care center, Amy's center. A man named Ed Conover was chatting with him about it while he showed Rick how to load and fire an automatic rifle.

"Oh yeah, it was bad news, y'know, 'cause we were trying to get that Jew-loving senator, but it turned out all right because of a couple different reasons . . . Okay, that's it, just push that magazine up in there, uh-huh . . . Well, yeah, it was too bad those kids got killed and all, but we hadn't planned for that to happen. Still, first of all, it let them know, the federals, I mean, that we weren't anything to mess with. Told 'em straight off that we had the technology and the know-how to get the explosives in where their big boys were, y'know? . . . All right, now just yank that slide back there . . . No, no, don't be so dainty, give it a good yank, it won't break . . . *There* ya go . . . And in the second place, Barnes—Satan take his black soul—did us at least one last favor when he said that patriots never woulda done anything as bad as blowing up a bunch of little kids, but the government already had at Waco so this was just one of *their* tricks to make the militia folks look bad. And you'd be surprised at how many people bought it.

"Okay, you're locked and loaded, pal. Now let's head on over to the range and—"

"Set for bear, huh?" Rip Withers said, interrupting. "I'll take him over to the range, Ed." Withers loaded a weapon in a tenth of the time Rick had taken. "Let's go, Guy."

They walked out of the building and toward the firing range. "Ed telling you about our 'explosive situation'?" Withers said, and chuckled. "That's nothing compared to what we got next. You came just in time, Guy. We already got our delivery crew picked but you'll be able to share in the glory."

"What, uh, what do you mean?"

"I mean the Olson building in Hobie—where all the government offices are. We got a real sweet treat going in there tomorrow. All the plastic explosive that we've been stockpiling for the past year, minus, of course, what we used for the day-care place. None of this fertilizer-and-petroleum crap. It's going to make Oklahoma City look like a cherry bomb. There won't be *anything* left standing afterwards."

"Tomorrow?" Rick asked. He could feel his heart pounding.

"Tomorrow morning we head out. Powder's finished putting it together. Stored in the magazine. Though, boy, if it'd go off I think we'd all turn into Jell-O." He laughed as he sat down at one of the shooters' benches. "Okay, let's practice firing at those targets right there . . ."

As he aimed at the black circle, Rick thought about what in the hell he could do. He could quickly turn on Withers and kill him and then try and make it to the powder magazine. But there were several other shooters on the range and he couldn't hope to shoot them all before they gunned him down.

And even if he could get inside the magazine, what then? Could he blow the whole damn thing up and himself with it before they got to him?

Probably not. Rick didn't know a thing about explosives. No, any quick attempt at sabotage would end up with him dead and nothing accomplished. At least the powder magazine wasn't locked. Maybe he could slip away and figure out some way to dismantle the device or get to a phone, although he hadn't seen any.

And maybe, just maybe, Amy would get here in time to do something to stop this plan.

36

Night had fallen at last, and Amy Carlisle looked at herself in the mirror. The camouflage was perfect. She would blend seamlessly into the night, and the fit was tight enough that she wouldn't get hung up on any branches. If thorns tore her flesh, it made no difference. The pain would pass and she would heal as quickly as the wounds appeared.

Levinson had bought everything she had requested and more. The boots she wore were masterpieces of engineering, lightweight but with sturdy soles with which she could move through the forest like a wraith. He had gotten her a combat belt for her knife and a second knife as well. "In case you leave the first one sticking in a tree or the ground or an insane extremist," he told her.

He had also bought extra magazines for both weapons which could be slipped into the belt. When a magazine was empty, all she had to do was pop it out and slam in another one. "This must have cost you quite a bit," she told him as he sat on the bed, watching her.

"It just came out of my extermination budget." He shook his head. "God, that sounds awful. That was the phrase the Nazis used about the Jews—extermination."

"The Jews were innocent. These people are guilty."

Levinson took out three small tins from a paper bag. "You still want the paint?" he asked.

Amy nodded and took them. She tied back her hair, then opened the green and the brown and began to rub thin layers over her face, mixing the two until her skin was the color of mud. It dried quickly and then she opened the white. "I want to blend into the darkness," she said. "And yet

I want them to see *something*. I think I want them to see their deaths coming."

She dipped a finger into the clown white and drew a thin line that outlined her lips. At the corners of her mouth, she brought the white line upward an inch on either side like a ghostly smile. Then she outlined her eyes as well and looked closely into the mirror. She shook her head. Something was still missing.

Then she knew what it was. She dipped her finger into the white and made one more line under each eye, straight down, like a pale falling tear.

"I'm ready," she said, and turned to Levinson.

The man shuddered and Amy knew that her face contained all she had hoped it would. It was a face that would inspire terror, a face of the dead that was one with the night, yet would shine out of the darkness like an angry star ready to burn away all those who tried to stop it.

"Yeah," he said. "I think you're ready." Then he smiled. "I just hope you don't get stopped by an officer."

"I'll just tell him I'm a little late for a Halloween party," Amy said, and smiled back, though from the look on Levinson's face, it probably would have been better if she hadn't.

He walked her to the car and they put the weapons and the heavy-gauge wire cutter into the trunk. Amy got behind the wheel and looked at Levinson. "I probably won't see you again. Thank you, David. I don't know what else to say."

"I don't either, Amy. I really don't. It has been . . . a unique experience."

"We never really talked about it," Amy said, "but are you religious?"

"I know where the local temple is but I haven't been there since I moved here. I'm afraid I'm pretty well one of those lapsed Jews." Levinson smiled. "But what I've gone through lately has made me wonder. I may be *re*lapsed."

"In any case," she said, "will you do me one more favor?"

"If I can."

"Will you pray for me? In your temple? Pray for my soul, wherever and whatever it is. And for the souls of those who died. The innocents."

She didn't say whether she meant those who died with her or those she had killed, but it didn't seem to matter to Levinson. "I will," he said. "I promise. For *all* of them."

That was good enough. She knew what he meant and that he had known what *she* meant. "Thank you. Good-bye, David."

The garage door opened and she backed out, then drove into the night, toward her purpose, toward the end of it all.

She drove well under the speed limit so that no policeman would stop her on the way. On the outskirts of Hobie she dropped the letter to Levinson in a mailbox and then left the lights of the city behind, threading the black Avanti through the twisting back roads and the dark forests.

The Crow flew before her, dropping in and out of her beams. Though she did not need it to guide her, she was glad it was there. " 'Prophet still, if bird or devil,' " she whispered, and followed.

When she reached the dirt road back to the compound, she drove the Avanti off the road and among the trees, fifty yards into a small clearing next to a patch of brambles. She ripped out brush and broke off branches to hide the car from sight, then took out the weapons and the wire cutter, loaded her combat belt with the filled magazines, and walked back to the dirt road.

The full moon made it easy for her to find her way. Its light fell through the nearly leafless trees onto the forest floor, making a pale path before her. It was even brighter on the dirt road itself. The night was windy and she thought that would help to cover the sound of her footfalls on the dry leaves. With luck, they would not know she was there until she was standing beside them, her knives in their backs.

Ace Ludwig was pissed. He *knew* he had seen this Guy character somewhere before. If he could just remember . . .

Ace didn't buy this fugitive-from-justice shit at all. The dude was too *clean,* almost as if he had done himself up to look shabby, like he was in a fucking movie or something. And when Ace had talked to him in the car on the way back to the compound, he had given all the right answers but there was something weird about the whole thing. The *words* were right but it was like he really didn't believe what he was saying.

If the guy was a fed, they could be fucked royally, even though Ace had lost the tail who had climbed on his ass somewhere on the interstate. But if he *was* a fed, how the hell would Ace have ever seen him before? Through the afternoon Ace had gone through the file of photos they had of feds whose covers had been busted, and there wasn't anybody who looked like this Guy Adams.

Shit. Maybe somebody he had been in the service with? No, the guy was too damn young to have been in the Nam and so fucking dumb when it came to guns that Ace knew he had never been through basic. Hell, he had probably never even been in a fight in his whole life. Looked like too much of a yuppie for that.

His hands were soft too. No matter what he'd told Rip, this was not a working man. Guy Adams was a desk jockey with a pretty wife, two cars in the garage, a deck, a couple kids in an expensive day-care . . .

Then Ace froze. That was it. Day care.

He walked into the rec area and started flipping through the videotapes Rip had made of the news stories about the bombing, and started shoving them in the machine. After twenty minutes of searching he found it and went looking for Rip.

It was dark by now but the flood lights illuminated the compound as brightly as if it had been day. Near the shooting range several of the men were positioning the cages for the bird shoot.

The search lights outside the enclosure were on too, lighting the dirt road coming up to the gate. They weren't usually on but Rip wasn't taking any chances of a last-minute covert attack by the feds. Anything was possible.

Ace found Rip in the mess hall, talking with some of the men over a cup of coffee. He leaned down and spoke into his ear. "Where's Adams?"

"I don't know," Rip said. "But don't worry, he's being watched."

"Good thing. I got something to show you about our new friend." He stood up and led the way back to the rec hall. Powder and Ray came with them. "Check this out," Ace said, and hit the play button on the VCR.

A reporter stood in front of the smoking rubble of the Making Friends Child Care Center. It was night not long after the explosion. The reporter was saying how everybody inside had probably been killed, and then she turned and said, "I believe this is the husband of one of the victims. Sir? Sir, would you mind telling us how you're—"

Then a man in a dark jacket appeared behind the reporter, crossing the screen with a woman. He looked toward the camera for less than a second and looked away so quickly that his brightly lit face was distorted by motion blur before it disappeared. But Ace hit the remote's review button and the image backtracked, then froze on the man's face. "Look familiar?" Ace asked.

There was no doubt in any of their minds that the man looking at the camera was Guy Adams. Ace let it play out. "I guess he has no comment," the reporter said, turning back toward the camera. "That, we believe, was Richard Carlisle, the husband of the owner of the center, believed to have died in the blast."

Ace turned off the machine and looked at Rip. The man's already florid countenance was reddening even further and Ace could see his jaw muscles clench as he leaped to his feet.

"That fuck! That lousy *fuck*! Find him, we gotta find him *now*!" Rip led the way outside but when they burst through the door they saw the man they now knew to be Carlisle and the two men assigned to watch him coming from the direction of the powder magazine. The two men were holding pistols to Carlisle's head.

"What?" Rip asked impatiently. "What'd he do?"

"Nothin', I hope," said the one man. "He went into the magazine and when we followed him he was messing around with the bomb."

"Shit!" Powder Burns barked, and sprinted across the area toward the magazine.

Rip walked up to Carlisle and looked him in the eye. "Richard Carlisle, huh?"

Carlisle smiled. Ace had to give him points for that. That took guts. Or maybe the guy was just stupid. "My friends call me Rick," he said. "You can call me Richard."

Rip backhanded him with a shot that staggered him. He fell back a few steps but didn't fall down. Ace gave him some more points for that too. It was one hell of a wallop. "You slimy *prick,*" Rip said. "You fucking traitorous *shit*!"

The other men were starting to gather now. Ace saw Karl come trotting up, looking worried. Rip looked at the boy, then at the other men. "We got a real treat here, men—an out-and-out sonovabitch *spy*!"

Karl walked uncomfortably up to Rip. Ace could tell the kid didn't want to say a word but felt that he had to. "Dad . . . he, well, he saved my life . . ."

"He saved your life to get in *here,* you dumbass! It was a setup—he was with the *bitch*!" He looked back at Carlisle with murderous eyes. "All right, let's take this piece of Jew-loving, nigger-loving crap to the cell and have a little talk with him."

Just then Powder Burns came back, looking pale and tired. "It's okay," he said. "He just pulled a couple wires, tried to screw up the timer or something, but didn't have time to do anything."

"He shouldn't have had time to do *shit,*" Rip complained, snarling at the two men who had been guarding Carlisle. "Is it all right?" he asked Powder.

"Yeah, I wired it right back up. Never any danger."

"I want extra sentries tonight," Rip ordered. "Not just at the gate but four more to cover the perimeter. Karl, you're one of them—go to the north end. Powder, assign the rest. Come on, bring him," he said, pointed to Carlisle, and stalked toward the cell half buried in the earth of the forest.

Rick's only chance now was Amy. If she didn't come he was dead, and he was probably dead anyway. At least then maybe he would be with her again someday, after this whole thing was finished. He had tried to dismantle the bomb but had no idea of what he was doing. The main danger was that it might go off, and if it did, that would have been all right too.

But no such luck. And now he was being taken to the cell Rip Withers had shown him earlier. And torture chamber? Rick wondered. He didn't know how Withers could resist.

As it turned out, he was right. They tied him to a wooden chair with leather straps and put another strap around his head so that they could move it, exposing his throat or either side of his head. There were four of them in the cell, Rick, Powder, Withers, and Ace, who had joined them after assigning the sentries. All were armed with guns in holsters, but it was a knife that Withers held in front of Rick's face.

Rick tried to keep smiling but he was scared shitless. He hoped that whatever happened he wouldn't piss himself, but was afraid he probably would. Wasn't there some involuntary reaction to extreme pain or terror? He knew that if he died, he would lose it all, bladder, bowels, the works, but by then he wouldn't care much. Let these bastards deal with the mess.

"See this knife?" Withers said. Before Rick could respond, Withers had stuck it in the hollow of his ear and jerked the blade sideways, slicing the flesh and the cartilage.

Rick couldn't help but give out a yelp, but the shame made him grit his teeth immediately. Flop sweat started to bead his skin and he could feel blood trickling down his ear lobe and dripping off onto his shoulder.

"It won't bleed much," Withers said. "Just wanted you to know that I'm serious. If you don't tell me what I want to know, I will disfigure you, I will cripple you, I will kill you. You are worse than the enemy, you are a spy and a traitor. You are less than *meat* to me. You're going to die and you can make it easy—*relatively* easy—or you can make it hard. Now the first thing I want to know is, who are you with?"

That was an easy one. "My partner." Partners in life, partners in death.

"Not the feds? Not the police?"

"They don't know I exist. Like I said, it's just me and my partner."

"All right—who *is* the bitch?"

Rick paused. "Yo mama," he smirked.

It was a stupid thing to say and Rick knew that it would only bring more pain. But maybe he would get lucky and this asshole redneck shithead would get so pissed he'd kill him right off. But the main reason Rick said it was that he was pissed. He hated this man and what he had done.

Apparently Withers had interrogated prisoners before. He didn't get mad, not raging mad anyway. His nostrils widened and his teeth showed and he moved the knife to the other ear and sliced again.

This time Rick was ready for it. A grunt came from deep in his throat, but goddammit, it was a *manly* grunt. Fuck this wanker anyway. Let him cut, Rick had lots of skin. And with both ears slashed, the drips had evened out. He was bleeding in stereo.

"I don't like it when you get smart with me, *Richard,*" Withers said. "Not a bit. I'm not amused and neither are my friends. Now I can cut your ears to make you look like a dog. I can slice your chest to give you hanging tits. And I can make a woman out of you in other ways too. You get my meaning?"

"I believe so," Rick said, breathing heavily.

"All right. Now I want to know who the woman is. The woman who killed Junior at the gun show, the woman who got Wilson Barnes to spill his guts."

"You know what else she did?" Rick asked. It had just occurred to him that he might as well tell this nutcase the truth, that it would scare the shit out of him and, most of all, that Amy would probably want him to know. It might also have the advantage of saving him from more torture. "She killed the guys on the stage—all of them. You had any other of your storm troopers killed in action lately?"

Withers looked serious as hell. "Yeah. A man in a parking garage and the mother of one of our men—in her trailer."

"Tell me," Rick said, smiling. "How'd they buy it?"

"The one was stabbed. The old lady's neck was broken and her trailer set on fire."

"Sounds like my partner's M.O.," Rick said, and chuckled. He wondered if he were going a little crazy. "She likes to leave things messy."

Withers grabbed the leather strap and yanked Rick's head back, exposing his throat. Rick felt the edge of the knife against it. "Who is she? Who the fuck *is* she?"

"You don't know?" Rick said roughly, his throat taut. "You ought to. After all, you killed her."

"What?" The knife moved away from his windpipe and the strap was released. His head slumped down and he looked back up at Withers, who was staring at him, confused. "What do you mean, I killed her?"

"My wife. Amy . . . Amy Carlisle."

Withers stared a moment longer. Then a smile bent one side of his mouth and he barked a phlegmy laugh, one that was afraid to be heard. "What are you talking about? She's *dead.*"

"That's right. But she's *back.*"

For a long moment Rip Withers looked terrified. Then his face became set with resolve and he lifted the knife so that it was less than an inch from Rick's right eye. "You're a fucking liar and liars lose things that are important to them."

"I'm *not* a liar," Rick said with as much fire as he could. "Your own son saw her get shot and keep walking. She fried your guitar player, took the juice herself, then walked away from it. You can't kill her, Withers." He smiled in the eye of the knife. "To paraphrase that tape Rush Limbaugh always plays for laughs, She's here, she's a feminist, she's *in your face.* But this time nobody's laughing."

Withers swallowed hard and the knife came slowly away from Rick's eye. When he spoke, his voice shook just enough for Rick to hear. "I don't care who the hell she is. If she comes here, she's going to die. If she tries to stop us, she's going to die."

"That'll be tricky. Like I said, she's already dead."

"And *you're* gonna *join* her!" Withers said as he stood up. "Right after the shoot, the one who gets the most kills gets to finish you, you little faggot! There's gonna be one more grave under the moss by morning!"

"There'll be a lot of dead people by morning, Withers."

"Get somebody to guard this motherfucker," Rip said to Ace, and spun on his heels and left the cell followed by Powder and Ray. He couldn't stay in the same room with this liberal piece of shit for another second. He was afraid Carlisle would push him too far and he'd kill him. No, he wanted him to live on for a while, to think about dying, about getting shot down in front of the people he hated most in this world.

Well, the feeling was fucking mutual. Rip hated these yuppie, government-loving lefties just as much as they hated him and probably more. There wasn't any answer, there was no compromise, there was no possible way for two ideologies so different to coexist in the same country. Congress was pulling itself apart and bipartisanship was a fucking joke. War was the only answer, war and extermination or banishment of whoever lost, and Rip didn't intend it to be his side.

"What do you think, Rip?" Powder asked. "About what he said."

He whirled around and put his face right into Powder's. "What do I *think*? I think okay, let Amy Carlisle come back from the dead. If she can hold a gun, we can shoot her and we can shoot her again and again and again until we blow her into so many pieces the cunt'll *never* be able to pull herself together!"

Ray looked down for a moment, the thoughts slowly falling into place, then looked back up. "But we already did that."

Rip's teeth clenched. Words failed him. He was angry and anxious and scared, about the spy, about the woman, and about the bombing the following day. There was just too much to think and worry about.

So he decided not to think at all. He would kill something instead. "Hey!" he shouted in mock joviality to the men standing around the cages near the range. "Who wants to shoot some birds!"

37

Amy was careful to put at least fifty yards between herself and the compound fence. The open area had been lit up like Steven Spielberg was expecting the mother ship to land and the light filtered into the surrounding forest, letting her see while remaining unseen.

She had decided the best place to enter would be at the opposite end from the gate. There was no reason for the Sons to think that anyone had discovered their location and if the bastards were as inept at security as they seemed to be at everything else, she should have no problem getting in.

And once she got in, the best way to handle things would be to do what she had done on the outside. Take them one or a few at a time. Even the gun show had been a close call. She had been assaulted with so much firepower that she had feared falling beneath it several times. If she had, and if they had been able to get chains on her or imprison her, she would have failed.

She might fail now against the sheer firepower of several dozen armed men. Best to come upon them like a white-eyed plague, one at a time, until none were left.

Amy wondered how Rick was doing. His mission had been braver than hers. She remembered Scrooge's protest to the spirit from *A Christmas Carol*: "I am a mortal, and liable to fall." He was indeed, and she wished that she could stop thinking and worrying about him so much.

She wished she could stop loving him so much.

She had told herself over and over that he and she were now on different shores of creation, though they had been face to face. That was why she had not fallen into his arms, not clung to him as though she would let nothing, not even death, pull them apart again. It was not fair to him. It was not even fair that she had let herself be seen by him. She should have remained a memory.

And yet, wasn't it somehow reassuring for the living to know that there was indeed something after death? That they might be reunited again?

Amy. And Rick.

And Nancy.

It stuck in her heart like a barb. If she had been passed over to wherever the peaceful spirits go when they die, she could have looked down and seen Rick and Nancy together and felt not only love for both of them, as she did now, but fulfillment, knowing that the one she loved was no longer alone. And wasn't that what love was all about? Not wanting the loved one to die so that they could join you, but wanting them to live happily and live loved.

It was not resentment she felt, but sorrow, and she had fought it as best she could. In a little while she wouldn't have to fight it anymore.

As she walked beyond the throw of the powerful lights, she moved nearer to the fence so that she could keep it in sight. Once she saw something moving on the other side and at first assumed it was a deer. But when she froze and looked more closely, she could see that it moved with the unmistakable gait of a man walking slowly and carefully.

So there were extra sentries out tonight. She would have to be more careful then.

When she heard the first of the gunshots, she dropped to a crouch, even though the shot did not sound near to her. Another shot followed, then more, and she realized that they were coming from the brightly lit area near the buildings. Perhaps Levinson and other policemen had followed her and she was hearing a gun battle.

But no, the shots were coming at too long intervals. They must be training or having a competition. At any rate, more than just the sentries were up and about and armed, and her caution increased even more.

At last she reached the place where the fence started to curve to the east, and she trod gently across the fallen leaves until she reached the ten-foot-high chain link fence. The razor wire at its top shone brightly in the moonlight. Though she thought about simply climbing over it, it would be too easy to get entangled in it. Her clothes, if not her flesh, would be torn to shreds. So she took the wire cutters and started snipping away at an open spot where the brush did not come right up to the fence.

The powerful tool cut the individual strands like dead twigs and in a short time she had made a hole big enough to climb through. She left the cutters behind. Her weapons were all she would need now.

Once within the fence she listened intently, but heard only the wind and the sound of the guns to the south. Her gaze searched between the trees but she saw no movement.

Amy could have headed straight south toward the buildings, through the trees in the center of the fenced area. But she reasoned that if she kept to the perimeter, she would come across the sentries and could take them individually. They would be looking outside the fence, not inside. So she began to follow the fence line, staying several feet from it, working her way south. Both weapons were slung over her shoulders so that her hands were free. She didn't want to draw attention to her presence yet, and the knife would be quiet.

Amy saw the first sentry after walking two hundred yards. He was a tall, heavy man, holding an assault rifle at port arms as he walked unconcerned through the trees toward her. As she had assumed, he was looking outside the fence for danger. Drawing her knife, she stepped behind a tree and waited for him to come closer.

It was almost too easy. His back was to her as he passed and she had to take only one step to reach him. Wrapping her left arm around his head so that the inside of her elbow pressed into the hollows of his eyes, she drew his head back and, with the knife in her right hand, scored the blade across his throat.

She didn't even feel the blood splash. She only felt the man spasm until she released him, and he fell straight down on his face, across the weapon he was holding.

Amy kicked him over easily. His finger hadn't even been in the trigger guard. Amy wiped her knife on the dead leaves, slipped it back into its sheath, and took the dead man's weapon. She didn't know the name of it but it looked deadly, and she decided to start her shooting with it and toss it away when it was empty. It would save her a change of magazines.

Shots continued to be fired from the other end of the compound as she dragged the dead man into the brush and kept moving south. She was about fifty yards away from where she had killed the sentry, when she stepped on something other than the loamy forest soil.

Before she had time to question what it was, the world burst into flame around her and an intense pain ripped at her body. She could feel her feet and legs torn apart and what seemed like fists of fire slamming into her torso, shredding her bowels like they were paper. She flew, her flesh ravaged, into the night sky, seeing her blood arc from her, the drops glowing like bits of jellied napalm, then, as the flame died, like glistening rubies in the moonlight. She fell, landing heavily on her back, her sundered face looking upward at the moon through the skeletal branches of trees.

Her throbbing brain knew that it was a mine. She had stepped on a mine and though she had not even heard it, it had exploded beneath her, the concussion stunning her and the blast smashing her to pieces.

Then her eyes saw, alighting on a branch so that its dark shape eclipsed the moon, the Crow. It seemed to look down at her, though its eyes were shadowed, and she knew that her mission was not over. She did not question. She did not lift her head and look down at her body to see if she was capable of rising. She simply sat up and got to her feet.

Her clothing hung from her in shreds but it covered her flesh, which was knit together again as though the mine had never been. The guns she had been carrying on her back had been wrenched from her by the mine's force, but when she picked them up, they seemed functional. They were made to take punishment, she guessed, although the weapon she had been holding had taken the full impact of the concussion and was twisted beyond use. She was glad to see that her knife still had its edge.

A rustle sounded overhead and she looked up to see the Crow flying south again, toward the sound of guns and the lights. Amy started walking.

38

Powder Burns looked up in alarm. "You hear that?" he asked Rip Withers, who was standing next to him, watching the shooting.

"What?"

"Sounded like something up in the north—a shot or explosion or something."

"Ah, you heard an echo, that's all," said Rip.

Powder thought about it. The sound had come right on the tail end of a shotgun blast. Maybe Rip was right and it had been an echo. But man, it had that *crump* quality to it, and the more Powder tried to re-create the sound in his head the more certain he became that it wasn't a shot, but one of his antipersonnel mines going off.

Hell, it happened now and then, but it had always been a deer that had made an unlucky step. A lot of the men were worried about it, though, and with sentries in the north, where they weren't used to patrolling, anything was possible, though they were told over and over not to go within ten feet of the fence.

Powder tried to get his mind off of it by watching the men shooting. There was a certain beauty to it, the bird being released and darting into the air lit by the bright lights, then the sound of the shot and the bird either flying away while the other men hooted at their comrade's lack of marksmanship or, as happened nine times out of ten, the bird exploding in a supernova of blood and feathers.

Now Ed Conover took his stance and yelled, "Go!" A dove shot into the sky, zigged and zagged for two seconds, and then Ed blew it apart with one shell.

As Powder watched the bird dissolve in the air, he thought about what his mines could do, and then he remembered that Karl Withers was up there, walking around the perimeter, within yards of those mines. Karl Withers, Rip's one and only son, one of the nicest if not the brightest kids Powder had ever known, and it was that not-so-bright aspect that now alarmed Powder. What if the kid had blundered into a mine. Odds are he hadn't, but oh shit, what if he had?

What the hell, it wouldn't hurt to check. He could get up and back in a half hour or so. He'd take a flashlight and whistle the Horst Wessel song all the way so that the sentries would know he was coming. Might as well take a pistol too, just in case.

Phil Riley knew damn well what that sound was, though he was a lot closer to it than Powder Burns had been. Somebody or something had stepped on a mine, and the hair on Phil's belly curled even more at the thought. He hoped to hell it wasn't one of his brothers, as he trotted toward where the sound had been.

Phil wasn't scared of the mines. Although he didn't know where all of them were located, he knew just how close he could come to the fence before he risked getting his nuts blown off. But some of his brothers were a little more careless than he was.

After all, it came with the territory. If you were an outlaw in the eyes of the Jew government, it tended to make you a little reckless. You knew you stood a good chance of dying before you reached a ripe old age so you tended to value your life a little less than you otherwise might have.

But not Phil. If Phil was going to die, he wanted to do it for a reason, for a cause. He wanted to go down taking as many Jews and niggers with him as possible. He wanted to make the bastards pay. The damn ZOG government took all his money in taxes for those raggedy-ass coloreds who didn't do shit except sell drugs to each other. Even now, in the cool night air, the thought made Phil Riley's blood boil. He wished he had a nigger to kill, one of those so-called poor, raggedy ones.

He walked more slowly as he approached the place where the noise had come from. And then he saw it in the moonlight. There was a small crater in the earth where he was certain that a mine had exploded, but there was no body anywhere. Now what the shit was *this* all about?

Phil leaned his gun against a tree and stepped gingerly toward the crater. No use in taking any chances, though Powder probably hadn't put his mines that close together. Phil knelt, looking at the crater, searching for any signs of flesh or blood when he heard leaves crackle behind him. He turned and standing between him and his gun was his worst nightmare.

The figure was dark. Its skin appeared black in the moonlight and rags hung from its thin frame. Its face was dark except for the eyes, two white circles with darkness at their core, and the mouth, a pale, painted smile. It looked like a blackface minstrel gone insane. And it had a big knife in its hand.

Phil couldn't even speak. His mouth moved but no words came out. Finally his mind cleared just long enough for him to reach for his survival knife and yank it from its sheath. The black figure still didn't move.

Phil lunged at it with his knife and tried to scream, "Die, nigger!" But the words came out choked and pinched. Still, the knife entered the raggedy nigger's guts and Phil ripped to the side and stepped back.

The nigger didn't move. It only smiled, and now he could see its white teeth rimmed by the white mouth. Then it spoke, in a woman's voice. "It's not nice to call names." The nigger's arm shot out and skewered him, sticking the knife in the same place where he had stabbed it. *"Redneck,"* it said, and slashed to the side, the same way Phil had done.

The effect on Phil was far more impressive. He put his hand to his side to try and stop his guts from sliding out over his belt, but it didn't work very well. Then he plopped down on his ass, trying with both hands to shove back into himself the warm loops that flooded over his hands and forearms like wriggling snakes. But goddammit, he couldn't *do* it, it wouldn't *work* and he didn't want to have to die this way, for nothing, and to have it done to him by a *nigger,* by some blackface *coon,* was more than he could bear.

So he died.

Amy wiped the knife on the leaves again. This was getting to be a habit. Maybe she should just leave it wet with their blood so it would slide into the next one more easily. She took the dead man's weapon, a good replacement for the one that the mine had destroyed, and started running lightly across the leaves.

She hadn't gone twenty yards before she saw another shape moving toward her from the south. Good, she thought. Another one. Line them up and knock them down.

Amy slipped behind a thick tree and waited. The shape came walking up, and when she glanced around the tree at it, she saw his face. It was only a boy, no older than seventeen or eighteen. His young skin looked smooth in the moonlight, his eyes were wide and frightened. The gun he was holding looked big and bulky in his hands. He appeared to be no taller than Amy and she guessed he might have weighed less.

He looked innocent. Young and guileless and innocent. There was no other word for it. And what had she promised Levinson? That no more innocents would die.

That was what had started all this, wasn't it? The slaughter of innocents had brought her back and the death of one more misguided child would not help to put the wrong things right. It would only make things worse, *perpetuate* the wrongs. No. It had to stop sometime.

But what could she do? The boy had a gun and if he fired it, it might arouse the others. Her plan to take them slowly had worked so far and there was no reason to change it now.

Then she would stop him from firing the gun without hurting him.

Let's see how innocent he really is, Amy thought, as she set down her guns. She staggered out from cover only a few yards from the boy, keeping her head down so he would not see her painted face, and moaning, "Help . . . please, help me . . ."

He *was* an innocent and came to her immediately, lowering his gun. When he was close enough, she wrenched it from his hands, then flung it away and raised her knife to his throat. "I don't want to hurt you," she said, "but I will. I've killed two men already."

The words panicked him and he staggered backward, turned, and ran. She was after him in an instant and leaped on him from behind, bearing him to the soft floor of the forest. He trembled beneath her and tried to roll over, turning his head so that his face came into contact with hers, cheek against cheek, flesh against flesh . . .

And images, more vivid than the most intense dreams, flooded from his mind into hers, and she knew his name, knew his father, saw his soul, what had made him what he was—

The raging, florid face of a man towering over him, fists, palms, open hands, fingers as hard as sticks. *Be a man, dammit, be a man, don't let those niggers push you around.*

The hands, those big hands coming down like thunder and lightning, pushing him away. *Daddy, stop, stop, don't hit her!*

A woman crying, tears falling down her cheeks, a bloody lip, bruised eyes. *Seen you looking at that ugly black stud, that fucking gorilla, you bitch, you whore, you nigger-loving cunt!*

Playing in the yard and Daddy, Daddy coming out yelling, *Get out of my yard, you damn Jewboy,* and saying, *He's my friend,* and Daddy's hands and *Jews aren't your friends, leeches running the fucking country, niggers, goddam niggers and Jews, that school's full of 'em!*

Jews, goddam Jews, all their fault, and the faggots and the niggers and the spics and the chinks and the gooks . . .

. . . and the and the and the . . .

Be a man Be a man I'll teach you to be a man!

Daddy's hands, Daddy's hands, Daddy's hands.

And then peace, a place of stillness, Mommy's arms and her voice, soft as a kiss as she cried and told him:

He's not yours, not yours, don't ever tell him, but he's not yours . . .

And then a name, the name of his real father, the name his mother told him to forget but that he never could . . .

Amy tasted it all, the bitterness of the boy's life, of secrets and hate and the venom that was fed to him every day until he gave up, succumbed to the poison, and let his soul die. It was easier that way.

She rolled away from the boy as though further contact would poison her as well. He lay there on his side and slowly his knees drew up, his shoulders hunched, and he started to cry in a way that would have brought a sneer to his father's face.

"It's all right," she said. "It's all right. I'm not going to hurt you." Then she moved him next to a tree whose trunk was a foot across and bound him there, as gently as she could, with the mesh and leather slings of her weapons so that he hugged the tree. She put a ball of torn cloth in his mouth and wound another strip of cloth around his head to secure it, making sure that he could breathe through his nose.

"When it's over," she said, "I'll come back for you." Then she started moving south again.

She was running over the dead leaves when suddenly the Crow appeared in front of her, fluttering down and standing on the forest floor as if to bar her way. She stopped and the Crow walked slowly in a circle. Then she understood, unslung her weapons and set them down, took out her knife and crouched in front of the bird as it rose into the sky again.

Amy used the knife like a pick, pressing it gently into the soil beneath the dead leaves until she heard a *tick* and felt the knife point hit a solid surface. It was another mine, and she prodded until she knew exactly where its edges were, then began to dig it out. She wasn't sure what she was going to do with it, but could picture herself tossing it like a Frisbee into the midst of the Sons of a Free America, and the image nearly made her laugh.

She had just straightened up, holding the mine, one hand on the carrying handle, the other on the base plate, when she heard a voice behind her. "Just hold it right there . . . Turn around slow."

She did as ordered and was rewarded with the sight of the widening eyes behind a pair of wire-rimmed glasses. The eyes and the glasses belonged to a long, lanky, scar-faced man whose greasy hair curled out from under his military cap. He looked, Amy thought, like the character Tom Courtenay had played in *Doctor Zhivago.*

"Greetings, Comrade Strelnikov," she said, holding the mine in front of her so that the pressure plate faced the man. "Or would you prefer Pasha?"

He started to back up but she followed, slowly closing the ten-foot gap between them. "Wait a minute!" he said. "Now just take it easy! If that thing goes off, it'll kill us both!"

"Are you so sure of that?" Amy asked with a light tone that belied the gravity of the situation. She didn't want to experience an exploding mine again but she had no real fear of it, and if she could bluff this skinny cracker out of his gun, it would be well worth the risk.

"Yeah, yeah," the man babbled. "I am *fucking* sure of that. I know my devices, okay, lady?"

"*Your* devices . . . ?" A thought crossed Amy's mind. "You planted this?" She walked closer.

The man tried to back up further but bumped against a tree. The contact made him jump. "Yeah," he said breathlessly. "Yeah, it's mine . . ." He looked about frantically for a means of escape.

"You're the bomb man," Amy said slowly. "The one who put the bomb into the center." The man didn't respond. He was too busy looking for an out. Then it hit her. "Powder . . . *gun*powder . . ." She looked more closely at the scars on his frightened face. "You're Powder Burns."

He neither admitted nor denied it, but started to slide his back around the side of the tree.

"No," Amy said, walking right up to him and making him freeze where he stood, his gun uselessly at his side. "Don't leave. I know some people who want to meet you, Powder. They want to welcome you home . . ."

She pressed herself against him then, the mine between them, and for the third time in her life and death and life, the world exploded.

This time she saw the results on someone other than herself. The charge blasted away Powder Burns's chest, leaving a downturned arc of shoulders from which ripped muscle hung like red streamers. For an instant Amy looked at the head that topped that arc, a face clawed away by shrapnel, which had driven the man's glasses into his eyes and deep into his brain. Then that face fell along with the shoulders, slapping the ground wetly, and Amy fell with it, ruined and shattered once more.

And once more, miraculously, she was healed. To her surprise, the damage was not as great as it had been the first time. The charge had been directed outward, toward Burns, and she had suffered the recoil, which was enough to make a crater in the earth and kill any living being. But as she reminded herself, she had the advantage of already being dead.

She picked up her weapons and began to walk, moving deeper into the forest. She had had enough of mines, and the sound of the last one, unmuffled by the ground, had surely been heard by the rest of the compound. Now they knew. Someone was inside and killing.

39

It was David Levinson's night off but he wasn't relaxing. He was scanning the police bands and listening for any news that he could connect to Amy Carlisle or a militia group. Fires in the woods, unexplained gunshots, explosions, you name it, he would have gone to the scene in a minute.

But it was a quiet night in and around Hobie. There was nothing out of the ordinary at all and that fact was driving him crazy. He wanted more than anything to help Amy Carlisle end this. He had been her accessory, helping her to break the law more than once, and even contributing to the deaths of innocent people, and he knew he would take that sin with him to his grave, where he would have to answer to . . . something.

Before this had all happened, Levinson believed that dead was dead. His forebears' Sheol was just that, the underworld, the place beneath the ground where bodies rotted and vanished, given enough time. But now he knew there was something more, some other place from which Amy had returned to do what she had to do.

He wanted to help her because he wanted to see justice served. But there was another reason too. As absurd and impossible and even blasphemous as it seemed, he was a little bit in love with the woman.

Jesus Christ, Levinson, he told himself, talk about going after the inaccessible. He might as well have had a crush on Marilyn Monroe. This woman wasn't just beyond him, she was on a whole different plane of being.

And maybe that was why he was fascinated by her. It was impossible, hence, it was safe. No commitment necessary. But still, she was here on his plane for now and he just wished that there was something he could do besides sit around and wait to help clean up the fireworks or, he thought grimly, hear about nothing at all.

He considered pouring a good stiff one but decided not to, in case something did come through on the scanner and he had to move fast. Instead he put a video in the VCR. It was a copy of the tape that an attendee had made at the gun show, the one from which the brief footage of Amy had been excised. He watched it primarily to see her, just get a glimpse of her from the back.

Yes, there she was. He could tell from the way she moved. He saw her for two seconds and then the camera moved away. He rewound it and watched again, then let it play on, thinking about her, barely seeing what was happening, at least not until Rick Carlisle crossed from right to left and out of sight.

Levinson grabbed the remote and backed it up. Yes, it was Carlisle. No doubt about it. What the hell was *he* doing there?

And then the thought occurred to him that maybe there were *two* vigilantes out there, one dead and one alive.

He looked up Carlisle's number and dialed it. If he professed an interest in guns, which Levinson doubted, all well and good. But if not, or if he denied having been there . . . well, Levinson would cross that bridge when he came to it.

A woman answered and when Levinson identified himself as *Officer* Levinson, he heard an audible gasp. Before he could say anything else, the woman asked, "Is he all right? Did you find Rick?"

Oh *shit,* Levinson thought, but only said, "I'm sorry, ma'am, who are you, please?"

"I'm Nancy, his wife. Do you know where he is?"

"No, I don't, ma'am, but I think we'd better have a little talk. May I come over to your house?"

After he assured her that he did not know where Rick was or *how* he was, she agreed and he got in his Blazer and headed to the address she gave him. He took along his service revolver, as well as a Winchester 1300 Defender pump shotgun with a seven-shot magazine that he slid under the seat. He didn't think he'd need it for the new Mrs. Carlisle, but God only knew what *Mr.* Carlisle might have gotten himself into.

40

When the second mine went off, the one that killed Powder Burns, Tom Danvers had just missed a pigeon which Ace Ludwig had then drawn on with his pistol and downed with two shots, just as it was about to disappear in the trees. People were teasing Danvers and congratulating Ace, and Rip Withers was thinking that he should bawl the man out since nobody was supposed to shoot at another man's target, when they heard the sound. It was much louder than the mines they had heard go off before.

"What the shit?" Rip said, looking around for Powder Burns and thinking that maybe Powder had been right and that it *was* a mine they had heard earlier. But Powder was nowhere to be seen. Oh fuck, and *Karl* was out there on guard duty.

"Ace," he barked. "Get some men out there and see what's going on—and don't get yourself blown up!" Ace nodded and picked half a dozen men, the cream of the Sons' crop.

Ace didn't complain about being taken away from the shoot. He had gotten a perfect ten out of ten, a score reached by no one else so far and not likely to be surpassed. No, it looked like Ace was going to have the pleasure of blowing away the liberal pigfucker tied up in the cell. He was sure Ace would make it entertaining.

Rip just hoped that it hadn't been Karl who had stepped on one of Powder's mines. He had thought about leading the party himself but was afraid of what he might find. If anything had happened to Karl, Rip would tear Powder apart.

Then he remembered what was going down the next day and decided that he would tear Powder apart later. Better yet, maybe he'd leave him tied up and gagged in the van so that he could feel the results of his handiwork.

Aw, fuck it, Rip thought. It probably wasn't Karl at all. Like everybody else, he had been told a hundred times not to go within ten feet of the fence. It was probably just a deer again, maybe that first time too, if it really had been a mine. Everybody was just too edgy, knowing what was coming tomorrow.

It was just a deer and Karl was fine and he wouldn't do a damn thing to Powder and tomorrow night they would all laugh and clap each other on the back and dance on hundreds of ZOG graves.

She heard them coming through the trees. If they were supposed to be stealthy, they needed a lot more training.

They were moving in a line, five or six across, by the sound of them, and Amy flitted through the trees, taking the knife from her sheath, moving to where the man on the right would pass her, and positioning herself behind a tree. She heard a slight rustle above her and imagined the Crow settling onto a nearby limb, her companion, her collaborator, her avatar.

When the man passed, she stepped out behind him, wrapped her arm around his head, and slashed across his throat. But unlike her other victims, this man had his finger on the trigger and jerked it spasmodically, sending a burst of automatic fire ahead of him, biting the bark off trees and filling the woods with a roar of exploding gunpowder.

Ace Ludwig had been well trained by the government he hated. As soon as he heard the first shot, he instantly fell prone, shouting *"Down!"* to the rest of the squad. The shots were on the right flank, where Tannahill had been. Then the gunfire stopped and in the moonlight Ace saw Tannahill falling and a shadowy figure slipping away from him behind the cover of the trees.

"Fire three!" he shouted to Andy Brett, meaning for Brett to fire three shots and warn the main party. Then Ace got up and ran into the trees after whoever had downed Tannahill. Behind him, he was dismayed to hear a near fusillade of shots. He turned around and yelled, "*One* of you, dammit!" then plunged into the brush after the intruder again.

He saw the shape dodge in and out from behind the trees but had no clear shot, so he ran faster in pursuit. He was closing in, and finally had enough of a sight picture so that he slammed his weapon up against a tree and waited for movement.

It came, higher than he had expected. For a moment he thought that maybe the attacker had climbed a tree, but before that thought had formed, he was already firing a string of shots at the black blur of motion. Ace heard the bullets smack wood and his heart leaped at the softer sound of them tearing into something wet and yielding.

He stopped firing. In the sudden silence there was a cry, a human cry that seemed to come from beyond the tree where he had seen the movement. Then he heard something fluttering and falling. From the sound it made when it struck the dead leaves, he thought that if it was a person, it was a damn small one.

When he reached the dying thing, the moon was bright enough to show him what he had shot. "Shit," he said when he saw it. "A fucking *crow.*"

The bird had been hit twice as far as Ace could see. One bullet had nearly chopped off a wing so that it hung by a thread of bone, and another had struck between belly and breast, leaving a large red hole. He thought he could see its heart beating, black in the moonlight.

"Fuck you," he growled, and stepped on its head, smashing it into the mat of dead leaves.

"Ace?" It was Andy Brett, gingerly coming up beside him. "What was it?"

"Just a nigger bird. A damn crow. But it's dead now. How's Tannahill?"

Brett shook his head. "Somebody cut his throat. He's dead."

"Fuck!" The others were coming now. Ace counted four with Brett. That meant Tannahill was the only one down. But where were the sentries? "Somebody's in here," Ace said, looking to all sides. "Somebody's killing our people and they're heading toward the camp."

He led the way south toward the buildings and the bright lights.

When Amy heard the shots, she thought she had been hit. There was a terrible pain in her right arm that made her drop the weapon she had taken from the dead man, and a jolt to her stomach that was like a fiery punch. It drove her to her knees and toppled her over and there was so much pain that she could only lie there wishing she were dead. But worse was to come.

Pressure suddenly seemed to build up in her skull as though her brain were expanding against the bone, and the only way to relieve it would be if her head burst open. The pressure increased. Her eyes felt as if they were being pushed out of their sockets, her ears were throbbing with the blood that pulsed behind the thin drums, demanding exit.

Then her head burst open and she entered the darkness.

* * *

When she awoke, she had no idea how much time had passed. Only a dull ache remained from the killing pain in her head. Her stomach felt as though it had taken a hard blow and her arm was stiff and sore.

There was something else too, some change that she couldn't name. She felt different, maybe weaker. Yes, that was it. She was tired, so very, very tired. She should try to end this, end it so that she could rest.

She heard something coming toward her from the north and pushed herself to her feet. The dead man's gun was on the ground and she picked it up, but was surprised at how much heavier it seemed. Then she started to run.

She *was* more tired. She was stumbling over roots, tripping in brush. The whole forest was like a covert ally of her pursuers, determined to slow her down.

Amy breathed a curse and pushed on. The lights of the camp glowed through the trees, and she shifted the gun in her hands so that the muzzle was pointing ahead, toward all those Sons of a Free America who she would soon put to rest in American soil. It had come to that now, just a firefight, her against them all. But her bullets would kill while theirs would only pass through. They would hurt her, but she had already been through enough pain for an eternity of hells. She could bear more.

Now she could see the buildings through the trees, see something moving, men walking, looking toward where she hid. Behind her, footsteps crushed the dead leaves as her hunters closed in.

It was time. She burst from the shelter of the woods, aimed at the men ahead of her and pulled the trigger, downing two of them. But they responded quickly, bringing up their guns and firing back. Suddenly something struck her arm and her weapon dropped to the ground. She stood there for a moment, hands empty, scarcely knowing what had happened, as more bullets whizzed past her.

Then the shots stopped, though she didn't know why. All she knew was the fire in her arm and the blood that was running down what was left of her sleeve. Something moved behind her but she had no strength to turn and see what it was.

Then her head burst into a ball of pain and everything flickered. And as she fell to the ground, these words ran through her mind:

I am a mortal, and liable to fall . . .

41

Nancy Carlisle was near panic when Levinson arrived at the home she shared with Rick. After he calmed her down, she told him all about Rick's obsession with finding Amy's killers, and that in his last call to her two days before, he had told her that he had gotten in contact with the Sons of a Free America.

"All right, Mrs. Carlisle," Levinson said, "I think you need to come down to headquarters and give us a statement. We've got to start looking for your husband as soon as possible."

"Do you think he's in danger?" she asked, her voice shaking.

"I think it's very possible, yes. The sooner we find him the better."

It made sense to Levinson. This was the way to do it. He would get the entire force looking, call in the feds and find not only Rick Carlisle but hopefully the bastards he was tracing, the very ones that Amy was on her way to confront right now. Maybe the police could only mop up after she was done, but at least it gave Levinson something to do besides sit on his ass and wait.

Levinson, Nancy Carlisle, and her daughter, Karin, headed for the police station in Levinson's Blazer, pausing to drop the girl off at a friend's house several blocks away. Levinson watched as Nancy kissed Karin good-bye at the friend's front door and felt a dull ache as he thought about the life that might have been his.

Their route took them by the empty lot where the day-care center had been. As always, it looked tragic and barren under the street lights that stood on each corner. Levinson turned and looked at the thick layer of dust that covered the site, and then without thinking, he slammed on the brakes.

Nancy, startled, asked, "What is it? What's wrong?"

Levinson thought he said *look*, but he only pointed to the blasted rubble until Nancy saw it too.

The dust was moving, although the wind had died down and no longer rattled the few dead leaves that still held fast to the trees. The pale dust and ash that had been the Making Friends Child Care Center and the people who had died there were gathering into what looked like individual waves that flowed together until a number of mounds had formed. The mounds rose and lengthened into rounded cylinders, with smaller mounds on top. They were, Levinson saw, taking the shapes of birds.

There were ten of them, and as Levinson and Nancy watched, their color darkened from ashy gray to a black so deep that they would have become lost in the night had it not been for the sheen of the feathers in the street lights' glow.

Then the birds spread their wings, and even through the closed windows, Levinson could hear a sound like dry paper being torn as the newly born creatures moved for the first time. They rose as one, their broad wings beating the night air, and flew north.

Without a word, Levinson began to follow them, and Nancy Carlisle made no protest.

"Wake up, you fucking bitch!"

The slap across the face brought Amy Carlisle back to consciousness. She felt cold, colder than she ever had since returning from her death. Her arm ached unbearably and when she tried to move it, to ease it into a more comfortable position, she discovered that her arms were bound behind her.

She blinked several times and saw that she was tied to a chair. Three men she did not know were standing before her. The one who had slapped her was breathing heavily. His teeth were clenched and his hands were balled into fists. He was wearing a gun belt from which hung a holstered .45; a sheathed knife hung on his left hip.

The other two men were dressed in camouflage like the first. One of the men was holding an assault rifle. There was a thin smile under his dark mustache. The third man was clean shaven and slightly resembled the first. His face seemed blank and Amy suspected he was mildly retarded.

"Awake, huh?" the first man said. "Look around, bitch, see anybody you know?"

Amy turned her head. Sitting next to her, tied in the same way, was

Rick. Before she even knew she was doing it, she said his name. "Rick . . . oh God."

"Rick, huh?" said the first man. "Well, Ricky, it seems you know our little friend here. Why don't you introduce us?"

Rick looked terrible. Both of his ears had been cut, and dried blood coated his neck. His face was bruised in several places and one eye was blackened. Still, he smiled at her. "You already know her," he said. "But for formality's sake, this is Ace Ludwig, Ray Withers, and his charming brother, Rip."

Rip Withers. The first name that William Standish had given her. Here he was right in front of her and she couldn't do a thing about it.

"And what's the cunt's name?" Rip Withers asked.

Rick kept smiling, but this time he smiled at Rip Withers. "Like I said, you know her. You killed her. This is my wife. Amy."

Rip Withers looked as if Rick were crazy, but then his face cleared. "I get it," he said. "I get it now. They never found your body, but that wasn't because you were blown up, it was because you were never in there to start with. You must've left before the shit hit the fan and played dead ever since, huh?"

"No," Amy said. "I died. And I came back. For you." She strained against the ropes but they held her fast as her arms throbbed with pain. She felt as if all her strength had gone, as if she were a different creature entirely from the one the Crow had brought back.

"Well, you had a good run, lady," Rip said. "But it ends here. Now you tell me, where the hell is my son?"

"Who?"

"Don't fuck with me! My boy was out there on sentry duty! My son, Karl! Did you hurt him?" The knife came out of the sheath, and Withers brandished it in front of her. "You tell me or I swear before Yahweh I'll cut your tits off and make Ricky here eat them!"

"Your son's alive," she said. "I tied him up."

"Now you know you're going to die," Withers said. "But if you hurt him, you're going to die slow." He turned to the man with the rifle. "Ace, I don't want a whole squad trooping through the trees, in case she brought some friends along. You're quieter in the woods than anybody we've got. Go find Karl, okay?"

"What if I find some of her friends?" Ace asked.

"Go ahead and kill 'em."

"All *right,*" Ace said. "I'd like to nail something tonight besides a goddam crow," and he slipped out the door.

That was it then, Amy thought. The Crow was dead. That was why her strength was gone, why she had been wounded in the arm and lost consciousness.

What would happen now? Would she die for a second time at the hands of this madman? If so, she would make sure that he would never forget her, that if she could not kill him, she could at least make him live in pain.

"All right, whore," Withers said. "Now tell me who else knows you're here."

"General Custer, the Sixth Fleet, the Terminator, Superman—" She had been about to continue with Nancy Drew and Jackie Chan, but Withers hit her with a vicious backhand that rocked her head and caused more pain to shiver through her wounded arm.

"Haven't you learned not to fuck with me yet?" he said, waggling his knife in front of her nose. "I can promise you a world of hurt, bitch."

"You know," Amy said, looking fiercely into Withers's eyes, "your son was a whole lot nicer than you. Doesn't that ever make you wonder?"

His eyes narrowed. "What are you talking about?"

"If he's really your kid? I mean, the way you treated your wife, don't you think it was likely that she sought . . . *comfort* from someone else? Someone nicer, more gentle? Someone who was always there at family gatherings and picnics and holidays?"

"Shut up," Rip said. "You just shut the hell up . . ."

But Amy knew that he wanted to hear more in spite of himself, so she kept talking to Rip Withers but turned her glare toward his brother, Ray, using the information that she had derived from her psychic link with the boy in the woods. "Personally, I think Karl looks and acts a whole lot more like his *real* dad than you, Rip. What do *you* think, Ray? Proud of your boy?"

Ray Withers looked confused and frightened and on the verge of tears, and Amy knew from his reaction that Karl's mother had told the boy the truth about his parentage. Rip was glancing from Amy to Ray and back again, and when his shocked face came to rest on Ray, Amy knew that the shot of pain she had just injected into his soul would gnaw at him as long as he lived.

"Ray?" Rip said, sounding angry and scared and so very close to losing control. "Tell this whore she's full of shit . . ."

It sounded like a plea but it found no pity in Amy. "You know it's true, Rip . . . It's why Karl was never as sharp as you. Why he wasn't as quick with his hands or his mind and why he never will be. Because he isn't even yours. He's Ray's. He's your dumb brother's boy. But your brother wasn't so dumb that he turned down some sweet, sweet lovin' when it was offered."

"Ray?" Rip said again. "You tell me that she's lying . . . you just tell me that and it'll all be all right." He gripped his brother's arm and swung him around to look into his teary eyes, his quivering face. Ray shook his head as if he didn't know what to do or say, and Amy guessed he didn't.

"Ray," Rip went on, and he sounded more dangerous now. "Did you fuck Elizabeth? You tell me that you didn't . . . You tell me the *truth*, Ray!"

"He can't tell you both," Amy said softly, feeling like the serpent in the garden. "Which do you want?"

"I . . . I . . ." Ray was saying and Amy felt sorry for him, but not sorry enough to try and stop what she had started even if she could have. "I . . ."

"You *what*?" Rip demanded, and Ray responded with two words that told everything.

"I'm sorry . . ."

Rip stared at him for what seemed like a long time. Then motion sprang from the stillness and Rip brought up his right hand, the one that held the knife, straight into Ray's belly and wrapped his left arm around his brother.

Ray gasped, his eyes wet and wide, and as his breath began to come in soft little puffs, he looked in disbelief at his cuckolded brother and put his hands lightly on Rip's shoulders.

"I'm . . . sorry . . ." he said like a child. "I . . ."

But what he intended to say next was never heard. His big body slumped in his brother's arms and Rip lowered it to the floor as the knife slid out.

"Did I hit a sore spot?" Amy asked gently. Though her strength was only mortal again, the flame of retribution burned strongly within her and she gloried at the pain she had caused her captor, the murderer of her children. As for poor, stupid Ray, she looked on him as just a dumb but deadly weapon aimed by maniacs. He was a dog with rabies, worthy of pity but meriting death.

Rip Withers stood up slowly, and the face he presented was one that should have been seen only in nightmares. "You . . . *fucking* . . . *BITCH!*" he said, the air hissing in and out through his clenched teeth. He held the bloody knife in front of him and seemed ready to plunge it into her face at any second. If she wanted to continue to live in this strange half-life of hers, she would have to respond quickly.

"You're what I expected," she said scornfully, showing no fear, for she felt none. "You're not a soldier, you're a sadist. You should be ashamed to call this a militia when you're nothing but a bunch of loonies. Just look at yourself. There's nothing military about you or your whole operation. Now you'll probably stab us too, won't you? Or will you torture us first to make you feel better." She laughed derisively, then stressed each word: *"You . . . sick . . . fuck."*

The speech had the desired effect. Rip Withers's face looked no less hateful, but some of the madness had withdrawn from it. "We're not sick," he said. "And we're not sadists—we're patriots!"

"Then why did you kill your brother?" Amy asked flatly.

"He was a *traitor*!" Rip strove to keep his temper. "He betrayed *me,* he would have betrayed the *Sons* sooner or later. He had to die. And so do you." He stood stiffly, a warrior again or so, Amy thought, he wanted them to believe.

"You think we're insane, but we're not—*you're* the ones who are crazy, to defend ZOG, a government that wants nothing more than to trample you and every other non-Jew citizen, unless you're one of the mongrel races they use as their soldiers against us. The time for outright war is coming fast—the first real blow will be struck tomorrow."

"How?" Amy asked.

Rick answered the question, probably tired of Rip Withers's speech. "They've got a bomb in their bunker that's going to blow up half of Hobie tomorrow morning."

"That's right," Withers said. "Centered at the ZOG government building. Too bad you won't see it. But you're two of ZOG's soldiers who will never raise up arms against true patriots again. You're going to die now, and you'll die as any spy would, by firing squad."

"What about the contest?" Rick asked. "I thought the winner was supposed to have first crack at me."

"That policy has just been changed," said Withers. "*Everyone* will have a crack at you—both of you." He opened the cell door and called out, "Prepare for firing squad detail! Jackson and Anders, bring the prisoners to the firing range!"

Two of the militia members appeared at the door with their guns. When they saw Ray Withers lying there, they looked with uncertainty at Rip but he looked back firmly. "Another traitor," he said in a tone that allowed for no questions. "Take the prisoners."

The two men undid the leather straps that were holding Amy and Rick to the chairs, but left their hands bound behind their backs. Then they grasped them by the right arms, but Amy winced and her guard took her by her left, unharmed shoulder. Withers led the way.

The entire open area was still brightly lit. Amy saw that the bodies of the two men she had shot had been zipped into body bags. They lay against one of the buildings and several of the men stood around them. Others sat on the shooting benches, their weapons across their knees, or returned from the barracks where they had gone to get their rifles for the firing squad. When Amy and Rick appeared, all the men looked at them with the same expression of undisguised hatred.

No wonder, she thought. They were spies and she, for one, had caused the deaths of several of their comrades. It didn't even enter their minds that they had caused the deaths of the children she had loved; and if what Rick said was true, they would cause the deaths of dozens, maybe even hundreds more tomorrow.

Oh God, Amy thought, when would it stop? If only she could have finished her work, just killed them all in a hail of gunfire, then it would have been over.

Yes, until the next group went too far, until another militia chose to become terrorists for whatever cause they celebrated. She knew that she couldn't end all the madness in the world, but at least she could have put a stop to the particular madness that had killed her babies.

She could have, that is, if the Crow had not been killed. Was there any way out, she wondered. When the avatar of death dies itself, how can the dead put the wrong things right? And if not, what happened to the dead who failed?

It looked like she was going to find out.

42

Rip Withers led Amy and Rick and their guards to the shooting range, but did not take them out to the end where the targets were placed. Instead he stopped only twenty yards out and turned to them.

"So," he said, "we're not going to tie you to stakes. You can stand here and meet the bullets. If you fall down before we fire, we'll just shoot at you on the ground. Your chances for a clean kill will be better if you stay on your feet. That's about it, except that I know you'll both burn in hell and I'll look forward to looking down from heaven and seeing that someday."

Withers turned his back on them and walked toward the rest of the men, the two guards in his wake. "Line up for firing squad duty!" he cried, and the men scurried to obey.

Rick turned to Amy and smiled. "I guess this is it."

"For now," she said. "I have no idea what's coming afterward."

"Maybe we'll both come back."

"No," she said, watching the men form their ranks in two rows. The front row knelt, the back row stood. There were over twenty of them. "I don't think I'll ever come back again. The fact that I got *one* chance to put things right was miracle enough."

"You're right," Rick said thoughtfully. "That *was* a miracle. But maybe the miracles aren't over yet, Amy. Believe." He smiled at her while the men prepared their rifles for firing. "I love you, Amy. I've never stopped loving you. I'm glad I'm with you now. I wished a thousand times that I had been with you then."

"Don't wish that. Don't ever wish for death. Life is too precious."

"Not when the one that makes it that way is gone."

She faced front, looking toward their executioners. She would not tell him that she loved him. She could not. He was still Nancy's husband despite the skewed realities that the Crow had caused. "I'm glad I'm with you now" was as much as she could say.

Still, she felt a dull fury that it should end this way, that these men should win and should wreak more havoc tomorrow, letting slip their dogs of war, a dirty, filthy war, waged in hate and fought in cowardice.

Rip Withers walked to the end of their ranks and barked out his order, "Prepare to fire!"

Amy looked up at the dark sky, far above the reach of their lights, and wished, prayed, hoped, *demanded* something to drop down from it, one giant black bird from the blackness to devour them all, one great Crow to put the wrong things right for good. Not all the wrong things, but the wrong things created by those wrong people who were all encompassed by a chain link fence on this small plot of earth.

Oh yes, now was the time for justice. Now, if ever, was the time for the Crow.

Her prayer was answered. She heard them before she saw them. At first it sounded like the distant cries of children at play. She could see the militiamen stiffen as one, their rifles to their shoulders, and the barrels slowly dropping toward the ground as the sounds grew louder.

Yes, she thought, they *were* the cries of children, the shrill laughter of Brenda Tran, Pete Grissom's teasing catcalls, the subdued giggles of DeMarole White as she clapped her hands over her mouth in a paroxysm of mirth. But as they grew louder, they changed, becoming the keening cry of birds, the raucous cawing of a murder of crows that grew louder and more demanding, insisting on being heard.

At last she saw them, set like black pearls against the topaz of the moon. They flew in a single line, straight across, unlike the delta formations of migrating geese. But their unity was unmistakable and, to Amy, their purpose certain.

They descended in the same line in which they flew, directly between Amy and Rick and the line of militiamen. When they landed, every one of them was facing the two ranks of riflemen.

Amy counted ten of them. Ten crows, one for each of the children who had died. Her heart leaped in excitement, but a cold fear crept along her flesh.

Then as she and Rick and the self-proclaimed soldiers watched, the crows began to grow and shift and change shape, lengthening here, broadening there, until with a chill of horror Amy saw her children, the toddlers, even the babies, all in a row between her and the soldiers,

She pictured them falling under the bullets as they had fallen beneath the bomb, and started to run toward them to shield their little bodies with her own. But they remained children only for a moment, just long enough for Amy to run up to them and see their faces.

They were faces filled with loss, children's faces laden with the adult knowledge that they would never grow up, never grow old, never see their own children run and play. They were faces of tragedy on features of childlike delicacy, and all the more terrible for it.

But those faces changed as Amy and the killers watched, became more adult and rose upward as the bodies beneath them grew. They were aging before Amy's eyes, living in seconds those years that no longer lay ahead, until there were ten young men and women, fully grown, possessing all the strength that loving upbringing would have given them, ten strong bodies, nude without sensuality, creations, not of life, but of some life beyond death, of some dark, feathered justice that refused to let things end with two bound corpses lying in their own blood on a cold field of dishonor.

They did not look at Amy. They walked past her, walked with purposeful and silent steps toward the two rows of soldiers. They walked with their heads high, their hands clenched into fists, and their eyes, alive for this night only, filled with righteous anger.

"Fire!" Rip Withers cried, but his voice cracked in fear. "Shoot! Shoot them!"

The riflemen aimed at the approaching figures and fired their weapons. The bullets tore through the flesh but did no harm, and in seconds the young men and women had closed in on their killers. The guards in the gate tower came down to help repel the invaders, but their weapons had no greater impact than did their comrades'.

Guns were wrenched from fearful, weakened hands and thrown far away. The soldiers fell to their knees as supernaturally strong fists pounded down on them. Some tried to run, but their pursuers, fast as the wind, pulled them down and wrapped wiry fingers around their throats.

In the midst of the attack Rip Withers stood, frozen in disbelief and shock, until a young man with Asian features and golden skin gripped his neck and began to choke him. And in the raging face of that young man, Amy saw the soft eyes of Charlie Tran, come back from the dead to avenge where she had failed.

"No!" Amy screamed, and was amazed to see the faces of all the young men and women look up at her. Their fists, ready to deliver death blows, paused in mid-air. Their fingers, digging into the flesh of thick necks, relaxed, letting air flow into windpipes, blood rush back to dying brains.

"Stop!" Amy said. "You can't do this, this is *my* battle. You can't stain your souls with these . . . fools' deaths! I'm the one who came back for justice, not you. Their deaths should be on *my* soul."

She looked at all of them, her eyes pleading. "I didn't come back to see you made killers—I came back for *love* of you. Please, don't do this. Give me your strength. Let me be your justice again . . ."

One by one, the ten children, grown to adulthood as they would never be in reality, straightened up, letting their adversaries fall to the ground, coughing and choking, shaking battered heads, nursing their wounds. Not a one seemed ready to fight again, after this attack by the invincible undead.

The ten figures now completely ignored the men on the ground. Instead they came walking slowly toward Amy, and she saw the eyes of a child shining from the face of every one.

When they reached her, they surrounded her, their arms on each other's shoulders, their heads close enough to hers that she could smell their breath, sweet and ethereal, like the purest incense.

She felt a love so overwhelming and so deep that it made her giddy. And she thought again of Scrooge, reborn, saying that he was "as giddy as a drunken man," and so she was, reborn too, giddy and happy and filled with joy and love at the presence of those she had never thought to see again in this world or the next. She felt there could be no higher state. She felt enfolded by love.

Then the youths began to vanish, and at first Amy thought that they were fading away. But she saw instead that they were turning to dust, pale dust that fell like snow to the ground and gathered in peaceful, rounded mounds at her feet. Her children. Her sweet children.

Golden lads and girls all must,
As chimney-sweepers, come to dust.

She didn't know what it was from but the words came to her as their requiem.

But there was no amen. Instead there was a cry from above, and when she looked, she saw, perched atop a round-roofed building half buried in the ground, the Crow.

The Crow. Alive. If that were so, then . . .

She strained at the leather bonds that held her wrists together and felt them come apart like paper. The strength was hers again. Her love for her children, and their love for her, had replenished her, and brought back the Crow.

43

Amy lost no time in freeing Rick and then picked up the nearest weapon, an assault rifle with enough firepower for her to mow down all twenty of the broken and battered men slowly picking themselves off the ground. Rick found a gun too, which he held on the defeated soldiers while he gathered any weapons close at hand.

Amy joined him in his work, and when they had piled all the guns together, she heard a sound of an engine from beyond the gate. In another few seconds she saw the lights of a vehicle approaching the compound on the only access road.

"Watch them," she told Rick, gesturing to the feeble remnants of the Sons of a Free America. Amy ran to the gate in time to see David Levinson climb out of his Blazer, a pump shotgun in his hand, ready for combat.

When he saw an armed Amy, he lowered his weapon, and his jaw. "What the hell," he said, as Amy opened the gate for him.

"How did you get here?" she asked.

"We followed the crows. But what—"

"We?" Amy's question was answered when the passenger door opened and Nancy stepped tentatively out. Their gaze met, and she saw first surprise, then joy, then shock quickly pass over her friend's face. Nancy turned white, and seemed to stagger.

Then the sound of shots split the night's regained silence. At first Amy thought that Nancy had been hit, but then she realized that the bullet had hit *her,* entered her back and exited her stomach. She barely felt a twinge of pain.

Amy whirled, heard another burst of shots, and then saw the boy,

Karl Withers, running from the forest, unarmed, looking back over his shoulder, yelling at someone to stop, stop shooting.

But whoever it was didn't listen. A bullet from the next burst caught Karl. Amy saw blood splatter from his left leg and the boy went down. Another burst spat up the dirt near him, and then everyone was running.

Amy dashed toward the trees from where the shots had come and heard Levinson's footsteps pounding behind her. To her left Rick raced toward the boy, firing blindly into the woods as he ran. Then he knelt, covered Karl with his body, and tried to pick him up.

Another burst shook the night, and Rick stiffened, then fell over onto the boy. Amy shrieked in rage and started to fire into the woods but stopped as something huge and black entered her sight. The Crow flew like an arrow behind a stand of trees, screaming its harsh cry, and Amy saw Ace Ludwig stagger sideways into the open as the Crow rushed by him.

Amy and Levinson fired as one. Amy's burst punched Ace in the stomach and Levinson's shotgun blast hit him in the neck. Either one would have killed him, but the result of Levinson's fire was more dramatic. The wad of shot severed the neck and the spine, and ripped off Ace Ludwig's head.

Immediately Amy swung the muzzle of her gun toward the rest of the militia, but they didn't move. Only Rip Withers was slowly walking toward where Karl and Rick lay. And it was to Rick that Amy was now running, still training her weapon on the deflated corps of madmen.

Karl had crawled out from under Rick and was ignoring his own wounded leg in his concern over the man who had tried to save him once more. It was all clear to Amy. The boy had broken his bonds and escaped, witnessed what had happened, and run from cover, trying to tell Ace to stop shooting, that it was all over. But Ace hadn't listened or, as was more likely, had looked on Karl Withers as a—

"Traitor!" It was Rip Withers who was yelling, moving toward the boy and Rick. "You traitor *bastard*!" he moaned, and there were tears in his eyes.

"That's far enough," Levinson said, pointing the muzzle of the shotgun at Withers. The man stopped, breathing heavily—his son, his army, his dream all gone.

Nancy and Amy arrived at Rick's side at the same time. He was beyond speech. Blood was frothing at his lips, and Amy knew he had only a few moments left to live. She nodded at Nancy, who, as if having received permission, knelt at Rick's side. Amy remained standing, looking down at them.

Nancy cradled her husband in her arms, oblivious of the blood that ran from the exit wound in his back. Rick turned his head slightly to look at her. A small smile bent the corners of his lips, and Nancy, tears rolling from her eyes, kissed his forehead, then his bloody lips.

His head rolled slowly back so that he was looking at Amy, but whether he had done it on purpose or whether it had been merely a gift of gravity, she could not tell.

Whatever the reason, the smile had fled his face, and in another moment life had left it as well. His lifeless eyes looked into Amy's, and she could read nothing there, not love, not the promise that they would meet again. They were merely dead eyes, as taciturn and enigmatic as the dead have always been.

Nancy's whole body shook with her loss, and she looked up at Amy, not knowing what had happened or how or why, knowing only that she would never really understand. Still, she strove to ask. "What . . . happened? What . . . have you . . . done?"

"I came back," Amy said, "to put the wrong things right." She looked back at Rick's face, and at the boy who had proven himself not yet beyond redemption, the son of her killer, who Rick had tried to save at the cost of his own life. "But it was Rick who did it." She shook her head. "All I can do is end it now."

She looked at Levinson, who had hoisted an assault rifle from the pile and stood covering the crowd with it and his shotgun. "David," she said, and he glanced at her. "Take Nancy and the boy out of here. Go get help."

"What about . . ." Levinson gestured to the men sitting on the ground or standing, their shoulders hunched in defeat. Their eyes, however, still burned with anger.

She walked up to him so that the others couldn't hear. "We'll lock them in that bunker," she said, gesturing to the half-buried building.

"What's in it?" he asked her.

"Nothing to worry about. I'll stay with them." She stepped toward the men and raised her voice. "Listen to me! We're going to imprison you for now. Then Officer Levinson will bring back more—"

Maybe it was the thought of imprisonment, or maybe it was being defeated by a Jew, but one of the men made a dash for the pile of weapons. Amy had anticipated such a move, and shot him in the chest before he had even gotten halfway. He fell without a sound.

"That's not something anyone wants to try again," Amy said calmly. "Now get moving. We're going to that bunker."

"Ma'am," said Karl Withers, as Nancy was helping him to his feet. "There's guns in there, and—"

"I know what's in there. There's not going to be any problem. I intend to be the chaperon for these gentlemen until the authorities come." She jerked the muzzle of her gun in the direction of the bunker and the men started walking. "Anyone makes a break for it," Amy said, "he's dead before he runs five steps. So make your moves wisely."

Amy noticed they were murmuring among themselves, and she was sure that the idea had gone through several of their narrow minds that they could get arms inside and turn the tables on the bitch with the gun. They did, however, think enough of her prowess that none of them tried to escape. Instant death was a strong persuader.

While Amy and Levinson herded the militiamen to the bunker, Nancy helped Karl as he limped through the gate to the Blazer. Amy preceded the men down the steps.

The inside of the building was far larger than its exterior suggested. A variety of firearms stood in racks along one wall and cases of bullets were piled against the other. Further back were wooden cases labeled GRENADES and near them were bins neatly loaded with dynamite sticks. There were also a number of glass jars filled with a gray putty, as well as packets of something sealed in paper.

But what Amy was really looking for was on a table near the entrance, next to the racks of rifles. She made sure that none of the militiamen went near it as she guided them over to the side of the building with the bullets. Let them have all the ammo they want, she thought. It was useless without the guns.

"Keep moving, gentlemen . . . that's it. Sit on those cases if you like. I'm sure you're all pretty tired. Just don't make any move for the weapons, please."

"Amy," Levinson said softly to her. "You're staying in here with them?"

"That's right." She kept watching the men. They looked edgy and dangerous. Rip Withers was standing, like most of the other men whose legs hadn't been injured in the attack. "But none of us are coming out." She glanced at him and saw he was looking at her with concern, and maybe a little fear. "Don't worry, though, they won't feel a thing." She pointed to a key that hung on a nail over the inside of the door. "Odds are that's to this building. Lock it from the outside. Now. And get Nancy and that kid far away, as fast as you can. Thanks, David." She smiled. "You're a *mensch.*"

Levinson tried to smile but something in his throat wouldn't let him. "And she speaks Yiddish too," he said huskily. "My dream girl. Shame we had to meet like this . . ."

He turned, grabbed the key, and went up the few stairs in a flash, slamming the door behind him. Amy heard the key turn, and at last beheld the situation she had been waiting for.

She waited for as long as she could. She pictured Levinson running across the clearing and out the gate, helping Nancy get the boy in the truck, if she hadn't already. He would fumble for his keys for a moment or so, then start the truck, panicking if it didn't turn over right away. But it would start. Then he would turn around carefully, avoiding getting stuck, and drive out the dirt road as fast as he could, expecting every second to hear something behind him.

There. That was time enough. He was safe now.

L'chaim, David Levinson. To life.

And now to death. The men were beginning to move. They could nurse their broken arms and twisted ankles and smashed noses only so long. It was inevitable that they would try to overpower her, even though some of them would have to be sacrificed to her bullets. Then they would break down the door and flee before the Jew returned with the feds. That was how they lived and how they thought. So she would have to entertain them.

Moving so decisively that they could only stand and watch, she walked past them, keeping her weapon and her eyes trained on them. She stopped at a carton of grenades, put her fingers under the wooden lid, and yanked upward. The nails shrieked out of the wood and the men gazed in wonder at what would have taken any of them a crowbar to accomplish.

The grenades were nestled like eggs in a nest of excelsior, and Amy plucked one out. She pressed the safety lever with her left hand, hooked her right index finger through the pull ring, and yanked out the safety pin. It was live now. All she had to do was to let it go and no one could call it back.

"Now," she said, turning back to the wide-eyed men. "If any of you were wondering just how I was planning to maintain discipline . . ." She held up the grenade in her left hand and her rifle in her right. "Behold. And don't bother to run for the door. It's locked." She strolled slowly back toward the front of the room and stopped by the table with the box.

"I'm sick of this," she said, unaccountably weary. She felt like sleeping for a very long time. She wanted to sleep in Rick's arms and then wake to see their children around her, but she didn't know if that would ever happen. She hoped it would.

"I died because of you," she told the men in the round-roofed room. "And I'm here because of you. I bring you justice. But I pray for mercy on your souls." She looked down at the grenade in her hands.

"Because if you're damned, then so am I."

Amy looked down into the large wooden box that held Powder Burns's final bomb. Then she released the safety lever of the grenade and jammed it into the multicolored jungle of wires and switches that sat hugging the bomb's payload, a hundred and fifty one-pound blocks of C–4 explosive.

There was only time left for the men to scream and for Amy to close her eyes, hoping that the darkness would remain.

Levinson saw the flash before he heard the sound, and he heard the sound before he felt the shock.

It sounded as though the entire forest was exploding behind him, and felt as though the ground were a giant quilt that someone had suddenly decided to shake out. He slammed on the brakes until the shock wave passed, but even a good half mile away, debris showered down like hail on the Blazer's roof. He wondered if there was anything left of the area within the fence.

Nancy Carlisle's trembling slowed and she said, "Amy . . . she's . . ."

"Yes, she's gone. They're all gone now." He looked at the boy. "All your friends."

There were tears in the boy's eyes. "They weren't my friends. None of them . . . *none* of them . . ."

It was a long road this boy was going to have to walk. Levinson hoped he could make it.

As they drove toward Hobie and its general hospital, passing the police cars that were coming the other way, Levinson told Nancy the story, as much as he knew of it. When he was finished, she was quiet for a while. Then she said, "I can't believe it. Amy couldn't have been dead in the first place. She and Rick . . . they planned this somehow." Her voice became thick with sorrow and humiliation. "I don't think . . . Rick ever loved me."

"What I've said is true," Levinson answered, "and I think that he did love you, as much as he could. But he loved Amy too."

"He's *with* her now," Nancy said, and he heard the grief and the anger and what he hoped might be love in the woman's voice.

He didn't answer, but he thought, I hope so. God, Crow, whatever makes these decisions, please let it be so.

44

The next morning just before dawn David Levinson was climbing into his Blazer parked outside the police station. Karl Withers was safely in the hospital, Nancy Carlisle was sleeping a sedated sleep, and Levinson had told his superiors and several federal agents much less than everything he knew.

The tale had taken hours to spin. He had told them that, to the best of his knowledge, Amy Carlisle had survived the explosion, probably wandered away afterward, having lost her memory, and upon regaining it had contacted her husband, now remarried. The two of them, without the new wife's knowledge, had then begun to hunt down the bombers, and ended their quest by dying in the explosion at the terrorists' compound.

The yarn probably had more holes than a pound of sliced Swiss but what seemed to be the linchpin was sturdy enough: the same gang of armed extremists who blew up a day-care center, then killed Wilson Barnes, William Standish, and his mother, had been blown up themselves by another bomb that they had built.

In Levinson's opus, Amy or Rick Carlisle may have been responsible for the killings of Sonny Armitage and Junior Feeley. However, a more likely scenario for the electrocution deaths in Eau Claire may have been a vendetta waged by the leaders of the terrorists against those whom they suspected of being traitors, in this case Chip Porter, though God only knew why.

So they were not only responsible for the deaths of those they insanely considered their enemies, they had also brought about the deaths of those sympathetic to their cause. The feds liked that idea a whole lot, and Levinson suspected it would stick in spite of any evidence to the contrary.

Well, he had done what he could to keep Amy Carlisle's memory as sacred as possible. He started his car and headed home, thinking that he would ask Trotter to help him go back for the Avanti. Trotter would ask no questions.

The former site of the Making Friends Child Care Center was not on Levinson's way home, but he wanted to drive by nonetheless, just to see if anything had changed. He was not disappointed.

Dawn was breaking as he pulled the Blazer up to the curb and got out. It was cold, but just the sight of the sun's rays pouring across the horizon made Levinson feel warmer.

Physically, the place had not changed. Or had it? There was something that had not been there before, some added piece, and it took him a moment to figure out what it was.

There were seedlings, three of them, that had pushed their way through the dust and the ashes, small trees growing from seeds the wind had brought and lodged in this spot. Less than a foot high, they stood in a rough triangle, several feet apart from each other.

As Levinson walked closer, he saw something that he was at a loss to explain. In November, on the cusp of winter and with the temperature close to freezing, the seedlings were sprouting small buds of green. Several tiny flowers had also grown and were blooming in the dust of the triangle the young trees made.

There were ten of them, their delicate petals all of different colors. They were moored in the dust and the ash, beauty born of destruction. Ten flowers.

Ten children lost.

Three trees.

Judy Croft. Amy Carlisle.

And her husband?

With Rick Carlisle's sacrifice, he had done as much as any of them. He had earned his place. He should have a tree.

Jesus, listen to yourself, Levinson thought. Signs in trees and flowers. Hell, it was coincidence, that was all.

But flowers and buds in November? In Minnesota?

He shook his head. Maybe now that the culprits were identified and after all the legal hassles were over, someone could do what nature had already started and make this a garden—a *memorial* garden, with some playground equipment, so that you could hear little kids laughing here again.

He looked up at the brightening sky, hoping to see a crow soaring dramatically out of the dawn. But instead, a few sparrows flew down, landed on the sidewalk, and began pecking at crumbs or pebbles.

Levinson chuckled and shook his head at his expectations. Always wanting more. Hadn't he seen enough miracles for one lifetime?

He watched the sparrows until they flew away. And then, keeping his promise to Amy Carlisle, he went to temple for the first time in many years. There he said Kaddish, not only for her, but for those who died with her, and those who died because of her.

He who maketh peace in his high places,
May he make peace for us.